UNWILLING CAPTIVE

"Why do you seek to prevent my marriage to Murdoch MacDougall?" Averyl asked. "What manner of man would abduct a maid upon her betrothal?" Then she gasped, feeling the blood drain from her cheeks. A knave would. A miscreant.

A maniacal butcher.

The truth of her captor's identity hit her like any icy sheet of Scottish winter rain, and she swallowed—hard. Her abductor's disconcerting gaze followed her every move.

"Oh, dear heaven!" Her voice trembled as she braced herself on shaky arms. "I know . . . You are the English murderer—the butcher of Lochlan MacDougall! You are Drake Thornton."

He drew in a deep breath, eyes blazing black fury. Beneath taut shoulders, he clenched large fists, sending Averyl's pulse into turmoil. Frantic, she looked across the room, toward the door and freedom. Before she could try to escape, he flew across the room and anchored his hands on either side of her head, trapping her. His presence, hot and looming, enveloped her.

"I suppose Murdoch told you that." His voice rumbled from his chest, much like the thunder above.

She nodded unevenly. "Why should you seek to prevent my marriage to him?"

The hard line of his jaw tensed again. "Revenge. He owes me a debt. You are my repayment"

Dear Romance Reader,

In July, we launched the Ballad line with four new series, and each month we'll present both new and continuing stories set everywhere from medieval England to the American West—the kind of passionate, romantic stories you love best, written by the most gifted authors. At the back of each book, we'll tell you when you can find subsequent books in the series that have captured your heart.

This month beloved author Jo Ann Ferguson completes her riveting *Shadow of the Bastille* series with **A Sister's Quest,** as a French schoolteacher embarks on a perilous—and passionate—adventure with a Russian count. Next, talented newcomer Elizabeth Keys offers the second book in her *Irish Blessing* series, **Reilly's Gold.** What happens when a man determined to find his fortune in America meets a spirited woman instead?

Beginning this month is a series from rising star Kathryn Fox. In 1874, three men—loyal, brave, and true—ride into the Canadian wilderness to fight for justice as *The Mounties*. In the first installment, a recruit trained as a physician will capture a bootlegger—yet *she* will claim his heart for **The First Time.** Finally, new favorite Shelley Bradley presents the second book in her breathtaking *Brothers in Arms* series, as a Scottish knight bent on revenge finds the power of true love with **His Stolen Bride.** Enjoy!

Kate Duffy
Editorial Director

Brothers in Arms

HIS
STOLEN
BRIDE

Shelley Bradley

ZEBRA BOOKS
Kensington Publishing Corp.

http://www.zebrabooks.com

*For Lesa Raesz, who was there in the beginning.
Don't give up!*

*For the talented and dedicated authors in my critique
group, Carol Rose Doss, Sylvia McDaniel, and Kathern
Shaw, who were there for me throughout and always are.*

*For Elizabeth Benway, who came recently to my
cheering section but has been loud and supportive
since she arrived.*

Thank you all!

Prologue

November, 1484

Dawn hid stubbornly behind Yorkshire's scarred hills, refusing to shed her light on the vicious scene below. Fires crackled as they blazed the surrounding cottages, illuminating the dark with an orange glow of dust and fog clinging to the pungent earth. The exhalations of warhorses and their riders created a poof of ghostly figures in the eerie dark as the air churned with bloodlust and greed.

Cursing his treacherous Campbell enemies, Drake Mac-Dougall turned to counter a challenge from one of his foes, his boots crunching on craggy earth. Arms tense from the long battle, he managed to wield his *claidmor* with a powerful swing, slicing through the morn's thick fog—and his foe's middle. Pulling his blade from the dead man's side with a desperate yank, Drake whirled to another sound, conscious of the metallic tinge of blood in the crisp, cloudy wind.

Suddenly, he saw the ax headed for his chest but could not counter in time. Before he could say his prayers, the man slumped forward, a thick lance protruding from his back. One of his brothers in arms, Aric Neville, emerged from the melee, through the dense air, to claim his weapon from the fallen man. Known through all of England as the

White Lion for his ferocity in battle and loyalty to the York-ist cause, Aric was a good knight to have at one's back.

Drake turned to his friend with a smile of thanks. Aric did not return his smile, but stared with bleak eyes, some-how aching and flat at once.

Scowling, Drake wondered what pain his friend hid.

Then a Campbell charged from Aric's side. Drake tensed. Aric diffused the challenge simply, nearly cutting the man in two, with a swing of his mighty arm. The soldier's dying groan hung in the air between them.

"Watch yourself, friend," Aric said, pushing the strands of his long, tawny hair from his sweat-streaked face, then disappeared down the hill, beyond the eerie orange light.

Where had the smiling friend of his childhood gone? Had the years of politics and power as the only nephew of War-wick the Kingmaker been so unhappy? Had the deaths of England's princes so afflicted his heart?

Shaking the thought away, Drake met the challenge of an oncoming Campbell, rending the vulnerable flesh be-tween the joints of his armor. The man clutched his useless, hanging arm and fell to the ground with an agonized groan.

Damn it, he hated the MacDougalls' feud with the Camp-bells, which had endured for generations. But the Campbells felt trapped between the highland MacDougalls to the north and Drake's grandfather, Guilford, earl of Rothgate, to the south.

When Guilford Locke's fatally spoiled daughter, Diera, had wed the powerful chief Lochlan MacDougall, uniting the families, the Campbells had taken the union as a sign of aggression. The fighting had commenced. Drake knew his father, Lochlan, regretted the marriage for more reasons than this incessant warring, but both would stand and fight—Lochlan out of duty and Drake out of affection for his grandfather—assisting old Guilford's sentries until the Campbell threat was removed.

With a *whoosh* of his broadsword and a whoop of excitement, Kieran, Drake's other brother in arms, leaped to his side, blue-green eyes full of mischief.

Drake smiled back, knowing better than to chastise his adventurous comrade. "How fare you?"

"The battle is near finished, and no one has killed me yet. That makes for a good morn thus far. And you?"

Drake sighed. "Ready to end this farce with the bloody Campbells."

Seeing a charging foe, Drake tossed down his *claidmor,* then retrieved the longbow from his back. He fired, felling the man. Beside him, Kieran repeated the process when another man behind the first approached.

Kieran laughed. "Lord, 'tis an excitement, besting your enemies, pitting your skills against mighty warriors."

"Killing is never fun." Drake couldn't help the harsh note that crept into his voice.

"Battle is the stuff of men and life," Kieran protested.

"Aye, but not of amusement." He grunted. "Do you find nothing else pleasurable these days?"

With a rogue's grin, Kieran replied, "How well you have forgotten me since I last saw you!"

" 'Tis right you are." Drake grinned despite his disapproval of Kieran's notions. "You always enjoy a good wench."

"At least one."

Shaking his head, Drake retrieved his sword and whirled away to discover another attacking Campbell. Kieran leaped in front of him and severed the warrior's head from his body.

His Irish friend let loose a battle cry.

Drake turned away, fearful the spirited fool would get himself killed if he did not watch his step.

At the top of the rise, Drake spotted his father. Lochlan took a minor blow to the leg from an opponent. Racing up the incline to his sire, Drake exhaled in relief when his father seemed to right himself, his broad silhouette standing proud against the orange-black sky. A man wearing his father's colors arrived to help dispense of the Campbell.

As the lowlander's body fell to the damp earth, Drake's father nodded, his expression one of concern. Drake nodded in return.

The sentry beside his father turned toward Drake. The dark-haired man was not one he recognized in the orange light. As the soldier spotted Drake, the man's gray eyes widened. With surprise? Apprehension? The stranger whirled about suddenly.

And plunged his bloody knife into Lochlan's heart.

With a cry, Drake raced to his sire as he fell to the ground. The unknown attacker fled over the hill, into the waiting blackness. Drake wanted to give chase, to slay the bastard. But he looked at Lochlan grasping his chest and feared for his father's life. At Lochlan's side, Drake placed his trembling hands over his father's jagged red gash settling around the deadly blade.

"Drake . . ." he moaned.

Panic welled up inside him. The wound was deep, the area a vulnerable one. Blood seeped around his fingers, hot, sticky.

Around him rose the cheers of Guilford's men.

"Bleedin' Campbell cowards," one shouted.

The battle had ended in victory, but Drake could only stare at Lochlan in horror.

"Father, I am here."

"You will do well . . . as chief." He ҫ   hed.

Chief? Nay! "Do not leave me! We wi   find some way to heal you."

Drake heard the desperation in his voice and could not stop it. Cold panic rushed through his veins. His father could not die! He had no wish to replace Lochlan as chief— or usurp power from his older half-brother, Murdoch.

Gritting his teeth, Drake knew the blade would have to be removed or his father would die. With a grimace and a pounding heart, he withdrew the knife from his father's flesh with one hand and pressed the other tightly against the seeping wound.

"You've been a—a fine son."

"Do not talk like the dead. Who loyal to the MacDougalls would plunge his blade into you?" he shouted. "Who?"

"Not mine." His father's voice was fading.

"Stay with me! Don't let the damn Campbells defeat you."

"The man . . . Murdoch's."

Lochlan fell limp at Drake's feet.

"Nay!" Drake shouted to the heavens. But his father's chest no longer moved with life's breath. Clutching the weapon of his father's demise, he could still scarce believe what his eyes told him—that his beloved father had been murdered.

And by one of his half-brother's men.

Drake cursed the sibling he had always hated, but never more than now. 'Twas no matter of questioning why. Drake knew better. Murdoch wanted power and wealth, both of which their father had been set to deny him as punishment for his misdeeds.

Somehow, someway, he would avenge Lochlan's murder. Drake vowed to repay Murdoch's evil in kind.

Footsteps rushed toward Drake. He restrained an urge to hide his father's body from prying eyes. God, how he wanted to go back in time even five minutes and keep his father safe from Murdoch's perfidy.

Gasps and curses lit the air around him. His father's most trusted soldier, Duff, knelt beside Lochlan's fallen figure, shock transforming his face.

Then he saw the bloodied knife in Drake's hand.

Duff leaped to his feet, fury and betrayal spearing him like a lance.

"Traitor! Murderer!" the man yelled as he scooped up the knife and held it up before the gathering crowd.

"Nay, Duff!" Drake protested. "I but saw him stabbed and rushed to give aid."

"By whom? Where is this fiend?" Disbelief rang from the familiar voice of Wallace, another of his father's castle guards—and one of Murdoch's allies.

"Gone. Ran over the hill." Drake pointed. "But perhaps you knew that."

Wallace looked affronted. Drake wasn't certain if he should believe the hard soldier's expression of blamelessness; he could not decipher it amid the shock and bewilderment swirling inside him.

"What would I know of yer misdeeds?"

"The misdeed was Murdoch's. My father recognized the man as one of Murdoch's!" Drake protested, unable to believe the spiraling horror of the moment. Did they really believe he had killed his own father?

None of his clansmen would meet his eye. Guilford's men only stood by shaking their heads.

Nay, this could not be happening!

Aric emerged at the fore, tall and sturdy, looking as powerful as the lion for which he was named. "Drake is innocent. His love for his sire is well known by you all."

Duff and Wallace both shouldered in to grab Drake's arms and roughly pull him to his feet. He resisted, only to feel Duff's blade at his throat.

Kieran pushed his way into the small circle, mouth hanging open in disbelief. "Pea-witted fools, Drake would never kill Lochlan! This you know."

"We know naught except we found this bloody knife in Drake's hand," Wallace spat.

A hush befell the crowd. All looked up into the firm, age-hardened features of his grandfather, Guilford, earl of Rothgate. "Release him. Drake murdered no one, least of all his own father."

Never my own father! He wanted to shout.

"My lord, he lay near the body wi' the bloody knife betwixt his fingers and claimed a stranger killed his faither," said Duff. "The Clan MacDougall maun judge him now, for I amna believing any tale of a murderin' stranger."

"I swear it!" Drake vowed. "I will swear it upon my father's grave."

It pained him to think of his father slain, of having a cold resting place within the earth, but Duff inched his blade closer to his throat with a curse. His thoughts turned to survival.

"Ye can swear it upon yer own grave," said Duff, "after Murdoch finishes wi' ye."

One

Scotland, June 1486

Drake crept along the middle bailey wall of Dunollie Castle like an intruder, inching toward the keep he had once called home. Cold anticipation settled into his gut as he spotted the kirk's elaborate spire through the early-morning shadows, then crept into the building.

The place of worship had not changed since his boyhood. The wooden benches and colorful stained glass above the altar called up memories of long-ago masses spent squirming beside his father while Firtha scolded him to behave. He shoved away the memory.

Only the present mattered.

Only revenge would suffice.

Success now might end nearly two years of hell and forever alter his life—as well as that of his murdering half-brother. This plan would gain him retribution for the unknown killer's blade in his father's heart, plunged there at Murdoch's order. Mayhap this vengeance could end the accusation of murder that hung about his head like a black cloud, for which he'd nearly died in this very castle's dungeon.

Most likely the scheme would also cost him his life.

Drake crept across the deserted chapel, then pulled the hood of the coarse woolen monk's robe about his face and settled onto the hard, narrow bench. Within seconds, Firtha, his old governess, trod into the holy place, always at dawn, her gait slow now with age. The golden glow of many candles illuminated her softly lined face as she slowly knelt before the white candle in the red globe and crossed herself.

"Firtha?" he whispered beside her.

She gasped, and he lifted a silencing finger to his lips.

"Master Drake! Oh—oh, thank the Lord yer alive!" she whispered.

He smiled, clasping her soft, worn hands in his, and helped her to her feet. "And no thanks to Murdoch."

"Why hiv ye not returned sooner?" She gasped, a wrinkled hand fluttering to her plump cheek. "Hiv ye been unwell, lad? The way his lordship treated ye—"

"My health is returned." Drake gritted his teeth against the reminder of his painful days in Murdoch's dungeon. "Coming here has simply been too dangerous."

"Aye, perhaps ye should not have come at all. 'Tis dangerous still. His lordship has offered a reward for yer head, lad, and still rants aboot yer mischief. Make no mistake, he vows to see ye dead this time."

"No doubt," Drake acknowledged, a grim turn to his mouth. "But if I'm destined for hell, I intend to take him with me."

Firtha clasped his hands. "Ye silly man, go to England, to yer grandfaither. Dinna let Lord Dunollie's hate destroy ye."

Drake began shaking his head before Firtha stopped speaking. "I will not hide like a coward while Murdoch enjoys the product of his treachery. All of his other deeds I could have ignored, but my father— Not that. Never."

"Then ye maun keep searching fer clues, something to prove yer innocence."

"If any such piece of evidence ever existed," Drake cut in, "surely Murdoch has destroyed it. He is no fool."

"Ni, but he is verra arrogant."

Drake released the old woman's hands and fingered his

father's silver cross hanging about his neck as a constant reminder of his love for and duty to his sire. "Aye, but 'tis unlikely we will ever know the truth."

The lack of other witnesses to his father's murder both puzzled and tore at him. The entire incident had been clearly planned to take place in the dark, among the thick branches of century-old trees, away from the melee. Aye, Murdoch had plotted carefully. Many of the clan's most important men could attest to the fact that Murdoch had been in Glasgow the morn of the brutal deed and had behaved with all appropriate shock upon hearing of Lochlan MacDougall's murder.

Drake cursed, wondering again why he had not expected his half-brother to plot something so ruthless. A foolish underestimation, indeed. One he would not make again.

"How did ye sneak in? His lordship haes posted a dozen men in the barbican to keep intruders out while the Lady Averyl is here."

He smiled. "I spent many years here, stealing in and out to avoid my mother's wrath, if you recall. Murdoch cannot stop me."

"Always a knave, ye were, since ye looked up to me knees." Firtha smiled. "If ye've an appetite, Alpina has baked a loaf of bread this morn."

He grinned as she clucked over him like a mother hen with her chick. "I shall worry about the rumblings of my stomach later. As for now, I must ask for your help."

"Ask? No askin' needed, lad. Ye ken I will help in whate'er way I can."

A shuffling nearby made Drake tense. He lunged for a darkened corner. At the sound of retreating footsteps, relief sluiced through him.

"Isna safe here," Firtha whispered. "Follow me."

Drake trailed Firtha down the steps adjacent to the kirk, then through a dim corridor. He opened the small portal, ducking to enter a little-used corner of the castle's vaults.

After using the torch on the corridor's wall to light the

tallow tucked away in his robe, Drake shut the door behind them. The scents of mildew and damp stone wafted in the air. The *plink* of a water drop in the distance filled the tense silence.

"I need information about Murdoch and the Campbell wench."

"Weel, Lady Averyl arrived but last eve. I hivna seen much of her."

Drake grunted in frustration. "From what you have seen, would you term her a half-wit?"

With a shake of her head, Firtha said, *"Ni.* Smart is that one. Knew it right off, I did."

"Good. Does she regard Murdoch like the demon he is, then?"

Firtha scowled. "Weel . . . *Ni.* Lady Averyl looks upon Lord Dunollie as if he were the blessed Lord Himself."

"So her strong opinions are backed by a weak mind. I expect nothing less of a Campbell." He swore. "And most like, she is vain and conniving as well." Just like his English mother, Diera. Drake shook his head, blood simmering with contempt. "Can you think of aught else to say of her?"

She frowned. "Lord Dunollie treats her wi' the charm of the devil himself."

Drake scoffed. "He can do naught else. The girl's father remains about, and Murdoch needs her lands, should he be planning to attack the Campbells, as I suspect."

"Ach, Campbell is a muddle-mucked oaf. He cares as much for the coin this marriage will bring as for the lassie herself."

"It is the way of landed daughters," Drake commented. "Is extra coin the reason Averyl and her father plot this marriage?"

"Aye. I hiv no doubt aboot that."

"And since she covets the match, 'tis likely Lady Averyl is as money hungry as her father. How like a Campbell to whore themselves for gold," he sneered. Clearly, Averyl Campbell and Murdoch deserved each other.

But such a union would not be their fate.

"Tell me what ye plan, lad," Firtha entreated. "Does it include Lady Averyl?"

Drake paced and listened to the distant groans of the chaplain and the willing wench Drake had paid to occupy him. Clearly, the holy man was more concerned with matters of the flesh than the spirit.

"The less you know, the safer you will be."

Firtha bit her lip. "Whate'er you plan, 'tis dangerous."

"Do not worry over me. Worry over Murdoch's state of mind when he discovers the Campbell wench not here to wed him."

With a gasp, Firtha crossed herself. "Yer plan, 'tis worse than I feared. Ach, lad, think! His lordship will kill ye."

"He will kill me, anyway," Drake said grimly. "But if I can prevent this marriage, he can never claim the inheritance for which he murdered our father."

"Ye can?"

"Indeed. When Murdoch fails to marry the Campbell girl by the day she turns eight and ten, according to my father's will, he will lose all his precious coin—and the keep."

"Still, ye should no' risk yer life so," she argued.

Drake sent her a grim stare. "My father would have done no less for me."

"The devil take Lord Dunollie fer what he's done to ye!"

"Someday he will, but you must not think like my father and lay the blame entirely at Murdoch's feet. Damn my mother, too."

"But yer father's death was his lordship's doin'. He hired the butcherin' fiend, not that English whore."

In his mind, he again saw Lochlan's attacker plunge the knife through his father's heart. Again, he saw his father collapse in death. Fury settled like a block of ice within him.

"Firtha, if my plan is to work, I need ask you to pack a satchel of the Campbell wench's belongings. Tonight, set it beneath her window."

"Drake, forget the past. Go to England and yer grand-faither. Find a lady love to care for ye."

He glared at her. "I have no desire for a lady love."

"But ye deserve happiness, no' death."

"Think you a woman will make me happy?"

He stared at his old governess as if she had lost her mind. "Should I wish for a woman to make me as happy as, say, my mother did my father?"

Firtha flinched, then opened her mouth to argue.

Drake pressed on. "I shall never be reduced to cursing a woman and crying for her in the same breath. Why succumb to love's tight fist, ever squeezing the life dry from a man, until he has naught left but the solace of strong drink and the inability to embrace a willing wench?"

"Isna like that fer most in love," she argued.

"Such happens often enough that I'll not take a chance."

Firtha sighed in defeat. "Weel, will ye return to Arran?"

"Aye, I am best hidden on the isle. Murdoch will not find me there."

"I pray 'tis so."

Silently, Drake prayed for that as well. Discovery meant failure—and certain death.

With her home, her heart, and her future at stake, Averyl Campbell couldn't help but fidget. How did a one sit idle, knowing she must somehow impress a virtual stranger—a man she had regarded as an enemy most of her life—now with the power to fulfill her dreams?

Determined not to contemplate the question, she cast an absent glance at the fresh rushes and spotless tables of Dunollie Castle's great hall. If he agreed to wed her, the chief of Clan MacDougall would prove he possessed at least some kindness and charity, like the princely heroes of childhood dreams. Even the Romanesque beauty and prosperity of his keep seemed out of a fantasy, much different from her barren but beloved home.

Today he would likely make his intentions known. Today, she must be at her best.

Tucking a wayward curl beneath her linen headdress with trembling fingers, she prayed Murdoch MacDougall would not refuse her despite the fact she was less than lovely. Much less.

"You've another curl here," her father whispered, pointing to her temple. "Tuck that . . . Aye. Much better, lass."

Averyl forced a smile. "Thank you."

He patted her hand. "I know how trying that unruly hair is. Your mother suffered the same hardship, bless her soul. Keep your tresses tucked away and no one will be the wiser."

Dejection pressed its heavy weight on her. Over the past seventeen years, she had accepted her homeliness. Today her father's familiar counsel hurt, especially now, when so much hinged on MacDougall taking a liking to her face and form.

"I dressed with care to look my best this morn." She smoothed a nervous hand over her pale dress, wondering if she should have chosen the green gown to match her eyes.

Her father's mouth turned down toward his sagging jowls. "No doubt that shade of yellow is bonny as a bloom. Mayhap if you pinched . . ." He clamped his thick fingers around her cheeks. "Aye, that gives you a bit more color."

With gritted teeth, Averyl turned away, her cheeks stinging. She was a waif, hopelessly pale and plain. Such mattered not—so long as Murdoch MacDougall made her his bride. So long as he protected her lands from other warring clans who would see peace destroyed, along with her late mother's much-loved keep.

Averyl drew in a deep breath. She could not worry further about her appearance. The MacDougall would soon enter the room, and she must act her best. Surely a man of his rank and maturity would appreciate a woman of strong convictions and mind.

Comforted by that hope, she eyed the castle's great hall.

Beautiful jewel-toned tapestries stretched along the walls above tables massive enough to seat easily one hundred. A pair of hand-carved chairs stood alone by the fire over a marble chessboard and, along with the prime condition of his keep, bespoke MacDougall's wealth. This, no doubt, thrilled her father, who was but a minor laird in the Clan Campbell. He had long since sold their tapestries and most of the furnishings to put crops in the ground and food in their mouths.

"Look at me." Her father interrupted her reverie.

Averyl turned to him and found his deep green eyes, eyes she had inherited, glowing with concern.

"Remember to watch your tongue, lass," he warned gently. "Lord Dunollie may not be accustomed to a woman who speaks her mind. And you must please him, Averyl, else he may not see this betrothal through and lay out the coin to repair our keep. We canna afford for your manner to displease him, particularly if your appearance does."

She balled her hands into fists beneath the embroidered hem of her sleeves. "I will endeavor to be most proper."

Refusing to think about the ruination her home would suffer if Murdoch MacDougall found her too plain, Averyl nodded. She would not allow Abbotsford, her last link with her beloved mother, to be ravaged again by enemies and poverty.

"Of course, lass. 'Tis simply that I am nervous. You've never been away from Abbotsford to learn the ways of others, and I canna rest until his gold warms my palms."

"Then why refuse cousin Robert's offer for me? As a Campbell, he would more likely—"

"Your cousin Robert is a penniless knave and wants only your dower lands, lass. He couldna help us save Abbotsford."

She frowned. "What of selling the east acreage? That would bring in enough money to save Abbotsford."

"We have trice discussed this, Averyl." His tone rang with impatience. "God's blood, I would not sell your dower lands to repair the keep. The land is your only chance of wedding well." He touched a fatherly hand to her shoulder. "Fret not. Lord Dunollie will agree to this marriage, despite your plain face, when you prove what a capable wife you will make him."

Capable, aye. But never comely, not with her mass of curls and her overlarge eyes dominating her pale face. Minstrels sang tales of smiling, pink-cheeked beauties, not waifs with little to recommend them but an active mind and steely pride.

Averyl jumped to her feet as the distinguished nobleman, dressed in blue brocade, emerged at the bottom of a rounded staircase. Beside her, her father rose and nodded in greeting.

She drew in a breath as she stared at Murdoch MacDougall. Despite his advancing years, he looked nearly every bit as dashing as the fantasy husband she had conjured up in her dreams. Lines formed by hard battle and good living bracketed his brown eyes. Russet hair shone in the soft light. He slid his gaze over her without a hint of disappointment as he approached on blunt-toed shoes. Dare she hope he would care for her? Come to love her? She swallowed, wary excitement bubbling in her.

"Hello, Campbell," The elegant chief extended his hand.

Her father smiled. As she stood beside him, Averyl's insides jumbled with anxiety. She clasped her clammy palms together.

"A pleasure to see you this fine evening," her father said.

He nodded. "Lady Averyl," MacDougall greeted, directing his dark gaze to her again. "You look fetching."

Averyl warmed under MacDougall's praise, praying he meant even a word of it. Could he be the true love her mother had vowed she deserved and instructed her to pray for?

"That she does," her father affirmed. "And trained to be a fine chatelaine from the time she stood at my knee."

His lordship's smile was all charm. "So you've said. 'Tis

certain only a fool would dally before making her his bride."

"Thank you," she said, blushing, hoping he meant such and would see to Abbotsford's needs as well as her heart's desire for love. Such possibilities made her more dizzy than mulled wine.

"Shall we adjourn to supper?" He led them to the raised dais at the head of the room. "The others will join us later."

Hazarding a glance in MacDougall's direction, she saw a faint smile cross his face as they took their seats. He positioned her to his right, in the chair she would occupy as his lady wife, should he choose to wed her. The gesture bolstered her confidence again. When she turned to thank him, she found his attention on two wenches hovering about, serving food.

Averyl tore her gaze from the servants—comely, at that— in silent rebuke. MacDougall sought a wife. Love would take time and patience. But his inattention revived her fear. She wanted more from marriage than an exchange of wedding vows for land. She yearned for untroubled days and joy-filled nights. To have a man admire her face as much as her mind. She wanted the kind of consuming love her mother had whispered of wistfully and often.

Focusing on her trencher, Averyl ignored the giggling maids. An array of dishes she considered ample food for two meals lay across the long table. The smells of warm meat and hot bread made her mouth water. How long since the people at Abbotsford had eaten aught but potatoes, leeks, and a scraggly hare?

One woman set sugared almonds and roast mutton before Averyl. Another server, a pretty redhead heavy with child, glared as she filled her cup with Spanish wine.

Was she the MacDougall's leman? No matter. If they wed, she would change that. Averyl reached for her eating dagger, determined at this moment to enjoy the feast.

MacDougall sipped his wine, then addressed her father.

"Tell me, Campbell, were your crops plentiful last harvest?"

"Unfortunately nae. Rain was the only thing aplenty."

At her father's tight-lipped response, MacDougall nodded. "Averyl's dower lands are in Campbell territory, are they not?"

"Aye, within its heart."

" 'Tis as I had hoped." MacDougall stuffed his mouth with mutton. "Peace must be maintained in Scotland. This foolish fighting between the Campbells and MacDougalls has gone on for far too long. 'Tis why my father desired this match, to make peace between our clans."

"Aye. Though some o' the Campbells are against your union with Averyl, once they see the prosperity brought by peace, they willna be objecting anymore, methinks."

He stabbed another peace of meat. "War is a foolish distraction. For my lands and my people, I desire even greater prosperity than my father enjoyed."

Campbell cleared his throat. " 'Tis unfortunate you came to possess these great lands because of your father's death. Despite being an enemy, he was the bravest of men."

MacDougall nodded politely. "Indeed."

"I cannot imagine your grief," Averyl said. "Though it must be of some comfort that you captured the swine who killed him."

MacDougall whipped his gaze to her, his dark eyes shadowed with a fury so raw and boundless, it seemed to eclipse the strong angles of his sun-weathered face. Averyl shivered.

"He escaped from my dungeons neigh on a year past."

She gasped, ice creeping into her veins like a winter chill. "Sweet mercy! I had no notion—"

" 'Tis true."

"How terrible! I hope you find the fiend," she said.

"As do I." He leaned closer. "Drake Thornton is an English butcher. A violent man with a volatile disposition."

How great Lord Dunollie's grief must be. She admired

his composure, knowing how much she still missed her
mother ten years after death and darkness had taken her.
"Murder is a terrible way to lose a parent."

" 'Tis truly dreadful, I assure you. The viciousness of
the murder shocks me each time I think upon it."

Averyl restrained an urge to touch his shoulder in a gesture of comfort. "Think you he might return to do you
harm as well?"

MacDougall turned a black gaze upon her. "The demon
will try, for his hate demands me also dead in a bath of
blood."

She trembled at the image. How terrible for Murdoch to
endure the enmity of a man so heartless and evil. She hoped
never to encounter the terrible beast.

"Does this Thornton fiend have a motive for such hate?"

"Averyl," her father warned. "Enough."

MacDougall swirled the wine in his goblet. "I've said
too much. Forgive me, lass. This discussion would be better
left unspoken. The story is a painful one not meant for a
lovely lady's ears."

She nodded, grateful to his lordship for smoothing over
the awkward moment. Perhaps MacDougall wasn't easy to
anger. Or perturbed by forthright conversation. That added
to her hope of a successful match. "Forgive me for speaking
of things painful."

"Of course," he assured with a tight smile.

Averyl nodded and cut into her meat. She could well
understand the pain of his loss. However, his refusal to
speak of his father's death baffled her. What could be more
shocking than a murder?

Evening shadows lengthened across Dunollie's garden
when Drake sneaked onto the quiet ground. He ducked behind the thick of a rosebush, waiting for the right moment
to steal inside the keep.

Tonight he would execute his plan. Vengeance would finally end this insufferable waiting. He could avenge his father's murder as well as repay Murdoch for his mistreatment in the hell of Dunollie's dungeon.

A movement, a blur of color to his right, made Drake whirl around. Between the waxy leaves of his cover, he tensed, willing his breathing to silence. He assessed possible escape routes as his gaze sought the source of his alarm.

An unfamiliar figure swayed down a nearby path with movements like a willow in a gentle breeze. Though distance and dim lighting obscured her face, the natural grace of her motions, along with her delicate silhouette, marked her a woman.

Curious, he slid from the hedges, closer, taking refuge behind the dyehouse a few feet from the garden's new occupant.

Drake watched as she wandered through the summer foliage. She fingered hyacinth stalks of various blues as they stood proudly, boasting delicate pastel petals, then plucked a climbing rose of perfect pale yellow.

By the flash of white teeth, Drake knew she smiled. His curiosity rose again as her smile faded, replaced by a melancholy mantle.

He shook the observation away, reminding himself he had come to exact revenge, not take in the garden's scenery.

Still, Drake did not remove his gaze from the woman as she raised the rosebud to her small red mouth. He noticed then a heavy bracelet encircling her wrist. The bauble had been that of Murdoch's mother. If a new woman wore it, 'twas likely a betrothal gift.

So this mystery woman was likely Lady Averyl Campbell—Murdoch's downfall, the key to his own success. 'Twas unfortunate indeed to find the Campbell woman beauteous.

The elaborate piece looked more a manacle than an ornament on her fragile wrist. Dismissing the fanciful thought, he watched Averyl stroll toward a riot of pink mums. She paused beneath a torch illuminating the garden and reclined against the stone wall of the keep. Holding the small bloom to the curve of her breast, she closed her eyes with a feathery sigh.

That sound shivered its way down his back.

Her fair skin glowed golden pink in the sconce's light. A delicate nose, firm, high cheekbones, and a small but stubborn jaw lent her a look that was both ethereal and sensual.

She tilted her head back, as if in worship to the moon. His gaze followed the arch of her neck, the stirring lift of her firm bosom as she inhaled a floral-tinged breath. He found himself drawing in a ragged breath as well.

Forcing his gaze lower made her no less enticing. Her body was tempting, womanly. Graceful shoulders rose above the inviting curve of her breasts above her small, tapered waist. A woman such as her would know how much she enticed a man. His English mother always had. Why should a Campbell whore be any different?

Despite his contempt, a lust coiled through Drake, pooling heat low in his belly. His enemy's woman was a surprise—not that such mattered. Lady Averyl was a part of his plan and would soon be a temporary part of his life out of necessity. Her role in this unfolding drama of vengeance was merely that of a pawn.

Averyl opened her eyes and looked about. He watched in puzzlement as she looked to her left and right as well as behind. Had she detected his presence? Cursing, he tucked himself tighter behind the dyehouse and glanced round the side.

A moment later, Averyl plucked away the white cloth adorning her head. With a shake, she moaned, and a cascade of soft curls tumbled down in touchable flaxen waves that ended at her waist.

His belly clenched. *Striking. Enchanting. Exquisite.* The words flowed from his mind.

As he shoved them away, Averyl lifted her tresses and

tossed them about, as if relishing freedom. She arched her lissome body into the evening wind.

Drake's pulse went into turmoil.

Murdoch was unfortunate indeed that he would never know this beauty, even if she was a bloody Campbell, as a wife.

He smiled with malice. Robbing Murdoch of Lady Averyl's wifely comforts would be yet another measure of revenge he had not expected but was more than pleased to deny his half-brother.

An older, unfamiliar man stepped into the garden. He raced to Averyl's side with all urgency, eyes bulging.

"Child, put your wimple on! What if MacDougall sees you? Though he will see all that hair soon enough, you must not reveal that . . . mass until after your vows have been spoken."

Mass? Drake gaped at the addled man's words. Her curls looked soft as down. Without them, she would seem somehow plain, Drake thought. The tresses gave her the appearance of innocence and innate sensuality at once.

With her money-grasping, Campbell-thinking ways, however, such was surely naught more than illusion.

"I am sorry, Father. No one was about, and I grew warm."

The portly man embraced her. "Would that you were a beauty, lamb, a tall girl with smooth hair and a more generous breast. It pains me to chastise you so. I hope you understand."

Averyl nodded stiffly. Drake found himself scowling.

"Now come inside," her father instructed. " 'Tis time and past you retired. Murdoch just informed me that on the morrow you are to be well and truly betrothed!"

A joyous smile lit up her face. She clapped her hands and gave a small shriek of excitement.

Drake wondered how much she knew—or did not know—about her choice of husband.

"Truly?" she asked.

"Truly. Now, get you inside, girl. You must look well for

your betrothal, and this damp air will only curl your hair more."

Some of the light left her eyes as she cast them down. "Of course, Father. I shall retire directly."

The aged lord stayed her when she would have walked away. "I am proud of you, Averyl. In spite of MacDougall's striking figure, you have not shied from your faults. You do me credit."

Averyl turned from her father. Moonlight settled across her solemn face. With a tight squeeze of her lids, she blocked Drake's view to her luminous, expressive eyes. She bit her lip to hold back tears.

Anger washed through him. It irritated him nearly as much as her father did. Ramsey Campbell ought to be beaten, at least until he could see the beauty of his daughter's face.

As he watched her disappear inside the castle, he shrugged the sensation away. Averyl's trials, whatever they might be, were of no concern to him.

Alone now, Drake looked about. Night had fallen completely, a storm was brewing in the angry sky, and the guard he'd gifted with a jug of ale had finally passed out by the wicket gate.

He had missed every possibly lethal clue while watching Murdoch's betrothed. Drake frowned at his lack of concentration, knowing he could ill afford such distraction. In two hours, the course of his life and Murdoch's would forever change.

But perhaps Lady Averyl's would change most of all.

TWO

The MacDougall wanted her for a wife!

Averyl's head swam with the notion, and her blood warmed with relief as she fingered the lavish bracelet of rubies he had placed upon her wrist. 'Twas a prelude to their betrothal, he had said. It mattered not that he wed her only to cease the wars between their clans. In the years to come, she would give him no cause to regret his decision despite her plain face.

Averyl entered her chamber in Dunollie's keep after the evening meal, as all the castle's inhabitants sought their beds. Though she doubted sleep would come this night, she vowed to try. She must look her best for tomorrow's betrothal ceremony.

Shedding her embroidered belt and its matching brocade gown, bought with the last of Abbotsford's funds, Averyl stood clad in her chemise, shivering at the room's chill. She frowned at the pair of weak flames seeming to hover above the candles in the corner, then stared at the empty grate beside it. MacDougall had ordered a fire for her. Wondering at his lazy servants, Averyl made her way to the door with every intent of calling for help.

A noise came, a shuffling behind her. She cast a quick glance at the two small windows. Neither was open to invite the night's breeze. And the shuffle had been too loud for a mouse.

As her heart began to thud, Averyl turned slowly to see what—or who—had invaded her chamber.

Suddenly, the meager light from the candles to her right flickered and died.

Averyl cried out, her heart pounding, as the detested dark enveloped her. The black she had despised since her mother's death closed in, choking the courage and logic from her.

Would she die now? Would it hurt? Would she live to see her marriage to the MacDougall?

The icy rush of her blood heralded prickling apprehension. Cold sweat beaded its way across her skin as her heart threatened to beat out of her chest. No brutal attack came— yet—as she struggled to peer into the frightening, endless black.

An intruder *was* here. She sensed it. Averyl listened, but heard naught except her blood churning in her ears, multiplied by the chilling silence. Saw nothing but shadowed night. Fear pulled at her as mercilessly as a stretching rack.

She glanced about the night-draped room again. Still, the murky gray-black revealed no one, naught sinister.

But the tingling sensation of a hot gaze upon her took root and grew.

Her heart pounded, quickening to a frenzied beat. Fear battled logic in the tense silence. Had her blessed mother felt this way before her death?

"Who comes?" she called, her voice shaking.

Utter hush met her query. The room stood still, clasped in the dark shadows of death. The wind gave a mean rumble outside.

The stare upon her intensified, like a hunter closing in on its prey. Even through the dark, she could feel someone's gaze upon her linen-clad shoulders, her bare legs. Her heart chugged faster as a low-pitched throb vibrated through her body, gathering strength.

Sweet Mary, where could she run?

Suddenly, a broad palm covered her mouth as a hot hand

seized her arm, pulling her against a large form in a coarse
woolen garment.

Terror washed over her in a cold, consuming wave. Gasping, Averyl whirled to face the threat, tried to struggle from
the harsh grip. She opened her mouth to scream but could
not force the sound past the strength of heavy fingers over
her lips.

Averyl strained over her shoulder for a glance of the
fiend. Silvery moonlight beamed through the window, over
a mere corner of the intruder's face. The fearsome specter,
draped in a brown tunic, hovered over her. Nature's light cast
harsh emphasis on his hard jaw and sprawling shoulders.

A moment later, the clouds blanketed the moon again.
The room fell into chilling darkness. A sharp clap of thunder followed, echoing her racing heart.

Defined by shadows, the man leaned toward her. A
scream tore at her throat, trapped still by his hand over her
mouth.

Lightning fast, the stranger backed Averyl to the mattress
and, with the press of his free hand to her shoulders, flattened her against it.

Nay! Her heart beating like a wild beast, Averyl squirmed
and writhed for freedom, kicking at his stomach, his shins.
He grabbed her ankles and clamped them between strong
thighs, rendering her legs immobile.

Bile and terror rose in her throat. Sweet Mary, who was
this villain? Why would he be *here,* staring with cold men-
ace?

How would she escape?

Averyl grunted, straining against his grasp as fear swallowed her. Lungs aching, heart pounding, she watched the
male figure bend over her, his palm still securely clamped
over her mouth, silencing her calls for help.

Fists clenched, she punched him, arms thrashing, landing
blows to his arms and face. He seemed not to notice even
when she pushed futilely against his solid chest. His insistent fingers merely seized her wrists and lowered her arms

to her sides. With her mouth free, she opened it to scream. His returning hand stopped the sound before she could utter it.

One of his unyielding arms reached beneath her shoulders. Trepidation burned through her blood. She turned her face away from his hand.

"Nay!" she screamed, but thunder muffled her cry.

"Not another word," he warned.

His voice told her he was Scottish, but it held a slight English clip. But who was he? Why had he come?

Averyl's mind raced as he fit his other arm beneath her knees and scooped her against him. In desperation, she writhed and screamed as he left the room, but he held her head against his shoulder, muffling her cries.

Fear burned her like a cauldron's fire as he descended the stairs. Where was he taking her? A creaking door precipitated the cool night wind, which served as her only answer.

She looked up, beyond his determined chin and strong nose, feeling his hot breath mingle with the howl of wind tugging at her cap. The garden. Mercy, would anyone see her here?

Knowing 'twas not likely, terror blazed her anew. Fingers bared, Averyl reached out to claw his unfamiliar face. He dodged her attack and set her on her feet.

She made ready to run, but the fiend grabbed her arms, holding them against her sides, then brought her body to his, trapping her thighs between his despite the monk's robe he wore.

His breadth and height eclipsed her, obscured her in black shadow. With little effort, he held her against his hard form and covered her mouth with his hand.

"I've no wish to hurt you," he said, his voice low, smooth.

Not believing him, Averyl jerked away from his touch. "You—you forced me from my chamber. If not to hurt me, why?"

"In good time," he promised into the wind's yowling.

Mistrusting the fiend, Averyl opened her mouth to scream. He slapped a warm palm over her lips once more.

"Do not make me gag you," he warned, then bent to his boot to retrieve a knife.

Averyl's heart bolted faster than lightning at the sight of his silvery blade. She bit into the salty flesh of his palm and tasted blood. With a curse, he tore his hand away. Into the stiff wind she screamed, fighting for her life. He clamped his hand over her lips again and searched about for intruders. To her shock, no one came to her rescue.

"I give but one warning, wench," he bit out.

The stranger reached toward her, a cloth in hand—a knife in the other. She couldn't breathe as she struggled, tearing at his hair, kicking his shins. She succeeded only in slipping to the mud below, falling to her knees before him.

Kneeling, he scooped her up until her feet were beneath her once more. She cringed in dread, panting, as he—and his menacing blade—loomed closer. Averyl wanted to run, but the vicious silver dagger glinted with danger in the stark moonlight.

Averyl closed her eyes, bracing herself for the tearing of her flesh, for the end of her life. Surprise rippled through Averyl when he merely bound her mouth shut, then ripped Murdoch's ruby bracelet from her cold skin with his blade.

Did he but seek to thieve it from her?

With his hot fingers clamped about her wrist, he dragged her over to the square building nearest the enclosure wall. She stumbled at his rapid pace, mud coating her bare feet.

He paused before the small structure. The kirk, she realized, spotting the pale cross gleaming in the moonlight.

The intruder held the bracelet to the dark wood and arched the knife into the enormous door. She started at the thump of the blade as he anchored the bauble in place, leaving it to dangle like a war trophy.

"Murdoch will know who has taken you," he said.

Averyl wondered how.

When he turned to face her again, her captor gathered her against his solid length once more. Averyl pushed against the steel of his chest, resisting his tight grasp as he crept to the wicket gate. He pushed her through it, then ducked to follow close behind, holding her about the waist all the while. Averyl nearly tripped on a pair of sentries lying against the curtain wall, each clutching a jug of ale in their drunken snores.

She would have no help there. Panic rising, Averyl tried to wriggle from his grip, only to find that task impossible.

Her captor clasped one strong hand around the back of her neck, then tore the lacy cap from her head with the other. As he coiled his fingers through her unruly curls, her gaze flew to his, punctuated by her shallow breathing. By the moon's light, Averyl could see the chiseled planes of the brute's hard face, framed by hair the color of midnight. His piercing dark eyes loomed dangerously close.

The wind wailed in the blackness. One of her pale curls lifted with the breeze to smooth across his cheek and skim his neck.

"You cannot escape me," he vowed. "You are only likely to injure yourself in trying."

Her every muscle trembled from exertion, from fear, as she yanked the gag from her mouth. "Y—you plan to k— kill me?"

Averyl had not thought her assailant could look any angrier. Not until she witnessed every muscle in his face tighten.

"If you die, 'twill not be by my hand." His curt explanation did not reassure her, and he offered nothing more.

The man placed the gag over her mouth again and rose. Grasping her wrists together tightly, he dragged her through a dark, dank tunnel for long minutes, then out into the storm's fury again, to a pair of horses tethered in the distance. She stumbled behind him, body stiff, resisting every step of the way.

Turning to one horse, the stranger checked the ties hold-

ing a satchel that looked to be hers. How had he obtained
her belongings?

Before she could begin to guess the answer, the knave
doffed the monk's robe and tossed it aside. Beneath, he
stood taller, broader than she first thought. He wore a simple black tunic and hose, perfect to become one with the
night, which seemed fitting.

The man mounted the dark gray animal, pulling her up
in front of him so that she, too, straddled the saddle. He
clutched her to his chest, preventing any further opportunity
to escape.

Gazing back at the stone keep so close, yet so far away,
her captor growled, *"Buaidh no bas."*

Conquer or die.

Sweet Mary, did he seek to conquer *her?*

The villain urged his mount forward. Averyl fought to
free her hands so she might jump and run. But he held
them too tight. She tried to scream past her gag and prayed
someone would hear and follow, that Murdoch would rescue
her. No one emerged from the castle as it stood stout against
the shrieking wind.

Dunollie Castle shrank in the distance behind them as
he took their journey at a canter. The dervish charted their
course from the main road and into a dense forest. Rain
began to fall, punctuated by an occasional flash of wicked
lightning as they rode farther and farther away from her
father, her future—and the only hope of saving her home.

The thought staggered her. Only his mercy stood between
life and death. Terrified, she sent a promise upward to do
whatever God wanted if only He helped her escape.

The man behind her must have felt her shudder, for he
covered her with his cloak, as if she were cold. As he
reached around her to fasten it, his fingers brushed her
neck. His scalding touch on her chilled skin multiplied Averyl's dread.

Loathing and fury overcame her. Summoning her energy,

Averyl squared her shoulders and stiffened her spine so she no longer leaned against the devil.

Minutes slipped into hours. Hours that became a cold, wet misery as they seemed to gallop toward the bowels of hell. Finally, the sun crept above the horizon, its slow pace mirroring her weariness. She scratched at her heavy eyes. Her back ached as much as her cramped legs. Pressing sharp nails into her palms to remain alert, Averyl straightened away from her captor once more. But she could not avoid the hard thrust of his thighs cradling hers.

As she fought to keep her heavy eyes open, his warmth lured her closer to his sheltering body, against all good sense. As if sensing her weariness, he touched an oddly gentle hand to her shoulder and settled her body against his before her heavy lids slid inexorably shut.

Averyl awoke, feeling a soft bed beneath her. The woodsy crackling of a fire penetrated her senses. How long had she slept?

The clink of a goblet alerted her to the fact she was not alone. Fear chased away the vestiges of sleep.

Opening her eyes, she found a man—her captor—sitting on a worn blue couch in an unfamiliar room. The golden light did naught to soften his features.

Hazarding a glance about, her gaze took in the shabby gray walls of a small room seemingly that of an inn, though not necessarily a reputable one.

The events of the night rushed her memory in an icy stream. Not only had he abducted her; he had not told her his plans now that he had her caged. Kill her? Rape her? Ransom her?

Or all three?

The glow of the fire thrust his hard, chiseled profile into stark relief. 'Twas clear the man had nothing soft about him, not in dress, face, or manner.

Rising above Lord Dunollie and her father, he was tall,

possessed of massive shoulders and hands. If he planned to
kill her, 'twould be no feat for him at all. How could she
fend off a man of such size and strength?

Suddenly, he turned to face her. Gasping, she willed herself to run. But he filled the small room as he stood and
settled dark eyes upon her.

"So, you have awakened."

Realizing he had removed her gag, she demanded, "Who
are you? What reason have you for abducting me?"

Her militant tone was overshadowed by the ill-timed rumbling of her stomach. Averyl pretended not to notice.

He peered silently as he turned to a table behind him.
"We have a lengthy journey ahead of us. Eat, then we will
talk."

Her captor handed her a flask of wine, a bit of bread,
and a small piece of reddish-yellow fruit she had never seen.
She bit into it and grimaced at the sour taste.

Scowling, he grabbed the fruit from her. "You must peel
this before you eat it."

"What is it?" she asked suspiciously, watching his deft
fingers peel back the rind with ease.

"Have you not seen an orange?"

He pulled the last of the rind away, then handed the fruity
orb to her. Not about to confess they'd never had the funds
for such exotic frivolities at Abbotsford, Averyl broke off a
section and gingerly took a bite. After all, she must keep
her strength if she intended to escape.

An unfamiliar tang burst in her mouth. A wonderful taste,
sweet, sour, and juicy at once. A droplet ran to the corner
of her lips. Tilting her head back, she mopped the juice up
with the tip of her tongue.

With a sigh of pleasure, she lifted the flask to her mouth
and found her captor's gaze upon her face.

If heat had an expression, his epitomized the word. He
stared at her mouth. His dark eyes flared above the taut
hollows of his cheeks. Time stopped. A heartbeat. Two. In
silence.

He looked at her as her father's men looked at the beauteous Becca back home, as if he . . . desired her. Averyl drew in a shaky breath, feeling her own heartbeat answer.

Then his look disappeared, replaced by an annoyed scowl that settled over his handsome face.

Averyl felt herself flush for her foolishness. No man would pine for so homely a maid as she—and certainly not a one so fine of face as her captor.

She took a self-conscious swallow of the sweet wine, then another, before she set the flask aside. "I demand you take me back to Dunollie Castle."

Her words engendered no reaction. "Why?"

She hadn't expected that question. "I am to wed the Mac-Dougall chief."

"Are you betrothed? Is that why you wore his bracelet?"

"Aye. He called the bracelet a betrothal gift, and the priest was to come this morn to witness—"

"Then you are not truly betrothed." A flicker of something—relief?—crossed his features. "I see no reason to return you."

The ruin her mother's beloved Abbotsford would become if she did not wed MacDougall taunted her. "But . . . I—I love him."

At that, her captor leaned indolently against the wall and scoffed in disbelief.

"Love is a word men bandy about to coax hesitant wenches into their beds."

" 'Tis not so!" she protested, eyes wide. "Minstrels sing prettily of love—"

"To entertain," he cut in.

"Chivalrous knights fight to protect their loves!"

"Think you men need an excuse to make war?" He raised a challenging brow.

His tone called her foolish and naive, and it raised her hackles.

"You must return me. My home—"

"Will still be standing when I am through with you."

"But its people—"

"Will not suffer in your absence."

"Stop interrupting me, you . . . you varlet, and hear me well. My people will suffer in my absence!"

"They will make due." Neither his face nor voice showed concern as he stood again. "What did you seek from this match?"

"You refuse to listen to me, so I've naught to say." She crossed her arms over her chest.

"Ah, I'm to believe this is a love match?" he said, disbelief heavy in his voice. "Is it his fat coffers that attract you most? Is that love to you?"

She glared at him. "Of course not. 'Tis more."

"But you do not deny that you sought his funds."

"Nay, but I think him a fine man,"

"Fine?" he grunted bitterly.

"He is, you fiend!" This knave would never convince her to think ill of the man she planned to wed.

"Thick-witted wench," he grumbled.

She raised her chin, refusing to heed his insults, his contempt. "You know me not."

"What little I know is enough," he spat. "Though why a wily wench like you should wish to wed a scoundrel like Murdoch befuddles me."

He peered at Averyl as if she were a puzzle he sought to solve. But she would not explain her dream of a caring husband, of a life filled with joy and love absent since her mother's death, to him. He would only mock her further.

"Do you believe yourself so unworthy that you cannot fathom a better man would want to wed you?" he asked.

Shock zipped through Averyl at his intimate knowledge of her fears. "How . . . how did you know?"

She did not realize she had blurted out her question until he answered. "I know much, my lady."

He'd invaded her life, storming her very soul, as he had Dunollie's defenses. She turned a burning glare on him, fury assailed her. "God's blood, what do you want with me?"

"Tell me precisely what you seek from this betrothal?" The flickering firelight revealed the determined heat in his fathomless, black-fringed eyes.

"It is my duty to marry as my father sees fit."

He shot her a suspicious stare. "Though you may possess many virtues, you've not shown me much obedience."

She resisted an urge to run across the room and kick him. "Why should I not wed a wealthy man with enough soldiers to protect my crumbling keep? I want a husband and children and money in our coffers. I refuse to wonder any longer if my home will fall about my feet and our vassals will starve come winter."

"Your conditions are harsh?" His voice reflected the same surprise evident in his frown.

"Entire families die each year we cannot feed them."

He paused, seeming to weigh her answer, and raked a hand through his dark hair. Finally, something seemed to penetrate his armor of arrogance.

"Could you not find another husband to provide all you require?"

"Not anyone wealthy enough to overlook our impoverishment." *Or blind enough to overlook my deficiencies.*

He looked skeptical. "No one else offered?"

"My penniless cousin Robert did, but my father refused him. You must understand, the MacDougall seeks my dower lands in the Campbell territory that once belonged to the MacDougalls. With them, he will bring more peace and prosperity between our clans."

The mean sound the man spit out could scarcely be called a laugh. "Aye, he will continue to tell you how much he desires peace with your kin up until the morn he attacks them."

"I will not believe such a lie," she said. "Murdoch MacDougall is a man of honor. *He* would never resort to thieving a maid from her bed for some nefarious end."

A tightness in his jaw and a momentary flattening of his full mouth betrayed his anger. Still, the violence she sensed leashed within him never surfaced. "You think not?"

"I care not what *you* think," she tossed back. "I demand you release me. I shall be ruined if you do not." The horrifying possibility of losing her home and her best chance at a contented marriage sank in with her statement. "The MacDougall might not wed me at all."

He answered with a cynical grunt. "He would wed you, ruined or nay. He needs you as desperately as you wish to wed him."

"Then return me," she near pleaded.

"Nay."

She placed belligerent hands on her hips. "Why do you seek to prevent our marriage? What manner of man would abduct a maid upon her betrothal?" *A knave would. A miscreant.* She gasped, feeling the blood drain from her cheeks. *A maniacal butcher.*

The truth of his identity hit her like an icy sheet of Scottish winter rain. She swallowed—hard. Her abductor's disconcerting gaze followed her every move.

"Oh, dear heaven!" Her voice trembled as she braced herself on shaky arms. "I know . . . You are the English murderer—the butcher of Lochlan MacDougall!"

He drew in a deep breath, eyes blazing black fury. Beneath taut shoulders, he clenched large fists, sending Averyl's pulse back into turmoil.

"You are Drake Thornton." Even her voice shook now.

Frantic, she looked across the room, toward the door and freedom. Before she could rise and attempt to escape, he flew across the room and anchored his hands on either side of her head, trapping her against the bed. Her mind racing, she tried to roll away and find her feet. The stranger caught her wrists and pulled her back against the mattress, this time bracketing his hands around her waist to prevent her escape.

The pressure of his fingers seared through her clothing,

into her skin. His presence, hot and looming, enveloped her. Dark, shaggy hair brushed the tops of his shoulders, longer than current fashion dictated, and framed a square, angry face. The corded muscles of his neck stood visible above the imposing breadth of his shoulders. The man was no one to trifle with.

Yet she had to risk everything for escape.

"I suppose Murdoch told you that." His voice rumbled from his chest, much like the thunder above.

She nodded unevenly. "Why should you seek to prevent my marriage to him?"

The hard line of his jaw tensed again. "Revenge. He owes me a debt. You are my payment."

She shook her head, imagining all the ways in which he might think to exact payment from her. "Do not touch me."

"I do not seek to claim your . . . charms."

That he seemed to believe she had none filled her with relief and anger at once. Still, Averyl hesitated.

Could she believe a fiend ruthless enough to steal a woman from her chamber, to coldly murder a man? Nay.

Thornton moved closer until he stood inches away. A curious tingling began in her belly. Danger, she was certain, and fear, for she felt it in every nerve of her body.

"Do you plan to kill me?" Her voice trembled.

Wrath and pain tightened his features. "I told you I do not. I have no lust to shed any blood save Murdoch's."

"Ransom me, then?"

"Nay. 'Tis not money I seek, unlike you."

She ignored his contempt. "Then why have you taken me?"

"So I can be certain you do not wed yourself with Murdoch before you turn ten and eight."

Though he seemed serious, Averyl could not believe such a tale. As if he would simply hold her at his side for the coming ten-month and expect nothing.

"You cannot mean to keep me for three seasons."

"I can and I will."

"And if I agree to wed someone other than MacDougall, will you release me?" If he said yes, she could simply return to Dunollie and wed MacDougall.

Her captor's dark eyes narrowed. "I must first be certain that you will not be . . . persuaded to accept Murdoch's suit."

She forced a laugh. "I have no wish to incur your wrath."

His gaze showed suspicion. "But you have no wish to give up such a match, either."

Gritting her teeth, Averyl struggled to find another tactic. She must escape the rogue. He seemed every bit as evil and heartless as Murdoch claimed.

"But I will. I vow it," she fibbed, desperate.

"You are a wretched liar. Mayhap I would accept your tale if you did not fidget."

"You make me nervous!"

"As you make me, so I shall watch you closely." With a grunt, he turned away. "Sleep now. We leave in three hours."

He returned to the other side of the room. When he found the couch, he lay on the too-short piece and shut his eyes.

"By the way, if you try to leave, I will hear. And if you escape, look over your shoulder. I will not be far behind."

Drake lay still for the next half hour, fighting the sleep for which his body ached. The fire had died to mere embers whose shadowy flames danced on the roof's bowed wooden ceiling. Across the small space, Lady Averyl lay, eyes gently closed. Her breathing told him she slept not.

Holding in a curse, he closed his own eyes, waiting for the Campbell wench to find slumber. Drake knew he had hoped in vain when he heard Averyl slip from her blankets and grab his cloak from the floor between them. With a quiet swish, she draped the garment about her, over her thin shift.

Opening his eyes a fraction, he watched her tiptoe toward

the door. Silhouetted by the gray mist of the dawn filtering through the room's small window, she paused and stared at her satchel lying on the ground at her feet.

As Averyl stole a nervous glance over her shoulder, Drake feigned sleep once more. A heartbeat later, she walked on, leaving her bag untouched.

Instead, she crept out the door and down the inn's stairs, treading as silently as the moon through the sky.

Drake rose and peered out after her, now convinced she had not arisen to answer nature's call. He followed, scowling.

Averyl darted down the stairs and faded into the dark of the inn's empty common room. With a curse, Drake hurtled down the stairs after her.

At the bottom, he found no one, heard nothing. Cautiously, he let his gaze circle the room. Damnation, she was small and quick and could probably find a thousand places to hide.

Behind him, a door squeaked open. By the sun's wan morning light, he watched Averyl dash outside. He gave chase, catching sight of her in time to see her sprint down a grassy hill.

Drake pursued her, though, truth told, her determination to escape surprised him. Hysterics he had expected, his mother's favorite tactics. Not Lady Averyl. Although she was lost in unfamiliar surroundings and had no funds or horse to see her back to Dunollie, she continued to vie for freedom. Murdoch's money and her keep, this Abbotsford, clearly meant something to her.

She stopped at the bottom of the hill and peered into the dawning landscape. "Nay, 'tis east?" she questioned, suddenly turning about.

As Averyl faced him, her gaze settled upon him. Her green eyes widened like endless twin fields. She gasped.

"I said there would be no escape." He grasped her wrist.

Determination stamping her pale features, Averyl yanked

free of his hold and darted away, into a thick copse of trees. Damnation, the wench was quick, he thought, following.

Spindly limbs tore at his face like a cat's claws. He swore and swiped at a streak of blood on his cheek, then sprinted after Averyl again, led by the sounds of dried twigs snapping beneath her bare feet. Though such must hurt her in the morning chill, she made no sound as she pressed on.

Flashes of the dark cloak she wore appeared, flapping in the cold air between the summer-green trees. He heard her panting, as if her lungs were near bursting for air. Putting one boot in front of the other, he gave chase, wondering when she would tire.

In the next moments, he realized his rapid footsteps were gaining him ground. Inches in front of him, she fought for another sharp breath. Drake reached out to seize her.

Wrapping his arm about her waist in an implacable grip, he yanked her to his chest. With his hands about her surprisingly small middle, she cried out in protest.

Panting, he turned her to face him. "Have we not struggled enough for your liking?"

She thrashed in his grip. "I will fight you until I die."

Drake brought her closer to still her. Her firm breasts met his chest. A scorch of sensation blazed through him. The rebuke on his tongue died.

She smelled like a trickle of rain on summer grass and some small flower he'd plucked as a child from his mother's garden.

Lust pierced him with a hot thrust, enveloping his body.

Beneath his hands, his stare, she stilled. As she tilted her head back to gaze at him with greenish pools of defiance, an urge to thrust his fingers through the damp waves of Averyl's pale curls and kiss her witless assailed Drake.

Frowning, he peered at her. How could he want *her?* He was no celibate monk pining after any woman's flesh. And as womanly charms went, hers were lovely, but she was his enemy's bride, his pawn only. She was the means to his revenge, not a woman he could slake his lust upon—even if she would have him.

"Damn you," he hissed. "I've had little sleep in three days, and you try my patience. Stop this foolishness."

"I would be foolish if I did not seek my freedom!"

Drake's only reply was a growl. He hoisted his captive over his shoulder and carried her back to the inn with teeth clenched. Past the innkeeper's shocked wife and up the dilapidated stairs they went, until he set her down on the bed with a disgusted grunt and tied her to its post. Shooting her stiff form a warning glare, he turned away to pack up their belongings and douse the fire.

When he'd finished, he approached Averyl. She sat defiantly on a brown woolen blanket. Her small form was nearly swallowed whole by his gray cloak. One bare ivory calf peeked out to tempt him. Her feet bore myriad cuts and scrapes beneath a thin layer of mud. He shook his head. She wanted escape badly to endure such self-inflicted wounds without complaint.

He pushed aside a flash of admiration for the Campbell wench. Despite her brave heart, she was naught but a captive.

Drake rubbed his gritty eyes, his body aching with fatigue. But he could not rest now, not after months of plotting this scheme. And although his captive clearly had her reasons to crave freedom, he must restrain her. The past must be avenged, his honor restored.

Murdoch could not win.

Cursing the cold rain and chilly wind, Drake dragged his small boat onto the grassy shore, anchoring it upon nearby rocks. He leaned down to retrieve Lady Averyl's sleeping form and held her against his chest, her satchel slung over his wrist. She trembled against him, drawing his attention to her unnaturally cold skin. Something like disquiet gripped his belly.

With a frown, he raced up the hillside, across the soft grassy plain, then down the next hill, into the ravine. Averyl lay still in his arms. Cursing, he pushed the gate open with his shoulder and darted inside his little hideaway, tossing Averyl's satchel carelessly into a corner. After laying her across his bed, he lit the dark room with several candles.

Exhaustion and cold pelted him in waves as discomforting as the night's rain. Across the room, Drake spied his slumbering captive. Wearing no more than a shift and a damp cloak, she was, no doubt, chilled to the bone.

He began a warming fire in the hearth, then returned to Averyl. She lay still, alarmingly pale. Fragile and drenched.

Something annoying nagged at him, something he could not quite place. Guilt? He shoved it aside and set his hands beneath the cloak, rubbing her arms to warm them as he cast his gaze about for a blanket.

The icelike chill of her skin could not be ignored; nor could the bruises on her thin arms.

Bruises he knew full well he had created in his urgency.

By the saints, he had not purposely hurt her. But he would have revenge, no matter the cost, even if that meant taking his place beside Murdoch in the ground outside Dunollie's chapel. True, Averyl would emerge from captivity unwed and of questionable virtue, but she would have her life and, someday, the knowledge she had not wed a murderous monster.

Until she learned of Murdoch's true nature, until Drake could safely release her to her family, he could protect her from Murdoch's schemes and her own foolish greed. And have revenge.

The irony did not escape him—a man accused of murder saving his captive from a highland chief. On another day, years before, he might have laughed.

Now he took her chilled hand in his. Snow could not have been colder than her bloodless fingers. The dratted damp wool cloak he had given Averyl during their journey could only be adding to her chill. He cast the garment away with a curse and fished a blanket from his trunk at the foot of the bed.

As he turned to spread the quilt over her, Drake made the mistake of looking at her.

Her heart-shaped face seemed fragile, somehow innocent, despite the fact she was a Campbell wedding a MacDougall for gold. The slight point of her chin hinted at the rebellion in her nature. Strands of her long, pale curls were plastered wetly to her cheeks and throat. Making his way to her side, he pushed the wayward curls aside to blend with those dotting her temples.

Past her pallid, frigid shoulders, his gaze wandered, to her breasts, visible through her transparent shift. His breath left his lungs in a hiss.

The rosy tips of Averyl's firm breasts stood taut with cold. Gently rounded, they were like twin beacons of seduction giving rise to the red embroidery of the low neckline.

Lust lurched into his throat, then sped into his loins. He swallowed to force it down and clasped his father's cross about his neck to remind himself of all that mattered.

Still, it did not stop him from gazing farther down her body, over her small waist, past the gentle flair of her hips. Drake stopped his perusal again, this time on her sleek, firm thighs and the light-colored thatch visible between them.

With lightning speed, desire slammed into him once more, shocking him with its strength. His only clear thought was that he wanted to lose himself there. He wanted those thighs around him, open and ready for his entrance.

Drake whipped his gaze away. He was not a randy boy lacking control. Averyl was cold; he could warm her. It meant naught.

Quickly, he sliced the wet, diaphanous garment from her shivering body, trying not to look—or think of all the possible ways he could touch her. But image after vivid image of her ivory skin and welcoming arms around him flashed into his mind.

Muttering an earthy curse, he tucked her beneath his blankets and turned toward the fire. Why her? He'd seen more comely women. Hell, even bedded a few. She was his captive, Murdoch's betrothed, and a Campbell. She would shrink from him in horror if she knew his gaze had touched her every curve.

Yet his body wanted her still.

Drake cursed, forcing his mind elsewhere. He had accomplished his first goal—to abduct the woman Murdoch must wed. Yet he'd come away surprised. Averyl had proven herself a strong, resourceful woman—no mere pawn.

Sitting back, he stared into dancing flames. Averyl had not been, as he'd assumed, living in luxury. Nor was she the spoiled and vain creature his mother had been. But she was still a fool. 'Twas admirable to seek coin for her home and people, to sacrifice herself to the ruthless Murdoch. Or did she simply love gold enough to bed down with the merciless man of means?

Drake stood. Averyl and her reasonings mattered not. Nor did his lust for her. His father's death, as well as his own torture, demanded revenge. When he released Averyl, he would give her enough funds to repair her keep and plant new crops.

If he still lived.

Frowning darkly, he prepared a pallet by the door. As for his lust, he must ignore it. Mayhap a bit of sleep would cure him of this want.

Averyl moaned in her sleep. Despite Drake's vow moments ago, his imagination reeled with images of their bodies damp with passion, limbs tangled in urgent need. Nay, he had no need to seduce the wench. But no matter how he told himself to forget the idea, long into the night that very male part of him ached to know how fulfilling such a seduction would be.

Three

Averyl woke, a soft featherbed beneath her. Something tugged at her, a foreboding that all was not well. Images rushed back to her of a tall brigand stealing her from her very bed. From her betrothal. Had a knave truly dragged her away from her future? Nay, could be no more than a nightmare.

Then she recalled his face, all hard angles and midnight eyes, as well as the angry chill in his manner.

Eyes closed, she frowned against memory. But she could not deny the truth. The man who had stripped her of MacDougall's costly gift, then carried her into the darkness, was real.

To a small inn he had taken her. The tang of fruit and his odd, heated glance lingered in her memory. His name . . . Drake Thornton. Lochlan MacDougall's murderer.

Her captor.

Averyl's eyes flew open wide at the truth. She scarcely had time to note the unfamiliar, old room and the heavy thud of her racing heart before she felt the warm quilt slide down.

Over her naked breasts.

With a gasp of shock, she jerked the covers about her chin. A thousand frightening images of what might have happened while she slept roared in her head, all too appalling to contemplate.

Averyl searched about for something—clothing, a clue, the rogue who had stripped her. Her gaze skated over a carved wooden chair. A blazing fire spit into the silence, hissing, cracking, lighting her spartan surroundings.

He held her in a cottage, she guessed from the walls of unbaked sod and the thatched roof. A battered table, a trunk, and the bed beneath her occupied the tidy domain. Simple and functional, the room possessed no colors, no softness.

Her satchel lay on a blackened hearth, near two sturdy black boots, which moved suddenly to face her. She swallowed as fear nipped at her composure. Her gaze traveled up a powerful pair of muscled legs outlined in dark hose, past lean hips. Her stare paused at his tapered waist and broad chest, covered by a simple dark green tunic, then slid upward over the might of wide shoulders to the remarkable face from her nightmares last eve.

A shortness of breath assailed her. Drake Thornton was no beautifully savage product of her imagination, but real flesh and blood—and genuine danger.

Her captor lifted a log to feed the hearth's dying fire. The strength apparent in the thick coil of his arms pricked her with a strange heated trepidation.

At least, given her homeliness, she would not have to concern herself with his lustful attentions. The desirous glance he had seemed to give her at the inn had been naught but an illusion, another reason to distrust the dark.

He dropped the log into the flames. Averyl's heart pumped furiously, nearly obliterating the sizzle and roar of the fire.

Thornton looked up. Their eyes met. Jet brows rose as his assessing gaze traveled her face, then dipped to take in her bare shoulders. Averyl clutched the blanket beneath her chin as a frightened child would a beloved parent.

"Are you well?" he asked.

"I have on not a stitch of clothing!" she shrieked. Eyes narrowing, she accused him. "You did this."

"You'll not find another soul for miles."

"You—you . . . For what purpose did you bare me, fiend?" She prayed he had not ravished her for revenge.

"My purpose was not lascivious, if that is your concern."

Lips curved up in a cool smile, he turned away. Averyl knew his denial should relieve her. Embarrassment flared to heated life instead. He, too, found her ugly, enough to laugh at the notion of touching her. She bit her lip, appalled that her pride stung so fiercely.

Knowing he thought her plain should set her at ease. 'Twas foolishness to feel aught else! She should be glad to be alive and unharmed, not worried what a murdering varlet thought of her.

Thornton stacked another log on the blazing fire that heated the dingy room. "I sought to prevent you from catching your death, Lady Averyl."

Her gaze flew to him in surprise. "You know my name?"

"That and more," he said, facing her again. His silky rasp set her nerves on alert. "You hail from Abbotsford, near the English border. You were born February twenty-fourth, 1469. Your middle name is Elizabeth."

She clutched her quilt tighter as he crossed the room to stand less than an arm's distance away. Thornton's dark eyes held her wide gaze captive with frightening ease. Her heart pumped faster. The air between them seemed scarce as she fought to breathe.

"You are Ramsey Campbell's only child," he went on. "Your English mother was sister to the duchess of Portsmouth. She died in September of 1475, when you were but six years old. You had almost become betrothed to Murdoch MacDougall, a stranger to you." He hooked a finger beneath her chin. "You are an impoverished innocent who believes herself plain."

Averyl twisted away from his disquieting touch, mouth wide open. Though she knew almost nothing of Thornton, he had whittled her entire existence down to a few curt sentences. He had ripped through the barrier protecting her memories and hiding her fears. Stripped her soul bare. Studied her life for his evil purpose. Exposed her in a way nakedness never could.

"H-how did you learn so much of me?"

He shrugged. "That is unimportant now."

Unimportant that her life had been examined by a stranger? That her most private, shameful beliefs were known by a murdering madman? She found nothing unimportant about having a sinfully handsome butcher stare at her as if she were an aberration of nature. "It bloody well is not! Tell me."

"You are in no position to give orders."

His unreadable gaze slid over her face, dropping to her bare shoulders, before he turned to the hearth. A vexing mix of shame and relief slid through her at his silent snub. Her bony shoulders would never tempt a man like him—and all the better!

"Where have you brought me?" she demanded.

He whirled to her again, his gaze slicing the distance between them. "To a heavily vegetated ravine on an isolated isle. If you hope a traveler will find you and take pity, you hope in vain. There's but one way off of this island, and I have hidden the boat. I also enclosed the ravine with a locked gate topped by pikes."

"Say you that I am trapped here until I hand you my future? Until my people starve and my home crumbles to the ground?"

Thornton returned to her side. His face hovered mere inches from hers, where she could hear his breath, scent something spicy and warm upon him.

"Until you turn ten and eight," he clarified. "Your father, if he pretends to be any kind of man, will find another method of fixing the ills of your people. Wedding his daughter to a wealthy man he scarce knows is common enough but foolish."

"My father sought a good match. He is a wise man—"

"But a blind one." Thornton strode away to tend the fire.

Averyl stared at her captor, a frown creasing her brow.

He clearly held the mistaken belief that MacDougall was some manner of villain. How, when Thornton himself had done nothing but act barbarously? And for what reason did he think her father blind?

Before she could question him, he turned to face her again.

"The gate has but one key." He paused to fish it from a small pouch within his codpiece at the apex of his hose. "Have no doubt, I would feel your touch, should you try to retrieve it. But then, if you put a hand in this pocket, I would assume you sought . . . something else."

"You have a depraved mind! I doubt you possess anything worth touching other than yon key."

Thornton shrugged as if her opinion meant naught to him. Likely it meant even less. Still, his gaze traveled over her shoulders, the swells of her breasts, once more.

Disturbed by his inspection, she pulled the blanket up higher. "Release me now." As hoped, her words returned his attention to her face. "I vow to wed someone other than the MacDougall, even cousin Robert, if 'twill please you."

He shook his dark head, clearly disbelieving. "You desire Murdoch's funds too badly. Besides, I need you here until your next birthday."

"This abduction is senseless," she railed. "Why do you care if the MacDougall and I are wed?"

His unnerving, unwavering gaze whipped back to her face. Refusing to back down, she glared in return.

"We have discussed this. My motives concern you not."

A new flash of fury seared her. Did he not understand the consequence of his actions on her life? Aye, he did. The heartless monster would end her hopes, crush any chance of restoring Abbotsford and enjoying a loving husband's arms. "Concern me not? Your selfish revenge will cost me my future!"

He paused, jaw taut. "When I am able, I will give you coin to save your home."

"When you are able?" she countered, clutching the sheet

below her chin in a tight grip. " 'Tis not enough. Even *if* our people survive the winter, I ask you, what husband will share Abbotsford with me? Whose children will occupy its halls? Your vengeful need will ensure I lose an honorable man willing to call *me*"—she pointed to herself—"his lady wife."

He approached again, face alive with anger. His penetrating eyes, tousled dark hair, and three days' growth of beard all lent him the look of a ruthless warrior. She refused to back away when he sat beside her, the mattress dipping with his weight.

"Honorable man?" he queried, grasping her arm. "You know naught of Murdoch. Do not be taken in by his pretty smile or his money. My revenge will see justice done, save the hides of your Campbell cousins, and rectify the damage of Murdoch's evil."

"His evil?" she countered, anger a hot flow in her blood. "Have you forgotten your own misdeeds?"

A chill slashed across his lean face, filling the dark contours with shadow.

"Murdoch put forth the coin for Lochlan MacDougall's murder and pointed the finger at me. I mean to make him pay for that."

Wildly, she shook her head. Such was not possible. Thornton had killed Murdoch MacDougall's sire. How could her abductor possibly claim Murdoch had been responsible?

" 'Tis not so. Murdoch said—"

"Murdoch said?" he countered sharply. "So it must be true?"

Drake stood, arms crossed over his broad chest like a warrior who had no doubt of a battle's outcome. The snug fit of dark gray hose and black boots accentuated long, muscled legs. His emerald tunic strained across the breadth of his shoulders, making Averyl aware that if he had lied and truly planned to kill her, she had little chance of stopping him.

Beneath an ominous scowl, his black eyes blazed with a riot of emotions. If Murdoch was a childhood fantasy, Drake Thornton represented a darker demon, the antithesis of all she'd sought in life, like the untamable dragon of old lore.

Just like those dragons, Thornton was immeasurably dangerous.

"At least he presented facts. What have you to say but threats and oaths?"

"Here is a fact: I was given not a moment to speak in my own defense." His tone was bitter, his eyes bleak. "No one cared how a blood-wet knife came to rest betwixt my feet. Within hours, your Murdoch convinced the clan of my guilt. They cheered like drunkards at a fair when he vowed to torture, then kill me."

Averyl did not doubt Murdoch's judgment had been correct, though the swiftness of his justice did seem abrupt. Still, she refused to be drawn into whatever game he played with his lies.

"How does preventing my marriage to MacDougall gain you revenge?" she asked.

He cocked a brow. "You know not about the will?"

"What will?"

He muttered a nasty oath and began to pace. "God's teeth."

Averyl winced at his curse. "What will?"

" 'Tis of no consequence now," he asserted, frowning.

Averyl knew from the strength of his grasp and the intensity of his dark eyes that he spoke false. The will was of consequence. Great consequence, she suspected.

"I demand you tell me what will you speak of!"

"You make too many demands, wench." His stern face reiterated that he would tell her no more on the subject now.

"So what will you do to me?" she asked.

His gaze brushed her face, her shoulders, before he

looked away. "I told you last eve I've no wish to harm you."

Averyl shook her head, refusing to believe Thornton's empty assurances. "And what of Lord Dunollie? You despise him."

"Aye."

The taut face and harsh eyes before her revealed his intent. "Enough to kill him, is that not so? *That* is your plan."

"Aye."

She needed to escape, to warn Murdoch, but how? Thornton had already defined her isolated prison hell. Somehow she would have to succeed, catch Thornton's guard down— if it ever fell.

He grabbed her bare shoulders with hot palms, pulling her frighteningly close. "Make no mistake, he will kill me, too. Upon his first chance."

Averyl scowled, and her mind raced between finding a way to escape and understanding Thornton's bizarre scheme. "You intend to kill Murdoch, yet you believe you will die as well?"

"Aye." He jerked his hands from her and turned away to pace.

"And believing you will die, you carry through with your plan?" Her sharp tone reflected her incredulity.

"Of course."

" 'Tis insane. Inhuman! Have you no wish to live, no regrets about killing others? Have you no feelings about dying?"

He whirled to face her, jaw clenched.

"I do not kill off the battlefield. For Murdoch, I will make an exception."

Shrugging the tension from his broad shoulders, he continued, "As for my own death, I have no life as a fugitive. If I have feelings about my death, they matter not. Emotions are a weak man's luxury I can ill afford."

Averyl could not stop her widening eyes or gaping mouth. "No one can extinguish their emotions thus. You cannot blow out the contents of your heart as you do a—a candle."

He sliced through her objection with a cutting glance. "You are wrong. Such feeling reeks like a pit of slimy water. Having seen others drown there before, I will not be dragged into those murky depths."

She was in a nightmare beyond her worst imagining. She'd barely believed herself abducted, but to be trapped with this emotionless ruffian? Unthinkable. He plotted to kill the man who would save her home, the man she'd waited a lifetime for. It could not be borne. She must escape, tonight!

Tears came to her eyes, constricting her throat. "Why in God's name do you plot this mad scheme?"

"As I've said, revenge," he answered tersely.

"A man so close to the grave does not need vengeance."

"I prefer to die in peace."

His statement hit her like an icy gust of wind. "You selfish cur! You destroy my life so you can go to your self-imposed death in peace? I would love to see hardship forced on you. Mayhap it would teach you to appreciate another's pain."

The hard line of his jaw tightened. "I understand pain. I *lived* it in Murdoch's dungeons. Now he will live it."

Thornton was cruel and barbaric, and if she knew how to curse, she would tell him how much she despised him in a way he could assuredly understand.

He rose and strode to the door. "Should you like to bathe, there is a pond outside. When you've finished, your clothing is in your satchel, which I set in the corner."

His suddenly cool tone rankled her. "Outside? How convenient. Had you planned to watch?"

His dark eyes slid over her bare shoulders and quickly swept her form, outlined by the thin quilt, before returning to her face. His eyes were no longer cold. Averyl's pulse jumped.

"Do you invite me?"

Fury rose, arming her words with fire. "I would not invite you to hell, though it's where you deserve to be."

He reached her in less than a heartbeat. His fingers twisted around her arm, pulling her close. Averyl struggled to maintain hold on the quilt.

"Open your saucy mouth all you like, but remember, I control whether or not you eat, bathe, wear clothing, speak—your whole life. And I control it indefinitely."

Dismayed, Averyl did not, could not, move. Two months ago she had been giggling with Becca, the daughter of Abbotsford's steward. Now she was the captive of a brutal stranger on an isolated isle. This nightmare that had ensnared her life swirled around her, creating a torrent of confusion. Naught made sense, least of all why Thornton had abducted her.

The will he refused to speak of was the key, but she knew nothing of the document, least of all who had written it.

Running bare through the chilly cottage, Averyl retrieved a shift from her satchel. Tears scalded her throat, but she refused to shed them. Instead, she settled the thin garment over her, wondering if the elusive will was tied to the sordid incident Murdoch had refused to discuss with her.

She could not think on that now. She must concentrate on the moment, seize any method of escape Thornton might have overlooked. For she did not believe he intended to do nothing more than keep her beneath his roof until she turned a year older. What her role would be, she did not want to contemplate.

Resolving she would not give up, Averyl searched her luggage for something to wear. Tossing out garment after garment, she sighed in frustration. Blast it, the bag was filled with only her finest dresses, those suitable to mark her as MacDougall's lady wife. Fragile garments that would not travel well and showed more of her small bosom than she liked.

Snatching a purple dress to her breast, she decided the choice mattered not. The display was not for Thornton. Her infuriating captor would not note if she looked well or care how much skin she bared. His searching glances meant naught. Perhaps he had merely wondered how a chief of Murdoch's ilk could marry a girl so lacking in womanly charms. Certainly a man as magnificent in face and form as Thornton could have any woman he desired. The unfeeling beast had no reason to spare her a second glance.

Worse, his imperious manner told her Thornton was accustomed to giving orders and having them obeyed. Tugging her dress over her small frame, Averyl vowed to be the most rebellious captive ever. With all her strength and courage, she would fight him until she found freedom—and her way back to the MacDougall.

For that, she'd need a weapon. Her gaze scanned the room. Nothing she could use to harm him rested in the basket of fruit on the three-legged table. There was naught ominous about the hearth, blackened by frequent use, or the motley collection of small pots, kettles, and wooden spoons dangling inside on a stick. And nary a knife in sight! She skimmed over an old spindle-backed chair, a cypress basin with a clay pitcher, and her satchel in the corner. Naught of use.

Then her gaze zeroed in on the thin object leaning in the corner. The iron poker he'd used to stoke the fire! Aye, she would knock him unconscious, steal his key, free herself from this ravine prison, and find his hidden boat. 'Twas so simple!

Averyl dashed across the room. Her fingers slid around the cold metal. Relief swelled inside her as she hoisted the weapon over her head. It weighed more than she had anticipated. But she could lift it once; once was all she would need.

A moment later, she heard the *thump* of Thornton's

booted footsteps outside. Averyl scurried across the floor, purple dress swishing about her legs, and moved toward the door. Then, climbing on the hearth, she hid behind the portal as Drake swung it open.

He stood motionless, towering in the doorway, the breadth of his shoulders spanning the door's frame as he scanned the room. Instantly, her breathing shallowed with his presence, her spine tingled with his nearness.

Pushing her anxiety aside, she took a breath behind him and lifted the weapon.

Four

With a grunt of effort, Averyl lowered the poker, aiming for the back of Thornton's shaggy, dark head.

As if sensing her intent, he ducked and dodged to the side. The poker struck his shoulder with a low thud.

Then he cursed as he turned to face her. Annoyance stormed across his angled face. With a scowl, he stared at her, then stripped the poker from her grip.

Though her stomach tightened with fear, she regarded him with unblinking defiance. "Though I am certain you glower at everyone who displeases you, you scare me not."

He returned her stare with a raised brow and silence.

"Do you practice that look in a glass, hoping to scare people from their sanity?" she snapped. "For it works not."

Besides extreme irritation, he looked somewhat surprised that she had dared such an attack. And intent that she should not hit him again by the way he gripped that iron poker.

His silence unnerved her until she began to feel like a child who'd been caught filching a sweet and now awaited punishment. She crossed her arms over her chest. Aye, she had never thought herself long on courage, but Drake Thornton would not cow her without a single word.

"More than once I have heard you speak, so I know you can." She sent a challenging stare his way.

The corners of his flat mouth began to curl, though she would hardly call such a smile.

"I can speak when I have need. I do not practice my

glowering in a glass. And you're a fool if you have not the sense to be scared of me, though I expect a lack of sense from a bloodthirsty Campbell wench."

After that, Drake resumed his silence. Why did she seem full of bravery one moment, then speak needily of love in another? And if she sought love, why did she wed for money? He shook his head, hoping to dislodge the mystery she presented, and gripped the iron poker between tight fingers.

Lady Averyl had opened the cottage's shutters to the morn's light. It filtered in with a brilliant summer cheer that lit upon her fair hair, seeming to alight it with a thousand different shades of gold as it tangled in a pale entwining and tumbled across one shoulder. She stood before him, seemingly determined to be brave.

Averyl reminded him of Botticelli's Venus, ethereal yet elemental. Lust pierced him like a longbow through armor despite the fact she had done her best to put a dent in his skull. Drake wanted to tousle her, engage the fiery side of her spirit. Arouse her, possess her. Bury his hands in her riotous curls and bed her.

Foolish. Dangerous. So unlikely to ever happen.

He must focus on his revenge, never forget that Averyl was an intelligent woman, gifted with perhaps an even craftier ability to entrance and confuse than his mother had possessed. For he saw now that Averyl's fragility was an illusion, just as his desire for her was a curse.

Drake held the poker between them. "Careful, else this could injure someone."

"If only it would, preferably by making a dent in your skull!"

Her dress clung lovingly to the slight curve of her breasts as she moved with furied conviction. A fresh wave of desire, thick and hot, settled in his loins. Why could Averyl have not been as plain as she believed? And meek besides?

Shoving the questions aside, he took the last step toward

Averyl, watching her eyes grow wider. With fear and fury, aye. But something new. What? Curiosity? Challenge?

"And I would gladly hit you again, harder."

How unusually honest she was. Tenacious and rampageous, too, just like his friend Aric's lady wife, Gwenyth. He frowned. But Gwenyth possessed not the tendency to sentiment and greed his captive and his mother shared. Averyl was indeed a puzzle.

Drake gripped the poker. "Then I consider myself warned and will put this from temptation's way."

"You cannot keep me here!"

"I can and I am."

The sound of her curse followed him as he made his way outside. That he ignored as he shut the door between them.

Then he heard a sob, quiet, muffled. Drake strained closer to the window to hear. Was that shrew-mouthed Averyl?

Again it came. Aye, 'twas her. Drake frowned as something foreign bit at his gut. It could not possibly be guilt. This revenge was necessary, his very life. Then why did he feel . . . badly?

Drake set the poker aside. Had he not learned to ignore a woman's tears from infancy? Aye, and why Averyl's should bother him, he could not fathom. Shoving his fingers through his hair, he searched for clarity, only to find a muddle where logic normally lived. Damnation.

Averyl sniffled. Drake's gut clenched. He rubbed the aching shoulder she had struck to remind him she was the enemy. But imprisoning her now seemed . . . wrong. Frowning, he wondered when he had deemed his act unjust. After he'd beheld those bright eyes in her comely face and saw her fiery desperation?

Drake paced. She was a pawn in his scheme. An intriguing pawn, aye, but a pawn all the same. True, she had a home to rebuild and vassals to aid. She had a right to a wedded life, if she foolishly chose it. And he wanted her in his bed. But all must wait until justice had been served.

* * *

Averyl crept outside minutes after Thornton. Within moments, she discovered he spoke true. Escape would be near impossible.

The ravine, steep as a cliff all about, was a narrow strip of land hidden by an abundance of wild heather and short grass, brambles, rock, and eternal Scottish mist. So far up did its vertical walls reach, she could scarcely see to the land above.

Giant oak trees sheltered the hideaway from prying eyes by fanning the sky with their far-reaching branches. The ancient trees swayed with the wind, their leaves forming a wall of lush green that convinced outsiders nothing lay below nature's display of summer. Beyond that, she heard the tempestuous crash of the surf against the isle's shore.

The gate he spoke of would indeed keep her trapped. Averyl stared up at its impossible height and the razor edge of the pikes atop it, lethal and smiling, as if inviting her to court death. Anger welled in her throat and burned her belly.

Thornton had her trapped, damn him. He had no right to intrude thus upon her life. What would become of Abbotsford, its vassals and gardens, should this captivity last? What of the village, her heritage, her father?

What would become of her?

The barbarian had ruined her plans to wed. If she wished to save them, she needed the key to the gate. He knew such.

She must steal the key. To accomplish such a feat, she would have to search his pocket—when he did not wear his hose. For that, Thornton would have to be asleep. She refused to put her hands anywhere near his powerful thighs and manly secrets. He was bold enough to believe she encouraged him and more than male enough to bed her, if only for sport.

Averyl bit her lip. She plotted rebellion against a known killer. 'Twas foolish, but she could not remain. If she did, her future would disappear like a drop of water in an ocean.

And the hate that seemed to permeate his every word and gesture might seep into her soul. Indeed, 'twas certain. Already she was learning to hate him back.

Murdoch entered the solar, striding past his leman's belly, with a curse on his lips. She scurried forward to greet him. He silenced her with a glare and proceeded to his chair.

"I hiv had a bath prepared for ye," she whispered.

One glance at her coy expression sent his temper soaring. "Back to the kitchen with you, wench! I've much to do."

Whores, every last one, from his first woman to this last. Naught changed. Each used their bodies for their gain.

Murdoch eyed the pouting redhead as she exited with a protective hand over her rounding belly. Aye, she'd made no secret of the fact she sought a husband of consequence to claim her and her brat.

He stripped off sweaty traveling clothes and sank into the warm water with a sigh. Though she'd vowed the child was his, Murdoch knew he had not been the only man between her thighs. And a fool she was if she believed the simple wifely act of preparing a bath would induce him to give up on Lady Averyl.

Damn his half-brother Drake! Averyl had been missing for nearly four days, and they had found only the sketchiest clues regarding her whereabouts. Still, he refused to rest. After scrubbing himself clean, he rose.

His bride no doubt looked for him each day with her lovesick gaze, awaiting rescue. He would not let her down.

Murdoch dressed quickly. His plan was in motion. When the two were found, Averyl and the wealth of land—which had once belonged to MacDougalls—along with the power that came with their marriage would be his. As for Drake, he sincerely hoped the whelp of his father's English whore found hell even more torturous than the slow death Murdoch vowed to provide.

After a brief knock, Wallace, his cousin and steward, entered the darkening room.

"Come in," he barked. "What news have you?"

"We have word from the west," Wallace said. "A man claiming connection to Clan MacDougall possesses information."

Murdoch stopped pacing. "Does he come here?"

"Aye, within the half hour."

Nodding with satisfaction, Murdoch clenched his fists. "And our soldiers, are they still searching?"

"Morn and eve."

"I have looked through filth and down countless dusty roads for Lady Averyl." He turned accusing eyes to Wallace. "Do not disappoint me with more failure."

Clearing his throat, Wallace assured, "We will see justice served for Drake MacDougall."

Anger roared until Murdoch heard it pound in his ears. "Drake is *not* a MacDougall. He is not worthy of any name but his whorish mother's."

"But your father was wed to—"

"Aye, my father married that English slut Diera and got a brat on her. But the son of such a woman will *never* bear the MacDougall name, not from my tongue!"

Wallace nodded. "As you wish, my lord."

The placating expression on his cousin's face annoyed Murdoch. But the business of capturing his half-brother loomed more important. "Drake cannot have taken Averyl too far, certainly not to that grandfather of his in England. Not yet, anyway. We must find them, and soon."

Wallace shuffled his feet. "With all due respect, my lord, what if Drake has killed her?"

"He would not," Murdoch growled. "Such an event would release me from my father's cursed machinations."

"Drake has always dared much," Wallace pointed out.

"On that we agree, but to kill her would achieve him naught and gain me everything."

"Could you not declare the girl dead? Such would give

you leave to marry another with more wealth and connections—"

"It must be her unless I can produce her corpse. My
father's will states that I will inherit only after I wed Averyl
and end this bloody feud with the Campbells."

"Ah, so you must find her and marry her?"

He clenched his jaw, cursing his father's manipulations
from beyond the grave. "Precisely."

Moments later, a castle guard appeared with an elderly,
stoop-backed peasant, a fisherman. He shuffled in, his slow
movements relating pain. His stark silver hair accented
black eyes that glittered with anticipation.

Murdoch chafed with impatience. "Well, what news do
you bring?"

The old man's gnarled fingers gripped his weathered
cane for support as he lowered himself into the nearest
chair. " 'Tis an honor to meet ye, me lord."

"Indeed." Murdoch ended the chatter with a glare. "Tell
me where to find my half-brother so I may say the same."

"Aye, me lord. I saw him two days past."

"Alone?" Murdoch hovered over the peasant.

"Nay. 'Twas with a woman he traveled."

"Describe her," he demanded.

"I dinna see her weel. She was a wee thing, mind ye.
Her hair was fair, as was her skin."

Murdoch nodded. The description seemed accurate
enough. "Which way did they travel? Could you tell?"

"Aye, me lord, I could."

After her bath, Averyl returned to the cottage as twilight
painted the Scottish sky a misty blue gray. Relief seeped
through her when she lit two tapers in the dark dwelling
and discovered herself alone.

Quickly, she ran a brush through her hair, braided it, and
tucked it beneath her cap. Frowning into the glass, she wondered why she bothered. Perhaps her mass of curls would

revolt her captor, ensure he kept his distance. Still, she hated to see them loose, to be reminded of all her faults.

With a sigh, she sat on the bed. Why had she not been born with silky hair and rosy cheeks like Becca? The mass of her pale curls next to an equally pale face made her look sickly. Her wisp of a figure did naught to dispel the image.

Bother! Her appearance mattered not. She would wed Murdoch, who had seemed pleased enough with her, when she emerged from this hell. And while here, she had no wish for Thornton to think her attractive. He was Murdoch's enemy, a murderer who would use her for his revenge at the expense of her future. He was no more than a hate-crazed beast.

Aye, but that odd moment of heat she had once seen in his eyes while she ate his orange made her . . . restless. No denying, he was sinfully handsome. Under other circumstances, he would never cast a second glance in her direction. Such a realization annoyed her.

Nay, she hoped Thornton thought her ugly. Returning to Dunollie and the MacDougall, to the match she might still make and the certainty that she could see Abbotsford's great keep prosper in her mother's memory—nothing more mattered.

Thornton entered the dwelling as the sun began to fall. Averyl turned to face him, only to find him bare-chested.

She felt her eyes go wide as her gaze covered him. The dark, golden skin of his impossibly broad shoulders glistened with water droplets. So did the powerful torso that tapered into a lean, muscled waist. Struggling for her next breath, she watched a droplet descend from his navel, down over his rigid abdomen, to the tangle of hair that narrowed into a thin line to the waist of his breeches—and lower.

The cottage suddenly felt smaller and warmer.

Without a word, he draped his tunic across the back of the spindle-backed chair. His thick arms were those of a seasoned warrior, corded and veined with muscle. Scattered scars appeared, a nick here, a gash there, all long healed.

As he moved, Averyl saw the play of hard-muscled flesh across his shoulder blades. She swallowed at the reminder of his power, which gave him the strength to hurt her if he chose.

He stepped beside the candle and bent to his boot. The golden flame lit on his wide back and the dozens upon dozens of puckered scars that crisscrossed there, some screaming red, some a painfully mute white.

She gasped.

Thornton whirled to face her, dark eyes glittering, hostile. "My scars offend you?"

"N-nay. I but . . . You . . ." she stammered. "I had no—"

"You can thank the *honorable* man you sought to marry for them. Murdoch does enjoy a hearty whipping."

Cold shock assaulted her system as she stared in silence. Nay. Could not be true! Hate merely deluded Thornton, devouring the core of his soul. He wanted her to think only the worst of the MacDougall.

What if Thornton spoke the truth?

She shuddered. No human being deserved such mistreatment, whatever his crimes.

Scowling, Thornton changed the subject. "Have you eaten?"

"Nay." Her voice trembled. "I have not an appetite."

His gaze sliced to hers, eyes narrowing as if to probe her thoughts. He strode toward her, a challenging glint in his eyes that did not bode well.

A voice within Averyl screamed to back away. Her pride would not let her.

"Do you find my scars so repulsive that you cannot eat?"

He was too near, his mood sharp and dangerous, like the edge of a blade. Averyl tried to control her uneven breathing, to break the hold of his dark gaze on hers. Thornton's stare stayed, allowing no retreat.

"I fear nothing about you," she answered, chin raised.

"Then why do you shake?" Thornton turned away and stalked across the room. "You've no need to skitter about like a frightened rabbit. You are safe with me. Unless you wish it, I will not touch you."

"Perhaps I would not *skitter* were your disposition more pleasant," she retorted through clenched teeth.

As he faced her once more, his eyes narrowed. " 'Tis a fool you are if you think I will behave any particular way so that you may regard me as pleasant."

"Then a fool I must be." She infused her voice with a razor edge. "I had supposed that a man with a beating heart, with feelings, would perhaps attempt some measure of civility in light of the fact my future is ruined." She paused. "Oh, but you haven't any feelings, have you? 'Tis doubtful you even possess a heart. How foolish of me to forget."

"I can see your father did not teach you to dull the sharp edge of your tongue."

"Nor would I have listened."

Jaw taut, he turned away once more. "Go to bed. I've no interest in sparring with you further this night."

"I've no interest in sparring with you at all!"

That said, Averyl whirled to the bed in the center of the room. Having conducted a tour of the small cottage, she knew the dwelling had but one other room—one that lay empty, void of any furnishings, much less a bed. She swallowed, then cast a surreptitious glance back at her captor.

"Where will you sleep?"

Wearing a smile, he dragged his gaze over the rumpled bed.

"You cannot!"

The smile widened. "Do you fear for your virtue?"

"Aye." Realizing she'd just implied that Thornton would want a homely maid like her in his bed, she flushed. "Nay."

She swallowed again. Would he take her if only because he had no other woman available to ease his manly urges?

With a resolute shake of her head, she clarified, "I know naught of your plans or thoughts."

"You know not if I desire you." He raised a jet brow. "Is that not the question?"

Heat, part excitement, part chagrin, coursed through her. She cast her glance to the uneven mud floor. Could he possibly want her? She opened her mouth, but no words came forth.

"Should I wonder if you desire me?" he whispered.

Averyl risked a glance in his direction. Her gaze followed Thornton as he smoothed a hand across his bare chest—and lower. His flat palm stretched over hard muscle. Her heartbeat quickened.

Did women caress their lovers in such a manner? The thought came, unbidden. Horrified at her musing, she dismissed the question.

The man possessed not a shred of modesty. Aye, but despite his scars, he had no reason to hide an inch of his well-honed warrior's body. Her face bloomed with hot color.

"Wonder not. I will never desire you," she swore. "Ever."

Thornton sent a challenging stare in her direction. But he did naught else. Said naught more.

"You swore you would not touch me," she reminded.

"I swore I would not touch you unless you wished it."

"That settles our issue, then. Does it not?"

He cocked his head, his dark stare questioning, measuring. "Perhaps."

"Unless you plan to rape me for your perverse pleasure."

"I've no need to force a woman to my bed."

The statement was direct, honest. Averyl did not doubt he had more invitations than he could keep. Her face burned hotter.

"If that is so, you have no need to force your way into that bed with me," she concluded, arms crossed over her chest.

He smiled darkly. "Instead, I will sleep on the floor, by the door, to be certain you do not escape."

Realizing she had possibly thwarted her own plan, Averyl turned away, fists clenched. Reviewing her options, she paced.

How could she escape this eve, without the key, as Thornton guarded the door? With the hated dark looming about her like a fiendish specter? Impossible. Still, she must try.

Suddenly, she caught Thornton's stare in the mirror. Across the barren room, in the flickering candlelight, he watched her.

For a moment, she beheld the unrestricted view of his golden chest without regard to its brute power. Never had she given any thought that a man's body might be pleasing. Had she not always felt one was much like another? Here Thornton proved her wrong. What she had interpreted moments ago as fear-inspiring power now struck her differently.

Through lowered lashes she studied the ornate silver-and-gold cross hanging around his neck, suspended from a thick silver chain. Below that, she examined the hard swells of muscle around his dark nipples and the ridged flesh across his abdomen. Was all of him built that powerfully?

"Come here, Averyl." His deep voice resonated about her.

His command was naught more than a soft challenge. She knew she should ignore it, ignore him. His glittering eyes would not let her.

Toward him she stepped, chin held high. "I assume this request has a purpose, for I am not your servant."

A smile curled the corner of his mouth. "A step closer, if you please. I am in the mood for talking."

Averyl snorted her disbelief. "I stand plenty close for talking."

"Not tonight."

His voice sounded warm, enticing—dangerous to one's soul. Gathering her composure, she stepped boldly toward Thornton. He seemed to thrive on her uncertainty. 'Twould be a hard-fought battle before she showed it again.

Mere inches separated them. The heat of his body, the scent of wood and musk, assailed her. He took her hand in his.

Averyl held in a gasp at his warm touch. When he began

stroking her palm with his thumb, she drew in a deep breath to calm her alarm. Even so, tingles of sensation assailed her, while his velvety eyes invited. She swallowed.

"Do you know the ways of men and women?" His voice stroked and incited her to something she had never felt. If he had naught but hate within him, how could his voice be so warm?

She raised her chin, hoping he could not see her tremble. "What I know or not is none of your affair."

"Perhaps I should ask instead if you wonder about the feel of a man's kiss. The touch of his hand where you ache?"

Lips parted, eyes wide, she stared at his dark face, into his knowing eyes. Yes, secretly, shamefully, on long, cold nights in her solitary bed, she *did* wonder.

"I—I . . ." she stammered, betraying her answer.

A smile curved his full lips, making him seem an entirely different man, one without anger or revenge dominating his heart. " 'Tis as nature intended."

The feather-light touch of his fingers teased their way up the bare inside of her arm. His words, his touch, shot a shocking ache from her center through her limbs. The drumbeat of her pulse erupted into a march.

"Have you imagined more?" His gaze, a flash of heat, pierced her with a sharp, answering want. "Wondered about the feel of a man on top of you? Inside of you?"

Gasping, she recoiled, face flaming, and tried to wrench from his grasp. "Nay! 'Tis unseemly."

Despite her protestations, his scent, of earth and man, rose up to confuse her, to plant carnal notions in her head.

What kind of lover would Thornton be? Demanding? Possessive? Or surprisingly tender?

She stared at his fine carved features, his incredibly dark eyes. She found no answers therein, only mystery, secrets he seemed to hide.

Disturbed, she sent her gaze down. She paused at his lips. The bottom one was fuller than the other, but as if to atone for this, the top lip dipped sensuously in the center, adding to his mouth's appeal. Somehow she knew he could kiss a woman senseless.

Her pulse soared with anxiety and awareness. She peered at him, wondering why her mind toyed with her thus.

"I can satisfy your curiosity." His tone said he could do that—and more.

Sweet mercy, had he read her very mind? "I want only freedom from you."

Cursing her breathy reply, she tried to withdraw her hand from his, to end the disturbing touch. He held fast.

"I could find more than one way to give you and your sharp tongue delight."

More than one way?

Averyl forced the instant vision of sheets and skin from her thoughts. She mustn't even consider such.

Tilting her chin upward, she still could not help wondering why he offered. Did he see something beautiful in her that other men, even her own father, did not?

Of course not. He merely sought to confuse and use her. She must not lose sight of that.

"Release me! I will not, for a moment more, allow this torture. Think you I wish to give my maidenhead to the swine who took me from my bed and family, then ruined my life? If so, sir, you hold entirely too high an opinion of yourself."

Thornton clenched his jaw and scowled. "I shall restrict myself from torturing you, as you put it," he said, releasing her. "But I suggest you keep your straying gaze elsewhere, else I will treat your stare as an invitation." He grabbed a blanket from the bed and strode past her. "Good night."

Averyl lay stiffly in darkness blacker than soot. She drew in a deep breath, refusing to succumb to the familiar frozen terror. Thornton had given her little choice but to seek escape during night's most shadowed hour.

At the base of the door, she heard his deep, even breathing. Though he slept, Averyl could not. Would not despite the comfort of the mattress beneath. Escape beckoned. And the location of Thornton's codpiece was crucial.

Straining to see her captor through the frightfully inky room, Averyl pushed her fear aside and rose from the bed. The cold earthen floor beneath her feet shocked her, and she made a mental note to grab her satchel before leaving.

Inching forward, she trembled, praying the corners of this dark, foreign room were not haunted by bloodthirsty demons or violent specters. Still, she dared not risk lighting a candle for fear of waking the mortal beast by the door.

She stepped on a rock and winced, biting her lip to stay silent. Thornton's deep breathing continued, and she crept on.

At his side, Averyl knelt and, like a blind woman bobbing for an apple, felt the floor around his body for the codpiece attached to his hose. She knew he'd placed it somewhere at his side, for she had heard the rustle of cloth as he'd disrobed in the dark. Averyl refused to wonder which other garments he'd removed, how much of his taut skin he had bared to the night.

After another tap or two, she felt a long length of cloth beneath her hand, thankfully void of a leg. Hope welling within her, she clasped the fabric and vowed to follow it until she found his codpiece.

She encountered a hard, hot, linen-clad thigh instead and jerked her hand away.

At her touch, Thornton stirred and rolled to his back. Face flaming at the intimacy, Averyl tensed and leaned away.

"Averyl?" His question was slurred with sleep, her own name hardly recognizable.

She did not answer. Moonlight penetrated the darkness through a crack beneath the door, which Thornton no longer blocked. Stark alabaster rays illuminated the floor, and Averyl seized upon the light as a sign from God. With it, she could see that no specters hovered near—as well as half of his hose.

The other half lay trapped beneath Thornton's hip.

Biting her lip, Averyl resolved to continue with her plan. She sat beside him and reclined on one elbow, hoping to gain better position to pry the pouch from beneath him. Stealing a glance at his face, she saw that he slept still.

Thankful for his slumber, she leaned closer, touching a trembling palm to the ridged plain of his bare abdomen. She drew in a sharp breath at the feel of his hard flesh and swallowed to conquer the urge to abandon her plan in the face of her pounding heart.

He moved not at her touch, and she continued on her quest, easing another hand beneath his thigh. The intimacy of her actions seeped into her. She'd never touched a man thus. Had never been this close to one.

Nor had she ever been abducted by a murderer.

Averyl forced herself to concentrate on his identity and nefarious plan, not the curious breathlessness she felt at the feel of his skin. Yet the warmth of his big body penetrated her anxiety with something stronger.

Bringing her hands closer together, nearer the codpiece, Averyl held her breath, trying to ignore the feel of Thornton's warmth upon her fingers. Another inch, mayhap two, and the pouch would be free. She resisted the notion that Thornton could hear the thunderous rhythm of her heart.

Her captor shifted again, giving her access to his pocket. Yanking it to her chest, Averyl slipped her hand into the scratchy wool, still warm from the most male part of his body. He had a good amount of coin, judging from the jingle within, but she resisted the urge to take any. She would find a way to Murdoch's side without resorting to Thornton's thievery.

Averyl reached, her fingers stretching. Finally, she felt a cold length of metal. She closed her palm around the long object and lifted it from the pouch. The slender beam of moonlight beneath the door told her 'twas a key.

Clutching it, she made to rise. Her captor shifted into her, throwing her off balance. Averyl fell to her back with a quiet thud.

She tried to find her feet, but Thornton draped the length of his battle-hardened arm over her stomach and rolled toward her, half of his big body covering hers.

"Averyl?" came the sleepy inquiry again, a whisper.

She lay completely still, save for the drilling of her heart. She must think of a way to leave his slumberous embrace without waking him—not of the scent of sandalwood and something muskier that clung to his skin.

Slowly, she inched away, grasping the key in one hand, eyes tightly shut. Thornton tightened his hold about her and sidled closer until more of his massive chest eclipsed her, pinning her to the floor beneath him.

He turned his head away from the door, toward her. His eyes remained closed. "Hmmm."

At his soft moan, her skin erupted with chill bumps. Heat swept through her. Why, under his touch, did she no longer feel her usual fear of the dark?

Shaking away the foolish thought, she chastised herself. Thornton merely slept, clutching his captive, the vessel of his revenge. He did not seek to protect her, and she must escape while defending herself against the dark's demons.

Averyl frowned, wondering, too, why he had not awakened.

Knowing she did not have time to solve that mystery, she lay still until his breathing deepened once more. Just as she moved to make good her escape, Thornton's hand lifted from the curve of her waist upward.

His warm fingers covered her breast.

She gritted her teeth to rein in a gasp. The foreign sensation, like a flare of lightning, erupted within her. A hot and cold ache pervaded her as her flesh tightened and her nipples pebbled beneath his touch. An urge to arch to him in offering blinded her for a moment. If he could give so much pleasure in his sleep, what measure could he give when alert?

Nay, she would not think so wantonly. The moment's surprise merely masqueraded as pleasure. She would learn if he slept still, then find a way to flee.

Easing from his touch, Averyl turned her face to his. He breathed deeply, evenly, with closed eyes. Did that not mean he slept on?

"Averyl," he whispered sleepily again.

She stilled as he wrapped his hand about her nape and drew her close, so close. Breath trapped in her chest, she felt his other hand slide up her waist, to cover her breast again. She jumped, startled—and found her mouth an inch from his. Assailed by the woodsy musk of his scent, the feel of his nearness and intimate touch, she froze in shock. And wonder.

He settled his mouth over hers. Soft, warm lips covered her own. Mingling breaths, a rush of sensation, an explosion of wonderment. His mouth swept over hers lightly, lingered and nipped, tasting of nightly ale and manly allure.

Averyl drew in a deep breath. The room seemed to spin about her. His lips, so tender . . . an utter puzzle. Could one so evil really taste so pleasing? Touch as if gentle?

He groaned, startling her. Averyl broke the kiss and eased away, then scrambled to her feet. Her lips tingled, and she placed cold fingers against them, aching for another taste of tenderness.

Nay! She must concentrate on escape.

Praying he did not awaken, she backed away through the hated dark, heart pounding, until her legs encountered the bed. Smothering a gasp, she scurried about the room, gathering her satchel and a quilt from the bed. She shut the door softly behind her, hoping the sound would not wake him.

Barefoot and shaking, her heart drumming, she sprinted through the obsidian night, up the steep hill to the gate, hoping to leave behind the demons of the dark—and her captor.

Her trembling fingers inserted the key and turned it. The gate swung open. Freedom was hers! She had naught to do but master her childhood fear, find Thornton's boat, and cast away from his prison isle. And she might be hours away before he woke to find she'd fled. She would be with Murdoch soon. They would wed. Abbotsford would be safe.

With a low cry, she burst through the thick shrubbery, into the night, a wild animal suddenly freed from its cage. At the top of the hill, she drew in a deep breath of pungent salt air and glanced above at clouds of ashen gray that obscured the moonlight to a faint, ghostly glow. Averyl clenched her fists as a damp sheen of fear bathed her face.

She must forget the villains and ghosts and remember Thornton's boat. Aye, it was most important now. She must have it to return to the MacDougall.

Averyl listened to the sounds of crashing waves about her, pelting her from all directions. Where would he hide it? A cave, most like. A black hole hiding the unknown. She cringed against the dark.

Then she squared her shoulders, vowing that to escape, she'd endure the pitch cavern. Staying could only be more dangerous. For with Thornton, she feared for more than her safety.

She rummaged through her satchel for footwear. Dresses and shifts she unearthed but naught resembling her shoes. Knowing she did not have enough time or light for a more thorough search, she tossed the blanket about her shoulders as protection from the chilly darkness and headed for the shore, scanning all about for bloodthirsty ghouls. If she must search the perimeter of the island, that she would do.

Upon reaching the rocky shore, Averyl found a scrap of sandy soil and began walking, guided by the milky reflection of the weak moonlight on the silver water. She scanned the land for anything that resembled a boat or a place to hide one, vowing she had not come this far and risked

Thornton's wrath for naught. Nor had she succumbed to the bewildering pleasure of a kiss she had enjoyed far too well to be thwarted.

Five

Drake rolled to his back and stretched, delicious languor flooding his limbs. Ah, such sweet dreams of Lady Averyl, of her fine berry lips beneath his. Her warm breast in his palm. He clutched the dream tight, clinging to the fantasy.

He reached for his pillow and encountered scratchy wool. His fingers followed the garment to its end, only to find his open codpiece.

Bolting to his feet, Drake's gaze sought the bed. Rumpled. And empty.

"Averyl!" he shouted as his fingers dug into the pouch in his grasp. Coin after coin he withdrew until the pocket lay empty. He cursed and made a quick search of the remainder of the cottage, only to have his fears confirmed.

She'd taken the key and her satchel and fled.

Pulling on his hose and tunic, Drake wondered how he could have let the vixen past him. Had he been so weary from three sleepless nights that deep slumber prevented him from hearing her escape? He thrust on his boots. Perhaps his wanton dream of Averyl had hindered him from waking as she fled.

Or had that been a dream?

He touched a finger to his mouth, determined to learn the truth. If she had used her wiles to escape him, he would make her regret it. His father had proved clearly the depths to which a man's soul could sink in order to win a lady's favor. He would not be manipulated by her perfumed flesh.

Aye, Averyl churned his blood. That he would not deny, but never would he allow his loins to transcend logic.

Making his way outside, Drake sprinted toward the ravine's fog-enshrouded gate. He must find Averyl before she discovered his boat and made good her escape. But his dream of her, soft and willing in his bed, would not leave him. Nor would the certainty she had used her mouth and his lust to manipulate him.

Troubled by the circle of his thoughts, Drake cursed when he found the gate flung wide. He surged up the steep incline and bolted to the top. There he halted.

The moonlight dodged in and out of the clouds. Scowling, Drake knelt and searched the moist earth until he saw the faint tracks of small bare feet. Frozen feet by now, no doubt. For even though 'twas summer, the night air held a chill.

With urgent steps, Drake followed the soft imprint of Averyl's footsteps. As he assumed, she had headed to the shore.

For twenty minutes he tracked her, gut churning with apprehension. Ordinarily, he would not believe anyone could so quickly find the cave in which he'd hidden his small boat. He'd carefully chosen the spot, secreted behind rocks and trees. Still, Averyl had proved herself no ordinary woman.

Soon the sand with Averyl's tracks skirted around an outcropping of boulders destined to endure nature's icy pounding for eternity. The moon disappeared once more beneath a black strip of angry sky, snatching the milky moonlight away. Blackness oozed where the muted light once reigned.

Skirting the rocky shore, he climbed slowly upward, past the ancient standing stones. At the edge of the heather-dotted cliff, he found Averyl bathed in shadow, a small mass huddled beneath a red blanket. Her hair whipped behind her like a sail in the screeching wind as he approached. Her satchel lay next to her, on its side.

Relief zipped through him. On the heels of that came

fury. He needed her here as much for her own safety as the success of his plan. She must understand that.

Drake stepped toward her, forming a tongue-lashing in his mind. Then the wind carried her cry to his ears.

Why did that cry bother him so? More this time than last?

Did she know he approached, and sought to win his sympathy? 'Twould be like a woman—all except Aric's Gwenyth. She would flail a man with her dagger tongue before showing him her tears. But with the fair Gwenyth settled happily into married life with his friend at Northwell, Drake did not believe he'd meet another woman with so forthright a manner. Particularly not a Campbell.

Drake crouched behind Averyl, ready to berate her. Before he could speak, her tresses whipped up to graze his cheek. She smelled of salt and those damned white flowers. He doused pleasure with anger.

"You cannot escape, Averyl. Give me the key."

She gasped at hearing his voice and turned. Drake expected many reactions, a struggle, a scream, another run for freedom.

Never did he expect she would throw her arms about him and press her small, trembling body against him.

Hesitantly, he drew his arms about her. She burrowed closer against him. An urge to protect her bolted through him, and he frowned against it.

"What ploy is this, little witch?" he whispered into the wind. "Do you seek to confuse me?"

She shook her head wildly. "I am frightened."

"Of me?" he asked, puzzled.

Her sob pierced his vexation. She sounded so distraught, so afraid.

"The dark frightens me even more than you," she confessed in trembling tones. "Please do not let aught hurt me."

The hard rock of fury in his gut began to crumble as the urge to protect her assailed him once more. He drew her tiny chilled body against him. She'd been out here minutes, perhaps hours, fearing what she could not see, and trusted *him* to save her?

He stroked the soft waves of her golden hair. "I will let naught harm you."

She nodded and relaxed against him.

For long moments she said naught, only clutched him as if he were a rope preventing her from falling to her death over a cliff. He held her only to ease her fears. He did not feel pleasure at her trust or arousal at the firm mounds of her breasts against him. He noticed not the silken slide of her tresses through his fingers. At least for no more than a moment or two.

Ach, what a fool. He did notice that—and more, like sounds of soft breath rushing from her ripe mouth, the satiny skin at her nape. He could scarce do naught but notice.

"How did you come to fear the dark?" he asked, breaking the dangerous spell of silence about them.

" 'Tis foolish," she demurred.

"No fear is foolish if it truly frightens you."

Averyl bit her quivering lip, then drew in a deep breath. "I . . . When I was six years, the MacDuffs lay siege to Abbotsford. M-my mother took me from my bed, up into one of the towers, for safety." She clenched her hands in her lap and pressed her lips together. "At—at the top, darkness abounded. A pair of rough hands wrenched me from her grasp. I heard her scream . . . but could see naught." After another shaky breath, she pressed on. "Hours passed while I cried her name into the silence. Come morning, sunlight revealed that she'd been strangled."

A pang hit him in the chest. A new urge to hold her assailed him, and he gave into it, much against his will. She'd been no more than a wee lass when such a tragedy occurred. Little wonder she'd clutched onto him as if her life depended upon it.

"No one will harm you here," he whispered. "This I vow."

"Thank you," she whispered into his neck.

Drake continued to hold his captive, swallowing against an odd need to hold her. Kiss her. Had he sampled that mouth once before? One simple taste would tell the truth.

"Averyl?" he called as the wind whispered around them.

She lifted her face to him, and the moon broke free from the imprisoning black clouds. Silver light illuminated her pure ivory features, the bright green eyes. Drake felt his loins tighten as he lowered his mouth and took hers.

She stiffened and froze. Despite the surge of hunger gnawing at him, Drake softened his kiss. He tasted the sea's salt on her lips as well as a hint of wine and something uniquely her. Something delectable.

Something *familiar.*

Though he had solved the mystery of his dream, Drake held fast, savoring her lips, again sweeping his mouth over hers. To his surprise, her mouth turned pliant against his own. If her kiss was a ploy, so be it. He would feel the pleasure before her machinations came.

But such thoughts were dangerous. His mother had nearly killed his beloved sire with her honey-laced cruelty. He must not forget that.

Drake tore his mouth away. "I did not dream of another kiss, did I?"

Even in the muted moonlight he saw Averyl flush pink. She wiggled free from his embrace, and he released her.

"I—In my search for your key, you reached for me."

Was that so? In his dream he had been the one to seek her mouth with his own, to seek satisfaction in her body, true. If their mouths had truly mated before she fled the cottage, had he been responsible, not her manipulation?

Drake swallowed his uncertainty. He was not an irresolute man, and though her reply made sense, he did not like that answer, one that meant she haunted him in his sleep.

"You did not find my boat, I take it?" he asked, changing the subject.

"Nay, as you can well see."

Her bitter tone incited that ill feeling in his gut again. Though 'twas not guilt, he vowed. Still, he had taken her from her family and future. 'Twas up to him to ease her plight.

"I recall long days in Murdoch's dungeon," he said softly. "Freedom was a fantasy. But on many days a ray of sunlight would penetrate the cracks of the castle walls. I would oft concentrate so hard on that light, on my remembrances of the outdoors, I could imagine myself there."

In the moonlight, her eyes grew wide with recognition. "Aye. When the clouds parted, I could see land, could imagine it beneath my feet, yet not reach it for the sea."

"The Mull of Kintyre is but four miles west."

Averyl shivered, and Drake draped his arm about her again. She stiffened until he drew her small icy feet in his grasp. Her sigh shivered its way down his back.

How could he feel anger, protectiveness, lust, and remorse within the span of minutes? Had he gone mad, or did Averyl bewitch him?

"Where have you put my shoes?" she asked, allowing him to keep her feet in his grasp. "I found them not in my satchel."

"I hid them for just this reason." He shrugged an apology.

Apology? Now he felt contrite? Nay, 'twas lack of sleep. Naught else. Certainly not her allure. Or his conscience.

" 'Tis time to return to the cottage, Averyl. I mean you no harm, but neither will you escape."

"So you merely mean to destroy my future and Abbotsford?"

Drake shoved aside the damned ill feeling her words engendered. "Murdoch will pay for his sins. You are his currency. Accept that, else we will spend many more nights here, playing this game you will not win."

* * *

The thud of footsteps outside the cottage woke Averyl. She sat up in bed, expecting Thornton to stroll into the dwelling with the knowledge of their kiss glittering in his dark eyes.

Flushing at the remembrance, she lowered her head into her hands with a sigh, then batted a hand at the sleep-mussed hair lying in a tangle about her. How could a tyrant without care for anyone but himself, without feeling at all, rouse her blood? Soothe her with his unexpected understanding of her fear?

Footsteps approached the door. Averyl's stomach fluttered.

She would not dwell on him or their kiss. 'Twas folly. He did not and would not have feelings for her. The kiss, her fears, meant naught to him. His patience could mean even less to her, for she would never desire, much less love, a man with no heart. That he'd aroused any feeling in her save hate was no more than happenstance.

Jumping from the bed, Averyl struggled to shove her hair beneath her wimple. Chiding herself for the foolish vanity, she grabbed her dress and thrust it on. Still, Thornton did not appear. Instead, to her amazement, she heard two men conversing. One voice, the more somber one, she recognized as Thornton's. The other was unfamiliar.

The strength of the voices grew as they approached Thornton's dwelling, until the men stopped just outside. Her heart picked up its pace. Who was this stranger? Might he help her escape?

Curiosity and hope soared within her as she crept toward the window and eased open the shutter. Silently, she crouched beneath, listening for any piece of information that might aid her escape.

"You look weary, my friend." She recognized the voice as Thornton's. "Did you travel all night?"

"Aye, most of it. But with a little sleep and a warm wench, I will be better than new," the stranger quipped.

"As always." An irony Averyl did not understand resounded in her captor's voice. "Tell me what news you bring."

"If you expected good news, I am bound to disappoint. When Murdoch discovered Lady Averyl missing, he bellowed like a wounded hound. He cursed you and the day you were born."

Surprisingly, Thornton laughed, a rich baritone sound that projected into the one-room cottage, flowing over her senses rather like warm honey.

"What then?"

"After he realized cursing would help him not in finding his bride, he began gathering his allies to seek you out."

"As I expected."

As he expected? Averyl felt shock reverberating through her half-clad body. Thornton sounded frighteningly calm, as if he abducted women every day.

'Twas possible, she acknowledged with a thud of fear.

Abduction was a common occurrence with daughters and wives. Many came to accept their captivity. Averyl knew she should do the like, if only for her safety. Despite his assurances to the contrary, Thornton might be provoked to rape or murder, as was the fate of many captives.

But she refused to accept her bonds.

"Murdoch has again demanded your death," the stranger said. "This time, on sight. He means to have your blood on his hands. Watch your back, my friend."

"His wishes mean naught."

"But as he searches for you, he travels with a priest."

"A priest?"

"Aye. One to perform his marriage vows to the Lady Averyl just before your last rites."

Averyl frowned at the terrible image. Would her gallant chieftain really order such a barbaric wedding?

"Murdoch would have starved or beaten me to death in his dungeons," Drake argued. "Should we come to combat, I am his equal. And if I die, 'twill be knowing I fought for honor and vengeance. At least with Lady Averyl in my keep,

I have a chance to best him by striking at the heart of his greed."

Greed? Of what did Thornton speak?

"We shall have to think of some alternative if you want to keep her. For upon your last journey to Dunollie, a member of the Clan MacDougall spotted you docking a boat at Ardrossan and told Murdoch such two days past. He is convinced you hide on one of these isles and will search each until he finds you."

A long minute of silence passed before her captor finally responded, his tone gravelly. "That is not good news."

Reining in a cry of glee, Averyl balled her fists and smiled. Thornton was trapped, as well he knew. She would be free of the handsome barbarian who imprisoned her, hid her shoes, kissed her until she could scarce breathe. Murdoch would find her soon and make her his wife. All would be well.

"Since Murdoch believes Lady Averyl harbors some measure of love for him and will make every attempt to flee, he is determined he and his priest will be waiting when she does."

Averyl's heart leaped again. Murdoch would aid and protect her once she managed to escape. 'Twas a hopeful sign that he cared for her.

"I will see that she cannot," Thornton replied flatly.

Leaning in for a closer listen, Averyl resisted her sinking hopes.

"Can you tell me she has not tried to leave?" He sounded doubtful indeed.

"Aye, and more than once."

"Then she may well succeed, my friend. If she wants freedom from you badly enough, she may find it."

Another long pause. Averyl stood stock-still, poised beneath the window in the hope Thornton might see reason and release her.

"Perhaps you are right. I shall have to think. Murdoch cannot be allowed to escape murder without punishment."

Averyl bit her lip mercilessly to hold in her outrage. Again, Thornton intimated Murdoch had participated in his own father's murder. 'Twas an insult! The MacDougall would not commit such a heinous act. Her captor merely had this stranger duped into believing his wicked lies. By his own admission, Thornton sought to kill Murdoch Mac-Dougall.

"I could kill him myself for his treatment of you," said the other man.

Thornton grunted in response. "Someway, somehow, I vow Murdoch's hate and lust for power will cost him."

"I shall help you. My ideas are always more interesting."

At that, her captor scoffed. "Always? I would hardly call peeking at crones bathing in the river an interesting idea."

"So you remember that? I thought in ten years' time you might forget."

"Never."

"I told you I assumed Guilford's younger maids would bathe as well," the stranger defended.

"You would know more of their bathing habits than I."

"These days, aye." The man's voice was mischief itself.

"Do you return to the village and Dunollie?" Thornton asked. "I could use the spy."

"Murdoch needs mercenaries and pays well besides."

"Learn what you can and send me word."

"I will, friend," the stranger answered.

"As always, I thank you."

"And I accept." The stranger's voice carried a note of humor. "And since we've concluded our business, you must tell me how you fare with your captive. I assume any bride of Murdoch's would be some manner of horned she-demon."

Thornton did not respond for long moments. Averyl tensed, and the pause dragged onward as he paced the hard-packed earth outside, twigs snapping beneath his boots.

"Averyl is not horned. But a she-demon . . ."

"So, she has been difficult?" the man asked.

"She is no weak-willed wench, but nothing I cannot manage."

"What is she like?" the man persisted.

"Always interested in the women." There was amusement in Drake's voice. "She is well-spoken and sharp-witted."

And though Averyl knew Thornton complimented her, it stung her pride that he found nothing else about her worthy of comment, particularly in light of their kisses. She shoved the feeling aside, refusing to care what the brigand thought of her.

"When do I meet her?" the stranger asked.

Averyl heard footsteps coming toward the door and tensed. Before she could act, Drake spoke again.

"Later. She sleeps, and 'tis best for now if she stays thus."

"As you wish. Pray tell me, what does she look like?"

"A young maiden," Drake replied without inflection.

But not a fair one, Averyl thought, and wanted to cringe.

The stranger laughed. "Firtha called her lovely. Has your pretty face finally failed you with a woman?"

"Kieran, I've no reason to charm the wench."

Tattered pride lacerated Averyl like a whip on the wind. Thornton thought of her as nothing but the means to an end. *What else did you expect, fool?* She clenched her fists, wishing she could ignore the ache his painfully honest remark caused but not understanding why she sought the miscreant's good opinion when she wanted naught but escape.

The stranger paused before teasing, "That means she is most homely or already besotted. Which is it?"

Thornton said naught.

"You are never one for many words, my friend. But such silence . . . I can only assume you want her badly."

"Kieran . . ." Her captor's voice held a warning.

"After fifteen years of friendship, do you not think you can tell me the truth?"

"God's teeth." He sighed heavily. "You know me too

well. Averyl is so damned fair, she knocks the breath from
me each time I gaze at her."

Beneath the window, Averyl stopped breathing as shock
wound its tingling tendrils throughout her. Did Thornton
speak true? Nay, he lied to ease his friend's curiosity, surely.

Then why had he kissed her last night, not once but
twice?

"Well, now. That is interesting."

"Her eyes are so wide and green." Drake cursed.

He had noticed the color of her eyes?

Thornton gave a resigned sigh. "I know not what to do."

"Of course you do." The other man laughed. "Bed her."

"She is my captive, not my leman."

"I do not see this as a problem. Would she resist you?"

Again, Drake paused. Averyl held her breath, wondering
if he knew how he repelled her, yet how often she thought
of him.

"With every breath she took. 'Tis not an option, Kieran."

"Nonsense. 'Tis always an option, my friend."

Minutes later, Drake and the stranger, Kieran, entered the
small cottage. Averyl's mind whirled in a confused daze.
Forcing aside her myriad questions about Thornton's belief
of Murdoch's guilt, she gazed at the stranger.

He was nearly as tall as Thornton, their broad statures
betraying them both as warriors. This Kieran appeared a
few years younger, but Averyl knew not if that was fact or
a product of the man's perpetual grin.

The stranger's hair was a dark mahogany, liberally laced
with auburn, his eyes a startling shade between blue and
green. His face held a hint of boyishness, confirmed by
dimples, then belied by the mischief dancing in his gaze.
He smiled, looking much friendlier than her captor, like a
man who enjoyed life.

Soon some pull induced Averyl's gaze back to her captor's dark visage. His intent stare held hers. Did Drake really think her beautiful?

'Twas foolish to wonder such. She should concern herself only with whether the stranger might be persuaded to aid her.

"This is Kieran Broderick." Thornton turned to the other man. "My friend, Lady Averyl Campbell."

With a smile, Kieran lifted her hand to brush his lips across her fingers. " 'Tis a pleasure to meet you, my lady."

Unaccustomed to such a flattering gaze, she withdrew her hand. "Greetings."

Then realizing only the rogue Kieran could help her escape, she offered him a smile. Aye, 'twas unlikely such a man would find her worthy of attention; a smile was all she had to offer.

Kieran surprised her by smiling back.

A pause settled in the air, blooming with tension. Drake broke the silence. "Averyl, go outside and retrieve Kieran's belongings."

" 'Tis your captive I am, not your slave," she snapped.

Kieran laughed. "An answer Gwenyth would give."

Who was this Gwenyth? And why did Drake scowl so?

Kieran added, "Well, 'tis clear our brooding Drake is unhappy. Lass, if you would gather my bag, I would consider it a favor."

A quick glance at Thornton revealed a scowl. Good. Her smile widened. "I shall see to your things right away."

Averyl let herself out the door. Drake watched, his gaze remaining on her alluring backside until she was out of sight.

Christ's blood, why did he want her so? Why had she smiled so sweetly for Kieran? Might Averyl be like his treacherous mother: another man, another conquest? Diera had never lacked a reason for her flirtations. What would Lady Averyl's reason be? And how would he stop her?

"Kieran," Drake began abruptly. "Averyl is here to serve my purpose. Do not trifle with her."

"Trifle?" His friend frowned. "I would not intrude upon your . . . claim."

" 'Tis no claim," he growled.

"Oh, aye. You desire her, do not wish to, yet want no other to have her."

Drake cursed. Kieran could be annoyingly perceptive. "She is a wench, and a Campbell one at that."

"Aye, as well as a fragile, wee thing whose only sin was in agreeing to wed Murdoch."

"Thus far."

Kieran sighed in exasperation. "Drake, you cannot punish her for Diera's sins."

Drake felt his composure crack from the foundation upward, spearing him with a bolt of anger. "No more than you withhold your heart from women because of your parents' doings."

"We speak of you and the lady." Kieran looked angry for the first time Drake could recall. "Averyl is not responsible for your pain. She did not destroy your father with betrayals. Diera did that alone."

"I need no reminder that my mother was a whore."

"Forget it. She is dead. Gone. Life is now."

Drake whirled away. Though Kieran spoke true, Drake refused to forget. He let his pain fester, hoping 'twould remind him that to trust a woman would be heedless. Diera had crushed his proud father's heart. At her hand, Drake had learned the perfidy of which women were capable and the depths of a man's anguish. But with Averyl he feared that lesson would be easy to forget if he touched her lush, fragrant flesh under a shadowed moon.

Never would he be such a fool. If he took the fair Averyl to his bed, his heart would remain untouched.

The following morn, Averyl awoke before the sun, hoping to sneak a private word with Kieran. True, he had given no indication he would aid her escape, but she prayed for it.

Grabbing her red silken dress from beside the bed, she slipped it over her shift, protecting her skin from the morning chill. A quick glance across the room proved her captor slept, his large body sprawled across the door. In the dwindling firelight, she saw one brawny arm strewn above his head, the other bulged across the lean power of his chest.

How would such mighty arms feel about her, holding her tight against a heart filled with love and devotion?

Her pulse picked up, and she crossed herself in reproach. Sweet mercy, she was a fool to desire the very man she must escape, to feel aught for the captor who thought her an inconsequential pawn in his vengeful scheme.

Averyl raised both hands to secure her wimple, then tiptoed around the corner, to the cottage's empty room, where Kieran had bedded down the previous night. She winced at the quiet click of the latch as it gave way beneath her fingers but did not hear Thornton rouse from his pallet to pursue her.

Inside, the room lay dark. None of the flickering firelight made its way into the gray-black depths before her. Cursing her lack of foresight and her fear, Averyl turned to seek a candle.

Drake Thornton stood squarely in her path, his broad chest bare, his dark hair mussed, his scowl grim.

"If you seek Kieran, look no more. He left an hour past."

Hope crashed to her toes with the impact of a boulder. Damnation! She had hoped Kieran would see her off this isle. But Murdoch was still coming, and until he did, she would do everything possible to ensure that he found her.

"Nay. I but heard an odd noise and thought perhaps—"

"Kieran might be awake to listen to your pleas for help?"

Averyl raised her chin and sailed past him, into the golden-orange firelight. "I've no need of his assistance, for Murdoch is coming to get me, is he not?"

As she turned to him with a triumphant grin, Thornton paused. A small half-smile raised the corner of his mouth. The gesture on another might have comforted Averyl. On him, the smirk sent a twinge of foreboding through her blood.

After a nod, her captor said, "Aye. He comes. You heard that when eavesdropping on my conversation with Kieran?"

" 'Twas hard not to hear you," she defended. "Besides, now that the truth is out, you can do naught but surrender."

"Naught but surrender?"

He lifted a dark brow, alarming Averyl with another slice of disquieting suspicion. She found herself taking a step back.

"Murdoch will find and kill you if you do not release me."

Thornton stepped forward and grabbed her arm. "You speak true. He might find me and kill me. But if I die, I will make sure he finds hell as well." With a jerk on her arm, he brought her closer, to the countenance dominated by night-shaded eyes and vengeful determination. "Do not think I will release you so easily. I have devised another plan, one that ensures Murdoch cannot win his greedy game even if you escape."

Averyl sucked in a shocked breath and jerked her arm from his grasp. "Of what nonsense do you speak? You have already abducted me. You cannot mean to defile me. Did you not say Murdoch would wed me, regardless?"

"Aye, he would wed you even if you were round with my child. You see, though he is chief of the clan now, he cannot fully inherit its riches or power until he weds you. 'Twas spelled out thus in Lochlan's will."

"Lochlan? Murdoch's father?"

Thornton's jaw hardened, along with the bleak cast of his eyes. "Aye, Murdoch's father. So I will not . . . defile you."

Averyl raised her chin proudly. More than like, his words to Kieran of her beauty had been naught but lies. She had always known that ugly truth.

She stifled disappointment and glared at him. " 'Tis good fortune that we will be spared so unpleasant a deed."

"Unpleasant?"

He reached for her. Refusing to back away from him again, she stood her ground, her heart pounding inside her chest. His palm gripped her cheek as his thumb caressed her jaw, down to her mouth, leaving a trail of tingles in his wake.

"I will not find bedding you an unpleasant task."

Averyl tried to ignore the whisper that made her stomach quiver and her legs unsteady and to concentrate on the words themselves. "I—I thought you . . . that we just agreed bedding me would gain you naught."

"Aye. Bedding you alone would gain me naught but pleasure. 'Twill be different when I bed you as my wife."

Six

"Your w-wife?" Averyl sputtered.

Drake nodded as her eyes widened with pure shock. Her face turned waxen, as white as her gown. Her dismay was to be expected. It meant naught. For him, he could mean even less if he wished to succeed.

"Aye, Averyl. I will bind you to me for the next year, irrevocably."

Horror spread across her face. He looked away from it. It should not anger him to be rejected by a Campbell, a wench who thought him scarred and guilty. But fury curled in his belly.

"We will handfast," he said. "If I survive until your birthday, you cannot wed Murdoch, even if he finds you or you escape. When our year of handfasting is done, I will free you."

She shook her head, denial spreading across her chalky countenance, radiating from the suddenly cool greenish depths of her eyes. "Release me. I-I will wed cousin Robert—"

"Nay." Drake reached out to vow they would wed, to tell her he would be no ogre who contented himself by beating his wife. As he touched her chilled fingers, she jerked away.

"Do not touch me," she hissed. "Ever. I will not call a murderer my husband!"

Before he could stop himself, he flinched against the one barb that had the power to sting. His hand fell away to clench at his side. Something cold and hard settled in his chest.

"I will touch you, Averyl, for we will consummate our union. Do not doubt that."

"Will you force me to your bed?"

"If that is your choice."

Her distress disturbed him, annoyingly enough. Why, when revenge left no room for mercy?

She charged him like a pained animal, head tossed back, teeth bared. "You despicable creature! 'Twas not enough for you to abduct, frighten, and threaten me. Now you would cut off any hope I have of ever wedding a good man, a chief with the coin to save my keep and the heart to love me. Instead, you force me to wed you, a murdering knave without a heart."

He held her against him, letting the familiar anger wash over him, revive his purpose. "Murdoch ensured I cut my heart out long ago. He would soon show you how dangerous are your foolish notions of love."

"You who seek a selfish end and a senseless death? What know you about the gentle matters of love?"

Feeling. Always such great displays of emotion and drama.

Drake cursed. "Why desire a sentiment that makes field mice of men and scheming felines of women?"

"Field mice? Felines?" Her eyes narrowed beneath the fawny arches of her brows. " 'Tis ignorant you are! I know of love's power, its ability to comfort the lonely, better the sick, heal the hurting, and humble the arrogant."

He arched a brow in challenge. "And which of those miracles do you believe love will wrought in you?"

She tossed her head back, a proud goddess shedding light in the predawn dim. " 'Tis no miracle, for I know that if I am looked upon with eyes of love, I shall never have to fear."

Of what did she babble? "Fear what?"

With a sigh of frustration, she stomped past him, toward

the cottage's main room. "I cannot explain such to a man who refuses to understand."

Frowning, he watched her small form retreat, her thick golden braid swishing across her back. Firelight penetrated the thin, cloudlike shift she wore.

He followed her, trying to keep his eyes off the velvet curve of her backside. "No man can understand when you speak in female riddles."

"Have you never felt less than perfect?" Before he could answer, she rolled her eyes and gave a frustrated wave of her hands. "A foolish question. You, I am certain, have never doubted yourself for a single of life's moments."

A remembrance of Lord Campbell's disparaging words to his daughter at Dunollie, at the tears they had nearly engendered, flashed through his mind. The fool thought herself ugly.

Sighing, Drake approached her. When she would have fled, he grabbed her hand and held fast. " 'Tis misguided you and your father both are."

"What know you of my father?" Suspicion clouded her face.

"Has he not always told you that you lack womanly charms?"

Averyl's eyes widened with dismay until the only color on her face was huge green orbs. "How could you know that?"

He waved her question away. "Your father is a dolt."

Averyl drew in a breath and bit her bottom lip, all the while regarding him with a questioning gaze. Drake knew she wondered if he thought her beautiful.

"Ask me," he said into the long silence, smiling at her indecision despite his irritation with the subject of love.

"Ask what?"

The innocent uncertainty of her gaze warmed something in his chest. Nay, 'twas only a sensation in his loins—lust.

"Do you not wish to know if I think you beautiful?"

She paused, hands clasped, then she shook her head. "Nay."

Drake stared at his intriguing captive. Did she speak true? "Most women plead prettily for compliments."

"I would not." Averyl frowned. "Though Becca, our steward's daughter, told me such tribute is . . . pleasant."

"Have you never received a compliment?"

Her delicate ivory cheeks bloomed with color. "I am not the sort of woman to incite others to poetry."

So unsullied she was. Unspoiled by hate or jealousy, betrayal or revenge, Averyl knew nothing of the real world—or her beauty. She knew only her father's blind ignorance.

At once eager and reluctant, Drake extended his hand to her face, faintly aware of his beating heart. He was going to touch her again. And though her eyes held wariness, she would not pull away this time.

Desire tightened its hold about his throat—and lower.

His palm closed over her cheek in a soft stroke. His gaze sought hers. Staring into the depths of her bemused green eyes, lust hardened him. The mystery of her floral fragrance teased his nose. Lilies? Irises? Heather? He wasn't sure.

"Averyl . . ." he whispered, barely hearing himself over the pounding of his heart.

The picture of modesty, Averyl cast her gaze to her hands folded in her lap. The set of her shoulders was as taut as a longman's bow.

"Averyl, whatever your father made you believe, you are lovely and worthy of any man's attention."

Her teeth caught her bottom lip. "You need not say such to me. Since you want us to wed, your efforts to set me at ease are understandable," she said. "But you need not lie."

"I do not lie. I have no use for—"

The wet slide of a tear down her cheek stopped his words. Averyl drew in a deep, ragged breath, and Drake cursed. Why did her tears move him in a way no woman's ever had?

"Do not cry." He paused for her response but found none.

He grasped for words. "You heard my conversation with Kieran. I admitted how beautiful I think you."

Finally, she raised her head to gaze at him with eyes the wind-tossed green of a stormy Scottish loch. He swallowed.

"Why do you say these things to me if not to coax me into giving my hand and my maidenhead?" she whispered, her gaze clinging to him like a spring-grown vine. "Why do you care?"

Why indeed? 'Twould be simple to confirm that his words seemed the easiest means to coax her into accepting their coming nuptials—and their marriage bed. But somehow there was more, something he could scarce name. Some warmth where cold had recently lived. Must be his conscience, he thought with gloom.

Drake looked away. The urge to touch her was strong. "I but speak a truth someone should have told you long ago."

He put distance between them, knowing he had said far more than he intended. He cursed when she followed.

"Such an admission of your feelings . . . puzzles me."

With a scowl, he glanced over his shoulder at her. " 'Tis not a feeling but an observation that I had hoped would cure you of the absurd fantasy that love will make you beautiful."

Averyl backed away as if he'd struck her, the white gown billowing about her legs. "I do not believe love will make me beautiful."

"That is what you said."

She shook her head. " 'Tis peace I seek. To know someone accepts the plain face and wild curls God gave me, yet still wishes me near."

He laughed. "Then it is not a man's love you want but his lust. You seek to know you can stir his blood upon your whim."

"Nay!"

" 'Tis what you describe." He advanced. "Besides, you cannot truly want love. It lies with a serpent tongue."

"That is not so!"

Drake grabbed her arm. "Forget what you dream. Accept the face God gave you. It will not change. And no paltry emotion like love will grant you the peace you seek."

"And lust would?"

He nodded. "It is more honest."

"But fleeting, you wretched beast," she spit in fury. "I will not handfast with you!"

She had not listened, had not absorbed one word. Still did not believe in her own charm. Stubborn Campbell wench.

"You are the last lady I wish to wed as well. You know naught of life and less of men and women. But fate has dictated we will be man and wife for one year—and without that deceitful sentiment you call love."

Stillness and mist blanketed the island's rolling green hills the next eve. Averyl lay awake in bed, her back to Thornton as he prepared to bed down beside the door. This night, as last, sleep would not come. She could not blame the dark, for Drake kept a candle beside her bed. Nor could she claim summer heat, for the nights had been cool, brushed by gray sea winds.

Instead, she dwelt upon Drake's proclamation.

How soon would he insist they wed? Who would witness their handfast union? How would she stop this farce?

Then there was Drake himself.

By the door, Averyl heard the rustle of clothing. The whispers of him disrobing roused her imagination. Somehow she could not prevent herself from envisioning him, muscle-hewn, completely male. Even as her stomach fluttered, her mind rebelled. Pictures of him stormed her— Drake tossing aside his simple black shirt and baring the golden angles of his powerful chest, stepping out of his breeches and displaying hard thighs.

This must cease! Upon her word, what had become of her vow to resist him, of feminine decency?

How could she despise and dwell on him at once?

Clutching her pillow in the firelit night, she could scarce deny that he dissipated her logic like mist in sunlight. Her mind told her he was capable of killing Murdoch's father. She had seen the tangible anger that ran swift and hot under his icy façade. But something within her protested the hasty judgment. Drake had not harmed her. His strong arms had even held her on the windswept cliff while she battled her fear of the dark. He had called her beautiful.

Chewing her lip, Averyl wondered which Drake was the real one. A depraved butcher no sane person would cross or a tortured man driven to retribution?

Averyl rolled to her side, tangled in her own thoughts. The contents of Thornton's soul mattered not. Even if he was innocent of murder, she would not wed him. Could not. She need only concern herself with convincing him that she refused to accept a husband with whom saving Abbotsford was not possible.

Still, the tang of ale and smoke mixed with the sweet smell of summer rain and damp thatch to form the scents of Drake's world. Closing her eyes, she inhaled deeply, finding the fragrance, different from that at Abbotsford, oddly pleasing.

"Why do you not sleep?" Drake asked from across the room.

Averyl sat up in bed, looking across the small room to him. She tried not to focus on the shadows caressing his bare chest—or her own flaming cheeks. "I cannot dismiss from my mind this foolish marriage you seek to make."

He sighed and leaned against the door, turning the golden expanse of his chest and abdomen squarely into her view. She dragged her gaze away.

"Foolish, mayhap, but necessary."

"I cannot conceive that you wish to wed and bed a

woman who wants you not. I've no doubt you could find scores of women willing—nay, eager—to agree to what you have proposed."

"Scores?" he challenged. "You think much of my charm, Lady Averyl, particularly since all Scotland believes me a butcher. Through you I will see Murdoch brought to justice."

"But you have already taken from me my keep, my father, my chances of wedding well. Do not take my dreams from me, too."

"Your dreams?" A moment later, his puzzled frown cleared to a scowl of annoyance. "Ach, love again. 'Tis tiresome."

"Only your refusal to believe in it is," she replied, teeth gritted. "Love is real. Will you not accept that?"

"If you have felt it not, why do you?"

She smiled. "My parents loved with such passion that even death could not tear my mother from my father's heart. I cannot settle for a union without that possibility."

"You speak with the naive eyes of a young girl."

And he spoke like a man who possessed no heart.

"I know my father loved my mother. He has not taken a leman since she died."

Drake laughed. "That you know of. Fathers do not often flaunt their mistresses before their well-reared daughters."

"Abbotsford is too small a keep to hide such secrets. He loved her too much to dishonor her memory with faithlessness."

Rolling his eyes, Drake said, "Only a eunuch of a man remains faithful to a dead woman for eleven years. That or a buffoon. Either could describe your father well enough."

"That is unkind! You know nothing—"

" 'Tis time to cease this prattle and sleep."

Averyl clenched her jaw. The insufferable oaf refused to see any view but his own. A eunuch? A buffoon?

"You are blinded by your hate for Lord Dunollie. Think

back. Did your own mother and father not love?" she quizzed.

The chill upon his indifferent countenance froze into icy anger. "Aye, until it became the death of them both."

She frowned at that riddle of an answer. "I do not understand."

" 'Tis not important." His scowl was deep indeed. Clearly, the subject was not one he liked.

"It is of import to me," she argued, leaning forward on the bed. "I seek to understand why you refuse me the simple request of leaving me unwed and untouched."

"Simple?" He grunted. "Such statements only prove how little you understand of Murdoch and his deceit."

Averyl stood and crossed the room, trying to ignore the golden tongues of firelight licking Drake's taut skin.

"Then make me understand," she challenged beside him.

Drake's expression closed up tighter than a keep under siege. The glare of his dark gaze held more chill than a Highland January.

Refusing to be daunted, she pressed on. He must see she would not wed where she could not love. "If your parents loved, they surely loved you in turn, did they not?"

Her only reply was the bobbing of Drake's Adam's apple as he swallowed and looked away.

Always sparse with his words, Averyl realized he was rarely this quiet. She frowned and crouched before him. All parents loved their children. Did Drake believe he had been unwelcomed?

She touched a hand to his arm, so rigid. With fury? Tightly held control? Curiosity and sympathy gushed over her good sense in a torrent. "You cannot believe your own mother did not love you?"

"I know she did not." His words were flat, unequivocal.

"That cannot be," Averyl argued.

He grabbed her shoulders and dragged her against him. She gasped when their gazes met; she felt his flashing rage—and something else. Pain? "Even mothers can be heartless."

The bitterness in his tone shocked her. "I do not understand what—"

"Understand that my mother was incapable of caring for anyone, particularly the child she never wanted. Or does that simply give you a clearer picture of me? An abductor of women so loathsome even his own mother could not tolerate him?"

His hurt reached out to her, wrapping around her heart with a pang. His mother's indifference had cut him. Averyl longed to reach out to Drake, to offer him comfort. After all, she'd suffered at times from her father's words. She knew the hurt such blows inflicted. Yet she'd always known he loved her.

She palmed Drake's whisker-roughened cheek. "I am certain your mother cared even if she did not express her love—"

At her words, Drake flinched and jerked away. "She told me I'd done naught but leave scars on her body and that she wished I had never been born."

Averyl faced the grim challenge on Drake's face, her heart crumbling for him. How could any woman be so cruel as to tell a small boy he was not wanted?

Reaching out, now tentatively, knowing he might reject her comfort again, Averyl touched his shoulder. "I am sorry."

His face tightened, the carved planes hard and closed. "I have not need of your pity. Just your hand and your virtue."

She withdrew her touch. "I will give you neither."

Averyl returned his stony expression for a long, seething minute. Thornton looked away first, swearing as he lay back on his pallet, lacing his fingers across the taut flesh of his abdomen.

"The terms of our marriage are not open for discussion," he told her, shutting his eyes. "Sleep."

At his command, Averyl returned to her bed. Now was

not the time to approach Thornton, or his wounded heart, to obtain release for her dream's sake. But she would find a way to escape. Certainly they would have to leave the island to handfast. Her opportunity must come then. Her life, her very soul, depended upon her not marrying a man with such a fortress about his wounded heart.

Averyl rose minutes after the sun to find Thornton gone, his blankets folded fastidiously on the table.

Dear God, what had Thornton demanded of her? Marriage. To him. A man almost certainly a killer who could not repair her keep and send her an army, much less give her any measure of love. And he had vowed to bare her body to his gaze, his hands, his mouth, to consummate a union she did not want.

She swallowed. From what she suspected of Thornton, Averyl feared he would demand her total surrender not only of her body but her soul. 'Twas clear he liked to be the master in all things. He would give none of himself that was not of the flesh. That she knew for certain.

She would give him naught!

The fiend entered the cottage, interrupting her reverie. He was large and restless, wearing a white tunic that looked stark against the dark plains of his face. When had she ever seen a more appealing man? Never. Nor had she encountered one with such a surly demeanor.

With shiftless grace, he dropped into a chair and sipped from a tin cup while studying her over the rim with a lingering gaze that made her too aware of their isolation, oddly conscious of her female and his male nature.

None of that mattered. She squared her shoulders. Today, now, she must find a way to dissuade him from this marriage that would ruin them both.

"I would speak with you," Averyl said, hands on her hips. "Where have you been?"

Drake stared, seeing her mood was less than pleasant.

Though he was not surprised, he knew that if he had any intention of convincing his captive to become his willing bride, he must begin the seduction now.

Murdoch and his roving band of murderers had not given them time for courtship. And mayhap he could charm her into forgetting his unfortunate, unaccountable outburst last eve. Cursing his mother and the institution of love was not the way to persuade Averyl to be his willing handfast bride.

"Did you miss me, then?" he teased.

"As much as I would a poisonous snake," she shot back, head held at a proud angle.

Her fiery visage, her blazing eyes, inflamed him, speeding thick blood into his loins. Drake itched to pull her into his lap, palm the weight of her breasts, encased in shimmering gold silk. To show her all the ways they could be good together.

Instead, she seemed bent on incessant conversation about the tiresome subject of love. Frowning, Drake wondered why he bothered to discuss it with her. Indeed, why did he speak to her, his captive, at all?

Because he wanted her. Because something about her would not leave him in peace.

Drake allowed his gaze the treat of roving over her—the pert lift of her chin, the sweet curve of her breast, the small indentation of her waist, the lush arch of her hip.

Even now, as she likened him to a serpent, he could easily imagine Averyl's dewy alabaster skin bared for his eyes, his hands, as she cried out with pleasure in his arms.

Aye, his want coursed more fiercely than he could ever recall. For now, he would seal her babbling mouth with a kiss.

"What do you know of desire, Averyl?"

"As much as I need." Her words sounded brave, but the quivering of her fingers and the wariness of her eyes revealed a woman fearful . . . or a woman wanting. Or both.

"I disagree."

With slow steps he crossed the room to her, the crunch

of his boots just a tinge louder than her breathing. Or was that his? He concentrated on the pulse beating at the base of her neck as he stopped mere inches away.

Her green gaze remained steady, even stalwart. Had she the physical strength, she would have made a formidable warrior, for she had courage aplenty. Aric would like her. And he had no doubt that Kieran thought her worthy of a tumble or two.

Averyl returned his stare stoically. Then Drake unleashed his hunger for her within his eyes. She drew in a soft gasp of breath but did not look away.

"Do you yearn to be touched, Averyl?"

"Nay," came her breathy denial as he curled his fingers around her wrist.

Its warm fragility sent his heart pumping. Averyl tried to twist away, but he drew her forward until her breasts nestled against him, shocking him with an instant of need, a surge of desire. When he slipped a hand around her waist, fitting it at the small of her back, he found that the soft femininity of her small body fit perfectly against him.

She wriggled against him for freedom.

Drake gnashed his teeth. Damn it, he had never been at a loss to find a willing wench. So why did one who resisted and hated him so stir his blood? Why could he not erase the taste of their last kiss from his memory even as he anticipated drinking of her mouth again?

In his arms, Averyl stilled and tensed. Then he reached up and removed her wimple.

"Nay!" she protested. "Give that back." She stretched across his chest, grasping for the headdress he held behind him.

"You've no need for it." He let his words whisper across her neck as he dropped the cloth to the dirt at his feet.

Averyl cursed him roundly. Driven by the feel of her in his arms, Drake turned his attention to the combs and pins enslaving the curls atop her head.

Handling her with care despite her struggles, Drake drew

out the restraints. His eyes widened in awe when the mass of golden spirals fell around her shoulders in a tumble. He slid his fingers into the glossy tangle of her sunshine tresses.

"Never wear this hideous scrap of cloth again." The words slipped out, raspy, almost reverent.

Averyl swallowed, saying naught. But her haunting eyes communicated such vulnerability. Drake ached to touch her, to somehow reassure her. Lord, he behaved half-cocked, felt utterly daft! He muttered an oath.

Drake could no longer deny he had been craving the chance to feel her against him. Her gaze touched his mouth, and he heard the nervous quickening of her breath. Good. She was not unmoved by him. Leaning closer, Drake anchored his hands in her hair and brought Averyl's face within a heartbeat of his.

"Do not do this." The militant tone she'd began with ended in a breathy rasp.

Drake ignored her, leaning closer. "Give me your mouth."

His intimate murmur arced between them. Her flushed face revealed both pleasure and uncertainty before she looked away.

"Do not touch me," she whispered.

"I scarce touch you now, Averyl."

" 'Tis not true. You do touch me." She swallowed.

He smiled. "Not nearly as much as I would like."

"Drake . . ."

He lowered one hand to her waist and urged her closer.

Averyl placed her warm hands against his chest, his beating heart. He saw the protest hovering in her mind, on her tongue. But she did not push him away.

Drake clasped her damp palm in his, interlocking their fingers. Averyl tried curling her hand into a fist, but as his thumb stroked her palm, her fingers slowly uncurled.

Their gazes met. Awakening and apprehension swirled together in the arresting depths of her eyes. A pulsing pleasure beat in the pit of his stomach. He checked an urge to ravage her mouth.

Averyl dropped her gaze to the dirt floor, tensing against his hold. When she said naught, Drake lifted his hand to stroke her jaw, trail down her arm, then wander to her waist. A hunger to touch her intimately, without the confines of clothing, kicked him in the gut and attacked him lower still with all the force of a one-million-man army.

Averyl quivered in his arms as he slid his hands about her neck and coaxed her face upward again. He scanned her eyes, feeling oddly breathless, and lifted his fingers to her cheek. She stared back, not uttering a word of protest.

"Do you know, Averyl, that you tempt me until I ache?"

Her eyes widened. Upon her face he saw a flash of surprise, then a desperate wish to believe him and a yearning for something he did not fully comprehend.

"That is untrue," she accused.

"I will show you how true it is," he vowed, lowering his mouth toward hers.

He touched her lips with an exploring brush of his own, demanding naught—yet. Beneath him, her berry-ripe mouth was surprisingly soft. An explosion of tingles kicked through him.

Drake groaned low in his throat and slid a calloused palm down her back, enclosing her further in his embrace. Then Averyl's arms circled his shoulders and clung tentatively. Her mouth parted slightly beneath his.

The feel of her, the taste of her, robbed him of breath and rational thought. A thick molten ache swelled through Drake's body. His hands clutched the back of her dress as his mouth delved into hers. And though shy and unpracticed, Averyl answered. With her small encouragement, he turned up the heat of their kiss into something blistering, potent. His lips stroked, beseeched, asking for more.

He followed that kiss with another that lingered and demanded. Averyl tilted to him like a flower seeking the sun. His loins tightened like a bowstring. Their fingers locked together; the warmth of her palm seared his as she nestled closer to him. His own desire was echoed in the fire of her mouth as he covered her lips again, caressing them.

Beneath his hands, he felt tension bunch in her shoulders, her back, as she strained closer to him. The scent of flowers, warm sun, and female touched his heightened senses.

Still, he needed more.

Lifting his head, he extended his forefinger toward her. She seemed spellbound, and he pressed on, placing his finger on her lower lip. "Open for me, Averyl."

A throb coursed through him as she nodded and did as he bid. He released a moan from somewhere in his chest and sank into her mouth again. Her lips parted further, not denying him. Drake touched her tongue, and she met him hesitantly with her own. Basking in the thrill of her response, he laved her mouth slowly, tasting each recess, the hint of wine within.

Averyl responded to his new demand beyond his expectations, matching his urgency. She moaned into his mouth. The sound reverberated through his chest, his body. The pulse in the pit of his belly surged dangerously.

He captured her mouth again, craving more of her sweet taste. His hand tightened about her waist, pressing her to his arousal. Averyl responded with a gasp. The primal vibration of Drake's need beat strong, coiling in his belly.

He clung to the feel of her small vibrancy in his arms, ignoring the weak protests from his rational mind that he wanted her too much. His exhilarated body pushed those protests aside with the seeming rightness of her soft form against him.

Drake caressed her shoulder before his seeking palm drifted down and delved into her bodice. Drake trembled for want of the weight and intimacy of her breast in his palm.

Before he could make that torrent of need real, Averyl jumped away.

"Nay!" She crossed her arms over her chest. "No more."

Drake stilled, stifling a wicked slash of disappointment. A long moment later, he stepped back. "For now, anyway."

She raised her chin proudly, struggling for breath. "For always. Are you not satisfied with taking me from my home, my family, and my future? And threatening me with a forced union?" Tears gathered in her eyes. She tossed her head angrily as if to shake them away. "Are you so cruel that you must hurt me more by—trifling with me and forcing intimacies?"

Whirling away, Drake hissed a breath of disappointment and stared into the now-empty hearth. He could remind Averyl that he'd used no force, but 'twould only raise her defenses more. "You cannot expect a man who plans to become your handfast husband to be blind to your . . . charms."

"I have no charms, as you well know!"

"You have them, dear lady," he returned, anger and need congealing into a dangerous challenge. "God's blood, your eyes alone could bring a man to his knees."

"I hardly see you upon your knees."

He impaled her with a furious, hungry gaze. "If I thought you would come to me willingly, I would fall to my knees now."

"That is naught but a lie!" she spat. "You only have to take what you want."

And he wanted her to give herself freely. 'Twas doubtful she ever would. God's blood, where was a stout ale when a man had need of it?

Anger tightened her pink mouth. "I am surprised you did not take me just now. You care for no one but yourself. You neither want love nor will you give it."

Drake stood silently. How could a simple truth he'd often relished fill him with an odd discomfort?

"I beseech you not to seduce me," she continued. "Do not whisper pretty words when you have no intent to take me into your life and your heart."

Then Averyl spun about and fled the cottage. Drake

cursed as she ran but did naught to force her back to his side. What would it accomplish but another raising of her defenses—or his own boiling need?

Damnation! Though he had kissed Averyl to introduce her to desire, to coax her into handfasting, he could not deny he wanted her—much too much. He craved her luscious red mouth. Her scent teased him to solve its riddle; her sweet taste lingered on his tongue.

And although she haunted his thoughts more than was wise, he must wed and bed her with all due haste.

Seven

"Open your eyes," Drake commanded as she lay awake in bed just after dawn. Gritting her teeth, Averyl feigned sleep.

Damn him. Such were the first words either she or Thornton had spoken since the previous eve. And they made her grind her teeth, for she was in no mood to be obedient to such a cad.

Averyl lifted her lids a fraction to peek at Drake. Indeed, a frown flattened his full mouth into an angry scowl this morn. What reason had he to be piqued? 'Twas she who had every right to let her fury simmer. He had used his experience, which must be considerable judging from his persuasive kisses, to seduce her, to bring her a step closer to forsaking her dreams.

Averyl knew herself a fool, for he had very nearly succeeded. No more. 'Twould be foolish to forget he but sought to sway—and use—her for revenge. His mood this morn only proved that he cared not for her.

"Get up," he demanded, his voice a low growl.

Still, Averyl refused to respond, though she felt his gaze upon her. Let him be annoyed. He certainly deserved such.

Yet she had spent the better part of a sleepless night wondering how a knave with such a wounded heart, who kissed like the devil, could speak words that touched her with the magic of an angel? Tempting, he had called her. She did not believe his lies, of course. Heaven above, she knew

better, but hearing the words spoken to her had been a foolish, dangerous thrill.

And his kiss . . . Zounds, but Drake had possessed her
mouth with all the fury of a man's fire, sparking a fluid
ache that had penetrated her body the moment their mouths
met.

Averyl swallowed a rising tide of remembered desire.
Again, she felt his lips covering hers, his warmth caressing
her. His touch had left her faint, confused, filled with yearning.

She had to escape as soon as they traveled to the mainland. True, she wanted to save her home from ruin and her
people from starvation. And once she was free, she would
do so by marrying Murdoch MacDougall—if he would still
have her. But a new sense of urgency to escape assailed
her. Averyl knew that only the unsettling emotions Drake
engendered could be at fault.

Clearly, she could not wed the man, live with him as his
wife in the most intimate ways, when he felt nothing for
her. Such would be a grievous error indeed. Unthinkable,
surely. Averyl frowned. Yet had she not been willing to wed
Murdoch MacDougall, then see where life and love led
them? Why did she find the same idea so abhorrent with
Drake?

"Get up now!" he barked. "Else I will take your presence
in bed as an invitation."

Averyl rolled over and fixed a glare on him before rising
from the warm sheets. "A good morn to you, too, lout."

He scowled at her sarcasm, his red-rimmed eyes betraying a lack of sleep that filled her with perverse pleasure.
"Dress yourself. I will await you outside. We travel within
the hour."

"To the mainland?" Had her time to escape finally come?
She dared not breathe lest hope flee her.

His eyes narrowed with suspicion. "Aye, and I will watch
you every moment. Do not imagine you will escape me."

Drake left the cottage then, and Averyl's heart began to

pound. They *would* travel to a town. A town with other people. A town off this island! She bit her lip to restrain her cry of excitement. Despite his warning, she knew this was her opportunity to elude him, perhaps her last. She must seize it before he forced a loveless marriage upon her.

She completed her quickest toilette ever and raced out to the morn. Drake unlocked the gate and held a strip of black cloth.

"Lean toward me," he demanded.

He meant to blindfold her. She panicked. Dark would settle upon her gaze. Blackness would rule.

Shaking her head, she backed away, eyes wide. "Nay."

Puzzlement overtook his features, then understanding tinged with regret and something softer than she had ever seen upon the harsh angles of his face.

"Naught will hurt you, Averyl," he whispered. "This I vow."

"But—"

" 'Tis only until I launch the boat."

His boat—he wanted to hide it. And she wanted light.

But she wanted freedom more and could not vie for it until they reached the mainland. Though it chafed her pride and her courage to do so, Averyl bowed her head. No need to alert Thornton to her plan. Besides, after today, she would have no need to learn where he'd hidden the vessel.

Semidark settled over her as the blindfold settled across her face. He left it surprisingly loose. Golden sun seeped in from the top and kissed her cheeks with warmth. Averyl sensed Drake close behind. And though such did not follow logic, the fear did not seize her when he stood near.

Drake helped her into the boat and heaved it into the sea. Within moments, the water lapped around the small craft as the breeze blew strands of her hair with summer and salt.

She felt his touch on her face, at the back of her head. Her heart picked up speed at his nearness. Then he lifted the blindfold away and cast her a searching gaze, real concern in his rich earth-brown eyes.

Knowing not what to say, Averyl nodded and looked away to the island retreating in the distance. It rose up from the sea, an abrupt cliff on one side, a rolling shore on the other. Green and mist-enshrouded, standing stones a tribute to its pagan past, the isle seemed a place of mystery, of secrets. The perfect retreat for a man like Drake.

Riding the choppy waves of breeze-blown water, Averyl calmed her roiling stomach with deep breaths of salty air and thoughts of escape. The rhythmic swish of Drake's oar through the sharp sway of the blue-gray waves brought her ever closer to freedom.

When the movement stopped and Drake disembarked on soft-packed earth, she strained to see or hear anything that would help her gain her bearings. Only Drake's footsteps sounded in the mist-damp silence. A small, still town lazed nearby.

After disembarking, Averyl studied the greenery and quaint cottages about. The air smelled of fish, pungent and strong. She made a mental note that Murdoch—and freedom—lay to the east.

Almost no one inhabited the streets. Where would everyone be on such a bonny day?

Before she could look about much, Drake gripped her hand, and not out of any affection, Averyl knew. As they walked through the *clachan,* passing several children who scampered about, chasing a yapping puppy, she searched her surroundings for an escape route. He squeezed her hand tighter and sent her a warning stare. Cursing beneath her breath, Averyl knew she had little choice but to wait to make good her escape.

When they came to the back of a tiny inn minutes later, Averyl shot him a questioning glance.

"We will spend the night here," he said. "I call many in this clachan a friend. No one will aid your escape."

"I had no such plans," she protested in a voice she hoped carried innocence.

He scowled. "You ought not to lie unless you do it well."

With that mocking advice, he knocked on the door. In seconds a balding, dark-haired man answered. His cheeky, red-headed wife stood behind him, gasping with excitement.

Drake greeted him. "Gordan, my friend. 'Tis good to see you."

The older man bellowed a hearty welcome. "Aye, and ye, too." The two men shook hands; then Gordan clapped Drake on the back. "Edina said just yesterday 'tis been far too long since ye visited."

"It has been. I apologize, Mrs. Gibson." Drake regarded the innkeeper's wife. " 'Twas kind of you to miss me."

The plump Mrs. Gibson blushed and waved his words away.

Averyl tried to close her gaping mouth. Never had she seen Drake smile so sincerely or imagined such reputable-looking folk would call him friend. Were they fools?

Or did they know something about Drake that she did not?

He smiled, then cleared his throat. "Gordan, Mrs. Gibson, this is Averyl."

To her shock, Drake brought her hand to his lips for a brief kiss. "She is to be my wife. We will be married this very day."

"I never consented to wed with you," Averyl hissed once they were behind closed doors.

"You would rather have Gordan and Edina believe you stay in this room with me as my leman?" he quizzed, dark brow raised.

She avoided glancing at the room's lone, white-quilted bed. "I care not what they think of me. 'Tis you I am curious about. What would they say if they knew you had abducted another man's intended and took her to wife?"

Drake paused; the angled planes of his face tightened in the harsh silence.

"Mrs. Gibson will expect us to share that bed," she argued, pointing to the pillow-laden mattress in the corner.

He towered over her, an unfathomable stare shadowing his face. "And so we will."

Averyl felt her breathing quicken. She dropped his heated stare, unable to hold it any longer. "Why? You do not love me. You care not for me beyond the fact I bring you revenge."

"I have told you 'tis not love that makes a marriage."

"For me it is, and I will not share a bed with a man whose heart is so closed."

She marched closer, hands perched on her hips. 'Twas a mistake. Averyl hated to admit his nearness made her knees weak. But denying such was useless.

Thornton's eyes leaped with something before he banked the light. He continued to stare at her, hands on hips, mouth irritatingly closed.

"Damn you, nor will I sacrifice my maidenhood to your hatred and your schemes!" She whirled away from him.

"Are you certain? I remember moments last night when you seemed willing enough."

With a gasp, Averyl did something she had never done to another in her life; she slapped him.

Thornton's head snapped to the side. His jaw tightened. Averyl expected retaliation in kind. A severe chastising, at the very least. Instead, he took her assault in silence, his face without expression. His lack of emotion stunned her.

"You really have no heart, do you?"

"You know well I do not."

His reply was so unequivocal, Averyl knew she would never rouse his compassion, much less any tender feelings. Why could he not care, at least a little?

And why did she care if he did?

Biting back fury, she vowed, "Enduring your touch is a mistake I will not repeat again."

So quickly it dazed her, Drake seized her by the waist and drew her flush against his solid length. Averyl drew in a sharp breath at the feel of his unyielding chest and rigid thighs against her.

"I've no intention of taking a bride in name only."

Something in her body weakened at the whispered challenge of his words, at their closeness. Senses leaped to life as she took in the breadth of his shoulders and his heated male scent. Her legs turned to warm butter as aching memories provided the salty-sweet taste of his kiss. Averyl's insides flared with heat.

"Your body was made for my hands," he whispered, sliding his palms down to cup her buttocks and bring her closer. "God shaped you capable of bringing a man supreme pleasure. You will fulfill that promise with me, not Murdoch. Never Murdoch."

Averyl closed her eyes and swallowed a lump of heat his words and nearness evoked. Nay! Despite his understanding of her fear of darkness and the fact he claimed to find her beautiful, she must remember she served but one purpose for him: Revenge. Why did that cold truth hurt so much?

"Never with you," she managed to choke out before she broke from his embrace and turned from him.

"Only with me," he whispered, his warm breath fanning the skin at her nape. Fire swept through her. Averyl wanted to run. She stayed rooted to the spot as his rich voice poured over her with the headiness of spiced wine.

"I want you in a way Murdoch cannot claim, and I intend to give you every soft pleasure for which your body was made," he murmured, his finger tracing a fiery path across her shoulder. "And as my wife, I will protect you during our year together and see to your needs. Murdoch would make no such vow that is not a lie. Think on that whilst I am gone."

With a nearly silent click of the lock, Drake departed. She drew in a shaky breath and sank to the bed. What did he mean about wanting her in a way Murdoch did not? What *could* he mean?

Averyl shook her head. It mattered not. Drake merely played games with his words. Aye, he might want her, but only as a symbol of hate, never as a woman. Never as one he could love.

No matter how sweet his kisses, that she must remember.

Drake reached the threshold of the kitchen and paused, drawing in a deep breath. Averyl was so damned determined to return to Murdoch. He saw that in her bright green eyes, and it soured his stomach. Much as he wanted to deny it, the thought of her giving herself to a craven miscreant like Murdoch turned his insides. In fact, the thought of her in any other man's bed left Drake scowling and ill-tempered.

Forcing the foreign thoughts aside, he watched Edina slice vegetables for her hearty soup. The aroma of roasting hen wafted across the room, and to her left sat several pastries, each designed to delight the tongue with their sweetness. No doubt she was preparing this feast to honor the marriage he must thrust upon Averyl—one in which her soft heart was doomed to crave an emotion he could not give.

A union he would not see end in disaster, like his parents'.

"Mrs. Gibson?" he called.

"Aye! Come in, lad. Come in. Why aren't ye upstairs wi' yer beauty of a bride?"

Drake cleared the lump in his throat, hoping it would dislodge the tightening in his chest. "I must buy supplies now, for Averyl and I will leave early in the morn."

Edina planted plump hands on her hips in disappointment. "Oh, ye canna mean to leave so soon. Where do ye go?"

" 'Tis better if you do not know. Should Murdoch and

his henchmen question you, they will be ruthless if they suspect you have information that could lead them to me."

"I willna lose my tongue around that devil. Ye canna stay? Ye bring Gordan such joy and laughter. We've missed ye."

Something in him softened. "I, too, have missed you, but if we stay longer, you would only be in more danger. Until I prove my innocence, I am still a hunted man."

"I know, but I was hopin' . . ." She paused. "Verra well."

"And if Murdoch found Averyl, he would use her in any way necessary to bring about my downfall."

He paused to touch the older woman's shoulder. "I've locked Averyl in our room, and there she must stay. She believes if I give myself over to Murdoch's mercies, he and the clan will believe my innocence."

"He haes no mercy!" Shock tightened Edina's kind face.

"And I have told her so, but she does not understand. For her safety and mine, could you see that she does not leave our room whilst I am gone?"

"Of course, lad. Once she haes been wed to ye for a year or two, she'll ken she must obey her man."

"Aye," Drake lied.

Even a lifetime together wouldn't engender obedience in Averyl. That he knew.

Odd, he'd always assumed a dutiful wife would please him, if ever he took one. Now such a paragon sounded dull. He frowned.

"When ye return, we'll have a feast to honor yer marriage," Mrs. Gibson offered.

"I wish you had not troubled yourself."

"No trouble. 'Tis excited we are ye've chosen a bride." She raised a red brow. "Surprised, mind ye, but excited."

"This marriage surprises me, too." Drake cleared his throat. At least that wasn't a lie. "But wedding Averyl is something I must do."

The older woman smiled softly. "I ken that, lad. She's a

beauty, and if ye seek to wed her, she maun hiv a good heart."

A woman with Averyl's beauty good of heart? Averyl *was* willing to sacrifice herself to a depraved demon to save her people and her home. And instead of demanding jewels and riches in return, she asked to be loved. Her deeds and wishes were definitely not the act of the kind of selfish shrew his mother had been. Diera had wanted money and constant attention. She had never cared if her son had been hungry or cold, much less deigned to think of the welfare of Dunollie's vassals.

A furrow settled across Drake's brow that matched the unsettling whirl of his thoughts. "You always see the best in others, Mrs. Gibson."

" 'Tis the truth I see, and dinna ye be forgettin' it."

With Edina's words in his ears, Drake left the inn.

Two long hours later, Drake unlocked the door to their chamber. Averyl lifted her gaze to meet his tense one. An uncomfortable moment of silence passed as he scanned her, from the braid wound about her crown to the pointed tip of her leather slippers peeking beneath the hem of her purple gown.

"Come," he said, voice hoarse. "The fair has begun."

"Fair?" she asked innocently, though her heart pounded.

"Aye, to celebrate Midsummer Eve. There we will handfast."

Averyl thought to protest leaving their chamber. But escape was impossible within these four walls. She managed a nervous smile, one she hoped did not appear too eager.

Ignoring his suspicious scowl, she approached Drake. As he enveloped her palm in the warmth of his, she noticed he had donned a clean tunic of midnight green that made his dark eyes seem as rich as fathomless earth before spring planting.

Feeling a rush of heat skip across her skin, Averyl looked

away, but not before she realized he had shaved away two days' growth of beard. In honor of their nuptials?

However, Averyl had no doubt that Drake would be much admired by ladies wherever he went. Today he would reign supreme over all other men at the fair, with his courtly dress and warrior's mien. His lips alone made a woman stare— and yearn for the feel of that wide mouth over her own.

Averyl raised her gaze to his profile and bit her lip at the tense set of his jaw and brows. Despite his words to the contrary, she could only imagine his reluctance to take such a homely lass as his wife. Well, she would never comply. A year of his loveless but tender pity was more than she could bear.

She followed him out into the bright sunlight, and he led her into the heart of the village. In the distance, waves churned against the shore, their sound competing with the merriment of voices raised in cheer somewhere within the dust cloud of shuffling feet.

The brown mist parted to reveal scampering children. Fair maidens sported ribbons in their flowing tresses while dancing around bonfires. Men set about to prove their strength in all manner of contests. The aroma of turkey legs, fruit tarts, and St. John's bread wafting through the air made her mouth water. Jugglers and fiddlers plied their trade. Above the din, a young boy announced the next showing of a revue of traveling players. His hand gestures alone portended the show's bawdy nature.

Awed, Averyl stared, wide-eyed. Never in all her years at Abbotsford had she seen anything so busy, so chaotic and magnificent, at once. Drake turned to her with a questioning glance. She answered with wide eyes.

Drake smiled with surprising indulgence. "You like the fair, do you?"

"I have never been," she admitted, "though I can most earnestly say aye."

A collection of gaily colored ribbons caught her eye. She gasped as a weathered man held out a strip of purple-and-gold satin that perfectly matched the hue and trim of her gown.

"A bonny bauble for a bonny lass?" he asked Drake.

Embarrassment heated her cheeks. She refused to look at Thornton beside her. "Good sir, nay. I have no need—"

"Give her the length of ribbon and be gone," her would-be husband instructed, tossing two pence over her head.

With disbelief, Averyl saw the coins land in the leather-like hand of the merchant. The man grinned and handed the scrap of satin to Averyl.

Her numb fingers closed around the ribbon. Drake had bought it for her. Why? Averyl raised her gaze to his, seeking an answer amid the churn of hopeful anxiety inside her.

Drake glanced into the crowd ahead. "The trifle will make you look more the bride if you tie it round your braid."

Before she could swallow her disappointment that his gesture was no gallant gift, he grabbed her hand again and pushed farther into the crowd, the ribbon pressed between their joined hands. Ale and wine flowed freely despite the early hour. Joviality and play ruled the afternoon as it settled into dusk, yet she could not revel in the mood, now reminded of the purpose for their visit.

Following Drake's lead past two gossiping women hovering about their pastry stand, they circled a pair of men arguing over a lady's honor. Beyond them stood a crowd of couples, many eagerly holding hands, a few risking a stolen kiss. Blushes and knowing smiles abounded. Here Drake stopped.

"Hiv ye come to handfast, like us?" a thin-shouldered blond man asked Drake.

Before Drake could form an answer, the shouting men behind them erupted in fury. One pushed. Another shoved, then followed with a fist. The stricken man stumbled backward, knocking her hand from Drake's.

A moment later, the crowd rushed to look upon this latest sport. Vaguely, Averyl noted that challenges were issued as women tittered and pointed to the champion of their choice. She spared the combatants no glance, only Drake, who stood on the other side of the crowd, scanning the faces about for hers. His intent, searching expression told her he saw her not. Her breath caught in her throat.

This was her chance for freedom, and she knew she must seize it—now.

Eight

Heart pounding, Averyl crouched low and crept from the fight. She ducked beside the pastry stand, then slid behind a weathered oak. A quick peek back revealed Drake nowhere in sight.

As she sneaked away, hidden in the crush of townsfolk, her hope soared. A juggler followed her, performing for coin. She waved him away and glanced over her shoulder again.

There she saw Drake, leaving the swelling roar of those eager to watch the fight. Tense, watchful, he searched about the pastry stand, then glanced behind the tree.

Grimacing when he again started in her direction, Averyl thanked God, for once, for her lack of height and curves and continued through the throng. She breathed so hard, she could scarce hear the lute player's musical routine beside her.

Glancing about, Averyl feared she could not run in the open spaces past the fair's perimeter without Drake's watchful stare spotting her. And from experience Averyl knew she had no hope of outdistancing him. She needed to hide quickly, until night fell, when she could assume her captor believed her gone.

A bright red tent decorated with golden moons and silver stars caught her eye. Beyond caring who or what lay inside, Averyl ducked within its confines.

At first, she saw no one within. She heard only the familiar sounds of vendors hawking their wares outside and the faint tinkling of bells. The pungent odor of spicy incense wafted to her. She turned to discover the source of the smell. Just beyond the edge of the faint glow, Averyl found herself looking into the oldest face she had ever seen.

"Come. Sit," she said.

The small woman had skin lined with knowledge and life. She gestured to the empty chair across the scarred, circular table.

"You are frightened." The woman's stare pierced Averyl until she looked away in discomfort. She glanced over her shoulder and through the curtain. Drake was nowhere in sight.

"Sit," the woman commanded again.

Knowing she had nowhere else to run, Averyl complied, slowly sliding into a huge dark-wood chair.

"You run from somebody?" the crone asked, her oddly accented voice crackling with each word. Before Averyl could reply, the woman amended, "It is from one man that you run."

Averyl gasped, her hand rising to her chest. The woman was a spaewife. Could such people really tell the futures of others?

The woman's eyes followed the gesture, and her olive-skinned face lit up in a mysterious smile. "Give me your palm."

When Averyl hesitated, the woman reached across the table, a bracelet of gold dangling from each wrist, and seized her hand.

Though Averyl was alarmed and wondered if the woman didn't belong in an asylum somewhere, she was intrigued.

The woman turned Averyl's palm up and studied it, tracing the sign of the cross with a silver coin. For several long moments the fortune-teller's gaze did not waver.

When the woman looked up, her eyes were focused at some distant point. Her face reflected a series of emotions before she settled on a smile. Her attention returned to Averyl.

"Ah, a fortune worth telling," she commented, her voice thick and exotic, clearly not Scottish.

The wisdom in her fathomless eyes disturbed Averyl. "Say naught. I do not wish to know of my health, wealth, or happiness."

"What of your future husband?" The crone smiled. "You wish to know of that, yes? Yes, you do. For now, I shall start with your past. Your mother has been dead many years."

"Aye," Averyl admitted, disturbed and frowning.

"You are betrothed, no?"

"Aye." How could this crone know such? Perhaps this spaewife did have special powers?

"But there is another. He is close, and he searches for you. He separates you from your intended." The old woman peered into the air. "It will be thus in the future as well."

A stab of dread pierced Averyl's stomach. Did the woman believe she would never find her way back to Murdoch MacDougall's side to become his wife? It mattered not, for no one could see the future. Could they?

Before Averyl could protest, the mysterious hag frowned suddenly, her cloudy eyes racing over Averyl's palm. "The past is vital. Learning it will unlock the key to your future. Then you will find the answer to your hopes for both coin and love."

Averyl bit her lip, her mind racing. Though everyone wanted to hear they would be happy and rich, Averyl paused, considering the woman's words. Had she not discovered for herself that the past drove Drake and the hate in his heart?

"My betrothed and the other man in my life, what has passed between them?" Averyl asked, surprising herself.

The woman paused, brow furrowing in concentration. "They have known each other for many years and share a common bond."

A bond? Before Averyl could decipher that puzzle, the woman's bony, bejeweled fingers snaked across the table and took Averyl's other hand in a surprisingly strong grip. The length of purple ribbon fell from her fingers, to the table. "The man you run from, who gave you this gift"— she nodded to the scrap of satin between them—"is your future. Your destiny."

Shock rippled through Averyl. Drake, her destiny? The crone must be daft. Yet she'd known of Drake's gift.

"You are much mistaken," she said, rising.

The woman's wrinkled grip tightened. "Sit, child."

Averyl felt compelled by the ageless knowledge in the woman's black eyes and complied.

"This cannot be!" Averyl demanded. "He cares not for me."

Her hacking laugh sent a shiver down Averyl's spine. "He cares. You will love him, and he"—she raised a dramatic jet brow—"will love you equally, if not more."

Love? The unconditional giving of tenderness and trust from Drake? Such was not possible. "Now you truly are mistaken."

Clucking her tongue, the woman shook her gray head. "Look beyond his words and deeds, deep into his eyes. Give him your trust. There you will find a treasure."

Confusion eddied and swirled within her. Only the worst kind of man could speak his words and commit his deeds. "I will not trust a murderer who would force—"

"Never would he force you to give of your body. Nor did he kill. Look to the face of another suitor for that."

Another suitor? She could only mean Murdoch. But 'twas impossible. Was it not?

Averyl bowed her head, her mind whirling. The soothsayer believed Drake innocent, as did Kieran and the Gibsons. Was such possible? Drake had maintained that Murdoch MacDougall had framed him for the heinous murder. Averyl sighed in confusion, wishing she could escape the old woman and her riddles.

Clutching Averyl's palm, the woman went on. "Yes, consider your lover's innocence. Once you realize the truth, you will give yourself willingly. This man will treasure your love and innocence. It is a gift he has had from no other."

Give herself willingly? While Averyl could not deny Drake's rousing kisses had the power to melt her, she would never bed down with the man. Not when she had the Mac-Dougall to return to, not when she had her land, her people, and her heart to save.

Averyl bolted up from her seat. "I must go."

The woman's worn grip on her hand tightened, refusing her leave. "The secrets of your lover's past are dark ones. Inside is a man with a tender heart and a needy soul."

When Averyl opened her mouth to argue, the woman spoke. "Let time unfold and do not fear your destiny. Go now. He searches for you."

With that, the woman released Averyl, then turned away. Still stunned, Averyl rose slowly. The shining purple ribbon lay bright and new on the table before her. She stared at it and thought of the man who had given it to her. Drake had not meant it as a gift, had felt no affection in the purchase. But something inside her refused to leave it behind.

Cursing herself a fool, she snatched the ribbon from the table and tied it about her braid as she exited the dim tent.

Outside, Averyl found that dusk had descended upon the fair. By all appearances, the townsfolk were still celebrating. Bright streamers hung from every home in sight. A ring of wooden poles had been stuck into the soil to form a circle from which lanterns hung, outlining a crude dance floor, now occupied by a handful of the town's drunken inhabitants.

Beyond the fair lay unmerciful darkness and no way to shield herself if its terrors preyed upon her. Trembling, Averyl lamented that she had not thought of such sooner.

She clung to a giant oak at the outskirts of the fair, making certain Drake was nowhere in sight. Men milled about everywhere, some with ladies beside them, others partaking

of ale and one another's companionship. None possessed
Drake's height or controlled carriage, inky waves or muted
elegance.

He was gone.

A sigh escaped her lips as she wondered if she would
ever see him again.

What foolishness! Relief should fill her, not a hollow
ache within her breast. He wanted her not as a woman, not
for her heart, but as a pawn. 'Twas the truth, despite the
crone's intriguing words.

Drawing in a deep breath, Averyl vowed she would not
miss him. Not for an instant beyond this one. Or this one.

She frowned. Drake would never miss her, and she must
concentrate on that reality, not some fantasy her imagination
and body clung to.

Pushing away from the tree, she made one last scan of
the crowd. Three men loomed close, soldiers judging from
the heavy swords swinging at their thighs. With a shrill
whistle and a lascivious leer, Averyl knew they had spotted
her—alone.

A blade of trepidation sliced her when one started in her
direction, his eyes never wavering. The other two followed.

Averyl ran into the dark, fighting her fear, hoping this
once the black air would devour her, conceal her. An anxious glance over her shoulder confirmed that they pursued
her. Indeed, one sprinted after her, while the others laughed
at the sport.

Her heart pounding, lurching against her chest, Averyl
picked up her skirts and ran faster. The flat ground beneath
her feet provided nowhere to hide. No tall bushes nearby
to give cover. And a quick scan behind her revealed the
men still followed—and gained ground.

Her toe connected with something solid, and without
warning, she tumbled to the soft earth in a heap of bruised
knees and scraped hands. Behind her, she heard another
chorus of laughter.

Ignoring her aches, she staggered to her feet. Before she could escape, a harsh hand grasped her arm. She screamed.

"What have we here, lass? All alone, are ye now? Ye canna leave before the party haes started."

"I—I search for my husband." She stared into a rough face of browned teeth and mean eyes. Her heart pounded in fear.

"Is that so? We dinna see any men here but us. So if your husband is fool enough to leave ye alone, we'd consider it our privilege, nay, our right, to be enjoyin' yer . . . company this eve." He brushed her breast with his fingers.

Behind him, his duo of companions laughed. Averyl struggled against them in horror, praying she could find an escape.

"As the lass's husband, enjoying her 'tis my right, and mine alone," the familiar voice cut into the silence.

Averyl looked beyond the miscreant to find Drake standing behind them all, sword drawn. Relief shocked every crevice of her body with a warm comfort. Now she would be safe.

Drake stood a head taller than any other. He eclipsed the varlets in breadth, and if Drake's scowl bore any truth, determination, too.

The fiend holding her wrist gave a sickly laugh, his smile slipping. The other men backed away. "Ach, we were just teasin', now, weren't we, lass?"

Drake speared her with a questioning glance. She answered with a wobbly shake of her head.

His jaw clenched in fury. "Be gone with you before I make you part of tonight's stew."

The rotten-toothed ogre opened his mouth to protest. Drake took a menacing step forward, shining silver blade clenched in his fist.

"Give me a reason," Drake invited silkily. The harsh look on his face welcomed violence.

The rogue slinked away.

For a long moment, Averyl stared at Drake, her captor,

her rescuer, her handfast husband-to-be. Though she'd found this trouble in trying to escape him, she knew only comfort at his return. She resisted an urge to throw herself into his sheltering arms. 'Twas not a gesture he would welcome, judging from the black blaze of his eyes and the white fury around his taut mouth. He sheathed his sword and grasped her face with his large, warm hands. His gaze traveled over her carefully, with concern, leaving no inch untouched, even the ribbon at her braid.

"Drake, I—"

He silenced her with a hand. "Later. Now, follow me."

Thornton took her hand in his and spun away, clearly assuming she would comply. And she did, for she had no other option. Tonight had proved she could not safely return to Dunollie alone. Indeed, she had not escaped the first town.

Straightening her bodice with her free hand, Averyl followed him, too frightened to stay behind. Though it seemed irrational to place her safety in the hands of a man everyone believed capable of murder, she did. Despite his fury with her, Drake still calmed her fear of the dark with his mere presence. And he had proven, once again, that he would not harm her.

And since he kept her safe, was there a chance the spaewife spoke true? Was Drake, perhaps, innocent of Lochlan MacDougall's murder? Was he her destiny?

Drake glanced over his shoulder, watching an oddly subdued Averyl follow. He suspected lingering fear quieted her, since he would never imagine her contrite. And though it pleased him not, Drake admitted he, too, would have run, given Averyl's chance.

Still, the admission did not make his mood less foul.

He sighed in disgust. 'Twas not anger at Averyl that soured his disposition, though her repeated attempts to escape annoyed him. Nor was it knowing what he must do now. Instead, he pictured her, again and again, at the mercy of the vile vagabonds who had captured her. Even now, fury erupted through his veins, tightening his hands into fists.

He had wanted to kill them. To engage each in hand-to-hand combat, then steal the life from them. What Drake did not know was why. Why such a violent urge? 'Twas ugly but common enough for beasts like them to overpower a woman. Even the rapes he'd heard in Dunollie's dungeons had not filled him with this illogical need for blood lust, a need he had curbed for Averyl's benefit as well as his own hunted hide.

Again, why? 'Twas as important to him to protect her as it was that she not see him as a vicious killer.

Why?

Pushing the haunting question aside as they reached the gathering again, Drake waited for Averyl. She stopped beside him and cast a questioning glance at him with wide green eyes.

She feared him, too. In a different way, but he still frightened her. And he liked it not. Something within his chest tightened, and he forced his temper to calm and his voice to gentle.

"Give me your hand, Averyl."

She stared at him for long moments, as if trying to guess his intent. Drake stifled the remnants of his anger to remove the severity from his expression. Finally, she put cold fingers into his.

He closed his palm around hers and gave a gentle squeeze. "You are safe. I will let nothing or no one harm you."

After staring at their joined hands for a heartbeat, she looked up with such stunning trust, he lost a breath. "I believe you."

Trust. Her words near shattered him. He'd not received that in so long, not since the bloody accusations of nearly two years past. She believed him. Her vow rippled pleasure through him.

"Come with me, then."

Without awaiting her response, he moved forward, hand clasped about hers, closer to the crowd. He spotted a couple bouncing a laughing toddler on their knees. They looked more than adequate.

"Excuse me, good sir, madam. Could you spare a moment?"

"Aye, indeed," said the man, handing the baby aside and smoothing down his shock of red hair.

Beside him, Drake could feel Averyl's puzzled stare. The feel of her hand in his urged him on with anticipation.

"I declare this lady and I are handfast."

Averyl gasped at his side. Glancing quickly at her frozen ivory countenance, Drake squeezed her hand as she tried to pry it away and rushed to address the couple. "You are our witnesses."

The young woman cradled the toddler and tittered with delight. " 'Tis so romantic." She smiled at Averyl. "I remember my wedding night." With a sigh, she added. "As will ye."

Sitting beside her, the man flushed.

Drake smiled, hoping no one would take note of the pale shock frozen on his new bride's face. "Thank you, kind sir, good lady. We are obliged."

Before the couple could say more, before Averyl could object, he tugged gently on her arm and led her back toward the Gibsons, where a feast awaited them—and whatever their first night as man and wife would bring.

Nine

On their silent journey to the inn, Averyl walked beside Drake, struggling to match his rapid strides. Everything about his tense posture and shuttered expression bespoke turmoil. Beside him, she bit her lip, feeling a cauldron of anxiety in her belly. Did her husband think of the coming night?

Their handfast union was so sudden. And unless her new husband perished, she would be unable to wed the MacDougall before the bitter winter and Abbotsford's ruin. Even knowing that, she could not bring herself to wish for Drake's demise.

Nay, to save her home, only two options remained, neither likely. Drake was hardly apt to give her any funds, no matter how prettily she begged. Nor was she likely to see Murdoch so that she might plead with him to save her home. But her home did not reign supreme in her mind now.

Chirping crickets, green fields, and a damp breeze reminded Averyl she had this summer night—her wedding night—to face before considering the harsh consequences winter would bring.

She knew what Drake would expect tonight, at least in the vaguest sense. Her belly clenched, winding as tightly as the ribbon atop her head. Aye, she would deny him at every turn. But what if she weakened under the gentle assault of his kisses? What if she foolishly surrendered?

Casting a glance at her new handfast husband, Averyl felt a new claw of anxiety. Upon her abduction two weeks ago, she would never have imagined Drake possessed even one redeeming quality. Yet she realized he had mostly shown her only the sides of himself he'd wanted her to know. The gentle comforting, his protective concern, those had slipped out, she suspected, only to be quickly covered again by his gruff impersonality or anger.

But she *had* seen those glimpses of a different man beneath. Was the real Drake not a criminal at all but a mere man fighting to win back his honor while struggling to accept his mother's rejection?

His granite profile and distant mood told her naught.

When they arrived at the Gibsons', Gordan and Edina were waiting. Mrs. Gibson hugged Drake as they walked in the door. "So pleased I am, lad. If anyone deserves happiness, 'tis ye."

Drake returned the plump woman's smile stiffly while shaking Gordan's hand. "Thank you both, for everything."

Mr. Gibson waved his words away. "Ach, get ye to the table so I can congratulate yer new bride."

Drake disengaged his hand from Gordan's and with a troubled glance left for the inn's private rooms.

"Lassie, such a long face on yer wedding day?" Gordan said as Edina hugged her impulsively. "Could be she is fretful, eh?"

The older woman admonished her husband with a gentle *tsk.* "Now dinna ye be scarin' the poor lamb." She held Averyl's shoulders and smiled. "Drake'll be gentle as a dove. I hiv seen how he looks at ye."

How he looked at her? If his regard were much different than that of a nuisance—and a homely one at that—Averyl would be surprised indeed. Instead, she smiled weakly, knowing not what to say.

Drake appeared again, and the small group assembled around the table. With a long stare, Drake poured her a cup of wine. She drank greedily, hoping the liquor would ease the edge of her disquiet. Then she extended her cup toward him for more.

This time, Edina filled it with a sideways smile at her husband. Gordan returned his wife's grin and winked.

The Gibsons' affection for one another was almost tangible. Averyl ached, wishing for that happiness. She swallowed another sip of the sweet wine, acknowledging that despite the spaewife's avowals, such a love would never blossom between her and Drake. 'Twas impossible. Though she could see goodness in him, he was still angry, too focused on revenge. And Averyl could ill afford to do aught else but concentrate on resisting her husband's fine face and form and saving Abbotsford.

During the long, uncomfortable meal, Averyl barely tasted the juicy haggis. Mrs. Gibson seemed more than happy to make most of the conversation, with brief responses from her doting husband. Drake said little, ate less, and left the table the moment it was marginally polite to seek ale in the adjoining tap room.

As Drake paced before a roaring fire, Averyl felt his restless spirit through the open door. The unsettled energy radiated, seeking release. Edina and Gordan seemed not to notice, but Averyl watched his swift, long-legged strides.

She wondered at the cause of his mood as he held his cup and walked the floor. Did he think on this night? Of the fury he would unleash upon her for attempting to escape? Or did he dwell on his revenge and the bloody murder behind it?

Finally, Edina looked at Drake. His stride ceased at her attention, and he dropped his moody gaze to the brew in his cup.

With a sly grin, Edina said, " 'Tis time and past for the bride and groom to be alone."

"Aye," Gordan chimed in with a knowing grin that twisted Averyl's stomach. "I ken an impatient groom when I see one."

Were they both addled and blind? How could they send

her upstairs with Drake, behind a locked door, when disquiet churned the air about him more surely than a windstorm?

"Not yet," Averyl protested. "I am enjoying myself."

Jaw hard, Drake's gaze pinned her to the wall with his stare and stilled her speech. Averyl tried to tear her gaze away, but his eyes held her, appearing to accuse her. Of what, she did not know. She swallowed, fighting anxiety.

Edina shook her head. "Come now, lassie. Ye maun no' be nervous. Ye hiv a groom to please."

Doubting she could ever please him, Averyl cast Drake an uneasy glance as he stood in the open doorway. The unreadable look upon his face as he moved closer did not comfort her.

"They are right, my love," he whispered. He settled his hand beneath her elbow, his fingers tight with tension. "You should make ready to retire."

His love, indeed. Such drivel, right down to his adoring tone. Still, she shivered at his touch, at what the coming hours might bring. Dear God, how she wished she could spend the night anywhere but behind a closed door with Drake—in a room possessing but one bed. Averyl closed her eyes.

Drake helped her rise from her chair, his hot fingers settling about her waist, conveying his warning with a squeeze.

"Do no' be shy," Edina said. "I will help ye prepare."

Averyl wanted to scream that Drake had no claim on her. But he now did, and the Gibsons would only think her daft. She wanted to shout that he might hurt her. Yet she knew her hosts would never believe Thornton cruel.

Her mind racing, Averyl sent a last terrified glance toward her captor and followed Mrs. Gibson upstairs to the room in which she and Drake were to spend the night celebrating a marriage that neither wanted.

* * *

With a smile, Mrs. Gibson released Averyl's hair from the confines of her thick braid, laying the ribbon Drake had given her on a nearby basin. She shivered when her dress came off next, leaving her clad only in a sheer white shift.

"Bonny as a bloom," the plump Mrs. Gibson declared.

Averyl managed a weak smile, her heart thumping.

The woman smiled back as brightly as the afternoon sun and withdrew a small bottle from her pocket. Averyl frowned when Edina opened it and doused her finger with its contents.

"Hold still, lass," Mrs. Gibson instructed, dabbing some of the pungent liquid at the base of Averyl's throat and wrists.

The scent, something spicy, wafted up to her nose in a pleasant drift, reminding her of hearth and home, yet signaling something darker. Aye, even passionate.

" 'Tis a blend of my making," her hostess said. "Cinnamon wi' my favorite blossoms mixed. Tonight ye shall smell so enchanting, Drake willna ever consider lettin' ye loose."

She wanted Drake to release her now. For if he truly induced her to his bed, Averyl feared he would demand her very soul. Certainly she did not wish him to see her so near to naked, smelling like temptation. No good could come of it.

" 'Tis for Drake I do this, ye ken? His past is so tragic, his road now so long and dangerous, I canna resist helping wi' his happiness where I can."

The woman knew something of Drake's past. Everything? Averyl's heart began to race for an entirely different reason. She wanted to know why Drake had chosen to destroy her life. She sought the reason for her husband's and Lord Dunollie's hatred. But most of all, she yearned to understand why Drake would tell her nothing himself.

"Indeed," she murmured. "I've often thought the same."

The older redhead nodded. " 'Tis why Drake canna turn himself in. Murdoch MacDougall will no' show Drake mercy. Ye maun kin the MacDougall haes none."

Clearly, Drake had the Gibsons believing him innocent. Reining in her frustration, Averyl encouraged Edina's further confidences.

"You speak true," she said with a sigh.

Her hostess touched a dab of the perfume in the valley between Averyl's breasts, then corked the bottle. "Aye, lass. Only the most heartless of men would seduce his faither's love for spite. 'Tis cruel, I tell ye, how the knave baited Drake after he found Murdoch, the swine, bedding his maither."

Edina wedged the customary willow branch beneath their bed to encourage fertility. Averyl scarce noticed.

Dizziness and nausea assailed her as the woman's words painted a vivid mental picture. *Murdoch bedding Drake's mother?* Murdoch would not be so vicious, would he? Surely not.

But what reason did Edina have to lie?

None.

Averyl drew in a worried breath. So Drake's mother was the source of his conflict with Murdoch. That and family pride. Had Drake intended all along to steal her honor in retaliation for the loss of his mother's? The thought washed her with another wave of nausea as Edina fluffed their pillows.

Her almost-betrothed and Drake's own mother. And Drake himself had discovered them. How terrible to find his mother cavorting with a man not her husband or protector.

Averyl could only guess from the bit she knew that the woman had been Lochlan MacDougall's leman. And Edina had said Lochlan loved her. Murdoch had clearly been in the wrong to seduce his father's woman. And Drake found them together, intimately. Had that shattered his motherly illusion?

"He was of tender years when that happened," Averyl baited, hoping her hostess would provide more answers.

"Aye, just ten and four. 'Tis awful, I tell ye."

Averyl's heart stopped, then thudded painfully. So much now made sense—the enmity between the two men, Drake's contempt for his mother. By the saints, how terrible. And Averyl was caught squarely in the middle, somehow a pawn to each man.

She frowned as Edina bustled around her. What reason would Drake have had to kill Lochlan MacDougall? Failing to protect his mother? 'Twas possible, but far more likely that if Murdoch hated his father enough to seduce his mistress, he may have hated his father enough to kill him.

Her thoughts racing, Averyl barely heard as Edina finally took her leave. Alone, she sank down on the soft mattress. Hugging herself to stop her trembling, she contemplated the enormity of her new information, praying she could somehow use it to arouse Drake's pity and escape. If not, the intimacies of marriage would not be a question of if but of when.

Drake reached a hand to the door separating him from his new bride but hesitated. Cursing softly, he lowered his hand.

He pictured Averyl waiting, wondering, fearing what this night would bring. Would she hate him come morn for what he must do now?

Appalled at his lack of resolve, he stared at the door wondering what his friends would do. Aric would watch Averyl, wait, find her vulnerability, and use it. He had patience. Drake lacked that, as well as time. And Kieran would use glib words and sweet phrases to charm her from her gown. Drake sighed. He had never had a charming day in his life.

He had only determination, desperation . . . and desire.

Pushing aside frustration, Drake knocked. Averyl's feelings mattered not. A consummation of this handfast union would put her beyond Murdoch's reach. Naught else could matter—not her green eyes, her pink mouth, or his urge to protect her.

When she made no reply to his summons, Drake eased the door open. Averyl stood with her back to his gaze, facing the open windows. A night breeze swept through, disturbing the folds of her flowing shift, made sheer by the moon's glow. The rumble of thunderclouds churned in the distance, mimicking his turmoil.

By the saints, how he wanted her. 'Twas not something he could deny, not when his heart raced and his palms turned damp at the very sight of her. Her hair, golden and soft, curled down her narrow back, ending just above the arch of her buttocks.

With slow footsteps, he came to stand behind her. The air about them hung charged, unsettled with disquiet.

She feared; he knew that. Drake also believed he could coax her into his bed this night—eventually. But the ugly question of tomorrow and the days that followed reared its head.

Aye, she would hate him for taking her innocence with no intent to give her the love she sought. Earning her enmity was not a new notion and probably no less than he deserved. Still, the day she turned eight and ten, she ceased to be important in his revenge. He had not taken a bride, as had his friend Aric, with the intent to keep her forever. Nay, only until Murdoch would be a poor man. Then Drake intended to use every means possible to kill the evil chief with the shameful knowledge of poverty and shame seared in his mind. And Averyl would be free.

But why did she feel most important tonight? As if her wishes and feelings should be honored despite the consequences?

And why did he want to touch her so badly?

Shrugging aside the foolish questions, he poured them each a new cup of wine. When Drake finished, he studied Averyl's stiff spine and for once wished she would say something.

Handing the cup in her direction, he leaned against the wall beside her. A long moment passed before she spurned the drink and faced him with an accusing stare.

"When did you plan to tell me that the man I nearly wed seduced your mother?"

Shock tingled its way through him. *Damnation!* Edina must have spoken of his past. But how much? And why tonight, when the past haunted him already?

Hissing an earthy curse, he glanced away.

"So, 'tis true?"

Drake saw no point in denying it. He nodded.

Her ire soared. "Did you plan to say nothing and simply take my virtue in exchange for the loss of your mother's honor?"

Drake swallowed, memories and guilt both eating at his gut. Though his mind told him that he owed her no explanation, somehow Drake knew that to be false.

Setting her wine aside, he forced his voice to even tones. "My intent to bed you has more to do with the fact you are now my wife than the recovery of honor my mother never possessed."

"She went willingly to Murdoch MacDougall?"

"Like the veriest of whores, again and again."

"Why?" Bewilderment choked her question.

"I can only guess about the whys of her faithless soul."

Averyl winced but forged on. "Then pray tell why did you force this handfast upon me if not to avenge her. Certainly not out of love, for you've refused to feel that."

Drake formed fists at his sides. "Averyl, you do not—"

"Understand? Nor will I. You seek to use me in the basest sense, then tell me nothing of your purpose. Do not think I can ever forgive you for that."

"I expect not."

Taken aback, Averyl stared in surprise. "Then what do you seek to gain from having my backside warm your sheets?"

"A wife, perhaps."

Averyl made a harsh scoffing that could not, even in kind moments, be considered an agreement. "A wife you would quickly leave once my usefulness was at its end."

Drake downed his glass of wine in a swallow and tried to determine the fastest words away from revenge. He wished to avoid her hate, so he turned his thoughts to seduction, to her sweet body beneath him, pliant and needy.

Suddenly he recalled the rogues who would have forced Averyl's maidenhood from her on a brutal dark field that eve. Again, he felt the violent urge to protect. What did such mean?

Naught. It could mean naught. He must claim her tonight. Now. Before she escaped or Murdoch found them.

Before his desire overwhelmed reason.

Shoulders taut, he checked an urge to touch her. First, he must make her understand that she could not escape alone.

"Did you never imagine when you ran from me that you might be harmed? Or killed? Or worse?"

Averyl said nothing at first. He could see her thinking, her mind turning his question over. Before she spoke, Drake realized such possibilities had not occurred to her, not until 'twas nearly too late.

" 'Tis over now," she said stiffly. "I am unharmed, and you are not without your captive."

Stubborn wench. Would she not understand? "Aye, you are unharmed. And 'tis lucky we are, *wife*. Do you know the unspeakable things those men would have forced upon you?" he growled. "They were drunk and lusty and cared not how much you protested. Their only interest was in sport and pleasure."

"And your plans are so different? Do you not seek to violate me as well?"

"Violate?" Anger made his jaw tight. "I would not abuse you so. Have I once harmed you?"

"Except to take me from my people and my purpose?"

she asked acidly. "And this night, whether you call it consummation, revenge, or rape, the end will be no different."

He stepped closer, hovering above her. Aching to prove her wrong, he wrapped his fingers about her warm, scented nape and pulled her closer. Averyl seemed to stop breathing as her green eyes widened and met his.

Their mouths a breath apart, he rasped, " 'Tis proof how little you know of desire. I could have raped you long ago had I wished it. But I want you willing, nay, eager, lass."

Averyl shook her head. "You cannot seduce me."

He smiled at her unwitting challenge. "I will, and for one simple reason, Averyl: You are not unresponsive to me."

She blanched white at his words, and Drake knew he had hit upon the truth. Though she shook her head again in denial, he sensed a new fear in her expression.

"I speak true," he whispered, his gaze delving into the heady depths of her eyes. "Do you know how I know that?"

She arched a pale brow. "Because you are arrogant?"

He smiled and loomed closer, a mere breath separating their bodies. "Because I see desire shining in your eyes." Averyl opened her mouth to rebut, but he stopped her with a fingertip against her lips. " 'Tis the truth. And I feel it in your mouth when we kiss." His whisper filled the charged air between them. "Surrender to that desire."

She turned away. "My surrender matters not. You will take what you want, regardless of my feelings."

He reached for her shoulders, surprised to feel her trembling, and whispered in her ear. "Nay, I will take you with every regard for your feelings. With every hope you admit you want to feel my mouth on yours, my body against yours."

Beside her, Drake watched her cheeks flush red. "I will not listen to your pretty lies."

His grip on her tightened. The charged energy leaping between them multiplied. "I do not waste my breath on lies."

The more Drake held her, the more he ached to have her.

Yet as she spoke, the more he feared his hasty possession tonight would pain her, not in body but in heart.

Before he could dwell on the unpleasant reality, his lips covered hers, softly demanding of her sweetness. She resisted, her warm fingers splayed against his chest as if to ward him off. Refusing defeat, Drake renewed his onslaught, reaping the honeyed harvest of her mouth. He gave desire free rein, drinking of her lips, drawing her stiff form closer.

His pulse quickened. His skin came alive with sensations of warmth and velvet. The faint scent of spiced flowers, of Highland rain, registered as he groaned and wrapped his fingers in her silken tresses, flowing loose and enticing. She could tempt the most pious of monks.

With a pained cry, Averyl moved to push him away. Drake held fast, possessing her mouth again, tasting, teasing.

Tearing her mouth away, she breathed, "Why?"

Drake let her gaze delve into her—deep—willing her to understand what he could not deny. "I want this. I want you."

Then he possessed her lips again, plundering.

Averyl's hands crept from his chest to his shoulders, then about his neck. Her mouth softened to him slowly. He courted, waiting for her trust, her need. She gave it in inches, melting against him, admitting desire. Drake rejoiced in each small surrender, in the long, velvety union of their mouths.

The kiss seized his breath. As if she knew her power, Averyl shyly touched her tongue to the curve of his lower lip, inciting a shiver.

Tilting her face up to his, he deepened their kiss and inhaled the feminine allure of her skin. Desire rose within him like the heat of an August noon. His tongue mated with hers, encouraging and insisting. Averyl returned every nuance of his kiss and heightened the flame of his need.

Their lips met again, urgency spiraling. Drake clutched

a handful of her chemise and used it to draw her close enough to feel every inch of his want. She melted into him, her fervor heating the air between them, stirring his lust-filled body.

He lowered his mouth to her neck, where he nibbled his way across her scented skin. Her soft taste sent a rain of sensation straight down to his aching shaft.

As he picked up hints of her essence with his tongue, she intoxicated him. Again, he devoured her mouth. Her fervent response held a heady mix of female innocence and a natural instinct to bewitch. And God knew, Drake was only too willing to fall beneath her spell.

Keeping her mouth captive to his, Drake lifted her against him, cradling her knees into the crook of his arms. The feel of her small, passionate form against him, seemingly so willing, sent his lust careening out of control.

Drake crossed the room with Averyl in his arms and set her upon the soft bed, where he planned to claim her this night until they both cried exhaustion. Lying her down, he followed her to the soft mattress, taking her mouth once more. She met his unrelenting demand as if she already understood the desperation of desire's throb.

Averyl moaned in his arms, and Drake felt her cry deep within him. He could wait no longer to have her, all of her.

With a brush of his hand, her shift fell from her shoulder. He gazed upon her milky flesh, the slopes of her shoulders, the soft rise of her breasts. He worshiped the flesh he exposed with his mouth, lips breathing over soft skin.

Finally, he pushed her chemise to her waist, sending his tingling palm over the small mound of her breast. He moaned as she arched into his touch. Drake closed his eyes at the dizzying feel of her beneath his hands, feeling lust pound in his body more strongly than the beat of his racing heart.

He leaned toward her and met her gaze. Desire pulsed in the air, potent, fast, consuming. Its rhythm doubled, pounded, when his mouth closed around the waiting tip of her breast and she cried out.

The green of her eyes flared with surprise and want. He stared at her, need roiling within him. Could one woman be so sweet? Could she truly make all those before seem like pale imitations? Aye, he thought as his hand grazed the curve of her waist, then drifted down to the arch of her hip, removing her silken shift in the process.

On fire, he reached for her hands and brought them to his shirt. "Undress me?"

At his ragged request, she lifted her eyes to him in uncertainty. She hesitated, biting her lip, swollen from his kiss. Cheeks red, breath fast, she stared, her gaze roving over his shoulders, his chest. Drake sat still, waiting, praying.

Suddenly, her fingers were in motion, working at his shirt. Inch by inch, she exposed his flesh. Her eyes widened before she consumed him in a heavy-lidded gaze of sultry wonder. He watched the rise and fall of her chest, heard her ragged breathing. Satisfaction seeped into him.

She pushed one side of the shirt off his shoulder. Drake trembled at the feathered texture of her touch, so light yet inescapable. Impatient, he jerked the garment over his head.

Slowly, she lifted shaking fingertips to the center of his chest, just below the gleam of his father's cross. The heat of her touch scorched him.

Talons of fire licking at him, Drake seized her mouth again, this time with a fervency he did not try to restrain. He whispered wicked suggestions, needful moans, as he touched her. Across her abdomen and the curve of her buttocks, around the heat of her thighs—anywhere she would have him. She gasped, arched, sighed—set him aflame.

Again, he devoured her mouth, begging and demanding her response at once until he felt certain she understood he intended to possess each warm inch of her.

Averyl did not shy away. Indeed, she returned his caress with a sweep of her glance, followed by the lingering touch of her hands up his arms, across his shoulders, until her fingers cascaded down his belly. Drake sucked in a deep breath of heat. With a gaze of eyes so green, she held his stare, as her fingertips made their way across the arch of his brow, the angles of his cheeks, over the sensitive curve of his lip. Drake had never imagined that such caresses could make him ache with such hardness.

Knowing he could passively endure her touch no more, Drake rolled her beneath him, eager to feel her soft body. Her harsh breathing matched his own, as did the want in her eyes.

Yet for all Averyl's beguiling ways, she was innocence personified. Like Eve before her fated walk though Eden, sensual but untouched. Pure and unspoiled.

Until this night. Until him.

The thought slammed into him. He swallowed hard to push it away.

If he took her now to satisfy his lust and revenge, aye, 'twould ease his aching manhood. But her virginity would be sacrificed on the altar of revenge. Even from afar, Murdoch would sully the one thing Drake wanted perfect between them. And she would come to hate him for the deed.

He lay motionless atop her, enduring her frown of curiosity. Still, he did not move.

Claiming her now would be tantamount to thieving the one gift he could not replace, one he had no right to, since he did not intend to remain her husband. Knowing this, could he defile her in the name of vengeance, make her a bride of hatred?

His mind raced. Her surrender was so clear, it seemed tangible. She desired him. Was that not enough? Could he not find good in the union of their bodies without a thought to the past? Or the future?

Into her eyes he gazed, seeing need and trust shining from their deep green depths. Could he really use her so ill?

Drake fought the answer, but it lay there like a serpent, coiling about his need.

"I cannot do this." He cursed roundly, then rolled away from her warm nudity.

"Cannot what?" Shock wound through her voice.

Drake reached for his shirt and breeches. Calling himself every kind of a fool, he thrust the garments into place. "I cannot touch you, not like this. I will not."

Before he could hear her reply or see the questions gathering in her wide eyes, Drake fled, slamming the door behind him.

Ten

Averyl opened her eyes to find Drake sitting beside her bed, staring. Though she heard the bustle and voices of the townspeople on the street below and saw the blank expression Drake wore, remembrances of the previous night rushed upon her mind like a blizzard—cold and unavoidable. 'Twas impossible to forget a rejection so painful.

Closing her eyes, she held fresh tears at bay. How easily Drake had walked away from her and their marriage bed. In no other way could he have told her so clearly she lacked beauty. All his pretty words and past denials to the contrary had been exposed as falsehoods. Lies surely designed to subdue her while he exacted revenge on the man she'd sought to marry. And like a fool, she had willingly played his pawn last night—nay, his whore—panting and aching at his touch.

When she opened her eyes, she wanted to look anywhere but at his tall, unreachable figure and the inky waves of his hair, knowing that he and his unerring stare would see her cowardice if she surrendered again to her hurt. Instead, Averyl brought the blankets beneath her chin and glared.

The withdrawal on Drake's sharp features told her naught had changed since the hours past midnight she'd waited for his return, finally succumbing to tears of humiliation near dawn when she realized he would not return. Aye, she had hoped to remain chaste but not knowing he found her unbearable.

"How soon can you dress?" he asked, his voice without inflection. "Less than the half hour?"

Did he have nothing else to say? Nay, she thought bitterly, what would he? She sickened him, even as a traitorous part of her pined foolishly for the burn of desire she had felt before he abandoned her to a lonely midnight. She still felt the slide of Drake's hands upon her skin, his earthy scent enveloping her, now taunting her.

She refused to be his fool any longer.

"Aye."

"Good. Gordan and Edina are surely awaiting us to break their fast."

Cringing at the thought of facing hosts who expected a couple in love, Averyl said, "Eat without me. I hunger not."

"We go together," he contradicted. "The Gibsons will have no reason to suspect their efforts to see us happy last eve were for naught."

Everything within her rebelled. 'Twas humiliating enough to have her own groom profess his revulsion of her, but to be ordered about as well— 'Twas not to be borne. "They will surely think ill indeed, knowing you spent your night elsewhere."

Averyl could have bitten her tongue the moment the words escaped. Drake merely stood, rising to his imposing height above her, and raised a stiff brow.

"I was in the empty room next to this. They know naught."

Averyl froze. Had he heard her pacing, her tears through these thin walls? She prayed to God that Drake had been deaf to the misery his scorn brought.

Of course, she could have welcomed his absence if he had used his anger to take her by force. But nay, he had nearly seduced her virtue from her, then brutally stripped her of pride when he had turned away.

She shrugged, feigning apathy. "They are your friends, not mine. I care not what they think."

But she did care, not only about the Gibsons and their

opinions but about Drake. In spite of his abduction of her, and her rejection, she felt he was a better—if broken—man beneath. Aye, he was misguided, thinking revenge would bring salvation, appearing to prize the screaming white scars upon his back as a reminder of his hate. But he was the same man who cared about her fear of darkness. The same one who had hurt naught except her pride. The husband who now looked at her with dark eyes that held naught—but for that something wild and needy he tried to hide.

Drake needy? She might as well have taken a potion that sapped her logic, for all she made sense today. What a fool.

Peace—she craved just a moment of it. And privacy, where she could collect her thoughts without the distraction of his presence, where she would not have to remember the soft magic of his touch or the hard scorn of his distaste as he rolled away.

Emerging from the bed in naught but her chemise, Averyl rose and paused to grab her dress, conscious of Drake's watchful eyes upon her. With all due haste, she thrust the dress over her head, then opened the door, lacing the garment as she entered the hall.

Drake swore and rushed to her side, pulling her back into the room. He slammed the door shut with a broad palm.

"Have you lost your senses? You cannot leave half-dressed."

"The state of my dress matters not to you. If I were now raped by the barbarians of last eve, 'twould matter not to you!"

He grasped her arm, then spun her to face him. "Do not put false words into my mouth. I would never let them touch you."

"Why? Because you do not want another trampling upon your property?"

He grabbed her chin and held it tightly. The expression on his taut face matched his black silence—something volatile, an explosion moments from erupting.

If she had angered him, it hardly mattered. Theirs was

not a real marriage. It never would be, not with his refusal to believe in love and revenge and revulsion lying between them. Averyl returned his scowl with a defiant stare.

Finally, he spoke in a controlled voice. "Until the next twenty-second of June, you are my wife. That is reason enough."

"I did not want the role."

"I do not recall *asking* if you would like to assume it."

" 'Tis true, you snake. You bullied me into surrendering my future and jeopardizing my home and vassals. For that, I shall never forgive you."

At that, he slowly released her. An emotionless mantle overcame his face. "I expected naught less."

Returning to their room after the morning meal, Averyl swallowed against the rise of breakfast in her throat. As she sat across from Drake while he had played the sated groom, her mortification could not have been more thorough or her hurt more acute. The Gibsons had merely smiled, seeming to take no note of her lack of enthusiasm.

No matter, for this visit had come to an end. She had naught to do but gather her meager belongings.

Of course, she must try to escape again. She'd come to that decision over breakfast. Legally wed they might be, but Averyl had no wish to live with a man who abhorred her and sought to use her for his own end. She could not remain, lest she truly begin to care for him. In fact, she'd come to realize last night had been a blessing, for her marriage was unconsummated.

Murdoch MacDougall could have it dissolved before they wed, should he still want her as his wife. She hoped Drake had spoken true in claiming Murdoch must take her as his wife to satisfy his father's will. If so, mayhap the MacDougall would welcome her without hesitation. Then Abbotsford would be saved, and she could cast the isolated, infuriating Drake Thornton from her mind.

To achieve that, she must concentrate on escape. And this time, she would be more prepared. 'Twas daylight, for one. And Drake's mood was nothing short of preoccupied. Best of all, she'd stolen a sharp knife from Edina's table for a weapon.

Tucking the blade within the folds of her skirt, Averyl gathered the rest of her belongings. She had turned for the doors, to find a way from the inn, when Drake strode into the room.

"You are packed quickly." His voice was deceptively calm.

Averyl merely gave him a regal tilt of her head, declining more answer than that, hoping he could not hear the pounding of her heart or the oath poised upon her tongue.

All but stalking across the floor, Drake paused before the open window, then faced her. "Averyl, do not think that I—" Sighing, he peered out the window behind him. "Last eve, I . . ."

Averyl turned away. Any talk of last night could bring naught but ill feelings and grief. Her life had been too full of those of late.

Drake leaned forward suddenly, then let loose a hearty curse. "What in hell's name . . . ?"

Shock infused his voice. Averyl whirled to its sound.

"This cannot be!"

She strode to the window, all else forgotten in the face of curiosity. Below she saw a large party on fine warhorses. Well-dressed men at arms rode through the middle of the street.

Murdoch MacDougall himself sat proudly at the front, not deigning to look at the town's peasants clustered about him.

Averyl gasped. Her savior was *here!* He would free her, explain what had led him to bed Drake's mother. He would save her home.

Before she could find the right words to shout, Drake

wound an arm about her waist, anchoring her against the wall of his chest, and clapped a hand over her mouth.

"You will not breathe a word, my good wife," he chided.

Fury rose within her, and she tried to bite the salty fingers covering her lips. Drake subdued her, his gaze trained over her head, on Murdoch.

Well contained, Averyl cast her stare out the window again, only to find Murdoch and his men stopping before the inn. Her eyes widened, and her heart raced as Drake stiffened and swore.

Had Murdoch discovered them here? If so, what would he and his men do to Drake? Maim him, kill him? She swallowed.

After dismounting, the MacDougall stretched and cast his gaze about. Then Averyl noticed a woman traveling with them, the kitchen wench with red hair, still round with child.

"Can you not waddle faster?" Murdoch snapped at her as she struggled to dismount, falling to her knees. No one moved to assist her.

The girl struggled to her feet and said something Averyl could not hear, something that caused Murdoch's long body to tense in fury.

"We have not the time to stop for you to relieve yourself again. You slow me down and yet have the nerve to complain of pains and discomforts? I grow weary of this."

Again the woman answered quietly. Averyl watched in outrage. Beside her, Drake dropped his hand from her mouth and shifted his taut arms more tightly around her.

Murdoch's vicious backhand across the woman's cheek caused her fragile neck to snap back—and Averyl to gasp. Such a blow would surely leave a bruise come morn.

Beside her, Drake's mouth twisted in a sneer of contempt. "There is the man you sought to wed."

Averyl flinched at that truth.

"You could help it very much by closing your legs to every man who walks your way," Murdoch sneered. "Re-

member that the next time you want a man to claim your
brat."

With a dismissive wave, he turned to a shorter man beside her. "Wallace, see to her care before she nags me to
death."

With a nod, the woman and the soldier disappeared, presumably inside the inn. Averyl felt cold with shock. True,
she'd wondered for some time if Murdoch was the dream
lover she sought, but she had thought him steadfast, kind.
His callousness toward a woman so clearly in delicate discomfort sent horror curdling in her belly.

" 'Tis cruel," she whispered.

Drake nodded. "Especially since the bairn is his."

"But Murdoch said—"

"That she made herself available to any man? No man
at Dunollie would be fool enough to dally with Murdoch's
leman. Few men find a tumble worth their lives."

Averyl took in Drake's words in solemn shock. Edina's
tale, along with Drake's warnings and Murdoch's actions,
painted an ugly picture of the man she'd nearly wed. A man
with whom life could not have been peaceful, much less
happy, particularly if he had killed his father, as Drake
claimed. As she now feared he was capable. She could nae
have loved a monster like that. And it stood to reason he
had no real wish to wed her, either, other than to fulfill the
terms of his father's will.

Such meant that if she could escape Drake, 'twould not
be to seek Murdoch. Marriage to such a man would be like
a descent into hell, permanent and fraught with evil. But
what to do now?

Swallowing a hard lump of truth, Averyl realized she
could not escape Drake's velvet prison. Not yet, for she had
nowhere to run. Abbotsford lay too far away, and her father
would only try to wed her off to the odious Murdoch again.
And there was that binding matter of her handfast to
Drake . . .

He had her well and truly trapped—but only for now.

"Where to, my lord, since we found naught on the western isles?" the man named Wallace returned to ask Murdoch.

Beside her, Drake smiled. Apparently, their hidden cottage had not been breached. Something that made little sense, that felt oddly like relief, slid through her.

The MacDougall paused, rubbing his thumb against the square block of his chin. "Ask the innkeepers within if they've seen the swine and that scrawny bitch."

Panic infused Averyl as she gazed wide-eyed at Drake. Looking shockingly unruffled, he released her and grabbed her valise. "We must be away."

"Where? They will find us before we can safely flee."

He shook his head, sparing another glance out the window. "Gordan and Edina will lie for us, much as I'm loath to see them do it. They will give Murdoch naught. But we must not linger in case he demands to search the inn."

"Aye," she whispered as he pushed her toward the door.

"They slept here just last night, says the innkeeper's wife," the voice outside told Murdoch.

Averyl froze. Were Drake's friends Murdoch's as well? Had they betrayed him?

"And?" the MacDougall barked with impatience.

"They left early this morn, headed north."

Drake smiled once more at the blatant lie. Averyl felt her tension ease.

After a pause, Murdoch added, "The Highlands offer many places to hide. But Diera's by-blow cannot hide forever."

" 'Tis true," Murdoch's henchman, Wallace, added.

Beside her, Drake tensed, nostrils flared, jaw strained. Without thought, Averyl placed her hand on his arm in a gesture of comfort.

"Let us search the rooms in case he left aught behind," Murdoch called, then ducked out of sight, through the inn's main door.

Averyl's heart lurched in her throat. Drake merely

glanced at her, brows raised, before he shot her a wolf's smile and dropped her valise.

She shivered as he crossed the room and withdrew a knife strapped inside his boot. Without hesitation, without flinching, he drew the blade across his palm, unearthing a ribbon of crimson blood across his browned skin. Stomach churning, mind racing, Averyl watched as he swiped his injured hand across the white sheet, staining it red.

When Drake turned back to her, mischief filled the corners of his smile. "Let Murdoch think what he will of that."

Bitterness rose. Nay, he wanted her not but would let his own blood to have others believe he did. Her belly clenched. 'Twas fury, she swore, not pain.

Drake wanted Murdoch to feel certain she had shared those tangled sheets with him like the most intimate of lovers. Why? As a statement of possession? Of revenge?

Still wearing a grin, her husband wrapped a kerchief about his hand and grabbed her valise with the other before showing her out the door and down the back stairs, away from the foul sounds of Murdoch's curses.

As Drake's hand rested protectively on the small of her back, Averyl found herself unaccountably grateful that he had taken her from Murdoch's clutches despite her resentment. Though she knew her new husband could not love her.

Upon a choppy but uneventful boat ride back to Arran and their hidden cottage, evening fell. With it, desire and memories of Averyl's soft body and willing moans rose.

Once inside the damp cottage, Drake turned his back to his virgin bride and sloshed ale into a tin cup. Her wide green eyes stabbed at his conscience, as did his memories of her midnight tears the night before. Raising the mug to his mouth, he downed the contents in one quick swallow, then poured more. He repeated the process twice within seconds, hoping at once to drown his lust and his guilt.

Aye, how he wanted her. Burned to possess her. Should, in fact, take her tonight—now—to make their handfast binding.

But he could not make himself do aught that might hurt her.

Still, he recognized that one could not be had without the other. Christ's oath, she wanted love, some fool's notion of devotion and chivalry that existed not.

A quick glance at her pacing near the door revealed a cautious expression; her greenish eyes still accused. Maybe she did not understand what love really meant, what it wrought. How could she? As a sheltered innocent, she could not know what he did, had not seen the devastation left in love's wake.

Drake paced, downing another long swallow of the bitter brew in his cup. He could tell her, aye. But would she understand?

Mayhap the problem was his. Averyl had never professed to love him, just to be seeking love itself. Perhaps he assumed more, since she would not leave his mind.

Since this morn, he'd begun to wonder what spell she had cast over him. Why could he not tear her from his gaze, absent her essence from his senses, free her from his thoughts?

Drake paused to refill his cup and empty it once again. "She nearly killed my father."

A frown wrinkled Averyl's brow. "Who?"

"My mother." Eyes narrowed, he turned away with a harsh grunt. "Her perfidy wounded him. The rest"—he shook his head—"nearly ended his will to live."

When Drake spun toward her again, her face was a study in turmoil. Warmth and liquid fire washed through him.

"The rest?" she choked out. "We spoke of your mother's seduction at Murdoch's hands. Is there more?"

He tossed back another long swallow of ale, his fingers tightening around the little cup. "The bairn."

"Bairn? Your mother conceived another one?"

He nodded, turning away so she could not see his face. Schooling his emotions, he waited for her inevitable question.

"Who sired—"

After a terrible moment of silence, Averyl gasped. Drake gnashed his teeth, thankful that she had spared him the humiliation of answering.

"Murdoch got your mother with child?"

Drake turned toward the horror hanging in her every syllable. "Aye."

Face white, she placed a trembling hand over her mouth. "What happened then? Your father must have been—"

"Furious," he slurred. "Hurt. Bewildered to be so betrayed." He nodded, tossing back more ale. "Choose any among them. Each fits," he said, making a sweeping gesture. "But that was not the worst. Not by half."

Looking into his empty cup, Drake swayed toward the ale and refilled it. "My mother knew there would be reprisals for her faithlessness." He stared moodily into his cup as if it foretold the past. "She tried to abort and died."

Averyl placed protective hands over her stomach. Drake saw the gesture, which warmed and irritated him at once. Still, the impact of his words on her soft face could not be discounted, though he'd begun to see two of her. Shock had replaced her anger, concern had overridden anxiety. A curious softness took up residence in his chest.

Raking a hand through his long hair, Drake was annoyed to find that it shook. "My father was a proud man. A fierce warrior who put fear into the hearts of many on the battlefield. My mother stripped him of that. He held Diera while she bled. He cried like a child as he chanted his love for her over and over, as if it were some talisman against death." Drake frowned, bitterness seething in his gut. "As she drew her last breath, she told him to rot in hell."

"Oh, Drake. How terrible," she whispered, her words like a soothing balm on the chafed surface of his soul. He closed his eyes against a suddenly swaying world.

"Aye," he said. " 'Twas bad enough until Murdoch framed me for a murder I did not commit, the murder of a man I loved well."

Trembling, Averyl rose and placed a soft hand on Drake's taut arm. He stared at her, his eyes anguished yet unfocused.

Sliding her hand in his, Averyl squeezed his warm palm. Her heart pained for him, for she understood now what a bitter threat he thought love to be.

Given his knowledge of Dunollie and of his nemesis, Averyl could only assume that the soothsayer at the fair had spoken true of some bond the two men shared. Perhaps Drake's father had been a soldier for Lochlan MacDougall, mayhap even one of his clansmen. Not only had his father most likely watched the more powerful Lochlan take to his mother's bed; he'd known she had also bedded down with the chief's son. A terrible tragedy for Diera's ambition or passions to have wrought.

She soothed a hand over Drake's clenched fist. "I am heartily sorry."

" 'Tis in the past, and I do not want your pity," he spat, wiping the melancholy from his sharp features. " 'Tis your body I seek now, the sweet surrender I should have taken last night."

He reached for her, the dark tones in his face matching his voice. His warm palm slid across her shoulder, gliding down her tingling arm, before he wrapped his fingers around her elbow. Averyl trembled with awareness, wondering why she always reacted to Drake this way—even when he presented the mask of an inebriated, irrational stranger, even when he lashed out in pain.

"You want revenge, not me."

Bitterly, he laughed. "I want you."

"But—"

"My mother showed me early that a man should never leave a woman's bed untended. Diera's passions were too strong to go long without a lover." He paused, his gaze invading her soul. "I will not be fool enough to make that mistake with you."

"I'm not your mother," Averyl corrected warily.

" 'Tis true enough, but you are more dangerous," he said huskily. "You make me feel."

Averyl absorbed that shocking news as Drake grasped her other arm and hauled her against his chest. His eyes, though half-closed now, gleamed with a golden, hungry light that made her heart pound. "I want in your arms. Your verra bed, lass. To feel your sweet mouth." He swayed, then steadied himself, "Your sweet mouth beneath mine."

He swerved again, his head rolling to one side, eyes closed. She scarcely had time to wrest the tin cup from his limp fingers before Drake sank into the chair behind him. His snores moments later told her there would be no more talk that night.

Eleven

Averyl lifted a quilt over her sleeping husband with shaking hands. Sleep softened his angled features, the hard slant of his mouth. He looked tired, and after speaking so much of the past, which he clearly hated, Averyl knew he needed whatever brief rest the ale could give him.

Disillusionment was exhausting, as experience had taught her. Hope, a brief, shining star against the backdrop of her life, always died a slow, wearying death, leaving behind only bleak reality. Learning to live without her mother, without her father's approval, and most recently, without a husband's adoration had taught her to understand such bitterness. Drake had learned, too, from his mother's rejection, Murdoch's cruelties, and the Clan MacDougall's murder accusations.

His self-imposed distance made sense now. After Diera's betrayal, he had sealed off his heart from any possible hurt that might mirror his beloved father's. Drake needed love. Instead of feeling the hunger for it, as she did, he guarded himself with mail-clad barricades so tight, he could not see that truth.

He seemed determined to believe he was utterly alone in this world and even more determined to convince himself that he preferred life in solitude. Only 'twas not true. Averyl saw now his great need, even as he continued to deny it.

A sad smile floated across her mouth. Drake could pretend evil, could try to convince her of his harmful intent.

She knew better; indeed she probably understood more than he wished.

A man capable of ruthless murder would not care for his captive's fear of the dark. Such a varlet would delight in her terror and pain, aye, even add to it where he could through brutality and rape. Would a violent killer tell her of his own past, of his pains, kiss her as if she was his world? Never.

But a man with a good—if reluctant—heart would soothe her fright, rescue her from certain ravishment by three strangers, and confess his scarred past. And as he had done so, Averyl had seen the humanity in Drake she felt certain he'd never intended to reveal.

With a light touch of her finger, she caressed his stubbled cheek. He needed the very comforts she sought: understanding, acceptance, to believe that someone cared.

'Twas her duty as his wife to provide them. But the burgeoning sentiment in her heart had only to do with a bond she now felt linked them. Aye, she understood him, *knew* him.

Cared for him.

'Twas a foolish feeling, one he would never return for many reasons, chief among them his scarred heart and her homeliness. Still, she clung to her notion like a treasured secret. She could treat him well when the rest of the world wished him ill and hope he held her in some regard. That seemed her only recourse, for to tell him of her sentiment would only drive a wedge between them the size of Abbotsford's debts.

Drake woke the next morning to the assault of sunlight and Averyl cheerily humming by the stove, clad in modest gray and one of those frilly white caps he hated. Groaning, he rolled away from his pallet, feeling as if a hairy creature had taken up residence in his mouth and a marching army now lived inside his head.

He also felt as if his senses had taken leave of him last night.

Turning to him, Averyl gazed at him with soft eyes and a face flushed. "Would you break your fast?"

Food? He grimaced and shook his head.

A moment later, she sat down with some heated wine and bread. Drake watched her, wondering when his head would cease aching and what Averyl thought of his foolish, loose tongue.

Aye, he remembered—with unfortunate clarity—what he had told her in his drunken state. Never, from the day he had taken Averyl from Dunollie, had he intended to tell her of the past, particularly the goriest of details, the kind that he'd revealed last night.

Then he'd seized her in his drunken grip, likened her to his mother, and all but told her he wanted to swyve her.

Damnation! Could he have been any more thoughtless?

Whispering a curse, he strode to the window and glared out. The late-morn air held a breeze. The sun shone upon the tufts of green grass swaying across the ravine floor. Drake sighed.

Averyl did not need to know of his past, of his mother and father, what motivated him to seek revenge. She had no notion what linked him to Murdoch, nor would he tell her.

More power over him Averyl did not need, for as the ache in his head subsided, the ache in his loins grew. A yearning to be beside her seized his logic. He wanted her in a way that went beyond mere desire. 'Twas not something he understood—or liked. But Drake feared nothing he did, short of lowering her to his mattress and taking her repeatedly until he could no longer want, would change his craving for her.

Still, he owed her an apology—more than one—for his behavior last night. For his surly mood of late. For allowing her to believe he'd thought her too homely to consummate their marriage.

"Are you certain you've no wish to break your fast?" came her soft inquiry from across the room.

"Aye," he said, facing her. "I must fish, else we will have no meal this eve."

A wistful yearning filled her eyes with green, just as spring did the land. "Aye."

On silent footsteps, he approached, softened by her expression, the lonely turn of her mouth. Averyl's melancholy disturbed him, even pained him in some silent way.

He frowned. "Averyl, I know when we were last here you did not leave this cottage much for the out-of-doors."

"True." Her smile looked tight and grim. "As a child, my father used to tell me I liked sun too much, for it gave me freckles upon my nose."

Drake pictured her, all blond curls, freckles, and mischief darting about the green Scottish hills, laughing, pretending.

He shook the image away, disgruntled by the thought he had taken that pleasure from her. "Would you like— You could walk along the beach whilst I fish if it would please you."

Her gaze flashed up to his, full of appreciation and excitement, like a child with an unexpected sweet.

"It would please me greatly."

Together they left the cottage. Ascending the steep hill to the gate, Drake turned and retrieved the key. He unlocked the barrier and let her through with a wave of his hand.

Her gentle smile, the one that curled her pink mouth and brought joy to her eyes, flashed across her face. Before he could stop himself, Drake found himself responding in kind.

With a shy duck of her head, she stepped through the gate, onto the grassy plateau above. Drake followed, watching the swish of her flowing gray skirts about her hips.

A recent rain had muddied the earth, bringing its scent, along with the Scottish wind and the sea salt about them. As he moved to stand beside Averyl, she cast him a blushing glance.

He felt an odd sense of contentment move through him,

warm, like a soft wind upon a hill in summer, or thick like honey on fresh bread.

"What did you do when you were younger?" she asked, peering at him. "Were you a stern child, always bent to study?"

Drake smiled at the image. "Nay, I made much mischief, so my father sent me to train as a knight when I was seven. There I met Kieran and another friend, Aric."

"You have been friends a long time?"

Drake found himself answering with pleasure as the years rolled away and he remembered the past. "As boys, we were ever wayward, thanks mostly to Kieran. Aric tried to remain the voice of reason. I . . . was always somewhere in the middle. I took my duties seriously but did not turn from frolic very often."

"You and Kieran and Aric are close still?"

"Very." He nodded almost to himself. "A man could not have better warriors at his back or friends beside him. They are like brothers."

Drake hesitated, wondering if he should say more. But something about the gentle harmony of the conversation lulled him. He much liked the idea of talking with Averyl without threats and ugly words between them.

"Aric and Kieran rescued me from Murdoch's dungeons. Had they not, death would have come soon."

Her gaze turned soft. "No wonder you hold great affection for them."

Drake sobered. "Aye. I owe them my life."

Together they began down the hill that lead to the quiet roar of the beach and the endless sea beyond. Averyl took a step upon the decline, then another, before she slipped.

While she wobbled to right her balance, Drake reached for her falling form. He caught her around the waist and set her upright once more as the soft flower of her scent washed over him.

He could not bring himself to take his hands off her.

"Drake?" Averyl sent him a questioning stare.

"I would not have you fall," he said, tightening his hold on the slight curve of her waist, fingers resting near her hip.

She seemed to relax at his touch. Drake glanced down as the summer sun pierced the clouds, shooting golden rays that lit the strands of her hair, peeking from beneath her cap. Sweat beaded his brow. Damnation and hell, how he wanted his own wife.

"I know of your mother, Drake. 'Tis sorry I am. Children deserve better."

"It means naught." Not wanting to discuss her, Drake shrugged her words away with a frown as they reached the shore.

Reluctantly, he released his grip on Averyl. The water lapped against rock and sand alike, and gulls wailed above. Averyl looked good beside the sea, like a water nymph resting upon land, letting the breeze play with her errant curls.

Shoving aside such fanciful thoughts, Drake waded out to the chilled water and dragged his nets to the damp sand.

"Did your father care, at least?" Averyl asked suddenly. "Were you close?"

All manner of feelings stirred, leaving him with a mood he recognized as grief.

"Aye," he answered. "He was steadfast and kind and caring. The very things your father should have been with you."

Averyl shook her head. "I could not be . . . the daughter he wanted. If I could, perhaps he would be proud to call me his."

Drake released the nets and gripped her hands in his. "You did not disappoint him. 'Twas his own foolishness that did not allow him to see the good in you."

She hesitated, contemplating. "Do you think so, truly?"

She wanted to believe him so badly, her expression said. All the yearning and uncertainty in her soft heart appeared upon her fragile face. He felt the strangest, strongest urge to kiss away her fears, assure her of her beauty.

Their gazes clung. Pleasure and want rippled through him.

"Truly," he murmured finally. "I am certain." ·

Then she smiled, something timid, yet full of hope and appreciation. He stopped moving, breathing, blinking.

"Thank you."

Though she squeezed his hands in appreciation, her eyes held a measure of care that spoke to him like a siren calling his name upon the wind. Desire pooled in his gut, along with something he did not recognize, something gentler.

Something disturbing.

He moved away and bent to his nets once more.

"Do you like the shore?" he asked.

" 'Tis peaceful here, as if we are a thousand miles from the rest of the world."

"Why do you think I chose this place?"

Averyl nodded, conceding the point. But a frown marred the ripe red of her mouth.

"If it pleases you, I shall bring you to the shore anytime you like," he found himself saying to ease her discomfort.

Surprise, then pleasure, cascaded over her features. "That would please me." She lay a soft hand on his shoulder that made him want to touch her in return. "That would please me much."

Back at the cottage, Drake wandered about as sunset fell over the ravine. Though he tried to think of aught else except Averyl—Aric and Kieran, Guilford, even Murdoch—no other subject held his mind captive as did his own wife.

As if his wishful thoughts had conjured her up, Averyl appeared as the pink-orange sky dimmed around them. But naught dimmed his view of her.

Gone was Averyl's unflattering headdress. In its stead, she wore a lone braid that slid over her shoulder and caressed the valley between the sweet breasts he remembered possessing with his hands, his mouth. His fingers itched to

touch her. His mouth burned to taste her. The rest of him—
Want did not fully describe how much he ached to possess
her.

She blushed pinkly under his scrutiny and turned away.
Drake fisted a hand to keep from reaching out to touch her.

"The fish is ready when you are," Averyl said, heading
back to the cottage.

The rhythmic sway of her slender hips beneath the folds
of her soft gray dress drew his gaze. Remembrances of their
wedding night assailed him, largely the moments when he'd
nearly possessed her, those trembling ticks of time while
he had held her body a quivering breath apart from his.

Shaking his head to clear his thoughts, Drake tugged his
tunic lower to cover his erection and followed Averyl inside.

They ate in silence. He could scarce concentrate on food,
so he ate little. But his stare remained on Averyl. The shy
return of his glances indicated she had taken note of his
gaze.

Wiping her hands clean, Averyl turned to him as if hesitant. "Drake, I must ask—" She sighed. "I am puzzled."

Puzzled. The word was rife with many meanings in their
context. Puzzled about their marriage? Their unshared bed?
His offer to walk the shore with her? His confession last
night?

"Are you?" he asked carefully.

She nodded her golden head, that twining braid rubbing
the side of her breast in a way that made him jealous. "Indeed. Why do you not confront Murdoch with the truth of
your innocence in his father's murder?"

His innocence . . . ? Her words penetrated. Cold shock
washed over Drake. He sat staring at her, open-mouthed.

"What say you?"

Even to his own ears, his whisper sounded raw and hesitant in the confined cottage's space. As he awaited her answer, body tense, he heard only the popping of a dying fire
and his own breathing. Was it possible she believed him
innocent?

"Why can you not confront Murdoch and the MacDougalls? 'Tis clear to me that no one who truly knows you would believe you capable of such a despicable deed."

He frowned even as hope leaped to life inside him that he truly had her good opinion. "No one who knows me? And you believe you do?"

Averyl cast an uncomfortable glance at the table between them. He crushed another urge to touch her.

"Enough," she answered. "You clearly respect your father, even from his grave, and sought affection from a mother not willing to give it. As your captive, you could have hurt me. No one would have naysayed you." She ducked her head. "Yet you have not. At times, you have comforted me, eased my fear of the dark, been kind."

Drake cast an amazed stare at her. He'd taken her from her family, dragged her to a remote island, only to threaten her and bully her into a marriage she wanted not. Instead of bitterness, she felt empathy. Averyl looked beyond his actions to the feelings beneath.

How?

"I do not mean to imply you have any feelings for me, of course," she rushed to assure him.

But he did have feelings for her. An abiding lust he could not shake. An intense craving that converged in the center of his gut, all but ready to explode.

" 'Tis just, despite what you wish me to think, I do not believe someone with your nature can be the kind of heartless monster who would stab a man to death without a fair fight," she clarified.

Still, Drake said nothing, but continued to stare. Would this woman's gentle temper ever cease to astound him? She believed in him, his innocence. And he had only hurt her at every turn, denying her the freedom he could not afford to grant, refusing the gift of her body she offered so sweetly.

Seemingly unnerved by his silence, Averyl rose and made for the door. With the scrape of his bench against the floor and the pounding of his heart in his ears, Drake rose and whirled after her. He caught her with a firm grip on her elbow. She faced him, soft surprise etching her ivory features.

Averyl was foolish. Too naive by half. And Drake knew he had never wanted anything, anyone, more than he wanted his amazing wife.

"Nay," he whispered hoarsely. "Do not go."

With a nervous swallow, Averyl shot him a cautious glance. "Did you need something?"

Nodding slowly, Drake memorized the green of her eyes, the soft rose of her lips. "You."

Before she could do more than gasp, he seized her delicate cheek in his palm and lowered his head to capture her tender mouth. A hesitant response lay upon her lips. He wrapped his arms about her, bringing her flush against the eager length of his body.

Within moments, she melted under his touch, as if she were made to mold around him. Fingers tangling in the hair at his nape, she moaned into his mouth. Her tongue touched his with a fervency that sent his clamoring passions into a tempest.

The compelling innocence of her kiss swept across his senses like a stormy summer breeze on a windswept moor. Her tongue matched his ardent rhythm, dancing with his in an intimate imitation of the act he hoped would follow.

Yet he wanted more, to feel every honeyed inch of her, to consume the alabaster pink of her flesh. The past, the future, their enemies, be damned.

Dragging his hands to her shoulders, one palm drifted lower, to the breast his fingers ached to encompass. Soft and taut, her flesh filled his hand perfectly, its weight infusing him with her heat. Brushing his thumb across the peak of her breast once, twice, he felt arousal in its stiff response.

Averyl clung to him, his name a whispered caress in the air. And he knew he could deny his desire no more. He anticipated her scent, her taste. He craved the feel of her around him in ecstasy, purging himself of this strange need.

Drake set determined fingers to the decorative hip girdle that began at her small waist. She shivered beneath his touch as he ripped the tasseled ornament apart and it fell to the floor.

Then he knelt before her, grasping the hem of her flowing skirt in his hands and lifting. Past strong calves, dimpled knees, firm thighs, he raised the dress.

When he stood with her skirt bunched in his hands at her hips, Drake brought her closer and met her wide green gaze. He read acceptance, even pleasure. No fear. Only trust and desire shone from her eyes. Aye, for this one moment, he would be with her, refusing to give thought to what had been or what would be if she learned the truth of his link to Murdoch. Tonight he would give in to his gnawing need and be a husband to his wife.

He placed a light kiss on her responsive mouth before lifting the form-fitting bodice past her waist. That indentation heated his hand an instant before the pouting curve of her breast slid into his palm. Pausing only long enough to rub the pebbled peaks with the pads of his thumbs, then take in the shallow gasp of her reaction, he hoisted her dress past her shoulders, above her head, to the floor.

Then he stared. Actually gaped at Averyl's pale glory. Her milky skin beckoned from beneath her white chemise, cut low enough to expose the upper swells of her breasts. The thin undergarment clung to every dip and curve of her body. The rosy, puckered flesh of her nipples stood visible through the fabric, reminding him of delights he yearned to taste again.

Fitting his hands beneath the transparent smock, Drake lifted it above her head until she stood naked, minutes from his possession.

Hearing his own labored breathing, he swallowed and reached for her. His kiss was wild, an expression of all his desire-muddled mind could not find the words to say. Averyl responded without hesitation or artifice. He nipped at the scented skin of her neck, and she rewarded him by arching that graceful throat for his pleasure. Into her ear he whispered his need to touch her, consume her. She moaned and clung tighter, leaving him to wonder why God had gifted him with such a beautiful bride in the midst of the ugliness his life had become.

As the thought formed, it flitted away. Drake concentrated on the perfect circle of her nipple as he drew his mouth closer to the floral scent of her skin.

The peak filled his mouth, accompanied by her soft moans in his ears. Her small fingers worked through his hair, down his shoulders, gripping, clutching, gasping.

Lifting her against his body, Drake carried her to the bed. He laid her across the straw mattress on which he'd dreamed night after agonizing night of sharing with her. The crush of their weight upon it filled his ears, its sound a heady seduction.

As he captured her breast in his lips again, wonder filled him. Averyl arched as his tongue worked at her turgid crest. A moment later, he smoothed his palm down the flat plain of her stomach, into the pale curls between her thighs.

He felt her momentary tensing and lifted his gaze to her. "I will not hurt you, my wife."

After no more than a moment's hesitation, she nodded.

"Open for me, love," he instructed. "Let me please you."

Seconds later, accompanied by the sound of rustling sheets, she did as he bid.

Her flesh beneath his fingers was warm and slick. Ready and willing. Fighting down a rising tide of primal joy, Drake fingered the nub of her desire in light circles. Averyl rewarded him with closed eyes and soft mews of encouragement.

Her body was flushed, damp. Still, he wanted to give her this pleasure in case her virginal body was too tense to feel it upon their first joining.

Patiently, he tightened the circle his thumb traced over her heated, hardening flesh. She rewarded him by clutching the sheets in her fists and calling his name.

"Aye, love. That's it," he encouraged.

Her knees bent and parted, her hips arched. He caressed her once more, twice more, before she quivered and cried out, a chant of pleasure in the dusk-darkened room.

Again, he pleasured her, twirling his finger about her sensitive nubbin. Seconds blurred into minutes, one release into the next until Averyl trembled, pleaded, perspired, her skin a flushed rose, her core cascading with the dew of her readiness.

Satisfaction and need swept over Drake as he lifted frenzied fingers from his bride to the lacings of his hose. Her hands joined his there. Together they tugged and pulled until the garment lay at his feet in a discarded heap.

Clamoring need consuming him, Drake divested himself of his tunic and braies. Her dilated green gaze wandered down his now-naked form. He stood a moment and let her look, though it cost him dearly in restraint.

Her stare encompassed his shoulders, past the battle scars of his torso, then lower. Her eyes widened.

"Will we fit?" she whispered.

In spite of the gravity of the moment, a gentle smile curved his mouth. "Aye. 'Tis as nature intended, lass."

She nodded again and lay back without another word. Clearly, she trusted him. *Him,* her abductor, her tormentor, her husband by force. What had he done to deserve this moment?

"Will—will you stay this time?"

Her hesitant question reminded him of their last intimacies and the ultimate pleasures he'd rejected. Regret pierced him, and he waited not a moment to assure her. "A whole field of warriors could not drag me away."

At her shy smile, he joined her on the mattress. He smoothed her grin away by nibbling her bottom lip, slowly drawing it into his mouth. Briefly he sucked it, then covered the rest of her mouth, reaping the instant passion of her response.

His mouth and hands covered her flesh again, claiming

her. Averyl lifted her arms about him and returned each touch. With the tender kisses he pressed to the damp skin of her neck and the caresses stirring the flesh of her thighs, he vowed he would make their first coupling the best it could be.

With a touch, he parted her legs and slid his knee between hers. Again he grazed her most intimate flesh. Her slickness and her responsive gasp sent heat reeling through him.

Urgency coiling throughout him, Drake took her mouth again, aware of her arching invitation tempting him, the musky moistness of her center shouting his name. The ache gnawed at him, chafed with impatience, stronger than he ever recalled.

As their mouths mated, he guided himself to her.

"I know naught of virgins," he confessed, sweat beading his forehead. "You must tell me if I hurt you."

"But surely you've—"

"Nay," he interrupted. "Not with an innocent."

Surprise floated across her soft face. "If I feel pain, I will tell you."

With a nod, he placed gentle hands on her hips and slowly drew himself inside. Tight and moist, she began to close around him in an exquisite joining that brushed the bounds of heaven. He fought to stifle a groan, knowing he must still break her barrier gently while his entire body clamored to thrust himself to the hilt.

Drake dragged in a deep breath and surged forward. Beneath him, Averyl gasped and tensed. He felt her body give way and open slowly for his passage like a spring flower to accommodate a bee. Shuddering, he sank down into her honeyed depths, completely within her, then gazed into her face.

Pain did not reside there. Surprise, perhaps, but no more.

"Averyl?" he asked despite the strain he heard in his own voice and the sweat bathing his chest

She touched his face, branding him softly. "I am not hurt."

"You are certain?" he asked one last time, though the delay began to feel like brilliant torture.

Beneath him, she rocked her hips, inviting him further within her silken body. Drake did not hesitate. He withdrew to stroke her again. Once more. Over and over until Averyl rewarded him with her responses, until he knew naught but her scent, her feel, her moans, her need.

About his waist, her thighs tensed and trembled. Her sheath gripped him without mercy, and he thought he might lose his mind. She clutched him tighter, demanding his mouth upon hers as her pleasure peaked and scattered over his senses, which felt already saturated with her.

Before he could stop it, satisfaction surged upon him. A shattering release consumed him even as her pleasure-filled cry echoed in the cottage, cleansing him of all but rapture, infusing him with a blinding bolt of something bright and warm.

Long moments later, he clasped her against him in exhaustion and awe. She placed tiny kisses on his face. Absently, he stroked her hair, oddly reluctant to let her go in the face of his sated bliss and her amazing sensuality.

Never had he wanted to hold a woman after partaking of her body. Such requests always irritated him for the intimacy they implied. Averyl asked for nothing, simply falling naturally into his arms when he willingly opened them.

This coupling somehow felt different, almost binding in its intensity, though the act itself was the same. Why?

Shaking away the odd thought, Drake lifted his head to ask Averyl if she hurt. He found her eyes peacefully closed, her breathing the even rhythm of sleep.

Into the lengthening shadows of darkness he smiled and held her. Tomorrow, this awe, this feeling of connection, would die. Tonight, though, he would forget all the reasons he could form no lasting attachment to her and enjoy the delight of his wife's body as many times as she would have him.

Twelve

Eyes still closed to the morning, Averyl yawned before her mouth curled up in a languid smile. She felt thoroughly touched, so wanted, her body pleasantly tender. Her mouth curled up further upon realizing she was truly Drake's wife.

She blushed with remembrances. He'd awakened her thrice last night to make love. Thrice! Each time, she'd fallen into his arms eagerly, basking in his single-minded attention.

'Twas a surprise to Averyl to open her eyes and find herself alone in their cottage.

Reminding herself that Drake often rose before the sun, she shrugged away disappointment and set about her morning ritual. Between braiding her hair and choosing a dress, Drake entered the cottage, golden filters of sunlight at his back.

A welcoming smile spread across her face. "Good morn."

Drake nodded, silent, his hot gaze sweeping over her chemise-clad form, resting finally on its low neckline. Though the garment covered the essentials, Averyl felt decidedly naked under his penetrating stare. Her cheeks heated as she felt her breasts tightening in response.

He wanted her. Again. Though she could scarcely comprehend such, she did not question the desire she felt, too. Instead, she raised her gaze to his, smiling in shy invitation.

He raised a dark brow. "Be careful, else I will accept what you offer."

"Surely that would not be bad," she teased.

"Later, when your body has rested," he said, his voice low.

Part of Averyl thrilled at his words. He did intend to take her into his arms again, and only concern for her prevented him from making love to her now. Certainly, she misunderstood his lack of expression or attention.

Yet uneasiness tugged at her. Of late, she had rarely seen Drake so remote.

"Drake . . . is aught wrong?"

"Nay," he answered solemnly, turning away to start a fire in the hearth.

Averyl frowned as anxiety rose again. Why was he behaving as if naught had happened last night? True, he had vowed never to love her, but today 'twas as if she were a stranger. Did he not remember what they had shared? Even now she felt his soft kisses on her nape, the scent of his musk on her skin, his soft words in her ear. All night, as he had held her, making her his wife, she felt a warmth in her chest spreading through her for this perplexing, troubled man.

Perhaps she made too much of her fear. His was not a tender nature, and she'd known better than to expect avowals of love. Though somehow, this morn, her heart wanted them.

"Have you broken your fast?" she asked. "I will be happy to make you—"

"I ate earlier."

His curt reply did not comfort her. Knowing not what else to say, she turned away and donned her dress of muted gray, which matched her mood of a sudden. Fastening the deep blue hip girdle about her middle, she caught Drake's eyes upon her. Again, they spoke of desire and damp skin, of midnight cries and moonlit skin. But nothing of the warmth she had seen yesterday on the beach or at the height of passion.

Averyl disliked this mood, for she knew he was likely to shut her out should she ask what plagued his mind. With a heavy sigh, she wondered how she, a woman who knew little of men, could coax Drake from his silence? Still, she must try.

"Drake, is all well?"

He shrugged, dark eyes turning impassive. "Well enough."

"You seem ill pleased by last night—"

"It was pleasing," he replied, awkward.

Pleasing. Not astounding. No mention of the silent connection, of the tender touches communicating care.

Drake thought little of the most amazing night of her life. A wave of mortification washed over her, leaving her cold.

" 'Twas pleasing," she agreed carefully, folding her hands together. "But I expected to be treated less like a stranger."

His dark eyes pierced her. "You wanted words of devotion and declarations of love."

How could she deny what she longed for in her heart? Given the scorn upon his face, how could she not?

"I seek them not," she said finally. " 'Tis simply that you seem . . . unhappy this morn."

"Not so," he answered, looking away to secure a long, thick knife to his thigh. "Now, with your leave, I must hunt."

Before she could reply or wish him safe, Drake was gone.

Three weeks later, naught had changed. Each night he came to her in fire, each embrace feeling somehow more desperate than the last. Just last night he'd propelled her to their bed before dinner, before the sun even set fully. He waited not to disrobe her, but lifted her skirts and took her in an ardent coupling of pants and moans, of tangled limbs and twined fingers. Then again, in night's blackest hour, he'd reached for her, his hands needy, his thrusts urgent. Responding to his magic, Averyl had given her body with ease, in trust.

Always during those hours he was caring and seemed at ease with their joining. Smiles came her way, as did the affection in his voice.

Then, when the sun rose, he would treat her no differently than one would a civil stranger. Certainly, any hint of the man who had shared his warmth, his body, and painful secrets with her was now gone, a mere phantom in her memory.

Feeling the recurrence of this morn's tears, Averyl willed them away. For the more she showed her pain and inquired about his solitary moods, the more Drake withdrew. She could give him no further cause to believe she cared for him. This foolishness was hers alone.

Now his endless dark eyes seemed not to display any feeling beyond lust. And she was a fool for hoping to see otherwise. She was no more than a convenient, if homely, body on which to slake his lust.

Averyl doubted Drake would ever love her. Even so, she had tonight devised a test. When he came to her, and he would, she planned to seduce him, pouring her heart into each touch, her care into every kiss. If, after such a fervent display of her feelings, he still did not respond with softness of emotion, she would finally know the truth.

What she would do then, she knew not.

Through the cottage's lone window, she noted the setting sun and lit two candles, placing them on the table behind her. Drake would return within the hour, and still she had not garbed herself for this eve's test. The dress, a scarlet gown with rich gold braiding about the waist and a low neckline, was among her best. She lay the garment across the bed, checked on their simmering stew, then braided her hair.

Drake entered the cottage well before she expected him.

He'd bathed in the pond outside, judging from the rivulets of water that ran from his damp hair, down the golden skin of his hard, bare chest. He wore a hungry expression on his face.

Averyl swallowed, trying to force down her desire. 'Twas nothing short of witlessness on her part to yearn for him so. Yet when his heated eyes traveled from her coiffed hair, down the slope of her shoulders, to take in her form beneath the transparency of her smock, his very stare singed her.

"Supper is nearly ready." Her hands trembled suddenly as she retrieved her gown. "As soon as I dress, I shall—"

"Nay." He was across the room in three steps. "Forget supper," his voice enticed. "Forget your gown."

He tried to take the garment from her.

Averyl held fast and opened her mouth to rebut, but Drake held up a hand to stay her.

His bawdy smile nearly stopped her heart. " 'Tis not your good cooking or pretty clothes that interest me."

Drake tugged on the dress again, and it fell from her fingers. After he tossed it across the bed, Drake turned her to the small mirror, fitting her back against the heated length of his body. The candles behind them illuminated their figures, from head to thigh, man and woman.

Against her buttocks, she felt the hard heat of his desire. Even as the answering flame ignited within her, she panicked. What of her plans to seduce him? She could not allow him to dissuade her from them. Yet as he glided one feathery finger across her jawline, down her throat, then descended into the valley between her breasts, Averyl felt her breath catch.

Determined to take control, she made to whirl about. His thumb brushed her distended nipple before she could move.

Averyl closed her eyes, fighting another wave of mind-numbing desire. Why did he always have this affect on her? No matter how great or small the stroke of his hand, she felt it all the way from her womanly core to her heart.

Nay, this could not happen. She must have her answer!

Turning to him, she opened her mouth to speak. Drake silenced her with a blistering kiss that seduced her, sapped her resistance. His tongue swirled; his lips possessed. He tasted of water and need and something so elementally male. And she felt herself melting against him like a candle too long lit, the scarcely covered mounds of her breasts pressed against the velvet steel of his chest.

When she moaned, he broke the kiss and turned her toward the mirror. The face that greeted her was nearly a stranger's. Her lips were swollen and berry red, her cheeks flushed, her eyes heavy-lidded. Her braid lay untwined about her shoulders.

Slowly, she turned to Drake in question. Inexorably, he turned her back toward the reflective glass.

"Nay," he whispered against her ear. "Watch. See what I see when we lay together."

His intent became clear to her when he cupped her breasts through the thin smock, rolling her nipple between his fingers. Her stomach clenched, both at the feel of his touch and the sight of his large golden hands upon her. The flesh in his grasp tautened to hard pebbles. She arched into his hands.

"Aye," he encouraged, reaching inside her smock to withdraw her breasts.

Averyl stared at the wanton sight of the dusky rose of her nipples and Drake's fingers teasing them. Heat curled deep in her belly. By the saints, how she wanted him. More than she had last week—or last night.

The gentle play of his fingers tormented her with one last shiver before drifting down the smooth plain of her abdomen, to the juncture of her thighs. Through the smock, his thumb made tight circles upon her moist flesh. Averyl reminded herself of her plan even as she gritted her teeth to stifle a cry. Drake must be made to feel the depth of her emotions in their joining.

Her resolution held until his teeth nibbled on the sensitive skin of her neck and her first release crashed over her senses. Averyl's eyes slid shut. Her control slipped, for Drake knew how to touch her, had spent these last weeks learning to play her as a musician would his lute. She drew in a deep breath, struggling not to allow the waves of desire to submerge her in their depths.

The sound of rending fabric and the feel of cool air on her skin brought her eyes open once more. Through half-open eyes she noted her own nudity and her torn smock hanging about her arms in shreds. The hard core of his arousal pressed against her back.

"The garment is not as important as this," Drake whispered against her ear just before his fingers began delving the slick flesh between her thighs again.

Her knees buckled as she watched her own ecstasy envelop her once more. Her breasts stood taut, and her flesh turned damp and rosy as he sent her closer to heaven. Her pale hair hung behind her shoulders, tangled, wild. She knew her dilated eyes no longer resembled her own.

And Averyl found that she could not care, not when fulfillment began to sluice and tingle its way through her body. Vaguely, she heard her own cry above her heartbeat roaring in her ears. Held upright by the strong support of Drake's arm, she let the waves of pleasure crash into her, one after the other, until she felt limp and warm and spent.

Behind her, Drake's face reflected hot triumph. The searing ebony of his eyes moved over her body. To her shock, Averyl felt an answering note within her belly.

After removing the vestiges of her smock from her, he guided her to the bed, then followed her down to the mattress. He reached to remove his hose. Somehow she found the strength to grab his hand and stay him.

Tonight Drake had shown her how easily one's emotions could be revealed during an ecstatic loss of control. She'd seen her own face and knew now she could never hope to learn Drake's true feelings for her when he maintained such command over his body and mind. Nay, she must drive him to the madness he'd sent her tumbling into moments ago.

"Let me," she whispered into Drake's questioning face as she rolled him to his back and reached for his hose.

His burning expression told her he found the suggestion pleasing, but when she grasped the edge of the garment and pulled down slowly, he grew tense. She moved her fingers tentatively over his hard male flesh. Drake clenched his jaw, appearing the picture of pain.

Averyl bit her lip in indecision. Did she stop?

Uncertainly, she removed the garment from his feet and tossed it to the floor. Drake answered her confusion by bringing her hand back to his shaft. Curling her fingers about his thick length, he guided her in an up-and-down motion.

Following his lead, she was soon rewarded with a toss of his dark head and a groan. She smiled. Aye, he could lose himself like this to her.

She moved faster. Drake's fingers curled around her thighs, clutching, biting.

Gratified, Averyl refused to relent, but watched his face. Cheeks taut, eyes shut, jaw hard, he looked magnificently aroused. She clenched her fingers around him more tightly.

"Look at me," she whispered.

Upon her command, his eyes flew open. The heat of a thousand infernos raged within their depths. She sent him a sultry smile.

"Nay," he rasped. "I will endure this torture no more."

Before Averyl could protest, Drake loomed above her and sent her onto her back. He entered her completely in one hard thrust, pushing, fingers grasping her hips as if to make his way deeper. She gasped as sensations washed over her, and she wrapped her legs about him.

"Now look at me," he said, voice strained, eyes probing.

Averyl met his gaze as he withdrew and entered once more. The connection of their stares she felt into the depths of her soul. The answering flicker in Drake's eyes filled her with yearning and hope.

Boldly, she kissed him. He answered with a sweep of his

tongue and a thrust of his hard body. 'Twas as if he wanted to be upon her, inside her, in as many places as he could at once.

He seared her with another lunge of his tongue, his body. She gripped his shoulders, nails cutting into his flesh as the sharp-edged pleasure rushed through her again.

With another push of his hardness, she exploded around him. Averyl fought to keep her head, even as the honeyed sweetness of her release lulled her mind and dulled her thoughts.

But her eyes remained open, enough to see the bright need in Drake's glowing eyes as he found his own pleasure. His hoarse cry and stiff body did not surprise her. 'Twas his eyes she looked to for answers. She saw a flash of something anxious and needy, warm but vulnerable. Something that reached out to her and wrapped itself around her heart. She smiled in relief.

Moments later, she lay a soft hand on his cheek to give comfort and sent a heartfelt gaze his way. Instantly, his shoulders and back turned stiff at her touch. He closed his eyes to her searching gaze, ground his hips against her once more, then rolled away.

Averyl felt his loss immediately. 'Twas more than the usual withdrawal of his body. A glance into his closed expression revealed the removal of his thoughts and feelings.

"Look at me," she whispered again.

Several deep breaths later, he complied. His black eyes reveled naught—no want, no satisfaction, no contempt. Their flat depths crushed her heart.

Averyl rose and dressed in the silence, tears clawing her eyes. Drake would never love her, she realized. Any feeling he had, he would ruthlessly stifle, never admitting it to himself, much less to her. He would give her pleasure. Lord knew he could. He would see after her, protect her.

But as Averyl dressed, she knew Drake would never allow himself to love her.

* * *

"Drake, I would speak with you," she said the next day.

The gravity of Averyl's voice behind him made Drake turn to her slowly in the fading daylight the next afternoon. Uneasiness slid through him as he lay his blade next to a pile of logs. The scent of wood hovered pungent about him.

Assuming a casual pose, he wiped the sweat from his brow. He tried not to notice her unsmiling regard. "Would you, my wife? About what?"

She cleared her throat. Folding her hands before her, she blinked several times, then wet her lips nervously.

Had she come to explain why she had turned away from his embrace three times last night and again this morning? Never since succumbing to the flame between them had she refused him the sweet solace of her body—until now. Why?

"I would talk with you about the end of our handfast," she said finally, interrupting his reverie.

" 'Tis barely begun." He scowled.

"Aye, but I would have you understand a few things."

"Would you, now?" he tossed back, little liking her tone.

She paced several steps before turning to him again. Shoulders tense within her muted blue gown, she stood fragile yet firm.

"When our handfast is at an end and I am no longer of any use to your revenge, I must insist that you give me the funds promised to save Abbotsford."

Her home. She worried over its walls, its people. 'Twas in her caring nature. That quality that made her different from his greedy mother, and drew him to her in a way that surpassed simple lust. Drake relaxed.

"As I promised." He caressed her cheek. "Unless I have gone to my grave, I will find a way to give you all that Murdoch agreed to lend your father. You need not worry on that score."

Averyl turned her face from his touch. Through narrowed

eyes, he watched her tense fingers clench each other in a prayerlike pose again.

"I also expect that there will be no further contact between us, that you will set me free in every way."

Glowering, Drake stared. Had he heard her correctly? She wanted nothing more to do with him? Everything within him rebelled at the thought.

Her greenish gaze crashed into his a moment later. She squared her shoulders, thrusting forward the firm mounds of her breasts. Of course, he did not wish her gone. Too many of her body's delights he had yet to sample.

He sidled closer, backing her against a nearby tree. "My dearest wife, you forget that the pleasures we have shared can often bring consequences."

Through stiff lips, she replied, "This morn I awakened to the proof that I did not conceive. 'Twould be to everyone's advantage if we kept it that way."

Resistance and regret sliced through him. Alarm followed, winding through Drake's body, centering in his suddenly tight chest. "Do you wish to deny me your wifely comforts for the better part of a year?"

"I wish to deny you the chance to use me at your will. 'Tis not me you desire but feminine companionship, and we would both be better served to avoid further involvement. Until June next I am your wife. Our marriage is consummated. Murdoch cannot dispute that. 'Tis what you wanted. You need no more of me."

The inflectionless precision of her speech stunned Drake. Where was the passionate woman he'd grown accustomed to having beside him? When had the caring woman he'd come to enjoy disappeared? In her place stood an unfeeling enchantress.

Turning away from her, he reached for his ax again and glanced blindly at the wood before him. An emptiness clawed at his belly, and he hacked at the branches to dispel the feeling.

"You will have your money or my death," he snarled.

"As for our marriage bed, do not imagine I will endure more refusals. I am within my right to take you anytime I wish."

"Use your conscience and leave me be."

Her cool voice poured over him like salt on an open wound. "You've known from the start I am a heartless bastard without a conscience. When I want you, I will have you, my lady wife."

Averyl's wide eyes dimmed with disappointment before she looked away. Drake stifled an emotion that felt too much like guilt for comfort. Long moments of silence ticked by.

Finally, she gazed at him once more, her face somber. "As you will. But do not expect me to respond."

Before his stunned mind could form a reply, Drake found himself glaring with incredulity at Averyl's retreating back. She would cast aside their marriage? Just like that? Aye, he'd never wanted the arrangement permanently, but never had he intended to treat it as callously as she.

"By God, you will respond to me, Averyl," he called after her. "You will respond every bloody night!"

She paused, turning until the last of the day's rays cast a halo at her back. Lengthening shadows of dusky pink accentuated her fair coloring, her luminous beauty. He wanted her. Now.

Drake took two steps toward her. She threw up a hand to stay him.

"Though you tell me you are a heartless bastard, I know better," her voice quivered. "Think well on the fact that if you make me respond to your touch, I will only hate you for it."

With that, she turned and disappeared into the cottage.

Thirteen

A week later, Averyl woke slowly, warm and languid—and aware of an insistent, heated tingle in her womanly core. Soft lips plied magic in the curve of her neck. On instinct, she arched toward them, seeking pleasure. She was rewarded with a hot hand upon her breast.

Fingers sizzled her skin as they caressed her through her smock and teased her nipple into a hard pebble. Something within her shouted warnings to withstand the artful mastery of those hands. Then she felt a mouth to her breast, and she moaned at the gentle friction of a warm tongue. Gasping, Averyl struggled to recall why she should resist this.

"Aye, lass," the voice encouraged. "Feel me."

Drake!

Fully awake now, she opened her eyes to find his gaze upon her, a hot black in the burgeoning light. Such utter male beauty never ceased to move her, nor did the depth of her desire. Swallowing, she fought the ache pulsing in her belly.

"This is good and right between us. We need naught else," he assured, his voice coaxing.

Except love, her mind shouted. Love he possessed not for her. Love he would never feel.

She pushed against his shoulders until he eased away, frowning. Averyl clasped the sheet to her.

"Where is my dress?" she demanded.

He glanced at the floor. " 'Tis an inconvenient habit you have of wearing too much clothing, my wife."

Averyl espied her gown beside the bed as Drake leaned closer, allowing her the feel of the velvet strength of his chest. She closed her eyes, praying for fortitude.

For ten nights she had rejected the arousing advances that curled her toes, the sensual suggestions that shallowed her breathing. Aye, how she wanted him, the sense of joining she always felt with him. 'Twas nothing less than torment to refuse that which she wanted so desperately—his attention, his tenderness, his touch. But her mind, her pride, refused her heart the bliss of surrender.

She would not become his whore, to be used and discarded as he wished. Though with each day, each kiss, he became harder to deny. Not only did her body respond to his seduction; her heart responded to his seeming confusion at her refusals.

His dark hair brushed her cheek as he slid closer. Before Averyl could turn away, his lips covered hers. The breadth of his hand encompassed her hip, wound around her thigh, raised her smock to her waist. Eyes closed, she clasped fistfuls of the sheets as she clenched her legs together to fend off the pleasurable onslaught of his nimble fingers.

"Do not touch me," she whispered.

"Your words say nay, but your voice breaks and pleads." He pressed his erection against her thigh. Her arousal climbed.

Sweet mercy, he was naked, completely. The warm expanse of his golden skin surrounded her, as did his manly scent—musky, wild, not to be denied—as he pressed against her again.

Averyl stifled a groan. How could she ache for him so badly when he wanted naught from her but her body? When he cared so little?

At the apex of her thighs, Averyl felt his fingers—gentle, insistent, coaxing. Her body felt as liquid as a river, her mind as empty as Abbotsford's fields. She must resist, for her future, for herself. She must.

"I say nay!" She pushed against him again.

This time, Drake sat up and stared at her through a dark scowl. He was very unhappy indeed.

'Twas no problem of hers. She had all she could manage resisting him, Averyl thought, rising to don her clothes.

As she dressed, she felt Drake's eyes upon her, intent.

"Averyl, why—"

"Hello?" called a vaguely familiar voice through the morn's heavy gray mist, ripping through their solitude. The owner of that voice stood just outside the cottage door.

Drake stiffened and cursed a string of unkind expletives before rising to yank on his hose and tunic, then open the door.

On the other side stood Kieran, wearing a lopsided grin. Holding the door, Drake stepped back, jaw tight, silent.

"Hello, Drake."

"Greetings," he intoned, closing the door as Kieran entered the small cottage and sat upon a nearby stool.

"Mind you that I used the key to let myself in your gate?"

" 'Tis why I gave it to you, dolt."

Averyl winced at Drake's abrupt answer. Kieran regarded him with a long look, then a raised brow in her direction.

"My lovely Lady Averyl, forgive my remiss," said Kieran, rising to take her hand. "How fare you with this rogue?"

She cast an uneasy glance at Drake, whose dark expression did more than hint at his interest in her answer. She could not answer. "What of you, after your last journey here?"

His answering smile was deprecating and charming at once. "I live to see another day of battle and beauties." Kieran began to raise her hand to his mouth. "Especially your beauty."

Drake stepped between them, taking her hand from his

friend's and grasping it with his own. "I'll thank you to cease fondling my wife."

"*W-wife?*" Kieran's blue-green eyes widened as his mouth dropped open in disbelief. All attempts at teasing disappeared. "You wed her? *You* took her to wife?"

Averyl blanched, wondering if Kieran was surprised that Drake had married or that he had tied himself to so homely a bride. She tried to pry her hand from Drake's.

He resisted, placing a hand about her waist to bring her against him. "Aye. What of it?"

Kieran said naught for near a minute. Even the birds ceased their songs.

Finally, a wide smile curled his charmer's mouth. "You rascal, I thought you would never take a bride, given Diera—"

"This is not a love match." Drake released her abruptly.

Again, Kieran fell silent. He glanced between Drake and herself, his gaze measuring, oddly disappointed. "Then why?"

"Murdoch cannot wed her if I have."

"True, unless he kills you, you dimwit!"

"He will do all he can to kill me, regardless. But if Averyl should escape"—he pinned her with a gaze that consumed and accused her at once—"Murdoch cannot wed her."

Kieran groaned. "You have provoked Murdoch enough. But to wed her . . . He will enjoy your death even more if he catches you."

"Why?" Averyl broke in. "MacDougall cares naught for me."

Kieran faced her. "Murdoch cares for no one but himself. 'Tis money he covets, which he stands to inherit a great deal of, but not unless he weds you before you turn eight and ten."

The infamous will again. Murdoch had the power of the clan behind him now but none of the funds, not unless he wed her soon. And only Drake stood between her and Murdoch's plans. Averyl trembled as she realized the added danger her handfast husband had placed himself in by speaking vows with her.

"And what if you live?" Kieran challenged. "What of your wife then?"

"We are but handfast. In a year's time, she will be free."

Kieran sighed, shaking his head. "Idiot. Your quest for revenge will ensure your death."

"I knew such when I started."

" 'Tis utterly irrational!" she cried. "You cannot mean to see your life's blood spilled over some dead man's money."

Kieran grimaced. "Averyl, Lochlan was like a god to his people. Such was doubly true of Drake, his—"

"No more," Drake hissed. "We are wed for the next year. No one, least of all Murdoch, can change that."

She looked from Kieran's chagrined features to Drake's tense expression. Another secret. She felt such, for the very words hovered on the tip of Kieran's tongue. How exactly had Drake and Murdoch's father known each other to form a strong bond of friendship? And why did Drake want to keep the secret so badly?

As much as Averyl yearned to know, she turned away. Until Drake could trust her enough to speak his secrets, until he could care for her as she cared for him, knowing meant naught.

Certain her wishes were futile, she left the cottage.

Drake stared at Averyl's retreating back, wondering why he should feel guilt for not sharing the shame of his secret with her. Aye, she was his wife now, but not forever. Nor, thank God, would she be witness to the fateful day when his past finally confronted him. He wanted her embroiled in neither such shame—or worse—such danger.

"Drake," Kieran began, snaring his attention once more. "Guilford worries for you. He is an old man now—"

"Not so old he cannot manipulate you into watching me more thoroughly than a nanny."

"That is so," Kieran said with a laugh. "But Aric and I worry as well."

"Do not. Aric has a new life with Gwenyth, while yours is that of a traveling soldier. Think of that."

Kieran scowled. "We did not rescue you from Dunollie's dungeon to watch you die."

"Revenge will make me whole again," argued Drake.

"Revenge can do naught but destroy you. Murdoch grows desperate and ruthless as the days become weeks," Kieran warned.

Drake paused. "Where is he now?"

Kieran grimaced. "I could not say. 'Tis as if Murdoch knows someone brings you information, for suddenly his lips stay as tightly closed as a nun's thighs."

That fact filled Drake with dread, for Murdoch had never been a fool. "And Firtha knows nothing?"

"Even less than I."

Drake smothered a curse. "Were you followed here?"

After a pause, Kieran replied, "I think not, but Murdoch is anxious. He suspects everyone."

Drake shrugged his dim thoughts away. "Mayhap you should go elsewhere for a while before returning."

"Aye. Mayhap you should consider the same as a safeguard. I overheard he has doubled the number of men searching for you."

Digesting that news with a slow nod, Drake answered: " 'Tis no less than I expected, since I doubt he will give up now."

Kieran sighed in frustration. "Nay, but what of you? Guilford and Aric think me reckless. But you, my friend, take risks I would not. Do you have naught else to live for?"

An image of Averyl in his arms this very morn, warring against her own desire, flashed through his mind. Such was hopeless. She wanted what he could not give. She wanted love.

Gritting his teeth, he faced Kieran. "I have nothing beyond seeing Murdoch burn."

Drake met Kieran's disbelieving stare with a hard glare of his own.

"Then God have mercy upon your soul—and my hide. For when Guilford hears you mean to see this through, he will likely try to change the shape of my head with his mace."

Later that day, Kieran found Averyl sitting by the shimmering pool at the bottom of the ravine, throwing rocks into the clear blue depths.

Beside her, he eased onto the short grass and plucked a nearby wildflower. When she looked up in his direction, he handed the blossom to her. She took it with a sad, silent smile.

"This abduction has been no easy ordeal for you," he began.

Averyl's mouth pinched tightly, unhappily. She wore so many emotions upon her young face: Hurt, hope, need, fear, anger. He hardly knew where one ended and the next began. Kieran wondered if she knew that herself.

And if what he suspected was true, Drake's choice of a mate surprised him. But it pleased him as well. A woman capable of such feeling, and displaying them without caution, might be exactly what his isolated friend needed to find his soul again.

And that Averyl was lovely, with her innocent eyes and fresh pink cheeks, only made Kieran smile more.

"He makes such difficult, for both of us," Averyl said.

"Of late, Drake has excelled in difficult, my lady. Fear not, he has a heart. He simply has trouble hearing it."

Averyl's head popped up, and she turned her wide green

gaze upon him. So much green. So much hope and sadness in so winsome a setting.

Kieran felt his interest stirring. He was, after all, a healthy man. Reminding himself that this particular beauty was not his, he smiled his understanding.

Suddenly, hope left her features. "He has no heart."

"Nay, he would only like you—all of us—to believe such."

She dropped her chin to her knees, now curled up to her chest. The waves of her golden hair shimmered over her shoulders, past her waist, skimming her hips. Aye, Drake was a lucky varlet to have felt the artless sensuality of her touch.

Beside her, he shifted his tight hose when Averyl spoke.

"I used to believe as you do, but now I am certain he truly is without a heart. I can see no other way he can hold me with such need, as if naught else in the world matters, only to revile me come morn."

The picture she created, along with the tears dusting her cheeks, made Kieran want to beat Drake senseless. Instead, he brushed her tears away with a thumb.

"As Aric's wife, Gwenyth, would say, he is a fen-sucked swine and deserving of a swift kick."

Averyl lifted her chin and laughed, her sudden smile brightening her face. "I think I like this Gwenyth."

"That looks better on you, love." He reached for her hand. When she gave it without condition, he squeezed it before raising it to his mouth for a chaste kiss.

"Thank you," she whispered softly.

A few feet behind Averyl, Kieran heard a rustling from the bushes. Alert, he turned—and spotted Drake standing just beyond the clearing. His friend's black gaze fell upon Averyl's loose curls; then her hand joined in his.

Raw fury settled on the abrupt angles of Drake's face. Thankfully, Averyl saw him not. Kieran pretended that he had not seen his friend as well and hoped Drake would not charge in.

Disengaging his hand from hers, he placed it on his belly and rubbed. "I fear I am near to fainting with hunger."

" 'Twill be my pleasure to help you, since you have helped me," she said, rising.

"You have my thanks, love. I shall be along directly."

After she made her way from the clearing, Kieran turned to the bushes. "She is gone. You can come out now."

Drake emerged into the clearing and grabbed Kieran by his tunic with angry fists and pulled him to his feet. "You would seek to bed *my* wife?"

Kieran considered his answer carefully. Though a healthy dose of jealousy might make Drake see his feeling for Averyl, it might also make him run from such.

Drake roared, "She is not an unwed lass you can chase for sport, to conquer without thought—"

"She is your woman, and I would never deny your claim," he vowed. "But if she is not a lass to conquer without thought, why do you believe she is a lass to conquer with hate?"

Drake regarded him with silence, scowling.

"Think carefully on that," Kieran advised, then returned to the cottage.

"I received word from Guilford last week," Kieran said over their simple supper of fish and leeks.

Drake did not reply; he merely glanced at his friend. Averyl wondered at his silence, which grew each minute.

"Aric does well with the new king, Henry. His skill as a warrior is valued," remarked Kieran.

"As it should be," Drake finally replied.

"Aye," said Kieran. "And Aric makes a fine diplomat as well, which King Henry has discovered and put to good use with those Yorkists left who would make war upon the throne."

In answer, Drake merely nodded.

"And it seems Gwenyth makes him addle-witted with her want of a babe."

Again, Drake glanced at her. This time, Averyl felt his gaze burn across her mouth, her breasts, her belly, before it slid away. "They will raise a babe well."

"Aye, 'tis the getting of one that seems to be the trouble. Gwenyth is impatient to conceive and insistent that Aric help her as often as he can spare a moment."

Finally, Drake directed a frown at Kieran. "And he complains of this?"

Kieran laughed.

Averyl flushed hotly when Drake's stare passed over her once more. She looked away, only to see Kieran watching her, the smile on his mouth turning questioning.

"Aric claims exhaustion, since the king keeps him so busy," Kieran said, "but he does not complain. And what of you? Any thoughts of a babe?"

"Nay!" exclaimed Averyl.

" 'Tis not possible," said Drake at the same time.

Silence fell across the table as they looked at one another. Averyl gripped her eating knife in her hand, absorbing the desire burning in Drake's black eyes. She glared in return.

"Soon that will change," Drake added.

His arrogant assumption, his callous conquering, packed fury into her response. "Never."

Pushing her trencher away, Averyl rose from her chair. "Pardon," she murmured to Kieran, then made for the door.

Emptiness gaped within Averyl as she realized Drake still wanted her for the easing of his lust. His heart did not call to hers and never would. She had known thus, but to be so reminded pained her.

She had no more made her way past the table when Drake followed, gripping her arm. "We have not finished with our meal."

"I am finished." Averyl hoped he understood she meant not only her supper.

After a stiff, silent moment, Drake slipped his hand

around her waist and brought her against his chest and the pounding of his heart. The urgency in his hands flowed into her body. A part of her longed to melt against him, to take the affection he surprisingly gave in that moment. But turmoil prevailed in her heart. Naught would change if she gave in. Drake wanted her available to his hunger, while he gave naught of himself. And if she let him, he'd shatter her heart—if he had not already.

"Release me," she whispered, hoping he could not see the tears gathering in her eyes.

Against her, Drake's body went taut and unwelcoming. A moment later he stepped away.

"You cannot run forever."

Averyl jerked open the door. "I have no need. You will discard me soon enough."

Stomach clenched with pain and fury, she slammed the door, knowing she must put him out of her heart or admit the worst had happened: that she had fallen in love.

As the door trembled in the portal, Drake stood mute. Disbelief, shock, and anger warred in his gut, along with something that felt like pain. He cursed, raking a hand through his hair. Did she no longer care about him? Had she ever cared at all? Had her fickle affection turned to Kieran already?

A moment later, he felt a heavy gaze upon him from across the room. When he turned about, he was surprised by Kieran's questioning stare. With Averyl's rejection, one that cut him deep, he had forgotten his friend. But Kieran's expression said he had been watching carefully his exchange with Averyl.

Slowly, Kieran spoke. "You care for your hostage bride a great deal, Drake."

"She is troublesome in her defiance and difficult in her insistence upon love," Drake defended.

"That may be so. But the care upon your face, your urge

to hold her for something other than sex, bespeaks feeling. 'Tis plain you are not indifferent."

Gritting his teeth, Drake made his way back to his chair and sank into it. How could he deny such a truth? "I wish to God I were."

Kieran leaned across the table, shaking his head. "The woman you held, your wife, *there* is your something to live for."

Drake steeled himself against the conviction in Kieran's words. "She is merely an *ablach*, a pawn."

The Irishman's disbelieving smile grated on Drake's nerves. "You lie, my friend. You seek to hold her close even when not bedding her. You seek to keep her only for yourself. Many years I have known you and never seen you display such a want."

"I—" Drake began as he rose and paced. "She . . ."

"You would not show such emotion if she meant naught to you."

"What say you?" Drake demanded. "That I grow soft?"

Kieran smiled. "Nay, my friend. I say you love her."

Fourteen

Two days after Kieran's departure, dawn crept through the cottage's lone window. And Drake called himself every kind of a fool as he held his wife while she slept.

He should release her from his embrace. Only a fool deep in the muck of love would hold her without cause, without seeking her body. And he was *not* in love, despite Kieran's suspicions.

I say you love her.

Why could he not dismiss those words from his mind?

Averyl was his wife, and he could hold her for whatever reason he sought. 'Twas his right. Just now, he enjoyed her softness, her scent. Men enjoyed such things.

Aye, his explanation was simple. Logical. Uncomplicated.

Then why had he dashed to her side last night when some manner of a dream caused her to cry out in her sleep?

With his silent comfort, Averyl had quieted quickly, and he could not dismiss that satisfaction. And sleep was one of life's necessities, especially while being chased by a pack of angry clansmen bent on execution.

True, all of it. Yet naught explained why he felt joy in helping his wife and reluctance to release her now.

Against him she stirred. Moaning softly, she rolled closer and pillowed her head against his chest.

Amid the intimate crinkling of the mattress, the mysterious floral scent of her flesh tugged at his loins. She snuggled the rest of her body closer to his length. He swallowed hard. The length of her arm across him, her unrestrained breasts beneath her linen shift lay against his chest, teasing his memories.

His manhood rose against her, hard, impatient. Aye, this was the reason he could not let her go. He was weak where her flesh was concerned. The soft thunder of her responses danced at the edges of his mind, taunting him. Drake knew he'd never held another woman like her, never reveled in the soft catch of another's moan, never felt driven to give every ounce of pleasure possible.

That did not mean he loved Averyl. Nay, he simply responded to her on a primitive level. Man to her woman, driven by the urge to claim her in every way possible.

But not because he loved her. True, her wit and spirit, while surprising at first, were not part of her charm. It only meant she was likely to have a scheme of some sort, and not one he liked. After all, she'd hit him with his own fire poker and had also rushed into the night to steal his boat.

Unbidden crept in the memory of her tears on the windswept cliff as she clung to him and told him of her mother's murder, of her fear of darkness.

Frowning, Drake resisted an urge to comfort her, stroke her bare arm, and ignored an odd warmth growing in his chest.

Without a doubt, Averyl was a disobedient wench, not the dutiful wife nearly every man wished for. Such was doubly irritating, Drake thought, for he had never wanted a wife, much less a hellion. Why, she had escaped at the fair under his very nose! While that proved her clever, it had also proved her foolish. She would have been raped by three drunken fools had he not been following her. Aye, and he would have loved to kill all three of those rogues for such intentions.

Realizing he'd squeezed Averyl more tightly to him, Drake loosened his hold. A small smile curled at the corners of her tempting red mouth. The warmth in his chest grew to an ache. He shifted on the bed to find a more comfortable position.

Indeed, she was a damn fool, believing herself homely. Aye, her father had planted the notion in her head, but she'd allowed it to take root and grow. Drake knew he'd been right to scorn such a ridiculous belief. Any sane man would.

And then there was her blind trust, her faith in him. Once, he'd been touched. Now he realized she was simply too naive to believe badly of the man she'd wedded and bedded. She knew him not. Not really, despite her words to the contrary.

God willing, she never would.

Certainly his intense desire for her sprang not from her devotion to the foolish concept of love. He found her dogged perseverance in the foreign emotion most irksome. Nothing short of a thousand-man siege could crush her belief. When she believed something, she did so fiercely, devoutly. Good qualities to have in the soldier at one's side, but in a wife? Nay. Though she was intelligent and loyal, who would love a bride possessed of such a wide stubborn streak?

Drake shrugged. There, he'd proved he could not want her for any reason but her body. And to prove further she meant naught more to him, he would resist even that. He could give up the sweet wine of her kiss, the sugary delights of her skin. And giving up other contact, conversation for instance, would be no struggle at all.

He would not miss her in the least.

"Good morn," she whispered, her voice heavy, bewitching.

At the sound, Drake jumped from the bed like a guilty child caught filching a tart, then chastised himself. The woman could hardly read his mind. Shaking off a vague sense of guilt, he reached for his tunic and scrambled to push the garment over his head to cover his erection.

"Drake?" she called huskily.

He gritted his teeth, feeling his manhood stiffen further.

How could she do that? How could Averyl, with a mere word, incite a pounding need to roll her on her back and make love to her from one sunrise to the next?

He grunted in reply and turned away to the hearth. Behind him, he heard the rustle of sheets as she left the bed, then the groan that accompanied her stretch each morn. Had it been only last week he'd teased her about her feline movements? And why could he see her body in his mind's eye reaching for the sun?

Drake looked down to find his hands trembling. With a curse, he thrust the kettle back to the hearth. "If you want aught to eat, make it yourself."

Air. He needed air. Fresh air, not that tinged with Averyl's floral-scented flesh.

Whirling around, Drake made for the door. Two, maybe three, strides and he would have peace. The urge to collect her against him, ravage her mouth, brand her forever, would blessedly leave him.

Averyl blocked his path, stopping his barreling gait by placing her small, warm hands upon his chest.

His heart pounded, and he cursed beneath his breath as his eyes slid shut. He'd had her, dozens of times now, more than he'd had any one woman. Why could she not leave his thoughts? Why could he not cleanse himself of this unruly desire?

"Wait," she entreated, pale curls streaming to her waist in a silken curtain. "I would talk to you this morn."

Drake made fists at his side in an effort to keep his hands from her. "I'm in no mood for talk, woman."

When he stepped around her, the image of her, ethereal, warm, burned in his mind. He clenched his fists harder.

Just before he reached the cottage door, he felt Averyl's hand at his elbow. "Why not release me?" she asked. "I will not wed Murdoch. You know I can never share a life with such a man, much less the intimacy of a marriage bed."

With a swift rush of indrawn breath, Drake admitted he could not even bear the thought of Murdoch's hands on her.

"Since our marriage is consummated, he cannot wed me."

What Averyl said was true. But the thought of releasing her inflamed a barrage of refusals within him. The issue of her safety remained. And he was certain, if he thought for a moment more, he could conceive other reasons why she should not leave.

As Drake looked at Averyl, it seemed to him as if she brought out something that opened the festering wounds of the past, ripped aside the barriers of his heart.

He felt. Not lust. Such was simple to classify. Nay, he felt a rush of too much at once. Guilt, desire, fear—all easy to note. But there was more. He wanted to turn to her, find succor in her arms. He yearned to cling to her, fit her against him and hold on until the tidal wave of feelings swept past him.

Drake knew he should run, flee her presence before he did something he would regret, something to make her believe he loved her. He should let her go. And he would—soon.

"Nay," he said finally. "You will stay with me."

"Why keep me? You care less for me than a rusty sword."

Gritting his teeth, he snapped, "Would I have bothered to rescue my rusty sword from three attackers?"

"Maybe you should have let them have me." She shoved a curl behind her ear. " 'Twould have saved you from plying me with lust that is naught more than convenient and fleeting."

"Convenient?" Had she no concept of the havoc she had wreaked upon his mind? "Oh, aye. 'Tis so opportune to desire you until I feel near exploding. 'Tis so fleeting, I spend entire days and nights hard for wanting you."

He grabbed her, brought her face beneath his. "I've spent hours of late thinking of how I could make you cry out beneath me, atop me, before me, around me. I dwell on using my hand to make you scream, my mouth to give you pleasure. And that's before I would use my body to completely make you mine. What say you to that, wife?"

Averyl stared, speechless. What could she say? Heaven above, were even half of that true— Nay, he had mentioned his lust, not love.

But Lord knew she was weary of denying her love for him.

Averyl chewed on her lip thoughtfully. Her mother's wisdom about seizing love when it appeared filtered through her mind. Could she, even if 'twas only for today? Even if he may never love her?

Such would be naught but foolishness.

Ah, but someday soon, he would leave her. What would she have of Drake then but memories? And even now, she felt certain he cared—at least a little. Had he not held her half the night with no intent to bed her?

Swallowing, Averyl stood locked in indecision.

"Well, what say you?" he barked, challenging her.

He claimed to want her. Lord knew, she yearned for him with pure ardor. Could she let him leave her forever without taking something for herself by which to remember him? Nay, and she wearied of resisting what she wanted more than her next breath, weary of denying the truth.

She loved him.

Now she wanted to express her love, satisfy her need to be whole with him once more.

Averyl stared at Drake. The white tunic he wore clung to his wide shoulders and sculpted torso, boldly outlining his ridged chest. She swallowed, transfixed by his beautiful, blatant masculinity. He smelled of man and earth and sun.

Averyl cleared her throat. "Do what pleases you."

Drake cast a shocked glance at her, the bronze power of his hands clenching at his sides. Images of those hands upon her, stroking, exciting her, sent pleasure rippling through Averyl.

"What?" he queried sharply.

"Aye, anything. Whatever you've been thinking."

Fingers trembling, she took his hand in hers and placed it upon her breast. He stiffened and cursed. But his fingers tightened upon her flesh in needy supplication.

As if her body had been made for his, she responded to his caress, her nipple tightening beneath his palm. The sharp hiss of his breath told her that he noticed.

"This cannot be real," he said almost to himself, even as he drew her closer to his heat. "Why?"

"I simply want you." She caressed the hand that covered her breast, noticing that he shook.

"You're asking me to swyve you?" He raised a dark brow.

"If that is how you choose to put it, then aye."

His eyes flared with confusion. Then he swallowed and stepped away, ripping his hand from her breast. "Why?"

"You said you wanted me until you felt ready to explode."

She stepped closer, pressing a kiss to the damp fabric covering his chest. Though his stoic expression reflected naught but uncertainty, Averyl felt his heart beat faster beneath her hands.

He grasped her wrists and thrust her away. "Why tempt me?"

Without awaiting her reply, Drake turned his back to her, raking a hand through his hair. Her smile felt bittersweet upon her lips as she took in his restraint. 'Twas as if he held on to the vestiges of self-control, afraid of what he might say or feel if he let go.

"If you want to make love to me, Drake, why do you resist?"

Muttering an ugly oath, he whirled to face her again. "You play a dangerous game, Averyl. Stop while you can."

She regarded him with a steady gaze. He met her stare, dark eyes defiant, angry. Aye, he wanted her—and wished he didn't.

So she gave, placing her palm over his rigid staff. Shock

and need vied for his expression. A groan escaped him. She curled her fingers around his length. Drake cursed.

Stepping up to the expanse of his broad chest, she whispered in his ear, "Once I thought to fight the pull of our attraction. But when we made love, you forced me to acknowledge my desire."

"And you think I owe you the courtesy of displaying mine like an untried boy?" His sarcasm cut through the air.

"Nay. Then you had what you wanted. Now I will have what I desire."

Though Drake's face remained blank, when Averyl stopped before him, heat burned in his eyes, setting her afire. She sent him a bold stare as she fit her hungry hands beneath his shirt, touching his fevered skin. After a sharp intake of breath, his heart began to pound with the force of a marching army.

Tortured desire loomed around his pinched mouth and hovered in his clenched jaw. And those eyes, hot, knowing, troubled, and angry. Clearly, he waged some battle within, one Averyl was determined he would lose.

She drew his mouth to hers slowly. With a mixture of desire and panic on his face, he leaned in. Averyl tensed, fearing he would stop her, refuse her this kind of control.

Finally, his taut arms rose to push her away.

"Kiss me, Drake," she murmured against his mouth. " 'Tis all I ask."

Expression rigid, his fingers clutched her waist. Averyl held her breath. Would he accept her or reject her homely face and body as he rejected her heart?

An infinite moment of silence later, Drake pulled her against him, fingers clutching her waist. Her head snapped back until their gazes met.

For an instant, silence held, broken only by their breathing. Desire had won. Averyl saw that in the blaze of his eyes. Elation swirled through her.

Then he claimed her mouth. Completely. With a ferocity

that forced the breath from her. Her elation turned to molten desire in the span of a heartbeat.

Parting her lips for his probing tongue, she groaned when he entered her mouth. He tasted of desperate hunger and need.

Again and again he exacted her response, his mouth urgent. Her own desire soaring, pooling between her thighs, she sidled closer and returned his kiss, measure for measure. She gave everything—her mind, her devotion, her love. Gave without hesitation, without thought, hoping only that he understood.

He propelled her backward, trapping her between the cottage's door and his body. He anchored his palms on either side of her head, pinning her to the rough wood. Primal hunger dominated his countenance. Averyl felt an answering chord within her, a savage, twisting desire that would not abate.

"Is this what you want?" His breath came hard, fast.

She arched against him. "Aye, and more."

He pressed his body closer until she felt each inch of his full arousal. "And this?"

Her voice trembled. "Aye."

His hand fell to the laces down the front of her shift. One, two, three; with speed and agility he unraveled them. His greedy palm enveloped the newly exposed skin of her shoulders. On a moan, he murmured something incoherent and kissed her neck.

A riptide of yearning swelled within her, drowning her in its intensity. Whatever burdens had held Drake back now dwindled beneath the onslaught of desire.

He murmured her name, his lips claiming hers again. No gentle need, this raging fire between them. His tongue slid against hers hotly, salty-sweet.

He took. Demanded. In return, he gave tenfold.

Averyl surrendered, clutching the bunched muscles of his shoulders, warm against his heart, wishing they could stay thus.

Drake's arms felt like steel as they banded about her. She felt his erection flush against her belly and arched wantonly to the temptation. He growled from somewhere deep in his chest as he rolled his hips against her in a fevered answer, a gesture of possession.

With impatient fingers, he tugged her smock above her head. Suddenly she was naked, her heated skin exposed to the morning breeze drifting through the open window. The savage desire in Drake's eyes made it worthwhile.

His gaze whispered across her sensitive flesh like a secret. She forced herself to stand still, shoulders squared, and invite him with her eyes to look his fill.

His black gaze lifted from her thighs, over her abdomen, and caressed her breasts on its way to her face.

To her shock, Drake turned her to face the door. With his heated chest at her back, Averyl felt his palm about her breast and his hot breath upon her neck. The sensation of feeling each exquisite touch, yet not seeing its source, heightened her arousal.

"Lass, how can you make me want you so?" he asked raggedly.

"I know not, for I am equally cursed to want you."

Drake's breathing was hard, labored. "Aye, 'tis a curse," he said finally. "Truly, you have bewitched me."

His hand left her breast to ignite a trail of fire across her belly, then down into her woman's flesh, damp with want.

She gasped as his one hand held her steady at the hip and his lips burned a path from the slope of her shoulder to the crook of her neck. The other hand found her pleasure bud with unerring ease. He circled the nub in rhythmic strokes. Tingles built to tightness, tightness to aching pressure. Matching the cadence of his heavy breaths, the aching pressure burst, and she cried out at the pulsing release.

He did not stop.

"Aye. Let me feel you again," came his warm command. Amazingly enough, with a few strokes of his fingers, pleasure exploded, awashing her again, leaving her trembling.

Before she could take a breath, Drake turned her to face him. Fingers of iron clasped her hips, lifting her. His mouth closed over her breast, the soft abrasion of his tongue like kindling to a fire. A whimper stuck in her throat as he pulled on her flesh with his lips and a gentle nip of his teeth. Averyl arched closer, drowning in his scent, something heady, musky, indisputably male.

His breath came in short pants as he tore off his tunic and worked out of his breeches and braies. "I can wait no more."

Hunger hung in the air between them, sharp and tangy, as he backed her to the door again. Against her belly, she felt him bare, rigid, urgent. She thrilled to the primitive realization that he meant to take her here, claim her now.

She met the thrust of his tongue earnestly as he filled her mouth with his taste, surrounded her body with his raw power. His fingers blazed like wands of fire as they delved between her thighs, urging them apart.

His lips teased the sensitive spot behind her ear when he plunged his fingers within her. She gasped, clutching him tighter, silently begging. The strength of her desire roared like a beast, demanding its way. She answered the call without remorse, glorying to the intensity of his need.

"Now!" she insisted.

"Aye, now," he groaned, lifting her, drawing her legs about his waist.

With one hard push, Drake was around her, inside her, filling her every corner with ecstasy.

Then she had no time to think. He found a rhythm, one uncivilized in its domination, ruthless in its ability to render her mindless. Excitement bubbled within her, erasing all thought from her mind except of Drake and this joining.

She tightened her arms about his shoulders, her legs about his hips, as sensation swept over her in a hot gush, crashing through her body without mercy. Arching against him with a cry, the feeling burst within her like an explosion of the sun, glittering, bright, brilliant. Drake drove into her again, then spilled his seed deep inside.

Averyl opened her eyes slowly as they sank to the soft carpet of earth beneath them. Drake still held himself inside her, with her above him. She wilted across his chest, listening to the rhythmic pounding of his heart and the chugging cadence of their breathing, accompanied by a lark's song outside.

Never had she felt so complete, the moment so perfect. He'd responded to her completely, holding nothing of himself back, even when he resisted sharing aught. She knew it. Felt it in his need *for her,* demonstrated by his mouth, his body, instinctively knowing he'd never before given this much of himself to anyone. By his own admission, she had bewitched him.

And *she,* homely Averyl, had been the one to unlock those feelings. She had been able to persuade this strong-willed warrior to share his emotions through his touch when he'd wanted nothing more than to keep such locked within his soul.

As he stroked her hair away from her damp temples, she felt a new truth dawn: She was not ugly—except in her father's eyes. Today Drake had taught her to believe differently, for 'twas clear he did, and she had been the fool for taking her father's opinion into her heart.

Relief soothed her like a mother's touch. Tears of repletion, of joy, welled in the corners of her eyes, spilling onto the hot flesh of his chest. She sniffled, trying to stop them, but it was too late.

"Here, now," he whispered, lifting his head to look at her. He wiped her tears away with gentle fingers. "What's this?"

" 'Tis nothing," she lied, even as his very tenderness caused the tears to come faster.

"Nothing makes you leak like a sieve?"

Against her will, she smiled at his teasing. "You are incorrigible."

"Me? Nay, 'tis you, my beautiful, wanton wife."

Her mouth trembled into a smile. "Thank you for making me believe that."

" 'Tis truth and always has been."

Drake placed the softest of kisses upon her forehead and stroked the slick skin of her back. Never had he been this tender after their lovemaking. Of great relief was that the haunted pain had left his eyes, replaced by a soft satiation. Mayhap she had succeeded in helping him see love's goodness.

Hope made her cry again.

"Ach, more tears. Why, Averyl?"

Chin trembling, new tears burning her throat, she stroked his cheek, her heart diving straight into the concern filling his dark eyes. She could no longer restrain the truth.

"Why?" Her voice shook. "Because I love you."

Fifteen

Those three words hung as heavy as an anvil in the **weighty wake** of silence. Even the lark beyond their window ceased his cheerful song. Averyl held her breath, heart pounding like a frightened rabbit as Drake stiffened below her.

After the wild, golden joining of their bodies and hearts, the fact that she loved Drake should not stun him. Yet clearly her admission of such had shaken him, down to his very core.

From the jolt of shock evident on his face, she saw that his peace was gone.

Though their bodies lay still joined in slick intimacy, Averyl felt an insidious separation sever the closeness they had shared, as surely as if he had taken his broadsword to a ribbon.

Something within her cried out as he set her away, his back taut, lending credence to her fear. Knees cushioned by pungent earth, Averyl clutched the hard span of his shoulders, yearning to hold him to her until he understood he had nothing to fear from her love.

Drake would not be held. With a shrug, he rose to his feet without a word, never meeting her questioning gaze.

Watching in painful silence as he hurriedly donned his clothes with little care, Averyl searched for the words to chase away the chill between them despite the warming summer morn. To assure him she would never crush the heart his thoughtless mother had scarred years ago. To convince him she would never misuse him, hurt him, cast him aside.

No words came to mind.

'Twas as if he refused to look at her, face her. Holding back hot tears, Averyl dressed, wishing she knew what to say.

The silence stretched on. The tense breadth of his shoulders told her eloquently there would be no discussion of her feelings. His fear, his rage, stood between them as effectively as a boiling ocean.

Still, Averyl could not let him walk away.

"Drake?"

Finally, his dark gaze reluctantly slid over her face before coming to rest on his boots. "I am sorry."

An iciness crept across Averyl's skin as she reached for him. "Sorry? Nay, you must not be. I seek nothing, but simply to tell—"

He cut her off with a sharp wave of his hand. " 'Tis but a matter of time before you would want your feelings returned. Even now your eyes plead. Nay." He shook his head, directing his angry gaze to the roof. "I have no wish to hurt you, but you must understand. Love is naught but a painful trap designed to twist a man inside out. I will not fall into it."

Averyl watched in mute pain as her husband walked out the cottage door. Dark clouds drifted across the sun, obscuring the sunlight, just as Drake had dimmed her hopes.

He withdrew further, in a way he had not done even in the earliest days of her captivity. She swallowed fiercely.

Aye, she'd known his views on love and hoped, perhaps without reason, that she could change them. The furious slam of the gate reached her ears and mocked her foolish dreams. Drake wanted nothing between them now but separation.

She stood on shaky legs, fighting the tears of despair that stung her tired eyes. The smells of burning wood, wine, and Drake triggered a barrage of memories. She recalled their first kiss so many weeks ago, Drake sharing his bitter fury at his mother's cruel betrayal, the times they had joyfully joined their flesh as man and wife, his tenderness upon witnessing her fear of the dark.

Drake was a hard man to know, complex, often hidden. But Averyl thought she had solved the puzzle, dug into his heart to find the hurt that pained him. She'd even thought to heal it.

This morn proved only that she knew nothing.

Deciding against any breakfast for her roiling stomach, Averyl prepared and poured fresh wine warmed above the dwindling orange fire. She sipped, scarcely noting the brew's bitterness.

And now that she'd confessed her love, she must face the consequences.

A gentle splash took her from her thoughts. A ripple in her wine, coupled with warm, salty tracks running down her face, slammed her with a new wave of despair.

One sob, followed by another, shattered her odd calm. The fist clutching her stomach tightened. Averyl thrust her lukewarm wine away and lowered her head to her hands, letting her tears flow unchecked.

By God's fury, why could Drake not love her? She groaned. Why did her caring have to hurt them both? Even now, she felt as if she had lay vulnerable her body and heart for his misuse, knowing he would do naught else.

And why, by the saints, did he allow the specter of the past to destroy their chance at any sort of future?

Four hours later, Drake had yet to return. Averyl tidied the cabin after she'd ceased her tears, then chopped some cheese and bread for lunch, her stomach rioting at their sour smell.

Pacing the cottage's small space, Averyl stared into the ashes of the morn's fire and realized Drake would not return for their midday meal. She grabbed a handful of her silken gown, anxiety rising within her.

Where had he gone? She prayed he had remained on the island, not venturing far away, particularly not to anywhere Murdoch might find him. Biting her lip, her imagination conjured visions that he had been hurt, even killed, because she had driven him away with her three revealing words.

Or, most like, he simply avoided her. The haunted countenance he'd worn after her confession more than told her how much her words had shaken him. How unwelcome they had been.

Yet she could not see what harm her admission had done. Though she wished he had returned the sentiment, she did not expect such. She had even told him so, only to be rebuffed.

Fine. 'Twould be a cold day indeed before she repeated such a heartfelt emotion.

As the sun waned in the dim afternoon sky, Averyl perused the perimeter of her ravine cell, waiting and listening for his return, vowing that when he did, she would keep all words of love, and any incriminating others, to herself until the time had come for them to part.

By nightfall, she'd seen no sign of him.

Again, she prepared their meal, pacing, cursing, crying. Concern remained, but irritation had joined as the hours ticked by, chafing like gritty sand against her skin.

Admittedly, telling Drake of her love had been far from wise, but he needn't have scurried off like a deer from a huntsman. 'Twas not as if she had demanded any display of his feelings in return. Indeed, he was hiding from her like the veriest of babes! And over three little words.

With a huff, Averyl sat down to a solitary supper, determined to enjoy her colcannon without him despite the fact she disliked cooked cabbage. Determined, in fact, to enjoy every moment of his absence. He would not be around to watch her, taunt her, tempt her to unrequited emotions. She could prepare for bed in privacy, enjoy the last of the wine.

Most like, Drake sat out on the island somewhere, huddled against the chilly fog rolling in, oblivious to all but himself, his wants and his selfish needs, as usual.

Pushing most of her brackish-smelling dinner away untouched, Averyl stood with a stomp. Her captivity, indeed their entire marriage, had been about Drake and his wishes. What of her? Her own needs? Her feelings? Doubtless Drake was too rooted in whatever foolish thoughts populated his head to realize she had thoughts and desires of her own.

That time, she vowed, had come to a halt.

She, too, had feelings, which ran as thick and sure as his. His past was littered with tragedy, but her own had been as well. Did she use that as an excuse to hurt others, to turn away from whatever love and solace was offered her? Nay. She accepted it, gratefully. Nor did she have any difficulty in admitting her own feelings in return.

So why did Drake believe himself different? Certainly even he had run out of tragedies and excuses.

Averyl paced the cottage's dirt floor and paused at the window. Clouds dimmed the moon's white glow, and she smiled.

Her errant husband, when he returned, would soon learn he was not the only one whose sentiments mattered.

By the position of the thin moon in the gray-black sky, Drake determined the hour somewhere close to midnight. Weary and troubled, he opened the ravine's gate.

His haunting thoughts of Averyl returned. Why had she spoken those damned words? Why had his pulse quickened in joy?

He was a fool, no more, no less, for hiding upon the shores of his own island, away from his own cottage, until he felt certain his bride was hours deep in sleep. He, who had never backed away from a necessary battle, never dismissed a worthy opponent, had left Averyl behind and hidden like a coward. The realization filled him with shame.

Still, naught had changed. In the morn, she would awaken, and he would tell her of his decision to leave.

Inside the cottage, he expected no more than the remnants of an evening fire to keep her fear of the dark at bay. But as he pushed the door open, nothing in his imagination prepared him for the sight of Averyl fully dressed before a roaring fire, candles lit all about the room, matching the determined flames in her eyes. Clearly, she had no intention of retiring soon.

"So you've finally returned?" she said acidly before he could even wonder why she did not yet sleep. "Have you finished brooding, or do you wish to sulk more?"

He winced at her sarcasm and realized he had once again underestimated her mettle. Once, Averyl might have curled up into a ball and cried herself to sleep over his callous behavior. Now she met him face-to-face, hands positioned upon her hips, clearly as ready for battle as any warrior.

Drake stepped around her, anxious to avoid a confrontation. He'd rarely known how to handle the sensitive and self-doubting girl she'd once been. He had even fewer ideas how to manage the woman spitting such resolution from her eyes.

"There is much you do not know or understand," he told her.

Though there was only one fact of which Averyl was unaware, 'twas a fact she would likely find terrible.

"Nay, I cannot understand," she countered, "because you refuse to tell me all. 'Tis only part of your tale you give, parts that make no sense. You hide from me in every other way, while you have demanded and coaxed until I have bared all my thoughts and fears."

"Averyl, I but spare you from ugliness."

"Nay, you selfish knave," she said through clenched teeth. "You keep me in darkness, telling me scattered tales of your past that make little sense when put together so you do not have to reveal yourself."

Drake turned to face her, the blood within his body suddenly very still. How had she stumbled upon that truth?

" 'Tis late, and I am tired. Rest—"

"I will rest when I have need to," she argued. "At this moment, I want answers."

"I have no more to give you."

"Can you do aught but lie? Or is that all you know?"

Her fiery green gaze blazed with determination, with fury. Again that sense of shame, the feeling that he owed her the truth, crept through him. Perhaps after all the trials he'd put her through, he did owe her something more. More, as long as the worst secret could remain his.

"Damn you!" she railed before he could recover from his guilt. "I do not dispute you were accused of murder or that you were blamed. But why you? Why not another member of the clan?"

Drake chose his words carefully. "Murdoch hates me most."

Averyl's delicate forehead wrinkled into a disbelieving scowl. "Why should he? 'Twas he who bedded your mother, not the other way around."

"Bedding my mother was just another way to show defiance to Lochlan and prove his hatred of me at once. But his loathing started long before then, when we were but children."

The suspicion shadowing Averyl's face showed she remained unconvinced. "You still speak in riddles, you rogue. Why should he hate you most, and how could one child come to despise another for a lifetime?"

Drake forced nonchalance into his shrug. "Only Murdoch possesses the answers to your questions. I do not presume to know what is in his mind."

Averyl clenched her fists. "You know, or at least possess, a very good idea."

Shrugging, Drake turned away, refusing to say more.

"Your revenge is against Murdoch, and you, too, hate him. Now, even if you say you know nothing of the reasons for his enmity toward you, you certainly know the root of yours for him."

He could hardly dispute her. " 'Tis true that I came to hate him while still a child."

"For . . . ?" she trailed off impatiently, clearly awaiting an answer.

Drake sighed wearily and sat before the crackling fire. Mayhap, telling her this little bit would hurt nothing. "For his cruelty to me, to Lochlan."

"For seducing your mother?"

"If Diera had not turned to Murdoch, she would just as easily have found another to warm her sheets. 'Twas her nature," he sneered.

"None of what you say makes sense," she declared, stomping closer. "Though I cannot say such surprises me in the least!"

Drake watched the swish of her skirt, heard the slide of her boots upon the dirt floor, and wondered what to say now.

" 'Tis the truth," he defended.

"Aye, but 'tis no more than your usual attempt to disguise the whole truth by revealing a few facts. Tell me!" she insisted. "For I cannot understand how this childhood hatred you describe, coupled with Murdoch's seduction of your mother, which you claim was not uncommon, anyway, would lead Murdoch to blame you for his father's murder. Or why you would seek to kill him. None of that adds up to your bitter rage and determination for revenge. Why did you not simply try to clear your villainous name and remember that Murdoch and your mother both enjoyed causing others pain?"

He stood and walked past her again, this time to the open-shuttered window and the fathomless inky night beyond. "There is ample proof of my guilt, none of my innocence beyond my word. I cannot allow Murdoch's deeds to go unavenged. Remembering that he and my mother were cut from the same cloth only inflames me further."

"Why?" she demanded, standing but a breath behind him.

The scent of her floral skin, the sound of her tortured struggle for understanding, suddenly coupled with memories of her lovemaking, of her tears. A hollow place in his chest ached.

Aye, she deserved better than he'd given her. She deserved the truth. But if he gave it, would she ever speak to him again?

"You cannot understand," he said finally, defeated. What plagued him to want her gone even as he craved her near?

"I tire of hearing such a truth, for I cannot understand what you will not explain! And I tire as well of your unpredictable behavior. Passionate one minute, cold the next. Caring come eve, remote by morn. Can you not see how this hurts me?" She crept closer until her breath was a whisper in his ear. "Or are you like your mother and simply do not care?"

Drake whirled to face her, a new fury roaring in his ears. "What did you say?"

" 'Tis not deaf you are," she challenged, chin raised. "I asked why you cannot find some way to resolve the past and get on with your future. Perhaps you are more like Diera than you realize. Mayhap you enjoy destroying others for the pleasure—"

"Damnation, never." His gaze bored into the depths of her troubled eyes. There he read anguish and anger, bewilderment and desperation. And need. That was his undoing.

"You seek the truth, my lady wife. As you wish. But 'tis sorry you will be."

He grabbed her arm and hauled her against his body, denying the niggling fear this might be the last time she allowed any such intimacy. She leaned into him, pliant, trusting. Inhaling, he filled his head with her soft floral scent. Slowly, he pressed against her, wondering how betrayed she would feel once he had revealed all and how much she would hate him for concealing so much for so long.

"Your betrothed, the man you nearly wed to save Abbotsford from ruin, we share a common bond. We share a father."

Averyl's concentration quickly dissolved into white-faced shock. "Lochlan? He was . . . ?"

"My father as well."

The blood drained from her face. "Then Murdoch is—"

"My half-brother," he confirmed.

Shock dominated Averyl's open-mouthed expression. After a still, awful moment, she writhed for escape, drawing out of his embrace. Drake let her go, regret and fury weighing upon him.

Drifting silently to the hearth, Averyl sat as if dazed. "Why would you use me so against your own brother?"

Drake sighed, running his hand across his tired face. He could almost see the disillusion crystalizing in Averyl's eyes. Remorse tugged at him.

"My father and mother wed several years after Murdoch's own mother met her grave. I know not why Murdoch always hated me, but he did. He tried to drown me when I was a boy of three."

Averyl gasped, disbelief and horror pasted on her pale countenance. Drake merely continued on.

"When I was but six, he abandoned me in the forest until my father found me two days later. In my tenth year, I visited home from my knight's training. He put a snake in my bed. At twelve, he poisoned my food. While a child, I endured his superior age and strength each time I came home, along with his unreasonable hatred, never knowing the reason behind it. I still do not understand it. That is God's truth."

"By the saints." Averyl's voice trembled.

Drake pushed on. "As I grew, the rows he and my father had became more heated. My father threatened to send him away, up north to an uncle of cruel reputation. In retaliation, Murdoch, then a young man, seduced my mother. Not because he wanted her or cared for her but because my father did."

"And you found them together."

Drake nodded. "He arranged the liaison in the solar, knowing full well I enjoyed spending my evenings there."

"He plotted just to hurt you?"

Pain and shock laced her voice. Drake refused to believe her tone or take succor from it.

"At first, I believed that. I later realized he arranged it thus so I would tell our father. I was the one person whose word Lochlan would never doubt."

"Why did Murdoch not arrange for your father to find them? Would that not have been simpler?"

Drake's sweating hands curled into fists. "Our father would likely have killed him on the spot, so great was his love for my mother. Murdoch is no fool; he knew that."

Confused, Averyl frowned. "What had Murdoch to gain by angering your father?"

"At first I could think of naught but pure spite for the threat to send him away. Later, after Murdoch left of his own accord for life at court, he and my father began exchanging letters. Murdoch made clear he only desired that Lochlan exile me and my mother and claimed that he had only bedded her to prove her a faithless bitch not worthy of our father's devotion. He was also quick to point out that the child of such a whore could only be baseborn and without honor."

Anger fired Averyl's expression. "Certainly your father did not succumb to such manipulation."

"Nay, as Murdoch discovered. After Diera . . . died, my father grieved for months—then rewrote his will, forcing Murdoch to wed you before you turned eight and ten."

"But 'tis a strange provision."

Drake shrugged. "Not really. The war between the Campbells and the MacDougalls needed to end. My father believed marriage for such a cause would help Murdoch mature into a better man. And until such an event transpired, Lochlan made me tanist of the clan. Had I not been accused of murdering him, I, not Murdoch, would have assumed the role of chief upon our father's death."

Comprehension began to dawn in gray tones upon Averyl's chalky face. "So Murdoch had Lochlan killed and you blamed."

He nodded. "After my mother's death, he arranged for some butcher disguised in MacDougall colors to attack Lochlan on the battlefield as we fought your kin. Murdoch was in Glasgow."

"Such explains why Murdoch sent for me, hinting of a wedding, months before we expected a summons." Averyl placed a trembling hand over her mouth.

"You refused him?"

"We delayed him. 'Twas just after Christmas when we received his letter. My father demurred, citing the harsh weather and the illness of my people. We were not able to travel to Dunollie until 'twas nearly June."

Drake nodded, wanting the conversation over. He had never told anyone so much, not even Kieran or Aric. The rest of the clan knew it not. Refusing to dwell on why he had spoken so to Averyl, he closed his eyes, feeling the ache of his muscles, the pounding in his head.

"So Murdoch had you falsely accused of Lochlan's murder so he could become chief?" she asked, disturbing the silence.

"Aye. He still had friends within the clan, powerful friends willing to believe the murder was all my doing, some English conspiracy with my grandfather to gain power. Once they convinced the others that I most stood to benefit from Lochlan's untimely death and produced the bloodied knife I pulled from my father's body, 'twas not long before I became a condemned man."

"And Murdoch, being your father's eldest son, was restored to power."

"Aye. He convinced them that no will written in grief over such a paltry thing as an Englishwoman's death was important enough to keep the rightful heir from becoming chief."

"By the blessed Virgin," she breathed. "So Kieran and Aric freed you, and you vowed revenge."

He nodded grimly.

"Oh, Drake. 'Tis a terrible tale indeed."

She placed her hand in his, her face solemn. Drake looked down at their palms, clasped together skin to skin. He felt something sharp and hot sting his eyes.

Gritting his teeth in effort, he pulled his hand away. "I do not seek your pity."

" 'Tis not pity I give you," she assured.

"Then what?" he asked, wary.

"Advice. 'Tis clear to me that you let past words and deeds rule your future. You must make your own," she urged. "Do not let your mother and father's enmity destroy you."

Confusion eddied through Drake. She spoke as if he had any say in past matters, as if he could change or forget them with a sweep of his hand. "Of what foolishness do you speak?"

"You need not shout," she said. "I but try to help. You see, I realized yesterday morn that I had allowed my father's opinion of me to color my belief of myself. I had allowed his words and deeds to control my thoughts and actions. You do the same, though you do not see it."

Fury and incredulity fought for Drake's tongue. "Am I to forget what's been done and pretend I am not wanted for my father's brutal slaying?"

She sighed. "Of course not. 'Tis a fact that nothing will change. But in the case of love, you allow your parents' bitter union to control your feelings, and it should not be so."

Wishing he could shake some sense into her, he grabbed Averyl's elbow. "Listen to me, woman. Love started this chain of events—my mother's death, my father's murder. What love did to my family now forces me to take my revenge, to see Murdoch into poverty before he draws his final breath. Aye," he said, answering the shock on her white face. "I want him to die knowing that all he has plotted to gain has been taken from him. When you turn eight and ten, he will lose the money and power for which he had our father murdered. Then I will kill him."

"None of that is love, but hate. Would you let hate and Murdoch end your life as well? What would happen then?"

Drake's jaw clenched. "The money and position transfer to our cousin Wallace."

" 'Tis not the money I ask about. Think of what Murdoch can do to you!"

"And should I run, hide like the veriest of cowards? Nay, I will see my revenge finished and end the damage love has wrought upon us all."

Averyl sat quietly, her expression grim. "Love did nothing evil. You but blame it for what you choose to do."

"You think love will grant you harmony? I have used you every chance I had. I use you still. That is love? That gladdens your heart?"

With a tight pinch to her ripe red mouth, Averyl rose and walked to the door. "Aye, though you cannot see it. I hope you soon realize we could have a future together despite this mess if you could free your soul from the past."

With that, she disappeared into the moonlit night, her anger apparently greater than her fear. Drake sighed raggedly, feeling the heavy hammer of his own pulse as he ran shaking fingers through his hair. 'Twas a tangle indeed.

Disjointed thoughts chased one another through his head, allowing him no peace. At the crux of his ruminations was Averyl and her words. Was his beautiful wife the sainted answer his hollow heart needed to heal? Or the ultimate pawn he and Murdoch would eventually destroy?

* * *

Drake fell asleep before the fire, awaiting Averyl's return. He awoke, knowing not what time it was. Only the grit within his aching eyes and the watery sun trying to penetrate the dirty window told him he had not slept long.

Rising, he stretched his stiff shoulders and neck, then cast his gaze to the bed, expecting to see his wife lying there in repose. To feel that rush of desire, of possession, she never failed to engender in him.

He found the bed empty.

Anxiety seared through his gut like a flaming blade. Had she escaped finally, driven away by the truth? Found her way through the locked gate and discovered the location of his boat?

His heart lurched against his chest as he envisioned Averyl, tall in courage but short on physical strength, trying to navigate his tiny boat across the choppy waters separating Arran from the mainland of Scotland.

Running out the cottage door in search of his wife, Drake pictured her drowning, dying, calling out to him for help . . . Sweat beaded on his forehead and ran down to his brow. His heart pumped faster as he searched the ravine, calling her. Panic rang with the peal of thunder in his ears when she made no reply.

A quick inspection proved the gate was still locked, the key still in his pocket. Drake took one breath, then another, assuring himself she could not be far, could not be harmed.

Parting the thick island foliage before him, Drake stomped through to find Averyl slumbering by the trickling green waters of the pond. He exhaled in relief, unclenching his fists, and sat on the ground beside her.

She looked in harmony with nature, her creamy skin the perfect foil against the lush Scottish grass, the sheen of her gold curls surrounded by the rich purple of heather. She resembled one of nature's blossoms, nestled here among the vibrant colors of God's land, like the lilies floating atop the water beside her.

His gut tightened with both desire and self-disgust. No

matter how much he denied the truth to Averyl herself, Drake knew, felt it deep within, that he had come to care about her.

Too much.

'Twas why he worried about her safety, why he'd made love to her when he should not. The reason he had wanted her to believe in her beauty. And the reason he'd told her, and no one else, the entire truth of his past.

'Twas the reason he was tempted to tell her he would try to love her in the way she had dreamed of since girlhood for at least as long as he lived. And why he could do no such thing, for she failed to see the truth: Animosity had plagued the love his parents shared. And Averyl's notion that he possessed buried fear that controlled his life was rubbish. Nor could he dishonor his father by forgoing revenge for love.

But that did not stop him from aching for her.

Drake sidled closer to his wife, resisting the urge to run his fingers through her tresses, glide his hand across the sunlit splendor of her delicate cheeks. His entire body clenched like a fist. His hand trembled at his side.

Revenge and the clan's condemnation did not allow for emotions, he told himself. He had never intended their marriage to be one of anything but convenience and revenge.

And the idea of opening what was left of his heart to Averyl and allowing her the kind of power Diera held over Lochlan turned his stomach to a cold block of fear. He could not endure the tumult of feeling flowing between them, wondering what he might do next to earn her displeasure, fearful that any day she might grow weary of his attention or of life on the run.

Aye, she claimed to love him today and clearly meant such. His mother had probably once uttered those same words to his besotted father.

Drake closed his eyes at the encroaching picture of such a bleak marriage that could only lead to his shattered soul.

Nay, he could not, would not, give Averyl that kind of power over him. He must put distance between them. Now, as he'd decided yesterday, after succumbing to his urge for her, they must part.

He woke Averyl with a gentle shake. Her eyes opened by degrees, revealing her splendid green orbs to him slowly. Her languid expression filled him with remembrances and lust. And resolve, for he must sever this tie between them now.

"Drake?" she asked sleepily.

He stood and cleared his throat. "I am sending you away."

She sat up slowly, confusion rampant in her expression. "Away? From here? From you?"

"Aye, to—"

"Do you still run from what you feel? Drake, do not—"

"I run from naught, least of all anything I might feel. 'Tis simply safer to send you elsewhere."

Averyl stood, denial on her beautiful face. "The Mac-Dougall has searched this island and found nothing."

"That does not mean he will not return. 'Tis for the best."

"The best for you," she shot back. "So you do not have to listen to me and risk facing what is in your heart."

"Hear me well," he ground out. "I have naught in my heart!"

"At least naught you will admit to me. Can you not realize your inability to love is the result of your slavery to the past? Do you not see—"

"Speak no more on this." He turned his back to her, determined they would never exchange words of this ilk ever again.

Before he could stalk away, a sudden noise split the air, an out-of-place crash that sounded frighteningly like the splintering of wood. Every muscle in Drake's body froze with foreboding a moment before the thunder of horses' hooves sounded inside the ravine. Instant white-hot fear stunned him.

"Come out, you bastard." Murdoch's too familiar voice whipped through the air. "I have you trapped!"

Sixteen

Shock pumped through Drake's veins. Sweating, he fought panic and glanced at Averyl. Her eyes went wide with horror.

"Come out, you worthless whore's son," Murdoch shouted. "You cannot escape this time!"

"What are we to do?" Averyl whispered.

Drake grabbed her hand, praying they would make it out of the ravine alive. "Run!"

Squeezing his hand, Averyl followed him, sprinting. Over the drum of his pounding heart, Drake heard Murdoch's men dismount and begin to beat through the surrounding green brush in their search. Hiding in the ravine's brambles and birches, clutching her small hand, he guided Averyl away from the men.

Turning her, he forced her stare to his. "Hold on to me, no matter what. Do you hear me?"

"Aye," came her whispered reply before they began creeping from the bushes as silently as possible.

Murdoch's men were visible everywhere but blessedly scattered and on foot as they searched the length of the ravine. Drake made a quick count and estimated there were probably a dozen and a half.

With a prayer on his lips, he sprinted toward the gate, Averyl's hand clinging to his as she ran beside him.

Within instants, a shout hailed that they'd been spotted. Murdoch's men gave chase. One leaped at them from a clearing, a long, wicked blade in hand, and made a quick swipe at Drake's chest. He arched, inching out of death's way. Over the sound of Averyl's sudden scream, he urged her on. The rest of Murdoch's men scrambled to return to follow while Murdoch himself shouted and gave chase.

Drake and Averyl bolted up the ravine's incline, past the splintered gate, and through the narrow opening to freedom. He heard the footfall of Murdoch's men gaining on them.

"Averyl, love, hold tight," he called in her ear.

She slumped against him in reply.

Fear slammed into Drake as he put his arm about Averyl's waist. Something thick, wet, and sticky greeted his fingers. In horror, he brought his hand before his face.

Red.

Oozing warm blood covered his palm and sheathed his fingers. Drake's gut churned as he realized the sentry's knife, intended to kill him, had maimed Averyl instead.

Nausea ground its way through him, along with bone-biting cold. And denial. She could not be hurt. She could not die. He would not allow it, by damned!

Sweating and cursing, Drake stopped before the small cave hiding his boat. Gingerly, he lay Averyl upon the soft sand, his heart racing at the pale shock of her face, her heavy, closing eyes. Wave after sickening wave of a prickly-cold sensation flooded him when he saw the side of her purple dress darkening at her ribs.

He cursed, knowing he must get them both away from this island now if he had any hope of keeping her alive. A panicked glance behind him confirmed that Murdoch drew closer and his men, all giving chase, were not far behind.

Drake's grip tightened about Averyl in fear. "Averyl? Can you hear me?"

"Hurts," she croaked, eyes cracking open. "Like fire."

Fear squeezed the air from his chest. "Do not move."

Her eyes slid shut again. She made no reply.

Both cursing and praying, Drake ripped into the cave's nearby opening, uplifting the camouflage of plants and rocks with lightning speed, and dragged the tiny boat into the water. A cursory glance revealed the oars within the bobbing wooden craft. Murdoch's own vessels were nowhere in sight.

After sprinting back to his wife, Drake cradled her against him as he darted for the little boat. Easing her down across the bottom, he pushed away from the shore just as Murdoch appeared atop the cliff above the beach, the one on which Averyl had confessed to her fear of the dark.

He vowed then she would not become another casualty. He would sell his soul if he must so she would not die.

Murdoch shouted, fist raised, as his men joined behind him. His half-brother's threats were gobbled up by the crash of the waves and the frantic beat of his own heart.

Drake absently noticed his adversaries turning away, no doubt in search of their own boats, before he turned his attention to his wife. How badly had she been hurt?

He squeezed his eyes shut, blocking out the pain and guilt that assailed him. This was his fault. His anger, his arrogance, might well cost this fiery woman with the heart of an innocent her very life. He should have plotted better, anticipated Murdoch's cunning, put Averyl out of harm's way once they were wed.

But he had desired her with him, beside him. He had thirsted for her, wanted her as a gasping man requires his next breath. And for his selfishness, his lack of restraint, she was paying the price.

In a terrifying instant, Drake knew anger, a helpless, clawing fear, a willingness to bargain with God, all of which mirrored his father's emotions as he lay over Diera's deathbed.

Was this searing pain the wretched love Averyl wanted him to feel?

Pushing his thoughts away, Drake ripped off his shirt and tore away Averyl's bodice. The jagged length of a gash see-sawed along her ribs, seeping blood. Panic bit into his gut, coupled with the brackish stench of sea salt. Drake placed his shirt over the wound and covered it with his trembling hands, then resumed his frantic rowing. He could do nothing more until they reached safety.

God's blood, she looked so fragile and unmoving, so painfully pale. Fear filled him with a sharp, serrated ache. He vowed then that if—nay, when—she recovered, he would guide her, and his own heart, from harm's path. No matter what the cost, he would shield Averyl from his perilous revenge, his dangerous desire. She would never be in jeopardy again.

If that meant he never saw her, held her, again, Drake knew 'twas his duty. He would do it.

After three hellish days with the Gibsons and a tensely slow week of travel, both marked by Averyl's fevers and his fear, Drake dismounted, his body leaden with exhaustion. Averyl still lay sleeping peacefully in the farm cart he'd bought upon reaching the mainland.

During those ten interminable days, he'd stayed by her side, providing sustenance, aid, and prayer as she recovered. During those bleak nights, he'd held her hand, sponged her face, and swore to himself he would never endanger her life again.

As long as he remained with her, she was not safe.

While Drake had kept vigil over his wife, he also watched over his shoulder, hoping Murdoch and his miscreants would not find him until he could get Averyl to safety. To his relief, they never caught his trail south.

Now Drake found himself in Yorkshire, staring through the early-morning gray at the massive stone doors of Hartwich Hall. His mood was as black as the threatening storm clouds.

A peace he had missed emanated from the walls of his grandfather's castle. Inhaling deeply, he let the peace soak into him, just as the sun suffused one after a long day indoors. He fantasized about such tranquility, dreamed of life without greed, jealousy, or hate.

But fate had decreed him a future of revenge, not peace, and 'twas foolish to dream of aught else.

Today he would say good-bye to his handfast bride, putting an end to the peril on her life—and his heart—for he could not stay without grave risk to both.

Refusing to dwell upon it, Drake scanned the ivy-draped walls, then the colorful riot of summer flowers amid the castle's quiet. Such reminded him of his grandmother, Matilde, God rest her soul.

During his boyhood years here, she had provided the motherly touches Diera never had, the soft voice over a scraped knee, the gentle smile over a deed accomplished. She had never needed to be the center of anyone's world, never demanded attention, as had his mother. Though mother and daughter, Diera and Matilde could not have been more different.

A fond smile tugged at his mouth. He'd missed his grandmother's generous ear and sage advice these last three years since her passing. Averyl, having been motherless for eleven years, would have appreciated the woman a great deal.

Averyl.

Drake lifted her still-sleeping form into his arms. Warm and dazed, she roused, asking in a slurred, sleepy voice, "What're you doing?"

He'd oft wondered the same thing over the past ten days. But he knew; he was leaving her. As he had told her he would.

Drake swallowed a lump of something thick in his throat and said, "We have stopped. Sleep for now."

Her green eyes lifted, half-open, slumberously stunning. "Where are we?"

"With friends."

Nodding tiredly, Averyl covered her mouth with a half-closed fist and yawned as her eyes drifted shut once more.

She laid her head trustingly against his shoulder and drifted back to sleep.

Her childlike gestures tugged at Drake's heart. With a gentle hand, he brushed a golden curl from her face, his fingers lingering upon her soft cheek, which had finally regained its healthy pink.

Holding in a sigh, he approached the castle, dread engulfing him like quicksand. His heart pounded. The urge to hold on to Averyl tightly swept over him like a Highland wind. Sense won out. To keep her with him would do naught but place her in more danger and submit his own heart to more of her bewitching. Neither consequence could be risked.

Shifting Averyl's weight, Drake approached the gatehouse entrance. The guard let him pass with a few words. Inside the garrison, the main gates remained closed against the night. A pair of well-armed soldiers admitted him through the wicket gate. His wife stirred restlessly in his arms.

Within moments, a young page met him in the courtyard, in front of the empty blacksmith's forge. Despite the pre-dawn's murky light, a fresh, friendly glow reflected from his face.

Drake wondered if he had ever been that young or innocent on his road to knighthood—and manhood.

"Sir Drake, I bid you welcome. You have come to see your grandfather?" he asked in gentle inquiry. His gaze traveled over Averyl's limp form, but he politely held his tongue.

"Aye."

"Step this way. I shall tell him you've arrived."

Drake followed him past the brewery and the joiner's workshop, where workers spotted him and stared. Drake veered through a garden gate, toward the majestic keep. Up several flights of stairs he trudged. Again, Averyl lifted her head groggily, only to put it down again at his soft whisper.

At the great hall, he watched the boy disappear up the

narrow torch-lit stairs, punctuated by gray stone walls. The young page returned long minutes later.

"His lordship is eager to see you. He awaits you in the solar."

In the dusky splendor of the hall, Drake held his sleeping wife a bit tighter and set upon the familiar trail to the solar.

With a dry throat and all the enthusiasm of a condemned man, he slowly entered the low-ceilinged domain of the fire-lit chamber. His gaze found the grayed man, his formidable figure now softened by old age and good living.

"Drake, it *is* you. When Lionel, my page, told me you had come, I was not certain if 'twas true. Are you well?" The old man's bushy gray brows slashed down into a frown.

"Murdoch has not yet stretched my neck, as you can see."

"Aye, and lucky for you." He glanced again at Averyl. "And the girl? She must be Averyl Campbell."

His gaze drifted down to the delicate lines of Averyl's face, pillowed against his shoulder. Drake felt a tight vice of pain in his chest as he realized this would be the last time he would ever hold his stolen bride.

Resisting an urge to clasp her closer, he answered, "Aye."

Something like approval filled his blue eyes. "Put her on yon bed, then come speak with me by the fire."

Drake searched for the courage to relinquish Averyl to his grandfather's soft, mossy-scented mattress—and a safer life. Though he had faced months in Dunollie's dungeon and armies of vicious men bent on seeing him dead, he found it nearly impossible to simply release her. But he did, gently laying her down with a brush of his thumb upon her cheek. Averyl stirred a brief moment before settling into the mattress. Drake covered her with a thick blanket folded at the foot of the bed. Reluctantly, he returned to Guilford.

The old man frowned, clearly choosing his words as he bade Drake to sit in a high-backed Romanesque chair. "Wine?"

Drake shook his head and sat. "I cannot stay. Murdoch's men hunt me still."

A furrow creased his forehead. "Unfortunate business. I did not like your decision to pursue revenge."

"But you understood it," Drake pointed out.

"True. Kieran arrived two days past, after Murdoch discovered his identity."

"Aye?" That was bad news indeed.

Guilford nodded. "He tells me Averyl is your handfast bride. If she is your wife and you intend not to stay, why have you brought her here?"

"I hoped you would hide her from Murdoch and his men."

Guilford scowled. "He will think to look for her here."

"That is so," answered Drake with regret. "But you can protect her. I no longer can."

"Why say you this?"

Drake glanced at Averyl with remorse, recalling with aching clarity the past ten days. "Murdoch's men nearly ended her life when they stormed my hideaway on Arran."

"Too wounded to travel further, is she?" Guilford asked, clearly skeptical.

"Nay. Simply dangerous. I must continue to hide until Averyl becomes eight and ten and I find a way to kill Murdoch." Drake rose to escape his grandfather's probing look.

"So you abducted her, then wed her. Is that correct?" Censure laced his voice.

Drake nodded like a contrite boy caught at mischief.

" 'Twas pure foolishness I hope you regret."

"Yet I know well Murdoch would have treated her very ill as his wife."

Guilford shot him a reproving frown. "True, but you should not have taken her. You had no right to force her from Murdoch's side. 'Tis doubtful she wed you willingly, either."

Cursing his grandfather's perception, Drake admitted, "Aye. And now I cannot give her the things she seeks nor can I protect her. Murdoch must not get his claws into Averyl, particularly before her birthday in February. So I have come humbly to you for help."

When Drake knelt at Guilford's feet, the old man laughed. "You've never had a humble day in your life, boy. Do not think to start now." He sighed. "What does the girl seek?"

"Money," answered Drake. "Her childhood keep falls about her ears, her people starve, and her father is a dim-witted dolt who knows not how to solve the ills of his vassals."

Guilford paused thoughtfully. "If funds for Lady Averyl's home will ease your mind, then I shall provide it. What else?"

With a sigh, Drake sank back into his chair. How could he explain a yearning he did not fully understand? "She seeks . . . affection. Her mother died when she was but a child. Her father convinced her she was homely and worthless."

"Ridiculous!" insisted Guilford as he cast another glance at Averyl upon his bed.

"To be sure, but she has grown up believing this and will need friends within these walls."

"Of course." Guilford granted the request with a wave of his hand, as if such required little effort.

Drake sighed in relief. Averyl would be happy here until her birthday. After that time, she could return to her father or remain here as his widow, whatever she wished.

He resisted the pain at realizing he would not be beside her as she lived out her days.

"Aught else?" the old man asked.

"Nay. I thank you for your help."

Guilford responded with a nod. "I sense something else troubles you."

He cursed his grandfather's perceptions. How could his elder know so much so quickly? Had Kieran told the old man about his suspicions of love? Pray God, nay. " 'Tis naught."

"Naught had you clinging to your wife like a babe clutches its mother as you entered the room?" he challenged. "Come, now. I may be an old man, but not so old that I do not recognize affairs of the heart. You care for her, do you not?"

Drake faltered for words, struggling to explain what he could not. "Our marriage . . . took an unexpected turn."

"Ah, Kieran speaks true. You do love her," he deduced. "Praise be! I never thought to see this day."

Drake regarded his grandfather with a probing stare, willing him to understand. "I love no woman. 'Tis simply that Averyl is intelligent and of good heart, as well as deserving of a life better than either her father or I can grant." He looked away. "I would simply see her safe from further harm."

"Including thus from your hard heart, Drake? Do you believe she loves you, then?"

He paused, wishing an end to this conversation. But Guilford would only pry the truth from him. "So she says."

"And you do not believe her despite her admittedly good heart?"

" 'Tis no more than a foolish girl's notion, one she will outgrow soon enough."

Guilford nodded in consideration as he rose and walked to the fire, boots heavy against the wooden floor. "Does believing thus make it easier for you to deny your own feelings?"

Drake drew in an impatient breath. "I do not deny that I have come to care about her welfare."

"And more, I daresay. I remember hearing similar denials from Aric not long ago." He shot Drake a skeptical glance from across the room.

"Their marriage was a different circumstance."

"Aye, instead of Gwenyth forced to the altar, they both were. What of it?" he demanded. "Drake, love would bring peace to your life. At last you have a woman worthy of your affection. Why not embrace her?"

Gritting his teeth, he replied, "Her life is in danger, and I swore to exact vengeance upon my father's grave. I will not sacrifice either to chase some foolish sentiment."

The old man paused, templing his hands beneath his chin. "Drake, your father, of all people, would have encouraged you to seize love whilst the opportunity is yours."

"Such love bought him nothing but despair and death."

"Do you think he was the only one hurt?"

Drake frowned, and Guilford continued: "Did no one ever tell you the story of your conception?"

Irritation coiled into his gut. "I assumed I was conceived in the manner of every other child. I am sorry to say it thus, but Diera was hardly the Virgin Mary."

Guilford smiled. "In some ways, you are wrong. Lochlan was quite enamored with your mother. She did not return his feelings." The other man paused, frowning. "I loved your mother. She was my daughter, after all. But I knew her shortcomings. And her greatest one was that she was fickle.

"She was a woman grown and a widow, since Lord Thornton's death in battle. In her mind, she could do as she pleased. When she met your father, the attraction was instant, and they soon became lovers."

" 'Tis no surprise. She granted her favors freely enough," Drake added.

Guilford pursed his mouth into a disapproving frown. "They were together mere weeks before your father believed himself in love with her. With his own wife dead for three years, it seemed natural that he ask Diera to wed. She refused that time and many others, though she continued as his leman."

Drake frowned. "Why would she refuse a position of honor with a powerful chief?"

"Because your father demanded absolute control over

everything and everyone about him, and Diera believed that control could not extend to her unless she wed him."

Knowing that Lochlan had always said control was his biggest ally, Drake froze, somehow dreading these next words.

"When another handsome Scot, a MacDuff, I believe, caught your mother's eye, she tried to leave your father. He refused to relinquish her despite her wishes, then locked her in his chamber. He refused to allow her to leave Dunollie. He restricted her visitors to women friends and family members."

Drake tensed in his chair, his hands unconsciously tightening around its arms. "My father would not have done something so heartless! How can you slur him in death?"

" 'Tis truth, Drake. Why else would your father come here to help fight my battles over the years if not to atone, to assuage his guilt?"

Drake had always assumed Lochlan fought because of his respect for Guilford, but now . . .

"And even after your father's attempts to keep Diera, she still refused to wed." With a heavy sigh, Guilford continued. " 'Twas then your father decided that, should she conceive, she would be forced to marry him. Eventually, he got her with you."

"My father forced her to bear me?" Cold disbelief sliced through him.

Guilford gave a sharp nod. "He made certain she had no way to prevent conception and seduced her repeatedly until the deed was done."

Drake gaped, his mind racing. His own father, so selfish? Why? Guilford's description hardly sounded like the honorable man he'd known. Yet his grandfather would never lie. Which left him to wonder, if his father had truly loved Diera, how could he have forced his dominance upon her without a care for her wishes?

"So she finally wed him," Drake said softly, frowning.

"She had little choice, for she could not bear the dishonor

to our family. Thus sated, your father continued to keep her under lock and key, then ordered her to be a proper mother."

"Which she was not."

"Nay, she was not, but surely you see that she acted out of anger and spite. She told me once that she wanted to love you but that you reminded her too much of your sire."

Drake sighed tiredly, pondering the ramifications of this tale. Had he known of his father's cruelty, he might have understood Diera's rejection and spite, perhaps made peace with her before her death. As it was, there was much left unsaid between them, most notably these facts.

"What does this have to do with Averyl?"

"Your father's unrequited love cost him his peace and your mother her life. She wanted to die; in fact, willed herself to die to escape the pain, the loneliness. Would you want to inflict the same damage on Averyl?"

"If not for Murdoch, I would never treat my wife as a prisoner."

"Desertion is but another prison, Drake. If you have any love for Averyl, embrace her."

Drake gritted his teeth, confronted by words he felt unprepared to face. "If this were a simple situation, I would consider what you say. But I am a bloody criminal in my clan's eyes. The most I could offer is dishonor, and she deserves far more than that. 'Tis a favor I do in leaving her."

"How noble," drawled Guilford. "Tell yourself that. See if it keeps you content as you grow old."

"If Murdoch has his way, I won't live long enough to grow old," Drake snarled.

"You will not let him best you. 'Tis Averyl I worry for now. Drake, you have used your wife in a very deadly game, and now you seek to abandon her like stale bread."

Stale bread. His entire being rebelled against his grandfather's words. Averyl was a treasure of goodness, hope, passion. But Guilford was right; Averyl would feel discarded—and again unworthy. Over the years, she would grow to hate him. 'Twas a thought he could scarcely bear, but bear it he must, for all too soon she would be another tragedy to add to his bleak reality.

He gave his grandfather a contrite nod. " 'Tis the only way to ensure she stays alive and out of Murdoch's grasp. She must not die," he all but pleaded.

Sighing, Guilford shook his head. "You are strong-willed, as was your father."

As Drake acknowledged that with a sad smile, Guilford crossed the room to place a comforting hand upon his shoulder. The urge to allow the old man to console him was great, but he did not. Some sense of manly pride and a reluctance to further burden his elder with his problems stopped Drake.

"Will you provide Averyl a safe home here?"

"Aye, and I will care for her for as long as need be."

"Her safety means . . . a great deal to me. Thank you. When she turns eight and ten, she should be safe to leave, if she wishes such, but not before."

Guilford rose, his expression sage. "As you wish."

Then he left the solar.

An agonizing moment of silence passed. Drake stared at Averyl, his chest aching, his mind numb, his body cold. Everything within him yearned to stay.

Fate had already proved that he could not.

"Godspeed, my wife," he whispered, then left.

Seventeen

Drake slammed his way out of the solar, anxious to be gone from Hartwich Hall—and Averyl. Instead, he ran into a living solid wall. Startled, he looked up to find his old friend Aric, massive hands upon his hips, scowling.

Before Aric could say aught, Drake said, "Greetings. Do you visit here from Northwell?"

Aric scowled more. "I but pass through on my way to do the king's bidding. I am surprised to find you arrived."

"Now I take my leave."

Aric raised a disapproving blond brow. "You cannot stay to exchange words with your friends?"

With a shake of his head, Drake angled past Aric in the narrow stone hall. "I must be away."

"Away from your wife, I presume."

At Aric's accusing words, Drake turned back to his mountain of a friend. "Kieran knows not when to keep his mouth shut."

Before he could turn away and continue on, Aric said, "He is concerned, as we all are."

"For no reason. I wed her to keep her from Murdoch's reach. Now I can only wait until she becomes eight and ten. Then Murdoch will lose our father's money and power, and I will kill him."

"And what will happen to Averyl?"

Drake sighed, impatient to be away before he changed his mind, stormed back into the solar, and claimed his wife for good. "I have just had these same words with Guilford. Should you wish to know my plans, ask him."

With that, Drake turned away and took long strides toward the stairs that would lead him down . . . and away from the woman who could make him perish with want.

"So you do love her," Aric called.

He stopped. " 'Tis a common misconception I shall have to beat Kieran for later."

"Then why rush to be away? If she means naught, you have no cause to run as if guilt chases you."

"I have Murdoch to kill," he said, facing Aric.

"But not until she turns eight and ten, which is . . . when?"

Drake gritted his teeth. "February."

"And 'tis now what, August?"

"Nearly September," Drake bit out.

He knew the words were foolish as soon as he uttered them but knew not what else to say. How could he explain the swirl of confusion, the reluctance to leave Averyl's kind heart, coupled with a grim impatience to be gone from the very distraction she presented.

"Think you it will take a six-month to return to Dunollie and stab a blade into Murdoch's heart?"

Drake knew it would not, just as Aric knew it.

"I cannot place her in any further danger," he defended.

"Aye, but methinks you protect your heart just as much."

Aric's knowing expression annoyed Drake. What did his friend know of pain in love, in marriage? He and Gwenyth had been sublimely happy for nigh on a year. They had found the Eden few did. Drake was unwilling to take a chance that he would be less fortunate.

"Averyl is not Gwenyth, and I am not you," he insisted, rubbing a tired hand across his gritty eyes.

"Nor are you your father or Averyl, Diera."

True, and based on his grandfather's words, Drake had known only the truth his father had told him, one not entirely accurate. But Diera's cruelty in the face of Lochlan's

grief and love was forever embedded in his soul. Even if
Lochlan had treated Diera ill, why did she hurt him by
bedding his elder son? Why could she not forgive his father
as she drew her last breath? Why had she nearly destroyed
his proud soul?

"I'll not take that chance," he uttered, then turned away.

Averyl woke slowly, eyes shut against the light beyond.
A sense of activity, a bustling prosperity, assailed her ears.
People chatted. Cows mooed. The bang of metal sounded.
Where were the sounds of birds and rustling leaves? She'd
grown accustomed to them in the past fortnight of sleeping
outdoors.

She rolled to her side gingerly. Lingering pain from her
gash stabbed her, but she noted with relief that the ache
lessened each day. Such would please Drake. For she knew
he needed to travel faster if he wished to continue to elude
Murdoch but had not for fear of her health.

She snuggled beneath an extraordinarily soft blanket, not
caring from whence it came. For some days, she had wondered why Drake put her recovery above his escape. At first
she had hoped 'twas because he truly did care for her. Such
was foolish, wishful thinking, she feared. His only concern
was to keep his conscience free of her death.

Frowning against the painful thought, Averyl turned to
her other side, realizing suddenly she had not hard dirt and
ground beneath her but a true mattress. At that, her eyes
flew open, and she regarded a well-appointed, unfamiliar
chamber of blue and gold. Alarmed, she sat up with a gasp.

" 'Tis a restless sleeper you have been these past hours,"
said a young woman of such stunning beauty, Averyl felt
her mouth drop open. "But I am glad indeed you have
awakened. Mayhap now Kieran and my husband can cease
their infernal pacing."

Averyl took her eyes from the unknown woman and
glanced about the unfamiliar, lavish room. "Who are you?

Where is—?" She broke off, not certain 'twas safe to mention Drake's name.

"Drake?" The woman's blue eyes narrowed with ire. "The hen-witted fool is gone. And more is the pity, for I should have liked to give him a piece of my mind."

"Gone?" She fought a rising tide of trepidation and asked, "When will he return?"

The other woman sighed, then threw a stare over her shoulder, where a cascade of silken black tresses lay.

Behind the woman, near the fire, stood an older man and a huge hulk of a blond warrior conferring in low voices. Kieran paced beside them, casting an occasional glance their way. Unease gripped her, showing her aching heart no mercy.

Finally, the old man came forward and took her hand in his warm one. "He says he will not return. He means to kill Murdoch, then release you from your handfast."

Though the graying man uttered the response Averyl had expected—and feared—somehow shock wound through her, anyway.

Gone? Forever?

"I know you are bound together as man and wife," the man said. "I told him 'twas fiercely wrong of him to leave you."

Averyl's heart sought to deny the truth she could not change. Drake had finally rid himself of the bride he'd taken for revenge. The bride he'd never wanted. Pain seared her.

"But, as through boyhood," the old man went on, "my grandson remains obstinate, at least for now."

"Your grandson?" echoed Averyl, taken aback.

"Aye. I am Guilford Locke, earl of Rothgate. You know Kieran, of course. The giant beside the hearth is Aric. And this sharp-tongued shrew," he said, putting a loving arm about the woman, "is Gwenyth, Aric's wife. As Drake's bride, you are welcome here at Hartwich Hall."

"You're English," she blurted.

"I trust you willna hold such against me, lass." He mocked a brogue and smiled.

Unwanted tears stung her eyes, tears she hated to shed. Drake had rid himself of her, as he had warned just before Murdoch's attack and her injury. She raised her watery eyes to the group whose kind gazes conveyed empathy without a single word.

" 'Tis from himself he runs," the old earl offered in a low, soothing voice. "He knows you love him, and it frightens him."

Drake must have told him—told them all—everything. The rest, Kieran had seen for himself.

Averyl sat up, clutching her blanket with tight fists. "I would not hurt him."

"One day he will understand," Aric assured.

She tried not to hear the optimism in the man's voice, tried not to believe because it hurt so much. To no avail. The more she struggled to rid herself of the feelings she had for Drake, the more she failed. And the more anger she felt.

"I must leave, return to Scotland." She made to rise.

The old man urged her to stay abed with surprising strength. "You've yet to heal completely, and you would be best served to keep clear of Murdoch, lest he hurt you."

Averyl understood such logic but hated it. Frowning against the rise of fresh, furied tears welling in her eyes, Averyl yearned to be alone, to think, to scream and rail at Drake's cruel desertion. How could he leave her so callously after she'd bared her heart? Apparently, he could and without thought simply abandon her upon a stranger's doorstep.

Her forehead fell to her fist. Why would the earth not open up and take her to the purgatory she felt within her?

Why did Drake have to care for her so little?

"Shh, child," the old man murmured as Averyl sobbed, then rubbed her shoulder with a comforting hand. "All will be well."

How Averyl wished that were so. Though she must try,

deep down she feared she could never cast Drake from her heart.

Sitting up gingerly among her blankets, Averyl squeezed her eyes shut against the sight of the small chamber next to Aric and Gwenyth's. Even after two months without Drake, the lack of his warmth and touch first thing in the morn tore through her heart like a jagged stake. And now she could add some strange illness that plagued her through each day. She felt tired even after a full night's sleep. Her stomach churned unpleasantly, rolling like waves upon a stormy sea.

Leaping from the bed as a sudden crest overcame her, Averyl searched out the pitcher she kept by her bedside and clutched it as she heaved forth the contents of her nearly empty stomach.

Gasping for air, she felt the sweat break out along her forehead, between her tender breasts. It only compounded the pain in her heart. She hated the reality of awaking without Drake each day, of being without him every night. Everything inside her wanted to cry, to protest that Drake's departure had stripped away half of her soul.

Averyl cursed her weakness, for given his continued absence, 'twas clear he did not reciprocate even a fraction of her sentiment.

Burying her face in her hands, Averyl felt tears constrict her throat, tearing the breath from her chest. How could he care so little for her? Apparently Diera and Murdoch had hardened his heart so thoroughly, he would trust no one with his emotions.

At the thought, her stomach rebelled again.

Through her misery, she felt a soft hand upon her hair, another supporting her back.

"Ill again?" came Gwenyth's voice. " 'Tis time you admit you carry Drake's child."

Averyl lifted her head from the pitcher, both exhausted

and embarrassed, and rose to her feet. Aric stood in the portal, gazing at her with concern. "It cannot be."

Though she knew such was indeed possible. Her memories flashed vivid visions of her and Drake, entwined in their pent-up passion, making love against the cottage door on a warm summer morn. Had they created life in one another's arms?

Averyl grabbed a blanket to ward off her anxiety and the hint of October chill, then faced Drake's friends.

"Are you not his wife?" Aric asked.

"Such means naught."

He smiled gently. "I know my friend well, too well to believe he is any sort of monk."

Despite her unsettled stomach, Averyl felt herself blush.

"So such is possible?" he queried.

A babe. A tiny life created by her and Drake. 'Twas an awesome thought. A child with Drake's dark eyes she would hold come spring. Both love and fear filled her.

"Aye," she whispered.

Gwenyth brushed a comforting hand along her back. "I know you feel alone and that Drake has hurt you. But we are here to comfort you. And since my husband is often gone in the king's service, giving us little time to conceive our own babe," she teased, "I shall have to dote upon yours."

She met the woman's blue eyes. Knowledge and wisdom shone from their lively depths. Disquieted, Averyl turned away.

"In truth"—Aric shot his wife an inviting stare, then turned her way once more—"his own actions have hurt him as well. It pained him greatly to leave you."

"Do not give me false hope. He cares little for anything but his revenge."

"That does occupy him greatly," Aric acknowledged, "but when I last saw him, I saw a side I thought long buried after Lochlan's death and his torture. I saw his heart again."

Averyl crossed the room to escape the pair and the insidious infusion of hope his words brought.

"Enough! He wed and seduced me, then discarded me. I was merely a way for him to settle his long vendetta with Murdoch."

Aric sighed heavily. "That was his plan. But he came to care for you, which warred with his mind. Understand that his example of marriage has not been a favorable one."

"I know about Diera, and while I think she behaved very ill, that does not justify what he did to me."

"Of course not, but he is afraid of caring, of pain. Lochlan's grief upon Diera's death affected him greatly, and he's allowed no one to get close enough to touch his heart until you. He knows not how to trust."

"Then he deserves no more than my pity."

Turning away again, Averyl peered out the window. A massive tree's leaves danced gracefully despite the biting autumn wind. The River Foss flowed a chilly blue in the distance.

"You love him," Gwenyth said softly. "Do you not?"

She hesitated. "Nay, no more."

"You cannot lie to yourself." Gwenyth closed the space between them in two steps. She placed kind hands on Averyl's shoulders when she would have voiced another denial. "When I was a girl, I lived near a place called Sweetheart Abbey. As legend has it, in 1273, a certain Lady Devorgilla grieved over her loving husband's death. To keep him with her always, she had his heart embalmed and set in a silver casket, which she wore round her neck."

Averyl arched a pale brow. "I would rather see Drake's head upon a pike."

Gwenyth laughed. "There are times he deserves such punishment, no doubt. But I think you miss him as much as Lady Devorgilla missed her mate."

Averyl cast her a dubious glance. "Think what you will."

"Drake needs your heart," Gwenyth pressed on. "You must look deep inside. Think not of the hurt but of all you shared, all that could be. Then you will find your love still abounds."

Her guilty gaze skittered away. "It matters not. We will never see one another again."

"You plan never to tell him of his child?" Aric asked, brow raised. "Perhaps your love and the babe can persuade him to give up this foolish revenge and certain death at Murdoch's hands. You could leave together, find peace elsewhere."

With incredulity, Averyl stared back at the tall warrior. "If he will not risk his heart for me, I'll not bring him to my side with a babe. For if he cannot love, he has no place with this child or with me."

Gwenyth sighed. "Drake needs time and your patience. Search your heart for forgiveness. He will return, I vow."

"As of now, I must devote my attentions to something more pressing than Drake's fragile heart. I know Guilford has sent funds for the people at Abbotsford, but I wish to go there, help in whatever way I can to see them through the coming winter."

"You cannot," Aric warned. "Were you to return home, Murdoch would certainly find you."

Averyl considered the truth in his words. "That is so, but still I wish to go."

"You and your babe will be in danger if Murdoch finds you, only to learn that you are wed and with Drake's child."

A fact, that. Averyl sighed, weighing her options. "But my people—"

"Will be well cared for," Aric assured. "Guilford promised such. Stay here. Now that Kieran plans to leave and join another army and I'm off again tomorrow on the king's business, there is no man we trust to accompany you on such a long journey. You would have to travel alone."

Remembering the would-be attackers Drake had saved her from at the Midsummer Eve fair, she shuddered. The brutal rogues would have thought little of taking her virtue for their pleasure. But the familiar faces of her childhood servants and friends, gaunt with hunger, swam before her eyes. She had to know they lived, not starved. And what of her father?

Aric crossed his arms over his massive chest. "If you go, you will not only jeopardize your own life and limb but all of Drake's plans. He has sacrificed everything sacred to him, most especially his heart, to achieve vengeance for his father's murder. Either you will die on the journey alone, allowing Murdoch to obtain his bloodied inheritance, or Murdoch will capture you in Scotland and Drake will die in trying to protect you from that butcher. Think of your marriage, your child, and your true feelings for your husband before you decide."

With that, Aric and Gwenyth left, hands clasped. Averyl turned back to the window, scarcely seeing the browning grass in the gray autumn chill. She saw Drake, his struggle against the evil of which he was wrongly accused, his inner turmoil. An image of his body lifeless as a cackling Murdoch hunched over him with glee assailed her, and she hugged herself in fear.

And no matter how much she had come to resent him for using and abandoning her, she knew she could place him in no further danger.

Until her birthday in February and the end of Murdoch's threat, she could do naught else but rely on Guilford's goodwill, feel her unborn babe grow inside her, and find a way to shut Drake out of her heart for good.

In the midst of blizzards and chill, the January morn dawned crisp and clear. Averyl rose from her bed and stretched, feeling more eighty and eight than nearly ten and eight.

The growing size of her belly added a new dimension to her sleepless discomfort. Soon the flowing gowns she and Gwenyth had made to accommodate her expanding waist would no longer fit. Though anxious to hold the precious child already kicking and turning within her, the thought of growing larger in these last three months of her pregnancy depressed her further.

Then there was Drake. 'Twas not that she missed him any longer, but he had stolen some part of her spirit when he'd left her here at Hartwich, some portion of her innards she had yet to recover. Listlessness prevailed daily, confusing the exultation of knowing she would soon be a mother with the somber ebbs of realizing she would do so alone.

A soft knock preceded Gwenyth's entrance. Her chatty cousin Nellwyn followed. "Good morn, Averyl."

"To you as well, Gwenyth," she said quietly. "Good morn, Nellwyn. How fares your daughter this day?"

"Margaret is merry and walking so well," began the round-cheeked woman. "Heaven above, I have even seen her climbing the tables in the great hall as if they are her personal mountain. Of course, I must watch her, for she's likely to fall, but Gwenyth is kind enough to help me with that, as you have been. And soon we'll have your babe to spoil, which I'm so looking forward to—"

"The letter," Gwenyth cut in with an indulgent smile.

"Oh, aye." Nellwyn handed Averyl a sealed parchment. "The messenger says it came from Scotland. I'm sure 'tis from your father again. He loves you fierce to write so often," said Gwenyth's cousin wistfully, whose own father had cast her aside after she left her cruel but wealthy husband.

"We shall leave you to read in peace," said Gwenyth. "Join us in the great hall when you are ready to break your fast."

Nodding as the women left, Averyl turned her attention to the letter in her hand. Her father's missives of late had brought many blessings. The people of Abbotsford now had food aplenty, as well as clothes and supplies to last through the winter, due to Guilford, bless his kind soul. Such eased her mind greatly, that the people of Abbotsford would not starve.

The parchment crinkled in her hands as she pried open the seal and unrolled the note. A single glance, filled with words written by an unfamiliar hand. She frowned.

Lady Averyl,
I keep Drake as prisoner in my dungeon once more. If you do not wish his blood upon your conscience, return to Dunollie within a fortnight. Wed me and I will set Drake free, as well as release him from blame of my father's death.
If you do not come, with great pain, he dies.
            Murdoch MacDougall, Lord Dunollie

For a full minute, Averyl stood rooted in place. Then she read the letter once more, praying she would find her mind had but played a cruel hoax upon her heart. But 'twas no such game.

She began shaking. Drake was again trapped in Murdoch's dungeon. Horror slid through her as she imagined all manner of hell the fiend could force upon her husband. And her own father had likely told Murdoch where to find her. Had he told Murdoch of her marriage as well? The note had given no such indication.

Averyl closed her eyes. What was she to do?

Drake might not love her. But she had been unable to cut him from her heart. And he needed her, as their baby would need its father. She could not allow Drake to die, especially not painfully at Murdoch's hands.

She had, in fact, one choice. 'Twas risky but necessary. Once, she would never have considered such a risk. Today she could imagine naught else.

With that, she turned and fled her room in search of Aric and Kieran. She found both training together in the lower bailey.

The *clink* of clashing metal greeted her ears as she found the two in damp tunics and chain mail engaged in swordplay. Kieran lunged. Aric parried.

"You are becoming far too careless," warned Aric.

Laughing, Kieran sliced, nearly nicking his friend. "I prefer to think of it as daring."

"A man deluding himself so young," teased Aric, switching his sword from left hand to right, then thrusting and scratching Kieran, " 'tis not wise."

"At least I am not soft and muddled by love." Kieran nicked Aric's arm with a *whoosh* of his blade.

Wincing at that comment, Averyl interrupted their play. "Kieran, Aric, I would speak with you."

At once, they turned to her; surprise, followed quickly by concern, crossed their familiar faces. Funny how she had come to know them over the months. Aric thought much and said little. Kieran said much and thought little. But of her, they had both become fiercely protective, and she was grateful.

"Are you well?" Kieran asked.

Aric's gaze echoed his friend's question.

With an unflinching gaze, she began, "I have not asked since coming here because I did not wish to know, but now I must. Has Drake sent you any word recently?"

The pair exchanged concerned glances that Averyl little liked.

"Nay," said Kieran as Aric shook his head. "Not in two months."

At Kieran's comment, dread plunged Averyl's stomach down to her toes. She had hoped Murdoch's letter was naught but a ruse. Now she saw that Drake's capture was indeed possible. Probable even.

Without comment, she held out the letter to the two men in a trembling hand. Kieran took it, and Aric leaned over his shoulder as they read. The warriors lifted their heads long moments later.

"We will go to Drake," offered Aric. "Fear not."

"Aye, we will," Kieran added. "He will not remain there long, love. We will make certain Drake does not die."

"Nay," she refused. "You cannot save him."

"Have faith, lass. Aric and I rescued Drake from Dunollie once before."

Averyl thrust a hand upon her hip. "Do you not think Murdoch will remember such and take different measures? He is not a fool. Cursed and greedy, aye, but not dimwitted."

Aric frowned. "If we do not go, what think you must be done?"

"You will go, and I will go with you as—"

"Nay!" protested Kieran.

"Never," vowed Aric.

" 'Tis for neither of you to decide." Averyl glared at them both. "Drake is my husband. True, he loves me not, but he is the father of this babe. I will not stand by idly when I have the power to see him freed."

"You cannot mean to give into this threat and wed Murdoch. Such is not even possible, since you are wed to Drake," Aric reminded.

"Drake and I are but handfast. By law, if Drake agrees to release me from the union and I say I wish freedom, we are wed no more."

"You would actually wed Murdoch?" Kieran asked as if she'd scattered her wits about Hartwich Hall.

"If I must to free Drake, aye."

"But what of the babe," Aric asked. "Murdoch will not want him if he takes you to wife."

"I know as much, but I will protect him. You worry about freeing Drake," she ordered, mouth set in an inflexible line. "Now, when I gain entrance to Dunollie, I can distract Murdoch and sneak you two inside so you might rescue Drake. Once he is free, I will try to leave Murdoch and return to Abbotsford."

"Much too dangerous," Aric said.

"I agree," Kieran added. " 'Tis more than daring, love. It is foolhardy, and the journey would be difficult besides. Best if you stay here and let us—"

"Perhaps you did not hear me," she broke in, determined.

"I will go back to Scotland and find a way to free Drake. If you leave without me, I will follow. If you think to deny me, I will travel alone."

Averyl feared she might have to carry out her threat. She remembered her brief moments of freedom just before her handfast, how dangerous and violent men could be to a woman traveling alone. But she would do what she must to see Drake freed. Maybe then she could set him from her heart and move on with her future.

Aric gripped her shoulder. "Averyl, please consider again what you plan. In your condition, you tire easily."

"I will fight it."

"Such is not good for you or the child. He may come too early if you do not rest well."

"Death is not good for his father, either," she argued. "I must do what I am able and pray to God to watch over my bairn."

Kieran took her hand. "Aric and I are trained to fight this manner of battle. I pray you, let us do this."

Averyl felt tears, all too common these days, burn her eyes. "Nay. I go, with or without you. And I leave come morn."

Eighteen

Nearly a fortnight later, Averyl, with her gown billowing about her legs, took in the formidable fortress that was Dunollie. Gloom fell over its towers and walls, drawn in dreary lines against the bleak gray morning sky. 'Twas as if the sun never fell upon its grounds, as if light and hope never dwelt within its walls.

"Are you certain you want to do this, love?" said Kieran, real concern visible beneath his rogue's charm.

"Aye. My bairn needs his father." *Even if his father needs me not.* Frowning, she rubbed a hand over her rounded belly.

"Let us do this," said Aric quietly.

But the reluctant respect in his eyes, and that she had seen in Guilford's before leaving Hartwich, spurred her on.

"Do you recall the plan?" she asked instead, needlessly. Aric would see to the details, while Kieran would risk all to see this rescue complete.

"Aye," assured Kieran.

Aric nodded, squeezed her shoulder, and released her.

Averyl took a deep breath to quell her quivering innards, then marched toward Dunollie. Determination beat soundly inside her as she prayed to God Almighty that her mission would be successful. Somehow, someway, this danger would pass. That she must believe or be doomed.

Still, what must Drake feel, locked up in a dank, dark

corner of Dunollie's dungeon for weeks now? Did he await death? Fight it? Or simply expect it?

Pushing grim thoughts aside, Averyl gathered a flowing cloak about her she hoped would hide her advancing pregnancy for a bit and approached Dunollie's gates with squared shoulders.

From outside, the castle looked devoid of activity, almost ghostly against the morn's fog. Averyl pushed aside her breath-stealing anxiety and, head bowed, trod toward the drawbridge.

"Who comes?" questioned a disheveled guard.

She swallowed, knowing she could not turn back now. "Averyl Campbell. I've returned to wed your lord."

Wide-eyed, in obvious shock, the man nodded and escorted her into the gatehouse.

As they passed through the stirrings of the lower bailey, then through the second gatehouse and the middle bailey, Averyl held her breath. A thousand things could go wrong with this scheme that had once seemed so logical. Today, with her stomach hopping and her heart pounding, naught of this seemed rational.

The snores of some lean gray hounds and the scuffle of a black cat chasing a plump rat broke the silence. Averyl shivered as the guard took her into the keep, up the stairs, and into the great hall to await Murdoch's audience.

"Sit, my lady." He sent another guard after their lord, then watched her, as if to make certain she did not leave.

The great hall, indeed the whole castle, seemed to seep a gloom she had not noticed before her abduction. Forcing herself to sit, Averyl wondered if she felt the keep's sense of tragedy now because she knew the history of its grievous inhabitants.

Fear roared inside her, adding an extra thrum to her heart. What if Murdoch wanted naught of her but her death? What if his letter was no more than a ruse?

What if 'twas not?

Clenching her hands into nervous fists, Averyl watched

the wiry sentry retreat upstairs. Would Murdoch come immediately? She prayed soon to know her fate—and Drake's.

The air about her thickened as she waited.

Into the fire-lit great hall entered a man, not Murdoch. His rolling gait and shorter stature told her that right away. Still, she found something familiar about his uneven profile and shaggy brown hair. But her concerned thoughts could not stray from Drake long enough to solve such a mystery.

The man turned to the table and saw her sitting there. Instantly, he gasped, staring as if he had seen some specter.

"Averyl?"

He knew her name? "Aye," she called, peering closer until recognition dawned. "Cousin Robert! What do you do here at Dunollie?"

Though Robert was the son of her father's brother, of late he had not been welcomed by her father or the rest of the clan. That, and his penniless state, had prompted her father to refuse him as her suitor. And now she found him upon MacDougall land?

"Your—father . . . he—" Robert shrugged. "Well, he wished me to come here and see if Drake Thornton had set you free or you had been yet found. And here you are!"

"Drake is a MacDougall," she corrected almost without thought, then frowned. "Why would my father send you? Why not come himself?"

Shrugging, Robert turned away to call for a mug of ale, then sat, head bent. "Too much to be done at Abbotsford, I am certain. So, you are looking well, even a bit plump for once. Drake Thor—MacDougall fed you well, I take it?"

Self-consciously, Averyl gathered the cloak about her middle and frowned. "Well enough. Have the Campbells and MacDougalls refrained from fighting whilst I've been away? Is that why you stay at Dunollie."

Robert gave her a vigorous nod. " 'Tis a good-faith gesture but one that is appreciated, I am sure."

Though Averyl was uncertain Robert could be trusted, he

was kin. Certainly he was more an ally than Murdoch. "Have you seen Drake since Murdoch captured him? Where is he?"

"In my dungeon, as I said in my letter," called Murdoch from the top of the stairs.

That low voice chilled Averyl. She gritted her teeth against the fear creeping within her as he descended the stairs.

"Leave us," he said to Robert without so much as a glance.

To her shock, the ever-unruly Robert rose to do Murdoch's bidding without a by-your-leave.

"Are you ready to wed me?" asked Murdoch once Robert was gone.

Nay. Never. "Aye."

He smiled smugly, victoriously. Averyl itched to slap him.

"A priest will be here on the morrow to perform the task."

The man she had almost been betrothed to possessed a piercing, crafty gaze. No doubt, he was clever and ruthlessly prepared to reap the benefits of his treachery. Why had she noticed none of this before?

Because she had been a child then. Drake had shown her more of life, of her own heart. He had challenged her to see the good—and bad—in others. For that, she would be forever changed.

"I must see Drake first."

Murdoch shook his head. "Why force yourself to see your tormenter once more, my lady? Do not think about Drake Thornton or his ill treatment of you another moment. Think of our future instead."

"Drake *MacDougall* is the only reason I have come."

Dark eyes narrowed, Murdoch tensed.

Before he could say aught, Averyl went on, feeling oddly calm and in control. "I know you have no interest in wedding me other than to receive the funds and power left to you in your father's will, the father you shared with Drake.

I know also that you duped this entire clan into believing Drake guilty of Lochlan's murder when, in fact, the crime is yours."

Averyl sat stiffly, heart pounding, awaiting Murdoch's reply. She expected fury. Denials, indignation, false assurances—all were the means he could try to disarm her.

Instead, he laughed grimly. " 'Tis a surprise that Drake would tell you of our dirty family history. I suppose you will ask me next why I swyved his bitch of a mother for a year."

Averyl tried not to flinch at such crudity. "Nay, that I understand perfectly. So does he. And naught you have to say on that subject will interest me. I came here to accept your bargain. Once I speak with Drake and be assured of his good health and his release, I will be your bride."

Murdoch shook his head. "You will see him after the wedding, not before."

Suspicion tightened her belly. Certainly Murdoch would take great pleasure in having her see Drake chained. Why did he hesitate, then?

"I fear, my lord, that will not do," she said with mock sweetness. "For you see, Drake took me as a handfast bride June last. So until he releases me from the union, I am not free to wed you."

The assured smirk on Murdoch's face slid off, replaced by a furious horror.

In two huge steps, he closed the remaining distance between them and grabbed her arm. With it he jerked her to her feet and ripped the cloak from her body.

His burning black gaze fell immediately to her swollen belly.

"You let him fuck you?" He shouted the curse. "Most like more than once if he got you with child."

With his free hand, he struck her violently across one cheek. "Whore! I thought you had merely gotten fat."

Pain exploded in her head, and Averyl would have fallen

to the stone floor if not for Murdoch's unyielding grip holding her upright.

Dangling, Averyl found her feet beneath her and swallowed a lump of bile in her throat. She must stand strong. She must not fail. Her life and that of her babe's, as well as Drake's future, was at stake.

"Did you hate him even as he rutted upon you? Or did you fall in love?"

Sensing the truth would only free the rest of the restraint holding in his anger, Averyl parried, "It hardly matters. I've come, as you requested. Let us see this thing done."

He wound his hand about her throat. "I'll not have you pining for the wretch after we wed. The clan will talk."

As Murdoch squeezed her neck, Averyl choked and gasped for air, trying to work up enough saliva to spit in his face.

"Do you hear me?" Murdoch squeezed harder. "Agree or I will cut this child from your womb and leave you to bleed."

She believed him.

"I agree," she choked.

Murdoch loosened his grip.

Collapsing to her knees, Averyl drew in huge drafts of air and shivered at Murdoch's evil stare. White specks whirled in her vision. Fear clawed her gut. She shoved it aside.

"Free Drake and I will wed you. I vow you will never see me pine for him. But if you ever harm my child—or hire someone to harm him—I will tell the rest of your clan what I know of Lochlan's murder."

As a threat, Averyl did not think it would scare Murdoch. After all, she lacked pertinent facts, like the identity of the man he had paid to see Lochlan murdered. She also lacked proof. But Murdoch knew that not.

Murdoch laughed. "This foolishness actually aids my cause, you Campbell slut." He released her as if he found the contact distasteful. "You see, I do not have Drake in my dungeon. In fact, I have no notion where to find him. I had hoped to bring you back to Dunollie, wed and bed you, then find that miserable wretch so I might end his life."

Averyl gasped. Relief, bitterness, and dread scraped at her like the edge of a blade. She had endangered herself and her bairn for a ruse, for naught. *Nay!*

"With you, I can lure him here to Dunollie," Murdoch went on. "He may not care overmuch for saving you, but he will save his bairn. Drake got his blighted sense of honor from our father, God rest his miserable soul."

With that, Murdoch made his way to the far side of the great hall and called down the steps. "Malcolm!"

A moment later, a hulk of a Scot, one who rivaled Aric in size, appeared. "Aye, my lord?"

"See our guest to her new accommodations—below stairs."

The dungeon! "Nay!" she choked, feeling the blood drain from her face.

'Twas dark there. Endless ribbons of black would abound, strangling her with fear. Specters—or Murdoch—could do away with her at any time. Aric and Kieran would have no way inside.

Before she could run, the burly, rough-faced man dragged her out of the great hall and down the stairs. She was no match for his strength. Averyl scarcely remained on her feet before one prodded her through another door, then toward a second steep bank of stairs that led into malodorous darkness.

Dread pounded in her heart. What would happen now? Would she live to see her babe born? To see Drake again? Would he come to rescue his bairn, only to die?

The giant all but pushed her down the narrow circular stairs. She scarcely kept her balance with the weight of the babe before her and darkness enveloping her.

At the bottom of the stairs, straw crinkled beneath her feet. A vile stench crept up her nose, seeping into her stomach with a nauseating intensity. The villainous guard pushed her into a cold stone corner, then shut the iron door behind them.

Her stomach clenched in fear. "Nay, please! Do not leave me here without light."

He said naught, simply left her alone with the darkness, memories of her mother's violent death, and her terrible fear.

She shivered, wishing for the soothing touch Drake had shown her on a windswept hill all those months ago, when she'd been overpowered by her fear of the black night. Blessedly, its remembrance calmed her. He had made light from darkness that night. And as tears rolled down her face, Averyl could not ignore the truth: Drake always would make light from darkness—at least in her heart.

Drake had come to find peace. And if he found it in death, so be it.

Aye, 'twas early by two weeks. February had scarce dawned, and Averyl had not yet turned ten and eight. But Drake had grown weary of waiting for the end, one way or another, of this cloying hate he and Murdoch shared.

Today one of them would die. Likely, it would be him. Murdoch had allies everywhere. And though older, Murdoch was a fierce warrior, noted as much for his cruelty as for his skill.

Drake knew if he, by chance, lived, the future held naught. His clan would never accept him again, believing him a killer. And his temporary bride surely hated him.

This revenge wearied him now, and he wondered if it had been worth all it cost him in pain. He wanted vengeance behind him—for good.

Confined to shadows and secret tunnels, Drake slid within Dunollie's walls past midnight. Most of the sentries present upon his abduction of Averyl were pleasingly absent on this night, making his trek through the winding passages beneath the castle nearly without risk or constraint.

Such was good fortune, for he would need to save his strength and wits for this last deadly dance with his enemy, his half-brother.

Stealing into the keep, he slid into the hidden opening at the mouth of the solar to await his prey. Drake's thoughts turned, as they often did, to Averyl. If he died today, would she mourn? He gritted his teeth. Most like, she would celebrate this final departure from her life. And why should she not? Someday she would take a lover or another husband, the kind, he hoped, who would love her as she yearned and deserved.

Drake swallowed, staring blindly into the room's dim surroundings, lit by a single candle. He wished his wife happiness in her future, but the thought of Averyl in another's arms made his stomach grind. 'Twas a foolish feeling, for she surely despised him. Such was no less than he had earned for wedding and abandoning her, turning away from her while recovering from a near-fatal wound, refusing to succumb to the feelings about which troubadours sang.

Where was she now? Still with Guilford at Hartwich? And whether he died this day or not, Drake vowed he would steal from Murdoch, if he must, to ensure Averyl received enough funds to keep her well forever. 'Twas the least he could do.

Suddenly, into the shadowed depths of the solar marched Murdoch. Beside him, he dragged a woman with pale curls. Averyl? Though he was certain such was not possible, he peered at the woman more closely, gut turning, suddenly sweating.

Her face was turned away. Her size was undeterminable, for the dimness and the gown that floated about her like a gray storm cloud. But that hair . . . Could she be another?

Murdoch shoved her to the ground, earning the laughs of three large guards entering the room, clearly willing and able to protect their master at the slightest hint of danger.

Drake returned his attention to the woman, wincing as his half-brother grabbed her tangled golden curls and slapped her face. Her back stiffened, and her head fell back from the blow.

Stifling a curse, Drake watched as the woman struggled against Murdoch's hold. Sneering, he held her down. With her hands bound behind her, she was no match for the scoundrel.

Murdoch laughed. "How I love to see someone else humiliated for a change. I wonder if that half-English bastard would want you in his bed if he could see you now?"

Drake's heart stopped at Murdoch's words. He peered closer at the woman, praying she was not Averyl, but could recognize naught from tangles down her back and an over-large gown.

Logic told him Murdoch had Averyl. God help her.

Rising a shaky hand to his mouth, he tried to rein in the panic bursting in him. What was she doing here at Dunollie?

In the silence, Murdoch slapped the woman again, this time harder. She moaned.

"Have you naught to say, whore?" Murdoch taunted.

"To such a worthless excuse for a man? Nay."

Drake's stomach lurched at the sound of Averyl's voice. His greedy gaze locked onto her even as fear burned in his veins. Dear God, how had she fallen prey to Murdoch?

And what was he to do?

Murdoch walked around Averyl in a slow, predatory circle. "Did Drake allow you to defy him like this?" When she said naught, he continued: "I know your father did, the fool."

"Say nothing bad of my father!"

"Why not? He was foolish enough to grant me use of your dower lands before we wed. Come spring, I intend to use it as a good MacDougall should."

"To attack the Campbells?" Her voice trembled.

Murdoch smiled. "What else?"

"Drake was right." Averyl shouted, "Barbarian!"

He scowled and grabbed a handful of her hair. "Be careful, whore, for I could yet decide to kill you for the sport of it."

Drake trembled with the urge to charge the room and rescue Averyl. But he would only fail now, with those three burly guards by his half-brother's side, and condemn them both to death. Nay, painful as it was, he must wait and plan—and pray for Averyl's safety.

"Brave words for a mere woman." Murdoch tossed her a speculative glare. "Perhaps I shall make you my whore as well," he said with wicked glee.

Drake felt another chill creep over his skin. Murdoch's idea of pleasure was harsh on any woman, but one with Averyl's ideals of love would no doubt find it unbearable.

Clenching his fists, Drake knew he must act soon.

"Aye, that might be an idea," Murdoch continued. "How that would torture Drake!"

"I will kill you upon my first opportunity," she vowed.

Murdoch grabbed Averyl's neck in a vicious vice. "Do not think I will be foolish enough to give you that chance."

"You are nae a man but a monster!"

With fury heating his eyes, Murdoch warned, "Watch your words well or I will prove you right in ways you never imagined."

"I have no doubt you could."

Drake shuddered at the hate in her tone. For that, Murdoch could punish her in terrible ways. He wished he could find some way to warn her against such reckless words without revealing himself. But such was not possible. He would simply have to find a way to rescue her before aught happened.

Murdoch sneered. "For your poison tongue, I will teach you the meaning of pain, but I will wait until Drake watches. Such torture to his mind will please me greatly."

"Rot in hell!" Averyl shot back.

Murdoch grabbed her arm, pulling her to her knees. "The

only one who will do that is your *husband*. When I find him and he learns of your captivity, he will save you."

"He will not," she argued.

Murdoch narrowed his dark eyes. "Once he learns I lured you here with a bargain to free him from my dungeon in exchange for wedding me? Nay, Drake's honor willna let you suffer long for your sacrifice. And when he comes, I will be waiting."

Drake clenched his fists so tightly, they trembled. Shock washed over him in a cold wave. Averyl had come to exchange her freedom for his? After all he had done to her? Dear God, why?

He felt stunned—and humbled.

And now Murdoch intended to use her as bait to lure him to his death.

Wanting to tear Murdoch apart limb from limb, Drake kept to the shadows, vowing vengeance for whatever ills he performed on Averyl. But such would have to be done without risk to her. And that required planning.

With one last cracking slap to Averyl's cheek, Murdoch slammed from the room, leaving a battered Averyl to be dragged away by Murdoch's mercenaries.

And leaving Drake more ready than ever to put his plan in motion tomorrow morn so he could have his revenge and save his wife.

Dazed, Drake wandered about Dunollie's shadows, watching the eastern edge of the predawn sky turn from black to a midnight blue tinged with gray. Suddenly, he found himself standing before his mother's grave.

Uncertainty swirling within, he stared at the stone marker for long moments before kneeling, knowing not what to say.

Slowly, he whispered, "Why did you never tell me the truth? Why did I never see your hurt?" He shook his head, his chest aching. "You let me believe the worst."

Drake was faintly aware of healing tears squeezing from the corners of his eyes, tracing hot paths down his face.

His very life had changed in knowing that perhaps his father had been as much to blame for the marriage's demise as his mother. His perception of the past, of the selfishness and deceit of women—all of that was in question now.

When it was too late to save his marriage.

Averyl's actions to save him seemed to reflect the true nature of love and cast a shadow over the marriage his parents had shared. Neither had given the other a moment of happiness, had never really given of themselves, to their own detriment. Had his parents loved at all or merely struggled for power in a relationship born of lust?

He sighed, his longing for Averyl growing stronger each day. Had he pushed her away foolishly, without cause? Had he endured wretched months of icy loneliness when he could have basked in the warmth of her love? Had he lost her to fear?

Aye, and 'twas likely that even if he lived to see this sun set, she would never take him back. Eyes closed, he let the pain of Averyl's absence, as well as the pain of his breach with his mother, seep into him.

The former he may never repair. The latter he could try.

" 'Tis sorry I am, mother. I knew not the truth."

Suddenly, wind whisked across his face, seeming to carry Diera's hauntingly familiar scent.

He whirled about, swearing he would find her there, so strong was her presence. Yet he saw nothing but a barren February winterland, white snow clinging to leafless trees.

"Mother?" he called, feeling her with him still despite the fact his eyes told him differently.

As quickly as the wind had come, it left, replaced by the bite of the cold dawn. Drake tingled with a certainty that Diera had both listened to his words and forgiven him.

From the nearby gardens, he retrieved a few wildflowers that had survived the winter chill and laid the snow-capped blossoms across her grave.

He knelt before the simple wooden cross and prayed to God to look favorably upon his mother and allow her past the gates into His kingdom. He asked forgiveness for his own wayward actions, including those to come. Most of all, he prayed for Averyl's future happiness and safety.

But now 'twas time to kill his brother—or be killed.

Minutes later, Drake shook Firtha awake.

"What— Who . . ."

"Shhh," Drake whispered. "I've no time to talk. Murdoch has Averyl."

The maid sat up. "Aye, he is using her to trap ye."

"I know. Where does he keep her?"

She hesitated. "The gatehouse."

Drake's mouth fell agape. "In the dungeon? Upon my word, I will kill him! She is far too delicate—"

"Praise be ye ken that!"

"Which is why we must not waste time. If you can, see her. Tell her I will not leave her again, not to Murdoch."

Firtha nodded. "I will find a way. Now, ye hiv to worry how to free her. Hiv ye a plan?"

"Of a sort. Know you how Averyl fares so far?"

"Our Lord Dunollie haes more desire to find ye than bed her. She eats and sleeps alone."

"Thank God," he muttered. "But still, I must tread carefully." Drake rose to pace. "Christ's oath, I must free her. And I want to cause Murdoch pain for every hurt he has done her."

Firtha took his hand. "Ye are in love, Drake. Ye ken that e'en if ye dinna like it."

He tried to ignore the burning in his chest as the acknowledgment of Firtha's words loomed. Aye, fool that he was, he loved Averyl. Six months away from her had changed naught in his heart except that the pain of their separation forced him to admit the truth.

Drake could never tell Averyl he needed her like food,

like water. He could give no one, least of all her, the key
to his soul. She could destroy him with it. She had cause
now.

"I ken that," he admitted to Firtha, "but now I must think
of Averyl's pain and Murdoch's death."

After bidding Firtha farewell, Drake wound through the
underground tunnels and emerged from Dunollie, mind racing. He scarce paid attention to the moonlit path.

Though he could not tell her of his love, Drake worried
about Averyl in Murdoch's dungeon. The fiend plotted to
rape her while forcing the man she had professed to love
to watch.

When he had imagined revenge, Drake had expected to
destroy only Murdoch and himself. Seeking this renegade
justice had cost Averyl her freedom. And he feared that
before this mad state of affairs ended, his revenge might
cost Averyl her life.

He cursed. Wondering about her while he lay this death
trap for Murdoch, knowing Murdoch had struck and threatened her—all of it stabbed pain in his gut, and his heart.

Aye, no doubt anymore. He did love her. Mayhap he had
from the start of her captivity, for she'd always drawn him.

And 'twas clear Averyl believed that she loved him. No
woman he knew, even Firtha, would be forgiving enough
to set aside her pain and fury over a man's abandonment
at her greatest hour of need and still return to an enemy to
wed him in exchange for her lover's freedom.

Had he ever been loved that selflessly? Mayhap by Guilford. And Aric and Kieran, perhaps. But even his father had
conditioned his love to ensure obedience. He had been a
good man, but one who demanded his wishes were met.
Had that been the reason his parents had known no harmony? Had his father commanded a submission his mother
refused to yield?

Had he mistaken their darker emotions and their consequences as love all along?

The minutes ticked by like centuries as Drake marched

his way through the tunnel, praying he could find some way to extricate Averyl from Dunollie without harm. He could not bear the thought of repaying Averyl's loving deed with Murdoch's cruelty.

The small, dank space of the tunnel finally gave way to the moonlit night. Drake inched up to ground and edged along the outer curtain wall to avoid detection by Dunollie's guards.

Instead, he felt a tap on his shoulder.

An alert determination, along with fear, coiled in the pit of his belly as he whirled to his attacker.

Instead, he saw Kieran. Aric stood just behind him.

"What in damnation—" he began.

"We thought you were in Dunollie's dungeon," Kieran said. "Did you escape?"

Drake frowned. "Nay, Murdoch did not have me."

Kieran and Aric exchanged glances. "He lied."

Drake nodded. "He has Averyl in his dungeon now and plots to use her to lure me to my death."

" 'Tis as we feared," said Aric, his voice a low rumble. "We must save her and return to England."

"After I give Murdoch the slow death he deserves."

Aric grabbed his arms. "Averyl must come first, you dim-witted dolt."

Drake might have pointed out that Aric began to sound like Gwenyth if the situation were less serious. "And she shall."

"With haste," Aric added with force.

Kieran nodded. "Unless you want your babe born in Dunollie's dungeon."

Drake's gaze whipped back to Kieran, who stood with wide arms crossed over his chest, his gaze challenging. Had he said . . .

"Babe?"

"Aye, in April."

"But . . . Averyl? I knew naught—"

"Because you abandoned her, swyving swine. And I am

furious enough with you to push a battering ram through
your miserable gut. You punish her for Diera's cruelty—"

"Kieran," Aric warned.

It fell upon deaf ears.

Drake winced.

"Think you Averyl would take one of your family to her
bed to spite you? Can you imagine such a deed from her?"
Kieran hissed. "If you say you can, I will punch you."

Stunned, Drake said naught. But his spinning mind considered the question over and over. Nay, he could not imagine such a thing. But when his father had first fancied his
mother, he doubtless never imagined such an event, either.

"Let us consider Averyl's safety now, hmm?" suggested
Aric.

Drake was all too willing to turn his mind to her rescue.
"You and Kieran free her from the dungeon, then meet me
by the tunnel entrance in the upper bailey. I will show you
its location when we get inside."

"And what will you do?" Kieran scowled.

"What I came here to do—kill Murdoch."

"Hellfire! Can you forget this revenge for once? It will
be the death of you!"

"If I forget it, what will happen?" Drake whispered as
furiously as discretion allowed. "Murdoch will hunt me,
hunt her. We will know no peace, no life, no future, as long
as he wants to see her as his wife and me in my grave.
Even after Averyl turns eight and ten, he may lose his fortune but not his power with the clan. He and everyone I
have known all my years will stalk me until I hang from a
rope by the battlements."

Aric, ever calm, separated him and Kieran. "If this is
your wish, we will follow it. What is your plan?"

For the next hour, they debated the possibilities, drawing
sketches in the dirt, arguing over the best strategy. An hour
after dawn broke, they formed a solid strategy.

Drake only hoped Averyl and his friends did not lose
their lives in the process.

Nineteen

Drake crept into the quiet of Murdoch's chamber. His guards were nowhere in sight.

Finally, now, revenge would be his.

Aye, but he felt all too certain such had cost him life with Averyl, the bairn she would bear—and his heart.

Pushing the thought away, he stared at his sleeping half-brother as moonlight spilled through the windows, bared to the coming dawn. And he hesitated. Why had he never been as close to the brother with whom he shared blood as he had with the warrior brothers of his heart, Kieran and Aric?

He frowned. Just as the biblical Cain slew Abel, Drake readied to kill his brother, too. Suddenly, he wondered if his father would be disappointed. And why he felt naught but dread.

Drawing from the anger he'd gathered during his life, Drake swallowed and drew his blade. Still he hesitated, uncertain.

Murdoch woke suddenly and opened his eyes.

Slowly, he focused on Drake. Their gazes locked.

"You!" Murdoch's eyes bulged with recognition. " 'Tis hoping I have been you would come for your death, my brother."

Fury tightening his gut, Drake shook his head. "No one here will die but you, and 'twill be by my hand!"

Murdoch spit in his face. "You will prove nothing but your own blood lust if you kill me."

"The clan already believes me dangerously mad, thanks to you. I have naught to lose by ending your worthless life."

With that, Drake charged Murdoch, who rose from bed clad in his braies and hopped to the floor. With a flash of an arm, Murdoch grabbed his own blade from the nearby trestle table.

Cursing, Murdoch charged, lunging with gritted teeth. Drake sidestepped the oncoming blade, then thrust at his half-brother. The short blade missed its mark by a breath.

Before Murdoch could recover, Drake rushed toward him and took a wild stab at his chest. Murdoch jumped from the knife's path and scrambled across the room.

"Where is your warrior's training now?" taunted Murdoch.

Drake knew his anger was building dangerously, had felt it from the moment Murdoch awakened. He drew in a breath, seeking calm. He found only Murdoch's sneer dominating his gaze.

Murdoch grinned. "How will you feel when I make your wife mine and take her to my bed? And I will, even if her belly is ugly and swollen."

A spark of an image, Averyl tied to Murdoch's bed, swept through his mind. Anger exploded in Drake's veins, and he gripped the knife tighter. By hell, the fiend deserved to die.

"You will never know," vowed Drake.

Attacking Murdoch once more, Drake growled at the man as he shifted in the shadows. His blade made contact with skin. Murdoch howled as his cheek bled onto his bare chest. He reached up to swipe the blood away, retreating.

The blood only gladdened Drake.

"Bastard!" cursed Murdoch.

Before he could move, Drake lunged again. Murdoch backed into a bench beside the fireplace. It crashed to the wooden floor, deafening in the early-morn silence.

A thick, still moment passed. Drake looked back to Murdoch, who lifted his blade again. Raising his own in answer, Drake made ready to fight once more.

Footsteps sounded in the hallway.

"Guards!" called Murdoch.

Fear sliced through Drake like a *claidmor* through flesh. If the guards came, he would be caught. His revenge would be incomplete, for they would slay him instantly.

He would never see Averyl again.

"Soon," he promised, sheathing his knife and darting out the door.

Two guards rushed down the hall. Drake elbowed one, who groaned in pain. Whirling about, he punched the other in the face. As the guard collapsed, Drake ran, blood pounding in his ears, his body burning for air, until he reached the tunnel.

There stood Aric and Kieran.

And Averyl.

The air completely left Drake, and his heart pumped faster at the sight of her, though he had ceased running. She looked bedraggled and tired, her ill-fitting gown torn and hanging off one shoulder. Her rounded belly nearly disappeared beneath her tent of a gown.

Relief, joy, an urge to possess her, all rushed warmth through his body. Drake dashed toward her and drew her into his arms. With an unsteady hand, he brushed the pale curls from her face. With the other, he felt their child growing.

"How do you fare, my wife?" His voice sounded thick.

Averyl looked at him, confusion and yearning tangled in that green gaze he had missed so for six months. He understood her emotions and felt connected by their touch.

Before she could answer, Kieran spoke up. "Drake, greet her later. The guards are searching the bailey now."

Whirling around, he saw that Kieran was right. Reluctantly, he released his wife but clutched her hand in his.

"Kieran," he said, "go first. Scout the tunnel for guards."

With a nod, Kieran jumped to the ground and disappeared.

"Drake, you next. I can fight the guards. You are exhausted. Take your wife and go."

"Nay, 'tis my fight. Go down and see Averyl safely out." Drake squeezed her hand again. She squeezed in return.

"Aye. Send her down. I will catch her." And with a reluctant sigh, Aric squeezed into the narrow opening.

"Follow Aric," he commanded Averyl, releasing her hand. "Hurry!"

Nodding, she sat at the opening and began to ease herself down with caution. But her swollen belly caught on the rim. Grunting, she tried to force her way through, but Drake could see she was stuck.

He knelt, frantically digging at the lip of the tunnel to widen it. 'Twas to no avail; mud and rocks continued to slide into place, preventing Averyl from escape.

She closed her eyes and bit her lip to hold in a cry. He could tell from her flush and the panic in her eyes.

"Go," she said, rising. "Do not let him catch you."

The idea horrified him. "I will not leave you here."

"You must," she argued. "Or Murdoch will kill you."

"I will not leave you!" he ground out, grabbing her hands.

Suddenly, she gasped. Before Drake could discern her trouble, a pair of rough hands grabbed his shoulders, jerked him about, and planted a fist in his face. Pain erupted in his head. The last thing he saw before blackness consumed him was Murdoch arriving to lead a screaming Averyl away.

That night, the guards of Dunollie brought Drake up to the solar, where Murdoch looked out the window at his ill-gotten domain. Averyl lay upon his bed, bound at the wrists and ankles. Firelight revealed a tired, pale face, but she appeared not to be ravished or hurt. She sent him a tentative smile as Murdoch's guards led him to his half-brother's side, then moved to stand outside the door. He smiled back through his pain, hoping she could not see the blood through his shirt from Murdoch's fresh lash marks.

The villain turned to face him, his mouth twisted with a malicious curve. "So, you've finally awakened. Feeling well?"

"Swyve off." His voice was flat, inflectionless.

Murdoch grunted. "Not yet, for I have a proposition."

"You have naught I wish for," Drake vowed.

"Freedom, perhaps." Murdoch strolled closer, measuring his steps slowly around Drake. "From pursuit. From blame in our father's murder."

The idea tempted Drake. Aye, he wanted that—so badly hope burned in his gut, roiling. He craved peace. He yearned for his clansmen to know of his innocence. But he also wanted Murdoch to pay for his guilt.

"Have you aught to say?" prompted Murdoch. "I offer everything you could wish for."

Not everything, not as long as Murdoch remained the respected Lord Dunollie. Still, he could play Murdoch's game. "At what price?"

"Relinquish Averyl from this fool's handfast. Once you do, I will see you freed and absolved of guilt."

"He agrees!" came Averyl from across the room.

Drake turned to Averyl in alarm. What was the woman thinking, consigning her future to a murdering monster?

"I will not release you," he refuted, then turned to glare at Murdoch.

"Drake, he will kill you if you do not let me go."

Though Averyl's voice held a pleading tone, he ignored it.

"You wanted me not, anyway," she continued. "Now you will be free."

She believed that, still. Drake closed his eyes and sighed. If she only knew how deeply, how completely, he wanted her now, forever.

"My wife is mine," he said finally.

"I can easily kill you and wed her," Murdoch reminded.

"You will likely do such, anyway, no matter what I say. Is that not right?" he challenged. "Kill me and let us end this."

"Drake, nay!" she cried. "Do not give up for me!"

"Say naught more, you Campbell slut," Murdoch commanded, then turned back to Drake. "Upon the blood we share, upon my mother's grave, I vow I will free you if you release her from your handfast."

Eyes narrowed, Drake studied Murdoch. Never had he looked more serious, and Drake nearly believed him. But even if Murdoch words were truth, Drake would never let Averyl go.

"Accept his vow, Drake. Go!"

Leave her here to suffer a cruel union with Murdoch? Leave her here to warm his bed day after day, year after year? "Nay."

"You would sacrifice your *life* for a Campbell wench?" Murdoch challenged.

"Aye," he whispered, feeling Averyl's gaze burn his profile.

"You love her." Murdoch's voice accused him.

More than anything, he thought, resisting the urge to look at her. "She is my responsibility. I will not see her hurt as long as I draw a breath."

"How noble," Murdoch sneered. "If you wish death, it will be so."

Crossing the room, Murdoch came to stand beside Averyl, then caressed her cheek with the back of his finger. Drake restrained an urge to race across the room and beat Murdoch into oblivion for touching Averyl. He restrained himself, knowing Murdoch only sought to infuriate him.

His half-brother smiled, then let his finger drift down Averyl's neck, to an enlarged breast. "When she came to me, willing to trade her freedom for yours, I sent notice to the rest of the clan we would soon have a wedding. They travel to Dunollie even now."

Averyl gasped as Murdoch flattened his palm over her

breast. She spit an oath at him and tried to roll away. Drake clenched his fists at his sides and fought his urge to save her. Too much caring from him would mark her a weakness. Murdoch would subject her to cruelties simply to torture him. Better this than rape or worse.

"I will simply plan your execution for the morn of our nuptials. 'Twill be the humiliation among the clan you deserved from the day Diera brought you forth from her whore's body. And the day you die a traitor is the day I will celebrate by bedding Averyl's offensively round body until she forgets about you."

"You cannot make me forget Drake!" she shouted.

Drake understood Averyl's bravery but wished she comprehended how vicious Murdoch would be if she did not begin to play the willing bride. Could she not see the fury mottling his face?

Aye, he might have eased her road by releasing her and making her hate him for the rest of his days. But Drake refused to give up his wife until God had taken him from this earth.

"And what do you think will become of Averyl and your child once you are dead?" he asked, his grin evil. "They will serve me no further purpose."

"If you kill them as well, do you not think the rest of the clan will be most suspicious?" When Murdoch did not answer in the next moment, Drake went on in bored tones, mastering his fear in the hopes of distracting Murdoch from that idea. "Are we finished here?"

It worked. Murdoch whipped his gaze to Drake, then crossed the room. Murdoch gave him a hearty slap on the back. Pain burst through Drake's body. The blood left his face, and he nearly stumbled to his knees.

"Drake?" cried Averyl, concern echoing in her gentle voice.

For her, he forced himself upright. "I am well."

"Good, I shall be down to see you later." The butcher flicked his wrist in a mock lash.

Gritting his teeth, Drake held in a groan. "I never doubted it."

'Twas obvious by Murdoch's scowl that he did not appreciate Drake's caustic response. "I swear I will keep you a bare inch from death, you bastard."

Averyl's mouth gaped open. Her eyes widened with concern and fear and love. Drake held in a curse, wishing he could spare her this truth.

" 'Twould hardly be the first time," he countered.

"Release her to me and I will spare your life as well as this pain," Murdoch demanded.

"Go to hell," Drake said.

He touched a stricken Averyl with his glance as he strode to the door, to the guards who awaited him and the long night of pain ahead.

A tormenting week passed, so slowly Averyl felt certain she could feel every excruciating moment of uncertainty and sorrow. Firtha, bless her kind soul, had been able to tell her each day that Drake lived. But Murdoch kept his promise to see Drake within an inch of death.

She paced the small chamber in which Murdoch kept her caged, hindered by the fine red silken dress Lord Dunollie insisted she wear for their wedding within the hour. Below, she saw clansmen milling about in their finery.

Faintly, she heard the ocean churning in the distance. Closing her eyes, she clasped her hands and prayed the plan she had devised in the wee hours of the morning would save her husband's life. 'Twas all she had.

"Lady Averyl?"

She turned to find Firtha standing in the door. Rushing to the older woman, she assisted her inside and closed the door.

"Have you news?"

Frowning, Firtha nodded her graying head. "I couldna find Aric and Kieran this morn to tell them of yer plan.

Hiv faith, though, lass, they are wise warriors. And Drake still lives."

Wringing her hands, she asked, "How does he fare?"

"Lord Dunollie hadna the time to visit the dungeon yestreen, with all the clan arrivin'. Drake is weak, mind ye, but he recovers."

Averyl sighed, rubbing sleepless eyes with her fingers. "Has this plan any chance at all?"

"If God haes any mercy, aye."

What Firtha said was true, but Averyl liked it not. She wanted Drake safe, happy, his life devoid of strife. She wished his life filled with love—her love. Yet he seemed to care not for himself.

"Why did he choose this, Firtha? For money and clan power, Murdoch might have honored the bargain to release him. Surely his life was worth the risk."

"His life, aye. But nae yours, lass."

Her brow furrowed in confusion. "Murdoch will wed me, anyway. Drake can do naught to change that. Why would Drake refuse to release me from this handfast?"

Firtha touched a motherly hand to her shoulder. "Ye ken that Drake haes been like me own son all his life. Always, haes he been stubborn."

"But 'twas not time for such stubbornness. He could have chosen his freedom and regained his life!"

"Over yours? Lass, ye ken the man he is. He wouldna leave ye to Lord Dunollie's cruelty as long as his life can spare ye."

"But—"

"Do ye not ken he loves ye, lass?"

Averyl's heart constricted, ceased beating. More than anything she wished to believe that love, not a sense of duty to her, resided in his heart. But now, with his life in jeopardy, it mattered not. She loved him and would do all within her power to save him.

The clatter of footsteps climbing the stone stairs stopped aught Averyl could say.

Instead, she pushed Firtha toward the door. "Go. See if Aric and Kieran have come for the ex— For this farce."

With a nod, the older woman was gone. A moment later, one of Murdoch's guards appeared and led her outside, into the crisp, brilliant February sunlight.

Tomorrow she would turn eight and ten.

Today, if Murdoch had his way, she would watch her beloved die and wed the heartless villain responsible. Aye, she prayed to God he would stop this impending disaster.

But saw not any way short of a miracle that He could.

She swallowed as the guard led her to the front of the crowd. The Clan MacDougall formed a circle of bodies, mostly men, across the winter-crisp green field behind Dunollie. Their mood was righteous, eager to see an innocent man die.

In the center of the circle, the guards parted. To her horror, Drake stood in the center, stripped to the waist. His face was bruised and cut. Blood smeared his mouth and tangled with the dungeon's dirt. One eye was swollen shut, and his bound wrists throbbed an angry red with rope burns—but nothing alarmed her more than the raw lash wounds open and oozing on his arms, chest, and back. He looked haggard, waxen, lifeless—and ready to accept death.

She glanced at the monster she had once sought to wed and saw blood lust in his eyes.

Averyl knew the instant Drake saw her. Time stopped, along with her heart. The air sizzled. She resisted the urge to run to him, heal him, tell him she loved him.

Before she could give into the urge, a passing chapman nudged her, nearly knocking her off balance. She scarce paid note to the peddler until he said, "Beg my pardon, good lady."

Aric! She whirled to him, scarce believing what her ears told her. But 'twas true.

She opened her mouth to say something. He shook his head in warning.

"We will save him," Aric whispered. "Fear not."

"Nay, 'tis a plan I have," she murmured in return. "One that might spare him and prove him innocent at once."

Surprise sharpened Aric's features before he smoothed them once more.

"What mean ye have no need for a bonny bauble?" he roared for the benefit of the nearby folk.

"Tell Kieran as well," she whispered, then spoke up. "I've no need for your wares, chapman. Be gone with you."

Averyl felt herself tremble as Aric blended into the growing crowd. On the other side of the circle, she spotted a monk who looked suspiciously like Kieran. A quick downing of his hood and a wink proved her right. She sent him a shaky smile before turning her attention back to Drake. No longer would he meet her gaze.

To her left, the impatient crowd parted, and Murdoch strode through the opening, stopping at Drake's side.

The evil wretch pushed Drake to his knees and, grabbing a handful of hair, shoved his face to the ground.

"Behold, my friends and my kin, a murderer. A traitor. Today he dies."

The crowd turned raucous, cheering, chanting. Averyl closed her eyes, wondering if she could even hope to win the support of the onlookers or if her cause was a hopeless one.

"He is an English whore's bastard and not worthy of his MacDougall name!"

"Aye!" shouted someone from the crowd.

Murdoch's squire made his way to his master's side then, dragging a huge, sharpened *claidmor*. Dread twisted in her belly until she felt both nauseous and dizzy.

Grabbing the weapon, Murdoch stabbed it into the ground at his feet, then jerked Drake's face to the crowd again.

"For your crimes against the Clan MacDougall and its last chief, Lochlan, your very father, the lairds have sentenced you to die."

"You and I both know I killed him not," Drake insisted.

"Silence!" bellowed Murdoch. "Your time for talking is done. Your time for dying is now."

Drake risked one last look at her then, his face lined and anxious. Averyl felt her heart constrict with pain, need . . . regret, denial.

Then the familiar warmth of his dark eyes was whisked away by Murdoch's cruel hand as he forced Drake's face to the grass.

Murdoch raised the sword above Drake's neck.

Averyl drew a deep breath and shouted, *"Wait!"*

Twenty

Instantly, all eyes turned toward Averyl. Annoyance, confusion, and shock burned in the gazes of the staring MacDougalls. She swallowed, her throat raw from screaming.

Murdoch faced her as well, masking his irritation so the members of his clan might not see his fury with his bride-to-be. 'Twould not look well only hours before vows were exchanged.

"What have you to say, my lady Averyl?"

His voice shivered down her back with its insidious smoothness. But the slight narrowing of Murdoch's dark eyes gave his anger away.

Still, she meant to save Drake's life and could not be cowed by the threat upon his face.

Briefly, she dropped her gaze to her husband. He tried to shake his head, as if to stop her actions, despite Murdoch's cruel hold upon his hair.

In return she gave him a slight nod, then lifted her chin. "What evidence have you that he killed his father?"

Murdoch groaned, as if disgusted with such a foolish question. "Witnesses, dear lady. A bloody blade in his fist."

She frowned and cast a quick glance at Drake. Even beaten and upon his knees he somehow looked proud and honest. Pain and dread clutched at her heart.

"Who are these witnesses?" she demanded. "What did they see?"

"My lady," said Murdoch with exaggerated patience.

"Duff and Wallace have already told the clan all they witnessed. This man is condemned to die for his crimes."

"What did this Duff and Wallace see?" she demanded, ignoring him. "Did they truly observe Drake stab his father?"

"*Ni,* ye Campbell wench," called one man. "But I saw the half-English bastard with the bloody blade betwixt his fingers."

The crowd murmured its angry agreement.

"Who are you?" she asked, trying desperately to hang on to her bravado. If the onlookers smelled her fear, her uncertainty, Drake would lay dead within moments.

"I be Duff."

She nodded, pleased. "And is Wallace here?"

"Aye," said another smaller man as he stepped forward, a frown upon his surly face.

"Did either of you witness Lochlan's stabbing?"

Both paused, hesitated. The crowd looked on in curiosity.

"We dinna," Wallace answered finally. "But who else had reason to kill our lord?"

"Aye!" chanted a few members of the crowd.

"He claimed another did the evil deed and ran over the hill, but I dinna believe such a falsity," spat Duff.

"But you cannot disprove that," she pointed out.

"*Ni,*" he said. "I canna disprove it, but—"

"In a moment," Averyl interrupted, holding up her hand to stay his protest.

"Hold yer tongue, ye Campbell wench. Ye canna prove Drake innocent," shouted a man from the crowd.

Rumblings of agreement, sprinkled with an occasional "Aye," sounded about her. Averyl repressed the urge to bite her lip or show any weakness these fighting men might pounce upon.

"And you cannot prove him guilty, either," she pointed out. "Before Lochlan's murder is there one of you who would have doubted Drake loved his sire with his whole heart?"

A pause settled over the twenty or so men about her. Silence lingered until finally broken by a *"Ni"* or two. A few shook their heads.

"When he was a wee lad, Drake wasna ever farther away from his father than a shadow," said one.

"Exactly," she affirmed. "As a man, he felt no less affection. But Murdoch and his father, did they not argue?"

"None of what you say is unknown," quipped Murdoch.

Still, a thoughtful still settled over the group. A few looked at one another as if for confirmation before casting speculative glances at Murdoch.

" 'Tis a fool's game she plays with words," he defended. "I wasna there when my father died, and well you all know it."

"Aye, but Drake did not say he saw *you* run over the hill that morn, but a stranger. Is that not so?" Averyl speared Drake with a glance that demanded an answer.

He hesitated. Murdoch tightened his brutal grip in Drake's hair. But Drake managed to nod, anyway.

"Did your father not make Drake his tanist in your stead?"

"Aye, 'twas why he killed my beloved sire," cried Murdoch.

"Or 'twas why you had Lochlan butchered and Drake blamed so neither of them might stand in your way."

Expressions of surprise and conjecture dominated the crowd.

"Mayhap the lass is right," said one man.

"Our chief hated his father somethin' fierce," came a voice from behind.

"Murdoch did hate his father," said Averyl. "Why else would he bed his father's wife, Diera, and get her with child?"

Loud gasps of surprise sounded through the gathering. The few women present crossed themselves. Apparently no one had known of that fact. Heart pounding, she praying for victory.

Averyl forged on. "Murdoch had reason and history to hurt his father."

"Be closin' your mouth, slut, or I will kill your lover," Murdoch yelled, holding the *claidmor* above Drake's neck.

Averyl's heart nearly ceased beating at the sight. The crowd murmured, rumbling in disapproval.

Forcing herself to go on, she shouted, "See, even now he resorts to murder!"

"What say you, lady?" asked a MacDougall from the crowd, a big man with massive hands, a short plaid, and a braided beard. "We canna simply let him go wi'out proof he is innocent."

"Then 'tis a contest I call for. A fair joust. God will give the man in the right the strength to be the victor."

On his knees, Drake looked stunned and weary and so bruised. Averyl hoped he still had fight within him.

" 'Tis fair," called a clansman to her right.

"Weel, I canna think of a reason to disagree," said another.

"Aye!" cried the plaid-wearing man. "Let them fight fairly for right. Let them fight to the death."

A scant few minutes later, Drake, in his armor, mounted his steed. To his shock, Kieran had appeared, dressed in, of all garments, a monk's robe. His Irish friend doffed the robe and stood at the ready with lances, a broadsword, and an ax.

Aric strode up to the duo moments later, dressed as a peddler. Drake frowned in question.

Kieran began, "We had a magnificent plan—"

" 'Twas adequate," interrupted Aric. "Averyl's is better."

Aye, Averyl's plan was brilliant. She was a woman of superior character, and it had taken him a long while to realize that. Now he ached to see her. Drake stared down the crisp February field for a glimpse.

But his vision blurred with fatigue. He saw only a crowd.

Murdoch, solitary against the sunlight, appeared moments later at the opposite end of the long field upon his own great mount. His bearing was of calm and readiness.

Damnation! Drake could feel himself shaking.

How had Averyl thought to suggest this joust? A victory would buy him freedom, and he thanked her making some of his clansmen see the falsity of Murdoch's "truth."

But Drake feared he was in too much pain to fight.

Every movement of the chain mail set his back afire despite the padded doublet beneath. His vision blurred again. He felt weaker than a newborn bairn.

Murdoch was a cunning warrior, and Drake wondered how he could best his clever half-brother with so little energy.

Ahead and to his right, he finally spotted Averyl clad in resplendent red silk, clasping her hands together in prayer. An unknown man stood beside her, arms crossed over his wiry chest. Drake turned his gaze back to his wife, wishing he could touch her now, in case 'twas the last time.

By the saints, how he had missed her. He loved her so much; 'twas as if his heart had ceased to live when he had been without her. But now he feared. What would happen to her, to their child, if he could not best Murdoch?

He shuddered, knowing the answer: Suffer until death.

"You will best Murdoch, have no fear," Kieran encouraged. "He is no match against all your fine training."

"But I am weak."

"Here," said Kieran suddenly, offering bread and water—his first sustenance in nearly a day.

Ravenous, Drake demolished the hunk of bread, washed it down with the crystal fresh water, and handed the flask to his friend. "Bless you for that."

Kieran flashed a tight smile. "Win. You are by far the better man. Then you can claim your wife, whom you do not deserve—"

"Shut your mouth, Kieran," Aric snapped.

"He speaks the truth," Drake admitted.

"As you see," Kieran piped up before turning directly to Drake. "Marry her in a church or I will do it myself."

Before he could block the vision out, Drake's mind flashed him a picture of Averyl in Kieran's arms, her sweet mouth open in surrender, her silken flesh accepting—

"No one touches my wife but *me,*" he growled. "And if you test me, you will surely find yourself missing that cock you're so furious proud of."

With that, Drake nudged his horse to the end of the field.

"God be with you," called Aric.

Drake prayed He was with him—and Averyl.

Aric turned to Kieran then. "Would you really wed Averyl?"

Kieran hesitated. Aric knew something devilish whirled in the Irishman's head.

"Unless Averyl and the babe would have suffered without a husband, nay. You know I will never wed." Kieran smiled. "But the idea certainly revived Drake with the fire of anger, aye?"

Drake glanced at Averyl from the stands. She had remained by his side, exchanged her freedom for his, proposed this tournament to save his life. Her actions alone told him she cared. What had he ever done to prove his feelings to her?

He vowed to show her in every way he could that he loved her, that his heart and soul were completely hers.

If he lived.

Kieran be damned.

Pushing away the grim thoughts, he thrust on his helmet. Moments later, he saw the signal given and charged.

The horses' hooves pounded the rich Scottish earth below, matching the nervous thundering of his heart.

As Murdoch drew near, each raised their lances. Closer, closer . . . Drake aimed for the center of Murdoch's chest and raised his shield as his half-brother took his own aim.

A moment later, Drake felt his lance spear something. Murdoch howled and cursed, and Drake looked back to see him grip his arm as the small crowd of fighting men cheered for blood.

On the next course, Drake did not strike Murdoch; he felt instead a sharp glance of his enemy's blade graze his thigh. Fire seared his flesh as he readied for a third pass.

Vision blurring momentarily, Drake prayed for fortitude. Kieran had been right those months ago: Averyl was his reason to live. Today he would fight for a future with his wife and their bairn, as well as for revenge and justice.

Urging his mount on once more, Drake made his way toward Murdoch. As they passed, Drake saw a small blade in Murdoch's right hand. He feinted moments before Murdoch might have planted it between his ribs. The crowd shouted for more.

At the end of the field, Drake glanced once more at Averyl, beautifully rounded with child, then the man by her side. Drake scowled. The man seemed oddly familiar—at least until his vision blurred once more.

"You look worse for the wear." Aric offered his flask.

Drake turned down his friend's offer of water and glanced at the blood trickling down his thigh. "Aye. I feel such."

He all but groaned as he made another pass across the field toward his enemy. This time, Murdoch stabbed his lance into the horse beneath Drake. The animal whinnied and crumbled beneath him, and he was forced to jump from the animal or be crushed.

Laughing, Murdoch jumped from his own mount and accepted the *claidmor* his squire brought.

Drake turned to find Kieran at the ready with a blade. He grabbed it from his friend's outstretched hands, then stalked toward Murdoch, ready for the fight. Ready for the end.

Neither man hesitated in the battle. Instantly, swords clashed, and grunts rang out. Sweat trickling in his eyes, vision blurring again, Drake focused on Murdoch's determined face, looked into his cruel eyes.

Before him lay the man responsible for nearly every misery in his life: his childhood pain, this terrible accusation of murder, his outlaw status, his wife's fear. *No more!*

A new strength roared into him, warming his veins, numbing his pain, his anger, his heart. All of those would come later, but not until this war was done.

Calling upon all of Guilford's training, Drake swung his sword at Murdoch, who raised his shield to counter the blow. With a flash of silver, he raised the blade to Murdoch again, on the other side. Murdoch staggered back, off balance. Drake charged forward and kicked Murdoch in the stomach. The blow ripped the air from the chief's body. Murdoch slumped to his knees. Drake used the opportunity to kick the sword from his half-brother's hands and tackle him to the ground.

With a clank of armor, they went down. Drake threw aside his blade and, holding Murdoch to the earth with a forearm at his throat, pulled his dirk from his boot.

His half-brother struggled, his face straining with effort until 'twas redder than his hair. To no avail. Drake felt naught but strength and rightness in his body, the power to win.

Gripping the dirk, Drake whisked it up to Murdoch's throat. "Tell me now whom you paid to kill our father."

"Rot in hell!"

"Nay, I will leave that to you, *brother.* I want the truth. Who killed him?"

Murdoch hesitated. Drake pushed the blade under Murdoch's helmet and chain mail, against his bare throat. Aye, 'twas vulnerable he was now, and well he knew it, for the way his dark eyes bulged with shock and alarm.

Still, Murdoch spat, "I will say naught."

A slow, killing rage overcame Drake. He wanted to push his blade into Murdoch's throat and be done with it. God had determined him the victor, at least according to this joust. 'Twould not be too difficult to convince the clan of such.

Breathing hard once, twice, Drake fought the urge to kill. God, how he ached to end Murdoch's life. But he could not, for he would have no peace until he had the truth.

"I pity you," Drake said finally. "I once believed you bedded my mother to hurt our father, but I know you did such to get his attention. 'Tis jealous you were."

"Ach! I simply made certain you did not receive money and power you did not deserve as a mere bastard."

Again, Drake restrained the urge to wet his knife with Murdoch's lifeblood. "My parents were married upon my birth."

"After you were conceived. Such hardly counts."

"It clearly does, or you would not fear that I could seize your position as chief. But 'tis certain I am that money was only a part of your reason you saw our father murdered."

Drake leaned toward Murdoch, daring him to refute the claims he next made. "You were jealous of the time I spent with Lochlan and tried to kill me rather than winning him yourself."

Murdoch reached up to push at Drake. "You know nothing."

Drake remained firmly planted over Murdoch's prone form. "You insisted that being firstborn should make you more loved, and he disagreed," Drake said, tone taunting. "So you discarded him before he could disown you."

The sunlight glinted silver to his right suddenly. Catching sight of the hidden dagger in Murdoch's hands, Drake moved to contain the threat. Behind him, Averyl gasped loudly. Gripping his half-brother's wrist and forcing it to the ground, he looked back at his wife.

"Nay," he heard Kieran warn. "He will only hurt you."

"Or use you to kill Drake," added Aric.

Drake cast his gaze to her, hot, searing, intent.

"Stay away," he warned, then looked back to Murdoch. "While I finish this feud—for good."

Icy, harsh rage filled his every nerve. He directed a killing glare at Murdoch.

Gripping Murdoch's sweat-damp hair in his hands, Drake shoved him against the pungent green grass. Upon Murdoch's grunt, he pressed the knife harder to his half-brother's throat.

"I have lost patience, you wretch," he growled. "You can tell me how you had our father killed. How did you arrange it?"

"I would rather go to hell."

Drake's eyes narrowed. "I vow I will send you there soon." His fingers trembled with the need for revenge. "You deserve to die for what you did to our father."

"Lochlan's heart was revoltingly soft," Murdoch hissed. "He loved flea-ridden kittens, that half-English bitch he called wife, and you."

"Whom did you pay to kill him?" Drake demanded, losing patience.

Murdoch opened his mouth, to lie, Drake felt certain. Fury sizzling through his blood, he sank the sharp of his blade just under his half-brother's skin, just enough to draw blood.

"Tell me now," he demanded. "Or you die in seconds."

"Drake, nay," Averyl called in warning.

Keeping Murdoch pinned to the ground with his blade, he turned back to Averyl. The stranger beside her took hold of her shoulder and kept her from the fight. Drake looked again at the unruly dark hair, the lean build, the gray eyes.

He had seen this man before.

Aye, he had! 'Twas dark then, and a battle ensued. His mind racing, Drake searched his memories until the truth hit him.

"You!" he barked, fury pulsing so hard, it stung him. "You killed my father. Release my wife!"

Around him, the crowd gasped. Whether 'twas over the announcement of the murderer's identity or Averyl's married state, he knew not and cared not.

"My cousin Robert?" Averyl asked. "How can that be?"

Drake frowned at her question. *Her cousin?* Had a Campbell killed Lochlan all along, and not Murdoch?

"I killed no one!" insisted Robert, looking most aggrieved.

Before Drake could release Murdoch and charge upon the guilty stranger, Aric and Kieran grabbed Robert and dragged him into the circle, beside Drake and Murdoch. Averyl followed.

As they came closer, Drake continued to stare at the man. But his mind told him naught different. Robert Campbell had stabbed Lochlan to death.

"You killed my father," he said slowly, still trying to comprehend.

" 'Tis not so," whispered Robert, who began to sweat.

He tried to jerk away, but he was no match for Kieran and Aric's hold.

"You did," Drake insisted. "With my own eyes, I saw you."

Robert returned Drake's stare, frowning as if in pain. Then resignation crept across his face. "Aye, 'twas me. But I killed Lochlan MacDougall at Murdoch MacDougall's order."

The crowd gasped again, loudly this time. Drake heard the sound explode in his head.

"Dear God," Averyl whispered.

Gaze whipping back to Murdoch, Drake turned in time to see denial spread across the chief's face.

Drake cut him off with a curse, a new fury consuming him. Tension gripped his entire body. "Robert spoke true, did he not, Murdoch?"

"Aye," Averyl cut in. "Such explains Robert's unexpected presence here. My father distrusted him, and I doubt he would have sent the scoundrel to see after me. He is here at Murdoch's bidding."

Mother of God, to hear of such evidence stunned him.

" 'Tis a lie!" said Murdoch finally.

" 'Tis he who speaks lies," Robert said with venom.

"Murdoch promised me land. Campbell land he would own after wedding Averyl. In exchange for it, I killed his father."

Drake growled.

Averyl nodded. "He wanted that land. That is why he offered to wed me!"

Robert nodded. "Your wretched father refused me and gave me no choice but murder or starvation, as I have no funds and my clan cast me out."

"And the murder of a good man was the only way you thought to survive?" Drake challenged, ready to kill.

"He held the knife, aye," began Aric, oddly soothing, "but remember who ordered its thrust."

Wallace approached Drake and stayed his blade with a hand. "Indeed, Robert Campbell's confession is enough to convince me that you are innocent, Drake."

"That is not true!" Murdoch insisted. "Drake did it! Do not believe the words of a Campbell. Who can trust them?"

"We both know he spoke true," Wallace contradicted quietly. "For I have long wondered if Drake could kill his own father."

"Robert Campbell lies," Murdoch ranted on.

He turned crazed eyes on Drake and let loose a savage scream, his expression a bloodthirsty snarl. The small blade in his hand gleamed cold and merciless in the sun as Murdoch raised the weapon and charged.

"Die, you bastard!" Murdoch shouted at Drake.

Drake watched in horror as his half-brother lifted the knife into his grasp. Without hesitation, Drake pushed Averyl out of the blade's path, then turned to his half-brother, dirk in hand. He scrambled away from Murdoch, trying to avoid danger, and swung his own blade at the exposed skin of Murdoch's neck.

Drake watched Murdoch surge closer, clutching his weapon in attack. As if seeing Drake's oncoming blade, he feinted to avoid its sharp tip at his throat, but 'twas too late.

The silver dagger sank to the hilt into Murdoch's neck.

Blood gushed from the wound, staining Drake's armor.

A moment of shock registered in Murdoch's dark eyes before they glazed over and he slumped to the ground, dead.

Silence, stillness, enveloped the field for a few moments.

Then Drake heard Averyl gasp as if from a distance as Duff and the others raced forward. Some seized Robert Campbell, calling for the dungeon. Drake regained himself and approached his brother, hate and regret beating in his heart.

He took the small blade from Murdoch's limp hand.

'Twas finally over.

Anguish carved into him like a dull knife. Beside him now, Averyl's green eyes misted with tears. Drake somehow resisted the odd urge to cry himself.

He moved to her side. He took her cold cheeks between his hands. " 'Tis over," he choked. "You are safe."

She put a hand to his cheek as a tear trailed its way down her face. "As are you."

"Drake?" Aric asked, his face quiet with concern.

His answering smile was both sad and hopeful. "All will be well here. And Kieran"—he addressed the Irishman—"forget your earlier offer. Averyl has no need of it. Find you own bride."

As Kieran laughed, Drake turned, wanting to be away from here, away from death and the disillusionment life had shown him today. "Come with me."

Averyl responded without question. He needed her now. Her gentle understanding, her quiet touch. Her. Not just for now, but forever.

He glanced at her trembling profile, unable to discern her thoughts. She'd once said she loved him. Did she still?

If he could love her, she would stay by his side, Averyl decided, savoring the feel of Drake's hand enveloping hers. Yet after what he'd been through today, could she expect him to consider such a matter? Nay, but soon the subject must arise. And then, if he could not admit any feelings for her, she would go. For living with an intimate stranger and raising her child with a father unable to express his love was unacceptable.

Before they could find privacy, Wallace sought Drake. "The clan has decided. You are free to lead, as you should have been since your father's murder. 'Tis sorry I am I doubted you."

Drake released her hand to shake Wallace's. "Thank you. I accept and hope to be a leader everyone can respect."

Nodding, Wallace turned away. Drake silently led her into Dunollie, far from the blood and memories. Duff and the other sentries followed them as far as the middle bailey, telling all what had transpired.

Within moments, a crowd of clansmen and servants began to gather about Drake, offering their humble apologies, most claiming they never believed him guilty at all. Drake seemed to accept their words with an impatient nod. Averyl wondered at his thoughts. Where they of Lochlan? Of Robert? The future?

Wearing a tense frown, his jaw clenched, Drake pressed forward. Averyl could see the emotion he fought now that his ordeal was over and he had been restored to the clan and made their leader.

Still, his triumph would never bring back his father or repair the torn brotherhood between him and Murdoch.

Drake continued to lead her toward the keep, shedding the joyous crowd of his clansmen behind. His step was urgent. Her stomach tightened with uncertainty. Why did he seek to be away from the very approval he had needed to live his life freely?

As they climbed the narrow stairs, her heart beat rapidly. She cast her apprehensive gaze to Drake. His pensive expression revealed naught of his thoughts or feelings.

"I am certain if your father could see you today, he would be proud," he said suddenly.

Averyl met Drake's softened gaze. "As would yours."

He smiled as they entered the solar. Then he went about shedding his armor and sat on what had once been his father's four-poster bed, wincing all the while.

"Averyl," he began. "I—"

"Drake!" Standing at his side, she saw the open lash marks crisscrossing his skin, many angry red and crusted.

Horrified, Averyl rose and shouted for a servant to fetch a bucket of warm water.

" 'Tis not important now," he said, reaching for her hand.

Mouth gaping, she insisted, "It is. You are hurt."

Averyl waited in the hall for the water. Her mind whirled. Would he recover? If he did, would he dismiss her from his life, send her away for good? Averyl did not think she could bear that again.

Finally, the water arrived. Bucket in hand, she approached Drake, who clenched his jaw. In impatience?

"I can have a servant tend this later," he ground out. "Now I—"

"I must tend your injuries before they do you more ill."

Averyl turned his back to her and applied the clean, wet cloth to his wounds. He hissed in a sharp breath. She repeated the process.

"I will make a poultice to help in the healing," Averyl offered.

"But—"

"Drake, 'tis my duty as a wife."

"Averyl, I wish to speak to you of that very thing."

She felt her stomach plummet, her body turn cold. Would he turn her away now?

"Our marriage has not been . . . common."

"That is so," she answered, then swallowed. Was he trying to say something or nothing at all?

What would he want of their marriage now that he was free?

* * *

Again, she pressed the damned cloth to his back. Aye, it burned like fire and needed tending, but could the woman not see he needed to speak with her now?

Reaching behind him, he grabbed her wrist and dragged her before him, bringing her small, now-rounded body between his legs. She looked afraid, uncertain. Guilt ripped into him.

Did she not know how much he cared, how much he wanted her by his side? Nay. And she would not be happy until he lay bare the contents of his heart.

She deserved no less.

And only a fool would let her get away.

"I want to marry you, in the church this time. I want you to stay by my side as my wife, my chatelaine, the mother of my children," he said with quiet certainty.

Averyl drew in a ragged breath, her eyes widening in soft surprise. "Why?"

Sweat broke out on his forehead, his chest. He loved her. Now he must overcome his fears and tell her or face losing her again.

She had trusted him enough to overcome her fears of the darkness, the insecurity of her own face, because he had urged her to do so. In return, she wanted only three little words he felt so deeply, it hurt.

The thought humbled him.

"You need a husband, our bairn needs a father. I need a helpmate. And I—"

"Release me." Averyl raised her chin, her face frighteningly devoid of all expression but fury.

Had he pushed her so far, waited too long, that he had now lost her love? Please God, nay!

He held her hand tighter.

"Release me, I say. 'Tis clear we are not suited."

Not suited? They were perfect.

Her support, her belief in his innocence, her gentle nature, had all earned his trust. Averyl made him want to be a better man. She had continued to give to him as a lover and a wife at moments when he had not deserved such. She made him feel so much. And still he wanted her. With the intensity of a fever, with the pitch of a crescendo. God, how he wanted her.

Loved her—and yearned for her to know such.

With a swish of her red gown, Averyl turned away.

By damned, nay! Not until she heard the truth, that he craved her, her sunny smiles, her trickling laugh, her floral scent. Needed her gentle soul, her trusting ways, and compassionate deeds.

He needed her love.

Drake grabbed her elbow, his desperate fingers wrapping about her arm until she faced him again. Then he took her face between both hands and sent his urgent gaze delving into hers.

"Listen to me, my stubborn wife! I love you."

She recoiled, her gaze sharp with suspicion. "Do you mean such or say what you think I wish to hear."

His heart raced, pounding hard. "They are hard words for me, but I say them because I mean them. I do love you."

She regarded him in silence, in uncertainty.

" 'Tis true." Tears hovered at the edges of his eyes. " 'Twas stubborn of me not to admit it sooner. But I feared you could hurt me, as my mother hurt my father, if you knew."

"I'm to believe after all this time that you now love me?"

Sarcasm and disbelief swirled thickly in her voice. Drake's gaze delved into hers, imploring.

" 'Tis difficult to believe, I know. But it is God's truth. I have loved you for months but was afraid to trust you."

"You have been naught but a wretch."

"Aye, and a selfish rogue, I admit. I had never known such a woman of good heart, of gentle spirit. You made me see love as it should be. You believed in me when no one did and gave of yourself when others turned me away. I treated you badly out of fear. I am sorry. But never again will I hurt you thus."

"You truly love me?" she asked, her suspicion easing.

He caressed her cheek. "Truly, I love you. Stay with me, as my wife, my love?"

She said naught at first. Drake feared he had waited too long, held the truth in for too many months.

Pain assailed his chest until he felt he might shatter. Still, he forced himself to say, "If you no longer love me, I . . . understand. And I will release you. You need not worry about Abbotsford. No matter what you decide, I will honor my vow to give you funds for Abbotsford. But before you decide, make certain you know, truly know with your heart, that I love you."

"What if I never hear those three words again?" She bit her lip in uncertainty.

Drake smiled, restraining an urge to cover those lips with his own. Instead, he swallowed, plunging ahead. "I will profess my love daily, even hourly, should you like."

Tears gathered in her eyes, turning them to grassy green. "Hourly? With those sweet words?"

Relief and love filled the whole of him. "Aye, lass."

"And with . . . more than your sweet words?"

Now desire flared to life as well. "Anytime, lass."

He gripped her hands in his, his gaze delving, cherishing, as he held back tears of his own. "Will you stay and love me as I love you?"

Her eyes softened with a radiant joy that warmed Drake's heart, completing him in ways no one else ever would.

Smiling, she murmured, "You've taken my heart captive. How could I not?"

ABOUT THE AUTHOR

Shelley Bradley, a native Californian, now resides in the Dallas area. Shortly after reading her first romance in college, she knew she wanted to write stories that readers everywhere would enjoy. To date, she has won or placed in over a dozen writing contests, including Romance Writers of America's prestigious Golden Heart, and has sold six historical romances. Closer to home, Shelley has a wonderfully supportive husband and a rambunctious little girl who is Barney's number-one fan. She loves chocolate, hates ironing, and lives for football season. (Go Cowboys!)

Visit Shelley on the World Wide Web at: www.shelleybradley.com. Or write Shelley at P.O. Box 270126, Flower Mound, TX 75027.

Dear Reader,

If you liked HIS STOLEN BRIDE, be sure to look for Shelley Bradley's next release in the Brothers in Arms series, HIS REBEL BRIDE, available wherever books are sold in March 2001.

To control the rebellious Irish, King Henry decides marrying them is one way to do it. Thus, half-Irish Kieran Broderick is sent to Ireland as the new earl of Kildare, there to choose a bride from one of the O'Shea sisters. Spirited Maeve is his choice—but Maeve is far from happy about marrying a hated Englishman, and refuses him his rights as husband . . . until she begins to want them herself.

<u>BOOK YOUR PLACE ON OUR WEBSITE AND MAKE THE READING CONNECTION!</u>

We've created a customized website just for our very special readers, where you can get the inside scoop on everything that's going on with Zebra, Pinnacle and Kensington books.

When you come online, you'll have the exciting opportunity to:

- View covers of upcoming books
- Read sample chapters
- Learn about our future publishing schedule (listed by publication month *and author*)
- Find out when your favorite authors will be visiting a city near you
- Search for and order backlist books from our online catalog
- Check out author bios and background information
- Send e-mail to your favorite authors
- Meet the Kensington staff online
- Join us in weekly chats with authors, readers and other guests
- Get writing guidelines
- AND MUCH MORE!

**Visit our website at
http://www.zebrabooks.com**

"Thrills from beginning to end. . . . *Fast Forward* is an appropriate title. . . . It was so good it seemed to take no time at all to get from beginning to end."

—Syracuse *Herald-American* (NY)

"Credit Mercer with a rare imagination . . . skill and wit . . . and a Machiavellian penchant for plot. . . . *Fast Forward* is a good yarn, well told."

—*Los Angeles Times Book Review*

"*Fast Forward* couldn't be a faster read if it tried. . . . [It] grabs the reader on the first page . . . and doesn't let go until the last, when all the loose ends are finally tied. . . . Perfect escapism, fantasy, and intrigue for anyone wanting to forget the world for a while."

—*South Bend Tribune* (IN)

"An irresistible new voice. . . . What raises this tale heads above the average . . . story is our heroine's pluck and indefatigable sense of humor. The result is a suspense novel with heaps of wit and not a little charm."

—*Alfred Hitchcock Mystery Magazine*

"A good shivery tale. . . . Judy Mercer has developed an appealing heroine for her first novel. . . . A pleasant page-turner."

—*The Pilot* (Southern Pines, NC)

"The reader experiences all the suspense, uncertainty, fear, and confusion that Ariel feels. . . . [You'll] find a gem in this well-written mystery with a twist."

—*The Gothic Journal*

"Engaging, fast-paced . . . with just the right combination of terror and compassion. . . . The ending, like the rest of the book, is a pleasing combination of the slick and the jagged."

—*San Francisco Chronicle*

"A natural born storyteller."

—Linda Barnes, author of *Snapshot* and *Coyote*

DOUBLE TAKE

"Stylish . . . inventive. . . . It's one of Mercer's triumphs that she ties the [plot lines] together without straining credibility. . . . She makes Ariel's predicament plausible."
—*San Francisco Chronicle*

"*Double Take* has it all—an amnesiac heroine . . . a guilt-driven, aristocratic Charleston family . . . a chance encounter with a stranger on a beach, [and] a mysterious disappearance."
—*Richmond Times-Dispatch*

"Mercer's second Ariel Gold thriller has a fetching cast and an ingenious plot device. . . . Mercer is a bright author with a fine sense of humanity."
—*Kirkus Reviews*

SPLIT IMAGE

"A tantalizing thriller. . . . [a] cunning game of truth or consequences."
—*People*

"Mercer hits her stride. . . . a tantalizing end. . . . Mercer manages wit and dialogue as well as ever. It's great fun to watch an intelligent author—and her intelligent heroine—advance."
—*Kirkus Reviews*

"Perfect for those who like their mysteries on the light side . . . [with] a bit of romance in the bargain."
—*Booklist*

Books by Judy Mercer

Fast Forward
Double Take
Split Image

Published by POCKET BOOKS

FAST FORWARD

JUDY MERCER

POCKET BOOKS
New York   London   Toronto   Sydney   Singapore

For
and because of
Larry

This book is a work of fiction. Names, characters, places,
and incidents are products of the author's imagination or are used
fictitiously. Any resemblance to actual events or locales or persons
living or dead is entirely coincidental.

POCKET BOOKS, a division of Simon & Schuster Inc.
1230 Avenue of the Americas, New York, NY 10020

ISBN: 0-671-89961-9

First Pocket Books printing June 1997

12 11 10 9 8 7 6 5 4 3

POCKET and colophon are registered trademarks of
Simon & Schuster Inc.

Cover design and illustration by Lisa Litwack

Printed in the U.S.A.

I am indebted to the following for their generous assistance: the Los Angeles Police Department and Detective Brian Mathews, Sgt. Bob Brounsten, Community Relations Officer Cathy Schuman, Sr. Police Service Representative Cherry Teter, and, especially, Officer Joe Yearwood and Detective Ralph Morten; the Los Angeles City Fire Department and Captain Richard Brunson and paramedics Gabriel Velez and Taylor Gaskins; Alfred J. Plechner, D.V.M.; Ira A. Greenberg, Ph.D.; Lawrence D. Brucker, D.D.S., and his staff; William F. Skinner, M.D.; Richard L. Coskey, M.D.; Karen Lee Copeland, Crystal Pyramid Productions, Inc.; Alex Paen, international correspondent; Colleen Dominguez, news producer; and my friends and advisors, Patricia Porter and Matthew Alper.

I am particularly grateful to Joy Harris, my agent, first for the pleasure of being able to say those words; no less for the counsel, encouragement and understanding that are her special gifts; and, finally, for her introduction to Dona Chernoff, my editor.

"There's no such thing as chance;
And what to us seems merest accident
Springs from the deepest source of destiny."

—*Johann Christoph Friedrich von Schiller*
The Death of Wallenstein

one

It was the dream that woke her.

Her eyes snapped open for the seconds it took to know the sounds weren't real. No one was there. No one was crying.

She took a deep, uneven breath and buried her face under the pillow. Body relaxing, heart slowing to normal, she tried to recapture the dream. It was gone, leaving behind a feeling of acute anxiety, profound loneliness and the memory of someone weeping. So sad. So hopeless. So real.

So get over it, she thought.

She uncovered one eye. Hazy gray morning light seeped into the room from under closed curtains. In fact, in the dimness everything looked remarkably hazy. Kicking off the covers, she swung her feet onto the floor and sat up, feeling heavy, sluggish, drugged. She peered absently into the mirror opposite the bed. And saw nothing but a blur.

She frowned, squeezed her eyes shut and tried again. A blur. Perplexed, she stood and crossed slowly to the mirror. She leaned close. The face grew clear.

Except that it wasn't her face.

The woman who stared back looked as panicked as she felt. Mouth open. Eyes wide. Face drained of color except for an ugly blotch of bruised purple. She raised her hand to

1

her cheek. The mirrored hand mimicked hers exactly. She spun to look behind her. There was no one there. She looked wildly around the room. It was a blur, it was a mess, it was a room she'd never seen before in her life.

And then she heard the noise.

Scratching. Loud, erratic scratching. It was the sound of claws gouging into wood, and it was coming from somewhere outside the room. Her scalp prickled. The image of a rat, a very big rat, leaped into her mind.

She groped around the end of the bed, her legs jelly, the blood that was pounding in her ears almost drowning out the rasping noise. She went toward the door, pulling up the heavy flannel granny gown that tangled around her legs, some part of her mind registering that she didn't own such a gown. She peered through the doorway. A long hall, as blurry as the bedroom, was empty.

She crept out. The scratching grew louder, more insistent. It seemed to come from behind a closed door at the end of the hallway. She inched her way to the door, stopped, reached for the knob. At that moment the door thumped heavily, reverberating in the frame as if something massive had been hurled against it. She stumbled backward just as the door crashed open, slamming against the wall, ricocheting back, swinging slowly open again.

The dog framed in the doorway was huge.

Ears back, hackles raised, teeth bared, he emitted a low growl as he gathered himself into a muscular crouch.

Obeying atavistic instinct, she remained absolutely immobile. She tried to murmur something placating. Nothing came out but a feeble keening. She tried again, managed foolish words. "Nice dog," she prayed. She swallowed, repeated it. And again, a mantra, over and over, having no idea what she was saying.

Amazingly, it seemed to work.

The dog, a German shepherd, had cocked his big head to one side, listening. His ears were up, his hackles down. He took a step toward her. She went rigid. He smelled her hands, her knees, her feet. Then he backed up, looking confused. He sank onto his stomach, made a peculiar whining sound and dropped his head onto his paws.

Her legs gave way. Slowly, she slid down the wall, keeping her eyes glued to the dog, resuming her incantation. Her knees splayed as she collapsed to the floor. The words poured out, dozens of words, cajoling, nonsensical words, edging toward hysteria.

"Good dog," she soothed, "You're a good dog. So big. So good. Yes, I know. You won't hurt me. No, you won't. Don't be afraid. See, I'm not afraid. I'm a nice person. I like dogs. I like you. I like dogs. I've always liked—"

She stopped. Whimpered. Her heart seemed to stop altogether as realization hit. She didn't know if she liked dogs or not. She didn't know if she owned a dog—or a cat. Or a gerbil. She didn't know if she was a nice person. She didn't know who the hell she was.

two

This time the crying was no dream.

It was real. It was her.

Arms hugging her chest, legs sprawled, she sat on someone's hallway floor and wept ugly, wrenching, painful sobs. Time was obliterated. Thought was obliterated. She rocked, paralyzed by fear, mindless with loneliness and grief.

Eventually, she realized that the room had become quiet. She didn't know how long she'd cried, nor did she remember stopping. Her head was resting against the wall as she stared, unseeing, at the ceiling. She felt chilled and stiff. One of her legs wouldn't move. Terrified anew, she looked down.

A large canine head rested on her knee.

With memory came a surge of adrenaline. She stiffened, started to shriek, started to scuttle away. Then she registered the expression on the face that peered up at her. The dog's brows were drawn together, the forehead slightly wrinkled. He looked worried.

The shriek became a giggle. The giggle threatened to erupt into hysteria. She stopped herself. Took a deep breath.

The dog lay still.

"Hey." Her voice was hoarse, strange to her ears.

The dog raised his head, his expression benign, inquiring. Tentatively, she placed her hand on the broad head. Patted.

"Take my advice, tough guy. Don't look for a job in a junkyard."

His tail thumped cooperatively.

"What's your name, boy?" Her lip quivered, and she felt her eyes begin to sting again. "Well, *one* of us ought to have one."

She turned the collar around to read the tag. On one side was a Los Angeles address and a phone number with a 310 area code. The reverse side read JESSICA.

"Jessica? Oh . . ."

She tried to see under the dog's belly. "My mistake, girl." She cleared the frog from her throat. "Excuse me. No, I meant that literally. Get up. My leg's asleep."

Clumsily, she pushed herself up, using the wall for support, pulling the gown from under her foot.

She felt so tired, so drained, so heavy. She stopped. Still bent forward, she slowly pulled up the bulky gown and stared at her legs in horror.

They were dimpled. They were generously rounded. They were *fat!*

She dropped the gown, straightened, looked down at her chest, and frantically clutched pillowy softness with both hands.

She bunched the gown's hem up around her knees and ran back toward the bedroom, lurching into a study of some sort before orienting herself and wheeling around the jamb into the bedroom. She stumbled to the mirror and thrust her face inches away.

"Oh, my God!" she whispered, jerking back, focusing.

This face was a mess. It had only dimly penetrated earlier, but now she saw that one of the cheeks was bruised and cut, and there was a lump on the high forehead. The eyes were red and swollen almost shut from crying. The face was full. Very full. The features seemed to her to be squeezed from the mottled flesh. The eyes were a little too widely set and the lips were too wide, the lower one too full. They were also elusively familiar. A small scar above the end of the mouth, however, was not. Equally strange were the heavy brows and the nose. Well, the nose wasn't that bad. Actually, it was pretty good. Perky. But it didn't go with the face. The chin—no, the *chins* were pointed, making the full face look like a big, fat valentine.

A big, fat, grimy valentine.

The face looked as if it had been used for a cleanup rag after a lube job.

She stretched the lips back, looked at the teeth and groaned. A tiny gap separated the two front teeth. Their opposite number below were slightly overlapped, atilt like little old tombstones.

And the hair, she thought. The hair! She pulled up a long, lank strand and dropped it. The haircut looked as if it had been done with a dull knife. The permanent, if possible, was worse than the cut, making the mousy brown look parched and dusty.

She dropped a hand to the dresser for support, knocking something to the floor. She peered down, saw an object next to her feet and picked up a pair of heavy, horn-rimmed glasses. One lens was cracked.

She held the glasses as if they were contaminated. She slid them on and looked into the mirror. The image was sharp.

She turned and looked at the room behind her. Except for the slightly weird effect created by the cracked lens, the focus was clear. She could have read the smallest print on an eye chart on the opposite wall.

Perfect. Just perfect.

In addition to being fat, maimed and funny-looking, she thought, I'm blind as a mole.

She threw the glasses back onto the dressing table just as a shrilling pierced the stillness. She spun toward the sound.

The telephone on the night table was ringing.

Reflexively, she reached for it, then drew back. She reached again, grabbed the receiver to stop the noise, lifted it slowly to her ear.

She held it, held her breath, listened.

"Ariel? Hello?" A pause. "Ariel, you awake?" A longer pause.

"Ariel?"

Her hello was a croak. She cleared her throat and repeated it. Waited.

"Ariel? Henry. What are you doing still home? Listen, Peacock was looking for you, some question he had. Since I didn't have you scheduled out, he thought I'd better call and check on you." The voice was pleasant, slightly raspy, older. And totally unfamiliar.

"A regular mother hen, old Peacock, right? Yeah, well, okay, it wasn't his idea. But I couldn't remember your ever not being where you were supposed to be. You don't have many virtues, but you tend to be—" The voice stopped.

"Ariel? Are you all right? Are you sick or something?"

Her mind was blank. What should she do? Ask for help? Try to explain? Hang up?

She needed time. Time alone. Time to think.

"Ai-i-i!" She sucked in her breath sharply as something warm and wet nudged her hand. She did a frantic two-step away, banging her shin on the bed frame and jerking the telephone off the table as she whipped around. The dog, startled by the rude reaction to a friendly lick, barked in reproach.

"Ariel, if you don't answer me, I'll get your address from Personnel and come over there! What's the matter with you?"

"No!" She sat abruptly on the bed, rubbing her shin. "I mean yes, uh . . . Henry? You're right. I'm sick. I think I've got . . . flu."

Stop babbling! she told herself. Get off the phone!

"I'm probably contagious, so don't come here, okay?"

Silence on the line.

"Well, if you're sure." His voice was edged with concern. Or suspicion.

"I am. I'm fixing to call the doctor right now."

"You're fixing what?"

"I said I'll call the doctor. I'll get back to you, okay?"

Another long silence.

"Yeah. Do that. I mean it, Ariel. You really don't sound like yourself."

She closed her eyes.

"Okay, I'll talk to you later then. In the meantime, I'll put Hodges on the immigration thing." He hung up without saying good-bye.

She sat motionless for a moment before replacing the receiver, sagging as her adrenaline again ebbed.

"Ariel," she whispered, gazing across at the mirror from which the wretched round face, unfocused, unchanged, looked back.

How do I know that's not my face? she asked herself. If I don't know who I am, how come I think that's not me? She frowned. I *know* I'm not homely as a yam and I know I hate fat! I've *always* hated fat!

She blinked. How had she known that?

If I know that, she thought, her heart beginning to race, I must know other things about me, too. All I have to do is remember.

Just think and remember! There's got to be some way to reverse this spell or whatever it is that's going on here, some way sane and rational and obvious.

Hypnosis?

Oh, good Lord!

Her momentary elation evaporated. Now, that's rational, she thought. I count backward from a hundred, fall asleep and *voila!* I'm back in the real world!

Get real. Get a grip. Get a life!

"You've got one," she said aloud. "It just doesn't happen to be *yours.*"

She pointed to the mirrored reflection. "You're probably just nuts, that's all. Crazy as a March hare." She made a demented face. "And here's the looking glass! But Alice doesn't live here anymore; *Ariel* does!"

She straightened her spine. "Enough of that! The first thing to do is find out who this Ariel person is." She put on the eyeglasses and surveyed the bedroom.

Sometime earlier in this hellish morning—ten minutes ago? a year ago?—she'd vaguely registered that the room was untidy, but housekeeping hadn't been a priority at the time. Now she saw the extent of the shambles.

"Good Lord, Ariel," she muttered. "You're a messy wench, aren't you?"

7

Drawers were pulled out, some dumped on the floor with clothes tumbling from them. A jumbo-sized bra was draped over a television set. A cachepot was overturned beside it, dirt and a very large peace lily spilling onto the carpet. Her eyes veered to the closet, where all the clothes still hanging were pushed to one side. Boxes that had presumably been on the shelf above were piled haphazardly on the floor.

"Why don't we just come back to this later," she said.

She left the wrecked bedroom and went next door to what she recalled from her earlier accidental entry was a study.

She stopped in the doorway, looking into a room totally ransacked. She took a step inside, pushing the door all the way open. The hair on her neck rose as she took in the disaster area. Papers, computer disks, books and cassette tapes littered every surface. File drawers yawned, emptied of their contents, which were dumped in a scramble on the floor.

She backed out. Turned toward the room that had held the dog captive.

One look at the kitchen from hell was all she needed.

She raced from living room to dining room. Trashed.

The bathroom was a fragrant confusion of powders and lotions. Bath gel made a small, dried green river from a bottle overturned in the bathtub. Dusting powder and coagulated liquids coated the vanity. The sink was half filled with jars, bottles and tubes.

Alarm bells were going off in her head. "I'm out of here," she breathed. "I want out of here now!" She turned and almost tripped over the dog, which trotted behind her as she flew back to the bedroom.

Where were her clothes? She grabbed a handful of garments from the floor, saw that they were slips and panties, threw them aside. The dog, sensing her panic, stood in the middle of the room barking. Hangers clattered from the rod as she ripped through suits, blouses and skirts that her short-circuiting brain registered only as large, wrong, alien! She wheeled to the bed. A pants leg protruded from under the covers. Jerking back the bedclothes, she found a crumpled sweat suit, smeared with dirt and what looked like oily smut. She picked up the shirt. A large stain on the front looked different from the others. It looked very much like dried blood.

She dropped the shirt as it if had burst into flame, then realized what she had seen under it. Gingerly, she pushed the shirt aside. Underneath was a small but very serious-looking gun.

She backed to the closet, snatched a coat from a hanger and plunged her arms into the sleeves. A worn sneaker lay on the floor. She forced in her left foot and dropped to her knees, scrabbling for the mate. She found it under a skirt, sat on the floor and crammed it on.

Followed by the barking dog, she ran to the kitchen and tried to wrench open what looked like an outside door. Locked. Her fingers slipping, fumbling, she unlocked first one and then a second mechanism. She flung open the door and lurched out into cold, drizzling rain. Stumbling across a patio and down a short flight of semicircular steps, she found herself in a large yard dotted everywhere with trees and shrubbery. It was completely enclosed by a high, concrete block wall. Seeing a path between the wall and the side of the house, she ran toward it, down it, toward the front of the house, where she was stopped by a padlocked gate.

She quickly retraced her steps back into the house, through the kitchen and hall, into the living room. The front door was also locked. She twisted the doorknob, freed a chain guard from its slot and tore through the doorway. A driveway to her left ended at a garage door. She ran to it and pulled on the handle. It wouldn't budge. Automatic, she thought. Where was the control? She found it back inside the front door, pressed it and hurried back to the garage just as the door whooshed fully up.

Inside was her car.

She reached out her hand in wonder, feeling as if she'd awakened from a nightmare. She started toward the car. And stopped, stricken. Recognition vanished. Familiarity became confusion. She touched the convertible top. Stroked the coarse fabric. For a moment, she thought, grief bringing an ache to her throat, for just one wonderful normal moment I thought I was me again.

She bent and looked into the ignition. There was no key.

She folded her arms on the roof, clutched her elbows, took a deep breath. The panic was gone, replaced by an abysmal sadness.

Where were you going, anyway, she asked herself. Home? Careening around the streets? To the police? What if that *is* blood on that shirt? Whose is it? How'd it get there? More to the point, who was responsible for putting it there?

She rested her cheek on her arm, her face turned toward the open garage door. The dog sat just inside the threshold, watching to see what she'd do next.

What would she do next? Think, she ordered herself. Just stop and think for a minute.

One, there's no one in the house now. Remembering the dried, coagulated mess in the bathroom, she mentally counted two—whoever was there is long gone. Three, whatever they were looking for—and it was obvious that someone had looked thoroughly, even desperately, for something—it wasn't something of mine. It's Ariel's. And maybe they found it. In which case, why would they come back? That's four and five. And six, if they did, there're locks on the doors. And a gun, seven. And a dog, eight. And, maybe, answers I can't get anywhere else right now. A big nine. And I want the answers, she thought, because I don't think I can stand this much longer without going completely insane. If I'm not already.

She closed the car door, stopped to slip her finger inside the shepherd's collar and led her through a quickening rain back into the house.

A moment later the garage door quietly descended.

three

From his vantage point in an alcove off the main room, the man could watch the entrance and the rain-smeared plate-glass window beside it. He'd come early to ensure just such a position. He wondered again if he'd chosen the right meeting place and again concluded that it was satisfactory. The diner was encrusted with the grease of generations, it was disgusting, but it was satisfactory for his purposes.

He'd been here before, several years ago, in the company of a woman with useful connections but quirky tastes. He hadn't been pleased with this particular manifestation of her eccentricity, but he was sufficiently interested in her favors to indulge any number of whims.

Four days ago he'd thought of the diner and the adjacent video store (where he and the woman had bought a rather primitive but inspirational tape) and driven here to make certain both businesses still existed. Glancing casually into the diner before entering the store beside it, he'd made his way toward the rear and seen what he remembered: a back entrance. It gave onto a parking lot shared by several shops, among them a newsstand. The newsstand also had a back entrance, as well as magazine racks from behind which one could see the street.

The escape route would probably be unnecessary, he thought now, but he was a man who preferred meticulous planning. He had reason to know its importance.

He took a sip of coffee. It was still too hot. The waitress refilled his cup every five minutes, asking if everything was okay with his breakfast and looking generally harassed. She was annoyingly attentive but, he noticed, she never actually looked at him. He shifted the bright red Abraham & Straus shopping bag beside the booth to make sure it could be seen from the entrance, leaned back and looked around. No one was paying him the slightest attention. He glanced at his distorted reflection in the metal napkin holder. The thick

11

moustache and hairpiece, both white, had been applied with an expertise born of experience, and they looked natural. He would be neither recognized nor remembered.

The envelope in his lap, hidden beneath the skimpy diner napkin, hadn't been as bulky as he'd thought it would be. But then, this project hadn't been as expensive as he'd thought it would be. In fact, he mused, it was rather shocking just how cheaply murder could be bought. While inflation drove the price of practically everything steadily upward, the value of human life was apparently in decline, with the cost of its extinction dropping correspondingly. Or perhaps it was just the individual for whom he waited, who was not, he suspected, among the elite of his profession.

He would have done the job himself and in a much more straightforward way but he'd discovered, curiously, that he had a distaste for the kill. Not the concept. The kill itself.

He looked at his watch. The agreed-upon time was ten minutes past. He'd give it five more minutes, he decided. The cretin had probably forgotten the appointment.

Their first telephone conversation had not begun reassuringly. "Rodriquez," as the high-pitched, slightly accented voice had identified himself, had sounded anything but capable. He'd sounded, as they say, "hopped up," his conversation disjointed. But he'd grown positively eloquent as he'd warmed to a theme. Explosives, it had quickly become apparent, were his favorite subject, his love, his passion. Bombs, in short, turned him on.

Perhaps, in the afterglow of ecstasy, it had slipped his mind that he was to be paid.

It was time to go. Just as he counted out a precise 15 percent tip, his peripheral vision caught movement at the door. He relaxed back onto the banquette.

The man who entered was a Latino. He wore a fatigue cap and a padded army jacket, unfaded patches on the sleeves indicating where single stripes had once been sewn. Dark, jittery-looking and a great deal heavier than the incongruously tenor voice had suggested, Rodriquez took off the rain-soaked cap and slapped it against his thigh, making dark stains on his faded jeans. He scanned the room. Catching sight of the man, he broke into a grin and hurried to the booth.

He sat, dropped his cap onto the table and ran a hand nervously over the bristles of his crew cut. "So," he said in the agitated, slightly effeminate voice the man remembered, "I finally get to meet you, huh?" He inclined his head toward the red shopping bag beside the booth. "Sure beats a flower in the buttonhole, which I gotta say might be a little out of place in this joint. Who's Abraham & Straus, anyway?"

The man across from him said nothing.

Rodriquez clasped his hands between his knees, rocking forward conspiratorially. "You saw the papers?"

The man leaned marginally away. "I wouldn't be here otherwise."

Rodriquez wiped his nose with the back of his sleeve, his eyes focused inward in loving recollection. "A minute and forty seconds flat, man, and it was handled. A couple of sticks, the caps, a little wire, then when she turns the key . . ." Rodriquez threw his hands up and out, making a plosive sound with his lips. "You should'a seen it, brother!"

"I'm not your brother, and we've discussed the procedure sufficiently. It's hardly brain surgery."

"Yeah, well, you better know what you're doing, and you better be careful with the stuff I got to you, you know what I mean? What are you gonna do with—"

A hissed "shut up" startled the Latino into silence.

The waitress had spotted the new customer and was hurrying to their table, pulling her order pad and pencil from her apron pocket. The man smiled and held up a hand to forestall her. He turned back to Rodriquez, his smile gone.

"There've been very few details released," he said. "Just the location and the color of the car. 'No identification possible at this time,' and so on. There's no question in your mind about the target?"

"Well, I didn't go up and introduce myself." Rodriquez frowned, rocking his body backward and forward. "You said a tall woman, thirtyish, with brown hair and that she'd be there at nine-thirty. You said she'd be inside the restaurant for, probably, a half hour max and that she drove an old red Thunderbird, right? A 'fifty-five, right? What do you think—there were a bunch of those there?" His voice had risen, thinning out in protest. "Lighten up, man! It was a cinch, everything just like you said. No car jockeys, that fence between the parking lot and the restaurant so nobody could see from inside—and dark? You got that right! But no sweat! Hey, listen, you hired the best, you got the best!"

"Keep your voice down! Reach under the table and take this. Put it away unobtrusively." The man held the envelope by one corner, avoiding Rodriquez's hand. "I'm going to leave now, but you will not. You will remain where you are for five minutes." He slid to the end of the banquette, retrieved the shopping bag and stood.

Rodriquez hardly noticed the small, securely taped bundle he crammed into his jacket pocket. Still aggrieved but unable to think of a clever parting shot, he glared as the man took an umbrella from the hat rack attached to the end of the booth and made his way, quite slowly, out of the café.

Wonder why an old coot like that needs somebody done, he thought. Looks like he'd be too tired for anything to matter that much anymore.

He picked up a triangle of cold toast left untouched on the plate across the table and folded it into his mouth, reliving the pleasure of the previous night. He hadn't mentioned to this dude that when he'd wheeled out of the alley behind the restaurant, he thought he had in fact seen another old T-Bird. But what were the odds? And the light was real bad in the whole parking lot, especially back there.

The money in his jacket, he knew, would keep him in blow for a real long time in Mexico. And he had an idea for how he could get some more before he left. It would be a cinch compared to what he'd just pulled off—a real no-brainer.

four

What's needed here is a methodical search, she thought. Or a bulldozer. She surveyed the upended living room. A bulldozer would be good.

" 'Who are we? Where are we?' " she muttered, shrugging off the coat and dropping it over the back of a chair. She toed aside a sofa cushion and turned a lamp right side up. She'd bent to retrieve an afghan from the floor when it struck her that she was probably disturbing a crime scene. It wasn't scruples, however, that caused her to straighten empty-handed; it was the hopelessness of the effort.

Every woman in America carries a handbag, she told herself as she stepped over a dark stain decorated with vase fragments and drying ranunculus. With any luck there would be one here, somewhere, and in it would be identification.

Seeing everything slightly out of kilter through the cracked lens of the glasses, she crept through the dining room and bathroom, glanced into the kitchen, avoided the study—the site of the worst devastation. She found the purse in plain sight, intact, on the seat of a bedroom chair. The seat cushion was pushed up against the backrest.

Deduction, she thought grimly: I almost certainly wasn't here when the place was tossed.

Which tells you what, Sam Spade?

She knelt and rooted in the purse. Pulling out a small black plastic box, she looked at it, trying to assess the implications. Why did she carry a tape recorder? She put it on the chair. A thick wallet was next. She ripped Velcro and saw that it was actually a combination of wallet, checkbook and several other little booklets—an organizer.

Inside, up front, were a number of slotted credit cards and a driver's license. The license belonged to Ariel Rose Gold, and pictured on it was the face from the mirror.

She sank onto her heels, took a deep breath, let it out slowly.

She read the data beside the photo. Sex: F. Hair: Brn. Eyes: Hzl. Height: 5–9. Weight: 142 lbs. Ha! she thought sourly; in your dreams, Ariel!

An appointment book was inserted to face the credit cards. As she began to turn the pages, she heard a crash somewhere in the house. Quietly, slowly, she rose, clutching the purse and wallet to her chest, and followed the sounds to the kitchen.

The dog, tail wagging, was busily consuming a cluster of grapes that lay among the jagged remains of a ceramic bowl.

"Hold it, girl!" Dropping purse and wallet on the table, she pushed the dog to one side. "You're going to get yourself a perforated gullet."

While she scooped pottery shards and what was left of the grapes onto the countertop, she scolded the dog defensively.

"I was going to think of feeding you. Sooner or later." A thought occurred. She considered the dog, who looked back with lively interest. "Speaking of doggy needs—You must have a bladder the size of the Hindenburg!"

She looked carefully through the window and, seeing no threat, reached to open the door. She'd forgotten to relock it. "Brilliant!" she murmured and yanked it open. Making inviting gestures toward the backyard, she said, "Come on, out you go. Pit stop."

The dog continued to sit where she was, panting attentively. The long, pink tongue dangling over her molars gave her a dopey but agreeable look as her tail swept spilled flour from side to side.

"Incredible." She eyed the dog in disbelief. "Well, maybe you went when we were flailing around outside. I didn't notice, being hysterical at the time." She closed the door, locking it this time.

"Tell you what, Tiny . . ." Her eyes scanned countertops and what was left in the cabinets. "I'll get you breakfast if you'll tell me where a person could find some coffee in this place." She looked through the refrigerator and opened the freezer compartment, both of which appeared undisturbed. "Well, I reckon they weren't looking for heroin or coke or whatever it is people hide in the freezer."

She pushed a half gallon of Häagen-Dazs to one side and,

with an exclamation of delight, spotted a bag of Colombian beans. Finding a grinder and filters, she rescued a kettle from the floor and proceeded with coffee-making. All the time, she kept up a monologue, whistling through the graveyard, comforted by the sound of her own voice.

"I know, I know. I said the 'breakfast' word, Jessie. You mind if I call you Jessie? I can't quite get my mouth around Jessica." She looked again through the cabinets. No obvious dog fodder. "You look pretty well-fed, so I don't think grapes are your normal diet. There's got to be something." She looked again in the refrigerator, then turned to a pantry. On the floor was a bag of Nature's Recipe.

"Looking good, mutt. Looking good! There's not even a question in my mind that you own a bowl. Aha!" Under the table was that object, overturned.

"So here I am," she chattered on, "in the middle of the wildest out-of-body experience in the history of California— and that's going some, sport!—inhabiting the corpulent body of someone I don't know from grits, who seems to have— or maybe has had—something somebody wanted pretty desperately, and I wake up in bed with a gun and an article of clothing that looks like it's got dried blood all over it. Plus some person named Henry who has access to this address could be over here any minute, and I'm worried about your diet and whether you've relieved yourself. So I reckon we've learned one thing about me."

She put the bowl, filled and mixed with warm water, on the floor. "I reckon I do like dogs."

She poured a mugful of coffee, swept the clutter on the table to one end and dumped out the contents of the purse. Thumbing through the organizer, she turned to the check register. A balance of just over two thousand dollars. Not bad, not good, not revealing. In the credit card section there were a couple of gasoline cards, a library card, Triple A and Blue Shield. Department store cards ranged from Saks Fifth Avenue to May Company.

The address book was pretty much a dead loss information-wise. Except for some innocuous businesses—Royal Dry Cleaning, California Consolidated Bank, a pharmacy, etc.—and two entries preceded by "Dr.," the people listed could have been anyone, friend or foe, villain or veterinarian. In the *H*s she saw a Henry, no last name, who might be the Henry from the telephone, and in the *P*s was a Peacock, no first name, who surely must be the Peacock mentioned—how many Peacocks would anybody know? Both numbers began with the same prefix; there were no extensions or other identification. With those two exceptions, the only thing certain about any of the names was that she'd never heard of them.

On an enclosed notepad was what at first appeared to be hieroglyphics or something written by a doctor but that on closer inspection proved to be a recipe for a complicated Rock Cornish hen dish.

From the utter lack of information so far, Ariel was either a secretive woman or she didn't have any secrets to hide.

She turned to the appointment book section. As she flipped through, she absently fingered the purse contents on the table. She picked up a pack of Marlboros, tipped one out and put it between her lips. She felt for matches—and froze. Aghast, she looked cross-eyed at the cigarette dangling from her mouth. She carefully removed it and stared.

The faint odor had been a subliminal presence from the time she awoke. It was an odor that seemed familiar, comfortable, but she felt positive—sort of—that *she* didn't smoke.

She found a lighter. Experimentally, she lit up, inhaled. Twice. Three times. She felt a rush of satisfaction. A flood of guilt. A wave of dizziness. She lurched to the sink and ran water over the cigarette, drowned it, dropped it.

For the first time she began to absorb the fact that not only was the body in which she found herself unknown, its *history* was unknown: its addictions, genetic makeup, illnesses, strengths, experiences.

Obviously, it had a nicotine habit. A disgusting eating disorder. And, judging from that little scar over the mouth, it had maybe had chicken pox somewhere along the line. Had it ever given birth? Had operations or broken bones? Was there, even now, ticking away somewhere in its DNA some awful disease? At the very least, it suffered myopia or astigmatism or both.

She ripped off the glasses and slung them onto the countertop. They hit the tile backsplash, and the upper half of the cracked lens popped out with a tinkle. And the mellifluous sound of chimes.

She did a double take. Chimes?

She realized as Jessie tore barking from the room that what she'd heard was the doorbell.

Her heart lurched into an arrhythmic drumroll as she followed the dog to the front door. Slipping the chain guard into its slot, she looked through the peephole to see a giant green-and-white umbrella. Under it, a tiny person stood, looking back toward the street.

She cracked open the door and peered around it. Jessie, sniffing eagerly, stuck her snout through the opening below.

"Um-m, that coffee smells wonderful," the person chirped, turning to face her, eyes widening. "Great heavens! What happened to you?"

"Um, I'm not . . . well," she said. She stared at the apparition on the porch, too distracted to be frightened. It struck her that she'd wandered from *The Twilight Zone* into a Fellini movie.

The person was female. Almost certainly. What could be seen of the hair peeping from under a multicolored knitted cap was an unlikely red-brown—the color designated Burnt Sienna in the Crayola box. The face was as wrinkled as a raisin. The lips were ambitiously painted, and bright red crept into the erosion of wrinkles around them. The body was enveloped by a yellow slicker so long it trailed to the tops of white, neon-striped athletic shoes. The arms held a miniature dachshund, his muzzle gray with age, and the hand that wasn't holding the umbrella clutched a folded newspaper.

Alert blue eyes returned her stare with frank curiosity and concern. "You do look a trifle under the weather, don't you?" She raised penciled eyebrows, creating still more wrinkles on her forehead. "You remember me, Marguerite Harris from two doors down? And Rudy?" In a series of movements approaching legerdemain, she managed to wag the dachshund's paw, test the elements with an upraised palm, snap the umbrella closed and hang it over her arm.

Squaring her shoulders in a businesslike way, she launched into a filibuster.

"I wouldn't have disturbed you—I've noticed you're a person who values her privacy—except for what happened last night. I was walking Rudy, and I thought I saw a light in your house, but it wasn't a proper light, more like a flashlight or a candle, flickering, do you see? And I only saw it for a moment. However"—she took a breath and plowed on—"I'd seen you drive away a little earlier, so it just didn't look right to me, so I went home and asked my husband—Carl, you know—to come down here and make certain that all was as it should be. Carl rang your bell and knocked, but no one answered, and—I'll be frank with you—it was his opinion that I'd imagined the light, but I saw what I saw. So when I took Rudy for his constitutional this morning and noticed that you hadn't picked up your newspaper"—she gestured vaguely behind her—"it seemed appropriate to look in on you and see that you were all right. Are you?" She stopped as suddenly as if she had slammed into a wall, and waited expectantly.

"Mrs. Harris . . . hold on just a minute, will you? Just one sec." Resisting the effort to slam the door and hide behind it, she ordered Jessie to stay and slipped the chain free. She stepped onto the porch, pulling the door closed behind her. "Mrs. Harris, this light you saw . . . what time was it when you saw it, do you remember?"

"Well, I can't be absolutely precise, but it was between nine-fifty and ten. I watch *Mystery!* Sunday nights at ten, and I always plan our walks to get home in time for the opening credits, which I enjoy almost as much as the program. Do you like *Mystery!?*"

"I wish I could answer that, Mrs. Harris. Did you see anything else? Or anybody?"

"Yes, but I don't know whether it's connected. When we set out on our walk thirty minutes earlier—which would make it between nine-twenty and nine-thirty, of course—I saw an automobile parked at the curb in front of the Shelbys'? The corner house? That would be four . . . no, three doors down. I only noticed because I know the Shelbys are out of town—visiting their oldest son Julian in Fresno, I believe I heard—and there's been no car at the house since they left, nor should there be, do you know? The car was still there when we passed your house and saw the light inside, and it was still there when Carl came over, but during the intermission of *Mystery!* I looked, and it was gone. Do you think it was connected?"

"Well, I don't . . ." The red, rapidly moving lips were making her dizzy. The grizzled little dog, on the other hand, was utterly still, an occasional blink the only sign that he was alive. She had the brief, mad thought that the two had some kind of reverse ventriloquist act going. She tried to focus. "Do you happen to know what the car was? What make?"

"I'm very much afraid I no longer know one automobile from another. In my day Imperials had fins and Buicks had those little round holes and Studebakers were shaped like a car that was coming and going at the same time, do you know what I mean? But today Cadillacs look like Hyundais or Hondas or whatever they're called. But it was dark gray, and it was a rental. Thrifty. I mean the bumper sticker said THRIFTY; I have no idea, of course, if the rental was economical or not. Do you know who might have been driving it?"

"Mrs. Harris, I'm clueless. Literally." She tried to think what else she should ask, but nothing occurred to her. "But I appreciate your . . . vigilance. If you see anything else out of the ordinary, will you let me know?"

"You can be sure, can't you, that if anything happens I'll see it." Mrs. Harris wiggled her brows in candid admission of her curiosity. "In the interim, you take care of . . . whatever ails you, won't you? Here's your paper."

Relieved of her news and the newspaper, she did an abrupt about-face and started down the porch steps.

At that moment an explosion split the air, short, sharp and shocking as a thunderclap. Mrs. Harris merely flinched, but the woman behind her let out an audible gasp and flattened herself against the door. Mrs. Harris's glance veered from a rust-eaten truck—trailing black smoke and an encore of flatulent pops as it rattled down the street—back to the porch, her blue eyes quizzical and concerned.

"It was just a backfire, my dear. Are you all right?"

"It sounded like . . . I thought it was . . . you know. A gunshot."

Without missing a beat or indicating that she found the reaction in any way peculiar, the little woman said, "You might want to skip the caffeine for a while, my dear. A little ginseng and ziziphus tea, I think, would be just the thing."

She popped the dachshund onto the sidewalk, took hold of his leash and marched away, the umbrella swinging on her arm.

five

All morning Henry had had that little blip on his mental Macintosh.

Too many years in too many newsrooms—print and electronic, from Boston to Los Angeles, with stops memorable and forgettable along the way—had honed the blip to damn-near infallibility. Too many times he'd been foolish enough to ignore it. One time had almost proved fatal.

It had been during a stint at the *Cleveland Plain Dealer,* one of the memorable stops back in his newspaper days. He'd gotten a call from an inept plastic surgeon whose imminent ruin was due mostly to Henry's tenacity. Unaware of the extent of the man's mental deterioration, of his intention to do away with himself and to take someone with him, Henry had agreed to meet the doctor to get his version of the story. All the way to the rendezvous, the mental blip was making like the airport at rush hour. Henry, lured by the prospects of another page-one, above-the-fold byline, had turned down the volume, tuned it out. Fortunately, the doctor was no better with a gun than he was with a scalpel. He'd missed Henry and only succeeded in making himself a permanent vegetable.

There'd been other professional occasions when Henry had regretted ignoring the blip. Like the times when, even after Legal had okayed a story, he'd known a fact ought to be checked one more time and hadn't done it. And there'd been personal occasions, like the morning the blip had nagged him to turn his car around and go back home but, anxious to pin down a source who was sounding itchy, he'd kept going. It wasn't the first time he'd forgotten to turn off a burner. It was, however, the first time he'd left a pan with bacon grease on a burner he'd forgotten to turn off. If his first ex-wife hadn't picked that morning to come by for a snoop, the fire would've been even more serious. And, speaking of Marjorie, there was the time the blip had warned him to watch her actually board the plane to her sister's before he used the pay phone to call Sheila, who later became his second ex-wife. But that was another story.

This time the blip had to do with Ariel Gold.

He didn't know Ariel well—no one did as far as he knew—but he'd talked to too many frightened people on the telephone not to know how that particular emotion resonated down the wires. And Ariel was frightened.

Henry had put the blip on hold until lunchtime—it had been the kind of morning when the alligators were running the swamp—but as he settled in with his egg and onion sandwich, he thought back over the conversation.

The woman hadn't sounded ill; she'd sounded on the verge of hysteria. He'd seen Ariel in some tight spots, and he couldn't remember a time she'd ever lost her cool. He'd never seen her scared of anything. Except maybe life, but that was just his notion. For all he knew, outside this building she could be the last of the red-hot mamas. He grinned at the image that idea evoked. Not likely, he thought. More like Margaret Thatcher without the aplomb and the polished exterior—not to mention the husband.

Henry caught himself. That wasn't accurate. Ariel actually *had* mentioned a husband one time. He remembered being taken aback by the idea of somebody marrying Ariel, and ashamed of being taken aback. She hadn't been explicit and, as usual, her demeanor hadn't invited questions, so he hadn't pursued it. His impression, as he recalled, had been that whatever it was or wasn't, it was past tense.

He massaged his left shoulder blade, the spot that always plagued him after mornings like this one—which was most mornings—and hauled his feet off his desk. He finished the last dill pickle while he looked up her number on his Rolodex. After four rings, the machine picked up, and Ariel's somewhat uninflected, matter-of-fact voice delivered the minimal information women who live alone are advised to divulge.

"You've reached 472-8762. I can't answer the phone just now. Please leave a message at the sound of the tone." Disregarding the request, Henry hung up.

Well, he speculated, she could be at the doctor. If he didn't hear from her by the end of the day, he'd call Personnel and find out where she lived. He shrugged away the discomfitting idea that he might actually be concerned about the woman.

It's the blip, he thought, just that unrelenting, undismissable, bleeding alarm signal.

He wasn't Ariel's keeper, and he was no more a mother hen than was Peacock. Ariel was just an employee. An unusually capable, conscientious employee who, as far as he could remember, had never been late, let alone not showed up at all, let *alone* not even called in, in all the time she'd worked there. It wasn't even that somewhere he felt a little kernel of pity for her. It was just that he didn't have anything to do tonight anyway. The Lakers were off, ex-wife number three had taken their son location scouting somewhere in the desert, and alimony payments had pretty much put him off romance for the moment. He was too old for that, anyway, he thought, rotating his shoulders, trying to ease the tightness.

He'd drop by her house and check out the situation—unless she lived in the Valley. He didn't go to the Valley unless he was being paid for it.

six

She closed the door. Locked it. Leaned against it. Realized that Jessie was still sitting where she'd been left, waiting patiently for further instructions.

"Oh, dog!" She knelt down, dropped the newspaper on the floor and scratched behind the erect ears. "You're *trained!* Lord! You can probably do all kinds of stuff. Well, stay tuned. Seeing as how I'm probably legally blind, I may need you to lead me to the nearest loony bin." She rested her head against the shepherd's, her hand on the muzzle, feeling too lonesome to think, let alone move.

The phone began to ring.

She stumbled up, heard a ripping noise. This gown has got to go, she thought, extricating her legs and starting for the bedroom. Before she could get there—or decide whether to answer the phone once she did—the ringing stopped.

She stood still, heard a slightly tinny voice as an answering machine picked up somewhere in the house.

An answering machine. Everybody had one of the bloody things! Why hadn't she thought of that last time? She listened, decided the voice was coming from the study and went into the room just in time to hear a click and a dial tone. A beep sounded. There was a portable telephone on the desk and next to it was the answering machine, partially hidden by an upside-down wicker in-basket. The machine busily snapped off, then on, and the light flashed on. She set the basket aside and looked at the machine speculatively.

Okay, that was a hang-up, but there might be messages. She rewound the tape. When she pressed play, a pleasant male voice inquired, "Ariel? You there? Guess not. It's Victor and it's, let's see, seven o'clock Sunday night. Missed seeing you yesterday morning. Nothing urgent. Give me a call when you can." The machine stopped. There were no other messages. She let out the breath she was unaware she'd been holding.

Forty-five minutes later, sitting at the kitchen table, she drained the last of her coffee and reexamined each item from Ariel's purse as she replaced it.

Keys. One that looked like a house key, two that were probably car keys and several others, unidentifiable, all on a brass key chain that read—she tilted it slightly and made out the worn engraving—"With thanks for your support. LASPCA." There was an empty eyeglass case. And, of course, the cigarettes and lighter. These she tossed in hurriedly, not liking the sudden urge they inspired. There was a matchbox-sized automatic garage door opener, a grocery store coupon pouch—she smiled as she dropped that back in—and the usual detritus. A packet of tissues. Breath mints. A lipstick (in a yucky shade of pink). A Sports Arena ticket stub from an L.A. Clippers game three nights before. Lint.

The organizer appointment book had been a disappointment. The entries all appeared to be of a personal nature and hardly sinister—a C.P.A. last week, a teeth cleaning two months hence, "game" jotted on the same date as the ticket stub and on a number of other dates past and future, "kennel" written on alternate Saturdays at 7:00 A.M. Those were the only entries. Of course, this was only the third week in February.

The 18th, to be exact. Presidents' Day. The fact that she knew that gave her pause. She wondered just what information her new, unimproved self came equipped with. She knew that she was in Los Angeles and that the local area codes were 213, 310 and 818. She was pretty sure that Hank Aaron was still the all-time home run champ. She'd known that the gun on the bed was a .38 automatic. She knew that Aden was the capital of Yemen, and she could spell *supercalifragilisticexpialidocious*.

Why, there was no end to the things she knew. She could go on *Jeopardy!* But she didn't know who her best friend was. Or if she had one.

She was putting the organizer back into the bag when her fingers brushed a small zippered side pocket she hadn't noticed before. She opened it, reached in and pulled out a mirror, then a metal card case. Inside were a dozen or so business cards that read "Ariel R. Gold. Producer, *The*

26

Open File. Woolf Television, Inc." In smaller print were an address, a telephone number and extension and a fax number.

Good grief. What in blue blazes did a producer do? Produce, presumably. Produce what? For the first time, it sank in that Ariel had a whole life all her own. That she might be bright, accomplished, even successful. Her perspective on the woman shifted; she recognized that she felt somewhat different toward her. She felt what? Respect? A little intimidated? And, whoa, what was that little twinge! Envy?

She sat. She thought. She wondered what in the devil the vague, dark rectangle low on the opposite wall was.

Squinting, she got up to investigate. A doggy door. She grinned at Jessie napping peacefully under the table. Well, at least one mystery was solved. But she was reminded of another, more pressing issue. She was still Mr. Magoo, and the glasses were history. If nothing else, she had to be able to drive a car. Anyone this nearsighted, she felt sure, would probably have a spare pair, but the prospect of searching through the debris was daunting.

She flipped through the address book and jotted the two names designated "doctor" on the memo pad. As she started to the bedroom phone, she noticed a wall phone beside the back door and, in a recessed shelf underneath, a directory. In the white pages she found Boeck, Neil J, MD and Pollock, Victor, DVM. Well, at least she could eliminate the last one, she thought, writing down numbers. She looked at the vet's name again. Victor? The man on the answering machine? she wondered.

She turned to Physicians, Ophthalmology in the yellow pages and saw that the other name was a Diplomate Amer Bd Ophthalmology. She dialed the number.

"Doctors' offices, Boeck, Bowles & Myer, this is Wendy. May I help you?" a cheerful voice inquired.

"Yes, I believe I'm a patient of—I mean, I *am* a patient of Dr. Boeck? I'm, um, Ariel Gold?"

Realizing that she sounded harebrained but soldiering on, she explained that she'd broken her glasses and needed new ones. Could a pair be made up and delivered? she inquired. Fast?

"We're associated with opticians who could help you, certainly," assured the receptionist. "Let me connect you."

The male voice that came on the line was equally confident until he checked his records.

"Oops," he said. "I'm afraid your frames are discontinued. You're going to need to bring in your old ones or come in to choose a different style."

"The frames. Well, the frames are cracked. I sat on them, poor things." She squinted across the kitchen to where the glasses, frames intact, lay. "Look, I can't drive blind, so just pick something similar. Or not. Whatever."

"But that won't do," the optician said, obviously having trouble imagining a woman so lacking in vanity. "You need to see them on. How they work with the shape of your face. Can't you have someone drive you? Or taxi down?"

When she'd finally convinced him that any style was fine, just fine and that, no, she couldn't possibly come in, when she'd given him the data from the Visa card in the wallet and assured him that the $20 delivery fee could be added to the bill, when she'd secured his promise that she'd have the new glasses within twenty-four hours, she hung up feeling sweaty with effort—and reminded of another priority.

Twenty minutes later, she'd scoured the bathtub and pulled a clean towel and washcloth from a linen closet as topsy-turvy as the rest of the house. Firmly locking the bathroom door, she removed the no-nonsense tank watch she'd just noticed she was wearing and ripped off the torn gown. Making certain to look neither at the mirror nor the body, she sank to her shoulders in water as hot as she could stand.

She closed her eyes. She felt like drifting into shriveled oblivion. She forced herself to cold, logical analysis.

The first possibility—she started her mental dialogue with the obvious—*you're crazy.*

But I don't feel crazy.

She sank lower into the water. *Ah, but do crazy people know they're crazy? Well, probably some do, some don't. But I don't want to believe I'm crazy, so I won't. For now.*

She sat up and began to soap herself, trying not to notice how peculiar it felt to wash an unfamiliar body.

Okay, what's the second possibility? Amnesia? I suppose

the facts do support amnesia. I remember general things but not personal things, and isn't that how amnesia works? I could consult a shrink. I must have amnesia.

Oh, come on! She made a wry face. *You conveniently forgot you were fat and homely? And think about this: if you've got amnesia, this is you. All of you. Outside and in. Your face, your body, your cellulite.*

She didn't much like that option, either.

She reached for the shampoo and lathered her head slowly, mulling over other possibilities.

How about possession?

Look here, if you were going to possess somebody, would you choose this body? Well, maybe you don't get a choice. Hmmm, do priests still perform exorcisms, or is that just in the movies?

And if this is possession, wouldn't that would make you a demon? A—what do you call it? A succubus? No, that's not right. That's something sexy. She snorted. This whole train of thought, evoking images of little girls with twirling heads spewing revolting green goop, was too fantastic to consider. But the situation was fantastic.

Steady on, dear.

Okay. What else is there?

Reincarnation.

But somebody has to die for that. She shuddered. I'd *have to have died!*

And the new person, the reborn person, has no memory of its past self. She frowned. *Well, I don't. All I have is a conviction that this isn't me.* And that conviction, she realized, wasn't quite as firm as it had been. She sank below the surface of the water, rinsing her hair.

But, wait a minute here. Back up. When you're reborn, you're a baby. So unless I'm Baby Huey, that's out. She wiped her eyes on the towel. This was getting out of hand.

What else is there? A time machine? A cookie that said "Eat me"? (Except I didn't shrink; I got bigger!) Transmutation? Transmogrification? Were they the same thing? Were they anything? I've got it! A wicked witch put an evil spell on me and the kiss of a handsome prince will turn me back into my beautiful princess self. I like it! And I can always

*use the yellow pages again. Look under Handsome Princes.
Have kiss, will travel.*

The water was cold. She opened the drain and reached
again for the towel. She wrapped the body, obscuring it,
telling it kindly, " 'This world surely is wide enough to hold
both thee and me.' " She searched for a toothbrush, trying
to convince herself that if these were *her* teeth—at least for
now—it was okay to use *her* toothbrush, but she was still
relieved to find a new one in an unopened package.

As she pushed the medicine cabinet door closed, she
glanced in the mirror. The bruise was even more livid on a
clean face. She studied it. She touched the lump just below
the hairline, felt a real goose egg, winced. And absorbed
the implications.

A blow to the head. Concussion. Amnesia.

*Must be. Had to be. Nothing else made any sense
whatsoever.*

Okay, fine.

You're Ariel Gold.

Live with it.

She glared at the reflection, eyes glittering with tears, de-
fying them to fall, losing the battle.

*You, Ariel Gold, are going to fill in all the blank spots.
You're going to find out what kind of person you are and
what kind of stuff you're made of. You're going to learn
everything there is to know about amnesia. You're going to
find out if you've done something wrong or if somebody's
trying to do something to you and, if they are, you're going
to find out who and why, and you're not going to trust anybody until you do.*

Tears made rivulets down her face, mixing with the water
that trickled from her hair.

"And, Ariel," she said aloud, "about this preoccupation
with the way you look? You're going to get over it."

seven

Darkness had come early, and the heavy rain promised by late afternoon's low, ominous clouds now beat a steady tattoo on the windows.

Ariel had put the house back in order, as nearly as she could judge it. Most everything looked right. Seemed right. She felt at home and not at home at the same time, a dichotomy she was too tired to deal with. It mightn't have been logical to go into the eternal, woman-as-nester mode, she supposed, but she hadn't questioned the necessity of doing it.

The bed was changed, the bathroom and kitchen swept and scrubbed, books replaced on shelves, rugs and carpets vacuumed. She'd hung up clothes and refilled drawers and cupboards and thrown away what was beyond repair. Two bulging plastic garbage bags now sat beside the back door.

She'd discovered a broken window in the dining room, where, evidently, the intruder (and a good deal of rain) had come in. In desperation, she'd taped a baking tin over the opening; not only would it keep the rain out, she reasoned, but it would make a bang-up racket if it was dislodged. Then she'd called several residential security companies. She'd answered questions and described her needs, the major one being immediacy. By tomorrow afternoon the company she'd selected would have the house wired, and the locksmith they'd recommended would have repaired the window and checked all the locks. She hoped she had a generous credit limit on her Visa card—or funds she hadn't yet discovered.

In the bedroom she'd found a small, padded box containing jewelry. The jumble of trinkets was modest, but like the three TVs, the expensive-looking VCR and tape deck, the computer and several undisturbed antique pieces, the jewelry was further evidence that the intruder's motive hadn't been theft.

When she could no longer put off tackling the study, she'd forced herself into the room.

Here, fury had reached fever pitch. Flowerpots smashed, plants and wet soil dumped on every surface. A jar of ink emptied over files, the blue-black mess exacerbated by what must have been a full pot of tea. The shattered pot would never hold tea again.

Feeling sick, Ariel had pulled out limp, filthy papers semi-buried beneath the dirt and destruction. Many were too ruined to decipher. Some hadn't looked worth the trouble. One had.

It was a letter, written in a messy, out-of-control hand on what had once been fine lilac stationery. Almost an entire paragraph at the bottom of the page was still legible. It was also vicious. Smoothing the paper gingerly, she'd made out enough to send her heart racing.

". . . accusations are very dangerous," she'd read. "Say any of your filth to anyone else, and I'll make sure you regret it. Everyone will think you're deranged by grief. No one will believe you because you're nobody."

Beneath that, a capital *M* was followed by a lowercase *i* and, a few letters later, what looked like an *l*. The beginning of another sentence—or a signature? Mitchell, possibly, or Michael? Or Michelle. She couldn't tell whether the handwriting was that of a man or a woman, although the lilac paper suggested the latter.

Ariel had sat very still, staring until even the legible words ran together. If there had been a date, it was part of the sodden smear that was the remainder of the page.

With a vengeance born of fear, she'd swept and scooped and scoured, bagging what was unsalvageable. Then she'd begun sorting through the rest.

Most of the papers were innocuous, the sort of records you'd expect to find in anyone's files. Insurance forms. A cable TV bill. Receipts from utility companies. There was a pile of tickets for Clippers basketball games; they were single-seat tickets. There was a partially completed book of acrostic puzzles and a much-worn dog collar with a tag that read MISSY, but there were no more letters, no greeting cards or postcards. There was no evidence of husband or offspring, but there was one photograph—or what was left of it.

It was a framed snapshot, the subject a nice-looking, casually dressed young man of about thirty. His expression was serious, and his arm was around someone. Ariel thought the second person was a woman, but it was impossible to tell. The face had been obliterated by a sharp object, possibly one of the jagged shards of glass she'd found beside the smashed frame.

Shuddering, Ariel had put the photo aside and turned her attention to a batch of computer printouts. Dirty and disheveled, some were double-columned documents headed "Split Slate Script," some seemed to be transcipts of interviews and some were timetables, the paragraphs preceded by sequential time notations—2:00, 2:16, 2:32. All, presumably connected to her work, appeared to relate to news events, most concerning illegal—or at least questionable—activities. Perpetrators, witnesses and victims, scams, abuses and even murders. None had recent dates.

When her stomach had begun to rumble, she'd made a peanut butter sandwich, damning the calories, and taken it into the study.

Leaning back in the desk chair, swiveling and eating, she'd contemplated the printouts. They were an unnerving reminder that she had to think about the immediate future, that she had to reenter the world outside this house. Ariel's world.

The choices, it seemed to her, were limited. She could seek out a doctor, describe her dissociation or whatever it was and hope that therapy of some kind would put her head and body back together and turn this mare's nest into something manageable. But therapy was a long and expensive process. Could she afford it? Did she have insurance that covered mental illness? Henry, with whom or for whom she apparently worked, seemed unaware of the previous night's events. She'd reasoned that unless he was involved and had reason to hide it, whatever had happened, was happening, was probably not job-related. Which would mean workmen's comp didn't come into play. What if she got fired because of her condition? Did she have the means to live without a job? Did she own this house or just rent it? She'd shivered off a sudden vision of herself as a fat, shuffling bag lady, wandering the streets asking people if they happened to know her.

She'd finished her sandwich, licking peanut butter off her palm. All those were practical considerations, certainly, but she knew them for the smoke screens they were. It wasn't destitution she feared.

It was what she didn't know.

Ariel didn't know if someone was out to hurt her. If such a someone existed, she didn't know who—or why. She didn't know whom to trust, whom to suspect. Clearly, there'd been an intruder. He'd been after something general or specific and he'd been angry.

She'd swiveled in a wider arc. What about the possibility of her own guilt? What if she'd stolen something that couldn't be legally reclaimed? What if she'd been blackmailing somebody? Or harmed somebody? Your average producer-next-door surely didn't pack a .38. Or come home bloodied. Until she knew more, she'd decided, the police were not an option.

But fear of punishment wasn't the issue any more than fear of impoverishment—or even bodily harm. (Well, not altogether.) What really made her insides feel as if she were on a plummeting elevator was her utter vulnerability. If she admitted her circumstances to anyone—doctor, lawyer, police or employers—she would, in effect, relinquish control. She'd be placing herself, her fate, in someone else's hands, and that she'd resist with all her soul. She didn't know why that concept frightened her out of her wits, but she knew it did.

So, she'd play out the hand. She'd talk to people and keep looking for answers and go to work. In a job she knew zilch about. She didn't imagine that she could keep up the subterfuge long—maybe about an hour if she was lucky— but she'd give it a shot. Besides, didn't amnesia wear off by itself sooner or later? Wasn't that how it worked in movies? Maybe she had the short-term kind. She'd wake up tomorrow and her memory would be back where it belonged.

She'd know how to "produce." And how to work a computer.

Ariel had eyed the word processor looming menacingly from its tiered caddy. She'd found the manual in a drawer. Paged through. Clearly, it had been written by a sociopath, a diabolical alien to whom English was a second language at best.

"A full pathname includes the drive, root and any subdirectory names," she'd read. "The subject search is a preselected character or characters used to find the subject of a document. Should the characters in the subject search text exist in the first 400 bytes of a document, the word or phrase following the characters up to a hard return is inserted as the Subject/Account heading in the document summary." Say *what?* Maybe, in addition to everything else, she had dyslexia.

Why couldn't she have been a grocery store checker or an Avon saleswoman? Something nice and simple she could bluff her way through. But a television producer? Who dealt with criminals and politicians and electronic equipment? Hands-on?

Hands . . . ? She'd looked at hers. Replaced the book and slammed the drawer closed. Just maybe . . .

She'd trotted to the bathroom, opening and closing the newly organized cabinets until she'd found what she was looking for. The Ace bandage had been used at some time and rewound into a neat, flesh-colored ball. She'd unhooked the little metal clip that secured it and unwound a foot or two, thinking furiously. People with a broken hand—well, okay, a sprained hand—couldn't use a computer. Or write. How long did it take a sprain, a *bad* sprain, to heal? She had no idea what Ariel did in the course of a day, but surely this would buy some time. She had put the ball of bandage on the counter, patted it in a friendly way and returned to the study feeling considerably better.

She'd found three looseleaf notebooks. They were filled with clear sleeves that contained newspaper articles, each dated by hand. The dates were at least two years in the past. The bylines were all hers. She'd begun by skimming, trying to get a feel for the author. "In every man's writings, the character of the writer must lie recorded," she'd quoted to herself, turning the pages curiously. Then she'd found herself slowing to read more carefully.

The writing was very good, very professional. As she'd read, a confusion of emotions stirred. Admiration. Wonder. Pride. I wrote these, Ariel had told herself. I'm *good!* But the emotions she'd experienced were a frame out of sync— once removed, as it were. She'd felt as she imagined a parent might on seeing the successful efforts of her child.

When she'd shelved the last notebook alongside other books rescued from the floor, she'd looked around, assessing what remained to be done. What she hadn't yet gone through, she'd decided, would wait until tomorrow.

She'd turned her attention to the cassettes. Scattered helter-skelter, their tapes pulled out and snarled like shiny brown fettuccini, they'd looked hopeless. Their labels, names and captions, like "Budget Amendment Takeout," were meaningless to her. The tape recorder she'd found in her purse had been no more helpful; there'd been a cassette inside, but it had proved to be blank. Finally, exhausted, dirty again and largely unenlightened, she'd emptied a shoebox from the bedroom closet and dropped all the tapes inside.

She'd showered, put on a clean velour caftan (an Omar the Tentmaker original, she'd scolded herself for thinking) and built a fire from a supply of logs by the fireplace. Now she lay on the sofa, watching the flames reflected in the blackness of the living room window. She sipped wine, a good Cabernet, from a rack she'd found undisturbed in the dining room.

Ariel was surprised to discover that, at least for the moment and against all odds, she felt something like content. The rain pelting the window was reassuring, creating an illusion of security. The gun on the coffee table was even more reassuring. Thoughtfully, she fingered the bright afghan draped over the sofa. It was lovely, she mused, granny squares on a black background. The whole house was lovely when it didn't look like a victim of blitzkrieg.

Built in the thirties, she guessed, the house had thick, plaster walls with rounded angles, arched doorways, recessed bookcases and wall niches, coved ceilings and hardwood floors—all the charming architectural features indigenous to Los Angeles homes, even modest ones, of that decade. While it had been remodeled—relatively recently, Ariel judged—the renovations had been appropriate, enhancements rather than incongruities. Some of the windows were the original, crank-out casements, but several had been expanded to floor-to-ceiling windows arched at the top. With these and the skylight cut into the kitchen ceiling, the house had been relatively bright even on the gray day now ended.

The bedroom was unusually large, leading Ariel to believe it might be the consolidation of two small bedrooms, the practical alteration of a woman who didn't expect to need a guest room.

The appliances were state-of-the-art, the range an AGA, built-in, and the refrigerator a matching stainless-steel colossus that would be right at home in a haute cuisine restaurant.

It was apparent that a sizeable sum of money had been spent, Ariel thought, by someone to whom "home" was an important place.

She gazed around the softly lighted living room. The absence of pictures, she mused, was odd. Other than the mutilated photograph, she'd seen only one in the house, a simply framed, candid snapshot of a dog—not Jessie—in the bedroom.

She pulled the afghan over her legs and reached for a less attractive but equally practical security blanket: the Ace bandage. Awkwardly, she experimented with winding her right hand. After several rather comical, lumpy tries, she held up her hand to gauge the effect.

The doorbell chime brought her upright. Almost before the echo died, the dog door flapped noisily, and Jessie came barking into the room, water slinging off her coat.

Moving in jerks, Ariel tipped over the wineglass, caught it as a few drops spattered the table, grabbed the gun. She joined the dog at the door and put her eye to the peephole. In a pool of yellow from the porch light stood Mrs. Harris, a wizened Mary Poppins under the huge umbrella. She still wore the yellow slicker but tonight she also wore matching Wellingtons, and she held not the dachshund but a cabbage.

Ariel slipped the gun into her pocket, ordered Jessie to sit and unlocked the door. She opened it to an aroma so tantalizing she almost floated on it like a rapturous cartoon character. It seemed to be coming from the cabbage.

"I was of two minds about intruding on you twice in one day," Mrs. Harris began without preamble, "but you really did look alarming this morning, and when I was putting away this cassoulet I made for dinner, I thought about you and wondered if you were eating right, do you know?" She proffered what was, in fact, a tureen cleverly disguised as a cabbage, and from a vent in its lid of green ceramic leaves, fragrant steam escaped. "Now I'm glad I decided to come, as it seems you've hurt your hand, too. How?"

Ariel felt the laughter bubbling up, threatening to boil over. She didn't know if it was relief at finding no one more dangerous than little Mrs. Harris at her door, if it was the woman's stop-on-a-dime conversational style or if she was just giddy with hunger, but she couldn't stop. The harder she tried to screw her face into a serious, appropriate expression, the more the giggles hiccuped out like a percolator gone berserk. Helpless with laughter, she leaned against the doorjamb, clutching her middle.

Finally, she was able to catch her breath. "Oh, Mrs. Harris," she began, "I'm so sorry! Please ..." The cabbage set her off again. "Oh, please, won't you come in," she gasped between convulsions, "and get out of the rain?"

Perhaps Mrs. Harris had worked in a lunatic asylum. Perhaps she and her ceramic cabbage made frequent appearances and often evoked such reactions. She stood with perfect equanimity, a pleasant expression on her face, waiting for the fits to subside. After an eon, they did.

"Thank you, Ms. Gold, but Carl's waiting and, as you know, *The Open File* comes on at seven-thirty. We often watch it. It isn't at all like those exploitation shows that pander to the lowest elements, is it? In my opinion, they're the electronic equivalent of the tabloids at checkout counters. 'Woman Marries 200-pound Man Who Turns Out to Be Transvestite Father.' That sort of thing, do you know? But *The Open File* is, for the most part, worthwhile. It must be difficult these days to avoid the temptation of sensationalism. Is it?"

"Beg pardon?"

"Is it difficult?"

Before Ariel could frame a reply, she was blinded by the sudden bright beam of headlights. A car, being driven too fast, pulled into her driveway, then braked abruptly. Almost before forward motion was arrested, the door was thrown open. A man leaped out. Bent over, he ran toward the women on the porch.

The man gained the steps. He was five feet away, moving fast. His face was hidden by a hat, one hand hidden inside his coat. The hand came out. It was holding something small, round, metallic. Grenade, screamed a voice in Ariel's mind. She heard an actual scream. Something very large and very fast shot past her from behind. Simultaneously, she heard a loud "whumpf" of impact, a yelp from Mrs. Harris and a crash as the porch light went out. There was another scream. Since the dog had made no sound whatever, and the man who now lay pinned beneath her was too terrified to utter, Ariel thought it must have been herself who'd screamed. For an endless second they were a tableau, frozen in darkness except for what little light escaped through the open front door. Then Ariel came to life. She plunged her hand into the caftan and closed her fingers around the gun. It caught in the fabric of the deep pocket. She pointed the gun through the cloth.

"Jessie, off!" she shouted, stepping away from Mrs. Harris to give herself clear aim. Frantically, Ariel's churning brain tried to process information. Should she shoot? What if she *had* seen a grenade? The man's hands were empty, one held motionless between Jessie's teeth, the other desperately protecting his face. Where was the grenade? Had he had time to pull the pin? Should she run? What about the other woman? Her eyes flew from shadow to light, straining, searching.

Something was rolling across the porch. She tore her hand from her pocket, reached for the grenade, tensed to throw it as far as she could. Confusion flashed through her mind in the instant her hand made contact with the cylinder.

Throw it! Throw it! Every instinct shrieked the order as her intellect countermanded it. She held the object, transfixed. It wasn't the right shape. It wasn't waffled. It wasn't a grenade.

It was a can of soup.

Dumb with shock and leftover adrenaline, Ariel turned back to see that Jessie hadn't moved. The shepherd was silent, her muscles tensed, her attention focused on the man beneath her. No more than a few seconds had passed, Ariel realized, since he'd reached the steps. It seemed like an eternity.

"Jessie, off!" she commanded again. The dog remained motionless. "Back, Jessie. Stop!" No effect. "Jessie, no! Cease!" The dog dropped the man's arm, stepped off him and backed to Ariel's side, where she stood panting. Ariel whispered, "Sit! Stay!" She watched the man. He didn't move. Had he had a heart attack? Oh, God, was he dead?

She walked slowly to his side, holding the can of soup to her chest, her hand actually feeling her heart lurching with dread. He lay on the ground beyond the steps. Perfectly still, his eyes closed, his hat upside down near his head. His face, wet with rain and getting wetter by the second, was long, thin to the point of gauntness and bearded—a short, kinky beard. His eyebrows were well-defined and dark, and his eyes, deep-set, were pouched. His hair was thinning, dark brown and, like the beard, gray-flecked. To the best of her knowledge, she'd never seen the man before.

She felt a presence. Mrs. Harris, still clutching the tureen, stood beside her. They looked at each other, looked down at the man. He opened one dark brown eye. It peered at Ariel. "A simple 'I don't care for canned soup' would have sufficed." The eye, blinking against the rain, veered to Mrs. Harris. "How do you do? Is that a cabbage you're holding?" He opened the other eye. "I don't believe I've had the pleasure. I'm Henry Heller. You'll forgive me if I don't stand up? I believe I've done something unfortunate to my sacroiliac." Nothing moved but his eyes. They darted left, then right. "Where's Cujo?"

"How do you do, Mr. Heller?" Mrs. Harris stretched her neck to look down at him over her tureen. "I recognize your name from *The Open File* credits. Supervising producer, isn't it? I'm Marguerite Harris, Ms. Gold's neighbor. I would help you up but I have my hands full, and I wonder whether you should try to move. Should you?"

He considered her question politely. "As much as I like it here, I think I will just struggle up and mosey along. Where'd you say the dog was?"

Ariel, shaky with relief, said, "Jessie's on a sit-stay, Mr., er, Henry. She won't hurt you. Did she hurt you?" She extended her right hand to help him up, saw the bandage, put the hand in her pocket. She held out her left hand, saw the soup can, put it into her other pocket. "Were you serious about your sacroiliac? Should I call 911?"

Henry propped himself on his hand, got his feet under him and, wincing, pushed himself up. He was quite tall. "Don't worry, Ariel, I won't sue. I also won't bring you chicken soup again." He reached down to retrieve his hat, winced again and put his hand on his lower back, massaging it gingerly. "Maybe I'll call next time before I drop by." He put on his hat, pouring a cascade of water down his face. He closed his eyes.

"Please, let me . . ." Ariel held out her hand helplessly. "Look, you can't go around all soaked like that. At least, come in and dry off a little." She turned to Mrs. Harris. "You too. Please. Let's don't stand here in the rain. Come in and have some coffee or a drink or something."

"Thank you, no; I can still catch some of your program. Although," Mrs. Harris allowed, her eyes twinkling, "you'll forgive me if I say that this has been a great deal more interesting." She handed Ariel the tureen. "You'll need to warm it up, I imagine. Don't worry about the bowl. I've never liked the thing, and I'm in no hurry to get it back. It was a gift, do you know? From a friend. A rather eccentric friend." Her red lips twitched almost imperceptibly as she nodded to Ariel, shook Henry's hand firmly and took herself off.

Henry watched her go, grinning. "Sharp little bird. Friend of yours?" He turned back to Ariel, who stood hugging the tureen. "You said something about a drink?" He started toward the porch. Jessie tensed. He stopped. "After you," he suggested.

Ariel, who wouldn't have invited him in had she not been sure Mrs. Harris's nosiness would've compelled her to stay as well, preceded him. "Come," she instructed Jessie as she passed her.

"Would you mind closing the door?" She ducked her head, her hair partially obscuring her face. This man might be accustomed to her looks, but she wasn't. Even in the kind glow of the single lamp and the firelight, she felt exposed, like someone who'd undergone a botched cosmetic surgery facing the world for the first time. She gestured with the bowl. "I'll just go put this in the kitchen and get you a towel."

She wanted her hands free. She wanted to be able to reach the gun, unimpeded. She wanted a few seconds alone to regroup.

"Uh, Ariel . . ." Henry stood uncertainly inside the door. He took off his hat, carefully pointed to Jessie with it. "Are you sure . . . ?"

"Jessie, down." The dog slumped to her belly, watching Henry. "Stay," Ariel commanded. "She's fine, really." She smiled at Henry. I'm pretty sure, she thought to herself.

She put the bowl away and went to the linen closet in the hallway. As she pulled a towel from the stack she'd arranged earlier, she realized that she felt no threat from the man in her living room; he seemed as harmless as Mrs. Harris. He looked . . . gentle. Careful, she cautioned herself, drying her face and hair, for all you know, you might be the world's worst judge of character. But she kept seeing Henry dumping water on his head with his funny fedora, and she just couldn't muster up any sense of danger. She might even be able to talk to him, to tell him . . . Nope! "Too much doubt is better than too much credulity," she warned herself and shivered. She felt enough doubt that, while she wanted very much to get out of the soggy caftan, she wasn't going to change clothes with him in the house.

She heard his voice from the living room, saying something unintelligible. "Just a sec," she called out. She draped the towel around her neck, pulled two more from the stack and hurried to the bedroom closet, where she put on the coat she'd worn that morning.

She found Henry standing where she'd left him, eyeing the puddle collecting around his feet. He held his coat and hat away from his body and, without the coat, seemed even taller. Ariel squinted, trying to bring him more clearly into focus. He was, she could see, thin, lanky, uncoordinated-looking. Ichabod Crane popped into her mind. "I said," he repeated, "you've got a nice place here. Cozy. Where can I put these things? They're pretty wet."

"Oh, just . . . over there." She motioned toward a coat rack. Averting her face, she handed him a towel and knelt, drying the dog with her left hand.

Henry hung up his things and wiped his face. "Didn't you want to change clothes?" he asked.

"No problem. I will in a minute." She didn't look up.

"Suit yourself. But for a person who's already sick, that's not too smart, is it?" He dropped the towel to the floor and stomped on it in an ineffectual effort to sop up the puddle. "About that toddy . . . ?"

"Oh, right. Sit down and I'll get it." She couldn't remember where she'd seen liquor during her housecleaning. She gave Jessie a last swipe and started toward the kitchen. Remembered. Made a U-turn to the dining room. "What would you like?" She opened the door to the sideboard. "I've got, um, Scotch and vodka and . . ." She frowned at a label. "Slivovitz?"

"Scotch. Straight."

When Ariel came back into the room, remembering to carry the drink in her left hand, Henry was standing with his back to the fireplace, his expression thoughtful. She gave him a quick, awkward smile, inclining her head slightly. He looked startled.

They started to talk at the same time.

"Do you mind if I ask . . ."

"Hey, what happened to your . . ."

"You first." She sat on the sofa, indicating the chair opposite. She pulled the coat around her, covering as much of her body as possible.

"I was just going to ask, what'd you do to your hand?"

Her heart skipped a beat. Here goes, she thought.

"I think I sprained it. Or maybe broke it. I'm not sure."

She smoothed the fabric of the coat with her bandaged hand, conspicuously, showcasing it. "That's why I wasn't at work. But I couldn't get an appointment with a doctor today, not until tomorrow, so I probably won't be in again. It depends . . ." she trailed off.

"I thought you said you had something contagious?"

"Contagious?" She tried to remember what she'd told him on the phone. "Oh, no. I said . . . 'outrageous.' Something outrageous." She leaned to pick up her glass, pushed her hair back nervously.

"Something outra . . . ?" He got a look at her face for the first time. "And look at you! Ariel, what have you . . . ?" His eyes widened. He started to laugh, pointing his finger accusingly.

"You did it, didn't you?" he marveled. "I don't believe it! It's karate, isn't it? You took up karate like you said you were going to!"

"Karate?" She touched her cheek, blinked.

"When we did that story about the little old lady who broke the mugger's nose with a karate chop and—how'd you put it?—'seriously compromised his ability to reproduce' with a swift kick to the *cojones*. You were impressed as all get-out, and you said if she could do it, so could you! Tell me you took up karate!" He slapped his knee, looking relieved. "That's why you've been acting so . . . bashful. So chagrined. You weren't being coy, you're embarrassed!" He grinned. "With your tenacity, you're probably a brown belt by now! Hey, what'd the other guy look like?"

The image of herself, stuffed into a . . . smock or whatever they called them . . . waddling around a mat, horrified her. And the fact that he was probably imagining the same thing and enjoying himself hugely made her furious. She felt her face flood with color as her back went ramrod-straight.

"Let me ask you something, my friend. Henry. Just what were you doing whipping your car into my driveway like Fireball Roberts? Running at us like some kind of terrorist? And what were you going to do with that—with this?" She groped in her pocket for the soup, slammed it down on the table.

Henry's grin faded. "Good God!" he said. "You act like

44

some kind of lunatic, screeching and letting loose the hound of the Baskervilles on me, and you're questioning *my* behavior? What in blazes has my driving got to do with anything? I drive fast, I get where I'm going faster. I get a ticket, I pay for it. And I have never, not once, not ever, had an accident. Why was I running? I was running because it was raining and, having sense—unlike some people I could mention—I wanted to get in out of it!"

He picked up his drink and put it back down, breathing heavily. "And what do you mean, 'What was I going to do with the soup?' I was going to give it to you, because that's what you do when people get sick. You said you were sick? I brought you chicken soup! With matzo balls yet!"

"Oh." A pause. "I see." Ariel smiled feebly. " 'No good deed goes unpunished.' "

"What? What in the name of . . . What'd you think I was going to do with a can of Manischewitz? Throw it at you?"

She looked at her lap, muttered something.

"What?" he barked. "Speak up."

She raised her head, looked away. "I said, I thought it was a grenade." The words were barely audible.

"You thought . . ." He palmed his beard, rubbed it hard, dumbstruck. His eyes narrowed. "It's the glasses. That's why you look different! You're not wearing glasses."

"They're broken." She raised her voice. "And don't start about the karate again!"

"And you're not smoking," he continued, not hearing. "Since when don't you smoke?"

"Since I hurt my head. It makes me dizzy. And right now," she vamped, worried by the turn this conversation was taking, "I'm dizzy with hunger, and I think I'd better eat something and get to bed early." She rose. "But do finish your drink before you go."

"Well"—he raised his eyebrows in mock umbrage and set his half-finished drink on the table—"that was pointed enough even for me. But, Ariel." His expression turned serious. "When you get your hand checked, have the doc take a look at your head, too. Those are nasty-looking bruises, and you've been acting a little . . ." He waved his hand, palm down.

"I reckon I could have thought of that all by myself." She gave him a sarcastic look as she retrieved his hat and coat. "And I'm aware that I might have reacted a little . . . strongly before." She was glad Henry had no idea how close he'd been to getting pumped full of lead. And she was also glad he'd supplied her with an excuse for memory lapses. But she had to admit that grenade business worried her. "I can't imagine why it ever came into my mind that the, um, soup was, you know . . ."

"Oh, that's easy, now that I think about it." Henry took his things. "The drive-by bomber."

"Ummm," noncommittally. Explain, she begged silently. Don't make me ask.

"You do a story on some psycho who goes around throwing Molotov cocktails out his car window, see the damage he did to those bystanders over and over while you're editing, you get a little schizo yourself. But . . . you still get your head checked, you hear?"

After exaggeratedly checking inside the crown, Henry put on his hat and started out the door. He noticed the shattered porch light. "The soup can do that?" He tsk-tsked gravely. "Those Manischewitz missiles are pretty dangerous, aren't they? Say good night to Cujo and call me when you've talked to the doctor."

Ariel watched his car back out of the driveway, too fast, and went thoughtfully to the kitchen. Too tired to warm up the cassoulet or even put it on a plate, she stood at the counter, still wearing the coat, and ate from the tureen.

Could she have remembered a story she'd worked on? she puzzled. Afraid (with good reason), disoriented (with even better reason) and worried about an intruder returning, could her unconscious mind have caused her to flash onto a "drive-by bomber" she'd done a story about? Maybe danger, or what her mind perceived as danger, had stimulated the memory?

After double-checking all the locks, she called Jessie and prepared for bed. She was about to turn off the light, when she remembered the gun. She found the wet caftan in the bathroom and took the gun from the pocket. Back in bed, she turned out the light and tried to turn off her thoughts.

Suddenly, she switched the light back on. She grabbed the gun and opened the chamber.

It was empty. Cursing herself for a total, unmitigated, inept moron, she ran around in circles looking for ammunition, realized she hadn't seen anything that looked like an ammunition box during the day, tried to think of any drawers or cabinets she hadn't been into. Ten minutes later, she found a tin containing cleaning apparatus and ammunition in the back of the study file drawer—the files she'd put off "until tomorrow." Well, Scarlett, she thought, that'll teach you. Tomorrow may be another day, but let's live to see it!

When she turned out the light for the last time, the gun was on the bedside table. And it was loaded.

eight

Henry sat at the stoplight at Westwood and Olympic Boulevards. The windshield wipers slapped back and forth, blurring his view. Got to get those replaced if this rain keeps up, he thought, his fingers tapping the steering wheel impatiently. He raised his shoulders, held them stiffly, let them drop. He stared at the traffic light, assessing the state of his mental sonar.

His blip wasn't at full pitch, but it was still sending signals. Questions clambered over one another in his head, and he didn't have answers for any of them. Not good answers, anyway.

The light changed, and he stepped on the gas. That bump on Ariel's head could account for a lot of odd behavior, he guessed. Like forgetting how to call her dog off. He'd seen his life passing before his eyes until she'd finally remembered the right command. But, he conceded, that could have been the excitement of the moment; if you weren't used to your dog trying to eat people, maybe you'd panic. Of course, he still wasn't sure why she'd sicced the dog on him in the first place. Could his actions have seemed that threatening?

He fingered his beard. Well, maybe to a real nervous Nellie. Which she'd certainly never shown any signs of being.

He turned on KNX. There was a sig alert on the 10 Freeway east, a big rig overturned on the 405 south, and the weatherman was calling for more rain tomorrow. Amazing for L.A., where the only sure thing about weather is that there isn't much of it. He flicked the switch to Off.

It was possible, he supposed, that he'd made Ariel uncomfortable showing up at her house unannounced—he'd never been there before, with or without an announcement or invitation. They weren't exactly chums. And her mannerisms had definitely been different. The way she'd kept her face turned away, kind of letting her hair fall over it, peeking at him from under her eyelashes. What was all that about? There'd been a time or two when he'd actually thought she was ... well, coming on. He felt his ears flame. Yeah, old God's gift, Henry Heller. He could read people pretty well, even women occasionally, and it was crystal clear he'd misread that one by a mile. Besides, he was old enough to be her father. Well, her uncle.

He pulled into the intersection at Olympic and Beverly Drive, waiting to make a left turn behind an indecisive old Plymouth spewing exhaust fumes. Which reminded him of an interesting suicide story he'd read about that morning. He made a note on the pad affixed to his windshield, blew his horn and gunned his car through when the Plymouth finally moved on yellow.

Like a dog worrying a bone, his mind returned to Ariel. It was possible that she was just embarrassed about the karate; she'd gotten pretty hot when he'd teased her. She'd also never said that's how she hurt herself, he realized. Which brought him back to the fear factor. Maybe somebody else hurt her. Although it seemed unlikely, maybe it was some kind of domestic thing. In which case he wanted no part of it. He'd heard too many stories about women who screamed bloody murder until somebody tried to get between them and their abusers.

He noticed his low-gas warning light, wondered how long it had been on, seemed to remember seeing it blinking that morning. Pulling into a gas station, he put his credit card into the slot on the pump and stared, unseeing, at the electronic instructions.

There was something about her voice. He couldn't put his finger on it, but there had been a cadence, some quality of intonation, that wasn't right. It was Ariel's voice, but it wasn't. What had she said that bothered him? Some idiomatic thing? He couldn't remember.

He unscrewed the gas cap and pushed in the hose. His glance wandered from the rain dripping off the shelter above the pumps to the lighted booth a few feet away. Inside, a swarthy young cashier sat watching television—probably some rock video, Henry guessed. Now, that's a job I can do when I retire, he thought, on the night shift. You don't have to pump gas, wash windshields or even process credit cards anymore. No sweat, no deadlines, no aching shoulder. Except, he thought glumly, I'd have to pretend I didn't speak English. He was ashamed of the thought but, brother! Did he miss the days when you could actually drive up to a station and ask directions. And get an answer. And understand it. He couldn't fault anybody who was willing to work but, dammit, there were so many American kids who couldn't find jobs! He wondered whether this guy had a green card. Or a visa that was still good. From what they were finding out with the story on expired visas, the INS . . .

Now, that was the damnedest thing, and he hadn't even thought of it before. Ariel hadn't mentioned one thing about work, about the visa story she'd been working on or anything else. Here was a woman who lived and breathed her job—who, he suspected, had little life outside her job—and she hadn't even questioned what she'd missed today.

Henry replaced the hose and looked back at the booth. He was hungry. The bacon-double cheeseburger he'd picked up after work seemed like a long time ago. He went up to the window and asked for a bag of pork skins—and grinned ruefully when the young man told him, in clearly understandable English, that they didn't have any and inquired whether he'd like something else. He bought garlic-flavored chips and, making amends to his conscience, asked the kid what he was watching.

"There's this really great documentary on KCET with Bill

Moyers about healing and how the mind can control it." The answer was eager, friendly. "This stuff is really amazing!"

"Right," Henry said, rubbing his beard. "Keep the change."

About two blocks away, just about the time he'd gotten up to forty in a twenty-mile-an-hour zone, Henry noticed a black-and-white behind him. He sighed and slowed as the lights began flashing in his rearview mirror.

nine

The room was completely white. Sheets shrouded everything. White sheets reflecting white lights. The lights were shining into her eyes, blinding her. They were intensely bright, dazzling, yet they threw no shadows. There was a coffin in the room. The perspective was such that it seemed to be miles away, yet she could see every detail clearly. It, too, was white, outside and in. Resting on the white satin lining was a body under a white veil. She couldn't make out anything about the corpse, just protrusions where the nose, chin and hands would be. She could smell the white lilies banked all around the coffin. Hundreds of them. Their fragrance was cloying, smothering, nauseating.

Someone was crying, distantly, softly. The sound was heartbreaking, and unutterably lonely. She could feel the loneliness deep in her own body. An almost tangible ache, older than time. The weeping voice grew fainter, thinner, more despairing. It was the voice of a very young child who's lost all hope of being comforted. It raised goose bumps on her arms.

Someone was talking to her. Someone close. Coaxing her. Trying to draw her attention away from the coffin and the crying child. "Beautiful," the voice murmured. "Very good." This was a man's voice. Persuasive. Hypnotic. It was punctuated by an insistent clicking noise. Over and over. The clicking was rapid-fire. "Turn toward me," the voice encouraged. "Here. Look at me. Good, good." The voice came nearer.

She felt a hand on her cheek. The clicking was faster, like an alarm clock at impossible speed. The hand tapped her cheek. The voice grew demanding, insidious. The tapping grew harder. The clicking was the sound of the hand tapping her cheek. Slapping her cheek. Light, stinging slaps. Her cheek hurt. Her head hurt. She couldn't turn her face away, couldn't move, couldn't escape the pain. The clicking grew louder. Faster. The bright, white lights exploded into a kaleidoscope that was both fractured brilliance and violent, earth-shaking sound.

Ariel jolted into consciousness, already halfway off the bed. It was very dark. She could see nothing, but her hearing was acute, every sound amplified. She could almost see the sounds. The blood pumping in her ears. The air rushing in and out of her lungs. And a low, steady growling, very near, which made the hair on her neck stand up. She heard a clicking sound. Erratic. Faint. Real.

She froze. Her ears strained to make sense of the clicks—which weren't there anymore. She heard the distant rumble of thunder. The "clink-clink-clink" of rain dripping off the eaves outside the window. Was that what she'd heard? Her eyes, adjusting to the darkness, could make out the two points of Jessie's ears. Erect. The dog lay between Ariel and the bedroom door, growling low in her throat. She came to her feet just as Ariel stood. Jessie was immobile for a moment, then began to move toward the door.

"Jessie," Ariel hissed, "stay." She groped on the table beside her, found the gun. She moved soundlessly to the dog's side. They both listened, every muscle taut.

There was a brief rattling, then silence.

Where had that come from? The gate to the backyard? That would be . . . a few yards beyond the bedroom window, she estimated. She could see nothing through the draperies. She started toward the window. Stopped. How secure was the gate? She closed her eyes, tried to picture it from her panicked early-morning flight. It was sturdy. It was high. It had stopped her, certainly. Padlocked! It had been padlocked from inside.

Ariel took a step backward. How long would it take her to get to the telephone, to dial 911, to give her address.

Oh, God! She couldn't remember the address! She stood uncertainly, listening. Could they trace emergency calls? How long would that take? She went to the bedside table, lifted the receiver, strained to see the numbers in the darkness. Putting the gun back on the table, within easy reach, she punched in the three digits.

"911, emergency operator 42," a clipped voice answered. "What is your—"

"My name is . . ." Ariel broke in. Faltered. For an interminable moment her mind was a void, white noise, a space devoid of all information. She didn't hear the urgent questions coming from the telephone. She heard the explosion from the dream, saw again the blast of light, the consuming brilliance. She heard herself whisper a name. "Ariel Gold. My name is Ariel Gold. I think someone's trying to break into my house."

"What is your address?" The voice was calm, matter-of-fact.

"Please, I don't know the address!" The rattling sound came again, from somewhere else.

"What is your telephone number?"

"Telephone number?" Ariel repeated stupidly. She looked down at the phone base. "It's here!" She leaned close to see the number, quickly read it into the phone. Out of the corner of her eye, she saw Jessie starting through the open bedroom door.

"Jessie, no," she whispered. "Stay!" The dog hesitated.

"Is your address 11742 Denair—"

There was another sound—from the direction of the living room, Ariel was almost sure. He was coming in, and help was too far away. "I've got to get out of the house," she whispered, overriding the voice. "I can hide outside!"

She dropped the receiver to the bed, picked up the gun and inched toward the door. She could hear the tinny voice, muffled but insistent, coming from the telephone. She looked into the hallway. Empty. Twenty-five, maybe thirty feet, she calculated. Hissing "Come," she ran to the kitchen.

In the faint light from the window, she could just see the locks on the back door. She jiggled the top one desperately, trying to undo it with one hand. Impossible. There was a splintering noise from the direction of the living room. She carefully placed the gun on the rangetop beside her, her elbow bumping a kettle on the burner closest to her. The clatter seemed deafening. She grabbed the pot with both hands, stilled it, held her breath. The dog was motionless at her side, attention riveted on the doorway to the hall.

Ariel heard the front door open.

From where she was, two rooms away, she couldn't see the dark shape that paused just inside the threshold, listening. The silence was broken only by the steady tick of a clock somewhere in the shadows.

Ariel slowly released the kettle. Touched Jessie's head to keep her still. She listened for a second and then, cautiously, tried the top lock again. It clicked open. She stopped, waited, her ears prickling. Lord! Why couldn't the security company have come today? Yesterday. Whenever it was. Her hands moved to the other lock. Intense white light flashed through the kitchen window, immediately followed by a crash of thunder. She gasped, jerking involuntarily, knocking the gun to the floor, hearing it skid under the table. She turned.

Someone stood in the hall doorway. The figure dropped into a crouch, a wrestler's stance, arms curved upward. Lightning flashed again. In that second of illumination, she saw that the figure was a man, a large man. She squinted to bring him into focus. She saw something in his right hand. She saw his dark face, his mouth opening in a silent scream as Jessie hit his body full force.

He went down hard, his head slamming against something solid as he hit the floor. She heard a grunt, a "whoosh," as air was forced from his lungs. He lay still.

Ariel fell to her knees, her hands frantically raking the floor under the table. She felt the gun, seized it and pointed it at the inert body. "Cease, Jessie," she whispered.

The dog released her hold on the man's hand and stepped away, staggering slightly.

Keeping the gun trained on the man, Ariel backed toward the wall, fumbling behind her for the phone. Just as she lifted the receiver, she heard a whimper. She glanced away from the man, saw the dog lying on the floor, her head raised, her stomach bloodied.

"Jessie!" she cried. She'd half-turned, unthinking, bending toward the dog, when she heard movement. She spun toward the sound. Something seized her ankle. Off-balance, she fell backward heavily, her leg twisting under her. Jolts of white-hot pain shot first through her ankle and then her left hand as it slammed against the rangetop. The telephone went flying into the air. She saw, or sensed, Jessie trying to rise. Failing.

The man loomed over her. The weak light from the window reflected off the knife in his hand. He reached for the gun she still managed to grip. She fired.

The explosion in the enclosed space was a physical blow. Blood in impossible quantities seemed to erupt from the man's head. He reeled back slightly, then fell forward onto her. Blinded, her ears ringing, the weight of the man suffocating her, she tried to push herself up with her left hand. She screamed with pain. Using every ounce of strength she possessed, adrenaline pumping, she shifted the man's weight. She was panting like a woman in labor, whimpering. She tried to stand. Cried out in pain as her ankle gave. On her knees, she reached for the light switch by the door and flicked it on.

The man lay still. There was blood on the back on his head, and blood pooled on the floor under him. She crawled toward him. Grunting with effort, she turned his upper body over. The face and upper torso were awash with red. The skin not covered with blood had a bluish cast. The eyes, she could see, were open, the irises half under the lids. Above them was a bloody hole.

There was no question in her mind that the man was dead, but she put her fingers on his neck, held them there. Felt nothing.

She edged backward, to the dog. Without taking her eyes from the body, she could see the tongue lolling out of Jessie's mouth. Could hear her panting. Crooning, Ariel caressed the dog's raised head, felt for her tags, turned them and read the address.

She staggered to her feet, to the telephone. The line was

live. "72 Laurel Drive," she whispered, her teeth beginning to chatter, her whole body trembling violently. Her chest, she realized, was drenched with blood, the pajama top sticky, viscid, horrible. She dropped the receiver. It swung in arcs, banged onto the floor.

Lurching to the table, she dragged out a chair, fell into it. Her head was lighter than air. Lighter than helium. Disappearing altogether. She closed her eyes. Her mind was a vortex, swirling, sweeping images into a distant pinpoint of light. She swayed, and put her head between her knees. She heard the wail of a siren. The sound swelled in the distance, died abruptly. Ariel clamped her teeth together. Her body slowly stilled. In the silence Jessie's panting was loud, rhythmic, a laboring steam engine. The voice from the dangling telephone receiver was a tiny, metallic clatter.

Someone knocked at the front door. A muffled voice called out, "Police officers! We're here!" The rapping came again. "This is the police! Is anyone inside the house?"

Ariel heard the door being opened. The voice was very clear. "Police officers! Is anyone in the house? We're coming in!" She heard erratic movements—shoes crossing the hardwood entry, silence, then the creak of a door opening. She raised her head, looked at the kitchen door, unable to move. Intermittent flickers of light came from the darkness beyond. Fireflies? she thought wonderingly. The voice, coming nearer, was repetitious. "Police officers," it kept warning. "Is there anyone in the house?"

First one, then two uniformed people filled the doorway. Each held a flashlight in one hand and a gun in the other.

"Place the gun on the table, ma'am," one of them said. "Very slowly."

She blinked at him and looked at her right hand, surprised to see that she was still holding the gun. With infinite precision, she set it on the table and raised her right hand. Her left hand didn't seem willing to cooperate.

"Now move away from the table, ma'am. Toward us, please. Very slowly."

Her mouth was cotton, her tongue a great swollen object glued to the roof of her mouth. She stood. The room tilted. The same policeman, smoothly dispensing with gun and flashlight, was at her side. Gripping her elbow, his voice urgent, he was asking her a great number of questions. They didn't seem to be in any language she knew.

The other officer—a woman, Ariel now realized—was talking into something in her hand. She, too, was speaking in alien tongues. "6 Adam 68 requesting tactical frequency. Request two additional units to 11742 Denair Street to assist in clearing residence. Code 2. We have a man down, a probable dead body." Ariel could hear every syllable clearly, but the words were meaningless. "Possible suspect in custody," the policewoman was telling her hand as she squatted beside the man on the floor. The man who was dead. The man Ariel had killed.

The man's hand was a claw. Beside it lay a knife. The blade looked black. Ariel's eyes moved to the bloody face. The eyes were bruised, as if he were wearing a mask. The lips were drawn back, showing an expanse of pink gum. The teeth looked unnaturally large. The nostrils, too, were huge. Great dark caverns. The skin was utterly white. Waxen. As white as the spongy matter that had oozed from the hole in his forehead. She saw all this with an amazing clarity. Then she didn't see anything at all.

She was lying on something. A sofa. She was in the living room. She was hurt. She couldn't sort out where all the pain was coming from. It seemed to envelop her.

A voice, gentle but persistent, was asking her questions. She opened her eyes. Something cold and damp was on her forehead, partially obscuring her vision. She could see a section of the ceiling. It was blue and red and seemed to be revolving. She blinked. Lights. Police car lights. Her exposed eye rolled to the right to see an officer kneeling beside her.

"Ma'am, can you tell me your name? Is anybody else in the house? What is your name? Do you know your name?"

She reached up her left hand to push away whatever covered her eye. She sucked in her breath in pain and lay the hand carefully on her chest. But something was wrong with her right hand, too! She raised it. A plastic bag covered it.

"Why . . . ?" She licked her lips, swallowed.

"Ma'am, do you know your name?"

"Ariel Gold is my name. Why is there a bag on my hand?"

"There are certain steps we're mandated to take, Ms. Gold. It's just procedure. We're getting you medical aid. Don't worry. The bag's to protect possible GSR. Gunshot residue. It's just policy. Not meaning you're guilty of anything, ma'am." He held something up. "I have a glass of water here. Take a little, okay?"

She could hear footsteps, doors opening somewhere. There seemed to be a great deal of to-ing and fro-ing both inside and outside the house.

"Jessie!" She tried to sit up.

"Is there someone in the house named Jessie?"

"My dog." She managed to sit up, dislodging the washcloth from her forehead and bumping her ankle. Through a dazzling jolt of pain, she gasped, "I have to see about Jessie!"

"Don't worry, ma'am. We're calling Animal Regulation. They'll take care of the dog."

"No! Please! Don't do that! Can't I call her vet? Will you let me do that?"

He hesitated. "Do you have the number?"

"My purse. It's . . ." She looked around wildly. Where had she left it? "In the kitchen. Will you bring it to me? And there's a portable phone in the study. The room before the bedroom." She shivered, suddenly aware of her state of dress. "And, please"—she pressed her bagged hand against her chest—"could I have a robe?"

The policeman called to someone. His partner came to the door. They consulted briefly, and the woman officer left again.

The man offered her water. He held it while she took several deep swallows. Over the top of the glass, she looked into his eyes. Sympathetic eyes, she thought. It was important that he understand what had happened. She tried to talk before he could remove the glass, choking when the water went down wrong. She went into a paroxysm of coughing. "I tried to get out," she was finally able to wheeze, her eyes streaming. "I tried to get away."

She leaned toward the officer. "I didn't want to shoot that man. Who is he? I tried to get out, but he tripped me. He broke in. Am I hurt?" She looked down at her pajama top, stiff and black. "Am I stabbed?" Her voice rose, quavered. "I didn't want to shoot him!"

He took out a notebook with a pen clipped to it. "Ms. Gold, we have medical assistance on the way. Now, I want you to be aware that anything you say can be used against you . . ."

She stopped listening. The woman officer was back, handing Ariel the robe, asking what she wanted from the bag.

Ariel pulled on the robe, wincing when her hand caught in the fabric. "Could you just . . . there's a wallet. With an address book?" Ariel reached for the phone and the wallet. Her right hand was trapped in the bag. "Will you look up . . ." Lord! What was the name? "Let me look at the little memo pad there, please. Pollock! That number. Could you dial it?"

The woman dialed, listened, said, "Just a moment, please," and held the phone to Ariel's ear.

"Victor Pollock? You're a veterinarian? My name is Ariel Gold . . ."

"Ariel! What's wrong? Who was that?" The voice was hoarse with sleep, alarmed.

"Jessie's hurt. Will you come here?" Ariel didn't think about the lateness—or earliness—of the hour or the unreasonableness of her request. She didn't know if vets made house calls or if this one knew where she lived. She just knew he had to come here. Now.

"I'm on my way," the voice said simply, and hung up.

"Ma'am. Ms. Gold?" The policeman leaned over her. "You want to lie back down?" He eased her feet back onto the sofa, sending a wave of nauseating pain through her ankle despite his gentleness. She closed her eyes, but a great clatter from the front door brought them open again. The officer's face had disappeared, and had been replaced by a new one. The new man wore a blue jumpsuit. MENDEZ was stitched in red on his chest.

"My name is Mendez, ma'am." He nodded at another jumpsuited man who was busy with equipment of some kind. "This is my partner, Sims. Can you tell me your name?"

As she did so, he placed his hands on her head. Ariel heard the policewoman say something to the partner, Sims, about fainting.

"We're just going to see if you're injured anywhere." He

pressed both sides of her neck gently. "You'll need to help us, though, if you can. Do you know what day this is?"

The other paramedic shined a light into her eyes. She admitted that she didn't know the day.

"How old are you?" The first man, Mendez, placed something under her arm. She tried to remember what the driver's license had said about her birth date.

"I'm sorry." She felt vaguely embarrassed.

"Do you hurt anywhere? How about your forehead? Does your head hurt?" He touched the bruise at her hairline.

"A little, but that didn't just happen now. That was yesterday, or maybe the day before. My hand is hurt, and I've done something to my ankle. My chest . . . I don't feel any pain in my chest, but it's all bloody."

Mendez's hands were very cool, very efficient, very busy pressing, palpating, probing. He talked constantly, reassuring, questioning. While his voice paused for her answers, his hands never stopped, touching her in one place, then another. "Now, I'm going to press here. Tell me if this hurts. Were you hurt internally? Were you assaulted sexually? Now, I'm going to just lift your pajama top to check your chest. Tell me if you feel any pain." She mumbled answers, watching his face anxiously. Her left hand was picked up, explored, splinted. Moments later her ankle was splinted as well. As they were lifting her onto a gurney, a new face appeared above her.

The middle-aged black man had tired-looking eyes under gray hair and a deeply lined forehead. He held up his hand to the paramedics in a signal to wait.

"Detective Massey, Ms. Gold. Officer Woodman tells me you had a break-in here tonight. Can you tell me exactly what happened?" He held a small notebook and a pencil.

She repeated what she'd told the first policeman, filling in details as they came back to her. Even so, it surprised her how little there was to tell. "He's dead, isn't he? That man? Who is—was he?"

The detective looked at his notebook. "His name was Rodriquez. Luis Rodriquez. That mean anything to you?" He was watching her face. Intently, she thought.

She shook her head, wondering if the name should mean

something to her. What if she did know him? For no longer than it took the thought to cross her mind, she considered saying that if she'd been married to Luis Rodriquez she wouldn't know him.

"I've never heard of him. But you should know that he may have been here last night, too. I wasn't here, but someone broke in. Through the window."

"You report that?"

"Nothing was missing." She winced mentally, hoping it was true. "There was no real damage done. I just ... well, I called a security company to put in a system." She made a miserable attempt at a smile. "They're coming today."

"You have any idea why someone would break into your house and leave without taking anything?"

It sounded stupid, even to her.

The detective pulled a little plastic bag from his pocket. In it was a scrap of paper. "Rodriquez had this on him. Your address is on it. Any idea why he was carrying around your address?"

"I don't know." For the first time tonight, she began to cry. The sheer weight of all the things she didn't know was overwhelming. She wiped away tears with her arm. "I just don't know."

She heard voices on the porch. A uniformed policeman she hadn't seen before came in and approached the detective, murmuring something. The detective nodded, and the policeman left again.

A moment later a man carrying an old-fashioned doctor's bag burst in, looking around in astonishment, and when he saw her on the gurney, he rushed over. Crying "Ariel! My God, what's happened?" he looked from her to the detective to the paramedics. He was wearing what looked like a pajama top under a cardigan sweater. His hair, fine and fair, was still wet where he'd slicked it down with water. Behind wire-rimmed glasses, his eyes were round and frightened.

The detective looked him over. "You're a vet?"

"Victor Pollock. A vet and a friend. Ariel called and said Jessie was hurt. She didn't say ... What's happened to Ariel?"

"The dog's in the kitchen, Mr. Pollock. You want to go on in there? I'll talk to you in a minute."

Yet another man, this one in a rumpled sportcoat, came to the gurney, said "Just a sec" to the detective and proceeded to remove the bag from Ariel's hand. "I'm just going to take a look at your hand here," he told her. "This won't hurt."

Ariel glanced at what he was doing, something with powder, and looked away. Her eyes followed the veterinarian out of the room.

The sportcoated man finished fiddling with her hand and went away. The detective nodded to the paramedics, telling Ariel, "We may need to get back in touch, Ms. Gold. You take care now."

She was whisked outside and into a red-and-white ambulance. One of the paramedics and the policewoman climbed in beside her, and the doors were pulled closed.

As they sped through the empty streets, Ariel willed herself to relax, to forget the last two hours, to block the horrific images that ran like a film through her mind. The struggle in the kitchen in agonizingly slow motion. The sound of the shot echoing, replaying, echoing. The dead man's bloody, waxy face drawn into a skeletal mask, no longer human. She shuddered, tried to concentrate on her companions. The paramedic and the policewoman were talking quietly, their heads together. She caught only an occasional word, but evidently the conversation was funny. The man snorted, suppressing laughter.

Good idea, thought Ariel. Think of something cheerful. The trouble was, her memories were in rather short supply, and they weren't jolly.

She wondered if the threat to her—if, indeed, there was a threat—had died with Luis Rodriquez. If it had been he in her house the night before; if it was his blood on the shirt. If he was the original intruder, why had he come back? Had he been interrupted by Mrs. Harris? And why had he come after her? Why, oh why, hadn't he just run? Or let her run? She couldn't have identified him—not if he'd waved to her from a lineup! What was he *after?*

She closed her eyes. Dear Lord, she prayed silently, if this was a typical day in the life of Ariel Gold, could you arrange for me to be somebody else tomorrow?

ten

After an interminable wait in an appalling emergency area, a thorough physical examination and another who-are-you-what-day-is-it session—during which she was apparently coherent enough to satisfy the intern that she wasn't in shock—Ariel was dismissed.

An overmuscled orderly, his biceps and pectorals seriously testing the seams of his uniform, wheeled her back to the emergency entrance, a walking cane across her lap. Ariel let her head drop back wearily. It bounced off the orderly's steely, washboard abdominals. She jerked upright. Every part of her exhausted body ached. Her ankle throbbed in an elastic brace not unlike the one she'd so cleverly wound on her own right hand yesterday. The cast strapped on her left hand reminded her to be careful what she wished for in the future.

She saw a featureless figure beside the exit. As she was wheeled closer, she saw who it was. The tired-eyed detective was waiting for her.

He leaned against the wall, arms crossed, one foot propped against the other, his expression impassive. He waited until the wheelchair was four feet away before he slowly unfolded himself. Seconds ticked away before he spoke.

"I'll drive you, Ms. Gold."

His smile was perfunctory, as tired as his eyes. He held the door for the attendant to push the obligatory wheelchair through.

Although dawn had come, the gray skies, threatening rain yet again, gave the emergency drive an amorphous quality. It could just as easily have been dusk, and Ariel wondered fleetingly if she'd lost another day. She stole a look at the detective and wondered if she was about to lose a great deal more than one day.

He opened the front door on the passenger side of a dark,

anonymous sedan, walked around and got behind the wheel. That was encouraging, Ariel thought as the orderly helped her from the chair; she wasn't to be locked behind a grille in the backseat. Still, as she hobbled her way into the car, she felt like an elderly, overweight Public Enemy Number One. She perched tensely on the seat, pulled her robe together as well as she could with one hand and stared straight ahead.

When the detective reached toward her, she flinched.

"Just going to buckle your seat belt," he said mildly.

Ariel cleared her throat. "Forgive me, but I've forgotten your name."

"Massey."

He started the car and pulled away from the hospital, saying nothing more. For what seemed like a very long time.

Block after out-of-focus block went by. Ariel squinted. They could be in almost any middle-class neighborhood in the city. They passed what she thought was a school. A coffee shop doing land-office business. She snuck a look at the stony-faced detective as he braked for a traffic light. "Silence," she thought, "is the most perfect expression of scorn."

However, she resolved and set her jaw, "Calumnies are best answered with silence." She watched a bundled-up old man shuffle across the intersection conversing with a companion only he could see. She shifted her weight and sat straighter.

The light turned green. The car moved forward. She cracked. Telling herself, "Ignorance never settles a question," she looked the detective straight in the right eye.

"Where exactly are you taking me, Detective Massey?"

He glanced toward her, and a grin spread across his face, including even his red-rimmed eyes.

"Home." He lifted his eyebrows almost imperceptibly. "Where'd you think we were going? The slammer?"

He made a left turn. "Hope it's okay that the vet stayed at your house after we finished up there. We were going to contact you to see if there was a relative or a neighbor or somebody you wanted, but the vet—what's his name?— wouldn't take no."

"Oh!" Ariel exclaimed. She felt as if she'd been punched in the solar plexus. She turned cold with apprehension and then hot with guilt. She hadn't thought of Jessie in hours.

"Is she . . . ? Is Jessie . . . ?" She couldn't say it.

The detective's eyes were on the street ahead. He frowned as a Jaguar almost clipped a bag lady pushing a grocery cart across the pedestrian crossing. Never turning her head, slowing or speeding up, the woman gave the car the finger.

Massey glanced again at Ariel, plastered against the door as if to distance herself from what he might say. A look that was part chagrin, part impatience crossed his face.

"Oh, for the love of . . . ! Would you lock that door before you go flying into the street? The doc didn't give me a report—I didn't ask for one—but the dog was definitely not dead when we left. In fact, he was walking around in pretty good shape, it looked like to me. Maybe limping a little but in pretty good shape."

He made a vague gesture with his hand. "I think he, the doc, stitched the dog up. I think he maybe has some stitches."

"She," Ariel breathed. "She's a she."

"Yeah, well. Whatever."

When she recognized what she thought was her street, she realized that it had been blocks since she'd paid attention to the world outside the car. Massey was talking again.

". . . and when I called in, I happened to talk to a guy I work with, Max Neely. He said to give you his regards. Said you were okay. A pain in the . . ." He glanced over again. "A monumental pain, is what he actually said. A bulldog, but straight. That's why I'm chauffeuring you home. A favor." The grin reappeared. "You don't think everybody gets escorted home by an off-duty homicide detective?"

They pulled into the driveway she'd never seen until yesterday. Massey cut the engine and turned to her. His expression was suddenly quite sober.

"Your account of what happened last night was clear. There's no question in my mind that this Rodriquez broke in, threatened you, scared you to death and you shot him in self-defense. No question. But I do *have* a question."

He unhooked his seat belt and leaned back against the driver's side door. He looked perfectly relaxed.

"The 911 operator said you didn't know your address. Why is that?"

She looked at the house, seeing it for the first time from this perspective. Primulas bloomed under the living room window and lined the walkway. A mock pear tree flowered in the center of the lawn. She felt a small, detached thrill of pride at the neat appearance. She wished she knew the address.

Ariel looked back at Massey, unconsciously straightening her spine. She was the rightful resident of this house. An unimpugnable, respectable, upright citizen without a secret in the world. A victim. As far as she knew, it was true.

"I was awakened out of a regular, normal sleep. I heard noises—what I *heard* was somebody breaking into my house. I was, as you quite accurately described it, scared to death. I haven't lived here long. I. Just. Plain. Lost it."

She believed herself. She maintained eye contact. She wondered how this was going over.

He waited a long moment.

"I'm curious about one other thing." He rested his right arm on the back of the seat.

"At some point—after they'd already traced the call—you got back on the line, and you did give an address. It wasn't this one. It was up in the hills. What was that all about?"

Ariel had no idea on earth what he was talking about.

"I have no idea on earth what you're talking about," she said with perfect frankness. "Could you undo this seat belt, please?"

His fingers drummed the seat for several beats. The drumming stopped with a decisive little thump.

"We'll let you know when we're finished with your gun," he said abruptly and unfastened the seat belt. He got out of the car, walked around and opened her door, then trailed her, hands in his pockets, as she caned her way across the lawn.

The lock on the front door was ruined, Ariel had time to see just before the door flew open. Victor Pollock rushed to help her in, talking, frowning and nearly twitching with solicitation.

"I called the hospital, and they said you'd been released," the veterinarian was saying as he reached first for one arm and then the other. Cast and cane making physical support awkward, he settled for giving her shoulder a pat and holding the door open.

"The police told me what happened. Ariel, how awful! How do you feel? Are you all right?" He looked very earnest and—still dressed in his pajama top, red-and-white-striped flannel buttoned to the neck—a trifle foolish.

Nevertheless, Ariel thought, taken aback by the extent of the man's concern, I don't know you, Mr. Pollock, and I'd sooner not be left alone with you. Planting herself, she turned to invite Massey (who might be intimidating but almost certainly wasn't murderous or a cat burglar or whatever) in for coffee.

The detective was backing his car into the street. He gave Ariel a sharp salute as he drove away.

She was standing indecisively in the doorway when Jessie bounded into the living room. The shepherd showed almost no sign of a limp and was—Ariel could swear it—smiling. Jessie smelled her thoroughly, decided she was welcome despite the lingering hospital smells and proceeded to lick the hand that rested on the cane. Tears pricked Ariel's eyes. It was inconceivable that she didn't remember this creature beyond yesterday. Maybe, she mused, when a dog saves your life it has a certain bonding effect.

Victor beamed. He plunged his hands in his pockets and rocked from heel to toe.

"She was a very lucky animal," he explained. "The knife went in high on her abdomen and, while the tip probably hit her spine, it bounced off with no permanent harm done. The effect is something like a concussion, producing a temporary posterior lameness, but, as you see, it disappears shortly. I just gave her a local and sutured the wound. They'll absorb, the sutures, so you don't have to worry about that. Oh, and you'll find antibiotics on the kitchen counter."

Ariel wanted to pet Jessie, she wanted a tissue and suddenly she wanted very much to sit down. She tottered. The vet was instantly at her side, berating himself. "Here, here! Sit! I'm a nitwit to go on like that when you must be on your last legs!"

"Leg," she joked weakly as she allowed herself to be led to the sofa.

He didn't smile. "How bad is it? And your hand? Is it broken?"

"It's just a cracked metatarsal bone," Ariel began. Victor was stuffing a cushion behind her back and smoothing the afghan over her legs. "Ah . . . the cast is just to protect it." His hands, Ariel noticed, were long and delicately shaped. "It doesn't, um, need stabilizing. And the sprain's mild, just . . . Victor, please! I'm fine. Really! I'm just . . . fine."

"You're sure?" He straightened. "Maybe I should bring an ice bag for your ankle?"

"I'm fine. Thank you."

He looked momentarily uncertain, then brightened. "Well, just let me know if you need anything. Anything at all. Now, I've fed Jessie, and there's fresh coffee, and I've got breakfast ready to go. You didn't have any bacon or sausage, but there were eggs and bread, so French toast it is."

Victor had started toward the kitchen when he hesitated. He turned back to Ariel, his expression that of a man about to be flogged. "Would you like to talk about last night?" he asked. "Would that be a good idea? Or bad?"

"The last thing in this world I want to talk about is last night. Someday, maybe, but no time soon. Thanks anyway."

He nodded, his face serious and understanding. His relief was almost concealed as he left the room.

Jessie lay down as close to the sofa as she could get, turning onto her side and giving a small moan of fatigue or contentment. A white bandage about six inches square covered a shaved area on her abdomen. Seeing it, Ariel felt a pang of leftover fear. She scratched the shepherd's head and leaned down to whisper extravagant and heartfelt thanks into her ear.

The aroma of coffee wafted in from the kitchen, and Ariel turned her thoughts to the man inside. Settling into the cushion and draping her arm over her eyes to block the light,

she surrendered the last vestige of suspicion. If he's got killing me in mind, she thought with a sigh, it'll be with
kindness.

She was just drifting into a light doze when the answer to
Detective Massey's last question popped into her head. The
address she'd given the 911 operator was the one on Jessie's
tag! If that wasn't the address of this house, whose address
was it?

She was about to call to Victor when he reemerged carrying a tray laden with enough food to feed the three of
them. Gingerly, he set it on her lap and straightened, watching her reaction. From somewhere he'd turned up a crisply
ironed tea towel and napkin (or maybe he'd ironed them
himself), and he'd artfully arranged the French toast on a
fragile china plate. It matched the cup and saucer, as well
as a bread plate on which orange sections neatly overlapped
and a small bowl in which a single red camellia floated, its
color matching the tiny posies of the china pattern.

Ariel eyed the vision on her lap and felt warmth creeping
up her neck; she knew she was as red as the flowers. Unless
this Victor was a compulsive aesthete, there was a message
being delivered along with breakfast, and the implications
were boggling.

Were they . . . ? Could they be . . . ? For the first time in
many hours she was acutely aware of how she looked—
which, she was reasonably sure, hadn't been improved by
the night's events. Could the man possibly be attracted to
her? She looked up at him through her lashes, trying to
read the status of their relationship in his eyes. He merely
looked diffident. Well, she thought, like the Red Queen said,
". . . sometimes I've believed as many as six impossible
things before breakfast."

"Please, Ariel! Eat before it gets—Oh! Should I cut that
up for you?"

"No, no! Oh, no. It's just so . . . grand! I hate to spoil the
effect by eating it. The food, I mean. Not the effect. Well,
you know what I mean. Thank you. Really! Aren't you having any?"

"There wasn't enough for two, not with your marvelous
appetite." He appeared to think he'd paid her a compliment.

"Ha-ha." She grimaced. "Well, 'Grub first, then ethics.'" She popped an orange section into her mouth.

"I'll just bring in the coffeepot and a cup and saucer for myself." He disappeared into the kitchen.

She'd finished one piece of French toast and the entire orange by the time Victor had seated himself across from her. He watched with relish. She found that she was no longer hungry.

"Thank you," she said, "not just for breakfast but for coming over here in the middle of the night, no questions asked." She took a sip of coffee and tested the waters. "I guess you don't usually make house calls?"

He dismissed her thanks with a wave. "Well, you're hardly an alarmist. At any rate, after all you've done for me it was the very least I could do, don't you think?"

Well, she thought, that wasn't particularly enlightening. "You left a message on my machine. I'm sorry I didn't have a chance to get back to you. You said you'd missed me?"

"At the kennel. Saturday morning." He became very busy removing the tray and replenishing her coffee. "You've never failed to cover your shift, and, frankly, I was a little worried. Not that it was a problem, of course. I didn't mean to imply any criticism. It's just that I've—we've come to depend on seeing you. Oh!" He stopped avoiding her eyes and smiled in genuine pleasure. "Patton was adopted Saturday. A really nice family with a little boy."

"I beg your pardon?"

"Patton. The deaf bull terrier." His smile slipped. "The poor old guy that makes such awful noises when he barks?"

"Oh, yes. Patton. Good. That's great." Ariel watched the vet's puzzled face for a moment, torn between relief that the two of them clearly were not an item, sympathy for the man who just as clearly wished they were (love truly was blind, some amazed part of her mind concluded) and anxiety as to how she could learn more about herself without sounding witless. No good plan came to mind.

"Victor, will you please tell me why Jessie's wearing a tag with the wrong address on it?"

He shook his head, his face pinched in disgust. "I was going to tell you about that. You remember the tag we ordered finally came with her name misspelled? When we didn't get the corrected tag, I called the company. They were full of excuses, but I'm sure they just misplaced the order, because we didn't get some other things, either. Anyway, I called again Friday and got a recorded message. The phone's been disconnected. I reordered from someone else, which is what I should've done in the first place." He looked miserable about his small failure. "I can diagnose problems other vets miss entirely and stage a campaign that gets three hundred dogs and cats neutered in six weeks, but I can't seem to get you a dog tag!"

Ariel was disconcerted by the flood of self-recrimination her question had unleashed, but she was even more confused. Then a horrible possibility occurred to her. Did Jessie belong to someone else?

"Victor," she asked, her stomach sinking, "whose address is that on her tag?"

Victor tilted his head, his face a study in puzzlement. "Hers. Where she lived before you got her, I mean. Ariel, don't you feel well? Well, of course you don't. Did they check that bump on your head at the hospital?"

Her reaction surprised even her. Touching her bruised forehead, she made an effort to look wan. She thought she probably looked like a dying calf in a hailstorm.

"Oh, it's not serious, but I am afraid last night's taking its toll. Victor, I wonder if you could just indulge me—let's call it a sanity test." Her smile beseeched him. "Could you just run over the details for me? Please?"

"The . . . you mean how you came to have Jessie? Sure. I guess." Uncertainly, as if he were the one being tested, he explained.

"When Mrs. Morgan, Jessie's first owner, died, her husband didn't want her—Jessie, I mean—so you adopted her."

"Well, yes, but what I'd really like to hear are the specifics. You know, the humanizing details. Just paint me a picture," she encouraged, holding out her cup for more coffee.

He poured her cup full and, looking more dubious than ever, obliged.

"There's not all that much to tell, you know. Mrs. Morgan

was going away, and she brought Jessie in to board her, and—did we give her her DHLPP shot, then? Well, that's neither here nor there, is it? Anyway, she was supposed to pick Jessie up the next day but, obviously, she didn't. We called and called, but we just kept getting her machine." Victor shook his head sadly. "When I think about that poor woman lying dead in her house all the time we were leaving messages ...

"So, anyway, after a couple of days Maxine—you remember the receptionist we had who went to work for one of the studios?—she read in the paper about Mrs. Morgan dying. When we finally reached the husband, I got the distinct impression he'd forgotten all about Jessie. She must've been strictly the wife's pet. He sounded really irritated and, if you can believe it, he not only didn't want her back, he didn't want to pay the bill either! Well, I realize he was bereaved and all ..." Victor looked sheepish. "I guess we really should've just let it go under the circumstances. But my point is, I was flabbergasted that he didn't want to pay. With all the money he's got now!"

Victor leaned toward her, his elbows on his knees. "That was one of your Saturdays, and when you heard that Jessie was up for adoption, you didn't hesitate a second. I've never seen anybody so anxious to have a particular dog. Of course"—his voice dropped—"I know it had been a while since you'd lost Missy, and I'd really hoped you wouldn't wait too long before ..." He brightened. "And you did have a sort of proprietary interest in Jessie."

"I did?"

"Well, sure. With your having named her, I mean, and knowing her owner."

"Oh. Right. I see what you mean." She was bewildered.

"Your starting to come in—becoming a client—right about the time Mrs. Morgan did and your being there when she was asking everybody in the place to suggest names for Jessie ... it's like destiny intervened in the whole thing, don't you think? The pup was just a bundle of fur and big paws, you remember? And people were coming up with all these lofty-sounding Teutonic names—Jessie being up to her snout in papers and all. I remember Jim Anson came up with Griselda, and somebody actually suggested Frigg. I think that was supposed to be a joke. And you said, 'How about Jessie?' " Victor's smile invited her to share his admiration for this stroke of brilliance. "When we asked 'Why Jessie?' you didn't seem to know yourself. Then you said the facial markings were like a little black mask, like a bandit, and you supposed that made you think of Jesse James. So, to make a long story short, Mrs. Morgan didn't seem to follow your logic, but she liked the name anyway. Of course, she's registered as Jessica Von something-something-something, but Jessie she is."

"But she's mine now, right? There's no chance this man could change his mind?

"Oh, he had no interest in her whatsoever. But you said you were going to contact him and get her papers. Didn't you do that?"

"Ummm." Ariel couldn't think of any sensible answer to that one. "You tell the story so well!" Lord! Was she saying these things? "It's unbelievable how you remember every little thing!"

He shrugged, a pink flush rising in his cheeks. "I guess I'm sort of ... attentive when you're around."

He looked at his watch. "Good grief! I've got to go."

Hurriedly, Victor took the tray to the kitchen, and she heard water running and the clatter of dishes being stacked in the dishwasher. When he returned, rolling down his pajama sleeves over forearms surprisingly well-developed and sprinkled with fine, blond hairs, he asked if he could call someone to come stay with her.

Ariel shook her head. "But I would appreciate it if you'd check to see if any of the locks still work."

"The chain's okay," he said. "I fixed it while you were gone. But I don't feel right about leaving you alone. Do you want help to bed? Or to the bathroom?" He looked stricken. "I mean, you must be dying for a shower." He looked, if possible, even more stricken.

"Victor, you're a gentleman and no doubt a scholar, but I'm fine. And you're right about that shower." She struggled up. "I'll just lock the door behind you. And, Victor, thank you again. For everything, but especially for Jessie."

He patted her shoulder, obviously wishing to do more. Just as he got into his car, a van pulled into the driveway. Victor was back in a flash, and he and Jessie both eyed the approaching messenger with grave suspicion.

The kid, who looked about fourteen and as threatening as Huckleberry Finn, read her name off a form and handed her a box imprinted EYE-SITE. When she'd signed the form (wondering if her signature was going to cause a problem—she hadn't thought of that), he wished her good day, rejected Victor's offer of a tip and left, whistling merrily.

"I couldn't have given him a tip anyway," Victor admitted, pulling out his pocket linings. "I kind of left home in a hurry." He stuffed the pockets back and rushed off, promising to check in later.

Ariel watched him drive away through the beginnings of another downpour. *That's the shyest human being I've ever met in my life,* she thought, and then realized the irony of such observations. Pushing the chain into its slot, she unwrapped her new glasses, put them on and sighed thankfully. The world was beautiful to behold when it wasn't growing fuzz!

She'd started limping toward the bathroom when a chilling thought brought her up short. The kitchen. Lord! She'd never be able to go back in there. Would there be a chalk outline on the floor? The face of Luis Rodriquez flashed through her mind. The gore. The clawlike hand. The knife, black with blood. She shuddered. She'd deal with it later, she promised herself. Sometime.

She'd finished her shower (having learned that certain parts of the body can't be reached with only one hand), semi-dried herself and exhausted her ingenuity winding the elastic back on her cantaloupe-sized ankle when she heard the doorbell. She secured the bandage, cursing the time it took, pulled on a robe, grabbed glasses and cane and hobbled to the door.

Shushing Jessie, she looked through the peephole. A man in coveralls waited with a tool kit. The name on his truck—which, praise heaven, she could read—was MASTER LOCKS.

Before the locksmith had finished with the dining room window, the security company man had arrived, and for the next three hours Ariel learned about dead-bolt locks, pick-resistant cylinders, door and window contacts, panic emergency exit locks and reinforced door plates. From her perch on the sofa she reiterated decisions made on the phone the day before, answered questions about the break-in, wondered whether she was locking the barn door after the horse had already been stolen (so to speak), worried about her credit limit, glanced through the newspaper Victor had left on the coffee table (discovering that she couldn't read with the blasted glasses on), iced her ankle and memorized her new security code.

When the workmen left, she felt ready to keel over with fatigue but bolstered by a blessed sense of safety. Now, she decided, was as good a time as any to brave the kitchen. She straightened her spine and limped to the door. The room was immaculate, glistening to within an inch of its life. Victor, she thought. Bless his heart.

She made sure the locks were locked, the alarm system activated and the answering machine set to pick up. She closed all the draperies in the house, disconnected the bedside phone and climbed into her unmade bed. Within minutes, she was asleep.

Sometime during the afternoon the phone rang. By the time Ariel had roused herself enough to recognize the sound, the machine had picked up. She was asleep again before the caller finished his message—so deeply asleep that, when the telephone rang again several hours later, she never heard it at all.

eleven

Henry stomped into his office and slammed the door. The gesture was more of a signal for privacy than a viable barrier to sight or sound since the door and the walls on both sides were mostly glass.

A clandestine tape buy set up for the night before had fallen through with a thud, Henry's courier having come up empty. The poor guy, clutching the $1,500 payoff and feeling as if he were making a drug buy, had waited in the rain for half an hour without seeing hide or hair of anybody. So much for that story, Henry thought, until he could make contact with the nervous, would-be seller again.

He was twirling his Rolodex, trying to remember the name of the chief coroner in Birmingham, Alabama, when his door opened and Peacock came in. The correspondent pushed aviator-style glasses atop sun-burnished hair and laid the magazine he'd been reading on Henry's desk. He pointed to a small article headlined "Stepfather Sought in Tempe Six-Year-Old's Disappearance."

"Did you see this? It looks like that kidnap in Arizona may be just another domestic grab-and-run with a slight twist."

Henry flicked the magazine dismissively. "That guy didn't take the kid. From what the mother said, the stepfather never had all that much to do with him. I hate to say it, but that little boy is probably lying dead somewhere right now, and I'm still betting this snatching is tied in to the one in Flagstaff and the one in Albuquerque. We'll do some more digging."

Peacock sat down in one of the mismatched wooden chairs just inside the door and propped a foot across his knee. The top two buttons of his crisply starched shirt were undone, his Hermès tie was loosely knotted, and his enviable pectoral muscles strained against the tiny polo pony on his chest. In the cramped office, his chamois-soft Italian loafer barely cleared Henry's desk. "Why don't you get rid of these spine-manglers and bring in normal chairs like everybody else?" he complained, tilting the chair onto its back legs.

"They keep me humble. Remind me of my days as Henry the Hawk, mean-mannered reporter." Henry twirled his Rolodex impatiently. "And people I didn't want to talk to in the first place tend not to prolong their visits."

"That in-basket looks like it hasn't been gone through in years. You've probably got a wire service rip about Nixon's resignation buried in there."

"That's one of the things people I don't want to talk to talk about." Henry pushed a haphazard stack of papers to one side of his desk and picked up a pile of magazines. Looking around for somewhere to stash them, he plunked them onto the floor. "I can put my finger on anything in this office, anytime I want to."

"Whatever you say, my friend; whatever you say. I heard last night was a bust."

"Yeah." Henry grinned. "And poor Mike said he felt like he was about to be. Busted." He shrugged. "We gave it a shot. We'll get the tape sooner or later, and if it's all the guy at the network said, it'll be worth the wait and the money and then some."

"I wonder if we should . . ." Hearing a noise behind him, Peacock craned his neck back to see who'd stopped at the door. His chiseled chin pointed up at his assistant, who leaned in casually.

"Your three o'clock's here." The magnificent-looking twenty-two-year-old smiled down at her boss's (and, Henry suspected, lover's) face. "She doesn't look happy."

"In a minute. Offer her coffee or whatever."

The girl sauntered away, Peacock's eyes following her departure. The front chair legs banged down onto the floor, and he unfolded himself and stood. "What's the latest on that car bombing in Santa Monica?"

Henry picked up the phone and punched in a three-digit number with a pencil. "Gerald. Henry." He waggled the pencil at someone in the room beyond the window. "What's the bomb squad doing with that restaurant hit from Sunday night?"

He listened, harrumphed and hung up.

"From what they're giving out, they found some numbers, partials, but the only license plate they came up with belonged to the car next to it that got pretty well totaled, too. Some bystander picked up a grisly souvenir, no doubt. The cops say they'll probably have something to tell us by tomorrow. The driver's a problem, though. They've got some teeth, and the blood's typed, et cetera, but so far there's no match to anybody reported missing or anybody in the computer."

"They've got more than they're saying."

"Probably."

"It's not street gangs, not in that neighborhood."

Henry shook his head in the negative. "More like gangland."

Peacock buttoned his shirt and tightened his tie. "Where's Gold? Did she ever come in?" He scanned the outer room.

Damn and hell, Henry remembered. The woman said she was going to call in today. For reasons he didn't stop to analyze, he didn't mention going over to Ariel's house. Or her odd behavior.

"Beats me. I've been out a lot."

"What's she working on? Anything in particular?"

"The disappearing border crossers. A retro piece. This and that."

Peacock gave Henry a sharp look, unnecessarily smoothing his shirttails into his trousers. "When you've got time, I want to show you a new cut on my segment for Monday-night-two-weeks."

Henry propped his feet on his desk and watched Peacock enter the corridor leading to his own office. Where's the justice? he thought. It's not enough the guy looks like Robert Redford in his heyday—minus the moles—but as Henry had quickly learned in the short time Peacock had been on the show, he was intelligent, he was good at his job and he was no rip-and-reader. You had to keep reminding yourself about that. With his labels and his looks, it was too easy to forget the man's smarts, too easy to assume he was just another pretty face. Henry would be willing to bet more than one poor, unsuspecting schmuck had regretted that assumption through the years.

He hauled his feet to the floor and began shuffling through a stack of pink message slips. He pulled one out to deal with immediately and threw the others into his in-basket.

There was nothing from Ariel.

He tapped the edge of the little pink slip on the desk. When was her doctor's appointment? He didn't think she'd said.

He began dialing the number on the slip, but a thought intruded. What if that knot on her head was serious? He slammed down the phone and flipped the Rolodex to Ariel's number.

Get it over with, he told himself—Papa Heller checking in on his chick. Ariel's machine picked up. Very sweetly, Henry left a message at the bloody tone.

"Perhaps you could find a moment to update me on when you might drop back by here?"

He hung up.

After glaring at the telephone for several distracted minutes, he again began to dial the number on the message slip. Again, he hung up. He went out into the huge, noisy room beyond his office where two dozen people put together the stories for *The Open File*. He perched on the desk of the young woman whose workstation was next to Ariel's.

"Boss man," Lisa Jolley said cheerfully, turning from her computer screen, "what's happening?"

"Not a lot, Lisa. Tell me, have you by any chance heard anything from Ariel Gold?"

"Nada. But, then, I probably wouldn't. You mean she hasn't been in touch with you? Isn't that kind of weird?"

"Was she working on anything special that you know of? Anything she hadn't brought to a story meeting yet?"

The redhead shrugged, shook her head. "Well, there's a three-strikes angle I heard her talking to somebody about. Oh! And I know she's hot on that Robin Hood story. You know, the bank heists in Tennessee or North Carolina or wherever it was? I took a call for her on that yesterday, some sheriff, but I couldn't even understand what he was saying—guy sounded like he was drowning in molasses. I don't know what else. Ariel's always got a bunch of irons in the fire, and she's not one to run things up the Maypole with the rest of us, you know?"

Henry's mouth twitched; he decided not to let himself be diverted. "Is she close to anybody at all? Does she go to lunch with anyone? Drinks after work? That kind of thing?"

"Not that I know of. I mean, she's friendly enough. But she's really serious and kind of private. Like, you know, I saw her at the AIDS walk a couple of months ago? And she'd never even mentioned she was going to do it. Some of us had been talking about it just the day before, and she never said anything.

"Hey!" Lisa pointed to Ariel's desk. "Just go through her file folders there in that stack. That's where she keeps stuff she's not ready to input or bring up in story meetings, I think. Playing her cards really close to her chest and all. But, well, it's not like it's confidential." She wrinkled her nose, making her freckles run together. "From you, anyway."

Henry collected the stack of folders. Riffling through them, he said under his voice, "Vest."

"Come again?"

"Vest. I think the expression is 'to play one's cards close to one's vest.' Not 'chest.'"

She was unimpressed. "But your vest is on your chest. At least part of it is, so it all comes to the same thing, doesn't it?"

Henry imagined that this sort of discussion wasn't new to Lisa. He waved the folders toward her computer screen. "That Hollywood cult segment's going to be good, I think. It's got all the elements. Celeb's kid. Thirties mystique. Cover-up rumors. And nobody still around to sue." He winked and returned to his office.

The contents of the folders, as he'd expected, told him nothing. There were a few typed transcripts, all unalarming, many telephone numbers, many names and titles, many cryptic phrases with question marks or exclamation points. They were the kind of notations perfectly understood by the person who makes them but largely meaningless to anyone else. If whatever was going on with Ariel had anything to do with a story she was researching, Henry couldn't tell it from these scribbles. He put the files on the credenza behind him and put the whole Ariel Gold matter on his mental back burner.

twelve

The sun struggled through the clouds just in time to set, casting a strange, orange glow over the saturated landscape. As the momentary brightness suffused the bedroom, Ariel stirred, cried out once in pain or fear and was still again.

When she finally awakened, groggy and sore in every limb, the bedside clock read 8:10 P.M. Her stomach was rumbling and the heavy robe was twisted into an uncomfortable lump under her side. She stretched, saying several unladylike things when her cast struck the headboard, sat up and looked around.

Well, she thought, I guess I'm still Ariel Gold.

But at least the room was as neat as when she'd fallen asleep, and the house was quiet. Jessie snored peacefully in her appointed place between bed and door. So yesterday was an anomaly. Right? she prayed. Please?

Thinking that if she didn't stay up for at least a few hours she'd never be able to sleep later, she retrieved glasses and cane and, stepping over Jessie, limped painfully to the kitchen. She rummaged through the cupboards. Finding a can of albacore and lacking the energy for anything more ambitious, she decided on tuna salad and put an egg on to boil.

She went to the study, intending to pull some of the few remaining unexamined files to peruse while she ate. The red light on the answering machine was blinking.

There was only one message, and it was a short one. Short and sweet. Listening to Henry's sarcastic request, she realized with a pang that she'd completely forgotten her promise to call. She grabbed the portable phone, found her address book and thumbed through to "Henry." It was way too late to reach him, but she could leave a message. At least he'd know she'd tried.

"Heller."

Ariel did a double take. Expecting a recording, she

couldn't immediately think what to say. "Henry. Hey. Ariel Gold. I'm glad I caught you."

"Ariel! So good of you to call. Glad you could find the time."

Uh-oh, she winced. Well, two can play at this guilt-trip game. She smiled grimly. "I'm really sorry not to've called earlier but, you see, someone broke into my house last night, and I've been a little busy with the police and the hospital and getting my locks replaced and so forth."

"What? Ariel, are you serious? Did they get the burglar? Did he take anything? Are you all right?"

Hearing the concern in his voice and remembering what had actually taken place the night before, Ariel regretted her mean impulse.

"Oh, I'm . . . okay." A stab of loneliness hit her. She felt a sudden, overwhelming need for human contact. To tell somebody what the last thirty-six hours had been like. To ask somebody just who she was and what she was like. The timer she'd set for her egg buzzed and, cradling the phone with her shoulder, she turned off the stove.

"Listen, Henry, do you know if I have any vacation time coming? I know this is probably unorthodox, but I think it might be a good time for me to regroup, kind of."

"I can't remember your ever taking any time off at all. You're probably owed a decade or two. Hold a sec."

Ariel was giving thanks for the electric can opener and trying to figure out how to open a jar of pickle relish with one hand when Jessie came into the kitchen. Luxuriously, she stretched forward, then backward, and flapped through her dog door. Ariel gave up on the relish, and Henry came back on the line.

"Nobody's left in Personnel tonight, but I've got an unofficial diary, and it looks like you've got at least six weeks coming. Do you want to take it all?"

She thought of a month and a half with little or no human contact. "I don't think I'll need that long. Let's say three weeks for right now. Is that okay?"

"It's okay by me. But look here . . ."

There was a silence, during which Ariel heard some shuffling and what sounded like a chair squeaking.

"Henry?"

"Yeah, yeah, I'm here. What I'm trying to say is, are you sure you're all right?"

She swallowed. Quietly she said, "Thanks, Henry, for asking. See you in three weeks." She pushed the disconnect button.

Seated at the kitchen table with her tuna salad, Ariel opened the first of a half dozen still pending folders she'd pulled from the file drawer in the study.

Labeled with an address, the folder held a sheaf of official papers headed Deed of Reconveyance. Her name was typed into the space indicating that she was trustor of a property with the same address as that on the folder label. Did that mean she owned a house? This house? She hobbled into the living room, intending to go outside and check the house number. In the darkness she could see the gleam of white papers scattered below a mail slot cut into the door. She bent awkwardly and scooped them up.

Back in the kitchen, she looked at the mailing label on a Lands' End catalogue. It was the address on the folder. On the Deed of Reconveyance. She scanned the document.

So and so and so "the undersigned as the present Trustee of Record of said Deed of Trust does hereby grant and reconvey" and so on "all the estate and interest derived to the Trustee in and to the property described in said Deed of Trust." She looked at the next document, a deed of trust, carefully. "Well, blow me down!" she crowed.

She owned the house!

Eagerly, she opened another folder, this one tabbed MUNSON.

Inside was another legal document, this one a Petition to Probate Will in Solemn Form, and it was she who was the petitioner. In paragraph number one she read that on a date in 1990 a person named Charles Lawton Munson had departed this life owning property in California. In paragraph three she read that she was the deceased's only heir at law. The will itself wasn't in the folder, so her imagination supplied dollar marks followed by multi zeros. Her excitement was unaffected by the fact of Charles Lawton Munson's demise since she didn't know who he was.

On a roll, she took a bite of salad and turned to the next folder. Cable TV receipts. Oh, well. And the next, a handful of current-year canceled checks. Probably tax-deductible, Ariel thought, glancing through them.

Jessie clattered back through her door, lapped up almost as much water as she dripped across the floor and collapsed at Ariel's feet with a mighty exhalation. When the dog turned onto her side, exposing the white bandage, Ariel felt sudden coldness ripple through her stomach. Her appetite gone, she pushed her plate away and tried to do the same with all thoughts of the previous night. She stroked Jessie gently and turned back to the business at hand.

The next folder contained several Blue Shield Explanation of Benefits forms, whereon were itemized line after line of payments. None of the forms was recent, the biggest batch dating from several years ago, and none was of interest to Ariel. The last folder, however, was.

Labeled PERSONAL, it included a copy of a birth certificate which declared that Ariel Rose Munson, a white female, was born at 8:20 A.M. on June 3, 1961, in St. John's Hospital, Los Angeles. The mother, whose maiden name was Gladys Anne Wood, had been thirty-nine, the father forty-one. His name was Charles Lawton Munson. Both had resided at the address she now knew to be hers.

Her parents.

Her father, obviously, was deceased. She felt a sense of deprivation, not over the fact that he was dead but that she could summon up no sorrow about the fact.

He had been, it seemed, the proprietor of a tire store, and her mother had been a Hwf. A housewife. Ariel stared at the paper. Was her mother alive? Surely not, or there'd be evidence of her existence somewhere in the house. Letters. Pictures. Something.

She read further. The number of children born to this mother was two. The number of children now living was one. She wondered whether she'd had a brother or a sister and when the child had died. She wondered whether the loneliness that gnawed at her soul had begun when she herself was a child, the only living offspring of two middle-aged parents.

She sighed and picked up the next document. The University of Southern California, it stated, conferred upon Ariel Rose Munson the degree of Bachelor of Arts in Journalism.

Ariel's mouth fell open. Somehow the disparity of names hadn't clicked in until now. How did she go from being Ariel Munson to being Ariel Gold?

Not but one way likely: she was married.

Her hand trembling, she turned the diploma over to reveal proof of her deduction. A marriage certificate issued in the State of California, Los Angeles County, certified that Jordan Michael Gold and Ariel Rose Munson had been united in the holy bonds of matrimony on the fourth day of December in the year of our Lord 1984.

Ariel gaped at the license, then looked beneath it. There was nothing else in the folder. Carefully, she closed it. She stacked it with the others, her mind a snarl of questions and speculations.

Maybe she was divorced, she thought. But wouldn't divorce papers be in the folder? Then maybe she and this man were only separated. Or maybe he was just away on business. Or something. She shook her head to clear it. Stupid! Other than the photograph she'd found—Jordan Michael Gold?—there wasn't one iota of evidence of a man in the house. No clothes, no toiletries, nothing with his name on it anywhere. But she was still Ariel Gold, so if they were divorced, she'd kept his name. For career reasons?

She swallowed. Or because they had a child or children? And it was unfair to them to have a name different from their mother's? Lord! That was even stupider! Where were they? Hiding in the cellar?

When the phone rang, she jumped nearly out of her skin. She picked up the portable, debated letting the machine take it, finally pushed the button. She said nothing.

"Ariel?"

She relaxed. "Victor, hello."

"I'm just checking in. I hope I didn't wake you?"

"No, no. You were so good to clean up the kitchen, Victor. Really, that was above and beyond. I can't tell you what it meant to me not to have to face that."

He made a sound of dismissal. "The police said it was okay to clean. How's Jessie?"

Ariel glanced down at the shepherd stretched on the floor, her eyes at half-mast, fighting sleep. "Fine, thanks to you."

"Look, Ariel, you're not going to be able to walk her for a while. How would it be if I dropped by there tomorrow after work? I could take a look at her and give her a good ramble."

When Ariel had made token protestation at the bother and Victor had assured her he'd like nothing better, they settled on six-thirty and said good night.

Immediately, Ariel pulled out the phone book and turned to the *G*s. There were at least two hundred Golds listed— and that was just in West L.A., Beverly Hills and Santa Monica! Her eyes caught an A. Gold with the now-familiar address, and an irrelevant thought popped into her head: maybe that was where Luis Rodriquez had found her. A listing with initial only usually meant a single woman. Maybe she was a random choice, one of many vulnerable women he'd victimized.

An even more disturbing thought occurred: maybe her elusive husband was tied into this whole thing somehow!

A ruined piece of lilac stationery came to mind, and what may have been a name. She retrieved the letter from the study and read again the chilling fragment.

". . . accusations are very dangerous. Say any of your filth to anyone else, and I'll make sure you regret it. Everyone will think you're deranged by grief. No one will believe you because you're nobody."

She tried once more to decipher the smear of a word that began with a capital *M*. She had no more luck than on the previous day. It could have been Michael. On the other hand it could be Minneapolis. Ariel returned to the directory and looked under "Gold" for Michael. There were seven, and one Jordan. She started dialing.

Half an hour later, she'd made contact with three wives whose reactions ranged from brusque to irate and whose husbands had never been married to anyone named Ariel; three Michaels, none of whom had ever had a wife with her name (but one who was interested in meeting her); and one answering machine on which a breezy woman identified herself as Michael. There was one no-answer. She made a note about that one.

Jordan was a second-grader with a phone of his own.

She fared no better with the single-initial *M*s and *J*s, excusing herself to a Malachi, a Marian and a Mimsy, two Johns and a very curious Judith. The last call got her an answering machine on which a female had recorded her number only, no name, but she used the pronoun "I" rather than "we."

There were no Golds with the combination initials *J* and *M*.

Feeling overwhelmed, she wondered how many Michael Golds there were in California. In the country. In the world. How could she in this lifetime find hers? She sat staring at the legions of Golds and remembered something.

She found the jewelry box where she'd stowed it after a cursory glance the day before. Rooting through now, she pushed aside a necklace with a tiny diamond heart, a defunct watch and pearls that may or may not have been real. She briefly examined a USC class ring from 1981 and another ring, platinum perhaps, with minuscule diamonds in an old-fashioned setting. It might be an engagement ring, she thought, but unless it was an heirloom, it probably wasn't hers. Then she lifted out a gold band, very simple but wide and heavy—and not inexpensive. It didn't look overly worn, and there was an inscription inside. Holding it under the bedside lamp, she could easily read the initials and the date: JMG to AMG 12/4/84.

Ariel slipped the band onto her ring finger. The cast prevented its progress, so she unbuckled the cast. The ring fit. She gazed at it, willing it to conjure up a few answers. Where was JMG now? And what, if anything, still connected them?

Another look through the folders in the study turned up none tabbed GOLD or JMG or DIVORCE. She groaned. There were too many questions and no answers to be had tonight.

Well, there's one thing to be said for being frightened, confused and frustrated, Ariel thought as she scraped her uneaten dinner into the garbage; it makes a powerful diet plan.

When she turned off the light, the little red signal of her new alarm system was glowing beside the back door. She wandered across the hall into the dark living room, noting that the signal's mate was beaming reassuringly beside the front door. She pulled the drapery open and looked out at the front yard.

Cold moonlight bathed the stillness. The mock pear tree's blooms were a ghostly cloud of white. Behind the windows of the house directly across the street, faint light flickered sporadically. Someone was watching television. Ariel's gaze wandered to the next house, where Malibu lights cast a distant glow on a parade of bedding plants along the walkway. Just then, headlights approached, and a car came to a stop in front of a dark two-story house on the far side of the television watchers. Ariel leaned against the sill, watching idly. She'd seen none of her neighbors save dear, nosy Mrs. Harris, and she was curious as to who they were.

The headlights died, and the scene became as still as before. No one got out of the car. It was probably someone waiting for the occupants of the house to return, Ariel surmised. She squinted, but all she could see was a mass of shadow, unmoving.

She found her glasses and limped back to the window. There was only one person in the car. Was he looking at *her* house? Reflexively, she jerked back, then realized she couldn't possibly be seen in the blackness. Chiding herself for being paranoid, she tried to quell the uneasiness that had raised goose bumps on her arms.

What color was the car? Dark. Could be any dark color. The moonlight rendered everything monochromatic. Were those the neighbors Mrs. Harris had said were out of town? Ariel didn't think so. She stood watching until her ankle began to throb. The car hadn't moved. The figure in it hadn't moved. Should she call someone? Detective Massey? And say what? Putting her faith in strong locks and electronic wiring—and wishing she had her gun back—Ariel backed away from the window and quietly closed the drapery.

She brushed her teeth and put on clean pajamas, reminding herself that she ought to wash the ones from last night and the sweatshirt, too, or the blood would never come out. Better yet, she decided tiredly, she'd throw them away.

She was fluffing the bed pillows when a tiny, almost imperceptible noise behind her stopped her cold. Slowly, she straightened and turned. And saw the VCR digital display click to life. A program was being taped.

Ariel felt the hairs on her neck creep to attention. Relief at finding herself alone battled the eerie realization that it was she, once upon some vanished time, who'd programmed the machine. It might as well have been in another life. She let out a stale lungful of air and sat down, hard. After a few minutes of staring at the TV, her mind as blank as the screen, an idea surfaced.

There were all kinds of gizmos beside the TV and, fortunately, instruction books as well. Flipping through the *TV Guide,* she turned to Monday's listings. She found *The Open File,* punched in the code and read the description of the program Mrs. Harris had been so eager to see. It was a magazine news show, from what Ariel had gathered from both her neighbor and Henry, and last week's edition had featured a prizefighter who'd died in the ring in 1956, a man who may have knowingly infected his lover with AIDS and a little boy who'd been lost in the Great Smoky Mountains and who claimed that a vision had guided him to searchers. Hmmm, she thought; no comment until I watch it for myself. She looked up daily shows in competition with hers and entered the codes to tape three tomorrow night. Then, curious, she looked to see what the machine was so industriously taping at the moment. The craggy face of Bogart, wreathed in cigarette smoke, almost brought her to tears. It was *Casablanca,* and she'd missed only the first few minutes.

She settled back on the pillows, rapt, occasionally mouthing the dialogue in sync with the actors. By the time Bogie and Claude Rains walked off into the night, however, she was curled into a fetal position, oblivious to the start of their beautiful friendship.

By that time, too, the dark gray car across the street had long since rolled away into the night.

thirteen

W̲ell, he brooded as he steered through a deserted intersection, that little stakeout was less than conclusive.

He'd had time to kill between this evening's affair and his flight departure time and, while he'd have preferred to spend it in more profitable pursuits, he'd chosen discipline over diversion—certainty, if possible, over doubt. So he'd driven to her house.

He'd been prepared to keep moving at the slightest sign of police presence—had in fact circled the block twice before parking in front of the only unoccupied-looking house from which he could observe hers—but he'd seen no one and heard nothing. The sorry fact was that while his reconnoitering had provided no evidence that she was dead, it had provided no evidence to the contrary.

He glanced in his rearview mirror as he slowed for a stop sign. The face that looked back was grim. All this speculation, he thought, was getting tedious.

Ever since his rendezvous with the late, unlamented Rodriquez, he'd had a certain ... unease about the entire Gold project. Rodriquez had been too much the wild card. Rodriquez had been, to put it simply, a mistake.

After today, he had no further doubts on that score.

He'd had a meeting with his attorneys, whose offices happened to be in the vicinity of the courthouse, and he'd been returning to his car when a man had approached, the last man he wanted to see.

"The Jack," as Daryl Benson was known—a tribute to his expertise in the hijacking trade—was an ex-con and recent "consultant," one of the resources he occasionally utilized for the background color that lent his own work authenticity. If Benson was one of the more bizarre of his contacts, he was no less useful. The hijacker was full of self-importance and, as long as it was off the record, willing to talk about his exploits. He was good at what he did, but not so good that he hadn't spent the majority of his adult life behind bars. Consequently, he knew a great many worthwhile people. He was a gold mine of information, and it was he who'd supplied Rodriquez's name.

Listening to a hypothetical scenario requiring a killer for hire, Benson had been eager to help. Not exactly in my line, he'd said, but here's a guy you could talk to. The solicitation had been subtle. It had been oblique. It had been neither subtle nor oblique enough, and Benson had remembered it.

This afternoon, after entirely too much hail-fellow-well-met familiarity, he'd wasted no time in bringing up his old pal and erstwhile cellmate.

"Hey," Benson had bleated, "is this some coincidence! You remember Rodriquez? The guy I told you about? He bit it last night, Rodriquez did. Got blown away by some broad. The sumbitch broke into her house or something, I heard, and she let him have it."

Looking back on the episode now, he marveled that he'd kept his composure. He'd feigned ignorance, made puzzled sounds. "Rodriquez? I don't think I recall . . . ?"

His alarm hadn't been feigned.

He'd cut the conversation as short as possible and, wishing the ex-con luck in his latest scrape with the law, hurried on.

Rodriquez, he conceded, had been an unknown quantity, not thought out. He should never have hired such a hopped-up incompetent, should never have let the need for haste cloud his judgment. He shouldn't, getting down to cases, have involved anyone else in Gold's elimination. Distasteful though it might have been, he should have handled it himself. There would have been no mistakes.

And no wondering now if she was alive and if Rodriquez had paid her a visit last night.

A stop sign reminded him to keep a part of his mind on his driving and, circumspect, he stopped. Though there were few cars abroad at this late hour—not in this neighborhood—the very emptiness of the streets dictated caution, and caution was second nature. He'd learned it young.

He'd never been called to legal account for any action, never been issued a ticket for a moving violation or even for an expired meter. He paid his taxes in full and on time. His public image was pristine, reinforced by high-profile philanthropism; he was generous, at least with his name. His indiscretions were conducted discreetly, and any associations less than socially acceptable were easily explained by his work. He was a model of rectitude, insofar as any living person knew, and he intended to keep it that way.

Which accounted for the last few hours of wasted time.

He turned onto the 405 entrance ramp and merged into light southbound traffic, mulling over the night's observations.

Each of the other houses on the woman's street had had trash cans out front, waiting for a morning collection. Hers hadn't. It might be significant, or she might simply be lazy. The exterior floodlights were probably on a timer, so their being on was meaningless. The same went for the lawn sprinklers, which at one point had spurted into action like Old Faithful, and for the answering machine that had picked up when he'd telephoned earlier—and hung up, of course, without leaving a message. Why, after all, would anyone have deactivated lights or a sprinkler system or disconnected the answering machine?

If the evil that man does lives after him, he thought in frustration, so do the machines man sets in motion. The house might go roboting on, untouched by human hands, until the power was cut off or the bulbs burned out.

In fact, he realized as if a bulb had popped on over his own head, the lawn sprinklers coming on might be significant. It had rained for the better part of three days. If someone were living at the house, wouldn't automatic sprinklers have been turned off?

He exited at La Tijera and, waiting for the light to change, drummed the steering wheel.

There was no reason to assume that the "broad" Benson had referred to was Gold. No reason to believe that Rodriquez had stooped to burglarizing houses, particularly since he'd just earned a fair amount of money in a completely different and more advanced area of criminal endeavor. Probably, the incident that had ended with his death was some sort of sordid dispute. Some woman he'd met in a bar, perhaps, who'd spurned his advances. Or something involving drugs—that was the more likely explanation. It was true, admittedly, that he'd given Rodriquez Gold's name and, thereby, access to her address. He'd regretted it at the time as a mistake, a slip of the tongue. But perhaps it hadn't been. Perhaps it was yet another example of the charmed life he had always led.

It had been unlikely that Rodriquez could connect him to the project; now it was more than unlikely. It was impossible. The man was out of the picture.

Making a left onto Airport Boulevard, he stopped at an all-night service station. While the dull-looking attendant topped off the tank, he mentally ticked off the facts one more time.

The brief follow-up story buried in this morning's Metro section had few new details to offer. Either the car had been demolished beyond belief or the police were being more closemouthed than usual. The victim, the paper had said, was still unidentified. But if Gold had been reported missing, surely they would've made the connection by now. So why hadn't anyone reported her missing? Had the woman no friends? No family? She was as troublesome in death as she'd been in life.

He cursed, not for the first time, that unfortunate interview. It had been so long ago! His little comment had been so obscure! It was incredible that she'd remembered and, with so little to go on for so long, that she hadn't given up. That was the most chilling thing, to learn just how long, unknown to him, that interfering bitch had been dogging him.

He wondered if she'd ever had any real evidence or if, as it now appeared, she'd been bluffing. He wished that his search of her house hadn't been interrupted, though evidence had never really been the issue. She was. What she would have done with what little he'd found hidden in her closet was enough to raise too many questions. The file of newspaper clippings, the interview transcript and the notes outlining her entirely too accurate conjecture would have been more than enough to damn him by innuendo if not official investigation.

By the time he'd paid for the gas and eased back into

slightly heavier traffic, he'd convinced himself that she was dead. She had to be! If the job had been bungled, he'd have heard from her by now, directly or indirectly. He knew she'd left her house at the appropriate time and driven off in the direction of the restaurant. He knew because he'd watched her go. If she'd been there and lived to tell the tale, she'd have a *real* tale to tell—considerably more than mere suspicions and circumstantial evidence. Unquestionably, fear would have impelled her to go to the police rather than continuing with her ill-advised Lone Ranger act.

He turned left onto Century. The more he thought about it, the more convinced he was that he could go on to New York without misgiving. Could put this episode behind him. Could begin to enjoy the rewards of his labor, unencumbered by worries from any quarter.

He pulled into the car rental agency and, before retrieving his hanging bag from the backseat, made a note of the mileage.

Still and all, he thought as he dropped his receipt into the slot and boarded the tram, it would be a relief when and if the police identified the bombing victim—just to wrap it all up neatly.

fourteen

$152,850.

She was worth $152,850!

Ariel still couldn't comprehend it. And she couldn't wipe the dopey smile from her face.

This morning she'd awakened, sorer than ever, from a gut-wrenching dream about skull-faces, white rooms and blinding explosions. She'd felt like a dog with distemper and looked like the dog's breakfast. The similes had moped through her mind as she'd fed and watered Jessie, and the second one had been confirmed when she'd gone to the medicine cabinet for aspirin. The mirror had caught her in midyawn. She'd closed her mouth and studied her reflection. It hadn't been uplifting.

The lump on her forehead had subsided, but the bruise on her cheek was now a bilious yellow-green. The skin around her eyes was fluffy from too much sleep. Her hair was lank with bad perming and the need to be washed. She'd downed her aspirin with a sigh.

She'd piled up on the bedroom chaise longue with her coffee, the last of the file folders and yesterday's mail to keep her company. When she'd opened the first letter, the morning had taken a dramatic turn for the better.

In an envelope from Coast National Bank had been the news that her CDs were up for renewal—her two $50,000 CDs. If the new interest rate wasn't thrilling, the knowledge that she didn't have to worry about her immediate future was.

The balance of the mail had reaped nothing more than regret that trees had been sacrificed to make the paper, but one of the folders had stopped her with the coffee cup half-way to her lips.

It seemed that she had five thousand shares in a Vanguard fixed-income securities fund, each worth $10.57. Simple multiplication told her that she was $52,850 richer. Hurriedly, she'd looked through the folder. The dates were current; there was nothing to indicate that she no longer owned the shares.

She sat now on the backyard patio, watching Jessie lolling in the sunshine, evidently none the worse for her wound. A hibiscus tree was in full, radiant flower. Along the fence pruned roses sprouted vigorous little red leaves in anticipation and, twining over a trellis in the corner, Japanese wisteria was beginning to bloom. Pansies nodded friendly heads around the periphery of the patio, and cyclamen staged an elegant show under the shade of a lemon tree drooping with fruit. The birds, cooperatively, provided background music, singing their cheerful little hearts out. It was a most beautiful and glorious morning, it was the most wonderful morning Ariel could remember, and the fact that it was only the third one was neither here nor there.

She owned a fine house in, from what little she'd seen, a fine neighborhood. She had $317 and change in her wallet, $2,224 in her checking account and $152,850 in additional assets. There was a classic car in the garage and, if she hadn't yet found the title, she had a sneaking suspicion it was hers free and clear—she seemed to be the kind of person who owned things free and clear. She was elated. She was euphoric. She hoped her gains weren't ill-gotten.

She willed all thoughts of blackmail and bank heists out of her mind and marveled at how despondent she'd felt just an hour ago. "Consistency is the last refuge of the unimaginative," she told herself, repressing a desire to giggle.

Jessie, ever vigilant, leaped up to evict a marauding squirrel, which streaked up a tree onto the fence. The cheeky rodent paused just long enough to offer a squirrel's version of a Bronx cheer before disappearing in a flash of fur. Ariel laughed and closed her eyes, every pore drinking in the warm sunlight. Behind her lids bright colors danced for a few seconds before settling into a steady red glow. It was the first conscious moment since this purgatory had begun in which she felt absolutely relaxed. She reached out a languid hand for her coffee just as the telephone began to ring.

The bubble burst.

Struggling up, she made it to the phone just before the machine could take charge.

Her hello was tentative.

"Ariel! Neely. Heard your party got a little out of hand the other night. That'll teach you to bring home every joker you pick up in those meat markets you hang in."

Neely? Who the dickens was Neely?

"Massey was going to call to tell you you could pick up your gun—we greased the skids on the check, but I said I would. Hey, you okay?"

Ariel's mind clicked through the conversation with Detective Massey. He'd mentioned a Neely, someone he worked with. Someone who knew her and thought she was painful, as she recalled, painful but straight. A bulldog, he'd said. She cleared her throat, trying to decide what tone to take. Was he someone she knew through her work? What if he was a close friend and, if so, how close? Unable to figure out how to evince camaraderie and neutrality both, she finally, blandly said, "Oh, I'm . . . okay, I guess. And you?"

"Fine. Great. Look here, you want to come down and

pick up the piece? Or I could bring it by the studio. I called there first, but they said you were on vacation."

"I'll pick it up. Thanks."

She was about to go into a somebody's-at-the-door routine when it occurred to her to ask about the intruder. Apparently, this man was a source of some kind who might be good for information. She tried to sound straight. Bulldoggish.

"Say, about the man who broke in here—this Rodriquez. What's the story on him, do you know?"

"Gold, Gold! Shame on you. What is this? A little subornation, maybe? There is such a thing as privacy, you know."

She winced. She'd asked something she shouldn't have. Her ignorance had given her away.

"But . . . for you?" Neely asked. "You do have a personal interest, don't you?" The hearty voice became official, as if Neely was reading something. "His current sheet's mostly drug-related. There were some B and E's a long time ago, and there was something screwy while he was in the army. He got section-eighted, I gather. Everything since then's been petty for the most part. Some arrests but no indictments. There was a biggie a few years ago. A bombing. He was brought in for questioning when a lawyer got smeared all over his Beemer. Seems that was Rodriquez's gig in the army. Explosives. On-job training opened up a whole new world for Luis."

Ariel heard what sounded like a snort. It might have been a laugh.

"The bad news is you and I paid for a psycho to learn a trade. The good news is, if he was the perp, it was a lawyer he took out."

She had no idea how to respond to that.

"Hello? Come in, Gold! You must really be feeling poorly, lady. I can't even get a rise out of you! From what I heard, this nutcase came after you with a knife. Your heart can't be bleeding over this thing? Come on!"

Ariel squelched sudden anger. "Maybe," she said, "you had to be there."

"Yes, well, I have, pal. Now you have, too."

"What was he doing out, anyway? On the street? If he

killed a law—a man 'a few years ago'? How many years ago?"

"*You're* asking me that? *You?* Well, well! Things do change when it hits close to home, I guess! Anyway, I didn't say he was charged, just questioned. But if you want to talk about in and out? About revolving doors? About the scum walking before we can get the paperwork finished? There was this mutt last week—Unh-unh! Stop! This is be-kind-to-ulcer week, and we're not gonna have this conversation. So, you going somewhere for your vacation or you just going to sit home and suffer?"

"Sit. Suffer. I guess."

"When do you want to pick up the gun?"

"I think . . . tomorrow. Is that okay? Who do I ask for?"

"Makes no difference. If I'm here, I'll see you, but you just identify yourself, you'll get it. No worries, as my Australian friends say. Gotta go. I'm late for court as usual."

"Wait! What's the address there?"

"You think we moved from these luxury accommodations? We're still on Butler as far as I know. Maybe I'll see you tomorrow—if you don't see me first and all that. Ciao, baby."

Ariel looked at the receiver in disbelief. Some genteel chums I've got, she thought. Criminy!

Absentmindedly, her mind still on the conversation, she began looking for something that might pass for breakfast. A trip to the grocery, along with several other errands, was definitely in order.

A black banana went into the garbage. Twinkies *Light?* She read the box. Only 130 calories instead of the usual 140 or 150 or whatever—a dieter's dream. And they were stale, besides. As she started to toss the offending sweets in after the banana, the doorbell rang, throwing off her aim considerably. She limped to the front door and looked through the peephole.

Rodriquez stared back at her.

She choked back a scream and jerked away.

It couldn't be. She closed her eyes and took several deep breaths, fighting panic.

He's dead. You saw him. The police saw him. Victor saw him.

She forced herself to look again.

The man on the porch was, indeed, dark-skinned. But he was, she saw now, younger than Rodriquez and slighter. Other than the fact that they were both Hispanic, this man actually bore little resemblance to the dead man.

She unlocked the dead bolt and, keeping the chain on, looked through the crack.

"Missus? You forgot to unlock," the man said politely.

He was wearing a dark blue coverall, gloves and a leaf blower. She looked beyond him to the front yard, where a second man, dressed similarly except for the leaf blower, waited beside a sputtering lawn mower that belched black smoke and obnoxious fumes.

She found her voice. "Unlock?"

"The gate. So that we can go into the backyard."

"You're gardeners?"

He smiled uncertainly, as one might at a person of unsound mind. "Yes, missus."

"Oh, yes. I see. I just didn't . . . I wasn't . . . I'll open the gate."

She closed the door and relocked it.

She found Jessie waiting at the side gate, her tail wagging eagerly. Well, I guess that settles that, she thought as she unlocked the gate. Feeling justified in her caution but foolish nonetheless, she watched the happy reunion of man and dog and then retreated into the house.

Later, munching a saltine, she watched the men going efficiently about their business, Jessie romping beside the one who'd rung the bell. Okay, she thought, false alarm. This time. But I'm still going to wait until they leave before I shower. And, she decided, I think I'll pick up the gun today instead of tomorrow.

When the leaf blower was activated, she retreated, covering her ears and scowling, into the bedroom. She searched through the closet; the contents did nothing to erase her scowl.

How could I have such an unerring eye in putting together this house and be so blind when it comes to myself? she wondered. The clothes were of good quality, admittedly, but undistinguished, their hues muddy, more camouflage than color. She fingered a suit—a highly unsuitable suit for her figure, such as it was. She must look like Idaho's best in that, she thought.

By the time the cacophony outside had stopped and blessed silence ensued, she'd put together black trousers, a black knit tunic and a fringed Spanish scarf that had probably graced someone's piano at some time or other. Black flats and tights completed the ensemble, which looked a bit eccentric, but not dowdy, dammit.

The doorbell rang again.

Leaning on her cane and stumping to the door like Long John Silver, she peered again through the peephole and opened the door to the gardener who was Jessie's bosom friend.

"Yes?"

"Can I get paid, missus? It's the second Wednesday?"

"Oh, of course. That's the usual amount, I guess?"

He wasn't helpful. "Yes, missus."

"How much, please?"

"Seventy," he said, looking more uncomfortable by the moment.

She found her purse and counted out eighty dollars. "Just a little bonus. The yard looks great. Thanks."

The very dim wattage of his smile increased somewhat. "You didn't put out the garbage cans last night," he offered helpfully, quid pro quo, "but it's okay. Next week."

Smiling, having done his duty, he took his leave.

Within the hour Ariel was dressed and ready to go. Her makeshift outfit looked pretty spiffy, her hair was washed and pulled back with combs into some semblance of style and the address of the police station was in her bag. It would be the first time she'd braved the outside world under her own steam, and she felt uneasiness, even dread, at leaving the house. Scolding herself for agoraphobia on top of everything else, she'd pressed the button to open the garage door when an unwelcome thought struck: what would she do if the car was a straight shift? She looked at her cast speculatively; there was no way she could steer and change gears, not to mention manipulate a clutch. Leaving the front door open, she went to the car and peered in the window. Automatic.

"Yes!" she breathed as she returned to the house, bade Jessie good-bye and, concentrating fiercely, activated the burglar alarm.

The car started immediately, and as it idled she familiarized herself with the dashboard, where everything seemed slightly out of place. The mirrors and seat, on the other hand, were positioned perfectly. Resting her left hand in her lap, she backed out.

She thought she remembered Detective Massey's route from the morning before. She didn't. Cautiously, she crept down one street and up another. Nothing was familiar. Then she emerged from the cloistered neighborhood onto a busy intersection that most definitely was. They hadn't been through here yesterday; Ariel was sure of it. She was just as sure that she had been here sometime. Scarcely breathing, she turned right and within seconds Wilshire Boulevard lay just ahead. She knew precisely where she was.

She pulled over to the curb. Ignoring horns and impatient drivers swerving around her, she stilled the knee that had launched itself into involuntary tremor. She knew the street, true enough; it was a major thoroughfare. But it held no personal significance. It was familiar in the way a map of the United States was, or Mount Rushmore or the Empire State Building. After a long moment, she took a deep breath and steered back into traffic. Pushing down disappointment, wondering at the curious selectivity of memory, she turned left, toward what she knew was Beverly Hills.

After a few blocks of keeping pace with the unremitting traffic, Ariel was limp with the effort. She was infinitely relieved to see the distinctive dome of the Beverly Hills Civic Center, her first stop.

She turned into the lot that served the library as well as city hall and a police department—unfortunately, not the one she needed to go to. Giving the attendant her best damsel-in-distress smile, she explained that a very recent accident made it necessary that she park in a handicap space. Please? And where, by the way, did one go to get a permit?

The attendant suggested city hall and waved her into a nearby blue-striped space with a conspiratorial wink.

Following signs, Ariel came to one pointing the way to city hall. She took a hard look at the stairs and curving, ascending walkways that led to that office and opted for the ground-level library first. Or maybe only.

An imposing marble sculpture in the foyer ("Fusion," according to a discreet plaque) should have prepared her for an atypical library, but when she pushed through swinging doors into a vast room reminiscent of Union Station in its heyday, she stopped short. Natural light quietly caressed marble and mahogany, multicolored tiles and muted pastels. The vaulted ceiling and skylights, the arched galleries and geometrical light fixtures were a pastiche of Moorish flourishes and art deco precision. And everywhere in the immense, hushed space were books, by the hundreds of thousands.

She was almost certain she'd never been here before. She was glad she'd washed her hair and dressed decently. Limping past a grand staircase, past paintings and sculpted torsos, she stopped to read a plaque. Rodin. She looked at the sinuous black bronze more carefully. Only in Beverly Hills, she marveled.

When she reached the first of several reference rooms, she stopped and looked around, puzzled.

"Excuse me," she whispered to a smartly groomed Asian woman behind the information desk, "but where's the card catalogue?"

Eyebrows were delicately lifted a fraction of an inch. The woman pointed behind Ariel to several computer screens. "If you need help, let me know."

Eventually, Ariel was ensconced on one of the plush mauve sofas, a stack of tomes on a low table at her knee. With whispered assurances that she needn't bother replacing the books, the helpful information lady glanced curiously at cane, cast and face and left her alone. Ariel opened the first book to the reference on amnesia.

"Caused by damage or disease of the brain region concerned with memory functions," she read.

Scanning rapidly, she learned that the condition "might result from a head injury such as a concussion (as she knew) or a degenerative disorder such as Alzheimer's disease (non-applicable, surely) and other forms of dementia."

In *Harrison's Principles of Internal Medicine* she read that in severe cases the failure to recall extended to all events of one's past life, including personal identification, and that it was often due to "hysteria or malingering."

She closed the book and picked up another in which she learned that hysterical amnesia is "a very real syndrome that is not under conscious control" and another that cited examples of amnesics manifesting dramatic personality changes, many behaving in a manner diametrically opposed to their former selves.

During the next hour she read about possible organic causes—infections like encephalitis, thiamine deficiency in alcoholics leading to Wernicke-Korsakoff syndrome, brain tumors, strokes and subarachnoid hemorrhage—and psychogenic causes: psychiatric illness with no apparent physical damage. She learned about retrograde amnesia (the memory gap extending back from onset of damage), which she apparently had, and anterograde amnesia (a gap extending from the onset of amnesia until long-term memory resumes—"if it ever does"—during which the patient may be unable to store new information), which she wasn't sure she understood.

Ariel was only marginally aware that someone had sat down across from her as she read and then reread a passage advising that if memory returned, the present—or that which occurs between losing one's memory and regaining it—might be wiped out. With her own recent behavior in mind, she read that the amnesic might be subject to extreme impulsiveness, might suffer rapid and frequent mood swings and might exhibit inappropriate behavior such as outbursts of anger, laughter or tears.

Finally, she read that either a cataclysmic or a simple event can suddenly bring back memory, that the results of using hypnosis to restore memory were generally disappointing and that consulting a psychiatrist was indicated "only if the amnesic can't cope."

As Ariel sat trying to sort through what was relevant and what wasn't, what she'd understood and what she hadn't and what she should do, if anything, she became fully aware of the woman sitting on the other side of the table.

She was a little younger than Ariel and quite pretty. When she bent to gather up her belongings in preparation for leaving, her glossy blond hair made a graceful little swoop forward, then fell back into place as if choreographed.

"Pardon me," Ariel whispered impulsively, squelching thoughts of aberrant, impulsive behavior that came belatedly to mind, "your haircut's really great. Would you mind telling me where you get it done?"

As would most people, the woman found such a complimentary question irresistible. She smiled in a friendly way, creating two deep dimples, and whispered back. "Thanks. It's a new cut, and I wasn't too sure about it. Here, I'll write down the name of the salon for you. It's near here, as a matter of fact." Glancing around, she grabbed a small white square of paper from the pile of books and papers in her lap and jotted down the information.

"Sean does me, but they're all supposed to be good."

She stood to leave, then glanced uncertainly at Ariel's cast. "Do you need any help?"

Ariel declined with thanks and watched the woman walk away, envying her tiny but curvy figure, her perfect, long legs, her confident, graceful stride. Probably dumb as a post, she thought, and felt mean as a snake for thinking it. She read the shop name and "Sean" beneath it. She flipped the paper over. Listed in the same neat handwriting were six or so scholarly-sounding titles, each with lots of colons and about ten polysyllabic words. They all seemed to be concerned with the Code of Hammurabi.

Feeling as if she might be about to exhibit some inappropriate laughter, Ariel hooked her purse on her shoulder and limped out of the library.

fifteen

Expecting something like the set from *Detective Story*—bleak, Spartan and pulsing with seedy, film noir life—Ariel was vaguely disappointed by the prosaic police station in which she found herself.

A dozen molded plastic chairs bolted in a neat row along a windowed wall were all empty. The linoleum floor was recently waxed. A poster beside a door on the far wall exhorted in italicized capitals that *THE POLICE ARE THE PEOPLE. THE PEOPLE ARE THE POLICE.* Behind a polyurethane-sealed counter a large black-and-white map delineated the precinct's sphere of responsibility, and beneath it were two desks, one empty except for basic equipment and a healthy philodendron. At the other sat not Kirk Douglas, nor even William Bendix, but an attractive, dark-haired policewoman, talking on the telephone.

She glanced in Ariel's direction and held up one finger. After making a note on a pad, she hung up. "Be right with you," she said, and disappeared through a swinging door.

Before the door swung shut and again when the woman reemerged a few seconds later, Ariel could hear an agitated din beyond it. Raised voices, ringing phones and the hollow clang of a metal door suggested that crime wasn't on hiatus; the bad guys were just being kept out of public view.

"Yes, ma'am," Officer Presnell (according to the pin on her chest pocket) inquired, "what can I do for you?"

Ariel gave her name and, feeling like a vigilante, explained her business. If the policewoman had any opinions on the subject of citizens wielding weapons, she didn't express them. She made a brief phone call and invited Ariel to be seated. Lieutenant Neely, she said, would be right out.

Before Ariel could discover a comfortable position in one of the plastic chairs, an extremely tall, extremely thick man came plowing through the swinging door, grinning broadly. He looked to be in his midthirties and had the type of thin, reddish-blond hair that waves tightly and naturally and comes with very white skin. His eyes, dark hazel under almost invisible eyelashes, were edged with the fine lines that usually denote a lot of time spent squinting or laughing—or in Neely's case, both.

"Hey, Gold," he cried, ducking through the opening under the counter, "I thought you said you'd be down tomorrow. Somebody you can't wait to shoot?"

He dropped her gun, still in a plastic evidence bag, in her lap and plunked into a chair two over from hers. Propping his ankle on his knee, he drew barely discernible eyebrows together and studied the evidence of her various afflictions.

"You look like a riot refugee."

"Thanks," Ariel said, averting her face.

"Still bleeding from the heart about offing the slimeball?"

"Well, I'm not planning to star in a remake of *Death Wish,* but I didn't harbor one either." She'd meant to sound defiant, but suspected she just sounded defensive. "Have y'all found out anything more about the dead man?"

"What I told you is what there is as far as we know. Guess Rodriquez decided bombs were too dangerous and decided to pick up his drug money in the usual way—B and E. Shows how wrong you can be." He pointed his forefinger at Ariel, thumb vertical. "Bang!" he mouthed.

The man's cynicism was beginning to make Ariel feel as if she needed a bath. She dropped the gun into her handbag and grasped her cane with great dignity. As this seemed to be the day for vintage movies, she thought of Gladys Cooper in *Now, Voyager.* Or maybe she was more Helen Hayes in *Anastasia.* Staring straight ahead, she said, "I understand that it was because of you that Detective Massey drove me home yesterday. Thank you."

Neely lifted a shoulder. "No big deal. I do what I can."

He cleared his throat. "Anyway," he said in a much quieter voice, "I owe you. It meant a lot, your sitting with Marcie those last nights in the hospital, knowing she wasn't by herself when I was working."

Mystified, Ariel cut her eyes toward the man, but now his face was averted. When he turned back, his grin was back in place.

"Enough of that. Hey, how'd you get down here? You're not driving with that bum hand?"

Wondering if she'd imagined the fleeting transformation in the giant beside her, Ariel admitted she was. "Yes. I didn't ... actually, maybe you could tell me something. I need a temporary handicapped-parking permit. Do you know where to get one? Or how?"

He winked. "Stay put."

Folding his bulk nearly double, Neely ducked under the counter again and disappeared through the swinging door.

She stared after him, her confidence in her people judgment seriously undermined. Under all that crude bluster and black humor seemed to beat, if not a heart of gold, at least a heart—and one that had suffered, apparently. She wondered who Marcie was. And what had happened to her.

Both Ariel and the policewoman at the desk jumped as the outside door banged open. A diminutive meter maid (meter person?) came in, trailed by a very vocal man in a goatee, ragged jeans and a sweatshirt with the sleeves torn off. He was dogging the woman's heels, waving a parking ticket and furiously demanding an answer to some question he'd asked before they entered the room.

"What sign?" he was yelling at her back. "Where? Show me a sign!"

A deafening clatter brought Ariel half out of her chair. Neely had suddenly materialized, slamming the drop door back onto the countertop. This time, he walked through the opening upright. Placing his huge hand on the bearded man's shoulder, he said, very quietly, "If you're looking for a sign, son, you'd better try a church. If you need something explained to you about that ticket, you ask nicely."

The irate citizen looked up. By the time his eyes met Neely's his head was tilted back so far that his beard, which jutted out belligerently, was parallel to the floor. Ariel could see his Adam's apple bob.

He nodded and took two steps backward before edging sideways and out the door.

The meter maid eyed Neely, her expression flat, her fingernails tapping the counter in irritation. "Thanks. I needed that. Not." She left through the door beside the Police Are People poster.

Neely, unabashed, leered after her.

"Feisty little morsel, isn't she?"

He reluctantly returned his attention to Ariel, handing her a large black-and-white card. "Your permit, madam."

"Is that all there is to it?" She took the card in surprise. "Don't I need a note from a doctor or to pay a fee or something?"

"Normally." Sucking his back teeth, Neely leaned against the counter and crossed his arms. "You'll notice I made it valid for a month; if that's not long enough, let me know. Also, I didn't figure you had my home number, so I wrote it on the back."

A long, awkward moment ticked by, and he looked relieved when a new subject occurred to him.

"So, you doing anything with what I gave you on Carroll?"

Carol? Ariel frowned. Who was Carol?

"Well . . . we'll see what we'll see." She couldn't imagine a more inane response.

He consulted the oversized clock behind him and whistled, slapping the flat of his hand on the counter emphatically.

"I'm out of here. Look, Ace, you stay cool and don't shoot 'til you see the whites of their eyes, okay?"

In midstride, he stopped. "You call me if you need me."

Within seconds he'd barreled through the swinging door again, leaving the room feeling empty as a vacuum.

sixteen

By the time Ariel had hefted the last bag of groceries into the kitchen, she was shaky with exhaustion. She dropped into a chair, panting and gathering her strength, and gave Jessie a rundown on the adventure in store.

"Victor's coming to walk you in a few minutes," she promised the dog, whose tail thumped a hint that she knew something was in the wind. "And in a day or two I'll be able to take you myself. Lord knows I need the exercise! You and I'll be out there parading up and down the street with Mrs. Harris and Rudy the Wonder Dog."

After putting away the perishables—yogurt and milk (nonfat), chicken (skinless) and a veritable truck garden of raw vegetables—she managed to slice an apple and cheddar into a somewhat cockeyed presentation. She arranged the snack with crackers and then hobbled into the living room, where she sank gratefully onto the sofa. Immediately, the doorbell chimed.

Victor looked considerably more professional in a sportcoat and tie than he had in pajamas.

"You're certainly looking better," he said, mirroring her thoughts. "But why're you so dressed up? You didn't go to work today?"

Ariel assured him otherwise, grinning along with Jessie as she greeted the vet. "Bless your heart, Victor, for doing this. I'll swear she knows she's finally going to get out of the house!"

"Well, we'll just get the show on the road then, and I'll check her stitches when we come back. Where's her leash?"

Good question, thought Ariel, who couldn't remember having seen one. "I don't know what I've done with it. Let me look ..."

"Never mind! You sit and rest. I've got an extra in the car and a flashlight and plastic bags, too, for, um ... in case."

She watched them vanish into the darkness and turned back to a house that felt very empty indeed without the dog's presence. She locked the door.

By the time they returned, she'd put away the remainder of the groceries, scoured the sink unnecessarily, freshened herself up, taken the hors d'oeuvres, which looked even sadder as the apple had started to turn brown, into the living room and turned on the news to kill the silence. Jessie gave her the briefest of greetings before trotting to the kitchen, from which grateful lapping and then the crunch of kibble was heard. The humans settled down to their own food, and Ariel slipped into her sleuth persona.

"We've never really talked about your practice," she

prodded, hoping it was true. "How you got started, what your plans are and so on. Tell me about it."

Looking confused and obviously feeling foolish, Victor gave short and modest shrift to his beginnings and then, frequently protesting that she already knew all this, described the clinic, which catered to small animals, and the regular kennel, which sounded not only humane but luxurious. Gently nudged by Ariel, he went on to talk about the orphans' kennel, clearly his great joy.

"You know, of course, that it's staffed by volunteers and also—I'm not sure if you realized this—by people who can't afford to pay for services. They work it off, which is good for both of us. Have I ever told you, by the way, that we've found a home for every homeless animal that's ever been brought in? Every one! And that includes the odd boa constrictor or gator, which goes to the zoo. So," he finished, "that's about it. Except that if it weren't for people like you, there wouldn't be an orphans' kennel. I'm just glad to be able to do something to repay you."

He bit into a cracker, looking as if he wanted to say more.

"What?" Ariel smiled encouragingly.

"You seem ... different. Do you mind my saying so? Is it just because we're out of the usual setting?"

"Different how?"

"You've just always seemed so reserved. So private." The words tumbled out, perhaps before he could lose his nerve. "So—what's the term?—uptight?" He faltered. "Or maybe just shy. I can certainly identify with that."

"Tell me what other impressions you've had about me."

"I always had the feeling that you were—do you really want to hear this?—that you were sad, somehow. I wondered if that was because of your marriage?"

Bingo! Ariel thought. "What made you think that?"

"I don't know, really. Just a hunch. You only mentioned once that you were married. Or at least that you had been?"

Who was pumping whom here, Ariel wondered. "I don't remember the reference ... ?"

"You know, it was when Mrs. Bonaccolto brought in her Shar-Pei. And her husband was with her? And he had on that kind of, you know, slinky silk suit and gold neck chains and that flashy pinkie ring. I mean, he was sort of a stereo-typical Sicilian. . . ." He shrugged. "Besides sounding like a bigot, I'm getting away from the point. You said something like he reminded you of 'Michael's business associates,' and when I asked who Michael was, you said, 'The man I was married to.' You didn't elaborate and, frankly, the way you said it didn't invite questions. No offense."

Ariel opened her mouth and closed it again. Her husband, or former husband, was associated with Mafia types?

"Ariel? Did I bring up bad memories? I'm sorry!"

"No." She willed her mouth into a smile. She had to give this one some thought. Big time. "I think I'm just a little overtired," she said. Also I think I'm going to hyperventilate, she didn't say. "Were you going to take a look at Jessie's war wound?"

When he'd done so and taken his leave, looking surprised but a great deal perkier when she kissed his cheek, Ariel checked every door and window and burglar control. Taking the gun from her purse, she ripped off the plastic bag. Once the gun was loaded, her breathing became easier, but her thoughts were still in turmoil. She couldn't begin to figure out what to do next.

Sensing anxiety, Jessie placed an inquisitive paw on Ariel's knee.

"It's okay, girl," Ariel prattled, comforting herself as much as the dog, "I'm just wallowing in paranoia again. Taking mental broad jumps from a few careless words—which Victor probably didn't even remember accurately—to Cosa Nostra lurking under the bed. And even if I did say what he said I said, for all I know Michael Gold may be a jewelry salesman. He's got the perfect name for it, don't you think? Maybe he peddles gold chains and tacky rings from the inside of a trench coat. Or hey! Maybe he's a tailor, and he specializes in slinky suits."

She felt the tiniest bit better. She even managed a laugh. It skittered into a shriek when the phone rang. "A little jumpy are you, dear?" she taunted herself as she lifted the instrument.

"Ms. Gold. Marguerite Harris. If this isn't a good time to call, please say so, but I had to make sure you were all right, do you know? Carl and I just got back from San Francisco—we were there for a revival of my first play, which went over well, I'm happy to say, but that's neither here nor there, is it?—and I heard from Anita Stroud next door that you'd had quite a bit of excitement at your house. She said there were police cars and an ambulance there in the middle of the night! Don't think I'm being intrusive, but I was concerned that you'd been hurt. Were you?"

Ariel, as always when talking (listening?) to Mrs. Harris, felt as if the conversation had fast-framed out of control. She'd managed to keep up with the rapid-fire soliloquy only halfway through. "Your first play? Are you an actress?"

"Great heavens, no! But some of my best friends are, and I try not to hold it against them. Do you realize that you seldom answer a question?"

"No." Ariel grinned.

"That's better. Now, tell me, are you all right?"

"I've been better, Mrs. Harris; I've been better." She was about to elaborate when she heard a tiny beep. "Is your telephone beeping?"

"I don't think so. Why?"

"Oh, wait! I must have Call Waiting. Could you hold for a minute?" Ariel pushed FLASH. Tentatively, she said, "Hello?"

"Henry here. I wanted to let you know—"

"Oh, Henry. Hold on." Back with Mrs. Harris, Ariel assured her that she was sound in mind and body and, apologizing, promised to see her soon.

"Henry! Sorry. All of a sudden it's communications central here."

"I thought you were supposed to be resting. In fact, that's why I'm calling. You do have the six weeks coming if you want it, even though you really should've forfeited the time you didn't take last year, but even so, you'd still have three weeks this year. Are you with me on that?"

"Thanks, Henry, I appreciate it, but I'll stick with the three weeks for the time being."

"You sound too quiet."

"Do I?"

Henry didn't reply immediately.

She heard the squeaking noise that seemed to accompany deep thought on his part. "You really ought to oil that chair," she observed.

"What? Look, the paychecks came down today, and I thought since I'm covering a meeting for Peacock in your direction tomorrow afternoon, I'd bring yours over. Notice I'm calling rather than just dropping in? I don't want to antagonize Fang."

"Oh, don't go to the trouble, Henry. Really. Why don't you just mail it?"

"I'll see you between five and six," he said, and hung up.

Ariel looked at the phone. "You really ought to learn how to say good-bye," she told the dead line, "not to mention how to take no for an answer."

How was she going to cope with that visit? she wondered. Henry wasn't Victor. She suspected that he was unlikely to be as accepting of her lapses and that her flighty-damsel act wouldn't play in his theater. Would he remember which of her hands was injured? She couldn't recall any reference to "left" or "right"; he'd been too busy carrying on about ka-rate. Well, she thought, she'd worry about that tomorrow. She could always sic Jessie on him.

Meanwhile, cutting back to the chase, how was she going to find out about her missing husband and his questionable associates?

If they'd been divorced in the city, she figured, surely she could locate the decree? She didn't know what sort of information divorce documents included but there'd be an address and, even if it wasn't current, wouldn't his lawyer be named?

She knew there were no files she hadn't already examined, but she looked through them anyway. She did come across one new item. For some unknown reason, the title for the car had been filed with gasoline receipts she'd ignored earlier. Nice as it was to know the car was hers—which had been the case for only a matter of weeks, she noted—it was hardly vital at the moment. She searched the drawers; no divorce papers magically materialized.

Feeling frustrated and cranky, she sat fiddling with the old collar that had belonged, she now knew, to a dog she'd owned before Jessie. Something that was nagging at the edge of her mind surfaced. Jessie's papers! That was something else she hadn't found and, while that wasn't vital either, she made a note to call the number on the shepherd's tag the next day.

Ariel gave up for the evening and made herself a light dinner, eating more out of duty than hunger. She felt wrung out but restless, and it was too early to go to bed anyway. She considered watching the shows she'd taped—doing a little research on the job she'd better know something about before seeing Henry—but she was too antsy, and she had all day tomorrow to do that. It looked like another oldies-but-goodies moviefest night. Halfway to the bedroom she stopped, peering up at the hallway ceiling.

There was a chain hanging there she'd never noticed before. An attic fan? Couldn't be—no slats. What the chain was connected to was a door. A trapdoor. Ariel could just reach the ring on the end of the chain. She pulled it. With only moderate effort, the door opened downward to reveal stairs built onto the underside. Steps extended to about stomach level, the last few still folded, and at the top of the steep staircase was a dark, rectangular hole about three feet by four or five feet. Her eyes on the ceiling, Ariel backed to the switch plate. When she flipped the third switch, the attic was illuminated.

She found a handle and unfolded the last few steps. Cautiously, she climbed into the attic.

Ariel paused on the top step. When she placed her hand on the rough framework to steady herself, she felt a sharp sting. She eased out a splinter and, sucking the tiny puncture, looked around her.

The attic's floor was finished, but wall and ceiling studs were exposed. Only the center area was lighted, and only there could one stand upright.

Scattered here and there were a steamer trunk, several cardboard boxes and a few derelict pieces of furniture. Ariel examined a table of the Danish modern variety. Veneer. A ladder-back chair was nicer, but the caning in the seat was half gone. A truly grotesque fifties-style lamp lurked in the shadows, its squiggle-painted fiberglass shade hanging dejectedly, and beyond it Ariel could make out the handlebars of a stationary bike left to languish in solitude, an unwelcome reminder of failed aspirations. Ariel wondered if it was in the nature of attics to be sad places.

The first cardboard box was filled with dusty paperbacks. Ariel picked up *The Sensuous Woman* and replaced it, rolling her eyes. When she opened the trunk, the odor of mothballs brought tears to her eyes. The clothes packed inside looked no more than ten or fifteen years old, if that. She lifted out a pair of trousers that looked as if they would fit her now, but the next garment, a midcalf-length dress, seemed too small. She pulled out a dozen garments, the ascending and descending sizes eloquent in their suggestion of a woman who lost weight only to regain it.

And there was something else suggestive about the clothes. Some were the tailored, no-nonsense sort she'd found downstairs, but others were girlish in the extreme. She held up a floral chiffon dress and a sheer georgette blouse dripping with lace. Either she'd been schizophrenic in her shopping, she concluded, or she'd been dressing to please someone whose taste was radically different from hers. She was thoughtful as she pushed the clothes back into the trunk and closed the lid.

A second box of paperbacks just about convinced Ariel that her attic discovery was a bust. Then she pushed the lid off the last box.

It was filled with papers. There were yellowed tear sheets from what might have been a high school newspaper and others, slightly less yellowed, from a different newspaper that also had an academic-sounding name. They all bore her byline. She glanced through a write-up of a USC-UCLA basketball game. UCLA had won. She replaced it and pulled out a spiral-bound notebook. Written on the cover was the name "Ariel Munson" and a date. 1973. She reached for another. Her name, followed by 1974. Ariel grabbed another. If she'd kept one for every year, mightn't there be information about one Michael Gold? But the most recent notebook was dated 1982, two years before her marriage.

Feeling a ping of disappointment, Ariel dragged the chair

over and, sitting gingerly on the raveling seat, opened the 1982 notebook to the last page on which there was writing. December 16th. She paged backward. The entries hadn't been made on a day-to-day basis; sometimes there were gaps of a week or more without any of the neat but oddly slanted handwriting. She turned back to the last page, angled the book for better light and read.

I understand M less every day.

He's so incredibly bright and well-read, so sophisticated. His background is so completely beyond my experience.

His feeling for me is one big contradiction. He assures me that he's proud of my intelligence, that he wouldn't care for me if I weren't intelligent, yet he often belittles my opinions. ('Puerile,' he described a comment I made the other day. It's the only time I've ever admitted to myself that he sounded pompous, but it made me love him more to know he's not perfect either.)

He tells me I'm the antithesis of his mother (the awful Muriel!), that he cherishes my lack of superficiality and my system of values. Yet he criticizes how I look and dress, and he was livid when I cut too much of my meat at one time at Muriel's dinner party last weekend. (I hate those trips to San Diego! I am so glad she's spending Christmas in Palm Beach!)

M's mood swings are bewildering. This morning he lashed out at me for being out when he called. He'd needed something typed, he said, and he was 'depending on me.' Of course, he hadn't told me anything about it beforehand. Then, tonight, he was a different person. At dinner with his friends he kept trying to draw me out, talking about my scholarship and regaling them with stories about what he persisted in calling my 'prodigious' memory (which in less happy moments he refers to as my 'idiot savant' memory). And later, when we were alone, he was so gentle.

When he lets himself be vulnerable, I feel as if I'm the strong one.

I wish that money and appearances weren't so important to him, but I'd be satisfied if he admitted that they were.

I don't know what he sees in me or what he wants me to be. Sometimes I suspect he doesn't know either. Although I'd never say this to him, I believe he's torn between what he thinks he should value and what he does, in fact, value.

I'm sure of only one thing: if it's within my power, I'll be whatever he wants.

Ariel closed the book. She had the most confusing sensation of trespass, yet she believed she understood what she'd read exactly, as if she'd written it herself. Well, why not? she frowned. She did write it herself!

On a purely practical note, that one page suggested two things. One, "M" was motivated by money to the degree that it had merited comment by her much younger self and, two, he might have been a resident of San Diego. Or at least it seemed that his mother was.

Ariel scooped up all the notebooks and took them downstairs. Piling them on her bed, she returned to the kitchen and made a pot of strong coffee.

seventeen

My mother died today.

It was the only line on the first page of 1973.

Experiencing the most extraordinary combination of empathy and sympathy, of pity and detached curiosity, Ariel turned to the next page, dated three days later.

I meant to write something every day but I've felt so funny since Mother died that I didn't know what to say. I've been trying to think about what I feel so it would make sense when I wrote it. What Anne Frank wrote always made sense even though she lived through such terrible things. My life's not dangerous like that but we do have a lot of things in common, I think. I guess the important thing is just to say what I feel the best that I can. It's not like I'm going to be graded on this or anybody else is going to read it.

The handwriting of the eleven-year-old child was less well-formed than in the journal of nine years later, but the peculiar curves and angles were essentially the same.

I think I loved Mother. I know that if it hadn't been for her I wouldn't have been allowed to read or study so much. She made Daddy give in on that. But I wish she would have been more like other people's mothers. I wish she'd have told me she loved me and hugged me sometimes.

I don't know what she died of even. She acted different for a long time. Sometimes her hands would shake and lately other things too. She'd forget things people told her and say funny things. I don't mean ha-ha funny. Then all of a sudden she was just gone. When I came home from school Daddy just said she'd passed. But he didn't act sad. He acted mad. He acts mad most of the time anyway so that's not a big surprise.

The way he acts and Mother too but in a different way makes me wonder why they even had me. He sure makes it plain that he wanted a different kind of daughter. One like Ruth. Sometimes I feel like I don't even belong here at all.

I wish Mother had said good-bye.

The entries that followed continued to be irregular, some no more than a line or two, but they were sufficient to evoke a bleak picture of a lonely, chubby, love-starved little girl.

"Ruth" was mentioned several times, a paragon to whom Ariel failed to measure up. Ruth was the neat one. The obedient one. The sweet one. Ariel deduced now that Ruth had been the Munsons' first child, the one no longer living when she herself had been born.

Schoolmates were also mentioned, but no reference suggested real friendship. There were grade comparisons, envious descriptions of what someone wore or said or did—the unfortunate fact that all of them, even the boys, were shorter.

There were allusions to a church, of which the father was a pillar. Although the sect wasn't named, it was plainly of the fundamentalist ilk and very strict, the sort that frowns on makeup, dancing and all things worldly. By the time she'd reached 1974, Ariel was thoroughly depressed and, if she'd been able to get her hands on the father, she'd have throttled him. He was a cold, controlling fanatic who disdained secular education and the diversions of a "Godless society." As she read the entries of the twelve-year-old, however, Ariel's depression turned to outright fury. What began to emerge was a man who'd progressed from sternness to perversion.

Apparently, the father had never felt any compunction about meting out punishment, including the physical variety. But Ariel realized from the terse, shamefaced descriptions that the episodes were escalating and becoming overzealous, to say the least. Switchings became paddlings, which became whippings. On one fine day she was made to bend over a chair and, stripped to her slip, was struck repeatedly with a belt.

The girl who'd been verbal became closemouthed, even to herself. The girl who'd been chubby became fat.

Crying freely, Ariel slammed the journal closed.

How could people, teachers and the clergy of this church, not have realized what was happening? How could she have continued to live with that lunatic? And how could she have ever moved back to this house, to the scene of such a miserable childhood?

She blew her nose and sat staring at the wall. Gradually, her breath evened out. She poured out the last of the coffee.

Even today, with all the awareness of child abuse, she knew there must be many more instances going unreported than otherwise. In that time and in those circumstances, the punishment might not have been considered extreme, might even have been condoned.

And where could a girl that age have fled? The local bus station? There was no mention so far of grandparents or aunts or uncles, and the glory days of Haight-Ashbury were over. Besides, she'd read enough to know this child, to know herself as a child. This girl was proud. She was self-contained. She was tough.

Ariel prowled the bedroom. She pulled back the drapery and looked out at a full, blue-white moon.

As to why she'd moved back here after her father's death, she could only speculate. Doubtless, the house had appreciated incredibly since he'd bought it; the financial consideration had to be a big one. The renovations looked recent. Almost certainly, she'd done them herself, perhaps an exorcism of sorts.

Ariel wondered how the old man had died. Well, he wasn't that old, actually. She calculated from his age on her birth certificate and the date of his will that he'd been only sixty-nine or seventy when he died. She hoped it was a lingering, painful death. And what about her mother? According to the birth certificate she'd been around forty when Ariel was born, and she'd died in '72. That made her fifty or thereabouts. Was there something unusual about her death that had provoked anger in her husband, or a reaction perceived as anger? Or was that just his natural meanness? Steeling herself, Ariel opened 1975.

The entries were both fewer and shorter than in any previous book. Her father was seldom mentioned. The writing became almost impersonal, some of it blatant fantasy. From one paragraph to another in this book and the next as well, the child flitted from the weather or homework to fantastic true-blue girlfriends and football heroes who recognized her unique qualities.

And then, after a long gap in 1977, the entries gained momentum. They were neither longer nor more frequent, but they'd returned to reality and there was an increasing involvement in extracurricular activities. On the school newspaper, it seems, she'd found her niche, and her writing style flowered. Naturally, it had grown more articulate through the years, but now it also became more self-conscious. Sometimes experimental. Sometimes amusingly affected.

The 1978 notebook was similar, although the language had settled down nicely, and 1979 provided the good news that she'd earned a full scholarship to USC. Things were looking up, particularly once she moved into a dormitory for the summer quarter of her freshman year.

The next notebooks were filled with accounts of classes and anxiety about maintaining her scholarship. She was still the odd man out socially, and unhappy allusions to her appearance and, particularly, her weight increased. There were occasional mentions of diets, which were marginally successful at best.

And then, in 1982, Michael Gold made his entrance.

Romance to Ariel was an alien creature, as exotic and suspect as Pan, and as irresistible. "Dr. McDermott always calls him Gold," began the first reference. "His first name, I found out today, is Michael."

> He's older than the rest of us and intense. You can't help being aware of him since he's one of the few people in Modern Poetry who ever volunteers an answer. He has no shortage of opinions, and he expresses them without a hint of uncertainty.
>
> I've always thought of him as cocky, but now I'm not so sure. What's wrong with caring? With having the confidence not to apologize for it? When I understand what he's said, I usually agree with him, and he is remarkably articulate.
>
> I've never met anyone like him.

The event of meeting Michael was minutely reported, every word and action and nuance. What he'd said, what she'd been wearing, her regret that she hadn't chosen a different outfit that day—one she considered more slimming—were all worried over. Smiling indulgently, Ariel read through the infinitely described details. Her smile faded as she slowed for the final paragraphs.

> We'd just left class, and I'd stopped to clip my shades onto my glasses when I heard, "Interesting comment you made about the Dickinson poem." I hadn't heard

him come up, and at first I thought he was talking to someone else. Then I thought maybe he was being sarcastic. "I agree," he said. "The first verse does say it all. The rest is superfluous." I mumbled something stupid, I have no idea what. I just stood there like Lot's wife until he introduced himself. Then I just said "Hi." He had to ask my name. Then he said "See you" and vanished into Bradley Hall.

What was that all about? He isn't interested in my notes or my help. One, he's too smart to need them, and two, he's only auditing the course. And, besides, he's good-looking. I've thought about it all afternoon, and I still don't get it.

There followed ever more frequent mentions of Michael while the vulnerable young Ariel wondered and questioned and, finally, still disbelieving but rapturous, succumbed.

It was hardly surprising that love had hit with a wallop. And perhaps it was inevitable that the man to whom she'd been so drawn was not unlike her father. As the increasingly intimate relationship was described, so were Michael's fits of temper and apologies, his declarations of need, his compliments alternating with criticisms. Gradually, Ariel became difficult to find. Subtly and too often, it was another voice that spoke from the pages.

Scanning the rhapsodizing and secondhand opinions impatiently, Ariel learned that Michael, five years her senior, was in his last year of law school. His father, a well-to-do furrier headquartered in San Diego, had died during his son's adolescence, and his mother, "the awful Muriel," was a tyrant whose attitude toward Ariel was flagrantly condescending.

Toward the end of the final journal came an unusually wrenching tantrum, after which Michael disappeared for two days. Anguished and confused, Ariel borrowed from the poet mentioned at their first meeting. " 'Parting is all we know of heaven,' " she'd quoted Emily Dickinson, " 'And all we need of hell.' " She'd gone on to say, hopelessly, that if there was to be no Michael in her life, she saw little point in living it.

Michael returned.

Ariel as a twenty-one-year-old had thought Michael Gold compelling; the present Ariel thought he was a jerk—a pedantic, self-absorbed, overbearing bully.

Her eyes scratchy with fatigue, she reached the last page, the entry with which she'd begun. At some point, Ariel realized, she'd come to feel a strong affinity for the girl who'd written the journals. No, something more than affinity—a oneness, as if she'd begun to come together with herself. Michael Gold, too, seemed familiar. Ariel felt as if she knew him, or someone very like him.

Reflecting on what she'd read, she conceded that he was very bright; that if he was domineering, he could be charming; that he'd loved her as well as he knew how. She suspected that the smitten young Ariel had been right in thinking Michael idealistic and in believing that his upbringing made for an uncomfortable conflict with his ideals. But the sophistication that had enthralled the girl seemed from a more mature perspective a poor veneer. Michael, she thought now, was a man with one redeeming virtue: an instinctive attraction to innocence.

She lay awake for a long time, and when sleep finally came it was fitful. A variation of the "white dream" returned, with the same brilliant lights and pervasive scent of lilies. This time, however, she could see into the distant white coffin with a telescopic eye.

The body inside was that of a woman. She was tall and slender and, although she wasn't pretty, she had an unusual beauty. The face was familiar to the dream-Ariel. She tried to call out to the still, cold woman, to make her voice heard over the pitiful crying, but she could force no sound from her throat. Then Neely's voice, close to her ear and menacing, said, "If you're looking for a sign, Gold, go to church."

Ariel struggled to escape the dream and thought she was in fact awake, but the voice persisted, taking on the oily, pious resonance of an evangelist. "Seek, and ye shall find," the voice intoned. "Knock, and it shall be opened unto you."

She had to get away. From the voice, from the room, from the dream. The light intensified, swallowing every image, sealing her in a white void. She knew that, at any minute, the cataclysm would come—an explosion of lights and ear-shattering sound. She fought her way into wakefulness and the silence of the dark bedroom.

She turned over. Unconsciously absorbing the knowledge that she was safe, she drifted. Minutes, or perhaps only seconds, later, she was asleep again.

She dreamed of a little girl, squatting, watching a gentle wave roll over her ankles. As it foamed away, it left sparkling grains of sand on her curled toes. Ariel knew that she was the little girl, but she wasn't sad or lonely. She was laughing. She was at the edge of a vast, clear ocean, playing in the surf and calling out to someone who waited on the beach. The water was warm and caressing, and she could feel the sun hot on her back. She could taste the salt on her lips, hear the gulls crying overhead, see the tiny, silvery fish flitting through the crystalline water at her feet.

The feeling of happiness induced by the dream was powerful. Memory of the dream itself faded, but the feeling lingered in her mind long after she awakened.

eighteen

Ariel had her first cup of coffee on the backyard patio. She'd expected to feel logy after her late night but, warmed by an inexplicable sense of well-being and the early-morning sun, she felt ready to take on the world. A little voice in her mind mumbled something nasty about amnesic mood swings; she chose to ignore it.

Her ankle, she'd found on waking, was mending nicely, and the bruises on her face were a less repulsive shade of yellow. The specter of Sicilian bogeymen had faded with the light of day, and neither did the specter of Henry Heller give her pause.

Jessie brought out a tennis ball, which she was eventually persuaded to relinquish, and Ariel threw it for her until the dog flopped, panting, beside her. Ariel gently patted the area around the bandage and gave the shepherd a nuzzle. She read the telephone number on her tag and went inside to settle this ownership question once and for all.

After four rings a male voice, plummy even on the answering machine tape, repeated the number and promised that her call would be returned if she'd be good enough to leave a message. The beep sounded, and Ariel was about to speak when she thought better of it. Gently, she replaced the receiver in its cradle. Having no tangible proof that she was now Jessie's legal owner, she was at a disadvantage. She'd give Mr. Morgan no opportunity to rethink his decision about giving up the dog. She'd wait until she could speak to him directly, when she could control the situation.

Ariel checked the time. It was still too early to find governmental offices open, so her divorce investigation would have to wait.

Singing little snatches, off-key, from *Song of the South,* she moved confidently to the next order of business: business. The "Zip a Dee Doo Dahs" were liberally laced with hummed "dum-de-dah-dums" as she prepared to watch the magazine shows she'd taped. "Everything's going my way," she sang in a monotone, pressing PLAY on the VCR.

Ninety minutes later she wasn't so sure.

What she'd just watched was, largely, sleaze. Was that what she did for a living? She hoped Mrs. Harris was right in her opinion that *The Open File* was of a higher caliber than the mayhem, innuendo and exploitation she'd just endured. She wished she'd had a chance to tape her own program.

Replaying the credits of the first show, she made notes of the titles rolling down the screen. Lord! There were a lot of them, and almost every one had a qualifier. "Executive" Producer. "Senior" Correspondents. "Managing" Editor. Just about the only position left unqualified was "Writers." Ariel wondered if that meant they were the most qualified. The hierarchy of the other two shows featured a whole herd of producers, and even the adjectives had adjectives: "Supervising" and "Coordinating" were liberally preceded and succeeded by "Senior" and "Associate."

Contemplating chiefs and Indians, she looked for the textbooks she'd shelved in the study. There were only a few, she discovered, and those were fifteen or more years old. She opened *Handbook for the Electronic Journalist* by O. F. Anderson. The first sentence didn't augur well for the book's helpfulness.

" 'Message,' " she read aloud, " 'infers that you have something to communicate.' What I infer from that, Mr. Anderson," she muttered, "is that you need a handbook of English usage." Dubiously, she scanned the book. There was a chapter on how television actually works. She decided that, while converting optical light images into electronic signals was no doubt fascinating, she'd save that subject for a rainy day. The chapter on TV makeup, ditto. And, since she probably wasn't required to actually man a camera, she skipped over a section on lens turrets and plumbicon tubes. Quickly memorizing the definitions of pan and tilt, dolly and truck, she wondered if any or all of this stuff was obsolete.

The second book was so old that color TV would've been exciting news to the author, and two other books, which dealt with ethics and power and politics in the newsroom, respectively, were not only outdated but beside the point.

Okay, fine. Back to the library. But first, Ariel thought, she'd do a little digging for Gold.

Dragging out the dog-eared phone book, she turned to the governmental listings. Where, she wondered, did you find out about divorce records? There was nothing that said simply Records or Divorce, but the very first listing under Los Angeles, County of was Administrative Offices. It seemed as good a place as any to start.

She posed her inquiry and was put on hold. At length, her call was routed and a woman answered, saying something totally unintelligible. She was put on hold again. She listened to silence for several eons, and just as she was about to hang up, a man's pleasant voice came on.

"Superior Court. Are you being helped?" he inquired.

"Not lately," Ariel responded, a bit testily.

"You are now. Walters here. How can I help you?"

"How does a person," Ariel asked, "go about finding out if a divorce has taken place?"

"Name?"

"Gold."

"First names?"

"Ariel Rose and Jordan Michael."

"Year?"

"Oh, well you see, I don't know. I don't even know if there was a divorce, to be honest. That's what I'm trying to find out," Ariel explained.

The patient Walters didn't miss a beat. "Do you know the decade?"

"Somewhere between 'eighty-five and now? Is that too broad to be useful?"

"We can take a look at the fiche and see what we come up with," he said, and seconds later he was reading down a list.

"Albert, Alfie, Andrew, Andrew, Andrew—Don't ever marry anybody named Andrew," advised Walters in an aside, "they don't seem to have much staying power. No Ariels." He apparently skipped to another section. Ariel could hear him reading under his breath.

"Wow! Here's a firm you don't want to do business with," he said. "They've been sued by everybody except you and me!"

"A firm?" Ariel asked. "Wait a minute, I thought we were looking up divorces?"

"We've got everything in here—domestic, civil and probate. Well," he told her, "no Michael preceded by a J. There are two Michaels, but one's got an Alonzo after it, and one's got the letter D in front. There's a Mike; that help you any?"

Ariel thought not.

"Let me try the nineties," he said—and came up dry.

"I tell you what," Walters said, "I can't really spend any more time with you on this, but you can come down and look for yourself if you want to go further back. We're at the Civic Center."

"Walters," Ariel assured him, "you've been a peach, but since the marriage didn't take place until the end of 1984, I guess that's it."

She thanked him and hung up, reviewing her options.

They could have divorced somewhere outside Los Angeles County. She could call around to Ventura County and San Bernardino and Riverside and Orange Counties and all the others. It could take forever—and there might be no listing at all. There might never have been a divorce.

She called San Diego information. No attorney Michael was listed, nor was there a Muriel Gold.

She had one last idea. She looked up the American Bar Association. Finding no listing, she again dialed information and got the Los Angeles Bar Association, which referred her to the state association. From Membership she learned that they could only tell her whether a given attorney was "entitled to practice" in California, not whether he or she was actively practicing, and no, she was told, no one by the blessed name Jordan Michael Gold was. To determine if he was practicing elsewhere, she'd have to call each state individually.

She couldn't think of anything else to do that she had time to do. She tabled the search and hurried to get dressed.

The same friendly attendant was manning the Civic Center parking lot, giving her a thumbs-up when he spotted the handicapped permit. Ariel thought he must have an unusual talent for remembering faces (or hers was unusually memorable) until his greeting made it obvious it wasn't her face he remembered.

"Nice vehicle!" He approached the car and, stroking the fender reverentially, commended her on choosing the 'fifty-five rather than the 'fifty-six. "The continental kit looked great, but it messed up the handling. 'Course, the 'fifty-six goes for more but—what the hey!—you're the one's got to drive it, right?"

An old hand now, Ariel bearded the library's computers and confidently typed in TELEVISION NEWS. There were three references. They were historical and/or biographical. They were checked out anyway. She tried every conceivable combination of terms and finally came up with seven books both available and, possibly, useful. Two were from the children's section.

Hours later she had writer's cramp, an esoteric new vocabulary and a firm appreciation for the people behind the camera. She also had sense enough to know she couldn't walk into a newsroom or studio and bluff anyone into thinking she could perform her job. Just how she was going to pull off that tour de force was an inspiration that hadn't yet come to her.

She moved on to the periodical room and something called InfoTrac, which she mastered with gratifying ease, and then microfiche, which gave her a headache and a desire to be elsewhere.

A reward for her labor was in order. Since some decent clothes were also in order, she stopped at Westside Pavilion on the way home.

When the doorbell rang at quarter past five, Ariel was scowling at herself in the mirror. The new outfit was okay. The line was supposed to be slimming, and the scarf at the neck was supposed to divert the eye. To the next zip code, she hoped.

Her impulsive shopping trip had ended at a cosmetics counter where an earnest, extremely young woman with no discernible pores had convinced Ariel that she understood her natural aversion to unnatural makeup and then, wielding her wares with a lavish hand, transformed her into Bette Davis in *Whatever Happened to Baby Jane?*

Ariel's face now tingled from multiple washings. Knowing better, she'd incurred the equivalent of the national debt buying various snake oils from the poreless person but, in point of fact, she'd ended up with some fragrant concoctions that probably did diddly but felt good.

She pulled her shoulders back and opened the door to Henry, whose glance lingered on her for far less time than all her efforts warranted.

"You're looking rested," he said unsatisfactorily. "Time off agrees with you."

Jessie prowled into the living room and sat squarely in the middle of it. Sensing no alarm, and therefore no need for her services, she dangled her tongue and gave them a dopey grin.

Ariel looked at the two of them and remembered that two nights before she'd thought Henry was a grenade-toting terrorist. Forgetting herself—her looks and her misgivings—she laughed out loud. "You can fix your own drink," she said. "The Scotch is thataway."

* * *

"You're really looking pretty good," Henry said appraisingly. "If that's what getting burgled does for you, you ought to pay the guy. Here, give him this." He took an envelope from the breast pocket of his well-worn corduroy sportcoat and waved it. "Your paycheck." He dropped it on the coffee table and, sitting in the chair opposite her, proceeded to use the envelope for a coaster.

"Little late for that," Ariel murmured.

"They didn't get him? Par for the course, unfortunately."

"Well, no. That's not what I meant. Actually, *I* got him."

"You? You mean you apprehended . . . ? You're joking!"

Henry's gape became a frown. He'd just spotted the cane leaning against the sofa arm.

"What have you done to yourself?" The frown deepened as he pointed an accusing finger. "That cast is on the wrong hand."

"I shot the man." Her voice was barely audible. "He's dead."

"You shot . . . ?" He did a classic double take. "What were you doing with a gun? Good God, I hate guns! You're not one of the mob that went running to the gun shops after the riots? Do you even know how to use one? Well, obviously you did." He pulled his beard. "Why didn't you say anything about this before? Did he hurt you?"

"Which question did you want me to answer?"

"Are you hurt?"

"Just a cracked bone in the hand. And a twisted ankle. I was lucky." She smiled thinly. "And I had Jessie."

As she recounted the ordeal, a measure of the horror of the night returned. "You know something I just thought of? The way he looked at me just before . . ." She saw the face in her mind's eye. "The expression on his face was shock. Or fear. As if he was as frightened of me as I was of him."

"Well, for—Why wouldn't he be? You had a gun." Henry jerked his tie loose. "Maybe he thought nobody was home. You surprised him and he panicked. Besides, and I speak from experience, when Rin Tin Tin there jumps you, it does tend to make you a little tense."

He leaned back and propped one long leg over the other. "In this case, I have to admit, the dog came in handy, and

I'm glad for your sake she wasn't hurt worse. It's also nice you had a friend at the local constabulary. Max Neely thinks highly of you, sounds like." His eye fell on the pay envelope.

"Oh! Before I forget, Personnel sent down a form for you to sign. Something about your vacation." He pulled out two or three papers from an inside pocket. Perching a silly-looking pair of half-glasses on his nose, he glanced through the wrinkled assortment of notes and receipts, picked one out and stretched to hand it to Ariel along with a pen from another pocket.

Preoccupied with the story she'd just told, Ariel glanced over the paper and found a place to sign.

"What? Did you say something?" she asked as she capped the pen and looked up. Henry was staring at her quizzically.

"I was just going to say that I forgot you couldn't sign with your right . . . hmm."

Whatever he'd been about to say, he'd apparently thought better of it. He reached for the form and looked at her signature. Folding the paper and removing his glasses, he replaced both in his pocket and relaxed back into his chair. "Gordon says to give you his regards," he said casually.

"Oh, really? Thanks." Ariel felt a little tingle of unease in her midsection.

"Yeah. Said he'd keep the old NewsStar warmed up for you."

"Umm."

Henry's lanky body had become very still. His mouth above the beard was a straight line.

"We don't have the NewsStar program; we have News-Maker. And the only Gordon I know is my ex–brother-in-law."

Ariel ran her tongue over her upper lip. The silence in the room became heavy.

Slowly Henry leaned forward. He rested his elbows on bony knees and pressed his palms together.

"I would very much like to know how a person who's left-handed can suddenly and conveniently sign her name perfectly with her right hand. Which hand, by the way, was sprained or 'maybe broken' three days ago and is now completely well. And how a smoker goes cold turkey with no sign that it's any problem, but she does *have* a problem because she doesn't know which computer system she uses almost every day of her life. I would like to know why a workaholic who's seldom talked about anything *except* work, ad nauseam, for as long as I've known her hasn't brought it up once. Not tonight, not the other night, not once on the phone."

He leaned closer. "And, finally, I would also like to know how a woman undergoes, in the space of a few days, a total metamorphosis in her personality and her handwriting and even the way she talks—not to mention the way she looks. And I'm not talking about new clothes and perfume! I'm talking about the way she moves and wears her clothes and looks out of her eyes at you."

Nothing in the room moved but Henry's eyebrows, which climbed almost to where his hairline must have once begun.

"I'd really like to know that," he said.

Ariel could hear herself breathing. "Which question did you want me to answer?"

He waited.

"Okay, okay." Ariel sighed deeply, with resignation and what she realized—despite a warning light blinking deep in her mind—was relief. She wondered where to start.

She wished for the diversion of lighting a cigarette. Not for the cigarette, but for the diversion. She waved her hand, vaguely.

" 'I can't explain myself, I'm afraid, sir, because I'm not myself, you see.' "

"Ariel . . ." Henry's tone warned.

"No, wait. Truly. Alice said it better than I could, but maybe you have to have passed through the looking glass to appreciate it." She took another deep breath and looked into Henry's dark, deeply shadowed eyes.

"On Monday morning, when I woke up, I had no memory. I didn't know who I was."

She could see the wheels turning behind the eyes. The skepticism. The wariness. Finally, he broke the silence.

"You didn't remember your name?"

"No."

"You had no memory at all?"

"No."

"You woke up with amnesia?"

"Presumably."

Henry stood up abruptly. "I think I'll just have another drink."

When he'd returned with his glass refilled, he didn't speak right away but continued to eye her speculatively.

"Any particular reason why you chose to keep this little development to yourself?"

"Sometime Sunday night someone broke into this house and tore the place apart—"

"Wait a minute. I thought the guy broke in..." He thought back. "I thought you said it was Monday night."

"That was the second time. Or a different man, I'm not sure which."

Henry worked to absorb the information. "So, this first break-in ... that's how you hurt your hand before?"

"Well, no. I didn't actually hurt my hand until the second time." Her voice dropped. "I made it up the first time."

"Why?" He gave her a baffled look.

"Because I didn't know anything about what Ariel Gold did or how she did it. And I can't work a computer, so I invented a reason not to go to work."

"Yes, well." He held up his hands. "Let's just go back to that for a minute. Granted that waking up to the discovery that you're an amnesic must be a little disconcerting—if not incredible." His raised eyebrow signaled that he hadn't bought that yet. "I still don't get why you didn't just say so. Why the subterfuge?"

"Look, pu, yourself in my place. I didn't know who'd broken in here or why. I didn't know *you!* For all I knew, the intruder could've *been* you—or anybody else. I didn't know who anybody was! Including me!"

"You thought I broke into your house? Good God, why?"

"That's just it! I didn't *know!* And I still don't, for that matter. And there's something else I haven't told you."

"Oh, wonderful! What next? You think you're Anastasia? You've spotted Elvis Presley? You think the CIA is after you? What?"

For four days Ariel had held herself together. She'd been

strong. She'd been resilient. She'd done it alone. Now tears stung her eyes.

"Do you want to hear this, or do you want to be a smart-ass?"

"Don't do that." Henry closed his eyes. "Don't you get weepy on me, dammit. I'm trying here. I am trying."

"Are you hungry?"

"Are you crazy?"

"That's another possibility." She got up to find a tissue. "If you do want to listen to this, it's going to take a while, and I thought I'd fix something to eat. You might just say, 'Yes, thank you' or 'No, thank you.' Or you could just take a hike and leave me in peace."

Sensing a story, Henry backed off. "What've you got to eat?"

Ariel led the way into the kitchen, leaning on her cane more than was strictly necessary. She offered Henry an apron. When he declined, she took it herself, asking him to tie it for her. She handed him a butcher knife and ordered him to chop.

Setting out eggs, a bell pepper, green onions and mushrooms, she said, "There's just one thing . . ."

"Don't talk to me right now," Henry ordered, concentrating as if he were cutting into the Hope diamond. "There're too many injured limbs around here already."

When he'd reduced the vegetables to chunks no more uniform than Ariel could have made them, he wiped his hands on his pants and commanded her to start talking.

"Now you can wait a minute yourself. Perfect omelettes need undivided attention. Why don't you set the table." She nodded toward a cabinet. "The plates are there, and I don't know where place mats and napkins are. Just look around."

When they were seated, each with half the omelette, she fixed her eyes on Henry's and said evenly, "There's one thing you must know first. If you repeat any of what I've said or what I'm about to say, I'll deny it."

"Yeah, yeah, yeah. Just talk."

Her food cooled as she told him about waking up in a strange house with a strange dog. She described the state of the house and why she surmised she'd been out at the time of the first break-in. Putting her fork down, she straightened her spine and told him about finding the gun and the bloody shirt. And admitted she had no idea whether she herself had used the gun.

"What'd you do with the shirt? Have you still got it?" he interrupted.

"It's in the clothes hamper. I forgot to throw it away."

"Don't. It definitely wasn't your blood?"

"Not unless this cut on my cheek was a geyser. My skin wasn't broken anywhere else."

"And you don't know where you were the night before, when the house was broken into? Or what they were after?"

"No."

"It didn't look like anything was taken?"

"Not that I could tell, but how would I know?"

"When you cleaned up the house, you didn't find any-thing—anything at all—that would warrant somebody break-ing in here? A picture? A letter? A tape? A name or address or phone number on a calendar? Notes for a story? Anything?"

"No matchbooks from bars either." She gave him a spare-me look. "I'd have said."

She tried to make him understand what it was like not to know what was being looked for. Not to know whom to suspect, and therefore being suspicious of everyone. She as-sured him that the locks had been changed and that an alarm system had been installed. She told him that her gun had been returned.

"You never said if you know how to use it, if you've had training."

Ariel waited for him to answer his own question.

"Okay, you don't remember, but you knew how to load the gun? How to release the safety? You're not going to blow your foot off or shoot the postman or anything?"

"Actually, once I got over the shock of finding the thing, I sort of felt comfortable with having it—a lot more comfort-able than when I was without it—so I think, maybe, I've had some kind of experience."

She stopped to think of what she might have overlooked.

"I've told you everything I know about the intruder, about

Rodriquez. Oh! Late the next night there was a car parked across the street for a long time—in front of what looked like an unoccupied house—and there was someone in it." She shrugged. "It's hard to know what's a threat and what's paranoia. For example, I've learned that I've been married and that, from all evidence, I'm not anymore. I don't know if my husband's involved in this or not."

"How'd you find out about that?"

"You don't look surprised," she observed. "You knew I was married?"

"You mentioned it once."

"I did?" Ariel grew excited. "What'd I say?"

"Very little, as I recall. The implication was as you say, that you no longer were."

"Oh. What else do you know about me?"

"Next to nothing, personally. Our relationship was strictly business. So how'd you find out about the ex?"

Disappointed, Ariel told about finding the marriage license and gave a heavily censored account of the diaries. She also repeated what Victor had said about "Michael's associates."

"Wait a minute. Who's Victor?"

"Jessie's vet, and a friend."

Winding down, she looked Henry in the eye. "Do you believe what I've told you is true?"

"It is, as they say, too strange to be fiction." He draped his arm over the back of the chair, crossed his legs and thought for a long time.

"I wouldn't worry too much about what you might've done with the gun Sunday night. In the first place, the police wouldn't have returned it if it were connected to any crime they knew about. In the second place, *I'd* have known if there was an unusual shooting—something other than the standard drive-by or domestic or whatever. And I also wouldn't worry too much about the mob. The reference your, um, friend Victor made is pretty flimsy, and if you'd had connections—knowing you—you'd have used them as sources. Okay"—he held up a hand to forestall her—"I mean if they weren't adversarial connections. But I still think that's far-fetched."

He thought a moment longer.

"I know you didn't make up the bump on the head because I saw it. Did you ever get that checked?"

"They looked at it at the hospital, but since it wasn't a fresh injury—since it wasn't sustained that night—they didn't really, you know, do any tests or anything."

He pointed a long, bony finger at her. "You're going to see a doctor tomorrow. You know him—knew him—a psychiatrist we use a lot as a source, a quote-unquote expert. I'm going to ask him to see you."

The warning light in Ariel's brain escalated into pyrotechnics.

"It won't do any good," she blurted. "I never had any symptoms of concussion or Wernicke-Korsakoff syndrome or—"

"Of what?"

Ariel synopsized what she'd learned about the organic and psychological aspects of amnesia. "So, you see, science really is at odds with itself about how memory works and, unless amnesia's organic, there's not much they can do, and my memory could come back anytime, anyway. I really don't want to do this."

"Nevertheless." Henry stroked his beard in contemplation. "Amnesia! I didn't believe it really existed outside of soap operas."

"It's not exactly on the level with the common cold in terms of ... commonness. One book said there were fewer than five thousand reported cases in the country, but that was sometime in the eighties. For all I know, there's been a full-blown epidemic since then."

Henry pulled out a little notebook and, flipping through it, went to the wall phone.

He dialed and turned back to her. "You picked up a considerable amount of information on the subject in a short time. One thing you haven't forgotten is how to do research."

"You ought to hear what I know about broadcast news after an afternoon in the library. I could teach a course."

Henry held up his hand.

"David?" he said into the phone. "Henry Heller here. How're you doing? How's Miriam?"

The answer was, evidently, amusing. Henry snorted a laugh and then quickly sobered and got down to it.

"David, I need a favor. You remember Ariel Gold from the show? Right. Well, she seems to have—don't laugh—amnesia. Can you talk to her? See what the story is?"

After providing a few details, Henry listened for a while. Then, putting his hand over the receiver, he said to Ariel, "Ten-thirty tomorrow all right for you?"

She nodded, still distinctly uneasy about this development. She was amazed that it was all being arranged so quickly.

"She'll be there. Thanks, Dave, I owe you one." He hung up.

"He's coming in on his day off to see you." Henry sat down and pulled out a notepad. "Some of what you said is true, according to David, but he also said you definitely need to get your head checked. For potential physical problems. He'll arrange the tests."

Henry looked up from jotting an address. "Can you drive?"

At her nod, he tore off the page and handed it to her. "Now, what were you saying about teaching a course in broadcast news?"

Sheepishly, Ariel said, "I thought I should know something about what I'm supposed to do for a living. Before you came over."

"In one afternoon you were going to become Diane Sawyer? Dazzle me with all your expertise? We were going to talk *shop?*" Henry grinned.

Ariel folded her arms across her chest. " 'Chance favors a prepared mind.' "

"That's one of the things you do that I don't remember you doing before!" Henry slapped the table. "What is it with these quotations? You sound like a needlepoint sampler."

"Well, excuse me! I wasn't aware of doing it. And how would *you* know if I did or didn't? You said yourself you hardly knew me except for work."

"And another thing. You never explained how you can all of a sudden write with your right hand."

"How do I know?" she cried. She slapped the table, mimicking him. "Maybe I'm ambidextrous. Huh? Did you think of that?"

There was a low growl, or maybe just a snore, from the corner where Jessie slept.

Ariel subsided. "So, what do we do about the job? At the end of three weeks, I mean?"

"Beats me. Let's just wait and see what David says."

"But you're not going to tell anybody about any of this? What about this Peacock you mentioned? Is he your superior?"

Henry gave her a wry smile. "In countless ways, no doubt. But, no, he's one of the correspondents, and he's out of town, anyway. I won't be discussing your plight with him. Or with anyone else ... for the time being."

"Why'd this"—she looked at the paper—"Dr. David Friedman agree to set this all up so quickly?"

"I told you, he knows you. You've worked together. And," Henry said with a shrug, "he used to be my brother-in-law."

"I thought your brother-in-law was named Gordon."

"That's a different one."

"Your wife must have a lot of brothers."

"Each one has only one."

"Each one? What are you? A Mormon?"

He tapped his plate with his knife. "Successive. The wives were successive."

"How many?"

"Three. And I don't want to talk about it."

"Do you have one now?"

"Not now and not again." He pushed his chair back and took his plate to the sink. "Walk me to the door."

She did. He stopped on the porch.

"Lock the door behind me. Call me when you get home tomorrow."

She held the door open.

"Close the door and lock it. And tell Jessie to keep her eyes peeled. And *that* was a concession, in case you didn't recognize it."

He waited until the door closed and he heard the click of the locks before turning to leave. He looked around the yard; the street; the quiet, respectable neighborhood.

He was surprised at how reluctant he was to walk away.

nineteen

Having been prodded and poked, blinded by intense little lights in darkened rooms, smeared with unguents and wired for sound, cocooned in a claustrophobic Jules Verne vision, introduced to a taciturn neurologist and to technicians whose functions she was too nervous to grasp and, finally, asked many odd questions about proverbs and inkblots, Ariel waited in a haphazard office for Dr. David Friedman, who'd instigated the whole circus.

She crossed and recrossed her legs and tried to put aside the morning's anxiety. She fervently wished for a cigarette. She looked around restlessly.

Someone, sometime, had expended a great deal of effort to give this office the panache of a successful Cedars-Sinai psychiatrist, but the occupant had thwarted the decorator. The forest green carpet was as well-tended as Augusta National. Ariel could see the whorls made by recent vacuuming, unblemished by any footprints save her own. But everything above ankle level was a different story.

Books, files, magazines and newspapers were stacked on every available surface except the chair in which she sat and the handsome leather chair behind the desk she faced. Despite the witty prints on the wall and the dusty objets d'art on the credenza, this office was not chic. But it was oddly comfortable and comforting, as was its customary occupant.

Ariel didn't remember Dr. David Friedman, but she liked him.

At least two inches shorter than Ariel (who was wearing flat shoes), thickset, almost totally bald but with cheeks heavily shadowed and arms covered with a pelt of dark hair, Friedman looked like a short, benign bear.

He'd met her with a face full of kindness, reassurance and a frank curiosity he'd made no effort to hide.

They'd talked about the unusual extent of her memory loss, what she could and couldn't remember. Driving, cooking, working the ATM at the bank (which she'd brilliantly figured out how to do, inputting the digits of her birth date) were no problem. Operating a computer was. Geography wasn't a problem; she knew where Hollywood and Beverly Hills and Santa Monica were. But her own neighborhood was uncharted territory until this week. Her grasp of current events was, more or less, normal; she could name the president, the L.A. chief of police, the host of *The Tonight Show*. She wouldn't know her ex-husband—she didn't think—if he rang her doorbell.

The questions Friedman had interjected between endless personality, screening and intelligence tests were succinct but not curt, and his tone somehow contrived to be both businesslike and warm. He gave off an impression of enormous energy but, on reflection, Ariel wasn't sure why. His movements were economical, neither quick nor frequent. His voice was quiet. His manner was deliberate. And she now noticed, glancing at her watch, he'd kept her waiting for nearly half an hour.

She'd understood that this was his day off, that he'd come in just to oblige his former brother-in-law, so what was he doing out there? Had the good doctor decided that since he was here anyway he might as well line up a few more patients and make it worth his while? Just as she was about to conclude that he'd fallen prey to greed and the overscheduling for which Southern California doctors—all doctors?—are justifiably famous, David Friedman pushed open the door and closed it behind him.

"Nada," he said without preamble, sitting behind the desk in the leather chair. Quite a few inches of the backrest were visible above his head.

"From what we've seen so far, physically, you're clean as a G-rated movie. No evidence of disease and, despite the bump on your noggin, no evidence of concussion. Psychologically, you're no more peculiar than average," he smiled, "and you've never impressed me as unstable." He propped his chin in both hands and gazed at her. "So talk to me. Tell me what you know about yourself."

Ariel looked into the dark, liquid eyes that were focused on her and knew where the impression of energy came from.

The man's attention seemed absolute. His look was penetrating, communicating an intense and unequivocal interest.

"Well, as I told you," she began tentatively, "I remember everything that's happened since Monday morning of this week. Firsthand, I mean. Before that, I don't know anything at all except what I've been told and what I've read about myself."

"What you've read about yourself?" The dark eyes blinked once; the face was deadpan. "I didn't realize you were famous. You think you used to be somebody before you forgot who you were? Did I miss something in the media?"

Ariel stared. What kind of way was this for a psychiatrist to act? Her tension dissolving, she offered her profile.

"You mean you never recognized me?" She cut her eyes back to the diminutive doctor and said, "Well, that makes two of us. As far as I know, I'm nobody. A total unknown, almost literally. I got my inside dope from some old diaries I found in the attic. Sad old diaries," she added.

"You sound dispassionate about the sadness."

"It was schizzy." She tried to think how to explain it. "I felt like a Peeping Tom even though I knew, intellectually, that it was my own private thoughts I was reading. I could understand what was written. Not just what was written but the nuances. I didn't know about any actual fact or event until I read about it but once I had, I could feel—or at least vividly imagine—the emotions I'd felt at the time." Uncertain, she looked at him. "I just couldn't *remember* them."

"And what you read was sad?" he persisted.

"Oh, yes, but it also concerned things that happened a long time ago, fifteen years and more. I can't believe that how I felt as a little girl or when I was a college student has any bearing on whatever's happening now."

One of Dr. Friedman's eyebrows may have risen infinitesimally, or Ariel may have imagined it. He removed his chin from his hands, but he didn't take his eyes off Ariel as he leaned back in his chair, linked his hands over his stomach and crossed his ankles.

"This fugue in which you find yourself, Ariel, isn't usual—

as you must know from your read-a-thon you told me about." He smiled. "Of course, severe amnesia in young, apparently healthy people isn't usual, and I'm not a specialist in the disorder. But, be that as it may, I'm surprised to see no evidence here of either an organic or a functional problem. In fact, in your case I'm surprised not to see both."

"Why?"

"Because of how you present—the extent and complexity of your memory loss." His expression had turned serious.

"You said you have no recollection of the events leading up to loss of memory or of your own identity. Obviously, that's not uncommon in amnesia. But you also said you had no recognition of anyone else, neither names nor faces. No two cases are identical, but that is uncommon. As is your loss of skills. While some skills may be forgotten in your garden-variety amnesia"—he flashed a brief smile—"you remember no complex skills at all, at least none connected with your occupation. You don't remember what your job consists of or how you function in it. I worked with you enough to know your expertise with all the tools of your trade: cameras and editing equipment and so forth. Yet you don't even remember how to operate a computer."

His look measured her. "Do I have that right?"

With a little sting of irritation, Ariel wondered if he thought she was going to change her mind. "Will I be able to play the violin again?" she asked.

There was a tic of movement at the corner of his mouth. "Could you play the violin before?"

"No," she said innocently, "but I was so hoping . . ."

"Ariel, Ariel," he sighed, crossing his ankles in the other direction. "You know," he said, "amnesics haven't been all that thick on the ground in this office. What few cases I've seen were caused by drugs or alcohol or by brain damage resulting from disease or degenerative disorders. Stroke, tumor, Alzheimer's . . ." He waved one hand in an et cetera motion.

He went on, "When amnesia's psychogenic in origin—and I'm talking now about cases of colleagues and those I've read about—memory loss is often short-term. Memory can return spontaneously without therapy. Sometimes, on the other hand—despite years of therapy—the loss is permanent, and the patient isn't necessarily worse off. Or, to return to the first scenario, patients whose memory returned have been known to continue in their new lives, anyway."

"So what are you telling me?"

"The first thing is that therapy's optional. At least in your case and in my opinion."

"And?"

"And I don't know that you'd derive all that much benefit from my taking you on as a patient—if that's what you had in mind."

Ariel wasn't sure what she'd had in mind, but she did know that what he'd said flattened her mood. She felt rejected. She wondered how quickly one fell victim to transference.

"Aren't you taking kind of an uncapitalistic attitude here?" she asked. Hearing petulance in her voice and getting no response anyway, she spoke more reasonably. "Why do you say that?"

Friedman sighed and sat up. Leaning his forearms on the desk, he asked, "You understand that 'hysterical amnesia' isn't a pejorative term?"

"I know that it's a genuine malady. That the victim hasn't consciously chosen to forget," Ariel said cautiously.

"It's my guess that you're suffering from that syndrome, induced by emotional trauma. But, as I told you, my experience is limited. Also, I know you personally. You'd do better with someone completely objective. If you like, I can set you up with a specialist, and you can see what happens under amobarbital or thiopental sodium narcosis. Shall I explain that," he teased gently, "or would you like to explain it to me?"

She gave it to him by rote: "A clinical tool. An uninhibited twilight state induced by drugs, whereby lost items of memory may be recalled and reproduced. Results, in general, disappointing."

"There's certainly nothing wrong with your anterograde memory," he congratulated her.

"I don't want to see another doctor. I won't see another doctor." Ariel was very firm. "I want you."

Friedman started to object, but Ariel interrupted.

"I should have said something about this earlier, I suppose. That first morning I found reason to believe that something out of the ordinary had happened the preceding night."

She didn't think it was possible for his gaze to sharpen. It did.

"There was a shirt, bloodied, and a gun. Both were on the bed where I'd slept. And someone had broken into my house, apparently when I was out. Apparently, when I was out with the gun, getting blood on my shirt."

"Ariel, that merely reinforces what I was saying. You should be talking to someone with experience in amnesia resulting from emotional shock. And you should also be talking to the police."

"This is confidential," she said, her voice rising. "You can't violate the confidentiality. Can you?"

"You know better."

"The police know about the break-in and the gun. They checked it and returned it to me and, as Henry rightly pointed out, they wouldn't have if there'd been ... if I'd used it illegally. Also, there was a second break-in, and I had to ... I shot the intruder. He died."

"Let me make certain I understand the chronology. The shooting took place after your memory loss?"

"Yes."

"Within the last five days, you've suffered a complete memory loss, discovered blood on your clothes from some unremembered incident, had your house broken into not once but twice and shot and killed an intruder."

"Yes."

"Your life is not uneventful, Ariel."

"No."

She watched the tiny movements of his eyes that suggested an internal conflict.

"You're serious in saying you won't see another physician?"

"Oh, yes. I'll simply handle this alone, which is what I was prepared to do anyway before Henry rode roughshod over me." She hesitated. "I'm not crazy about the idea of putting myself in someone else's power, so to speak. But I find that I trust you, which is why I told you what I just told you."

"What I suggest"—he visibly pulled himself up—"is that we look further at the tests and we set up an appointment for next week, Monday if my schedule allows. In the meantime, I'll think this through. You do the same. And if anything changes, if you need me, call me."

Knowing the answer, prolonging the moment, she asked, "What about another blow to the head. Could that restore my memory?"

"Hollywood."

"What about hypnosis?"

"Same as drugs, basically. A crapshoot. It's been known to work."

"Have you used hypnosis? Yourself?"

"On occasion."

"Will you try it with me?"

"If you like."

"There's one other thing I suppose you should know."

"Tell me."

"When I woke up, not knowing who I was, I didn't just not know who I was. I wasn't ... me."

She wasn't playing for time anymore. She was having to think about the process of breathing, which suddenly seemed very complicated. In. Out. Slowly.

"I was ... repelled by myself."

He leaned back again. Said nothing.

"I was fat. And ugly. But I knew I wasn't. *I* wasn't!" Her lower lip quivered. She stilled it. This wasn't coming out right. It sounded stupid and superficial. Neurotic whining. Wishful thinking. She hugged her chest, chafing her elbows in frustration. "I don't know how to make you understand how ... foreign this body felt. I couldn't see properly! I couldn't move properly. It wasn't just that I couldn't remember. It was that I wasn't me."

The room was very quiet. Somewhere, a clock was ticking. The sound seemed to be filtered through dust. Through some strange phenomenon of suspended time.

"How would you feel," Ariel whispered, "if you woke up

to find that you weren't you anymore? But the worst part is you don't know who *you* are? You're gone." She clasped her hands, tightly. "You're just ... gone."

David Friedman didn't move.

"Interesting," he finally commented.

Ariel's hands relaxed. She took a deep breath. "It isn't the word I'd have chosen," she said.

twenty

So what you're telling me is that we don't know any more now than we did last night," Henry complained. He'd had another backbreaker of a day. He'd finally gotten around to returning Ariel's call in the late afternoon, and now his irascibility grated through the wires.

"You're really one of those half-empty kinds of people, aren't you," Ariel suggested sweetly. "We know nothing of any importance except that I haven't had a stroke and I don't have a brain tumor or a concussion and I'm not—at least in your ex–brother-in-law's opinion—a complete nutcase. Other than that, the day was a total waste."

"Humph."

"I really like David Friedman, incidentally. Is his sister as terrific as he is?"

"I don't want to talk about it."

"Sheesh! What a grouch!"

Ariel had felt indescribably and perhaps illogically lighter since leaving the hospital. The psychological journey she and Dr. Friedman would begin on Monday might be painful. She might learn things she'd prefer not to know. Or she might learn nothing at all. But she was doing something, and she wasn't doing it by her lonesome.

Which was, she thought, how this evening was stretching out before her. She was suddenly aware of how much time she'd spent in isolation during the past five days and that the prospect of another such evening wasn't appealing. Victor, she'd learned from her message machine, had received

Jessie's tags and would call later in the weekend but, meanwhile, he'd driven to San Luis Obispo to pick up some equipment he was buying from a retiring vet. She didn't know anyone else, literally.

"What are you doing tonight?" she surprised herself by asking.

From the slowness of Henry's response, she gathered he was no less surprised.

"Taking my son to a basketball game."

"Your . . . ?" Ariel faltered as her spirits sank. She'd slipped into camaraderie with Henry Heller so quickly, so naturally, she'd forgotten that she knew little about him. That she was an employee, an overweight employee with emotional problems. She felt a flush crawl up her face.

"That's great!" she exclaimed. (A little overdone, Ariel, she told herself. And let's watch those mood swings, shall we?) "How many children do you have?"

"Just one."

"Ah. Which game?"

"Lakers. Ted, the gaffer, gave me two tickets."

"Is there really a 'Ted the gaffer' or is he another brother-in-law?" (Lightly, lightly, Ariel. Very good!) Her face hurt from smiling.

"Hold on just a sec. I've got another call." With a click, Henry's end of the line blossomed into Tchaikovsky's Sixth Symphony, the *Pathétique*. Ariel rolled her eyes, and her smile became genuine. Too perfect, she thought.

There was a click, and a soaring, tragic note was cut off in midswell by an expletive from Henry.

"What's wrong?"

"Oh, we were well into developing a feature about a housepainter in Little Rock," Henry groused. "Disappeared in the late seventies. Well-loved, family man, etc. And he just evaporated one fine day—all that good mystery stuff.

"I just got word," he fumed, "that a fellow deacon in his church walked into a police station yesterday and confessed to murdering the man and burying him in the basement. Said his conscience had been keeping him awake for fifteen years, and he couldn't take it anymore. Seems the painter had tried to seduce this fellow's wife. Blast the man! Why couldn't he have stayed awake another two weeks, 'til the show aired, before he relieved his conscience. Wouldn't have hurt our ratings any."

"I don't suppose having your faith in human nature restored counts for much here?" Ariel asked dryly.

"Not a lot." Henry's tone changed abruptly. "What're your plans for tomorrow morning?"

That stopped her. "I don't make plans," she replied. "My life's been a little too unpredictable for that lately."

"I think we should talk about the show. About work. Don't you?"

"What do you mean?"

"It sounds like this therapy with Dave could go on for a while and, from what you said, you might not get your memory back regardless. Obviously, you can't just pop back into your job, but you might want to know something about it. About whether you might want to stay in the field in some capacity if the worst should happen. So I thought I could, sort of, describe the show and the process of putting it together, maybe give you a tour. What do you think?"

"Why? Why would you do that?"

"You were good," he said simply.

"Oh."

"Well?"

"Please. I'd like that. Would you . . ." Ariel considered whether she was about to give the wrong signals. "Would you like me to fix brunch? Say around eleven?"

"I'm not chopping. Make sure your doors are locked."

Henry hung up.

Wandering out to the patio, Ariel sat on the steps. Somewhere in the twilight distance the tinkling tune of an ice cream vendor played and replayed over and over. Absently, she tried to identify the tune as she mulled over the conversation with Henry.

It was good, if totally unexpected, that he was willing to counsel her. But that was tomorrow, this was tonight, and she felt low. She was due, she thought, for a spot of self-pity.

Jessie thought not.

She dropped her tennis ball into Ariel's lap and ran into

the yard. Whipping around to face her owner, the shepherd dangled her tongue over her side teeth and waited.

The way the game worked was that Ariel tossed the ball to Jessie, who caught it and brought it to Ariel, who then cajoled Jessie into giving it up so she could throw it again. Ariel noticed that a great deal more time was spent in discussion than in retrieving.

When it grew too dark and too cool to continue—in Ariel's opinion, anyway—she went inside. Sighing, she found the note she'd made and called the last local Michael Gold again. This time he was at home. He had a heavy, Germanic accent, and his wife, who was deceased, had been named Ilsa.

Ariel apologized, interrupting a panegyric to the late and much-lamented Ilsa, disconnected and listlessly punched in the number from Jessie's tag. By now, she'd memorized the number as well as the first half of the message, which was all she listened to. She was hanging up when, apropos of nothing, she remembered her own basketball tickets. She looked through the window at the darkness beyond. The thought of going out anywhere, at night, alone, caused her stomach to do a thrilling little flip-flop. But, she thought, if anyone was still around who meant her harm, they were certainly keeping a low profile. There was no question that the feeling of threat had diminished with each uneventful day.

But there was another consideration. If there did happen to be a local game, the part of town she'd be driving through wasn't exactly Sunnybrook Farm. She weighed the risks against the alternative, a long, empty evening by her suddenly intolerable lonesome. Common sense fought for a foothold and lost.

Where were the tickets? Visualizing the afternoon she'd found them, she went to the study, rummaged and located the red, white and blue stack under a box of paper clips. Shuffling through, she found today's date. The god of lonelyhearts had not only provided a Clippers game, it was at home!

So, murderers, vandals and imagination, she thought, heading toward the shower, do your worst. I'm going.

Spruced up nicely, Ariel arrived at the Sports Arena unmolested. Her seat, she was pleasantly surprised to find, was midcourt and just high enough to afford an unobstructed view of the action. Ingesting a lukewarm hot dog with everything on it (including onions, a consolation prize for being alone) and an outrageously expensive beer, wedged between a loud-mouthed father and his pint-sized son (lustily imitating the father's catcalls in a soprano shrill) and a furiously gum-chewing woman who seemed to be a self-appointed statistician, she surrendered every vestige of tension and yelled as loudly as her neighbors.

Despite the fact that the L.A. team almost blew an eighteen-point lead in the third quarter and didn't seem to find blocking shots or rebounding particularly important, Ariel thoroughly enjoyed herself. As she walked through the parking lot after the game, her cane swinging from her arm, she felt more cheerful. She was glad she'd made the effort to come.

She'd just passed beneath the jaundiced glow of a sodium lamp when she heard footsteps behind her.

Wishing that this section of the lot weren't so deserted, she began to walk a little faster. The footsteps matched her pace. She cut through a line of parked cars. The follower made the same detour. Ariel could hear dragging sounds, as if he wasn't picking up his feet, as if he was struggling to keep up—or to close the gap between them. She heard grunts, belligerent and too close. She whipped around, clutching the cane. The man behind her was only steps away. His face was terrible, his eyes wild, his jaw slack. He was reaching for her. She raised the cane, ready to strike, and then she heard heavy footsteps from another direction. She was being closed in, cornered. As she wheeled, searching for escape, the second man spoke.

"Let's move on, brother."

From deep shadow a uniformed policeman emerged. He looked very young but able. His voice was matter-of-fact.

Ariel swallowed a cry, then turned back to her accoster. She saw that the outstretched hand was beseeching, and filthy. That its owner was clad in layers of disheveled clothing.

"Come on, pal, move along," the policeman suggested again. He came to a halt, hooking his thumbs in his belt. When they'd both watched the vagrant shuffle away muttering something unintelligible, he turned to Ariel.

"Which one's your car?" he asked.

Not trusting herself to talk, Ariel pointed.

He took her arm and they began walking in that direction, she knock-kneed with relief, he full of reproach.

"That guy's a fixture around here," he warned, "cracked but harmless. A lot of them aren't, though—you know?— so you make sure somebody's with you from now on. If you don't have an escort, you ask a cop.

"We don't like muggings," he said as he helped her into her car. "The paperwork's a pain."

twenty-one

Following a whirlwind trip to the market for the makings of an Oriental chicken salad, Ariel fried won ton skin strips and tried to remember how much peanut oil to use for the dressing. It would be interesting to know, she thought, where amnesia leaves off and just plain forgetfulness begins.

She'd drained the won tons and was chopping lettuce when Jessie clambered through her door. The dog sat under the pullout cutting board, watching hopefully for something to fall and reminding Ariel by her presence to try to reach her former owner. For the dozenth time.

Ariel dialed and, cradling the phone on her shoulder, counted the four rings as she continued to chop. When the resonant voice came on the line, she was about to hang up automatically when she realized she wasn't hearing the usual message. The voice had simply said hello.

Rescuing the receiver, which had buckjumped off her shoulder, Ariel mentally kicked herself for not having thought out what to say. "Mr. Morgan? Excuse me for bothering you, but—"

The voice, sounding irked, interrupted. "This isn't . . ." There was a pause. "Who is this, please?"

Rats, Ariel thought, don't tell me I've been hanging up on the wrong number for days! "Is this 470-3342? The Morgan residence? I'm trying to reach my dog's former owner. I mean her husband, her, um, widower?" Lord, Ariel! she winced. Smooth!

She felt even worse when the silence on the line deepened.

"Forgive me if I've been insensitive," she faltered, "but have I reached the right number?"

Sounding considerably thinner with strain, the voice finally said, "What did you say your name was?"

"Oh, Lord! I'm sorry! I didn't say. My name is Ariel Gold."

She waited. "Hello? Are you there?" What if she'd already gotten the papers, she worried. He'd think she was a lunatic!

"Yes. What exactly did you want?"

"Did I catch you at a bad time? I could call back."

The voice hadn't quite regained its former timbre, but it did manage détente. "Perhaps you'd be kind enough to give me your number, and I could call you back when I'm free."

"Of course. Perhaps that would be better," Ariel agreed. She gave him her number and replaced the receiver with damp hands. Wiping them on her apron, she tried to decide what she'd say when and if the poor man did call back. If the matter had been taken care of, she strategized, she'd pretend she knew it and had misplaced the papers. Then she'd ask for the breeder's number and get duplicate papers. Jessie must have come from a breeder, she reasoned; surely she hadn't come from a pet shop.

Victor! she thought. Maybe he'd know.

She found his number and reached a recorded message that gave business hours, an emergency weekend number and a number where, on Saturday mornings between eight-thirty and noon, one could reach the orphans' kennel. At that number she found a friendly female who regretfully informed her that Dr. Pollock had decided to stay out of town overnight but would be calling in. Ariel left her name.

Shredding chicken, Ariel continued planning her campaign. If this Morgan hadn't heard from her before, she'd explain that his wife's vet—his wife's *dog's* vet—had given Jessie to her and suggested that she obtain the documents, but that she'd been away (an understatement) and couldn't call until now. Whatever he did or didn't say, papers or no papers, there was no question in Ariel's mind that the dog would stay where she was.

She was patting butter into molds for the sourdough rolls when Henry arrived. In worn jeans, a plaid shirt and a Cleveland Browns sweatshirt so often laundered the letters could barely be read, he looked both younger and even more lived-in than usual.

"Smells good," Henry said, actually petting Jessie. "You want to eat first and play 'Mr. Heller's Neighborhood' after?"

"Eat. I saw in the paper that your guys lost last night," Ariel taunted as she placed iced tea by his plate and waved him to it. "My guys won."

"Your guys?"

"The Clippers. I inherited tickets from myself, so I reckoned I might as well use them."

"Hmm," Henry grunted in disapproval—whether of her choice of basketball teams or the food, Ariel couldn't tell.

Delicately picking a sesame seed from between his teeth, he said, "Not too smart going out alone at night, is it?"

"Oh, I had a police escort," she hedged, and changed the subject. "The Clips could go to the play-offs this year, you know."

"If they ever get their act together. They've got the talent. So do you," he added. "I didn't know you were so handy in the kitchen."

"Couldn't you tell by looking at me?"

"What does that mean?"

"Obviously, I spend a lot of time there."

Henry had just forked in a mouthful of salad when he grasped her meaning. He sputtered in amusement and had to swallow tea before he could say, "You mean because you're a little zaftig? Funny, I never heard you do that."

"What?"

153

"Refer to your, ah, voluptuousness."

It was Ariel's turn to choke. " 'Voluptuousness'? Please! Anyway, amnesics often behave very differently from their old selves, or so I've read—and I'm talking a hundred and eighty degrees. As to my handiness in the kitchen, 'If you throw a lamb chop in the oven, what's to keep it from getting done?' "

At his look of mild puzzlement, Ariel grinned mischievously. "Joan Crawford said it, in *The Women*. Another one of my infamous quotes—the other thing you don't remember me doing."

He buttered a roll and said, too nonchalantly, "You really are very different. This amnesia thing has its points."

"If that was a compliment, thanks. What was wrong with me before?"

"It's not a matter of wrong or right. Just different."

"Methinks you're hedging."

"Well," Henry said, "I didn't know you except as an employee, so I can't say what you were like privately. Could be among friends you were the life of the party, but at work you were all business. As much as you *could* be in that situation, you were a loner."

"Oh, great!" Ariel rolled her eyes. "That's what they always say about mass murderers! I suppose I was shy, too. And quiet."

"Matter of fact, you were. You spoke when you had something to say, and you said it in as few words as possible. And I never heard you joke. I didn't even know you had a sense of humor, let alone about yourself. You were, ah, a little defensive at times."

Henry wiped his mouth, considering what else he might say, trying to think of something more positive. "You were, as I told you, good at your job . . ."

"Great epitaph. 'She was good at her job.' "

"In fact," he went on, giving her a you-asked-for-this look, "I'd say you were driven. Relentless. And resourceful. You made good contacts, and you handled them well, especially on the phone." He cupped his chin, massaging his beard, which Ariel noticed had been recently trimmed.

"I hadn't thought about this," he mused, "but I guess you

did have a side none of us at the studio knew about. Max Neely said something once, I don't remember what exactly, but I gathered you'd been pretty helpful in some personal crisis of his. And Lisa," he said, cutting his eyes her way, "a real person—no brother-in-law—whose desk is next to yours, mentioned that she'd seen you hoofing it in an AIDS walk." He harrumphed in some embarrassment and found an interesting spot to study on the wall behind her head.

"How long have I worked for you?"

"About two years, give or take."

Henry stretched his long legs underneath the table and folded his arms. Clearly, he'd had enough of the personality analysis.

"So talk to me about what it's like to be amnesic," he ordered. "I think we've got a story here. Not about you—don't panic—but it's been a while since anybody did amnesia."

"Who's the 'driven' person around here?" Ariel teased. Then, seriously, she said, "It's impossible to describe losing yourself. Not to resort to quotations again, but there's a passage in *Tropic of Capricorn* that goes—I think I have this right—'Something had killed me, and yet I was alive. But I was alive without a memory, without a name . . . I had no past . . . I was buried alive in a void . . .' That pretty much says it." She swallowed some tea and made a stab at lightening the mood.

"There're all kinds of amnesia. There's even one where all you forget is faces. Face agnosia, it's called. You can't recognize your mother or the president, but all your other mental functions are intact. Some people, particularly after head injuries, start at ground zero, having to be taught how to dress themselves and to not eat with their fingers; others simply forget what happened to them. Some forget who they are but remember everybody else, or at least their faces. This one woman didn't know herself or anybody else but remembered a phone number from when she was little, and another person, a man, remembered zilch but came up with the address of a mechanic he'd used years before. One story I read, a true story, told about an amnesic who picked a name at random from a shop, a dry cleaner or something.

The name on the sign was James Williamson. Turns out the amnesic's real name was William Jameson.

"Mine's pretty severe, obviously. I remember general things—how to read and and drive and so on—but I don't have a clue about my life before. I wasn't even certain in the beginning if I was suffering from amnesia or something even weirder."

At Henry's suddenly alert look, Ariel laughed. "Hold your horses! Don't tell me it's been a long time since somebody did possession or witchcraft or whatever! No, I think what we've got here is your standard-issue amnesia. And"—she waggled her fork—"an interesting side note is that if I do regain my memory, I may forget everything about this interim period. I might regain my past and lose my present, and you'll have your humorless but philanthropic and capable old Ariel back. How d'you like them apples?"

Henry ignored her question. "I want to get into this in more depth sometime, but right now we'd better play school. Why don't we start with what you do know." He was definitely smirking when he asked, "What did Ariel learn at the library?"

As she verbally regurgitated all she could remember, Ariel watched the smirk fade. She interspersed bits and pieces of history with ethics and technology, objectives and personalities. She talked network, cable and syndication, shot lists, formats and pre- and postproduction. While her recitation wasn't always to the purpose, it was impressive for its sheer length alone. Finally, Henry held up his hand. If there was still a trace of humor in his expression, it was mixed with respect.

"Enough already. You didn't remember any of that?" he asked. "From before? That was all from one day's cramming?"

"A few hours, actually," she said a trifle smugly, and finished her tea.

"Okay." Henry smiled, the corners of his eyes crinkling. "Some of the jargon is about on a par with calling a plane a flying machine, but apart from the anachronisms, not too shabby."

He chewed the inside of his cheek and gave her a speculative look. "If you had practically total recall before, I wasn't aware of it. I wonder if this photographic memory of yours is somehow or other a by-product of the amnesia . . ."

"One more case," Ariel said, "of your ignorance about me." She took off her glasses and cleaned them with her napkin. "There was something in one of the diaries I mentioned to you about my having an unusually good memory. How's that for ironic? Anyway, whatever ability I have now, I apparently had before—thus, the quotations you enjoy so much. Now, it's your turn. Let's have the lowdown on *The Open File.*"

Picking at the last of the salad with his fingers, Henry told her that the syndicated show's format was, obviously, that of an investigative magazine and that it focused on unresolved cases, criminal and otherwise. "If we have evidence that a death-row appeal has merit, we look into it. Or that an election was fixed or that somebody got a bad rap from the rumor mills. Unsolved murders. Mysterious disappearances. Uninvestigated injustices. Unexplained phenomena, natural and human."

"In other words," he explained, "we try to hit a balance between current and historical, human interest and straight news. We're not exploitative like the tabloids, but we're sometimes controversial and often confrontational. We don't stage stuff or edit in sound effects, and nothing's reenacted or dramatized. We aren't totally innocent of practicing checkbook journalism, but who is?

"Let's see." Henry closed one eye and looked at the ceiling with the other. "What else? We sometimes use hidden cameras but we are, I hope, sensitive to when they're gratuitously invasive of people's privacy. We're in a hundred and fifty markets or thereabouts. Our ratings are good enough to keep us on the air but not as good as they'd be if we were more into T & A."

He shrugged. "We try not to let a good story get in the way of the facts, we've managed to avoid doing a show on Bigfoot or the Loch Ness monster, so far, and I can sleep most nights.

"Look," he said, unfolding himself, "why don't we drive over to the studio, and I'll show you around."

Ariel grabbed a jacket and her cane and was about to deal with the alarm control when the phone rang.

"Just a second," she told Henry, "I'm expecting a couple of calls I'd like to take."

The voice was back to its plummy self, confident and charming.

"Ms. Gold? Sorry to be abrupt earlier but, as you can appreciate . . . Fiona's death was unexpected, you see, and it's been difficult. Now"—the tone became brisk—"how can I help you?"

Ariel apologized again and explained. "So do you have the papers," she finished, "or do you think you could locate them?"

"Oh, I think so," he assured her. "Fiona was organized when it came to her animals. Would you like me to bring them over?"

"Well, that's . . . extraordinarily generous of you! But I'm just about to go out, actually, and there's really no need for—"

"How about later this afternoon?"

"I'll probably still be at the studio. Look, Mr. Morgan, don't go to any trouble. Why don't you just drop the papers in the mail?"

When he protested that he'd really like to meet the dog's new owner, that he felt he owed that to his late wife, Ariel suggested that she go there, and they agreed on the following day at three o'clock.

Before she could remove her hand from the phone, it rang again.

"Ms. Gold?" a strange male voice inquired, "Ms., ah, um, Ariel Gold?"

She said yes, whereupon the caller identified himself as George Mueller, a partner in the firm of Mueller & Lupo, Attorneys-at-Law, San Diego.

Apologizing for intruding on her weekend, Mueller explained that he was leaving for a month's vacation and was clearing his desk of last-minute items, of which she, it seemed, was one.

"This is in regard to a client of ours who passed away several weeks ago, Ms. Gold. Ah, I don't know if you're aware of her unfortunate passing and I'm sorry to be the bearer of sad tidings if not. Muriel Coskey Gold? A relative, presumably?"

There was a delicate pause.

"Muriel ... ?" Ariel repeated. "Oh! San Diego. That's my husband's mother. She died?"

"Your mother-in-law. I see." Clearly, from the lawyer's puzzled tone, he didn't.

There followed a great clearing of throat and, more rapidly, Mueller resumed. "Yes, well. I am the executor of Mrs. Gold's estate, and I've come upon a letter among her effects, a letter marked 'private' and addressed to you. Affixed was a note requesting that our firm forward the letter on her demise."

"A letter? To me?"

"Indeed. May I confirm your current address, Ms. Gold? Do you still reside at 11742 Denair Street?"

Mueller assured Ariel that the letter would be sent along promptly, via registered mail. He was murmuring further condolences when she interrupted excitedly.

"Mr. Mueller, can you tell me anything about Michael? About Muriel Gold's son?"

"Her ... ? Your husband, do you mean?"

"Yes."

There was a moment of silence before Ariel heard a sigh and the sound of papers rustling. Mueller, plainly, was longing for the links or cruise ship or wherever he was headed.

"I'm afraid there's nothing in the file pertaining to a son."

"Oh. Well, then, you can tell me if Mrs. Gold said anything to you about this letter? By way of explanation?"

"As I said, I merely found the letter. There was no conversation. Mrs. Gold had only recently become my client, you see. I'd had occasion to meet with her, but those meetings were on matters relating to her will. Now"—he sounded hopeful—"if you haven't any further questions ..."

"To whom did Mrs. Gold's estate go?" Ariel persisted.

"The bulk of the estate was bequeathed to the University of California at San Diego to set up a memorial scholarship," said Mueller. "Now, as I mentioned ..."

Offering a telephone number and the name of a partner in

his firm should Ariel think of any further questions, Mueller wished her good day with audible relief that one more chore could be crossed off his list.

Ariel hung up, flummoxed. She returned to find Henry tapping his foot and looking put-upon.

"It seems my former mother-in-law died," she told him, "or so I'm told by a lawyer named Mueller."

"Don't tell me you're a beneficiary?"

"No, and nor was Michael, according to Mueller. But she did leave me something."

"Must be a different kind of mother-in-law from any of the ones I've been saddled with," Henry said. "None of them would've given me anything while I was *married* to their daughters, let alone after the divorce. Except bad advice."

Ariel set the alarm, locked the door and made her way to Henry's rather tired-looking Oldsmobile. Removing a wadded-up fast-food bag from the passenger seat, she got in, still bemused by this new development.

"Are you sure this lawyer's on the up-and-up? I never knew a lawyer to work on Saturday." Henry burned a little rubber leaving the driveway.

"He certainly sounded like a lawyer. What's boggling is that Mrs. Gold left practically everything to a school. Why on earth wouldn't she have left it to her son? Her only son?"

Ariel silently pondered the situation. Did Michael Gold have so much money of his own that his mother felt he didn't need hers? Or had mother and son had a falling-out? What could have been so terrible as to justify disinheritance?

"Does the name 'Lupo' sound Italian to you?" she asked Henry.

"Does what?"

Trying to ignore the speed with which they were zipping through the shade of overhanging jacaranda trees, Ariel told him the name of the law firm. "I just wondered if Lupo was an Italian name."

"Why? Are you xenophobic or something?" Then enlightenment dawned. "Oh, it's *Sicily*-phobia! Anything to do with your ex-husband"—he glanced across at her in great amusement—"and you start having visions of horses' heads in your bed!"

At her startled and horrified look, he said, "Oh. Don't remember the movie, I guess. You're probably too young to have seen it. There was this scene, see, in *The Godfather* where . . ." He sighed. "Never mind, it doesn't bear telling."

As they sped through an intersection, the Oldsmobile suddenly swerved, narrowly missing a car crossing from the opposite direction. Ariel was thrown sideways, the door handle gouging her ribs.

"Ow!" she cried, and looked back at the fast-disappearing scene of near-disaster. "He had the green light! You like to have gotten us killed!" She glowered at Henry and locked her door. "Criminy!" she said. "With friends like you, I don't need burglars or the Mafia!"

Unrepentant and unperturbed, Henry asked, "What's with this 'like to have' expression? Have you been watching reruns of *The Andy Griffith Show* or what?"

"Don't try to change the subject," grumbled Ariel, who couldn't think of a comeback or an answer to the question.

"Folksy," Henry chuckled, "but kind of cute."

He whipped the car into a driveway and, stopping at a gate, inserted a plastic card into a slot. After the gate swung open, he wheeled into a space stenciled HELLER and cut the engine.

"So, Ms. Gold, anything look familiar?"

"Oh, Mr. Heller"—Ariel put her hand to her head—"I do believe it's all coming back now." She gave him a disgusted look. "Let's try to stay grounded, shall we? If I don't know my own face, and your unforgettable countenance didn't ring any bells, why in the world would I recognize a nondescript cinder-block building?"

"If you don't ask . . ." Henry said philosophically. "We don't know where you were Sunday night. Could've been here. You could've been working on a story that precipitated whatever happened."

She undid her seat belt and opened the door. "There is that," she allowed. "But, no. No flashes of memory or insight."

Henry unlocked the studio door and, while he performed

some complicated maneuvers with an alarm system, Ariel wandered through the reception area. The room beyond was huge, receding into shadow-filled infinity, and Ariel's first impression was one of suspended animation. The two dozen or so workstations seemed to hum with silence, with an impatience to resume their normal, frantic pace. Track lights hung from skeletal rafters under a matte-black ceiling, and everything else in the room was gray or neutral. There were blank, waiting TV screens and monitors everywhere; every workstation had at least two. Notebooks, magazines and newspapers were stacked on every surface. The room bristled with the absence of activity.

She turned to Henry. "Where's my desk?" she asked in a near whisper. It struck her that she'd placed an emphasis on the possessive pronoun.

"This is where all the researchers and editors and producers work," he replied in a normal tone of voice, then indicated a workstation. "That one's yours. Take those folders home to look through when we leave. See if anything there does ring a bell."

Henry pointed to a glassed-in booth that looked like the control room of a grounded spaceship. "Over there's central control, and at the far end, there, is where the studio portion of the show's taped."

He walked in that direction and Ariel followed, her cane clumping on its rubber tip. Several cameras were aimed at a long desklike structure in front of a logo-emblazoned backdrop and, as Ariel had envisioned, nests of lights depended from the ceiling and cables snaked across the floor.

"In here," he said as they entered a hallway, "are the edit bays where we cut the stories."

A half dozen glass-walled, closetlike rooms lay to their right, shrouded in darkness. Henry reached inside one and flipped on the light.

"This is an editing machine. Sit down there." He pushed a button and the console came to life, blipping and blinking.

"Flight 999 to tower." Ariel couldn't resist. Using the knob of her cane as a microphone, she held it in front of her mouth and deepened her voice. "Flight 999 requesting permission to take off."

"Settle down." Henry gave her a look. "Now, I know you've read about editing, but it's a little . . ."

The rest of his sentence was drowned out by a clamor outside the little room. Lights flooded the area and before Ariel, blinded, could register exactly what was happening, something filled the doorway, blocking out the lights.

The something was a someone, a man, and he held a club of some kind in his upraised hand. Ariel's arms flew up to protect her head as Henry jumped to his feet behind her, and his grunt of surprise was echoed by the man at the door.

"What the devil . . . ? What do you think you're doing?" Henry shouted at the same time the other man yelled, "You scared the hell out of me!"

Amid much chest heaving—and, in Ariel's case, abject terror—the two men stood rooted, glaring at each other.

Then Ariel heard a choked exclamation, and Henry, his voice an octave higher, demanded, "Is that my Louisville Slugger? That thing's signed by Wade Boggs. Give it here!"

The tall, blond man, his body still rigid, had switched his gaze to the frozen Ariel. His face was unreadable, but at least he lowered the baseball bat. After several seconds during which his muscles gradually relaxed, he handed the bat to Henry.

"It was the only weapon at hand," the man said. "Hello, Henry. Ariel. Obviously, I'm surprised to see you here." His well-formed jaw unclenched. "What, exactly, are you doing here?"

In belated awareness of her state, Henry glanced at Ariel. He rested a hand on her shoulder, lightly, as he said, "We're working, Peacock—or we were before you scared the living daylights out of us. Ariel's leaving for vacation, so we were settling some details on the, um, Alaska plane crash segment."

"Sorry." The apology was curt.

Ariel saw the man's—Peacock's—mouth curve into a small, tight smile. His lids lowered slightly over extraordinary light blue eyes, giving him a watchful look. He was impeccably dressed in a charcoal-gray double-breasted suit that might have been not only tailored but designed for his body alone, and the pinstriped shirt underneath looked crisp enough to cut paper.

"I thought the Alaska story was Carol's." he said.

"True enough," Henry agreed, noncommittally. He watched Ariel watching Peacock, her expression still wary. "What, by the way, are you doing here? I thought you were back East."

Peacock appeared not to have heard the question. "So, Ariel," he asked, relaxing against the doorjamb, "you're on vacation?" The pale blue eyes were brought to play in the smile, giving it considerable wattage. "Are you doing anything exciting?"

"Nothing to top the last few minutes," she said, "I sincerely hope."

"It looks as if you already have. What's happened to you? Is that a cane?"

"So it is," said Ariel, who hadn't realized she was clutching that object. "Guess I couldn't put my hands on a baseball bat."

Peacock's eyelids dropped another fraction of a millimeter. He remained motionless for a beat or two before straightening to easy but perfect erectness.

"Right." He glanced at his Rolex. "I'll let you two get back to it." With another appraising glance at Ariel and a sketch of a smile at them both, he left.

Henry broke a long moment's silence. "So now you've met Peacock. And if you don't remember him," he added dryly, "no question you need your head examined."

twenty-two

Henry was serious, Ariel discovered, about reacquainting her with her job.

At the editing machine, he explained and demonstrated capabilities and hands-on postproduction in mind-numbing detail. He reviewed logging and time codes, the source as opposed to the record VTR, chroma keying, graphics and supers, voice-overs and dubbing.

On the set, he talked sound bites and clarified preliminary interviews as opposed to main interviews. He identified the TelePrompTer, microphones—boom and hand-held and la-valiere—and pointed out different types of lights and gels and reflectors. He showed her basic motion language and ticked off some of the verbal jargon: cuing and rolling and what's meant by "light" and "heavy" and "taking." He listed who does what and when: the correspondents, the in-vestigative teams and the various producers and editors, writers and researchers. He mentioned that she'd been espe-cially good with the technical crew, whose functions he described.

At her desk, he accessed NewsMaker and compared the merits of other information systems, Nexus and Basis and NewsStar. He talked about satellites, scanners and the value of the tape room as well as more old-fashioned but con-stantly used idea sources: newspapers and magazines of every ilk. Then came the paper blitz; he showed her scripts and formats and tape pages, talked about what seemed like dozens of lists: master checklists and equipment lists, crew lists and location lists, prop and shot and edit lists.

Then, just as Ariel thought he was winding down, Henry had a brainstorm.

"Come with me," he said, grinning mysteriously.

"This," he said as he popped a tape into a VCR, "is boo-boo time. We've put together outtakes from our show and some less-than-perfect moments from the competition, and we add to it on an ongoing basis. We're going to do a little quiz here where you tell me 'What's wrong with this pic-ture,' okay?"

Some of the bloopers were hysterical and obvious. Some were boring but subtle. A few were beyond Ariel altogether; I guess, she thought, you had to be there.

"Okay, what's the problem there?" Henry would stop the tape after each of the less blatant gaffes and wait expectantly.

Getting right into the spirit of the thing, Ariel would re-spond. "All we see are backs. The reporter should've stepped in front of the subject and stopped her." Or "The interviewer jumped in too fast. If she'd kept quiet a second longer, the junk bond guy would've blown it." Or "The terms are too esoteric, too 'in.' Half the viewers won't know what she's talking about." Or "He's talking too much. The pictures are already telling the story."

One hidden-camera segment left her openmouthed and red-faced. "Did they really tape that?" she asked Henry in amazement. "Lord, no wonder they call it trash TV!"

Between one clip about a child prodigy conductor in which the voice-over identified the closing selections as "Eenie Kleenie Night Music" and another in which a reporter's question was so long that the politician being interviewed only had time to answer "No," Henry heard his office phone ringing. When he returned, he seemed preoccupied, and it took a shot of Tammy Faye Bakker to bring him back to the present.

Finally, Henry inserted a different sort of tape. The last item on the agenda was an interview with a ghetto mother whose son had been killed in a gang shoot-out. It wasn't a jolly way to end, but Ariel found the questioning technique masterful.

"Listen to that," she commanded Henry. "She makes the toughest questions inoffensive. How can she sound so incisive and so sympathetic at the same time? Who is that, anyway?"

Henry's mind was somewhere else again. "Hmm? What?"

"Who's that?" Ariel pointed to the screen.

"Carol Lloyd," he answered absentmindedly.

"Is that the same Carol Peacock mentioned?"

"Yeah. Why?"

"Just curious." Ariel frowned in concentration. "I heard the name Carol somewhere recently, but I can't remember ... yes I do. Neely mentioned a Carol. Somebody he said I asked about."

"Why would you ask Neely about Carol Lloyd? Look, why don't I pick out a few more masters with interviews for you to take home and study—you have a VCR, don't you?—and, in the meantime, grab those folders on your desk. Let's hit the road. I'm thirsty."

Neither of them noticed an unremarkable dark gray sedan fall in behind Henry's car as they left the parking lot.

On the drive home, Ariel tried to keep her mind focused on the past few hours. The session had been fascinating, but she couldn't concentrate on it because her life kept passing before her eyes—which in her case, of course, didn't take long.

"Would you slow down!" she demanded for the third time in fifteen minutes. For the third time in fifteen minutes he did—until his mind wandered and habit took over again.

Clutching her seat belt and reflexively braking every few minutes, Ariel leaned her head back and closed her eyes.

"All right, all right! Put your rosary away." Henry eased up on the accelerator infinitesimally and made a show of signaling a turn with both blinker and outstretched arm.

The turn signal of the car half a block and two cars behind them began blinking.

Casually, he remarked, "You never made any comment about Peacock. Were you rendered that speechless?"

"What was I supposed to say?"

His eyes slid in her direction. "Oh, come now."

"Look where you're going! Why would I talk about Peacock?"

"Most women do. You ought to see his fan mail."

Ariel was finally distracted. Through a broad grin, she cried, "You're envious of that conceited clothes hanger! I love it!" The grin settled. "Why don't *you* talk about him? You obviously have opinions."

"Peacock's smart. He's capable. He's aggressive. And I don't think it's conceit—I think it's confidence."

"Well, I think he's aptly named." Curiously, she asked, "Do you dislike him?"

"I don't know him well enough to like or dislike him. I don't think he's exactly Mr. Warmth."

"You don't like him," Ariel said decisively. "I don't know that I did either, actually. He's good-looking, of course, but he is slightly on the reptilian side, isn't he?"

Henry glanced at her. "Interesting reaction," he commented. He didn't expand on what he found interesting.

They made another couple of blocks without incident. "It's not his fault he looks like that," Henry eventually said, sounding reasonable. "If they'd never invented mirrors, he could read the message in every female face. Emily—my last ex-wife—met him once," he said, adjusting the rearview mirror unnecessarily. "She came down to drop Sam off . . ."

"Sam is your son?" Ariel guessed.

"Emily acted as if she'd just been zapped with a stun gun when he gave her that . . . look."

Ariel didn't ask for an explanation. She knew which look he meant.

"You can't blame him for capitalizing on it. The look. The looks," Henry conceded.

"Is Emily David Friedman's sister?"

"No." He twirled the steering wheel, turning onto her street.

"Come in?" she asked when he pulled into the driveway. She'd stopped worrying about mixed signals; she simply didn't want him to go away.

"I guess not." He turned off the engine.

"What did you mean about my reaction being interesting?"

Henry drew his eyebrows together, lost.

"You said my reaction to Peacock . . . I don't know if you were referring to 'reptilian' or what, but you said my reaction was interesting. What did you mean?"

"Oh. It just came to me that you've always been totally nonreactive around Peacock. Period. Like he was—there's no way I can explain this. It was just an impression," he tap-danced verbally.

They heard a drone and were momentarily in shadow as the Goodyear blimp lumbered over Ariel's house. Henry watched its ponderous progress before he spoke again.

"See, you never have responded to Peacock, not to his looks, his charm, whatever. Women usually flirt or dissolve in helpless adoration—not you, though. There was zilch, not even a flutter. Before, I think it was because he was one of those physically privileged people that . . . Well, you didn't respond because of some kind of innate, preconditioned lack of expectation."

Ariel looked thoughtful.

After a moment she said, "I get it. I see what you're saying. 'Water seeks its own level.' If you have good judgment, you learn by osmosis what to expect from life. And I had no expectations of anything from one of the 'beautiful people.' "

"Yeah, I guess so."

"But today was different?"

"That's the point, see?" In spite of himself, Henry pursued the insight. "Today—once you got over being freaked—you were just ... cool. If you didn't respond, it was simply because he didn't impress you.

"There's a world of difference," he said, "and it's pure reflex."

Their eyes locked for a long beat before Henry looked away. "Where'd all that come from?" he asked. "And who needed to hear it?"

It was as close to an apology as Ariel ever expected to hear from Henry Heller.

She unfastened her seat belt. "What was that phone call you got at the studio? It must've been something juicy."

"It was, sort of." Henry fingered his beard. "There was a bombing last weekend, a car bombing in Santa Monica. It got my interest because the bomb squad guys really seemed to be sitting on the story, giving out next to nothing. Today, I found out why.

"A cop I know, a guy who owes me, heard that the car's been identified as belonging to a retired Florida senator. Former Washington big wheel, chaired a dozen important committees. Never had a breath of scandal connected to his name."

Thinking out loud, Henry went on. "They can't find the senator, but they know he wasn't the driver of the car. That, it seems, was a female, at least thirty years younger. And they still don't know who she was."

"How do they know that? Her sex and age?"

"Teeth," Henry said succinctly. He gave her a steady look. "A hand, with manicured nails. Other things."

Ariel shivered. "Do they think—do you think—that it was some sort of mob hit?"

Henry snorted. "I might've known you'd drag in the dons! Come on, I'll carry those tapes and files in for you, and then I've got to go."

They were walking to the door when the gray sedan, which had been idling patiently several houses away, made a slow pass, continued on and turned left at the end of the street.

As Ariel unlocked the door and deactivated the alarm, she asked, "Does Peacock have a first name?"

"Winston. His friends call him Win." Henry's mouth twisted ironically. "Naturally."

twenty-three

That stupid, bumbling, hophead defective!"

He turned on a lamp. Snatching a pillow from the brocade sofa, he threw it savagely across the room. The tinkle of breaking glass enraged him even further, and he stormed into the library, seized a decanter and poured a crystal tumbler full of amber liquid.

He lifted the glass and considered it for a long moment. The contents spattered when he slammed the drink, untasted, onto the polished brass surface of the bar.

"I'm glad the son of a bitch is dead," he muttered between clenched teeth. "I wish *I'd* killed him."

Focused on Rodriquez and the woman who hadn't died, he gave no thought at all to the anonymous woman who had.

Rodriquez had been killed, he was reasonably certain, by the woman whom he'd claimed to have killed. By the woman he'd been paid to kill—"a cinch," he'd called the job. There was an irony here that, in other circumstances, he could have appreciated. He paced to the window, stared out unseeingly, paced back.

Somewhere at his core he'd known all along that the job had been botched. He'd deluded himself into believing the Gold woman was dead. He'd allowed himself to maintain the illusion against nagging doubt. When he'd seen her today, when he'd heard her voice and then actually seen her, he'd been shocked. He'd been furious. But he hadn't really been surprised. Still, it had taken every ounce of control in his being not to panic. Her reappearance had simply confirmed what he'd known in his heart for long, uneasy days, what had made his trip onerous and triggered his early return.

"What were those two plotting?" he whispered. She and that bearded . . . Softly, repeatedly, he brought his fist down onto the bartop. They had to be up to something! Something about him!

But the woman's behavior, her actions, made no sense. That's what was maddening; that's what had made him feel in these last few hours as if he were living some kind of fantastic hallucination.

The accursed woman had acted as if the events of two weeks ago never happened! What sort of game was she playing? What had she been doing all week? Why had she done *nothing* all week? What could she possibly intend to do?

He stared into the whiskey bitterly before pouring the contents back into the decanter and replacing the stopper.

There was something about her that was very different. Her voice. Her demeanor. And then there was that cast on her hand, and the cane. What were those all about? Rodriquez might have gotten in a few licks, he speculated, before he met his demise.

He wondered if Ariel Gold knew how close she'd come to dying today. God knows, his rage and panic had almost gotten the better of him. But with the two of them together . . .

And then, later, when he'd followed them back to her house and they'd both gotten out of the car, all he could do, obviously, was keep driving. She'd have been left alone soon enough, presumably, but he'd seen something that hadn't been there Sunday night. "Westside Systems," the sign in the front yard read; "Armed Response." Entering her house wouldn't be the easy matter it had been a week ago, and it was unlikely that she'd just let him in the front door. Or would she? His mind was going around in circles, and where it kept returning was to the woman's baffling behavior. The truth was he had no idea what she'd do.

Perhaps she'd decided that her speculations alone were too weak. Perhaps Sunday night's fiasco had misled her into thinking he'd do something stupid to seal his own doom, something suicidally reckless. Perhaps *she* was suicidal.

And this, he told himself, is serving no purpose. He strode to the telephone to cancel his evening engagement, for which he no longer had appetite. He'd know soon enough, no doubt, what was in her mind. He wouldn't act rashly this time. He'd play it by ear. And, soon, in his own time, he'd kill her.

twenty-four

Ariel had been struggling through nightly half sit-ups for the last four nights. After manhandling the bike down from the attic, she'd bored herself silly pedaling the thing. Now, with her ankle almost back to normal, she decided it was time to start walking. Down to Marguerite Harris's was a good first venture, she decided.

She looked up the number, arranged to drop by, put the cabbage tureen into a string bag to return and snapped on Jessie's leash.

"Today I'm getting your papers," she told the ecstatic, too-long-housebound shepherd. "It's just a formality, of course. You're mine, and that's that. But I think it's a good idea, don't you?"

Jessie either agreed or just wanted to get on with the program. She stood at the door, tail wagging, looking over her shoulder impatiently.

The Sunday morning was golden and glorious. The air smelled of lemon blossom. The dog almost pulled Ariel to her knees in her desire to get going.

"Heel!" Ariel commanded, and Jessie did. Sedately, they walked to the Harrises', and as Ariel still felt up to it, they crossed the street, walked another block, then doubled back again.

Although the Harris house was of the same thirties vintage as her own, it was larger and more imposing, situated on at least a lot and a half. The property was bordered on

the west by an eight-foot ficus hedge and on the east by
eugenias of the same height. There was a huge liquidambar
tree in front, its branches empty of everything but cockle-
burs, and Ariel imagined that it would be splendid when the
leaves were changing. She climbed steps to a curved, stucco-
walled porch and pressed the doorbell.

The man who opened the door was tall, white-haired and
erect in a way that one associates with the military. Ariel
put his age at seventy or so, impressively preserved. His
cable-stitched sweater was a sunny yellow, the navy-and-
white-striped shirt beneath expensive-looking but frayed just
enough to be comfortable. Fancifully, Ariel wondered where
his ascot was. He would've looked natural wearing one.

"Ah, Ms. Gold. Carl Harris," the man said in a voice that
belonged to Hollywood circa 1940. Slightly British, more
studio voice coach. "We met once years ago. Won't you
both come in?"

Brushing protestations aside, he led her through a long
hallway on which stretched an Oriental runner, its colors
mellowed with age. He stopped at a light-filled living room
and waved her in.

"Make yourself comfortable there," he invited, indicating
a sofa slipcovered in a palmetto print that might have graced
the set of *Casablanca*. On a bamboo table before it, a silver
tea service waited. Tiny napkins were tucked beside a saucer
of lemon wedges, and the creamer held real cream. Miniature scones were stacked on a plate beside a crystal bowl of
coarse-cut marmalade.

From a pocket, Carl Harris produced a dog biscuit.

"May I?" he asked Ariel before inquiring of Jessie, "What
must you say, my friend?"

The shepherd sat up, delicately took the treat in her teeth
and then lay on her stomach, chewing in a most civilized
way. A great sigh escaped her.

Ariel looked around and saw that every available wall
surface was lined with bookcases. There were books by the
score, interspersed with objets d'art: a bronze bust, chinoise-
rie plates, framed photographs and a half dozen brass-and-
wood objects that looked like antique navigational instru-
ments. Atop the bookcases primitive dolls perched between

plants and, strangely, a gargoyle. Grouped on a grand piano were more photographs and a tall vase in which long-stemmed white calla lilies were arranged. The room was eclectic, a mixture of beauty and quirky personal touches.

"This is all so . . ." Ariel was trying to think of an adequate adjective when movement in the next room caught her eye. She pushed her glasses against the bridge of her nose and looked again.

Through an open archway was what appeared to be a sunroom where, upthrust between a wicker settee and a gigantic fern, were a pair of small, bare feet. They hit just about where Marguerite Harris's head would have had she been right-side-up. The feet disappeared, and the improbably colored hair replaced them.

"Be there in a tick," called the familiar voice. "Just let me grab a towel. Carl? Would you go ahead and pour?"

The distinguished-looking man did. He passed Ariel her tea and, with the faintest of twitches at the corner of his mouth, gravely said, *"Sarvangasana."*

"I don't think I quite . . ." Ariel tried to make her face completely neutral, leaving her options open. She didn't think he'd find any humor in, say, a terminal disease, but then she didn't know the man.

"Sarvangasana. The shoulder stand," explained Carl Harris. "Yoga." He filled his own cup and stirred in a generous helping of sugar. "I believe that particular asana is thought to revitalize the thyroid and have some beneficial effect on those suffering from hemorrhoids, digestive disorders and varicose veins."

He took a small sip and said, "I suppose it must work since Marguerite suffers from none of those ailments."

The twitch became a full-blown smile. "How're you coming along with your injuries? And the poor dog was hurt, too, I see. Are you both healing well?"

Before Ariel could answer, Mrs. Harris reappeared. Without makeup, she looked somewhat younger and decidedly less eccentric.

Taking up a cup, she said, "I was relieved when you phoned, Ariel. May I call you by your given name? And you must call us Marguerite and Carl. We've been worried, and I've really had to sit on my hands to refrain from calling again, but one can only push acquaintance so far, isn't that so? What happened?"

Ariel had to change gears to get into the rhythm of Marguerite Harris's conversation.

"A break-in," she said after a beat. "I'm fine, though, and so's Jessie, thank God. But I don't want to talk about me. You left me hanging when you called the other night! You're not an actress, you said, but you mentioned 'your' play. Now, forgive me if I should recognize you, but what *do* you do?"

"Playwright. Playwright emeritus, if I'm to be honest, as these days I mostly just lecture and do the occasional talk show so people can say, 'Is she still alive?' " Her expression was wicked as she went on, "It's great fun to be introduced to people at parties and see the shock on their faces when they realize I'm not moldering in the grave, don't you know?"

"At least, darling," Carl told his wife as he offered Ariel a scone, "you don't get the inquiries I used to get. My favorite was that irascible little old dowager in Cincinnati who demanded, 'Didn't you used to be somebody?' "

"Did you?" Ariel asked, impudently.

"No one at all, my dear, no one at all." He pronounced it as one word: a*tall*. "Many years before you were a gleam in the eye, I did trod the boards briefly in the East, and I did make a few films out here. I enjoyed a modest success in the midthirties playing second leads; the earnest but invariably unsuccessful suitor."

"The midthirties?" Ariel calculated rapidly and astonishment overcame manners. "But that would make you nearly eighty!"

"Thank you, my dear," Carl Harris said dryly. "I shall take your surprise as a great compliment. In actual fact, you'd be closer to the truth if you dropped the 'nearly.' "

"No!"

"I was known—or largely unknown—in those antediluvian days as Herbert DeForest."

"I remember you! You were Joseph Cotten's brother in—

what was it?—something about privilege. You died, very nobly, of some wasting disease. Isn't that right?"

"*A Privileged Life*. Very good, indeed!" He smiled. "It's gratifying that someone of your tender years would remember such a fossil of a film. More tea?"

Ariel held out her cup. "What did you do later? After your movie career?"

"You mean after I grew up? This and that. I did patent a little widget I'd been playing around with for years. Nothing terribly glamorous. You know—a nuts and bolts sort of thing. You probably have one of them gurgling away in your powder room plumbing right now."

Ariel nodded, beginning to understand the large, lovely grounds and the large, beautifully furnished house.

She turned to an uncharacteristically silent Marguerite. "Tell me about you. Might I have seen any of your plays?"

"Possibly"—the little woman was matter-of-fact—"if you were fond of the theater as a very young child. Or if you're a buff of old movies and hang about for the screenplay credits. Do you?"

"Well," Ariel hedged, "the latter, anyway." She hoped she'd heard of at least one of the titles, or could give a convincing act. "Give me a for instance."

"Let's see," Marguerite said, slathering a scone with marmalade. "There was *In Mixed Company*. That was one of the first. And *Cartwheel* was the last."

"But those were written by Marguerite . . . Lambert," Ariel finished, awestruck.

Looking nothing like a theater legend, Marguerite Harris, née Lambert, wiped marmalade from her chin.

Ariel shook her head wonderingly. "As your grandmother character in *Whistling Dixie* so often said, 'Well, I swan!' "

"You do the accent well," Carl said. "Are you originally from the South? Or have you done a bit of acting yourself?"

"No on both counts," Ariel replied, knowing at least one of the answers was true and thinking the other highly unlikely. Her uncertainty reminded her of one of the reasons for this visit.

"Tell me, have you lived here long? I can't really recall."

"Since, let me see, the mideighties. 'Eighty-four, was it?" Carl turned to his wife for confirmation.

"March 1985," Marguerite replied. "Remember? Just before Cynthia graduated? A godchild," she started to explain to Ariel, and then paused to greet the phlegmatic Rudy, who'd come waddling in. The dachshund gave Jessie a token sniff and jumped onto an ottoman, tucking his stubby feet beneath him.

"We married late," Marguerite continued, "too late for children, but we enjoyed visits—sometimes extended ones—from any number of nieces, nephews, and godchildren. Cynthia, as I said, was one of the latter, the daughter of a dear friend who was an excellent actress but a lackadaisical mother. Why?"

"Why was she . . . ? Oh. I just wondered if you knew my father."

Ariel's question didn't receive an immediate reply. The couple looked at each other in silent communication before Marguerite said, "We knew him to say 'Good morning' or 'We got some of your mail by accident,' that sort of thing, but we weren't exactly his cup of tea, I thought. Why?"

"Curiosity," Ariel said vaguely. "You seemed hesitant about answering."

"One doesn't like to speak ill of the dead," Carl said gently, "and the poor man did suffer a rather pitiful last few years. I hope," he added, "that his faith was a comfort to him at the end."

"I see. I wasn't around much," Ariel fabricated, "when he died of . . . ?"

Marguerite gave her a keen look. "Huntington's disease," she supplied. "Dreadful affliction. Yes, I gathered at the time—neighborhood gossip, you know—that you two were estranged. He wasn't easy, was he? If I may say so, though, you've been almost as much a recluse as he was since you moved into the neighborhood. These recent incidents, disturbing as they must have been, have caused quite a metamorphosis. You seem like a different person—are you aware of that?"

"Do you think so?" Ariel smiled disarmingly and changed the subject. "You didn't know my mother, obviously."

"No," Carl said. "She'd been gone for some years, of course, by the time we came on the scene. But I'll tell you who did know her—and, I think, well. Anita Stroud. She's lived here since the sixties, as you may remember."

Ariel stood up and Jessie, who to all appearances had been sound asleep, immediately got to her feet as well.

"I've taken too much of your morning," Ariel said, "but I've enjoyed myself. And the cassoulet was great. Oh!"

Offhandedly, as if it were a throwaway line, she asked, "You never met my husband, did you?"

The two elderly people stood, too, Carl towering over his immediately alert wife, who said, "No. Why?"

"Oh, no reason." Ariel adjusted Jessie's collar unnecessarily. "Just something I thought of. Thanks again."

After many admonitions from both Harrises not to be a stranger, Carl saw Ariel to the door.

"You've certainly weathered your injuries well, my dear," he complimented her as they said their good-byes. "You're looking marvelous, in fact. If I were forty years younger and Marguerite weren't so sexy"—he winked—"I'd suggest a spot of hanky-panky."

twenty-five

Driving east on Sunset Boulevard, Ariel plotted what she'd say to Mr. Morgan in order to get Jessie's papers with the least amount of complication.

She'd managed, amid much swearing, to let the top down on the car, and she was enjoying the sun on her face and the wind in her hair as she imagined a variety of scenarios. All the "what-ifs" were, she hoped, superfluous, but she didn't want to be caught flat-footed a second time. Besides, she wanted to get in, get the papers and get out, and on her return home from the Harrises', she'd been given a perfect, legitimate excuse to do just that. Her answering machine had blinked with a message from Victor. He'd be coming by later to drop off Jessie's tag.

Ariel turned left onto Benedict Canyon Drive and wound her way upward. Making another left and then a right, she was suddenly presented with a vast, breathtaking view of the city. She risked only a quick glance of appreciation. It was a good thing, she thought, that she'd left home early; these narrow streets were convoluted, and many were dead ends. She slowed down slightly. At intervals the road shoulders were almost nonexistent, and the drop into the canyon below was precipitous.

Easing onto a shoulder, Ariel consulted her map and the address she'd copied off Jessie's tag and saw that she'd passed the street. Carefully, she turned the car around and backtracked, found Laurel and made a right. She drove for another mile or so before spotting the number. It was affixed to a white-painted, seven-foot-high brick wall interrupted by an even taller wrought-iron gate. Curlicues traced upward to graceful twin pineapple finials in the center, and an intercom beside it waited for her to declare her business.

Awkwardly, she reached her right hand out the window and pushed a button. After several dead seconds, the voice she'd heard so often on the answering machine said "Yes?"

"Ariel Gold, Mr. Morgan." Ariel wondered if she had to keep the button depressed while she talked. Apparently not. She was greeted and invited to come in. The gate slowly purred open, and as she accelerated up the tree-lined drive, she heard it clank shut behind.

She brought the car to a stop in a herringbone-bricked courtyard, in the center of which was a fountain. Water spurted from the top and trickled down over gradually widening tiers into a shallow pool at the base.

Jessie, old girl, she thought as she looked around her, you've certainly come down in the world.

The house itself would have qualified as "a stately old home" in anybody's book. While she'd hardly expected a hovel in this neck of the woods, this place was truly grand— and by Los Angeles standards, old. Two-storied, constructed of gray stone and wood, it had the look of a French château. A big French château. Ariel was climbing from her car when the front door opened.

The man who emerged was handsome in a smooth, conspicuously cultivated way, and younger than the "widower" her imagination had conjured. The silvery jogging suit he wore was made of parachute silk and sported, Ariel saw as she neared, some designer's logo. Although he looked trim, Ariel couldn't picture the fastidious Mr. Morgan sweating out a jog. More his style, she thought, would be an exclusive private gym, probably with a personal trainer.

He greeted her from where he stood and waited until she was mounting the steps before he invited her in. His tone was a trifle cool, Ariel thought, but she reminded herself that he was recently bereaved and that she was probably a nuisance right now.

Closing the door behind them, Morgan silently extended his hand toward a room on his left. Their footsteps echoed across the round, marble-tiled entrance hall to marble steps that led down into a huge, sunken room. The far wall was composed entirely of floor-to-ceiling French windows. Through them Ariel could see a verandah and an enormous lawn sweeping down to a distant stand of eucalyptus trees; there were no other houses in sight. Between the room's entrance and the windows were acres of very formal living room. She stepped down, carefully maneuvering her cane on the polished steps. When her feet sank into Aubusson carpet, she turned to her tight-lipped host.

He looked to be around forty, but his hair was beginning to go gray at the temples. The little wings of gray were so perfect, in fact, that Ariel wondered fleetingly if they were dyed. Or perhaps the rest of the rather longish hair was dyed.

"What a very beautiful home you have," she said, smiling.

"Thank you," his mouth smiled back.

This man, Ariel decided, was either exceedingly reserved or exceedingly unfriendly.

"I don't want to take up your time, Mr. Morgan, so—"

A flicker of some emotion—annoyance?—crossed his face before he interrupted. "Please. Why don't you just call me Philip."

"If you like," she said uneasily. "Now, as I was saying, I'm sure you have more important things to do, so why don't I just collect my papers and get out of your hair."

"I have nothing to do that can't wait," he said, and suddenly his expression changed completely. His face was transformed by a smile, and his voice was cordial as he said, "My manners are awful, and you look too fragile to be kept standing about."

He took her arm and guided her to one of the immaculate white sofas. "Did you have a skiing accident? Or a car crash?"

"More of a domestic accident," Ariel said, taken aback by his about-face. Then it occurred to her that if her injuries could effect such a sympathetic reaction, she might as well play them for all they were worth.

"I had a break-in at my house, actually. I wasn't seriously injured—or at least not as seriously as the intruder intended."

"No! You didn't!" he cried. "And the burglar? Did the police catch him?"

"Mr. . . . Philip, that is, I'd rather not talk about it just now. And, in fact, I mustn't take your time—"

"Oh, no, Ariel—you don't mind if I call you Ariel?—you're not getting away that easily!" The smile reappeared. "Really, do stay and visit for a few minutes. Humor me, if you will. With Fiona gone and no staff about, I rattle around in this mausoleum, as you can imagine. Now let me organize some coffee for you. Or a drink? I make a wicked Bloody Mary."

Ariel wanted no coffee, and she certainly didn't want a drink before tackling those serpentine canyon streets again, but she also didn't want to offend this mercurial man. Dr. Jekyll might be the tiniest bit unctuous, but he was infinitely preferable to the granite-faced Mr. Hyde.

"Coffee, then," she agreed, "if you're sure."

He clapped his hands together. "Coffee it is. It'll just take a minute. Make yourself at home in the meantime."

Ariel sat where he'd placed her, listening to his footsteps recede and pondering the man's—Philip's—baffling behavior. Well, she thought, people in mourning have a right to behave oddly.

She noticed an elaborately framed photograph on the table beside her and angled it for a better look. Depicted was an unusually short, slightly built woman posed beside a racehorse. The woman—Mrs. Morgan, Ariel supposed—looked to be more or less her husband's age, but either she had no interest in current fashion and hairstyles or the picture wasn't recent. She was smiling happily, looking up at the horse. The horse sported a collar of roses, and he looked pretty pleased, too. Ariel positioned the picture as she'd found it and stood up. Restlessly, she went over to the French windows and looked out at the immense grounds. She wondered how long it was since Mrs. Morgan had died. Did Victor say? She thought not, but it was her impression that it was recently.

Finding the windows unlocked, she stepped out onto the stone balcony. The property was beautifully maintained, the lawn nearest the house neatly trimmed and the flower beds lovely, if a bit formal for her liking. The areas nearer the trees had been left in a more natural state, well-kept but uncultivated. Fifty or so feet to the left of the house, Ariel noticed, was a two-story garage. The ground level looked as if it could comfortably accommodate four cars and the upstairs, she guessed, must be servants' quarters. No one stirred, and she recalled Philip's saying there was no staff on the premises. Except for birdsong, it was utterly quiet.

" 'Money is better than poverty' "—Ariel sighed—" 'if only for financial reasons.' "

By leaning backward over the balustrade, she could see up to the roofline and to both ends of the house. From the front it had looked like a simple rectangle, but she saw now that it was E-shaped. The balcony where she stood formed the middle bar, and wings on each end extended rearward. The wing now to her right—the end nearest the garage—was asymmetrically shorter, and from it several high windows faced her. She squinted. For a moment she thought she'd seen movement behind one of them. She blinked and looked again. She saw nothing but shadow and reflected light.

She meandered back into the living room, thinking that Philip must be making a real production of the coffee. She hoped he wasn't stalling—that he did, in fact, have Jessie's papers. It came to her then that he hadn't once mentioned the dog.

She'd just picked up a magazine when Philip returned, apologizing for the delay. He had indeed gone to trouble. The silver tray he balanced was laden with the finest of Wedgwood and, she thought, Georg Jensen. He placed the tray on a low table and looked it over critically. As he straightened, Ariel noticed that he carried himself well, and that he was, as she'd first judged, really a handsome man. It must be my day, she thought, looking at him over the translucent cup and saucer he offered, for distinguished gentlemen and high-toned refreshments. But this distinguished gentleman wasn't forty-odd years older than she.

Philip caught her studying him. "Yes? Have I broken out in spots?" He smiled to temper the slight sharpening of his tone.

"I didn't mean to stare. It's just that you look familiar." She realized as she said it that it was true.

"Strange you should say so; I was thinking precisely the same about you. Could we have met?"

Ariel shook her head thoughtfully. "No, I don't think so. I'd have remembered you if we had." And I've met only a limited number of people in the last week, she said to herself, so why do you look familiar?

"Well, it's my loss if we haven't. Your turning out to be an attractive woman is an unexpected pleasure, and I intend to take full advantage of it. So tell me about yourself, Ariel. You mentioned a 'studio' yesterday. Are you in the movie business?"

"I'm a producer for a TV show," she said, feeling like an impostor to hear herself say so. "Have you heard of *The Open File?*"

"That's your show? Quite well done, on the whole. Perhaps I've seen you on television? Could that be why you look familiar?"

"Oh, good Lord, no!" Ariel started at the thought of herself on the air. Wasn't TV supposed to add ten pounds? "I'm just a behind-the-scenes person."

"Yes. A producer, you said. Now, as a producer, what do

you do exactly? I imagine your function isn't the same as, say, a Broadway producer or a motion picture producer."

Ariel rattled off what she'd recently learned about what she, theoretically, did.

"You're something of a sleuth, then? Are you working on a particular story now?" Philip asked with what seemed to be genuine interest. "Anything cloak-and-daggerish? Dope fiends? Dishonest officials? Nefarious villains?"

Ariel thought it probably wasn't the right time to point out the redundancy of his last question. "Well, not that I can talk about, no." She smiled. "What do you do?"

"At the moment I seem to be working full-time at clearing up my late wife's estate. And other unfinished details."

If her question hadn't elicited an especially informative reply, Ariel thought, it had served to forestall any further questions about her own work.

"It's incredible how many odds and ends there are," he said, "all sad. Obviously, this house is far too big for one person, and the maintenance is ridiculous, so I'm putting it on the market. I'll just keep the pied-à-terre in town." He smiled grimly. "The real estate people are barracudas, almost worse than the lawyers! And listen to this. Next week I'll finalize the sale of two thoroughbred racehorses. Can you believe it?"

"You're into racing?"

"Fiona was at one time. I know zero about horses. I've never even gone near one of the unpredictable creatures."

And speaking of creatures, Ariel thought, looking at her watch surreptitiously. As pleasant as this visit had come to be, she wondered how soon she could politely remind him of the reason for it.

"Did you know my wife?"

The question caught Ariel by surprise.

"I . . . met her. Once or twice, I believe. At the office of the veterinarian we share. Shared. Why do you ask?"

Philip's shrug was casual. "Do you know anything about her death?"

Ariel was even more startled. This conversation was taking a decidedly morbid turn. "I'm sorry, should I have . . . ? Was there something unusual about her death?"

"Oh, I've made you uncomfortable. I'm sorry." Philip slid forward on his chair, clasping his hands between his knees. "Fiona wasn't terribly social—she seemed to prefer her dogs and horses to people, frankly—but her name was well known hereabouts. Her death did receive some publicity, and I thought with your being in the news business you might have read about it."

He sat watching her, scrutinizing her, in silence. Her uneasiness returning in earnest, Ariel was about to mention her mission when he spoke again.

"Are you certain we've never met?"

"I can truthfully say that if we have, I don't remember it."

"This familiarity is tantalizing, isn't it?" he persisted. "Think. You've never seen me before? I've never seen you before?"

Ariel slowly shook her head no. "Why on earth wouldn't I say so if we had? You know, Philip, I'm expecting company; a friend's coming over in just"—she looked at her watch openly—"half an hour. I told him I'd only be here a few minutes. He's going to think I'm awfully rude, which I hope you won't think, too, but I really have to go."

She stood, and he looked up at her for a moment before rising as well.

"Well, then I must let you go, mustn't I? I'll just find those papers for you."

He left the room, and Ariel fumed. Did that mean he hadn't even looked for the blooming things yet?

Philip wasn't gone long before returning empty-handed. "You're going to be annoyed, I'm afraid, but the file isn't where I was absolutely sure it would be. And I've made you waste a trip."

He took her good hand in both of his. "Listen, Ariel, I'll turn the study upside down if I have to, and I'll find the dog's papers and deliver them personally." His apology was disarming. "I'll even throw in whatever dog food's still here. I know my wife always bought in bulk, so who knows how much there may be? Will that put me back in your good graces?"

Ariel swallowed her irritation. "It's a deal," she said. "Just give me a call. I know this is a bother, but for health rea-

sons—breeding history and all, in case Jessie ever got sick—
I'd really prefer to have the records in hand."

Ariel was back in her car and fitting the key into the
ignition when she heard her name being called. Philip came
hurrying down the steps, smiling and shaking his head.

"Your address," he said. "You forgot to give me your
address. I have to know where to find you, don't I?"

twenty-six

Sure enough, Ariel found Victor waiting when she arrived
home. He was leaning against his car with his eyes closed,
his arms folded and his ankles crossed. There was a smile
on his face. There were also earphones on his head and a
portable tape player hooked to his belt. One foot tapped
rhythmically.

As she turned into the driveway, Victor's eyes opened.
He turned off the tape player and, removing the earphones,
tossed the machine through his car window.

"I was about to send out a posse," he joked, coming to
help her from her car. "I don't think I've ever known you
to be late before."

Apologizing profusely. Ariel led him into the house,
where both were greeted with great enthusiasm.

"Hey, Jess!" Victor said. "Shake!" He pumped the proffered paw. "I've got a present for you," he told her, and
dangled a little metal tag for her inspection. "You belong
to this address now, and your name's even spelled right.
You're official at last, complete with all your impressive doc-
umentation. Right?" he asked Ariel.

"Afraid not," she said. "It turned out to be a wild-
goose chase."

She took Jessie's new tag from Victor, thanking him, then
tsk-tsking when he refused to let her pay for it.

"It seems," she said, "that the papers are among the missing, but Philip says he'll locate them and bring them over.
Now, let's find some pliers, and we'll get this tag on."

"Philip?"

"Mr. Morgan. Lord, if I'd known this was going to turn into such a project . . ." Ariel plundered through a drawer. "Well, I don't know what I could've done differently. Not just everybody gives away an expensive pedigreed dog—a well-trained pedigreed dog—and I don't want some son or daughter coming back at me a month from now . . ." She handed a pair of pliers to Victor. "Actually, he didn't say anything about children. Do they have any, do you know?"

"Beats me. Mrs. Morgan wasn't much of a talker." He knelt to remove the old tag. "But you talked to her for quite a while that first day she brought Jessie in; she didn't mention any to you?"

"Oh. No, I can't say that she did," Ariel said, and wondered what she'd talked to the dead woman about.

Giving the S-hook a final twist, Victor handed the pliers back. "I have no idea. Sorry." He gave Jessie a "down" command. When she complied, he took off her bandage and, after a brief examination, taped a new one on. "Looking good, girl," he said, scratching her rump as he stood.

"Have you ever met him?" Ariel asked. "Philip Morgan?"

"Nope. Not that I recall."

"You wouldn't happen to know if I ever met him, would you?"

"Haven't a clue. Why?"

Ariel shrugged. "He looked familiar. I really don't think we've ever met before, but he said I looked familiar to him, too. I don't know; it's a puzzle. *He's* a puzzle, for that matter—old school, kind of, and very charming, but . . ."

Ariel broke off as a surprising thought surfaced, bringing a tinge of pink to her face. She wondered just how bereaved Philip Morgan was. One could—certain women would— have interpreted his manner as a little, well, flirtatious.

"What?" Victor asked curiously.

"Oh, nothing. Nothing at all." It's probably just Morgan's way, she told herself. Another beautiful person who exudes charm out of lifelong habit, a knee-jerk reaction as natural as breathing.

"Victor, what do you say to taking Jessie for a walk? Do

you have time? And while you're gone, I could pick up some take-out food for us. How about it?"

Later, Ariel turned the little portable TV toward the kitchen table and they watched *60 Minutes* over their El Pollo Loco chicken.

"Have to keep up with the competition," she half-joked. "Ha! Don't we wish we were in their league. But then," she said, showing off her newfound knowledge of magazine show trivia, "it took them something like seven years to hit pay dirt."

"How long has your show been on the air?"

"Not that long," Ariel said evasively, wiping her greasy fingers and turning her attention to Mike Wallace.

After Victor had gone, first insisting on helping to clean the few utensils they'd dirtied, Ariel watched the interview tapes Henry had loaned her.

This Carol Lloyd was really good, Ariel thought, although, these being preliminary interviews, she wasn't actually seen. When the tapes were aired, Henry had explained, the TV audience would see only the interviewees and one of the show's three correspondents. But it was clear from the off-camera questions that the interviewer knew her facts and that she knew how to pose questions so the subjects didn't feel threatened. It was Ariel's impression that, caught off guard, they frequently said more than they'd meant to.

Ariel ejected the tape, wondering again if this was the Carol she'd asked Neely about. It seemed unlikely.

Sighing, she thumbed through the files Henry had taken from her desk. The scribbled, cryptic notes were as meaningless to her as they'd been to him, but in a hefty folder tabbed "N.C. Robin Hood" she found a batch of typed interview transcripts she had no trouble reading. Immediately, Ariel was caught up—obviously for the second time—in the legend of a thirties-era bank robber of rare magnanimity. Right after each heist, according to reminiscences by the local citizenry, needy families in the surrounding North Carolina countryside had found themselves in possession of chickens or a pig or a heifer. The robberies had stopped abruptly. The largesse had, too, and the benefactor had never been identified.

The volume of material and a raft of travel receipts indicated that she'd been heavily into developing the story, and as Ariel read, she suddenly remembered the "folksy" expression Henry had teased her about the day before. The reminiscences were liberally peppered with Southern colloquialisms. "Hey," she suggested to Jessie, grinning, "maybe it was catching! Maybe I've solved a minor mystery, do you *reckon?*"

Pleased with her deductive powers, Ariel wandered into the bedroom and, noticing the diaries stacked where she'd left them, decided she might as well put them away. She was replacing the notebooks in their attic storage box when she saw what looked like a different sort of book under the brittle newspapers. Sneezing from the dust, she uncovered an old-fashioned photo album.

At last, she thought—pictures!

Such as they were. Her family obviously hadn't been into saving their meaningful moments for posterity, and it appeared that even the perfunctory effort had ended with Gladys Munson's death. Wedged into the little corner tabs were mostly black-and-white photographs, yellowing toward sepia. The only studio portrait was of a serious-looking young man and woman posed before an arty, out-of-focus set, circa 1940s. A wedding portrait, Ariel surmised.

She studied the faces, but could see no resemblance to herself. The little girl whose photos began to appear, however, looked very much like her mother. This was Ruth, Ariel guessed, the sister who'd died. Judging from the child's dresses and a car in the background of one shot, she'd lived her short life in the mid-forties and early fifties. She looked about eight or nine in her last photo and, as in most of them, she was smiling.

Feeling sad, Ariel turned the page to see an older Gladys holding an unsmiling toddler. The small, sober face looked no more like either parent than did the adult Ariel. And there was something off-key about the face. When she came upon a color photo stuck in between two blank pages, Ariel realized what it was. This last picture was of herself in a cap and gown, and the plump face—even allowing for age—wasn't quite the present-day face she saw in the mirror.

Taking the photo downstairs, Ariel compared it to her reflection. It was the nose. She'd had a blooming nose job! She looked at the rather long nose in the photo and then at the one in the mirror, and she figured she knew just whose bright idea that had been. Remembering the diary contents and the wildly inconsistent clothing in the attic trunk, she saw the fine, critical hand of Michael Gold.

Rats! she thought. That nose had character! The most she could say for the one on her face was that it was perfect. She turned off the light, full of pity for her needy young self, so lacking in confidence and so eager to gain approval, whatever it took.

That night, fragments of the dream came back in even more bizarre variations. Ariel tossed in her sleep and finally, anxious and teary, she awakened. According to the clock's glowing red numbers, it was 3:16 A.M. She got up and drank a glass of water. After straightening the bed, she lay back down and consciously tried to relax. Eventually she was able to stop thinking about the dream.

Instead, for the hour it took her to get back to sleep, she worried about the next morning's session with Dr. David Friedman.

twenty-seven

Fully a third of the fifty-minute session was up before Dr. Friedman began to talk about hypnotherapy.

They reviewed her physical tests, which confirmed the neurologist's and Friedman's own first impression: there was no organic basis for her amnesia. He asked about her first responses to her predicament, the panic and how she'd coped; about the diaries she'd found; about the break-in and its traumatic conclusion.

Ariel grew more and more comfortable with the unorthodox David Friedman as they talked. How could anyone, she wondered, be so low-key and so intense at the same time? And how did one get to be so totally nonjudgmental? She was even able to distance herself somewhat from her experience, answering his questions without qualms or anxiety.

Finally, Friedman leaned back in his chair. Fixing his eyes on her as steadily as always, he folded his hands on his stomach.

"There're as many schools of thought about how memory works as there are researchers in the field," he began. "We could talk theories and ramifications for hours—the cognitive unconscious and implicit and explicit memory . . ." He waved his hand in a vague, all-inconclusive gesture. "Cybernetics and RNA and so on and so forth. The field's wide open and, basically, up for grabs."

His hand returned to its comfortable perch.

"One point on which there's general consensus, however, is that whatever's happened to an individual during his lifetime remains in the unconscious mind, in detail. That's not to say that there's a specific, physical part of the brain that acts as a storage place for memories. There isn't—as far as we know. In your case, Ariel, and for our purposes, we can simply say that the electrical system—the limbic system, in actual fact—has gone on the blitz." He smiled. "Due, presumably to emotional trauma, all the messages regarding your past can't get through your circuitry right now. Okay?"

"Okay," Ariel agreed, nodding wisely. "I see what's coming. Last week you wanted to pass me off to another doctor; today you're going to tell me to call an electrician. Why do I have the feeling you're trying to get rid of me?"

He gave her a long-suffering look and continued.

"As I was about to say, we have several tools to help with retrieval—or rewiring, if you will. There's traditional therapy, of course, with or without drugs. We can utilize ideomotor responses, with or without hypnotherapy. There's hypnotherapy alone, which might be a viable shortcut. And might not be."

Friedman leaned across his desk toward her. "That's what I want to emphasize, Ariel. Hypnosis isn't magic. It's not a cure-all by any means. But in a trance state, the subject does become open to suggestion and may be able to recall deeply repressed memories."

"What if I can't be hypnotized?" Ariel asked, frowning.

"Then we'll proceed to other methods of therapy. Or, as we discussed, you may decide to let nature take its course, to let your memory return at its own pace. Or not."

Ariel opened her mouth to speak, but Dr. Friedman held up his hand. "Just let me finish.

"It's my opinion, Ariel, based on your tests and on observation, that you're functioning well in a very difficult set of circumstances. You show no signs of clinical depression. Your behavior's appropriate, your attitude positive, and it doesn't appear to be forced or obstructive or diversionary. You're a little flippant, but I think that's a natural defense mechanism for a strong personality protecting its integrity. In short, you seem to be coping, and coping well."

"That may be," Ariel said, "and I'm glad you think so, but waiting for Godot isn't an option I'm comfortable with. It's at least possible that whatever happened, whatever caused this problem, might pose a danger to me. I admit I'm not as convinced of that as I was—it's been a whole week since anybody tried to kill me, after all—but what if I was right to start with? I'm not willing to just do nothing." She set her jaw.

"Okay. I don't disagree. What I suggest, then, is that we give hypnosis a try. We do a little preliminary work today and follow up with it in subsequent sessions. Then, depending on how things go, we can make a decision together about what treatment you wish to continue. Fair?"

"Fair." She sank back in her chair. "Do you think it'll work? In my case?"

Friedman shrugged and, recommending that Ariel make herself comfortable on the sofa, handed her an extra pillow. "Bright people, generally speaking, tend to make better subjects, as do strong-willed people. You're both. I, on the other hand," he admitted, "was a dud. Couldn't stop critiquing."

He closed the blinds. The only light in the room was the warm, yellow glow of the desk lamp.

"I've read," Ariel said with determined nonchalance, "that you're still in control of yourself—you know, during hypnosis?"

"Absolutely. I vill never haf you in my power, *mein liebling.*" He wiggled his eyebrows. "The operator is simply a guide. You'll be completely aware, and you'll say only what you choose to. I know that losing control concerns you, Ariel, and in fact, I may ask if it's all right for you to remember a given answer. You can freely tell me if you can't—or don't want to."

"Well," Ariel said, settling herself, "bring on the candle or pocket watch or whatever. Let's get to it."

"Why don't you just focus on that picture on the wall there," Friedman said quietly, "and on my voice." He seated himself behind her. "I want you to relax as completely as you can. Completely relax and just let go. Breathing slowly and deeply, concentrating on your breath, concentrating on my voice. Inhale, exhale. Inhale, exhale."

As he repeated the words, his voice slowed, became even more soothing. At length, she was no longer aware of the sound of her breathing. His voice became the only sound in the room.

"Your feet can relax now. Your feet are relaxing. Your feet are completely relaxed," he suggested. "Your legs can relax now; the ankles, calves, thighs, one by one, are all relaxing. Your legs are relaxing. Your legs are completely relaxed."

As he verbally moved up her body, naming each part in turn and spending the longest time on her shoulders and neck, Ariel ceased to notice the repetition of the words. At his direction, she pictured the parts of her body and watched them, felt them, gradually lose tension.

"You can feel yourself growing warm, as if you were lying in gentle, warming sunlight. Think about yourself at the beach. You can feel yourself being at the beach. Lying on a soft, buoyant float on the water. The sun is warm and caressing. You can feel the sun's warmth. Feel the brightness and warmth of the sun. You can hear the sound of the surf on the shore. Regular and soothing. Soft and steady. You can feel the gentle undulations of the water under your body. You're very, very drowsy, floating, buoyed by the gentle rhythm of the water, as light as a leaf upon the water . . ."

Images of the dream she'd had several nights before drifted through Ariel's mind. The happiness she'd felt as the little girl at the shoreline. The feeling of utter safety and well-being. She could see the limpid water. She could feel the sun's languid caress. Her eyes closed. Her breathing was deep and regular. The muscles of her face smoothed out.

"You're feeling completely relaxed. So pleasantly, completely relaxed and drowsy. You're sleeping. You're falling deeply asleep. Deeper and deeper . . ."

Ariel still heard the voice, but the words were unimportant. She was no longer aware of her body, no longer aware of anything but a feeling of pleasant lethargy. Moving in any way would have been far too much trouble.

"When I count to three, you'll be unable to open your eyes. One—your eyelids are shut. Your eyelids are heavy. Your eyelids are too heavy to move. Two—your eyelids are glued fast . . ."

Soon, or perhaps it wasn't soon—Ariel had ceased to feel the passage of time—the voice said, "I want you to raise your arm. Hold it straight out from your body. That's right. I want you to hold your arm rigid, as if it were a pole attached to your body. You'll be able to hold your arm in this position for as long as you like, and you'll feel no discomfort. Your arm will not become tired. It will feel very good. It will feel surprisingly pleasant."

Ariel thought of her arm. Felt it rising. The arm was light. There was no sensation of effort. As the voice continued, it eventually told her to lower her arm and suggested that she think about waking up that morning.

"You're now going back in time to this morning. Turning back in time and space. You're drifting back in time to this morning. And when I ask you, you can answer my questions. You're waking up now, and it's this morning. Monday morning. You can feel the pleasant sensation of stretching . . ."

Although she moved no part of her body, Ariel felt the pleasurable release in her arms and legs.

"Tell me what you see."

Ariel heard her own tentative voice.

"I see the light behind the draperies."

"What else do you see?"

"I see . . . my dog."

On and on the voice continued until Ariel could see everything in her bedroom as it had been that morning.

"All right," the voice murmured, "now rest and relax. We're going further back in time to yesterday, to last evening . . ."

Ariel described—or in some cases was just asked to think about—a moment in several of the days of the week that had just gone by. She pictured the people, the places, the voices. She experienced her feelings in infinite detail.

"All right, now rest and relax. We're going further back in time to Monday morning, one week ago. It's Monday morning, one week ago. You're waking up, and when I talk to you, you can answer my questions. You're waking up last Monday morning. What do you see?"

"Um . . . everything's blurry. I can't . . ." She felt herself beginning to tense.

"Just rest and relax. Just relax. What's your name?"

"Ariel. Ariel."

"How old are you?"

"Thirty-one."

"Where do you live?"

She hesitated slightly. "11742 Denair Street."

"Where do you work?"

There was a longer pause. "Woolf Television."

The questions went on. If she began to feel anxious, innocuous questions were alternated with more probing ones. Her answers were sometimes immediate, sometimes hesitant.

"Now rest and relax. We're going further back into time and space. We're going back to the day before Monday. We're going back to the Sunday before last. You're waking up on the Sunday before last. What do you see?"

Ariel's eyes fluttered and opened. She didn't answer.

After many reassurances, the voice coaxed her to remember the evening of that Sunday.

"If it's all right for you to remember that evening, you'll remember and be able to answer my questions. It's Sunday night. What do you see?"

"Nothing. Nothing."

"What's your name?"

There was no answer.

Suddenly her eyes widened as if in wonder.

"Jessie?" she whispered, and then, immediately, terror flashed across her face. "Jessie, please!" she cried. "The lights!" She threw both arms over her face, covering it. Her body thrashed briefly, violently, before it became perfectly still.

"Who is Jessie?"

Ariel said nothing. Her body remained motionless.

"You said the name 'Jessie.' Who is Jessie?"

Again, there was no response.

Friedman leaned toward Ariel, and his voice was infinitely soothing as he asked her to rest and relax. "Everything's fine," he reassured. "I'm with you here, and you're perfectly safe, you can relax . . ."

Gradually, Ariel lowered one arm. Her face was very pale, her skin clammy. As the words went on, encouraging, lulling, she felt her body begin to relax again, felt the blood returning to her face and hands. She felt very tired, very confused. She wanted to go to sleep and be left alone, but the voice continued.

". . . All right. Rest now, and clear your mind. Clear your mind completely. You're going to return to the present. You're going to return to the present time and place. I'm going to count backward from five to one, and when I reach one, you'll be wide awake. You'll feel relaxed. You'll remember everything you want to remember of the last few minutes. You'll feel wonderfully relaxed and clearheaded. Now I'll begin to count from five to one, and when I reach one, you'll awaken and you'll feel wonderful. Five . . . four . . . three . . . two . . . one. You're completely awake."

Ariel looked into dark, smiling eyes. As promised, she remembered everything. As promised, she felt alert and remarkably relaxed. She wasn't even sure she was disappointed at the lack of revelation. "Well, no news is no news," she said.

"Hypnosis isn't a panacea. No form of therapy is."

"Why did I say my dog's name?"

"Is Jessie your dog's name?"

"Yes."

"Was your dog—could your dog have been with you Sunday night?"

"I don't know. I don't think so."

"Are you very fond of her?"

Ariel smiled. "Considering I've only known her a week, I'd say inordinately so."

"Maybe," he said, considering, "you were just expressing your concern for her. You did say she was injured defending you."

He stood and opened the blinds. "I'm particularly intrigued by two things. First, the lights you mentioned. Do you have any idea of the significance of lights?"

"Maybe. But the time sequence is wrong." She frowned, concentrating. "I've had the same dream—well, similar dreams—several times, and one of the things that recurs is the brightness of the room in the dream. And this sort of explosion. Dazzling ..." She groped in her memory. "No, more powerful. It's like a volcanic eruption. But the thing is, the first time I remember having the dream was Monday night. That's what woke me when the ... when my house was being broken into. That was Monday night, not Sunday night."

"Interesting. I want to talk about that dream more next time."

She sat up. "What else? You said *two* things."

"Yes, the other thing. On Friday you said that, initially, the situation wasn't so much that you didn't remember who you were but that—I believe your words were, 'I wasn't me.' Let's talk about that next time, okay?"

twenty-eight

How would you feel about going on a local assignment with me this afternoon? Just as soon as you can get down here?"

Ariel had called Henry to report on her latest session with David Friedman as soon as she'd returned home, but she'd hardly begun when he put her on hold. When he clicked back on the line, he popped the question.

"Me?" Ariel was dumbstruck. "Why would you want me to go?"

"It's a chance for you to see some action. This thing came up unexpectedly, and I've just gotten word we're set to go. All the producers are either out of town or otherwise unreachable, so I'm it. What d'you say?"

"Well," she said doubtfully, "I'd just be an observer, though? I wouldn't actually be doing anything?"

"An innocent bystander," he promised, "relearning the ropes."

When Ariel agreed, they arranged to meet in the studio parking lot in twenty minutes. They'd be traveling in the van with the crew, Henry told her. After making sure she remembered the address, he hung up with typical lack of ceremony or sign-off.

This time when Ariel arrived at the studio, there was no helpful Henry with parking pass in hand. It didn't turn out to be a problem. The guard who peered out of a little booth she hadn't noticed on Sunday smiled in recognition, and the gate swung open.

Not knowing where her designated parking space was or if she had one, she pulled into a slot marked VISITOR, locked up and stood beside her car looking around uncertainly. There were no official-looking vehicles, nothing that looked like an equipment van.

"Hello, Ariel."

She turned toward the greeting, but it wasn't Henry. It was Win Peacock—"Winsome," as she'd mentally dubbed him on learning his first name.

"Hey, that's quite a car you've got there." He ran an admiring hand down the fender and then leaned his backside against it. "I thought you were supposed to be on vacation."

Smoothing her already smooth hair, Ariel thought fast. She couldn't say she was going with Henry on assignment. If she was willing to give up her off time, why would she need Henry? If he was going anyway, why would he need her? She opened her mouth, wondering what was going to come out.

"Ariel!" Henry came striding toward them. "It's about time you got here. Hi, Peacock. You coming or going?"

"Going. I was just about to ask Ariel what's so important that she had to interrupt her vacation."

" 'It is impossible to enjoy idling thoroughly unless one has plenty of work to do.' " Ariel injected fond reproval into her voice and, winking at Peacock, linked her arm with Henry's. "Come on, helpless. I'll find that file for you."

"Those quotes do come in handy," Henry said as they walked purposefully away, "especially when they mean *bubkes.*"

"Just keep walking. Where're we going, by the way?"

"Through the front door, hang a left at the corridor and detour to the loading dock. The getaway van's ready to roll."

"What did you tell the crew about why I was going along?" Ariel asked.

"Nothing. I'm the boss; I don't have to explain my some-times cryptic but always sage actions. Just keep quiet, stay in the background and they'll forget you're there."

Ariel's greeting to the two men waiting in the van was offhand and, she hoped, typical of her. They hi-yourselfed in friendly fashion and went back to arguing about, if Ariel heard right, the Mighty Ducks. By the time they'd gone a block, Henry was able to work their names and functions into the conversation fairly unobtrusively. Freddy the camer-aman was sitting shotgun, she learned, and Perc, the driver, did sound and lights.

As she looked around at the efficiently packed equipment, Ariel felt thoroughly intimidated. When she learned what the assignment was, she wanted out of the van.

"We're going to the home of a man who just learned that his wife's been blown to pieces?" she managed to shriek in a whisper. "Thanks a lot, Henry. I'll get you for this!"

Henry allowed as how she had to start somewhere and explained the urgency.

People in the early stages of grief, he said, sometimes grant interviews before the shock wears off. Then they clam up. That's why he was pushing this meeting with the hus-band, why he couldn't wait to go through all the normal procedures.

"Hit 'em while they're vulnerable," Ariel said nastily.

"Right." Henry pulled a notepad from his packet and added a question in some indecipherable code.

"I hate this."

"Right." Putting the pad away, he said, "Now. Here's the deal. You remember the car bombing I told you about—the car they traced to the retired Florida senator? And the Jane Doe they couldn't match up to any missing-person reports? Well, they finally found the senator. Turns out he'd taken his sailboat down to the Keys, somewhere fishing, for ten days. Had no idea the law was looking for him. And the car, in actual fact, wasn't his anymore. Not technically, anyway."

Henry crossed his long legs, trying to get comfortable in the cramped space.

"The way I understand it," he said, "the senator had sold the car, but he sailed away to Islamorada or wherever without the title being transferred. And the person he'd sold the car to was with him on the trip. Are you with me so far?"

"I think I've managed to grasp the gist of your narrative," Ariel said.

"So the cops catch up with the two of them, these two old guys. The other one, the one who bought the car—who happens to be a retired magnate—said he'd given it to his granddaughter. A gift. When they took off, so did she, driving the car and headed for California. The thing is, she never made it home.

"But this is the kicker." He uncrossed and recrossed his legs. "The granddaughter's a model, a fairly big name. She lives—did live—here in L.A. with her husband, who's not exactly unknown himself. Robert Macaulay's one of the more successful stockbrokers in town, so we've got quite a cast of characters."

"And Mrs. Macaulay was the female, I take it, who died in the car?"

"According to the coroner and the forensic dentist, yes."

Ariel looked Henry in the eye. "How do you do this?" she asked in a low voice. "How do you confront a man who's just lost his wife and ask him to tell you all about it? How it feels to have your wife blown to smithereens? Any comments for the press? Are we going to zoom in and get the grief up close and in your face so America can gawk at it over dinner? Maybe he'll really break down! Everybody can enjoy his misery and say 'there but for the grace of God' and burp and wash the dishes. Good Lord!"

She got no reply.

Arms crossed, foot tapping, looking away from Henry at the blank wall of the van, Ariel wished she were somewhere else, anywhere else. She wanted no part of this.

A block or two passed.

"Why didn't the husband report his wife missing?" she asked.

Henry smiled.

When the van rolled to a stop, Ariel bent to look through the front windows. And froze. In that split second her skin prickled with an electrifying sensation of familiarity. Of déjà vu. Then the connection clicked into place. It's just the gate, she thought, unnerved by the force of her reaction but able to breathe again. The gated entrance at which they waited was, indeed, very similar to the one she'd encountered the day before. The scene around it, however, couldn't have been more different. The Morgan property had been all rustic tranquillity; here chaos reigned.

Visibility from inside the closed van was limited, but Ariel could see enough to know the circus was in town, and it wasn't Ringling Brothers. The media was here in force. Voices shouted, demanded and begged. Faces, limbs and equipment moved in and out of her field of view, and the noise level was frantic. When a guard admitted the *Open File* van, the tumult became even more aggrieved before it faded behind them.

"Why us?" she asked Henry.

"Luck. I got a wake-up call from an old drinking buddy who's at the *Herald* now, Ham Snyder. Ham was with the welcoming committee, with Miami homicide, when the senator docked this morning, so I got the L.A. reconnection before anybody else out here. I got on to Macaulay within minutes after he was notified, before he stopped answering the phone."

He interrupted himself to instruct Perc to let him out at the front door and then, to Ariel, added, "Macaulay ran the gauntlet at Parker Center this morning, but his lawyer just no-commented everybody. For now, anyway, we've got the only interview."

Perc kept the van idling while Henry got out to make arrangements. Four or five minutes passed in idle chitchat before he reappeared at the driver's window. Ariel couldn't hear all his instructions, but she did catch something about setting up in the living room and being sure to get footage of a painting.

The motor was turned off, equipment hauled out, and the crew set to work with no wasted time or motion. Ariel trailed behind, watching carefully and staying out of the way as instructed.

The house was a fine one, as befitted a prominent, successful stockbroker with a wife successful in her own right. Ariel followed the crew through double doors into a foyer where almost everything was white or the color of corn silk. A white urn under a massive chandelier held white and yellow lilies and gladiolas and irises. A white-banistered staircase led past a large round window at the first landing to a second-floor gallery. It was an elegant entrance hall, but inviting.

Hearing her name, Ariel went through a wide doorway into a living room, where Perc and Freddy were busy finding outlets and setting up. Henry was off to one side, talking to a man in a charcoal-gray suit. He beckoned her over and introduced her simply as his associate and then, by continuing the conversation where he'd left off, diverted the man's attention away from her.

Robert Macaulay was tall, at least six-foot-three or -four, and nicely built. Brown hair swept back from a broad forehead, and his gray eyes were large, even a little exophthalmic, and intelligent. His jaw was protrusive, giving him a look of determination. Or arrogance.

He'd barely acknowledged Ariel when they were introduced, but as she wandered in the direction of the crew, she became aware that his eyes were following her. She looked directly at him. His expression was preoccupied, the look of someone trying to place a face. He didn't look particularly grief-stricken, Ariel thought, and for unfathomable reasons, he made her skin crawl.

She turned her back and found herself facing an almost life-sized oil portrait. She stared, rapt. The sadness that overwhelmed her was surprising in its strength. This was Mrs. Macaulay, and Mrs. Macaulay was dead. She took a half step closer, trying to study the portrait objectively.

The woman depicted wasn't precisely beautiful, Ariel decided, but once encountered, she wouldn't be forgotten. She was, in fact, hauntingly familiar to Ariel. Who now gave herself a little shake. The lady was a well-known model, she reminded herself. It was hardly surprising that she'd look familiar.

She was tall and very slender. By some trick of light or artistry, her short, fair hair seemed almost incandescent. The bones of her face were finely sculpted, the cheekbones prominent, the chin deeply clefted.

The expression she wore was grave, Ariel thought. Then she saw the almost imperceptible lift to the wide, mobile mouth, to one delicate brow. A glint of mischief lurked behind the extraordinary green eyes. Either the artist had an exceptional gift for vitalizing his work, Ariel judged, or his subject had been exceptionally vital. *Vital.* Her mind framed the word. It was inconceivable that this woman, so full of life, no longer existed.

Had Henry even said her name?

Hearing the men's approach, Ariel reluctantly tore her eyes away and found an inconspicuous place to station herself.

Macaulay was watching Perc affix a lavaliere mike to his tie. He nodded at some question posed by Henry and then sat in a wing chair just to the side of the portrait. Henry sat in the chair's twin, consulted with Freddy briefly and said, "Roll tape."

In a monotone Henry said, "Monday, February 25, 1993, interview at the home of Robert Macaulay, subject Robert Macaulay, Henry Heller producer. Shot one, take one."

The camera held on the portrait for several seconds, then Freddy slowly panned to Macaulay. He looked composed. His legs were crossed at the knee, his hands at rest, his fingers loosely interlaced. Two deep, vertical lines carved the center of his forehead, and his mouth was stretched into a flat line.

With practice born of long experience, Henry began, his voice quiet and uninflected. The camera never shifted his way and he became, even to Ariel, almost a disembodied voice.

"Early this morning, Mr. Macaulay, you learned that your wife was the victim of what the LAPD has confirmed was an explosive device. What do you know about the circumstances of her death?"

Macaulay cleared his throat, looked down at his hands and back into the camera. "Dynamite, I'm told, was wired to the ignition system of the automobile. When Jane turned the key, the bomb was detonated." His composure was stony. "She was killed instantly."

Jane, Ariel thought, looking back at the portrait. Her name was Jane.

"There's no room for doubt that the victim actually was your wife, Jane Macaulay?"

"There has been a positive identification."

"Mrs. Macaulay was a fashion model?"

"Yes. She'd been a successful model for several years. Although she was less involved in the field since our marriage."

Ariel was no longer cognizant of the lights, the camera or the men who wielded them. Henry had become her voice. She was completely focused on Robert Macaulay's answers.

"How long had you been married?"

"Three years."

"You were asked to go to police headquarters this morning?"

"Of course, as you'd expect. I've given the officials as complete a list as possible of Jane's friends and associates. Many people, certainly, will be questioned."

"Do the police consider you a suspect?"

The question was asked as quietly as those that had preceded it. Ariel watched Macaulay closely.

He didn't seem unduly concerned. "They do not," he said.

"Why is that, Mr. Macaulay?"

"Because of the . . . spectacular nature of the . . ." The man hesitated and began again.

"There were a number of people in the vicinity at the time

of the explosion. Obviously, there's no question as to when it occurred. My whereabouts at the time were confirmed."

"A car bomb isn't a weapon ordinarily associated with person-to-person homicide, a direct method of murder. Wouldn't you agree that a third party is often involved?"

Again, the question, though loaded, evoked no obvious reaction.

"The police appear satisfied that I had no motive," Macaulay said evenly.

"The obvious question: why? Why would your wife be killed, and why in such a particularly dramatic way?"

Macaulay looked directly into the camera lens. "There is no one, to my knowledge, who would have any reason to wish Jane harm. There's no doubt in my mind that her death was accidental. I don't mean that the bomb wasn't meant to kill. I mean that whoever placed it in the car didn't intend Jane to be the victim."

"Why wasn't Mrs. Macaulay reported missing?"

Ariel's attention focused even more sharply.

"My wife had flown to Florida to visit her grandfather. It's my understanding that he accepted an invitation to go on a spur-of-the-moment sailing trip, and that she declined to go along. Jane . . ." Macaulay shifted his legs slightly. For the first time he seemed ill at ease. "Mr. Coulter, Jane's grandfather, had made her a present of an automobile, and she decided to drive home in the car. 'To get the feel of it,' is what I was told she said."

Macaulay paused, appearing momentarily to look inward. He looked back at the camera.

"I knew nothing about this change of plans until this morning. I knew nothing about the car. I didn't know she'd returned to California. As far as I knew, she was enjoying a visit with her grandfather."

"Her grandfather is B. F. Coulter of Coulter Industries?"

Ariel recognized the name of the company, if not that of the man in question.

"Yes." Macaulay was again imperturbable.

"Why do you think, Mr. Macaulay, she would have gone to Anthony's, to the restaurant where she met her death, rather than driving straight home, here to this house?"

Ariel noticed that Macaulay's fingers tightened their grip on each other.

"I have no idea. It was a restaurant Jane and I occasionally patronized. We celebrated our first anniversary there, if I recall correctly. But why she would have been there that night . . . I just don't know."

Before Henry could pose another question, there was a clamor, coming from both the foyer and the opposite direction.

Out of the corner of her eye, Ariel caught movement. She turned to see a very tall, very bulky man standing in the entrance hall. He was breathing heavily, scrutinizing the scene in the living room. The expression on his face was unmistakable. It was scorn.

From the other direction, from whatever room lay on the other side of the living room, there was a scuffling sound and a shriek. The door was pushed open, and a smallish dog of indeterminate breeding charged into the room. His nails skidded on the hardwood floor as he slid to a stop, chuffing, wagging his tail and looking about wildly. He ran directly to Ariel and leaped into her lap, barking and bathing her face in a pandemonium of welcome.

All hell, if it hadn't already, broke loose.

Ariel heard Henry say, "Stop tape!" Macaulay thundered, "Nancy!" and the man in the foyer yelled something that sounded like "Stonewall!"

twenty-nine

The hindquarters of the shaggy, lion-colored dog slipped half off Ariel's lap, but he didn't move except to stabilize his position. He curled himself more securely, making himself smaller, trying, it seemed, to make himself invisible.

No more than thirty seconds had passed since the furor erupted, but Ariel's shock at finding a dog suddenly perched on her person and herself the object of all eyes quickly vanished.

"I know how you feel," she muttered. "Let's vamoose."

Scooping the dog into her arms, she stood and smiled at the men, all on their feet now, their expressions ranging from mirth to mystification to rage.

"Why don't I just take my friend here somewhere less crowded?" she suggested to the room at large.

The uniformed maid who'd come running in after the dog cast a mortified glance at her employer and hurried to Ariel, her arms outstretched helplessly.

"I'm so sorry," she said. "He opened the door and came in before I could stop him. Here, I'll take him."

But the mutt was having none of it. He put his paws around Ariel's neck and dug in.

"Why don't you just lead the way," Ariel said.

"But your arm . . ."

"It's okay," Ariel murmured. "Lead on."

The woman hastened back the way she'd come, glancing over her shoulder in gratitude.

Ariel followed. The outsize stranger in the foyer—who'd said nothing except the one word, whatever it was—stomped away, disappearing into some other part of the house.

When they were safely into the next room with the door closed firmly behind them, Ariel released her charge, who immediately tried to clamber back up her shins. She scratched his head and asked his name.

The maid eyed the dog warily. "Stonewall, he's called, and a right devil is the aggravatin' creature. If you don't mind," she asked in a tremulous voice with a hint of Irish, "will you go along until we can get him outside? He'll follow you, I think."

She led Ariel through a huge kitchen and out a back door into the yard. Stonewall trailed eagerly.

"Bless you!" The maid wiped shaking hands on her apron. "Could I offer you a cup of tea, miss, or do you need to go back to the others?"

"My name is Ariel, and I'd love tea, thanks."

"And I'm called Nancy." The broad face relaxed into a smile. The rosy flush that had colored it from forehead to neck settled into the cheeks, where it was, Ariel imagined, a natural feature. "Why don't you just stay here and enjoy the sunshine, and I'll bring your tea."

Ariel sat on a plumply cushioned lawn chair and gave the funny Stonewall a pat. She knew she should return to the business inside, but she was reluctant to do so. It was comfortable out here; curiously, she felt at home. Breathing in the freshness, she looked around the grounds.

There was a kidney-shaped pool with a sort of waterfall affair built into the far end. Beside it was a small, neat cabana, and beyond that a tennis court. The landscaping was gorgeous, a riot of bright flowers alternating in shadier spots with the lush green of ferns. While this property wasn't as secluded as Philip Morgan's estate, tall camellia trees flowering around the periphery gave an illusion of privacy.

Seeing the results of a great deal of effort and thought, Ariel wondered how involved Jane Macaulay had been. The sadness and shock she'd felt looking at the portrait returned, and when a cloud briefly passed over the midafternoon sun, she shivered with more than chill in the sudden coolness.

Stonewall, tired of being ignored, clamored for attention. Barking and wagging everything from his withers to his tail, he proceeded to bring her a variety of trophies, one at a time. An eight-inch-long beef bone, a Wiffle ball, a Frisbee and a rubber banana were all piled at her feet when the back door opened again. To Ariel's surprise, it wasn't the rosy-cheeked Nancy who emerged, but the large man from the foyer. He was an elderly man, she now had time to observe, and he was carrying a tray.

"Nancy's busy making coffee for your pals in there," he rumbled in a slow, deep voice as big as he was. "Down, you yellow heathen!" This last was addressed to the dog, whose exuberant leaps threatened to send the tray flying. "She's got too much to do, has Nancy, so I volunteered to wait on you," he went on, unconsciously imitating the maid's turn of phrase as he set the tray on a table.

"B. F. Coulter." He held out a beefy hand, grudgingly. A few strands of his white hair were lifted by a passing breeze.

"Ariel Gold." Her eyes widened. This ponderous, contrary old man in a rumpled black suit and open-necked white shirt wasn't her idea of a tycoon. "I'm so sorry about your granddaughter, Mr. Coulter."

As he gave her hand a single, perfunctory pump, Ariel

noticed a nick where he'd cut himself shaving and a bristly, dime-sized patch of white stubble he'd missed entirely. She also noticed that his eyes were red-rimmed and that he smelled strongly of alcohol. Beside the tea accoutrements on the tray were a glass and a bottle of Jack Daniel's. Sippin' whiskey, thought Ariel, eyeing the bottle. She suspected he'd been doing more than just sipping.

The old man sank heavily into the chair next to hers. "That mangy animal seems to have taken a shine to you," he said, keeping his eyes on the dog and ignoring her condolences. "He's not known for his taste. No offense."

Ariel took none, despite the fact that he didn't sound at all conciliatory. "He probably just smelled my dog," she said mildly. "Figured me for a patsy."

Coulter let out a massive sigh and said nothing. He slouched farther down into the seat, his legs straight out in front of him. The tip of a dark, wine-colored tie hung limply from the breast pocket where it had been carelessly stuffed.

It was a day for potent first impressions, Ariel mused, and this was the strongest yet. She didn't question it. Pouring sour mash into the glass, she positioned it near his elbow, made a business of preparing her tea and let the silence be.

"What's the matter with your hand?" He didn't seem particularly interested in the answer.

"Cracked a bone," Ariel replied, just as carelessly. "It's mending."

Slowly his gaze traveled over the grounds, preoccupied, seeing something, or someone, who wasn't there.

"Jane did all this," he said. "Thought it all up. Did a lot of the physical labor, too."

"I thought she might've."

Silence descended again. Ariel sipped her tea.

"She was as much my daughter as she was my granddaughter," he finally said, more to himself than to Ariel. "I raised her."

Surprised by the confidence, Ariel let a beat go by before she asked, casually, "Are her parents living?"

"Her mother—my daughter—died when Jane was a baby."

Ariel wondered about the father but thought it better not

to press. She listened to the music of the waterfall. Watched a hummingbird consider a feeder hanging from a tulip tree and then dart away again.

The big head turned toward her. "I'm not my grandson-in-law, and I'm not interested in being interviewed," he warned apropos of nothing. "I don't need vindicating."

Ariel scratched the dog's stomach, which he'd helpfully exposed in her direction.

Coulter drained the whiskey in one swallow. He rested the empty glass on his massive stomach and stared into the distance.

"If that's a technique," he said sourly, "it's wasted on me."

"Pardon?"

"I don't mind silence." His speech had slowed, but there was no sign of slurring. There was a trace of a drawl, or maybe it was just contempt. "There's not enough silence as far as I'm concerned. I'm not going to fill it up for you."

"Mr. Coulter." Ariel set her cup and saucer on the tray. "If you'd prefer to be alone, I'll oblige you."

Appraisingly, he cut his eyes her way. "What did you say your name was?"

"Ariel Gold." She'd slid forward and was about to stand.

He looked down at the dog stretched on his back at Ariel's feet. "She got that creature at the pound, Jane did. Girl had been raised with some of the best bird dogs that ever drew breath, and she goes to the pound and gets him."

His mouth twisted. "The husband would've been happier with a confounded Dalmatian or whatever's the trick to have these days. Something inbred." His expression softened. "Stonewall's okay. From day one he loved Jane. And she was nuts about him."

"I can empathize."

"Don't bother." The suspicion was back.

"I just meant that my dog's adopted, too," Ariel said mildly.

"Oh."

"Jessie."

"What?"

"That's her name, Jessie."

"Humph," he said, reminding her of Henry.

"Why 'humph'?"

"Nothin'."

"What's wrong with 'Jessie'?" Ariel asked, curious and beginning to be amused.

"Nothin' wrong with it. It just reminded me of something out of left field."

"What?"

Coulter went without speaking for so long Ariel was convinced that, this time, he wasn't going to answer. She sat still.

"When I first got Jane after my girl, my own daughter Suzanne, died . . ." He cleared his throat and wiped his mouth with the back of his hand, impatiently. "When I got Jane, she was just . . ." He held out the hand, palm down, about two feet from the ground. "She was about a year and some, just startin' to talk. I didn't know what to do with her. Little old baby girl like that."

He fell quiet, leaving Ariel sad for him but wondering what this all had to do with her dog's name.

"When Suzanne was little, see," he began again, "I wasn't home much. Too busy gettin' rich. But with Jane, I was retired—or as retired as I'll ever be—and I was with her a whole lot more than I ever was with her mother. A whole lot more."

He shook his head and brought himself back to the present. Pouring a generous slug of whiskey, he peered at Ariel from under bushy white beetle-brows.

"Don't worry," he growled, "I'm not senile. And I'm not drunk. Yet. I'm gettin' to the point. Like I said, Jane was just startin' to talk, and those first weeks she was miserable and scared, callin' for her mama and cryin'." He frowned. "She kept sayin' something that sounded like 'yessa' or 'yessy.' Something like that. She'd cry and say that over and over."

He took a sip, rolled it around, swallowed. "I don't know why I thought of that. Hadn't thought of it, I guess, in thirty years. Never did know what she was tryin' to say unless it was 'yes sir.' Kids in the South still say that, you know. Too

bad the Yankees down there rapin' the place haven't picked
up the custom."

"You're from Florida?" Ariel asked unnecessarily.

"North Florida," he differentiated. "What's left of it."

Coulter hauled himself to his feet, a laborious effort.
"You're not too bad for a Yankee yourself, Ariel Gold. Nor
for a confounded media person."

He glared down at her from his impressive height. "But
if I hear one word on the TV of what I've had the poor
judgment to say out here"—the drawl had all but disappeared—"I will personally make you regret it."

Ariel stood and drew herself up to her own, not unimpres-
sive height. She was close enough to smell Old Spice and to
reel from the alcohol fumes mixed with it.

"Mr. Coulter," she began firmly, and stopped. She
grinned. "I'm on vacation."

The bloodshot eyes narrowed, then slowly crinkled. "You
sure you're a Yankee?"

"Thank you," Ariel said dryly. "I guess I'd better get back
in there."

They'd begun walking toward the back door when Coulter
came to an abrupt halt.

"Hey, Ariel Gold, do me a favor. Tell my grandson-in-
law that when he finishes giving autographs, I'd appreciate
it if he'd let me know. There're some arrangements to be
made when he can spare the time. Tell him I'll be out here."

Returning to the chair he'd vacated, he lowered his bulk
into it. As Ariel closed the back door, pushing a whining,
determined Stonewall gently back outside, she saw that the
old man was pouring himself another shot.

On the drive back to the studio, Ariel tried to pay attention to the men's enthusiastic interview postmortem, but her
thoughts kept returning to her conversation with B. F.
Coulter.

While she'd felt only halfhearted sympathy for Macaulay
(downright antipathy, she admitted to herself, was closer to
the mark), her heart had gone out to Coulter. She wished
there were something she could do, some way to lighten his
grief. There was nothing, of course, and any gesture on her

part—stranger that she was and, worse, stigmatized by her profession—would be misinterpreted.

"What?" She realized that Henry had asked her something.

"Where'd you go back there?" he asked in a low voice. "You were supposed to be paying attention, learning from the master. Where'd you and Bowser disappear to?"

"Oh, around. I talked to the grandfather for a while."

"Coulter?" Henry's dark eyes lit up. "You talked to the old man? What'd he have to say? Anything interesting?"

Ariel gave him a disgusted look. "Nothing to the point. Except . . ." She paused, remembering the snide allusion to Macaulay and vindication. She considered what could be said without betraying the ramblings of a heartbroken old man. "I don't think he's too fond of his grandson-in-law. Which reminds me: I'm curious about why Macaulay agreed to do this interview. I don't mean with us in particular; I mean at all, with anybody."

"You wondered that, too? Yeah, well, my formidable powers of persuasion notwithstanding, so did I." He pondered for a minute and said, "My being the first to call, I think, was the key. Once he realized that our show won't air immediately, I've a hunch he regretted saying yes. He wanted a forum, in my opinion as soon as possible, to establish himself as a loving, bereaved husband who's in the clear as far as the cops are concerned.

"His idea was to distance himself from the murder right away," Henry conjectured, "and I think he wanted the most controlled interview situation possible. He knew the press would go after him, of course; it's too big a story. But he wanted to avoid a press conference or one of the more sensational talk shows where he'd be pushed hard on a couple of points and, if he didn't answer, get tainted by innuendo."

"Like where was he when the car exploded?" Ariel supplied.

"Like that. I pushed him on it myself, but he sidestepped like Ali in his prime."

"There was something there." Ariel remembered the extraordinary composure just marginally eroding at the question. "Guilt," she said, decisively. "He may not be guilty of her murder, but he's feeling guilty about something.

"Tell me what I missed," she said. "Did he happen to give any reason why he and his beloved wife hadn't communicated for at least a week? Or longer? When did Jane leave Florida, anyway?"

"Thursday afternoon, twelve days ago. Yeah, he said he'd called her two or three times, and nobody answered the phone. Coulter, it seems, has no message machine on his personal line. Has a thing about it."

"And he didn't wonder where everybody was? He wasn't a teeny-weeny bit concerned?"

"You're not overfond of Macaulay yourself, obviously," Henry said, acknowledging the sarcasm. "But you can't really come down too hard on him on that. They're out fishing or sunning or drinking orange juice or whatever you do in Florida. From what he said, the spontaneous sail into the sunset wasn't unprecedented. They'd done it before and, while he'd have been surprised, he said, if she'd gone off on a jaunt without telling him beforehand, she was with her grandfather, after all. As far as he knew." Henry shrugged.

"Well, still and all, he didn't reach her. She didn't call him. For such a loving couple it's a little strange that they don't talk for nearly two weeks, and he's not worried."

"Maybe in your experience," Henry said.

She gave him a look. He looked at his notes.

"Let's talk about logging in," he said.

When they got back to the studio, Henry was all business. He, Freddy and Perc huddled, and then he started into the building.

"Aren't you coming?" he asked, noticing that Ariel was lagging behind.

"No, I don't think so," she said. "It's been a very long day, and I'm going home if you don't mind. I am on vacation, remember?"

Henry walked back down the steps he'd ascended at his gangbusters speed.

"You okay?"

Ariel stuck her thumb up. "Aces. I'm just tired. And Coulter really got to me. Does this stuff get easier? Dealing with people at the worst moments of their lives?" She really wanted to know.

"It's a fine line," Henry said, understanding, realizing that hard as it was for him to keep in mind, today had been an unprecedented experience for Ariel. "It's a fine line between empathy—feeling empathy, creating empathy—and invading privacy. Capitalizing on the emotion. You achieve a certain amount of distance eventually, and hopefully you don't become inured beyond redemption." He gave her a weak grin. "Whatever that is."

"Why'd you want me to go along?"

The question was put simply, bypassing all the rhetoric. They both knew she hadn't been invited just to further her education.

"I still hate it," Henry admitted, answering in kind. "I've done it a thousand times—talked to people who've just lost their wives, their fathers, their sons. People who, for all I know, just *killed* their wives, their fathers, their sons."

He sat on the steps of the loading dock. "I did it for years. Girded my loins, took it on the chin, absorbed all that suffering. But for a long time now, I've been in a position to assign the grief to somebody else, to lurk in the studio, working with tape, not people. Today, I couldn't find anybody to hand it off to. I'd have done it," he assured her. "Wouldn't have hesitated a minute. But I thought, why not have a little support? A little distraction? I had no way of knowing, of course, that Macaulay would be an iron man."

He grinned. "You just happened to call at the right time, and you did get a taste of the glamorous world of magazine news, didn't you? Hey!" He was glad to change the subject. "You started to tell me about seeing David this morning. How'd it go?"

"It didn't." Ariel sat down beside Henry. "The hypnosis took, but I couldn't remember anything I didn't already know. It'll take time, he says. Now, let me ask *you* something." She took off her glasses and, holding them up to the waning light, inspected them for smudges. "Why're you doing this? Playing along and not telling Peacock or anybody about my . . ."—she waved the glasses— ". . . situation?"

Henry had to think about his answer. His reaction had been too automatic to qualify as a conscious decision.

"Call it perversity," he finally said. "I've never been much of a company man—which has been known to work to my detriment. Besides . . ." He pushed her knee, draped his arm over it. It was the first time she remembered him touching her. "I've always wanted to play Pygmalion. It's fun."

" 'Women,' " Ariel said solemnly, " 'upset everything. When you let them into your life, you find that the woman is driving at one thing and you're driving at another.' "

"Oh, God, spare me! Another blessed quote. What's that from?"

"Pygmalion. You brought it up, Henry Heller; keep it in mind. Now go play with your tape. I'm going home."

thirty

Win Peacock was lying in wait. Henry had no sooner reached his desk than he spotted the sleek blond head through the glass walls of his office and the control room beyond. Almost immediately, Peacock appeared at Henry's door, the expression on his tanned, annoyingly perfect face one of respect. He lounged against the jamb, his suit coat draped casually over one shoulder, hooked on his thumb. Henry could see part of the Hugo Boss label inside the lapel.

"So what's this I hear," Peacock asked by way of congratulations, "about an interview with Robert Macaulay? The one and only interview, yet. Not bad. So what's the scoop? I hear they're still in the dark about why the wife was killed. Is that right?"

"Macaulay's convinced, or says he is, that it was a mix-up. The wrong lady, he says."

The fine eyebrows came together. "Pretty unlikely, isn't it? She was inside the restaurant for a while. . . ." Peacock carefully hung his jacket over the back of a chair. "Obviously, long enough for the car to be wired. And it wasn't exactly your run-of-the-mill car, was it? That won't wash."

"Yeah, I know. If it was a contract hit—which it just about

had to be—and the hiree didn't know her, I can see that he might've gotten the wrong woman with a gun. But mistaking the victim and the car ... ?" Henry waggled his hand side to side. "On the other hand, Coulter told the police that to his knowledge his granddaughter hadn't called her husband before leaving Florida, that Macaulay didn't know she was on her way back or what kind of car she was driving."

" 'To his knowledge,' " Peacock repeated, examining the chair for dust before sitting down.

Henry acknowledged the validity of the proviso. "Macaulay also says the cops are satisfied he's got no motive. But he's blowing smoke. We all know they're just getting started."

He propped his feet on his desk. "But I'll tell you something, Win: I'll be surprised if it turns out Macaulay did have anything to do with this, for two reasons. One, I've heard rumors that Senator Osborne's not going up for reelection and Macaulay's one of the people being looked at as a possible candidate for the seat. And that he's not exactly disinterested." Henry paused for effect.

"So let's look at this scenario. Here's a guy who's got to be clean as the pope right now. Let's say, for the sake of argument, that his wife had something damaging on him, okay? He'd be a lot more likely to buy her off than bump her off. And even if for some unknown reason he did need her dead, there're a lot less conspicuous—and more efficient—ways to get it done."

"Get serious! In the first place, Jane Macaulay wasn't hurting for money. But more to the point, you and I both know that murder's seldom logical. If murderers were as shrewd in real life as they are in the movies, even fewer of them would be caught. The fact is, most quote-unquote well-planned murders are anything but, and most murderers are incompetent. Look at the Menendez brothers. The boys kill their parents—no witnesses, no problem. A fourteen-million-dollar inheritance is all theirs. Right? Wrong. One blabs to a psychologist, and he puts it on tape. How about the wacko from the World Trade Center bombing? He gets caught because he returns an incriminating van to get his four-hundred-dollar deposit back. And I'll give you an even better example."

Peacock leaned forward. "What about that feature we did on the lawyer in Atlanta? What was the name? Tokars! Here's a man who's got brains, money—he's even got underworld connections. So, allegedly, he conspires with an associate who's so brilliant he goes around publicly shopping for a shooter. *Interviewing* people, for God's sake! And this rocket scientist ends up with a junkie who royally bungles the job. The punk's hiding under the bed when the SWAT team comes for him!"

Peacock relaxed in the chair, tilting it backward. "It takes a rare individual to plan a murder and an even rarer one to execute the plan."

"But . . ." Henry pointed a pencil, waggled it. "You're talking about the ones who get caught, and you said yourself that too few do. Besides, you didn't ask the other reason I don't think Macaulay did it." He smiled as if he were holding a royal flush. "The old, finely honed Heller instinct. My gut says he knows no more about why she's dead than we do. And I'll tell you something else: it won't surprise me one bit if we never find out who blew the woman up."

"If it was some kind of random thing," Peacock argued, "I'd go along with you. Someone with no connection to the victim. Some nut who got a message from aliens that Macaulay's wife was in league with Satan or who just wanted to see all the pretty fireworks. But I don't think that's what we're dealing with. My money's on Macaulay, and that's *my* finely honed instinct talking. Anyway"—he stood and slipped on his jacket—"I hope you're right about one thing: I hope they don't find out who did it, at least for a while. This is our kind of story, in spades. And, thanks to you, we've got the only interview in town with the man who's got to be the primary suspect."

Peacock was halfway out the door before he turned and asked, "What's with your friend, Ms. Gold?"

"What do you mean, 'What's with my friend, Ms. Gold?' "

"You're not going to tell me you haven't noticed?"

"Noticed what?"

Peacock dipped his head, giving Henry a sardonic look.

"Ah, Henry . . . that's not the same woman who's been occupying that desk," he said, pointing to it, "during the two months I've been working here. Now, is it?"

Henry merely looked quizzical.

"Has the stolid Ms. Gold—incredible as I'd have thought it—found love, perhaps?" Peacock raised an eyebrow.

"How would I know? Why're you asking me?"

"Judging from the amount of time you two've been spending together, I thought you might be her confidant. Or the object of her affection?"

"Get real," Henry said curtly, hauling his feet off the desk and becoming busy with the blizzard of paper on his desk.

Peacock leaned against the door again.

"Really? Then I guess you wouldn't mind if I called her myself?"

Henry looked up sharply. "You're kidding!"

"You have a problem with that?"

Henry couldn't decide from the man's impassive face whether he was serious or not, but he'd never thought of Peacock as being much of a humorist.

"What is it with you, Peacock? Notches on your gun? Some kind of quota you have to meet?"

"Well, well. Sounds like maybe you do have a problem with it."

Henry just glowered.

Peacock chuckled and straightened. "Good night then. Oh, we still haven't looked at that cut I mentioned to you. Tomorrow, okay?"

He strolled away.

thirty-one

Ariel's answering machine had been busy in her absence.

Philip Morgan had called to ask whether it would be convenient for him to drop off the dog's papers the next day, Victor had called with no message except to give him a ring when she could, and David Friedman's receptionist had called about changing Thursday's appointment to Wednesday.

She told Morgan via his machine that tomorrow would be

fine and to let her know what time; she chatted with Victor, who, as far as she could tell, had called for no other reason than to chat; and she assured Dr. Friedman's machine that Wednesday was no problem. She hung up from the last call thinking that B. F. Coulter might be on the right track with his aversion to answering machines, that R2D2 and his cohorts were taking over the world.

Speaking of which, she programmed her VCR to record *The Open File* so she could study the program at leisure.

Thinking about the show turned Ariel's mind again to B. F. Coulter, which was an exercise in futility. There was nothing she could do. Restless, she argued with herself about the advisability of going for a walk in the dark, then poohpoohed her trepidation. She grabbed the leash and a jacket, reset the alarm and marched into the front yard, vowing to stop dwelling on imaginary danger, number one, and, number two, to buy a canister of Mace tomorrow. Then she saw that all the debate was academic anyway—she had company. Marguerite Harris was coming down the sidewalk dragging Rudy, who was determined to get one last whiff of a fire hydrant.

They circled several blocks together, Marguerite slowing her fire drill pace in consideration of Ariel.

"You're really doing better, though, aren't you?" the little woman asked. "I see you've dispensed with the cane."

Ariel was about to agree when she heard a tiny, ghostly voice from behind an azalea bush immediately to her side. She let out a gasp and jerked involuntarily on the leash, but Jessie, strangely, showed no alarm, and neither did Marguerite.

"Anita!" she exclaimed, smiling. "Show yourself! What in the world are you doing back there in the dark?"

A flashlight snapped on, pointing skyward. Caught in the eerie, vertically angled beam was a white-haired specter.

"Snails." The beam shifted, and the specter became a fragile-looking very old lady in a silk kimono. "If you get them before they breed," she said, aiming the light at the ground, snatching something up and hurling it into the street (where Ariel heard a sharp crack), "you don't have the poor, disgusting things eating everything in sight come spring. It's this alyssum," she complained. "So enthusiastic, but it does give the creepy little snails sanctuary."

The flashlight beam was briefly flashed on Ariel's face. "Why, Ariel Gold, isn't it?" the ancient woman exclaimed in apparent delight. "It's been years! How are you, dear? Recovering from your ordeal?"

Guessing that this must be the neighbor both Marguerite and Carl had mentioned, Ariel started to answer, and for the second time in half a minute was left with her mouth hanging open.

"Speaking of which, Anita Stroud," Marguerite scolded, "I've got a bone to pick with you! You were supposed to call when you got over your flu. You promised you'd come for a meal or tea or something. Explain yourself!"

"Stop bossing your elders, Marguerite. Ariel, come inside in the light so I can see you. Bring the dogs in, too."

So saying, she marched away, trailing her dragooned guests behind her.

Ariel raised her eyebrows at Marguerite, but all she got in response was a "Good! You've got a treat in store" and a rather firm push toward the neat stucco house, where the porch light gave her a better look at their hostess.

Her face serene, her smile sweet, her voice only slightly quavery, the little old lady looked frail, but Ariel had the feeling Anita Stroud took orders from no one.

She herded people and animals alike into a most remarkable living room. The only furniture was a low, red-lacquered table surrounded by floor cushions. The floor was hardwood stripped to the pale, natural grain, and all the walls were white, the one opposite the front door composed of sliding panels with delicate wooden frames and panes of translucent paper. In a corner there was an odd alcove in which hung a silk scroll painted with two blackbirds against a dusting of cherry blossoms. A vase on the raised floor beneath held three aspidistra leaves, and a wooden post in the alcove served, as far as Ariel could see, no purpose at all.

Anita seemed oblivious of the effect of her home. She slipped off her shoes and gave Jessie's side a pat and a keen look. She asked no questions. Instead, observing that the sun was well past the yardarm, she said, "I'm going to have my martini. Shall I make a pitcher, or would you prefer something else? Ariel? What would you like, child?"

"Fine. A martini's fine," Ariel answered a little breathlessly. This neighborhood was full of surprises, and a perfect Japanese room lurking behind an ordinary pseudo-Spanish facade was one of the better ones. She telegraphed a question to Marguerite, who, next to their hostess, seemed like a spring chicken. Marguerite only smiled and said, "Count me in."

As Anita exited through a swinging door, Marguerite ordered Rudy to sit and stay (an order he ignored) and said cheerfully, "Can't think when I've had a martini, and didn't I love them once! Well," she shrugged, "we're not driving, are we?"

"What's this all about?" Ariel hissed.

"Just hush and enjoy it. I went along because I wanted her in out of the chill, but now that we're here, let me show you something."

Walking over to the paper wall, she slid a panel aside to reveal a picture window. With an abracadabra flourish, she flipped a switch, and a Japanese garden materialized in the floodlit backyard. Giant succulents nestled beside huge rocks. Spiking above fleshy jade plants and echeveria and portulaca were dozens of regal agapanthus stalks. There was even a scaled-down arched bridge over a tiny, cleverly contrived stream.

"Oh!" Ariel said.

"Yes, isn't it?" Marguerite was thoroughly enjoying her surprise. The door popped open, and the octogenarian (nonagenarian?) Anita emerged with a glass pitcher.

"Showing off again, I see," she said. "Make yourself useful and fetch the glasses in the freezer and the other things, would you, Marguerite?" She set the pitcher on the low table and gestured toward the cushions on the floor. "Sit. Your back's all right, isn't it? You didn't hurt that, did you?"

"No problem," Ariel assured her, settling awkwardly and worrying about how the two much older women would manage.

Anita sank agilely to her knees, and Marguerite, bearing

frosty martini glasses and a saucer of olives and cocktail onions, was so graceful she appeared to alight. Intertwining her legs in the lotus position, she put a glass in front of Ariel and Anita, plopped olives into her own and rubbed her hands together in anticipation.

"*¡Salud!*" she said when her glass was filled.

"*Kanpai,*" said Anita.

"May you live all the days of your life," Ariel contributed. She sipped the clear, icy liquid, eyeing her barefoot hostess over the rim. The white hair was thick and pulled back into a chignon, the eyes behind rimless glasses a pale gray. The delicate face was angelic and looked almost as translucent as the paper panes of the sliding panels. The surprisingly few wrinkles, Ariel observed, radiated from the corners of the eyes and the smiling mouth.

"You're looking wonderful, Ariel, and it's so good to have you here at long last," Anita said kindly, stirring her drink with an onion-laden toothpick.

"I guess I've been kind of antisocial." Ariel wondered why she'd been such a hermit when she had such lively neighbors. "But now that I'm here, please, tell me about your house."

"My house?" The old woman's confusion made Ariel wonder if she was a little less sharp than she appeared.

"Ariel's talking about your rather unusual decor, Anita," Marguerite interjected. To Ariel she said, "She doesn't realize that this might look just a hair eccentric to other people. Or like the repo men have been here, don't you know?"

"Oh, that!" Anita popped an onion into her mouth. "Well, I lived in Japan for two years after my Felix died. I'd always wanted to do that after I retired from teaching, but Felix was a bit short on curiosity. He thought you needed a visa for a trip to San Francisco, bless his jingoistic heart. So, I buried him, leased out the house and bought a one-way ticket to Tokyo." She smiled benevolently, and then her forehead creased as something seemed to occur to her.

"I was there, in fact, when your father died and you moved in, Ariel, which is why you got no condolences or welcome from me. May I extend both now, belated as they are?"

"Thank you. And your timing's just fine," Ariel said with a touch of irony. "Now, go on—tell me about your house."

"There's not all that much to tell, child. The truth is that, although I do admire the simplicity of the traditional Japanese home, it wasn't appreciation so much as practicality that convinced me to do all this." She waved her empty toothpick vaguely. "I was just plain tired of dusting tchotchkes and nursing that big back garden. All that out there now's drought-resistant, you see. I've got better things to do," Anita said seriously, "and I'm not as young as I used to be."

"What's that little alcove there?" Ariel asked, shifting from one hip to another. Her feet had gone to sleep.

"That's called a *tokonoma*. It's where you put your decorations." With a finger hardly thicker than a chicken's claw, she pointed to the post. "And that's just a focal point, for the beauty of the wood. Although in a Japanese house, it would probably be helping to hold up the roof. Are you really interested in all this, or are you just being polite?"

"Don't fish, Anita. Go on." Marguerite patted the bony hand.

"The panels are *shoji*, and they're made of *washi*, or rice paper. Oh, to go back to the *tokonoma*. The arrangement in the vase there's in the classical style known as *sho-ka*, which follows principles that are centuries old. No doubt you know that flower arranging's taken seriously in the Orient. An arrangement doesn't just look pretty; it tells a story."

"Explain," Ariel said, entranced.

"You come again, young lady, and I will. I don't want to use up all my lore on your first visit."

Ariel straightened numb legs and waited for the needles and pins that signaled the rush of returning blood. " 'Unbidden guests are often welcomest when they are gone,' " she sighed.

"Shakespeare?" Anita guessed.

Marguerite interrupted the chatter. "Before we go, Anita, let me ask you a question." Her tone was no longer lighthearted. "What was it Ariel's mom died of? Do you remember?"

"Good heavens, Marguerite! You do know how to end an evening on an up note, don't you?" Anita gave her friend a look of mild rebuke, then thought for a minute. "I'll answer your question by asking Ariel one: how much do you remember or did you ever know about your mother's death?"

"Very little." Ariel had been as surprised by Marguerite's question as Anita had. She'd completely forgotten that Carl had said her mother and Anita were friends.

"Is Marguerite asking about this for your benefit? Do you want me to be frank?"

"Yes." Ariel's stomach felt suddenly leaden.

"Well, I don't remember because I never knew. For a fact. Gladys had a degenerative disease, I know that, even though she wouldn't talk about it and took pains to hide that she was sick at all, let alone how bad it was." Anita's sharp eyes softened in memory. "She tried valiantly to hide the trembling, but it got progressively worse, and I could see that she was affected not only physically but mentally. She began to forget things. Badly. To be despondent.

"Your father would've been dutiful, of course, but Gladys would've been miserable being taken care of by him. It was always the other way around, you see. They grew up together—you knew that, I suppose—in some tiny community upstate where everybody was related to everybody else. She was always the strong one, although you wouldn't have known it. He was just—forgive me, Ariel, but Lawton Munson wasn't an easy man to like—he was just more overbearing, that's all."

Anita fell quiet, her mind twenty years in the past.

"She was a proud woman, my friend Gladys, and I'm sure she was . . . desperate about her illness. About what the future held for her. I think she decided to cheat the disease."

She gave Ariel a level look. "I think, for her, that was the only decision to be made."

Ariel felt very sad, but more for Anita than for herself. She didn't remember the woman who'd been her mother, but this woman had been her friend.

"Had you known her for a long time?" she asked.

"Well, of course. Don't you remember all the time we used to spend together? I knew her from when you moved into the neighborhood, when you were just a toddler. And what a grave little thing you were! Not at all like the sprite you were named for. Oh! Your reference to Shakespeare reminds me: do you know about your name?"

Ariel shook her head.

"Lawton named you Ariel, Gladys told me, because he'd heard that it meant 'lioness of God.' She went along, but it was her little private joke that she had the other Ariel in mind."

Anita became brisk. "Well, all that was a very long time ago, wasn't it. And I'm glad, Ariel, that you don't have bad memories."

Getting to her feet with little effort and no apparent stiffness, she exclaimed, "Isn't that dog of yours good, lying there so patiently? The only reason Rudy's still is because he's asleep."

"Oh, leave the poor old thing alone," Marguerite said good-naturedly, kissing her friend's cheek.

Once Marguerite and Ariel and their dogs were out again in the now quite chilly night, Marguerite became unusually quiet. At her own sidewalk next door she said good night and turned away.

"What's the matter?" Ariel asked. "Is something wrong?"

Marguerite pivoted in her tracks, her face a mask of indecision. "Oh drat! I have to ask. Have you been tested for Huntington's disease? Hearing Anita describe your mother made me think of it. She can't have had it, too, God forbid, but even with just your father having the disease, you've got a chance to have it, too. You must know that." Her voice faltered. "Have you? Been tested?"

"Well . . . don't worry," Ariel said lamely, "and thanks for tonight." Impulsively, she embraced her neighbor and went off, sinking further into anxiety with every step.

Having other, more pressing things on her mind, Ariel hadn't considered how her father's illness might affect her. And what if her mother had, incredibly, had the same thing? Wouldn't that mean that she herself was a sure bet to have the gene? Cold fear squeezed her heart. From what she'd just heard, the town her parents had come from had been inbred; they could've been cousins or something. Or had Anita just said that about everybody being related as a figure of speech?

As she let herself into her house, Ariel tried to organize her thoughts. It was immaterial whether one parent or both had the disease; she'd have to be tested, and right away. Suddenly, she remembered something she'd seen when she was cleaning the study. It stood to reason that she'd known about the risk she faced. Surely she'd been tested at the time! In a flash she was at the desk, flipping through folders. She pulled out the Blue Shield file and checked the date on the Explanation of Benefits forms: 1990, the year her father died. She scanned the entries. If they indicated what she'd been charged for, Ariel couldn't see it, but a lab was named as well as a doctor. She'd call tomorrow, find out what they were all about and proceed accordingly. In the meantime, she decided, she'd stop worrying.

Sure.

Jessie began to bark seconds before the door chimes sounded.

Marguerite, thought Ariel; she's remembered something she wanted to tell me. She hurried into the living room and looked through the window. A long, dark sedan sat at the curb. Quickly, she drew back, her heart beginning to thud. She moved to the door. Cautiously, as if the person outside would be able to see her, she looked through the peephole.

Standing on her porch, his huge bulk blocking out everything behind him, was B. F. Coulter.

thirty-two

Ariel Gold. I hope it's not too late to pay a visit."

Ariel held Jessie's collar, whispered "Sit," and stared through the doorway.

The old man's eyes were even more bloodshot, his suit even more rumpled. His hair looked as if he'd been caught in a high wind, and either the porch was swaying or he was.

B. F. Coulter, Ariel realized, was drunk as a lord.

"Mr. Coulter, I don't mean to sound ungracious, but what on God's green earth are you doing here?"

With the mournful look of a maligned basset hound and great dignity, he said, "Paying a visit. I believe I just made that clear."

Ariel shivered in the chill night air. "Well, I suppose you'd better come in," she said. "This is my dog, Jessie. I told you about her."

As Coulter went past her into the living room, placing his feet with exaggerated care, Ariel noticed movement in the car parked at the curb. She craned her neck and peered into the darkness but could only make out that there was someone behind the steering wheel.

"Who's with you?" she asked, relieved that he hadn't driven himself.

"Just Roy. He'll wait."

"Who's Roy?" Ariel closed the door.

"My chauffeur."

"Your . . ." Ariel looked back toward the door. "Are you serious?"

"Why be filthy rich if you don't take advantage of it?" he asked, dismissing the subject.

"But I thought you lived in Florida? Did you fly your chauffeur to California?"

"Who said I just had one resi . . ." He paused and thought for a second. "Residence," he finished with satisfaction.

Listing dangerously, he looked around the room. "Very nice," he said politely. "May I sit down?"

"Please. By all means, sit down." She refrained from saying "before you fall down."

"Mr. Coulter, if you don't mind my asking, how did you know where I lived?"

"Man in my position can find out pretty much whatever he wants to. I called your boss and asked."

"You called Henry?" she asked in disbelief.

"Who's Henry? I called Bill Silverstein, and he called somebody else, who probably called somebody else. Anyway, I found out, didn't I?"

Jessie was sniffing his knees. "Nice dog. What's the matter with her belly?" He scratched the shepherd's head.

"Who's Bill Silverstein?" Ariel was thoroughly confused.

Coulter closed one eye, the better to focus the other one on her. "Billy Silverstein. The chairman of Woolf Television."

"The chairman of ..." Ariel closed her eyes. "Give me strength," she muttered.

"How come you don't know who Billy Silverstein is?" he asked.

"Never mind that. Listen. Why don't you tell me why you went to so much trouble to find me. In other words, to put it straight out on the table, why're you here?"

Coulter scratched his ear, grimaced and gave it some thought. "Tell you the truth, it's been so long ago I thought of it, I don't honestly remember. And we did stop at a bar or two on the way."

His voice thickened. "I wasn't about to stay over at Macaulay's house and listen to all those strangers talkin' about Jane in whispers, so I went home. But she was everywhere. Pictures of her on every wall and table, stuff . . . gifts she'd brought me from jobs all over the globe. Her room. Well, it's a guest room now, but it used to be hers."

His gaze roamed the living room, unseeing, Ariel thought.

"I didn't want to be around anybody that knew her, and I found out I couldn't tolerate bein' alone either." Coulter turned bleary eyes toward Ariel. "There was something about you this afternoon, kind of reminded me of Jane. So it seemed like the only thing to do was come here."

"I? Reminded you of *Jane?* Mr. Coulter, I think you need some coffee. And something to eat. When have you eaten?" She half-rose.

"No," he said. "I'll go directly and let you get on back to your business, but just sit here a minute and talk to me. Why'd you say that like that?"

"What like what?"

"You acted like I'd said something ridiculous when I said you made me think of Jane."

"Mr. Coulter." Ariel was torn between sympathy and exasperation. "Your granddaughter was a successful fashion model. She was beautiful. She was *very* slender."

Ariel sat still, wordlessly inviting him to look at her, letting her presence—all of it—speak for itself.

"What?" He seemed genuinely puzzled. "I didn't say you were her spittin' image; I said you reminded me of her. Fact is, a good bit."

The muzziness had dissipated, at least marginally.

"What's your problem, Ariel Gold?"

"What problem?" she asked, uncomfortable with the turn this conversation, such as it was, was taking. "I'm fine. Fine as wine. Right as rain. I'm just not exactly on a par, physically, with cover girls."

Coulter frowned, looking Ariel over as if she were a bird dog he was thinking of buying. "Nothing wrong with you that losing five or ten pounds wouldn't fix. Take off those glasses," he ordered.

"Mr. Coulter! Please! Let's get off this. I know what I look like."

"Nothing wrong with my eyes. You're the one wearin' glasses, and you'd look better without 'em. So did Jane, for that matter."

"Well, she had amazing eyes to show off, didn't she? I never saw such a beautiful green."

He snorted. "You'd see 'em in the mirror if you wore colored contacts like she did. Anyway, you talk like you think you're not a nice-looking woman. How bad *are* your eyes?" He glared at her, his face a tragicomic study in indignation.

"Listen, Jane wasn't beautiful. Why"—his arm swept the air in a wild gesture that made Ariel fear for the lamp beside him—"she was downright peculiar-looking when she was a kid. Too tall, her nose kind of long, and her mouth was too big for her face. And gawky? One time she fell and cut her chin open on a can of Vienna sausage—like to scared me to death, but confound it if it didn't heal up into that cleft that ... well ..." Coulter pointed a shaky finger. "Point is, I made sure she knew she was special and beautiful to me, and she grew into her looks like a lot of little girls do.

"We fixed everything that needed fixin'—spent a confounded fortune on braces. Got her into ballet and gymnastics. And was she death on weight! Kept after me all the time about low-fat diets and I don't know what all. I think that's why she had a tough time when she gave up the weed; she was afraid she'd put on weight."

Ariel relaxed, glad to get the topic back to Jane. Realizing what he wanted and needed, she hugged a toss pillow to her stomach and said, "Tell me what she was like."

The room was quiet for a long time, so long Ariel thought the old man had gone to sleep.

Coulter squinted at her. "I'm a fool to be here. I know that," he said quietly. "To be talkin' to you, a media person. Foolish."

"I can give you my word," Ariel said just as quietly, "with no reservation whatsoever, that anything you say in my home won't go beyond it. And if you'd feel better not talking," she added, "then don't. I'll fix you something to eat."

"I'd a lot rather you fixed me something to drink."

"I don't suppose it'll do any good to remind you how you're going to feel in the morning?"

"See," he said, making his point, "that's just the kind of thing Jane would've said. And, no, it won't do any good."

Ariel found an airline-size bottle of Kentucky bourbon. Well, she thought as she poured it, at least it's Southern.

"That's the best I can do," she told him. "And that's all there is, by the way."

He thanked her, took the glass and studied it for a while

before draining it in two swallows. Jessie, who'd long since stretched out at Coulter's feet, sighed. A forepaw quivered as she dreamed.

"Jane," he finally said, his sigh echoing the dog's, "was kind. She was a good-hearted little girl who grew up into a good woman. Hattie and I can both take credit for that."

"Hattie?"

"What? Oh. My housekeeper. Got her when my wife died, long years ago. She raised Jane as much as I did.

"And, Lord have mercy, when I had to break it to her this morning . . ." His face seemed to grow older before Ariel's eyes.

"I'll tell you this," he said softly. "Jane was real. Not a false bone in her body. Good-natured, easygoing. She loved to read, Jane did. And working her puzzles . . . studying recipes. In fact, I guess you could say she was kind of, I don't know . . . passive, in a way."

Jessie, dreaming of who knew what adventures, began to whimper, and Coulter bent to comfort her.

"She could get by on her looks, you see," he went on, wheezing with the effort of straightening back up. "And her brains. She didn't have to work all that hard mostly, didn't have to make all that much effort. Things came her way.

"She didn't have any . . . passion about anything yet. No causes, no real calling. That well was still untapped."

He pondered for a long moment.

"But she was full of life and humor and, I thought, confidence. I thought she was strong, and she was in some respects.

"Jane was no baby when she married, you know, but I think she'd got to where she wanted out of the single life, where she wanted children. I'd hoped that waiting so long, she'd end up with somebody as straight as she was. As easy. But it went just the other way."

Coulter's faced hardened. For almost the first time, Ariel could see a hint of the man who'd built a megabusiness and masterminded it ruthlessly.

"Macaulay's a bully, and she let him run her," he said, his voice bitter. "I don't know if it was pride—that she couldn't admit the marriage was all wrong or what. Maybe she couldn't face starting over, admitting she'd made a mistake. She was proud, no doubt about it, and stubborn as a goat. When she did set her mind to something, she wouldn't be stopped by a herd of Huns.

"Or could be," he considered, "it was simpler than that. Maybe she was looking for a daddy, somebody to give her direction. Lord knows she never had a 'father figure' "—he pronounced the term mockingly—"except for me."

"What became of her father?" Ariel asked.

"Oh, Harrison was another winner! Bright enough, but weak. Naive. Got his ideals from song lyrics instead of life. I don't mean he was a bad kid—and they were just kids, he and Suzanne, when they ran off together. If we hadn't forbidden her to see him, maybe . . ."

"What?"

Coulter pulled a face. " 'Maybes' are for fools."

"Tell me."

"Her mother and I didn't hear from her but once in nearly three years, from somewhere in Colorado. I had somebody looking for her, naturally, and he almost caught up with them then. Traced 'em on out here. Then nothing."

Ariel waited silently.

"Well, one fine day Harrison showed up back in Florida, with the baby. By then my wife had passed on—never even knew Jane existed. I wasn't home, but Hattie was. The boy was doped up on something, she said. Said she couldn't get any sense out of him, just that Suzanne had . . . that she'd died. Hattie tried to hold him, but he took off, claimed he'd come back for Jane when he could take care of her. He didn't—not that I expected him to—and I couldn't find him. Couldn't find out what happened to my daughter."

"You never heard from him again?"

"Oh, yeah, indirectly, three or four years later. I got a call from a hospital in Canada. Figure he was avoiding the draft. They found my phone number with his things after he died of an overdose.

"So much death," he said. "And now Jane . . ."

He stared at Ariel, through Ariel.

"I'd pay money," he said, "to know what she was doing

at that restaurant. Why she didn't go straight home, *if* she didn't."

His gaze focused. "If I weren't satisfied that son of a bitch was ignorant of Jane's whereabouts and the car she was in, he'd be dead now. If I find out different, he will be."

There wasn't the smallest doubt in Ariel's mind that he meant it.

Coulter fell silent, brooding.

Ariel sensed that she'd let him say enough—more than enough. That when he remembered the conversation, if he remembered it, he'd regret it.

"Look here, I'm going to get us some food, okay? I haven't eaten either, and we could both use it."

She got up. "I won't be long. You just keep your seat."

He seemed unaware that she was leaving the room, and when she returned with coffee and sandwiches, she found B. F. Coulter slumped even farther down on the sofa, his head resting on his chest. He was snoring.

Ariel took the food back to the kitchen. She brought a pillow and half-coaxed, half-manhandled Coulter into lying down. She took off his shoes and tucked the afghan around him.

Remembering the chauffeur, she went out to the big car and knocked on the window. The man inside, sound asleep himself, jerked his head up and, turning on the ignition, pressed the automatic window control.

"Yes, ma'am?" he said, blinking himself awake as the window slid down.

"Roy, isn't it?" Ariel asked.

"Yes, ma'am."

"Mr. Coulter's fallen asleep on my sofa, and I don't think there's much point in waking him up. I'm not sure we could, to tell you the truth. Why don't you just go on, and I'll have him call you in the morning."

"Well . . ." The long-suffering Roy scratched thinning gray hair and looked at the dashboard as if for guidance.

"It's all right," Ariel reassured him, chafing her arms against the cold. "Would you like some coffee before you go?"

"Can't drink it this late," he smiled, "but thanks. And,

miss? I'm sorry we came over here like this, but he can be real stubborn. I've been with B. F. eighteen years, and I've never known him to be dissuaded when he's made up his mind."

Roy put the car into drive and turned on the headlights, then reached into his pocket and pulled out a calling card. He handed it to Ariel.

"You call me up if you need to for any reason. Otherwise, I'll be over here around nine tomorrow morning if that's all right with you."

thirty-three

While B. F. Coulter found temporary oblivion from his grief, a man several miles away kept vigil.

He sat in darkness. The only sound that disturbed the silence was an intermittent click, the only movement that of restless fingers toying with an old-fashioned pocket watch, the lone legacy of a mother long buried and unlamented. Absently, he snapped the engraved cover open and closed. The name inscribed on the watch wasn't his or that of his mother, who'd stolen it from one of her tricks. It was the only thing of value she hadn't pawned to buy liquor; he'd stolen it from her before she could.

He was only peripherally aware of the object in his hand; his mind was focused on the problem of Ariel Gold.

His fury had long since cooled, and he was himself again: deliberate, careful and calculating. Especially the last. Everything he'd seen and heard pointed to one unbelievable but inescapable conclusion: the woman remembered nothing. The most accomplished actress in the history of theater couldn't have played the scenes of the last few days, couldn't have read the lines that convincingly. She wasn't acting.

Moreover, there was no reason for her to feign ignorance. What could she hope to gain? Why would she put herself at such risk? And why would she hesitate to make her accusations known? They would be sufficient to create a very public scandal at the least, to resurrect questions about long-dead issues at worst. The woman herself was the danger, and everything pointed to the fact that unless she had miraculously forgotten what she knew, he wouldn't be sitting here in peace.

He didn't bother speculating about how this state of affairs had come to be; the point was, it existed. He wasted no further time vilifying Rodriquez for his ineptitude or berating himself for involving Rodriquez. There was only one issue, and that was what to do about the woman. The unavoidable reality was that, whatever she did or didn't remember today, there was always tomorrow. She was a loaded gun.

One thing he had reason to know was that some circumstances are beyond one's control. Even for a person of his intelligence, even with the shrewdest of plans, even with the coolest of execution, the perfect crime didn't exist. But the unsolved crime did.

He had reason to know that, too.

It just took thought. He had to have time to think. Ms. Gold would find out as had others before her that he would not be threatened.

He relaxed his head against the chair, allowing his mind to drift, to savor the first time. Creighton Arnold.

His lips curved as he remembered the cuckold, with his inflated sense of importance, his belief that money and *breeding* made him superior. Oh, Arnold had had his short-lived revenge. It had been because of Arnold that he'd been forced to change his identity. That in itself hadn't been the problem. Experimenting with camouflage was amusing. With the finesse of a chameleon, he could look older, younger, invisible—but more important, he could actually change himself. He could be whoever and whatever suited his best interests, whatever fulfilled the needs he sensed in others. Expediency was everything, and in the aftermath of Arnold he'd simply resorted to the expedient of cosmetic surgery. Oh, he'd done nothing radical. The new chin line was firmer, more suitable really, and he'd erased a year or two around the eyes. He'd regretted shaving his moustache, but that, too, had made him look younger.

No, the physical alterations hadn't been the problem. Because of Arnold, he'd had to do something far harder; he'd had to suffer the galling indignity of starting over, of inventing himself yet again. He'd emerged with a new name, a new career and another asset: he'd looked even better. Better and, he'd thought, unrecognizable. He'd found out different.

He felt cold even now when he remembered that long-ago benefit dinner he'd had the bad luck to attend. Things had just been starting to break for him once more, everything falling into place beautifully. And then the woman who'd invited him as her escort, a woman who'd been quite useful at that time, had taken his arm and said she had someone she wanted him to meet, someone important. He'd turned, smiling, welcoming an opportunity, and found himself looking into Arnold's eyes. He'd seen recognition dawn. He'd seen Arnold's mouth tighten, seen him turn on his heel and walk away, seen his carefully reconstructed life crumble in that one moment.

He'd also seen opportunity.

Arnold's wife had been more than useful.

Through her he'd obtained the perfect weapon, the very one with which Arnold had been foolish enough to threaten him. Through her he'd learned Arnold's plans for what would be the last night of his life.

That night Arnold had learned something, too: that all his money and all his connections did him no good at the end.

That episode had been nothing more or less than self-defense, and the same was true now with the troublesome Ariel Gold.

If the woman hadn't talked to anyone before this extraordinary memory lapse—and he had every reason to believe she hadn't; she'd wanted too badly to get him herself—then he was safe. Because she'd made it her little personal vendetta, there was nothing incriminating to connect them. It was important to maintain that distance. The best plan would be to make her death appear to be random. If that could be managed, fine. If not, he'd make sure that it couldn't be connected to him. He'd find out more about her; he'd give himself just a little time. He wouldn't proceed until he'd thought things through from every angle. The planning, after all, was the best part—the challenge. The killing itself was just a necessary evil.

thirty-four

When chimes echoed through the house at 8:00 A.M., Ariel hurried to the door, trying to stop the noise before it woke the still-snoring Coulter. She found not an overanxious Roy, as she'd expected, but a postman who, on obtaining her signature, presented her with an envelope from Mueller & Lupo, Attorneys-at-Law. With a little thrill of apprehension, Ariel slit the envelope. Inside was a second envelope, pale lilac, on which were written her name and the words PERSONAL AND CONFIDENTIAL, underscored three times.

The lilac paper, weighty and expensive, rang a bell. So did the sprawling handwriting. At last she knew who'd sent the ruined letter she'd found that first day. Taking a deep breath, she opened what was literally a message from beyond the grave.

The letter from the late Muriel Gold was dated August of the previous year, and the greeting was simply "Ariel." There was no embellishment.

"You'll probably be very surprised to receive any communication from me," she read, "particularly under the circumstances. I don't know when you'll be reading this, but I don't think it will be too long from now.

"Knowing that your time is short makes you look at things differently, and I want to get something off my conscience.

"This has to do with the things I said the last time I saw you and what I then wrote to you. Naturally, I was in shock, and with you doing the sort of work you do, you can't blame me for assuming that you were trying to capitalize on the violence. I have no choice but to admit I was wrong.

"If the authorities can be believed, at least some of your ugly allegations seem to have been true. I still don't know how Michael could have become associated with such vile and dangerous people, how he could cause me such humiliation and ruin my life.

"At any rate you've kept your silence, and I have to pre-

238

sume that you haven't pursued your investigation. I don't know, of course, what your reasons were, but your decision was wise. Some things are better—and safer—left alone."

Ariel's first reaction was vindication: she was right, and Henry was dead wrong. She didn't know who Michael was mixed up with but, Mafia or not, they were "dangerous people." Almost before fear dawned, something else did. This letter was written six months ago, and the first one was even older. The time lapse confused her, and she knew what the cynical Henry would make of it. She reread the letter. When she'd finished, what she felt was disgust.

Was this grudging little epistle supposed to be an apology? Ariel fumed. This wasn't expiation; it was indemnification—a self-serving woman hedging her bets as the specter of death loomed.

Ariel stomped, quietly, back to the kitchen, where she'd been making coffee before the doorbell had interrupted. Wanting to wham the grinder onto the counter and bang the kettle back onto the burner, she restrained herself. Jessie, who'd been lying in a peaceful puddle of sun, gave her a wary look and left the room. Finally, deep-breathing, Ariel sat and stared into her coffee cup. She blew out her breath and wiped her mouth and shook her head.

Where was Michael? she wondered. What was this all about and what in the world had the man done?

Hearing sounds from the living room, she threw a raw egg into the blender with tomato juice, pepper, celery salt and a tot of vodka. She whirred the concoction, which she'd made up on the spur of the moment, and poured it into a glass. Eventually, B. F. Coulter, looking like judgment day, wandered in, Jessie trailing.

"Good morning, Mr. Coulter," she said. "Drink this and don't mess with me. I'm mad."

Coulter rubbed his chin and sat down. He smelled the contents of the glass and decided not to ask what was in it. He took a tentative sip, then downed it.

"Stop calling me Mr. Coulter," he said, his voice a rumble. "God knows I'm old as dirt and I feel every minute of it, but you'd do me a favor to call me B. F."

"What does that stand for?"

"Nothin'," he said. "That's my name. It was my father's name, too, matter of fact. I'm B. F. Junior." He frowned at the sunlight streaming into the kitchen and tried to slick a few white hairs back down onto his skull. "You can call me Junior if you want to."

"Well, B. F., I don't think I will call you Junior. Now, how about if I fix you some breakfast? Roy'll be here in about half an hour. You've got time."

While Ariel fried bacon and scrambled eggs, Coulter sat trying to focus. Neither said a further word until she'd put his plate on the table.

"I've got some low-cal apricot jam, but I advise against it," she said. "I think honey's what's called for here."

She didn't wait for agreement. She put toast and the honey jar in front of him, along with coffee. Warming up her own coffee, she asked in a slightly less belligerent voice, "What happens today?" She grimaced. "I mean, there won't be services yet, will there?" Abruptly, she sat down. "I'm sorry," she said. "I'm being a jerk."

"Did you get out of bed that ill or did I miss something?" B. F. inquired with his mouth full.

"It's not worth talking about. Sorry you got the brunt of it."

"Your dog gave me a wake-up call—her nose in my face." He managed a feeble grin. "I think she was lookin' for reinforcements. Did you bless her out, too?"

"Not likely." Ariel gave the shepherd a hard scratch on the rump. "If it weren't for her, I probably wouldn't be here this morning."

At his quizzical look, Ariel gave him a synopsis of the break-in and Jessie's heroic role in it.

His bushy white brows drew together. "Look here, Ariel Gold, are you sure it's safe for you to be stayin' here? I've got a big ol' condo on Wilshire, and there's more than enough room for both of you. Why don't you come on over there 'til the police get this thing solved."

Ariel told him the part she'd omitted, that she'd been forced to shoot the intruder.

"No lie!" B. F. smiled in open admiration. "Good thing you knew how to use a weapon!" Melancholy flickered across his face. "I taught Jane to shoot when she was just a girl, with a revolver and a rifle. She lay waste to quite a few Mason jars—she got mighty good—but I never could get her to hunt."

Impulsively, Ariel covered B. F.'s big, rough hand with her own.

"Listen, B. F., I know you don't know me, and you've got no particular reason to trust me, but if there's anything I can do, if you just want to talk or whatever, I've got plenty of time on my hands right now."

Quick tears brimmed in his eyes and almost as quickly disappeared. "You've done enough," he said; "shoe's on the other foot. I don't expect you make a habit of lettin' strangers bed down on your settee—drunk strangers at that. I'm not goin' to apologize. I'll just tell you I appreciate your not throwin' me out. And lettin' me rave on. You said you're on vacation. Does that mean you're not workin' on the story you people are doin' on Jane?"

Ariel was about to answer in the negative when it occurred to her to question why he'd asked.

"You said you wouldn't repeat anything I said," B. F. answered, "and I'll hold you to that, but I could tell you some people you could talk to officially. If it would benefit you directly, you understand?"

"Well . . . I don't know—"

"Here," he said gruffly, "get a pencil and some paper, and I'll give you some names."

By the time the chauffeur knocked on the door, B. F. had finished his breakfast and all the coffee, and Ariel had the name of the owner of Jane's modeling agency and the first names of four models she'd worked with often as well as the name of her hairdresser, of several friends, and of her gardener and two other members of her staff, including the maid, Nancy.

"Who knows," B. F. said, "maybe you'll come up with something the police miss. I'll be in touch." He rubbed the top of her head, rubbed Jessie's in much the same way and lumbered out to join Roy in the waiting Cadillac.

Ariel watched him cross the yard and then stared at the list in her hand, wondering what to do with it. She looked up Henry's number and dialed it. Win Peacock answered the phone.

"Good morning, Ariel. What an unexpected pleasure," he said when the startled Ariel identified herself. "I was just looking for something on Henry's desk, which, heaven knows, is a challenge. He's not here right now. Will I do?"

Her mind a fuddle of possible replies, she mumbled a "maybe" and considered what to do. She might have something of real value to contribute, and time was certainly a consideration. Win, of course, was part of the show, but still . . .

Stalling, she asked when Henry would be back.

"Somebody said he flew up to Sacramento this morning early," Win informed her, "and I don't know if he'll be back in the office today. Are you sure I can't help you?"

"Well, the thing is, I've gotten access to some names relating to the Macaulay feature, and I was going to see what he wanted me to do with them."

" 'Do with them'? Why, talk to them, what do you think! Oh, you mean because you're on vacation? Well, that doesn't seem to have made much difference so far. What kind of names? Whose names?"

"Friends, staff, her hairdresser . . . like that. Maybe Henry already has some of them?"

"I don't know, but even if he does, duplication's better than not reaching them at all. How'd you get them?"

"Sources," Ariel said, almost giggling at the unlikelihood of what she was saying. "Please leave Henry a note, would you? Say I'll be working on this just until I hear from him."

"Fine. Fine," Win said impatiently, "but in the interim, you call in with anything worthwhile. In fact, I'll give you a call later just to see what's what."

Ariel's Call Waiting beep sounded, and she excused herself, her palms starting to sweat at her audacity.

"Ariel, good morning," Philip Morgan's unmistakable voice said. "I hope I'm not calling too early?"

"Oh, you'd be surprised at the activity that's already gone on around here," Ariel replied. "So, you found the papers? That's great. But do you mind delivering them? You're sure you wouldn't rather just mail them?" She hoped he'd say no. She was tired of all the lollygagging.

He obliged her. "Not on your life! I've got some dog food for you, too, remember? A little too much to drop in the mail. Actually"—he paused—"I was wondering if you might be free this evening? I feel I owe you dinner at the least." There was another brief pause before he continued, sounding uncertain. "The truth is, you'd be doing me a favor. I'm feeling a little blue, and I'm beginning to talk to myself up here. Please?"

"Well, you certainly don't owe me anything, but I'll have dinner with you if you like."

They agreed on a time, agreed that it would be casual and agreed that he'd have no problem finding her house.

"There's just one other thing," Philip added. "Would you mind not mentioning this to anyone? Not to anyone at all? There are people, unfortunately, who would misconstrue."

Again, Ariel agreed. She hung up the phone and stared at it briefly, lost in thought, before going to retrieve the insurance forms from the night before. It was time to find out whether she'd been tested for Huntington's disease.

The doctor named on the forms had retired, Ariel learned, and another doctor had taken over his practice. His nurse couldn't seem to get past the idea that, since Ariel would be a new patient to the new doctor, she'd have to come in for a checkup. Even when she finally managed to grasp the situation, she insisted that Ariel would have to speak to the doctor, and he was at a medical conference in Houston. Besides, the files would be too old to be in the computer. They were warehoused, the woman said, and it would be days before they could be retrieved.

Stymied, Ariel left her number and called 411 for the number of the lab on the other forms. There was no current listing.

She looked up Anita Stroud's number and, after thanking her again for her hospitality, came to the point.

"I know my mother never told you what was wrong with her but, I wonder, did she ever happen to mention the name of her doctor?"

Anita was unable to help. She was also curious as to why Ariel was asking the question.

Muttering a nonanswer, Ariel changed the subject, and they chatted briefly about inconsequential things. When she hung up, Ariel growled in frustration and snatched up the list B. F. had dictated. Her debut as a newshound could be put off no longer.

thirty-five

The first call, to the owner of Jane's modeling agency, was the most difficult.

Ariel had written down how she would introduce herself as well as a list of questions just in case she got a chance to ask them, but she couldn't overcome the feeling that she was flying under false colors and she couldn't altogether quell the tremor in her voice when she asked for Eleanor Ashby.

"Please tell her," Ariel said to the receptionist, "that B. F. Coulter suggested I call."

The name had power.

Ms. Ashby was on the line in a twinkling, asking in a gracious and heavily accented voice how she could help.

"And how's Mr. Coulter doin'? How's that pore ol' thang holdin' up with all this tragic business?"

Texas, thought Ariel, unless I miss my guess.

"Just about as you'd expect," she said. "Ms. Ashby, we'd like to do what we can to find out why Jane Macaulay was killed, and I wonder if you could spare a few minutes to talk with me about her. As soon as you could work me in."

"Be glad to, sure. But I can tell you right now it had to be some kind of mistake. There wasn't the first reason in the world for anybody to kill that girl. Now, you not talkin' about comin' down here with cameras and all, are you? You talkin' about just you and me or what?"

"Right now, I'm talking about just you and me." Ariel was pretty sure that was how it was supposed to work. "I'm looking for some background: what Jane Macaulay was like, what her life was like—that sort of thing. Is that all right with you?"

"I can see you at . . ." Ariel heard the faint murmur of Ashby conferring with her secretary—"They're only in town for the day" followed by "He can wait" and "Set him up for one of those times tomorrow"—and then the voice was briskly back.

"I can see you at three o'clock this afternoon for half an hour; will that work with your schedule?"

"Excellent," Ariel said, then asked if someone could provide last names for the models B. F. had given her. Ashby supplied three, all of whom she represented, as well as the fourth, listed with a competitor but well known. Ariel was then transferred to a hireling who added phone numbers and the information that one of Ashby's models was out of the country, but the other two, she said—Pepper Sills and Marianne Milke—were in town.

The former agreed to see Ariel at one o'clock at her gym. The latter was booked for the afternoon and all the next day. "But now's good," Marianne Milke volunteered, sounding breathless and a little ditzy.

With all the bravado she could summon, Ariel said, "Great! Now, I'm going to put you on speakerphone so I can tape this, okay?" Eyeing the tape recorder nervously, she scanned the questions she'd prepared for Eleanor Ashby and ticked off those that were appropriate to ask the model.

"Let's start with how long you'd known Jane Macaulay," Ariel suggested, settling on the simplest beginning.

"Oh, gosh. I guess about a year. No, longer. Maybe two. I met her right after I came out to L.A. It was on one of my first jobs, and was I nervous! Jane was so nice. I remember she said that with my eyes and skin, I'd do just fine, She even told the makeup guy—nicely, I mean; she wasn't rude or anything—that he ought to soften up my lip line . . ."

Ariel soon realized that getting the model to stop talking would be the challenge.

Twenty-five minutes later she turned off the recorder, feeling as if she'd been slogging through cotton candy. She'd heard more about hair and makeup than about Jane, and she knew she had a lot to learn about steering an interview. The only thing of interest she'd heard was that there were some "sour-grapey" models who'd been jealous of Jane, who'd felt that with all her money, she ought to move over and let other girls have a shot. Marianne didn't agree, of course, but she did allow as how "Jane was kind of old, and maybe she'd have retired pretty soon, anyway."

Ariel left a message for the hairdresser, who was "doing a color" and located a number for the last model, the one who wasn't with Ashby. Her cleaning lady told her in broken English that "Miz Coe at yob. You call back." The gardener she found only after speaking with several other people named Hashimoto, and he hung up on her after protesting in great agitation that he knew nothing. Neither of the other domestic staff members was at home. Ariel assumed they were at Macaulay's and, since she certainly wasn't going to call them there, decided she'd try them again in the evening.

She was about to dial the first of Jane's friends when the doorbell chimed. A florist van was parked in her driveway, she saw through the window, and a deliveryman holding a white box and a vase of colossal sunflowers stood at her door.

Ariel took the box and asked him to set the vase on a table. She was about to fetch a tip when, smiling as if at a great joke, the man said, "Don't go 'way!" He trotted back to the truck and emerged with a shallow brass container of jonquils, a bowl of narcissuses and a crystal vase of freesias. On his third trip he carried a brightly flowering azalea bush and a gigantic basket full of yellow tulips.

Transfixed, Ariel watched his progress. When he'd gone—after refusing a tip, explaining that it had been taken care of—she gazed around her living room. It looked like a greenhouse. She opened the box she was still holding. The small Quimper pitcher inside held a bunch of pansies but no card—that she finally found in the tulip basket.

"All these mournful white wreaths at Macaulay's are getting me down," it said. "These looked a whole lot more cheerful."

It was signed "B. F."

She arranged the floral bounty, touching the petals and

breathing in the pungent aroma of the freesias. The pansies she put on her kitchen table to bolster herself while she made the remainder of the calls.

They proved productive.

The first friend—a yoga teacher, according to B. F.—was named Laya, and she was amenable to meeting with Ariel at four-thirty at her home. The second, Mindy Gorham, was disinclined to talk but agreed to think about it. Then the hairdresser returned her call. Raoul (who sounded suspiciously like Inspector Clouseau) was not disinclined to talk. His salon, the very same one recommended by the pretty blond in the library, was near the Ashby agency in Beverly Hills, so Ariel arranged to meet him there at two. The last person on the list, another friend, was out of town but, according to a roommate, would return the following night.

With time to kill, Ariel watched the *Open File* she'd taped the night before. She was immensely relieved to see that, as advertised, it did manage to entertain without sensationalizing. Even after jotting a few comments and questions for Henry, she still had time for a walk with Jessie before dressing, which she did with special care. She packed a notepad and the tape recorder in her bag and, giving herself a thumbs-up for courage, set out.

Pepper Sills's gym was on Sepulveda, only five minutes away, and Ariel was early; the very tall, very sweaty Pepper was only halfway through her session on the StairMaster. While Ariel waited at the juice bar, questions about how (and whether) she should be proceeding with the upcoming interviews tumbled around her mind like clothes in a dryer.

The towel-draped model who soon joined her did nothing to quell her doubts. Pepper was surprisingly plain, nothing like the glamorous cover girl Ariel had expected, and her demeanor was equally plain. Blunt to the point of curtness, she made it clear right up front, and not quietly, that she had no intention of "dishing" Jane.

"She was straight-up, and she was a friend of mine," the redhead declared, "so don't waste your time with me if you're looking for some seamy secret life or anything like that because, as far as I know, it didn't exist."

With that, she drank half a bottle of mineral water,

plunked the bottle on the table and began patting her neck and breastbone with the towel.

Aware that several curious faces had turned their way, Ariel glanced around uncomfortably, trying to figure out how to defuse the situation. Her gaze fell on a line of framed and autographed photos above the counter, all studio shots of gorgeous men and women. She looked more closely at the third one from the end, then back at her companion, her expression a question mark.

"Yeah, it's me. Amazing, isn't it, what a little makeup can do? The one on the end's Jane." Pepper twisted around to look at the photos, and her back was to Ariel when she said, "Sorry to come down on you. I just—I don't think anybody getting killed that way could've shocked me more than Jane." She turned back, composed and purposeful. "Listen, the reason I agreed to talk to you is to make sure you know her death was some kind of hideous, stupid mistake. It had to be."

"You could be right." Ariel spoke quietly but rapidly. "Her husband certainly agrees with you. But if it wasn't a mistake, we want to find that out. And even if it was, we want to do whatever we can to make sure the killer's found. So help me here, okay? When was the last time you saw Jane?"

"Two days before she was leaving for Florida. We did a fragrance shoot together. She was joking about coming back with tan lines. That," she explained, "is a no-no for a model. Jane was always joking. She was very professional, very efficient, but she thought the whole business was a crock. Jane was smart. A lot smarter than the average model, including me."

"Did she ever say anything to you about any threat? Any unexplained phone calls? Any admirers she may have found strange?"

"Never."

"What about disappointed suitors? Jealous boyfriends?"

"I didn't know Jane before she was married but, no, she never mentioned anybody like that, and if she did any fooling around I'd be surprised. Jane was pretty old-fashioned. She was even modest, which is practically unheard of in this industry, especially after years of dressing and undressing a dozen times a day with makeup and hair people running in and out and stylists making rather, shall we say, intimate adjustments on your person." Pepper made a face. "Maybe it was her Southern upbringing."

"Did she ever say anything about her husband? His business? Could someone have it in for him, punishing him through her?"

"Look—what was your name? Ariel?—Jane and I weren't close personal friends. We didn't spend time together outside of work or anything, so it's not likely that she'd have told me or any other model I know of about anything like that. When she wasn't in front of the camera, she was usually reading or working one of those crossword puzzle things."

Ariel asked the few other questions she could think of and gave the now considerably more civil model a card with her home number written on the back. She hurried through the gym looking neither right nor left, feeling overweight and guilty.

By the time she'd found a parking space three blocks away from the beauty salon and walked back, Ariel was a few minutes late for her second appointment. Breathlessly, she asked for Raoul.

A very short, thin, outrageously dressed man was pointed out, and she watched as with a great flourish he whipped a plastic cape from the shoulders of his customer. The pixie pressed his cheek to the woman's, looked into her eyes in the mirror, lightly caressed the coiffure he'd just created and whispered something. Whether it was styling advice or gossip Ariel couldn't tell, but the customer was nodding vigorously and smiling. Raoul gave meaty shoulders a final squeeze and, slipping a folded bill into his pocket, nudged the woman toward the cashier. With a sigh, he turned to Ariel and extended a hand almost too fragile to shake.

"I shall take a break now," he announced in an imperious tenor. "We will go next door to the café for a café au lait."

Once they were seated under a striped umbrella on the patio next door, Raoul's entire posture and demeanor abruptly changed. He ordered plain black coffee in a perfectly normal, unaccented voice, propped one leg atop the knee of the other and lighted a scarred briar pipe, asking Ariel after the fact if she minded. She managed a deadpan no. Feeling as if she'd just watched something akin to a frog becoming a prince (a queen becoming a prince?), Ariel became very busy with her equipment. She was halfway through a question when he blew out a cloud of aromatic smoke and began to talk.

She learned that Raoul, whose name was actually Ralph, had had a crush on Jane for years. He'd worshipped the ground she trod, he cheerfully admitted, but he'd known that he didn't stand a chance with her and that they'd look ridiculous together anyway.

"She was your height," he chuckled. "I barely reached her shoulder. Can't you just see her bending down to kiss me good night?" But Ralph seemed at ease with his height and, for that matter, with himself.

"Jane was a good Joe," he said, "unaffected and friendly as she could be. She almost never talked about herself, though; she always asked about me. What I was doing. What I wanted to do. Why"—he grinned slyly—"I acted like a pouf. When I told her I was dating Margaret, my fiancée, she wanted to know all about her. Wanted to meet her. We never got around to that." His grin faded.

"So I can't tell you much if anything about Jane, you understand, since she didn't run on about herself like most of my customers, and if she'd told me anything personal, I wouldn't repeat it. But I do have something I want to tell you. About her husband.

"I was invited to a party at their house last summer, much to Macaulay's disgust, I think. He acted as if he couldn't remember who I was from one minute to the next and couldn't understand what I was doing there in the first place. Maybe the man's a real charmer—there had to be something there or Jane wouldn't have married him, I guess—but he sure never showed me any of it. Anyway, to make a long story short, I spotted him in a car, a red Porsche, about a month ago. He was sitting at a stoplight, and the woman in the car with him wasn't Jane."

Jolted, Ariel set her coffee cup down. "But that doesn't

necessarily mean anything," she said. "The woman could've been his sister. A client. Anybody. We can't jump to conclusions."

Ralph pointed the stem of his pipe at Ariel. "Well, if she was his sister, somebody better explain to him about incest. They were in a clutch like something out of a porno flick. The guy behind Macaulay had to blow his horn twice when the light turned green."

Ariel opened her mouth and closed it again. She cleared her throat. "You're sure it was Macaulay?"

"I was waiting on the corner for Margaret. The guy wasn't four feet away from me, and the top was down on the car."

"Forgive me, but I have to ask: you're sure the woman wasn't Jane?"

"She was small, she looked to be in her early to midtwenties and she had very black hair. A pretty good cut, too.

"Look, I've got to get back to work, but I wanted somebody to know about what I saw. Macaulay may be nothing worse than a philanderer, but if he had anything at all to do with Jane's death, I don't want him to get away with it."

Ariel gave him her card, again with her home phone number, and walked him back to the salon.

"Why *do* you act like a pouf?" she couldn't resist asking.

"Well, it started out as a bet." Ralph glanced through the plate glass window of the salon, saw that his next customer was being shampooed and turned back to Ariel. "I was working in this kind of second-rate shop right out of school, and I wanted to move up. I'd tried three posh salons as myself and couldn't get arrested, you know? Friend of mine put up fifty dollars. He bet if I flounced around a little, I'd be hired, and he was right—on the very next interview."

He plunged his hands in his pockets and said ironically, "Reverse discrimination, what can I tell you? Hey, you need a haircut, bad. Call me sometime; I'll give you a free one."

Ariel learned nothing new from the formidably well-groomed, midsixtyish, steel magnolia Eleanor Ashby except that she wanted to be the next Mrs. B. F. Coulter. She didn't come right out and say so, but Ariel got the drift.

"B. F.'s a charmin' man, isn't he? Always was. He and

my late husband used to go off on these weeklong fishin' trips," she told Ariel. "Least, that's where they said they were goin'. Some of the fish they brought back with 'em weren't native to these waters, I don't think."

Her accent grew less pronounced and her pace brisker as the interview wore on. Ms. Ashby's husband, Ariel came to learn, had been a sometime business associate of Coulter going back for a number of years and, following John Ashby's death, the widow and widower had occasionally socialized. It had been Eleanor who, when she decided to start up a model agency, encouraged Jane to go into the business.

"She had an unusual look, an insouciance, that the camera loved," Eleanor reminisced. "That mouth, the cleft in her chin, even the nose. She didn't have the height to be a supermodel, or the drive, for that matter. The modeling thing just came her way, and she went with it. But, privately"—Eleanor raised frank eyebrows—"she called it a stupid way to make a living. Said if she let herself dwell on it, she felt like so much meat on the hoof."

The woman shook her silver, perfectly coiffed head in fond recollection. "I had to ride her like the dickens to keep her portfolio updated and to get a new head-sheet every once in a while. She hated casting calls like poison, and she was known to turn down a booking if she had something she'd rather do or if she didn't like the looks of it. But," Eleanor emphasized, "if Jane did take an assignment, she left smilin' faces behind her. The girl was mighty good and mighty easy to work with."

Ariel left the agency feeling she'd learned little, wondering what other, more cogent questions she should've asked. She consoled herself with the thought that, if the story aired, she'd laid the groundwork for a good side interview by someone else.

Laya-no-last-name, the yoga teacher, lived in an apartment complex in West Hollywood. Pressing the button beside the unit number she'd been given, Ariel envisioned an exotic Eastern lair scattered with floor pillows and pungent with incense. As she was buzzed in, she pictured an ebony-eyed Laya draped in a sari, a gem twinkling from her pierced nostril, a dot of red on her forehead.

The tall black woman who opened the apartment door wore gym shorts and a T-shirt, and the apartment behind her could have been transplanted from the Bronx or Hannibal, Missouri, so lacking was it in distinction. Laya looked like a feminine version of Sidney Poitier and, while her voice held traces of an exotic accent, it was West Indian rather than East. The look she gave Ariel was long and appraising.

"Have a seat," she said, "and don't mind Arthur." The marmalade cat she indicated blinked lethargically. "He's too fat to do anything more dangerous than shed on you. I've got a class in a little over an hour, so why don't you tell me exactly what you want from me."

Ariel turned on the recorder and began asking the now-familiar questions. Laya wasn't particularly reticent, but neither was she chatty. Noncommittal was what she was, and Ariel began to get the definite feeling that she herself was being sized up, that the woman was taking her time deciding what she would or wouldn't say. When nearly half the allotted hour was up and Ariel was reaching the end of her resourcefulness, Laya interrupted mid-question.

"You mentioned Jane's grandfather. Did he really suggest that you talk to me?"

"He gave me your name," Ariel said. "I wouldn't have known you existed if he hadn't."

"Why?"

"Why did he give me your name? I should think that's obvious. B. F. Coulter, probably more than anyone else, wants to know why his granddaughter died."

The handsome black woman made a dismissive gesture.

"I can tell you that right now. Jane died because someone evil was also tragically careless."

"How can you be so sure she was the wrong victim?"

"For one thing, Jane didn't live the kind of life, didn't know the kind of people, to put her in that sort of jeopardy. For another, if she'd been frightened or in trouble, I'd have known."

"She'd have told you?"

"She wouldn't have had to."

Unsure what that was supposed to mean, Ariel merely said, "Ah."

Laya said nothing.

"When was the last time you saw Jane?" Ariel asked.

"When did I last see her or when did I last talk to her?"

"There's a difference, I take it?"

"Oh, yes."

"Let's start with the last time you saw her."

"In class, two days before she left town."

"And when did you last talk with her?"

"The night before she died."

Ariel's heart stuttered. "She called you?"

"Yes."

"From where?"

"From a hotel in Phoenix."

"Will you tell me what she said?" Ariel felt as if she were trying to pull teeth from a bulldog with his mouth clenched shut.

"Why should I?"

Deliberately, Ariel said, "I can't think of a single reason. Except that it might shed some light on what she was thinking, what was going on in her life, why she and her husband don't seem to have spoken to one another in nearly two weeks, and why she drove clear across the country and then went to a restaurant rather than going to her own home. Was she meeting someone there? Someone who may have seen something? Heard something? Who may know something we don't? Who may have even been the intended victim?"

Ariel took a breath. "Maybe you're absolutely right and Jane's death was a mistake. Maybe where she's concerned, 'There is no truth to be discovered; there is only error to be exposed.'"

The dark eyes widened. "Did you know Jane? Were you ever around her?"

"No. Why do you ask?"

Laya blinked and seemed to collect herself. "It's not important. Who were you quoting just then?"

"Um, Mencken, I think. Why?"

Unexpectedly, Laya smiled. "I wonder if you're this intense about all your stories. Or if this one could be special for some reason."

"If I say it is, will you talk to me?" Ariel returned the smile. "I'm being flippant; forgive me. You're quite right— it is special, for several reasons. One of them, which you might find hard to credit, is personal, but I hope you'll believe that I like Mr. Coulter a great deal. I'd like to see him find some kind of peace with this thing."

"What I'm going to tell you wouldn't give him peace. Quite the contrary. And I'm going to leave it up to you whether to make it part of your program. I hope you won't."

Ariel said nothing.

"Despite the fact that Macaulay is a very careful man, very . . ." —Laya looked away, searching for the word she wanted— ". . . circumspect, Jane had been suspicious for a month or more that he was having an affair. She didn't have proof, and she didn't confront him. I think she was a little afraid of him, frankly. I don't know that he was ever physically abusive, but he was autocratic and he could be mean. Too, Jane felt her commitments very deeply, and she was committed to that marriage. She hoped that if she was patient, if she kept her own counsel, that the affair—if there was one—would die a natural death. And she believed that if they had children, Robert would return to the fold of his own accord."

Laya watched Ariel closely as she said, "Jane had been trying to get pregnant for a long time. She found out just before she left Florida that she was."

"Oh, my God," Ariel whispered.

"She bought one of those kits. It was positive."

"But why didn't she say anything? To her grandfather? Or her husband? Why didn't she call her husband and tell him? Or did she?"

"She wanted to tell Macaulay the good news in person, to see his reaction. Also, she said she wanted verification from a doctor before she told anyone, even her grandfather. I don't think she could quite believe it herself."

"Then why'd she tell you?" Ariel asked bluntly.

"She was too excited to hold it in any longer; she had to tell somebody. And, besides"—Laya smiled a knowing smile—"I didn't need a kit, and I didn't need Jane, to tell me. *I* told *her*. That last day in class. Oh, she didn't believe me—said it was just another of my 'otherworld epiphanies,' as she called them. She said her period was due and that it would be right along as usual, unfortunately. Jane wasn't much for metaphysics. When I told her things I had no way of knowing, it spooked her."

Laya gave Ariel a level look. "So what are you going to do with this information?"

"I don't know," Ariel admitted, and she didn't. But the thought of B. F. Coulter's face if he knew gave her a pretty good idea. "Let me ask you another question: Why'd she go to Anthony's Restaurant that night? Do you know?"

"I know one thing, and this isn't from any sixth sense. Plain old common sense tells me that Jane drove straight home first. She couldn't wait to give her husband the big surprise. Several things could've happened then. The three most likely are that, one, he wasn't at home or, two, he was but for some unknown reason asked her to go ahead to the restaurant, planning to meet her there later or, three, what I think actually did happen: he wasn't expecting Jane, and I think she was the one who was surprised. Unpleasantly."

"Oh. Dear." Ariel felt her heart twist with pain for this woman she hadn't even known. "But why the restaurant?"

Laya consulted a small clock on the table between them and began speaking more rapidly.

"They used to go there when they were dating and early in the marriage, before things started going sour. It's where Macaulay proposed. Jane told me on the phone that she'd spent some of the happiest evenings of her life at Anthony's and that she planned to tell him about the baby there. She wanted things to be the way they used to be, to stir the embers of romance and all that." Laya ran a palm over her closely cropped hair. "If what I think happened did happen, I can only guess about why she went on her own."

"So guess," Ariel said.

"Suspecting that your husband may be fooling around and seeing him with another woman are two different things. Jane would've been horribly hurt, of course, but she'd also have been angry. She'd have seen Macaulay, at last, for what he was. Knowing the way she thought, I believe she went to Anthony's to complete the circle. To have a last, ceremonial drink and say good-bye to her marriage."

Sad silence blanketed both women for a moment, and then Laya stood. "I've got to go. Sorry. Come on, and I'll walk you out."

In the elevator, Ariel said, "You realize that at least one of your scenarios for Sunday night allows for the possibility that Macaulay knew Jane's whereabouts, and two out of three for his knowing what kind of car she was driving."

Laya gave her a dry look. "He just happened to have a bomber on call?"

"Well ... but you did say she was afraid of him."

"I'm just a yogi; you're the researcher."

They shook hands, and Laya was walking away when Ariel called to her.

"Why'd you decide to tell me what you did?"

"I want the murderer caught, too. You'll see that I'm right—Robert Macaulay didn't kill his wife. But I believe you'll find out who did."

Ariel was astonished. "Why do you say that?"

"I don't know what you think your reasons are for considering this case special, but I think you'll find there're other, much more telling reasons." The yoga teacher flashed a quick Cheshire cat grin, hoisted her gym bag and disappeared into the building's underground parking garage.

thirty-six

Good grief! What are you doing here?"

Ariel invited Win Peacock into her living room and commanded Jessie to cool it. "I'm sorry. I'm not usually quite that rude, but I just didn't expect you. Obviously."

Win whistled at the floral display. "Some admirer you must have. Or admirers."

"It is a bit lavish, isn't it." Ariel looked around with some embarrassment. And a twinge of something else, something she recognized as self-satisfaction. She was glad for what the flowers implied, and she was also glad she'd had time to change and freshen up before this surprise visit.

He turned the full power of his smile on her, his incredibly white teeth—a testimony to genetics or bonding—flashing. "Is it your birthday? Or is there something I should be congratulating you for?"

"No. Nothing like that. Would you like to sit down?"

He did so, tweaking his pants leg up half an inch as he crossed his legs.

"I wouldn't have dropped in without calling, but the fact is I've been trying to call all afternoon. Your line was busy every time. And since I don't live that far away, I just made a slight detour. The way you've been burning up the wires, I thought you might have something on the Macaulay segment."

Ariel didn't tell him that she hadn't hung up her telephone properly when she'd made the last call of the morning and only discovered it a few minutes ago.

"I just got off the line," she fudged. "I was talking to the Macaulay maid."

"So, what've you found out? Anything new?"

"Not from her. She's quite ... circumspect about her employer," Ariel said, borrowing the word Laya had used for the womanizing Robert Macaulay. "The only thing I got out of her was that she was given Sunday night off, and it wasn't one of her usual free nights."

"What about the other people you talked to?"

The phone rang, saving Ariel from answering the question.

"Why in blazes don't you get Call Waiting? I've been trying to reach you for an hour."

"Hi, Henry. I was just talking to Win Peacock, who happened to drop by," Ariel said sweetly, smiling at Win.

There was a moment of dead air.

"What's he doing there?"

"We were just talking about the interviews I've been doing on the Macaulay story. Didn't you get the message?"

"Ariel, what're you up to? Where'd you get these names Peacock left me a note about? Who, would you kindly tell me, is this 'source'?"

"We can go into all that later, okay? I don't have a lot of time here. I'm going out tonight." She made a moue of apology to Win. "Do you want me to tell you—both of you, of course—what I found out? Or do you want to speak to Win? Or what?"

Henry said nothing for fifteen seconds. Ariel could hear the man fuming, the wheels cranking, the curiosity winning.

"Go ahead," he said.

She handed Win the portable phone. "I'll pick up in the kitchen," she told him over her shoulder.

When the three of them were on the line together, Ariel said, "I want to make sure of one thing: you tell me that you won't do anything with what I'm going to say unless you discuss it with me first. I want a guarantee on that."

"Naturally," Win said as Henry barked, "Get to it."

"I think I know why Jane didn't go sailing with her grandfather and drove back here instead. And why she went to the restaurant. And why Macaulay tensed up when you asked about that, Henry."

In the next seconds Ariel discovered the meaning of the phrase "The silence was palpable."

"You mean you didn't find out who killed her?" Henry finally growled.

"Not yet, but I've been told I will." Ariel would have enjoyed the moment a great deal more if the phantom of B. F. hadn't been lurking at the back of her mind.

"Well, what're you waiting for? A formal invitation?" Henry asked as Win said, "Ariel? Do you want to tell us?"

Grimly, she told them what she'd learned.

"Jane Macaulay had just found out she was going to have a baby. She was rushing back to tell her husband. She was hoping the news would cement what was, apparently, a less than blissful marriage. She almost certainly drove straight home when she got back in town, and she may have found Macaulay in flagrante delicto. That last bit's speculation, but she did suspect him of being involved with somebody and he had been seen, by a third party, with a woman in a compromising situation."

Both men began talking at once. Ariel said, "Wait a minute! I already asked myself these questions. Yes, he may have known she was back in town and, yes, he may have known what kind of car she was driving—which was what, by the way?—but where would he have found a handy hit man on such short notice? And what was his motive? You don't kill your wife just because she discovers you may be— that's *may* be—unfaithful. It's not as if he were poor and she had all the money. He must have as much as she'll have—would've had—someday."

Whatever Henry started to say was interrupted by someone in his office. Ariel heard two or three disgusted grunts, and then Henry was back. "We can talk about this later," he said to Ariel. "I'll call you. Oh, you said you were going out." There followed the sound of a chair creaking. "It might be a good idea for you to check in with me when you get home," he said, his tone laden with meaning. "Now, let me talk to Win for a minute about Sacramento."

"Yessir, boss." Ariel hung up without saying good-bye.

"I'll take off," Win told her when she returned to the living room, "since you've got plans. With the sender of all the vegetation, I presume?"

"Actually, no. Sorry to rush you, but I do have one or two things to do before my, you know, company's due."

Win was driving away when he noticed a car slowly pulling to the curb in front of Ariel's house. Curious, he looked in his side mirror, but he was too far away to see the occupant.

Philip Morgan, too, was duly impressed by Ariel's bower, and he seemed no less impressed by her home and her appearance. He was so thoroughly charming, in fact, that Ariel could barely recall the tense, unfriendly man she'd first encountered.

"The dog's papers," he said, presenting them with a bow and a stiff click of the heels. "And I have enough food in the trunk to feed the beast for a month."

Unmindful of his immaculate trousers and blazer, he hauled in an unopened, twenty-pound bag of kibble and went back for a case of canned food from which only a can or two were missing. Ariel noticed he'd gotten a smudge on his jacket, but he brushed at it with complete unconcern.

She smiled to herself, imagining the spiffy "Winsome" Peacock in the same situation.

"I thought that if it's all right with you," Philip suggested, "We'd try a little Polish restaurant I've heard about. It's off the beaten track and, although I've never been there myself, I hear the food's excellent and the prices reasonable."

When Ariel readily agreed, she got her first surprise of the evening. The car to which he led her was new—that wasn't surprising—but it was far more modest than she would have expected so wealthy a man to be driving.

"I'm not sure where . . ." Philip rooted between the seats for the other half of her seat belt and found it with an "aha" and an explanation.

"I've had this car less than a week," he said, "and I'm still locating things."

As he drove to the restaurant, he went on to say that one of the first things he'd done after his wife's death was to sell both her car and one she'd bought for him.

"Outrageously pretentious, both of them," he grimaced, "and invitations to thieves. Being a native New Yorker— and I still spend a good deal of time there—I'm not into this West Coast 'You are what you drive' mentality, you know?"

The restaurant, too, was unprepossessing. It was divided into separate rooms of different sizes Ariel suspected had once been the living room, dining room and so forth of a private residence. This one, she speculated, looking around the small room in which they'd been seated, had probably been a guest bedroom. There were only two tables, and the other one was unoccupied.

The food, however, was delicious, and Philip's conversational skills were just as impressive. He talked very little about his own life ("too disheartening right now," he said), but he seemed genuinely interested in everything Ariel had to say about herself. His interest was beguiling. While she was hard put to dredge up enough facts about herself to answer his questions at any length, the occasional lulls in their conversation weren't uncomfortable.

Cozy with the candlelight and the muted Chopin wafting from an overhead speaker, Ariel told him a little about her job and the interviews she'd conducted that day. She was careful to reveal nothing inappropriate, chatting instead about the challenges of technique in general. Philip asked intelligent questions and listened attentively to the answers. His deportment, Ariel thought, was exactly right for a recently widowed man. He was courteous, even gallant, but she felt no pressure. The only time he'd touched her was to help her from the car, and the questions he asked about her personal life would have rated the strictest duenna's approval. If he had a shortcoming, it was that he didn't always get her attempts at humor. Maybe, Ariel thought, I need some new material.

Philip was refilling her wineglass over her protestations—she noticed that he hadn't touched his own—when he suddenly stopped, the bottle poised, his expression rapt. He was listening, Ariel realized, to the music.

"Fiona used to play that on the piano," he said. "It was one of her favorites."

"It's beautiful. One of the nocturnes, isn't it?"

Philip resumed pouring and changed the subject, but the brief moment lingered in Ariel's mind. He'd looked so vulnerable, so bleak.

When he said good night—doing nothing more intimate than clasping her hand, his decorum impeccable to the end—she remembered that moment when his composure had slipped. Impulsively, she kissed his cheek.

"This has been lovely," she told him sincerely, "and I'm glad you couldn't find the papers on Sunday. You're all forgiven now, so if you get lonely again, you call me. Next time it's my treat."

"Then there'll be a next time," Philip said. "I'm glad." He gave her a long, measuring look, squeezed her hand again and was gone.

Ariel had already reset her burglar alarm when she remembered something.

"Drat," she said to Jessie. "It's garbage night, if I recall correctly. Old . . ." She realized she didn't know the gardener's name. "Old whoosis will have a fit if I forget again."

As she dragged the barrels one by one to the curb, it came to Ariel that it was now more than a week since she'd found herself in this unknown existence. The day she'd encountered the gardener and earlier, when she'd explored the house and met up with Jessie and then Marguerite and Henry, all seemed like a very short time ago, in a way. Her life as she now knew it was embryonic, after all. But those experiences also seemed distant. A lot had transpired in a short space of time.

She stood at the curb and looked back at her house and then around the neighborhood. Smelling the ripe aroma of the garbage cans, she smiled.

The threat she'd been living with seemed remote at the moment. Dropping her guard wasn't necessarily reasonable, she realized; there were still far too many unanswered questions. But the fact was, she felt at home.

Ariel stopped woolgathering and noticed to her disgust that Jessie was following a snail's progress across the sidewalk. The shepherd's inquisitive nose was an inch away from the slimy thing.

"Off," she ordered. "Stop acting like a dog."

She went back inside and, as ordered, called Henry.

thirty-seven

After unruffling Henry's feathers about interviewing without a license, so to speak, Ariel filled him in further on the information she'd gathered. He finally gave a grudging seal of approval on how she'd handled herself and by the next morning was moving full steam ahead on the story. He'd work it personally, he told her, to avoid the obvious difficulties of involving staff until Ariel had gained experience. While he dealt with the "experts"—the police, the coroner and any insurance ramifications, plus Robert Macaulay and his associates—he wanted her to continue pursuing the people she hadn't yet reached and to try poking around at the restaurant where Jane had been killed.

"I never turned in the vacation form to Personnel," Henry admitted, "so you've been on the payroll all along."

The next busy days flew, reminding Ariel of the old movie

gimmick of pages ripping from a calendar and swirling across the screen. By the following Monday she'd talked to all the restaurant employees as well as the few customers she could locate. She learned nothing of consequence, however, until she ran down Martin Sprague, a sometime bartender who'd been working relief the night of the bombing and who'd been on a fishing trip ever since.

The droopy-eyed, mustachioed bartender looked as if he'd heard one too many hard-luck stories—or maybe he was just wishing he were back in a boat with a pole in his hand. At any rate, he looked doleful. He didn't look as if he wanted to be on the balcony of his Venice pier apartment talking about Jane Macaulay's death.

Ariel turned her back on the motley parade of humanity strolling the boardwalk below them and watched Sprague checking the contents of his tackle box as he told her for the third time that he really didn't think he could contribute anything useful.

"I can't tell you anything more than what I told the cops," Sprague insisted as he fiddled with a garish lure. "I wish I could. I really liked Mrs. Macaulay."

"You sound as if you knew her," Ariel said.

"Oh, yeah. I used to work the dinner shift at Anthony's full-time back a few years ago. She and her husband came in pretty often then. She always had a margarita. Cointreau instead of triple sec."

"The night she was killed, how'd she seem to you?"

"Well, it's like I told the police . . ." Sprague paused as his busy hands made a deft, conclusive-looking motion. He put the lure into the tackle box at his feet, pulled out another and continued. "She was quiet. Not friendly and sociable like she always used to be. She just sat at the bar, looking around like she was trying to memorize the place and nursing her margarita. A virgin margarita, I remember."

"Then she didn't seem anxious? Or afraid?"

Sprague's lower lip protruded in a "nah" expression, and he shook his head in the negative.

"Sad. She looked sad. She asked me if I was married. When I told her I had been once, that my wife had flown the coop with a guy that worked for the water and power, she just nodded and sort of laughed. I don't mean like she thought it was funny, more like 'What can you do?' You know?"

"Did you notice whether anyone else in the restaurant that night spoke to Mrs. Macaulay? Or even approached her?"

"Just the maître d'. She told him she wouldn't be eating."

"Did you see anyone behaving suspiciously? Watching her, maybe? Or anyone who just looked unusual?"

"Ms. Gold, I tend bar in southern California. I'd more likely remember anybody that looked regular."

Ariel conceded the point. "Did she say anything else?"

He squinted, looking even more miserable. "Yeah. When she got up to leave, she said, 'Good-bye, Martin.' "

The bartender's hands became still. "I didn't think anything about it right then, but later—you know how you do, after the fact?—it seemed like she'd said it real final. I don't mean like she knew she was about to die or anything like that. I just mean like she wouldn't be coming in again."

"Do you remember anything else that Mrs. Macaulay said or did that night? Anything at all?"

"Matter of fact, yeah. I didn't mention it to the cops because I didn't remember it until one afternoon when I was fishing, and it just popped into my head. While she was sitting there at the bar, she took off her wedding ring and dropped it in her purse." Sprague watched a skateboarding giantess in short shorts and halter wheel away beneath the balcony before he continued. "She didn't make any big deal of it or say anything. It was like . . ." He shrugged. "Like she just didn't care for it anymore."

Later, Henry and Ariel chewed over the bartender's recollections. Certainly, they seemed to confirm Laya's theory that Jane was through with her marriage, that something, possibly just the scene the yoga teacher had imagined, had brought her to that decision. But even if Jane had discovered Macaulay in a compromising position, even if the marriage was on the rocks, all they had was speculation. There was no evidence that the marital situation had any bearing on the killing, and when Henry called Macaulay's office to try to set up another interview, he got nowhere.

Ariel went into the studio several times during the week to observe the progress being made on the story. Mute, smiling vaguely and keeping in the background, she watched the editing of Henry's early interview with Macaulay and those later taped by Win with Sprague, Ashby, Laura Jennings (the model who'd been out of the country), Laya and Jane's reticent friend Mindy Gorham.

If her coworkers wondered why she was hanging around during her vacation, they kept their questions to themselves. She was given the occasional curious look or distracted smile, but after one or two visits was no more noticed or commented on than if she'd been another piece of equipment. Except by Win Peacock.

One afternoon when Ariel was watching a last-minute edit on one of the current week's stories, she looked up to find him watching her.

"Good, isn't it?" he asked, nodding toward the screen. "They're giving it an extra forty-five seconds, cheating my segment." He kept his slightly hooded eyes fixed on her. "You watch that control board as if you can't wait to get your hands back on it. I'm a little confused. Are you or are you not on vacation?"

"Not so you'd notice, I guess," she hedged.

Win gave her a quizzical look and turned his attention to the monitor, on which one of the other correspondents was interviewing a white supremacist. "Now this," he pointed and stepped closer, "is good. This is where Kathryn really gets down to it."

He was directly behind Ariel's chair. When he placed his hands on the armrests and leaned down, his head above hers, Ariel was intensely aware of his proximity. She could smell his subtle aftershave. She could feel her body stiffening slightly. A very long time seemed to go by before he spoke again, his voice soft.

"Do you ride?"

Ariel barely stopped herself from blurting, "Pardon me?" She tilted her head back and found his pale eyes inches away from her own. She managed to inject a question into her smile.

"Horses," he explained. "Would you like to go riding with me sometime? Take a lunch? Get out of the city?"

Ariel found herself mesmerized by his pupils, which at that range seemed enormous. She'd forgotten the question.

He placed his hands on her shoulders and held them for the space of several seconds. "Think about it."

The eyes disappeared. When Henry came into the edit bay shortly afterward, he had to call Ariel's name twice before he got her attention.

Ariel's private life was as full as her burgeoning professional life.

At B. F.'s request, she attended the memorial service for Jane. The media were kept at bay by sawhorses and the police, but even at a distance, their behavior caused Ariel to cringe with shame at her profession. Her worst moment came, though, when she entered the small chapel. The overpowering scent of lilies was an assault, and for one shocking instant the "white dream" was real. It required an effort of will to keep walking normally and find a seat.

The chapel, she saw, was packed to the rafters. Among the somber crowd was each of her interview subjects as well as obvious business associates of Macaulay, even more obvious fashion models, several individuals she guessed were domestic staff, and many disparate and less easily identifiable people. The dignified black woman who sat beside B. F. clutching his hand was, she surmised correctly, "Hattie," the housekeeper who'd helped raise Jane.

When Ariel saw B. F. and Hattie off at the airport afterward (he was taking her back to Florida but would be back, he said, in a week or two), she couldn't help noticing how the middle-aged woman studied her. Hattie was light of skin, flinty of eye and tight of lip. Ariel hoped that she wasn't being pigeonholed as an opportunist, but she didn't know what she could do about it if she was.

Her car, which had been idling roughly, conked out altogether on the way home from the airport. A mechanic advised a complete overhaul, and Ariel left it with him, seeing dollar marks before her eyes as she rented a car for the duration.

The doctor who'd taken over the practice named on her insurance forms finally called. Ariel had to do some fast talking to explain why she was asking about it again, but she did get him to confirm that she'd been tested for Huntington's—and to tell her that the results had been negative. A small, hard knot of fear, the existence of which she'd denied, dissolved. She was glad she hadn't known until then that there'd been a 50 percent chance of a different outcome.

She caught up on errands like getting Jessie's belly checked ("good as new" was Victor's verdict) and getting her own injuries checked ("coming along" was that verdict; she could forgo the cast at her discretion as long as she was careful), and she finally got around to looking for the Mace she'd promised herself to buy. She discovered that it was off-limits without a license, so she settled for cayenne pepper spray—not to be used on humans, the label admonished.

Victor, full of plans about a seminar in Boston, came for dinner, and the next morning Ariel took her turn at his orphans' kennel. It was a bittersweet experience. Only by steeling herself did she manage to come home without a half dozen dogs.

She followed up, unsuccessfully, on an idea she'd had in connection with locating her ex-husband; the USC alumni association had had no communication with him in years. Whatever Michael had done, Ariel surmised, it must have been a lollapalooza. He seemed to have vanished.

She went out with Philip twice more, both times to out-of-the-way places he chose in order to avoid encountering disapproving friends. Despite his reluctance to talk about himself, Ariel gradually learned a little more about him, and she liked what she learned.

He was in every respect a gentleman, his behavior polished, his manner of speaking unfailingly correct, his style of dress conservative and unremarkable. He wasn't in the least ostentatious. On the contrary, he behaved like a man with anything but the pots of money he evidently had. His correctness, no less than his frugality, suggested to Ariel he might have grown up poor, and one incident suggested as well that it had been a struggle.

It was the evening of the day she learned about the medical test results, and Ariel was in high spirits, even giddy with secret relief. She and Philip drove to Malibu, to a restaurant perched over the ocean's edge, and as they were walking from the car she gazed up at an inky sky and let drop one of her quotes.

" 'Moonless, starless and bible-black,' " she declared mock-dramatically, "to borrow from the redoubtable Dylan."

"Dylan?" Philip asked. "You mean Bob?"

Ariel actually giggled.

"No, not Bob and not Matt either," she said. "Thomas."

They reached the entrance just then, and Ariel happened to glance at Philip's face.

"Hey! What's wrong?" She smiled and touched his arm, surprised to find it rigid.

"I'm glad you find my ignorance so entertaining," he said stiffly. "Maybe we didn't all have your opportunities."

The hostess approached at that point and once they were seated, Philip acted as if the uncomfortable moment hadn't happened. When Ariel tried to apologize, to explain that she hadn't been laughing at him, he merely remarked on her unusually good mood. Clearly, he was embarrassed by his show of defensiveness; obviously, he didn't want it pursued; wisely, Ariel let it go. And, deftly, Philip turned the conversation back to her.

Then as always, he was deferential. He was an excellent listener, and he remembered what he heard. He paid Ariel compliments, but they were thoughtful, never effusive. He gave her glances she could only interpret as admiring, but he never touched her except in the most innocent and casual of ways. He was sober, literally and figuratively, and there was something about him that was rather old-fashioned. The former quality, certainly, was appropriate to his circumstances and the latter, Ariel realized, she found touching.

When she once observed aloud that he paid cash for everything, he explained with some chagrin but more conviction.

"I don't like the idea of my personal business floating around in people's computers," he said, then added, "and why take the chance of missing a payment and throwing away money in interest—as Fiona did repeatedly, until I convinced her to cut up her credit cards."

It was one of few references he ever made to his late wife. An impression Ariel formed, that she'd been the older of the pair and that they hadn't had a lot in common, stemmed from nothing he actually said; never was a negative word spoken about Fiona Morgan.

Ariel also continued to see Dr. David Friedman, until one morning when she realized that it felt superfluous. If she was making progress, it was toward acceptance rather than revelation.

To begin with, hypnosis continued to be fruitless and she could be regressed no further than she'd been the first time. It was as if she'd been born on Monday, February 18. Then, when Friedman brought up the "white dream," Ariel found that her memory of it had become vague and that, in fact, she had no recollection of dreaming at all in recent nights. On the subject of the diaries, Friedman had to admit that while they explained much of the appearance and behavior of the Ariel he'd known from *The Open File*, they seemed to have no relevance to the woman he was now treating. With that dichotomy in mind, he listened as Ariel once again tried to describe her early alienation toward her body.

"Your not recognizing yourself," he said after a long moment's reflection, "is par for the course, I suppose. But what I'd like to talk about is this repugnance you describe. Or— let's take it a step further—how do you feel now?"

Ariel considered the question and was more than a little surprised to realize it was no longer an issue. She'd grown comfortable with the face and body that had seemed so offensive. They were hers; they were her.

"I guess," she said, "it's sort of like when I hurt my hand. At first, I was constantly aware of it. I had to stop and think about how to do every little thing, and everything was unfamiliar and awkward. Now I hardly think of it at all." She shrugged. "That's just the way it is."

"Ariel . . ." Friedman smiled his penetrating smile. "I wonder if you're simply beginning to allow yourself to accept reality, to see yourself as you really are. The reaction you describe was extreme, to say the least. As if you were disfigured. You remind me of an anorexic: a walking skeleton looking in the mirror and seeing a fat person."

Ariel laughed. "You're not going to tell me I'm skinny!"

"No," he said composedly, "but you're working on it, I notice. And even though you persist in talking as if you have a big weight problem, I also notice you're able to joke about it." He placed his hands in their favorite position, clasped on his own ample stomach.

"I once had the pleasure," he said, "of meeting a lady who had the reputation of being a great beauty. She was in her seventies at the time, and she still had some indefinable . . . let's say 'allure,' for want of a better word. I asked her what she thought made a woman beautiful. She didn't hesitate. With utter conviction she said, 'Wit, charm and grace.'

"The thing is, she wasn't physically beautiful—never had been. You, on the other hand, Ariel, are an attractive woman. Yet when I first knew you, before the onset of the amnesia, you acted as if you didn't know it. Your posture, your body language, your defensiveness were those of a woman who perceived herself as undesirable. That's no longer true. You have those three qualities I mentioned, and confidence as well."

He rocked in his chair for a moment before asking, "Am I off on a tangent? I just find it interesting how dramatically you've changed, Ariel. It's a phenomenon not uncommon in amnesia—one of the compensations, you might say."

Ariel shook her head. "I thought psychiatrists sat around looking pontifical. Umming and aahing and making the patient talk."

"Is *that* why I'm not rich and famous?" David Friedman asked. "I guess I just never got that right."

"I think you know I'm fixing to sail off into the sunset. I think this is some kind of stratagem."

"Are you?"

"Am I what?"

" 'Fixing' to sail off?"

"Yeah."

"Bon voyage." He flashed his warm smile again. "Tell me why you've decided not to come back."

Ariel looked at her hands and then at the psychiatrist. "I believe that whatever threat there was is gone, so the urgency to remember's gone, too. The man I shot—Rodriquez?—he broke in, he got scared off and he came back the next night to finish a burglary. He's dead now. Finis. The gun I found? Probably I came home and saw that somebody'd been there and got the gun out to defend myself. I don't know about the bloody shirt, but that could've been anything. Maybe I clipped one of Jessie's nails too short. They bleed like crazy, you know. And the blood was dried. Maybe it was from an old injury. Or maybe I stopped to help an accident victim that night—that could've even been the trauma that induced the memory loss. But who knows? Maybe some little synapse in my brain just went blooey."

Her fingernails tapped a thoughtful, rhythmic tune on Friedman's desk. "Every bit of that could be true, you know—it's even plausible!—and I want to get on with my life. If my memory comes back, some of it or all of it, fine. If it doesn't, it doesn't. There're advantages," she said, "to starting with a clean slate."

It was Saturday the 9th of March when Ariel finally had time to take Ralph up on his offer of a haircut.

As it turned out, a haircut wasn't all he had in mind, and with only minor misgivings she put herself in his small hands. The results were unanticipated. At first she was elated; then she studied her image more closely in the salon mirror. The sad permanent was excised and her short hair shone, several shades lighter and gleaming with ash-blond highlights. But something struck her more forcibly than the vast improvement.

"That's Jane Macaulay's cut," she accused, "and her color!"

"You're right," Ralph agreed, "precisely. And I should know; I invented it for her years ago. It suited Jane, and it suits you. Or don't you agree?"

She couldn't disagree, and she also couldn't shake a feeling of uneasiness.

"And I'm going to suggest something else." He glanced around to make certain no one was within earshot of his specious accent's disappearance. "There's a woman here who's really good with facials and makeup and so on. She's free about now, so let her do something about those awful hedges you call eyebrows, will you?"

Late that same afternoon, Henry stopped by Ariel's house, interrupting her at work in the garden. Whatever he'd come to say died a quick death when she opened the door.

"Ariel?" he asked dubiously.

"Is that an 'Ariel, you look nice?' or an 'Ariel, what've you done to yourself?'" she asked, feeling pretty dubious herself.

"You look . . . different."

"Lord help, Henry! Try not to be so effusive." Averting her face, Ariel was reminded of her discomposure the night she'd met Henry. She felt even more uncomfortable now. She stomped out to the backyard, leaving him standing in the doorway.

In a few minutes he trailed out and sat in a deck chair, staring.

"What've you done to yourself?"

Ariel firmed the earth around a newly planted cyclamen and didn't reply.

"You do realize who you look like?" Henry asked.

"Not that much, really. Superficially, maybe." She didn't look up.

"Ha!"

Ariel took her eyeglasses from her pocket and put them on.

"What's that supposed to be?" Henry asked sardonically. "A disguise? Why'd you do that . . . to your hair? And your face? *How'd* you do that?"

Stabbing the trowel into the ground, Ariel fixed Henry with a killing look and said, "It wasn't my idea. I went to get a haircut, period. I just happened to go to Ralph—Jane Macaulay's hairdresser—and to a cosmetologist who worked with her. If anybody's being morbid, it's them, not me!"

"Okay, don't bite my head off!" Henry relaxed slightly. "It was just the shock. And you do look damned fine, by the way—I guess I should've mentioned that—but I can see you're the same old Ariel ... or at least the Ariel of recent weeks. You're sure nothing like the *original* Ariel!"

"Whatever that's supposed to mean. What did you want, anyway?"

Relaxing further, Henry got to the point of his visit. He told her that he'd ambushed Macaulay in the parking lot of his office building and, eventually, had been able to bluff an off-the-record pseudo-confirmation of their suppositions.

"I'm convinced," Henry said, "that he never even saw Jane that night, that he guessed what she'd seen, just as we did. To tell you the truth, I think he's suffering. Nobody gets that angry and that heavily into denial unless the guilts are eating them up."

"You didn't tell him about the pregnancy, did you?" Ariel asked in alarm. "I told you I don't want B. F. getting wind of that!"

"I said I wouldn't, didn't I? I'm not the voice of retribution." Henry slouched and crossed his endless legs at the ankles. "The coroner didn't say she was pregnant—I guess there wasn't enough left of the poor woman to know about that—and I won't either. Even though it adds poignancy to the story." He gave Ariel a speculative, hopeful look, shading his eyes from the setting sun. "But if you change your mind ... ?"

"Forget it," Ariel said tersely. She peeled off her gardening gloves and dropped them onto the chaise longue. "I hate to run you off, but I've got plans for the evening, and I want to take a long, hot bath."

Henry gave her an irritated look.

"You're awfully mysterious about your social life. What's the big secret, anyway?"

Ariel merely said, "You're a busybody. Come on. Off you go."

"All right, all right. But while you're playing in your bubble bath, I want to catch the news—a break in a kidnap story we've been watching. It'll be too late when I get home."

They went into the kitchen, where Ariel flipped on the portable TV. An old, syndicated nighttime soap was playing, and she was about to switch to the news channel when her hand stopped in midmotion. She stared at one of the two tiny figures on the screen. The camera cut to a close-up of a hard-eyed, negligee-clad brunette and then went back to a wide shot. The man who seemed to be threatening the brunette was quite distinguished-looking. He wore a smoking jacket and held a bottle of champagne and two tulip glasses. His expression was very familiar.

Henry looked at Ariel's face and then at the TV.

"What?" he asked. "You miss that installment or something?"

"But that's ..." She pointed, openmouthed.

Henry looked again at the screen. "That's dreck," he said. "Don't tell me you're a secret *Tulsa* fan."

"No! That man, that's Philip!"

"Yeah. Philip whats-his-name—Carroll. Soap star extraordinaire, mediocre actor. So what?"

Ariel turned sharply. "Philip *Carroll*? Are you sure?"

"Ariel," Henry asked impatiently, "what is your problem?"

"Nothing." She took one more look and switched the dial. Taking two glasses from a cabinet, she poured them each a lemonade, dropped in ice cubes and sat down.

Henry kept one eye on the news and the other on Ariel's closed face until the story he'd wanted to see was over. He snapped off the TV.

"I thought you were going to take a bath?"

"Well, I don't need you to scrub my back."

His ever-present curiosity aroused, Henry strolled around the room, hoping she'd say more. She didn't.

"What's this?" he asked, fingering a notepad beside the telephone. "Why're you calling the USC alumni association?"

"Henry!" Ariel said in exasperation. "Turn off your radar! It's none of your business, and it's nothing anyway. I told you I was trying to locate my ex-husband, and I just made one last stab at it. He's hiding out in Brazil or somewhere for all I know. Weren't you about to leave?"

He looked thoughtfully at the note she'd jotted on the pad.

"You know, Ariel, about that . . . there's one possibility you don't seem to've considered. He may be dead."

She stared, forgetting her snit. He was right. That possibility had never occurred to her.

Henry lifted the telephone receiver, punched in a number and waited.

"Gil Chen," he said, and then, after a moment, "Gil. How's it going, buddy?"

After a little old-boy networking repartee, Henry said, "Yeah, I know I owe you one for that. Thanks. But, actually, I need another favor. Could you punch up a name for me in the obits? Michael Gold, an attorney—local, I think."

To Ariel he said, "What was his full name, do you know?"

"Jordan Michael."

Henry repeated the name, nodded a time or two and gave Ariel's phone number. "About fifteen more minutes," he said, and hung up.

"A friend at the *Times*," he said in answer to her unspoken question. "You go ahead and do whatever you need to do; I'll wait here." He gave her a Groucho leer. "Unless you changed your mind about my scrubbing your back."

When the phone rang twenty minutes later, Ariel (who'd opted for a fast shower instead of a leisurely soak) was back, wrapped in a terry-cloth robe. She answered and handed the receiver to Henry.

"Yo," he said. He listened for quite a while, his eyes avoiding Ariel's. Finally he said, "Yeah, I remember now. I'd just forgotten the name. We might do a story, you never know."

He thanked the reporter, hung up and faced Ariel. His expression confirmed what she'd already guessed.

"What happened to him?" she asked.

"He was killed. Murdered, in fact. He and another man, a passenger in his car, both were. And you were right: Gold had some pretty unsavory chums. There was talk he was into money laundering among other things, and the police looked into it with a good deal of interest, but they never could prove anything. It's still open and, Ariel, it's old news. I mean, it happened four years ago." His eyes edged away again. "You weren't divorced, by the way. You were listed as the surviving spouse."

They both sat silently until Ariel came to herself with a jolt. Looking at the wall clock, she said, "I've really got to dress, Henry."

As she walked him out, Henry draped an arm over her shoulders.

"You must feel peculiar," he said with accuracy, "finding out that a husband you don't even remember is dead."

Ariel stopped at the door. With her hand on the knob, she gave him a bleak smile. "Well, there's one good thing, isn't there: it is, as you say, 'old news.' He and his 'unsavory chums' are specters I can banish. Thanks to you, it looks like I've about run out of villains."

thirty-eight

Why would you let me go on believing your name was Morgan? Why the big secret about who you are?"

The dinner paraphernalia had been cleared away, the coffee poured, and Ariel had finally asked the question. She'd waited because she found the whole situation at least as embarrassing as it was perplexing. She'd been made to feel foolish and she anticipated that Philip might feel the same, but, surprisingly, he looked angry. That impression came and went in an instant. What she'd seen, Ariel decided, was only shadow play as the candles flickered. When the flame steadied, she saw that Philip's expression wasn't one of anger, but regret.

"I never said my name was Morgan, you know. That's an assumption you made, and I just . . . didn't correct it." He smiled sadly. "Once I saw that you really didn't recognize me, well . . . you can't imagine how seldom I have the opportunity just to relax and be myself. Not to worry about what I say. About whether some misinterpreted action is going to end up on the front page of a tabloid."

"I don't mean to offend you, Philip, but I didn't recognize

your name any more than I did your face. I mean, I'm sorry, but, while you did look familiar, I couldn't place you. Obviously. Just how well-known are you, anyway?"

"Ariel, dear, you're obviously not a fan of prime-time soaps, but hundreds of thousands of people are. During the four-year run of *Tulsa* I was written up countless times in—*People* and *Cosmopolitan* and so on. Of course, I had a respectable list of credits before the success of *Tulsa,* and I've done a movie and a number of TV guest appearances in the months since it ended."

Philip seemed rather piqued, Ariel couldn't help thinking, for a man who'd just been extolling the joys of anonymity. As if he'd read her mind, he gave her a slightly abashed grin.

"I admit I was surprised—and, okay, a little irked—when you didn't know me. I assure you that's unusual.

"It's outrageous," he went on, "how the press pries. And how rude fans can be. That's another reason I've taken you only to out-of-the-way places—dimly lighted and untrendy, as you may have noticed—so we'd be left alone." He looked up from the cup he'd been turning in slow circles. "Being with someone who likes *me*—not some role I've played or an image created by the press—has been like a gift. And I'm not wrong, am I? You've enjoyed these last two weeks, too?"

Ariel studied Philip's earnest face. The reputation actors had for being insecure was evidently well-earned and universal. Here was this handsome man, rich as Croesus, successful in his own and others' estimations, and he was asking whether she liked him.

"I wouldn't be here otherwise," she answered.

"That's fine, then." Philip nodded in satisfaction, then frowned. "But, Ariel, keeping my private life private is something I feel very strongly about, particularly now, with Fiona's death so recent. I hope I can continue to rely on your discretion. Promise me that."

Ariel, rather disconcerted by his intensity, swore she wouldn't breathe their friendship to a soul, and he nodded again, a pact sealed.

"Good. Now, let's talk about something more interesting than my foibles. Like how lovely you look. I was serious when I told you that with your new do, you remind me of that poor Macaulay woman. I've figured out, by the way— it was impossible not to, you know, despite your prudence— that it's the Macaulay murder you're working on. How's it going?"

"Comme ci, comme ça." She waggled her hand, smiling, and the remainder of the evening passed agreeably. It was only when she mentioned Henry, perhaps one time too many, that the harmony they'd regained was briefly threatened.

"He must be quite the detective," Philip interrupted. "What does he look like, this Henry?"

"Henry? Tall, bearded. Thin. What's his appearance got to do with the price of rice?"

"You're fond of this Henry?"

" 'This Henry' is a good friend, yes," Ariel said, very slowly. Then it occurred to her what the edge in Philip's voice suggested. "We have a good professional relationship," she said neutrally, and changed the subject.

They were in his car before an obvious question popped into Ariel's mind. She turned to look at Philip's fine profile, illuminated at just that moment by passing headlights.

"Why," she asked, "was your wife called Morgan? Why not Carroll?"

Philip touched a dial on the tape deck, and Placido Domingo was relegated to the rear speakers.

"Why do you ask?"

"Loose ends bother me."

"Yes. The newslady in you, I suppose." Philip's expression tightened. "Fiona enjoyed a small success as an artist. Horses were her specialty, painted against California land-scapes, and the tourist galleries loved her. By the time she died she'd pretty much stopped.... But, to answer your question, for the sake of her career, her art, she retained her maiden name. Through both her marriages."

"I didn't know she'd been married before," Ariel re-marked. "You've really told me precious little about your-self. Your life. Your wife."

He glanced at her as he slowed to turn onto her street. "I could say the same about you, you know." He parked and turned off the engine. "Are you aware," he asked, "that you seldom talk about your past? I don't even know if you've ever been married."

"Widowed." Ariel felt her insides shift as she revealed what she'd only just found out herself. "Like you."

"That's a sad thing to have in common. Recently?"

"No." She tried for a lighter mood as she fished for her keys. "We're both going to have to turn in our California citizenship if we can't manage to talk about ourselves more openly. I don't think I'm up to baring my soul, but I'll tell you about my psychiatrist if you'll tell me about your astrologist, okay?"

Philip didn't smile. "I don't have one. I think we make our own fates, don't you?"

"Good Lord, Philip, who knows?" Ariel laughed. "I can't say I'm on top of mine, especially. If we're going to talk philosophy, I think I'll go with 'Thou art slave to fate, chance, kings, and desperate men.' At the very least."

"Why do you say that?"

"I didn't, technically speaking. John Donne did. Would you like some more coffee? I made a practically nonfat cheesecake this morning. Mocha chocolate. Will you come in and have some?"

"I think it's better if I don't." Philip turned fully toward Ariel and regarded her with a hesitance unusual for him. "Don't think less of me for saying this—and you don't have to tell me it's inappropriate—but what started out as a pleasant way to escape loneliness is becoming something else. Maybe too fast." He clasped his hands between his knees and rubbed the pads of his thumbs together, unaware, Ariel thought, that he was doing it.

"I haven't said much about my marriage, you're right, but the truth is it wasn't all I'd have wished. I'm not faulting Fiona; she was devoted. But her health, emotional and physical . . . I was lonely for a long time before she died."

His last statement hung in the air, heavy with implication. Ariel was surprised, but not for the reason she would've been just two short weeks ago. Her surprise stemmed not from any feelings of inadequacy but from her appraisal of Philip's character. He was, she thought, a man not given to intemperate emotions or spontaneous admissions. Thoughtfully, she examined her feelings for this man who was still, in many ways, a stranger.

There was no question that she found him attractive. And there were many things about him she admired, his restraint not the least of them. She could easily imagine a growing relationship, discovering more about each other, learning to care for one another. But she had someone more important to get to know first. Herself.

She leaned forward and placed her hand on his cheek. His hand covered hers and held it there.

"You're right, Philip," Ariel said softly, "it's too fast, for more reasons than the obvious one. There's plenty of time, and I don't think either one of us is ready."

Philip kissed her, a light, lingering touch of his lips to hers, and released her hand. When she said good night at the door, she was convinced she'd been right in her assessment, that it was too soon. Or nearly convinced.

It was four hours later, when she awoke with the scent of lilies fading and a cataclysm of lights bursting into oblivion, that the memory clicked into place. Instantly wide awake, she asked herself: what if Max Neely hadn't said "Carol" that afternoon in the police station? What if he'd said "Carroll"? She dredged up the question that had so mystified her at the time. What he'd asked was, "Are you doing anything with what I gave you on Carroll?"

thirty-nine

What little sleep Ariel had achieved after her revelation (her stupidly delayed revelation, she told herself in disgust) had been fitful. At six o'clock she gave up the effort and made a pot of coffee. With a legal pad in front of her, she wrote down her thoughts, trying to make sense of them before she called Neely.

The big question, of course, was whether the detective's offhand question had referred to the name "Carol," presumably female (who could be the Carol Lloyd at Woolf Television or any of legions of women yet unencountered), or "Carroll," of whom Ariel knew only one.

If it was the latter, the next questions became equally important: why had she asked, what had she asked, and what had Neely's answer been?

David Friedman—and maybe Hermann Rorschach, too— would've appreciated the free-form shapes that blossomed on Ariel's pad as she thought. The more she reviewed her association with Philip, the more she wondered whether they'd met before their apparent first encounter three weeks ago. If they had, their whole relationship was a grotesquerie.

She tried to remember what Victor had said about when she'd adopted Jessie, but all she could resurrect was the impression that it hadn't been long after Fiona Morgan died. When was that? Had there been time to contact her husband? She'd told Victor she was going to, she recalled his saying, so if she had, why had Philip acted as if they'd never met or talked before? Why hadn't he questioned why *she'd* acted as if they were strangers?

A thought curled its way into her mind. If they had met prior to three weeks ago, Philip had to know she was amnesic. Or pretending to be. Or wacko. Yet, incredibly, he hadn't questioned it. He was even attracted to her. The insidious thought branched into a Hydra. He was an actor. She knew almost nothing about him.

She remembered the day she'd met him, for what she'd thought was the first time. Vividly, she pictured his face when she'd arrived at his house. The behavior she'd thought unfriendly she now saw as hostile. Tense. Suspicious. His questions about whether she knew him—the questions he'd asked relentlessly, it seemed to her now—were those of a man amazed not to have been recognized. Not because he was a celebrity desirous of anonymity, but because he knew they'd met before.

And then she remembered the gentle way Philip had kissed her the night before. The courteous way he treated her. The thoughtful observations he made, never prying, always sensitive to her mood. Henry had dismissed him as a mediocre actor, but if Philip had been acting for the last two weeks, he was a long way from mediocrity; he was Academy Award material.

All her misgivings, Ariel thought as she shaded in the question marks on the notepad, were based on guesswork and a casually mentioned name, the spelling of which she still didn't know. They were the misgivings of a screwball who'd fantasized about the Mafia because her husband's business associates might have been flashy dressers. Who'd briefly entertained the possibility, for Pete's sake, that she was possessed!

She dialed the precinct station where Neely worked. He had the nine-to-six shift today, she was told. She left a message. Then she remembered that she had his home number. She located the handicapped-parking permit on which he'd written it and, resisting an impulse to cross her fingers, punched in the digits.

"Sure it was *C-a-r-r-o-l-l,*" Max Neely said. *"P-h-i-l-i-p* Carroll. You asked for everything we had on his wife's death, and the name of the coroner who did the autopsy. What's with you, Gold? Have you got amnesia or something?"

"Yes," Ariel surprised herself by saying. "As a matter of fact, I do." She was too dispirited to make up a credible story. "But I'd appreciate it if you kept it to yourself. And if you'd tell me again whatever you told me before."

Neely's jocularity petered out. "You're serious, aren't you. What the devil's happened now?"

"Neely, if I knew what's happened, I'd tell you. I was abducted by aliens and zapped into the depths of Lethe, for all I know. What did you tell me about Philip Carroll's wife?"

"The depths of what?"

"Lethe. The river of forgetfulness in Hades."

"You know the screwiest things, hon. But what about this amnesia. That's not for real?"

"I promise to give you a play-by-play, Neely, next time I see you, but in the meantime—please? Carroll's wife?"

"Well, it's been a while." It was obvious from his tone that Neely was leaving the subject of amnesia unwillingly.

"Let me think a minute. Hey! I just might still have a copy of the notes I gave you before. I know I brought 'em home then."

Ariel heard drawers slamming, papers rustling and Neely exercising his considerable vocabulary of expletives before he came back on the line. "Fiona Morgan—she didn't have the same name as her husband, for some reason—was found dead by the aforementioned husband somewhere between one and two days after her demise of, according to the coroner, one W. Sparks, natural causes."

"Why was there an autopsy?"

"As far as could be determined, she was alone in the house when she kicked off and since she didn't die of old age and didn't have anything terminal that her doctor knew of, we had to look into it. 'Death unattended by a physician' and so forth. Could've been suicide, but it wasn't."

"So what was the cause of death?"

"You really don't remember any of this stuff, do you?" Neely asked wonderingly. "Heart failure's what the coroner said. Informative, isn't it? It does say here she had some kind of heart problem. Hold it, let me read this."

He muttered to himself for a minute, then said " 'Athero-sclerotic arterial disease,' according to her doc. They'd done an angioplasty a couple of years before, and she'd checked out okay the last time he saw her, but that was four months before she died."

"So you—the police," Ariel amended, "were satisfied there wasn't any foul play involved?"

"No reason to suspect any, looks like. No sign of forced entry. No robbery. No visible wounds on the corpus. No poison. Nobody with a motive we could find. Except the husband, of course; he came into a bundle."

Her stomach rolling with dread, Ariel asked, "He was a suspect?"

"We asked around, naturally. Nobody'd ever heard of any trouble between them. They'd been together three years and, while it must've been kind of a long-distance marriage—Carroll was gone a lot—neighbors said she was nuts about him, real devoted. He's clean, recordwise, but all that's kind of academic, anyway."

"What do you mean, 'academic'?"

"He was three thousand miles away when she went to her reward."

Ariel sat down abruptly. She closed her eyes and swallowed hard. "You're absolutely sure about that?"

"Gosh, no, Ariel, we just took his word for it," Neely said. "Carroll had just flown into L.A. He had his ticket receipt, his seat was occupied, and two stewardesses identified his picture. Fact was, they'd recognized him without the picture. It was Carroll on the plane, all right, and trust me, the wife didn't get as fragrant as she was in just the hour or two after his plane landed."

"How do you know he didn't fly here earlier? And go back to wherever he was?"

"He was working on a movie in New York, and anytime he wasn't working his whereabouts were accounted for. I don't have the details, but I could get 'em."

"No." Ariel switched the phone onto her shoulder, wiping her clammy palm on her robe. "If you all say he was seen certain times and places, I'm sure he was."

"Let's look at the timetable, just for the fun of it," Neely suggested. "We're talking about, say, eleven or twelve hours round-trip flying time to and from any New York airport or Newark, plus driving to and from the airport on each end. In L.A. alone that's got to be at least forty-five minutes each way even in the dead of night, so we're talking roughly fifteen hours in addition to whatever time he's at the house here. No way."

"Okay, then," Ariel said, "that's that. Oh, wait a minute. You didn't say when she died."

"Yeah, I did. Sometime between one and two days before Carroll found her, which was Friday, February first, at ten P.M."

After doing her best to convince Neely that she really didn't know why she'd asked about Philip in the first place and promising that she'd tell him, sometime, why she was asking again, she thanked him for going through it all with her.

"It's okay," he grumbled. "Hey, let me know next time you go see the Clips play, okay? My brother and I go some-

times when I'm not working nights. We could ride over together, have a wienie at halftime, breathe onions on each
other. How about it?"

"Maybe. I might just do that."

"And you can tell me about this amnesia thing," Neely
said. "There just happens to be a game Wednesday night."

Ariel spent the rest of the morning on the back patio
absorbing the sunshine and mulling over what Neely had
told her. That Fiona had been dead five weeks left two
weeks, pre-amnesia. It was inconclusive. Until she knew
when she'd gotten Jessie, she couldn't know if there'd been
time to contact Philip. She'd left a message for Victor. He
wouldn't be back in town until Tuesday, and only he could
pinpoint the timing. And something else. Chewing at the
edge of her memory was something Victor had said that first
morning, after the break-in. But she hadn't been cooking on
all burners then, Lord knows, any more than she was now.
It wouldn't come.

Just before noon the sky began to darken and a brisk
wind whipped up, riffling the pages of the neglected Sunday
newspaper beside her and raising chill bumps on her arms.
Jessie preceded Ariel inside, pausing for a quick, purely ceremonial lick at her water bowl before collapsing sluggishly
onto a rug. Her head on her paws, she gave Ariel a doleful look.

"I know I'm no fun today, Miss Jessie," Ariel agreed.
"What's frustrating is I don't know where to go from here.
Philip's innocent as far as I know, of anything except waf-
fling, but I wish I could be sure whether we'd met before.
And I'd sure like to know why I asked about his wife's
death to start with."

The sharp ring of the phone cut through Ariel's one-sided
conversation. She had the instant conviction that it was
Philip, and she wasn't even remotely up to talking to him.
She ran to the answering machine and waited through her
message. An irascible male voice said, "Confound! I hate
these things!"

Ariel grabbed the receiver and pushed the PAUSE button,
saying "Wait a second" as a screech from the machine

286

nearly annihilated her eardrum. "Are you okay?" she asked. "I'm sorry about that."

There came a long-suffering sigh, pregnant with disgust. "If that thing'd gone off on the ear with my hearin' aid, I don't think we could be friends anymore," B. F. Coulter said.

"You don't wear a hearing aid."

"Well, I ought to. Is there any chance a'tall you're not busy tonight?"

"Every chance," she said, feeling conspicuously better than she had two minutes before. "Are you back in town? Do you want me to make you dinner?"

"Yes, and no. You're coming here. I'll send Roy at six."

Ariel hung up with a big grin on her face and called Jessie. "Come on, sweetie! We're going for a hike!"

A long walk, a long soak in the hottest water she could stand and a longer nap later, Ariel regarded herself in the mirror. The Jane-look-alike hair wouldn't do: B. F. would have a stroke. She plundered until she found a jar of mousse and experimented. Minutes later her hair looked slick, literally. Plastered down in something approximating what she thought was called "the wet look," it appeared darker. It also didn't look like a style Jane—or probably any self-respecting woman—would wear. She downplayed the makeup. She slid on her glasses. She donned an outfit that had looked stylishly oversized in the store dressing room and now just looked too big. She pronounced herself adequately the good old Ariel.

Roy was prompt to a fault, and when she handed him the cheesecake she'd baked the day before, a neatly cellophane-wrapped host gift, he smiled wickedly.

"That's right beautiful, ma'am, and B. F.'ll be glad to see it. Sarge doesn't let him near much in the way of desserts."

"Who's Sarge?" she asked the back of his head as they drove away.

"Sarge McManus," Roy said, "cook and self-appointed bodyguard."

Ariel slid forward and propped her forearms on the back of the seat. "Unusual combination, isn't it?"

He laughed. "No offense, but *unusual* is a word you could use on most anybody B. F. takes a notion to associate with."

"Unusual" was an understatement.

The man who opened the penthouse door to Ariel was shaped like an old-fashioned icebox, just as solid and not much taller. His hair was cut in a severe crew cut through which she could look down on most of his scalp, and his head seemed to grow straight out of his rectangular body. There was no neck to speak of. He looked to be about sixty, but Ariel didn't imagine that many thirty-year-olds would be eager to mess with him. Judging by the size of the biceps that emerged from his pink golf shirt and the formidable expression on his face, she wasn't sure she much wanted to either.

"Ariel Gold?" he asked. It sounded like a challenge.

"Well, who do you think she is?" bellowed the man's employer from somewhere behind him. "Golda Meir? Quit giving her the evil eye and let her in."

The compact, aging linebacker in the doorway stood his ground just long enough to establish that he wouldn't be ordered around, then stuck out a meaty hand.

"McManus. Come on in. B. F.'s right in there."

He jerked his head toward a room behind him and waited until Ariel had gone into it before he disappeared in another direction. B. F. was lying supine on the floor.

"Are you all right?" Ariel cried, rushing to him. She stood looking down at the huge old man. "I guess you are; you're smiling. What in the world are you doing on the floor?"

"What did you do to your hair?" he asked.

"Answer me."

"Backache. I'll get up in a minute. Meantime, fix yourself whatever you want. The bar's six feet that way." He pointed.

When Ariel had poured herself a glass of what looked like sinfully expensive wine, she raised her glass to her recumbent host. "Did you want me to join you down there, or could I just do something peculiar like sit in a chair?"

"Sit here where I can see you." He pointed again, to an oversized leather chair. "Tell me what you've been up to."

Ariel took her time complying, looking around first at the huge room. The wall beyond the streamlined dark green leather bar was floor-to-ceiling shutters, closed. Remembering the length of the elevator ride, she had a good idea what lay behind them.

Everything in the room was oversized, and what could be overstuffed was. Deep, golden-yellow touches here and there kept the predominant dark green from taking over, and furniture had been kept rather minimal so that the feeling of spaciousness wasn't just from the size of the room. A large oil painting, spotlighted above the fireplace, was the focal point. B. F.'s request forgotten, Ariel crossed the room to stand before it.

The subject was a young Indian man—a Seminole, unless Ariel was mistaken. He was kneeling, his face inclined as if he was listening to something in the distance. How a few lines and a few strokes of color could convey the complexity of sadness, resignation and fierceness that Ariel saw was mystifying. And awesome.

"Who is he, do you know?"

"No, and I'd just as soon not know. He's either a very old man or dead by now. I'd rather keep him like that, wouldn't you?"

"What about the artist?" She squinted at an illegible signature.

"Dead," B. F. said brusquely. "That's another story. Now come on and sit. What have you been doing worthwhile since I saw you last?"

"Well, sir, let's see." Ariel couldn't suppress a little thrill of pure devilment as she sat and crossed her legs. "Speaking of death, I found out yesterday that I'm a widow."

Owllike, B. F. blinked. "I didn't even know you were married."

"I hardly knew it myself."

"Takin' kind of a cavalier attitude, aren't you?"

"Well, you see, it's been several years since my husband died."

"And you didn't know it until yesterday?"

"Right."

"You were, er, estranged?"

"Not that I know of." Ariel's mouth twitched. "But I don't really remember, having amnesia as I do."

"It's probably just as well I'm lying down," B. F. said after some deliberation.

Ariel refused to fill the silence.

"I'll bite." He looked steadfastly at the ceiling.

"This could take a while."

"Do you have plans for later? I don't."

By the time they'd gone through broiled catfish ("Fried's the only way they oughta be eaten," groused B. F.), creamed white corn ("Silver Queen. Sarge put it up last summer"), green beans with Vidalia onions ("The beans are undercooked again," he yelled through the dining room door) and incredibly light, short biscuits, Ariel felt like Scheherazade. Her tale finished, she wound down, and even with a full stomach, she felt lighter.

"What can I do for you on any of this?" B. F. asked straight out.

"Not a thing I can think of." Ariel hadn't mentioned Philip. Talking about her doubts on that score seemed too much like slander, and without more information, which she hadn't figured out how to get, it just didn't seem fair.

"About Michael, I guess that's simply a fait accompli, but I'm still curious. I'll go to the library tomorrow and look up the coverage of his death. Fill in some more blanks in my memory."

"I could hire an investigator."

"Well, I'm supposed to be one, of a sort. Remember?"

"Yeah, but *you* don't. You might've been a whiz at research once upon a time, but the plain truth is you're a novice right now. Isn't that right?"

B. F. slid his chair away from the table and draped his arm over the back. "I'm not easy with all this, Ariel. Something bad enough happens that you forget everything, immediately on the heels of which your house is broken into not once but twice—that's not usual—and then you find out your husband was murdered. Well, okay—that unfortunate event might be totally unrelated. Probably is if it happened that long ago, but we don't know, do we? And they never found out who did it."

His jutting lower jaw ground slowly back and forth as if he were chewing over the problem.

"I don't like it, Ariel Gold, and I've got a suggestion. My business here in L.A. won't take long. Let's you and me take a trip. Europe or South America. Australia. All of 'em—why not? You're supposed to be on vacation anyway, and I could stand to get away from my troubles. You'd be doin' me a favor. I'll talk Hattie or some other female into goin', too, so you won't have to worry about your reputation."

This last was said ironically, but Ariel knew he was dead serious about the rest of it.

"What d'you say? I've got a fair-sized yacht, or if you don't like water, we'll fly."

Ariel didn't trust herself to speak around the ache in her throat. She swallowed it, and even managed to smile on answering.

"I say 'Later.' I want to be in on the finish of the story about Jane. And there's another matter that's a little worrisome, a . . . well, that's not worth talking about." She smiled again, a brisk dismissal of the subject. "Anyway, I mean to do something about finding out who I am, not just biologically but the rest of it. I'd like a past I remember, whatever I told the psychiatrist."

B. F.'s shake of the head was the smallest of movements. "You're too bullheaded for your own good. You remind me of Jane when she got her teeth into something. I just wish she'd lived long enough to find something worth her grit, something besides her confounded marriage."

Ariel felt an irrational stab of guilt about the things she knew about Jane and her husband that B. F. didn't. She was convinced she was right to suppress them, and she shuddered at the thought of the wrath and sorrow that would be unleashed if she spoke. Seeking distraction, she looked around the room again, realizing for the first time what wasn't there.

"Why aren't there any pictures of Jane?"

"Put 'em away for the time bein'."

So much for that conversational gambit, thought Ariel, looking at the man's shuttered face and feeling worse. She pulled off her glasses and, playing with them, said, "Yes, well . . . about Jane. I want to thank you for giving me the names you did. It was really helpful to me personally, and I—"

"You know," B. F. interrupted, "without those goggles on and thinnin' down like you're doin', you really do look a—"

Just then Sarge plowed through the swinging door from the kitchen, a bantam Sherman tank bearing the cheesecake as if it were a coiled water moccasin.

"Roy gave this to me." The statement was the next thing to a snarl. "B. F. needs it like he needs arteriosclerosis."

He plunked the dessert on the table and returned momentarily with plates, forks and a serving knife.

"I had some nice raspberries," he grumbled.

Ariel kept her face straight, with an effort. "It's about three grams of fat per serving, Sarge. Won't you have some?"

"Three grams?" he asked suspiciously.

"And a fraction, maybe."

He sliced into the cheesecake and, after serving theirs, put a minuscule slice on the third plate he just happened to have. He sat across from Ariel and took a bite. He made no comment.

"The dinner was excellent. Thank you." Somebody, Ariel thought, should have some manners.

Sarge did. He swallowed politely before he gave Ariel a look that would have made Torquemada proud.

"Where'd you meet B. F.?" he demanded.

His employer (who clearly had a rather unorthodox relationship with his help) rolled his eyes. "Lord have mercy," he beseeched the ceiling, but he said nothing to Sarge or to Ariel, believing, she presumed, that she could take care of herself.

"At his son-in-law's house, where we were doing an interview," Ariel innocently replied, and then drove in the metaphorical knife a littler farther. "I'm in the news business."

The sparse hairs on the cook's head bristled like antennae. As he carefully put his fork down, his eyes boring into hers, Ariel had the definite impression that he was about to launch himself across the table. She deeply regretted her flippancy during the split second that her body froze against the onslaught.

"Sarge. Down." To Ariel's amazement, B. F. was laughing. "I don't know why you persist in thinkin' I'm a fool. Have you noticed," he asked, indulging in a little devilry himself—"how much like Jane Ariel Gold is? Doesn't she kind of remind you of Jane?"

Sarge whipped his head around in alarm. His thoughts were transparent.

"I'd only thought she *acted* a lot like Jane," B. F. turned serious as he continued, "but now that I can see her eyes, I think she even looks something like her. Don't you see it? The mouth? And especially around the eyes?"

Ariel had never seen anyone, as far as she knew, on the verge of an apoplectic fit, but one looked imminent.

"Stop it! B. F., that's not funny. Sarge"—she turned to the cook, whose face was the color of the raspberries he'd intended to serve—"I'm harmless, truly. I have money of my own, and I have no designs on that big dope financially, professionally or any other way. Furthermore, I'm sure neither he nor you sees any resemblance between me and his granddaughter."

Before B. F. could protest, Sarge cut in. "That's not true," he said, looking as if he was surprising himself. "There's obvious differences, of course, but you do look more than a little bit like Jane. And nobody I've ever known except her would've had the nerve to call B. F. a dope."

He forked in the rest of his cheesecake, said, "I'd like the recipe for that, okay?" and left the room with much less force than he'd entered it.

"Well." B. F. watched the door swing closed and turned to Ariel with comically widened eyes. "A conquest, I believe. Do you really have money?"

"Nowhere near your league, but enough."

"Where'd you get it?"

Ariel gave him a sideways look. "If you're trying to provoke me, don't bother. I don't know where I got it. From working lots of years, I suppose, and from my father's estate, maybe. Or my husband's. Or both. Once I stopped believing I might've robbed a bank, I gave up worrying about it."

B. F. again became serious. "This psychiatrist you were seeing—are you satisfied that he was okay? Would you like me to ask around, get the name of the best?"

"I liked him just fine, B. F. In fact, I miss him. Stop trying to do more than you're already doing by being my friend. Now, tell me, how's Stonewall? And how's Cap?"

"I'm thinkin' of taking the mutt back to Flor—"

The old man stopped, his mouth ajar. It snapped closed, and his eyes narrowed. They looked malevolent.

"What did you just say?"

Ariel was so disconcerted by the strength of the reaction, she honestly couldn't remember for a moment.

"I just asked about Jane's dog and about Hattie," she said faintly.

"You said 'Cap.'"

"Did I? I guess I did. Why're you angry at me?"

"Where'd you hear that name?"

"From you, I guess. Isn't that what you call her sometimes? Look, I'm sorry if I was too familiar. I wouldn't offend you for . . ."

But B. F. was no longer listening. He'd pushed himself up and left the table. He kept his back to her as he folded open the shutters, revealing the brilliant view of the city Ariel had guessed would be there. She glanced at it, but her eyes went immediately back to B. F. She couldn't believe how much it hurt to have him upset with her.

When he turned around, the anger was gone. In its place was more despair than Ariel ever wanted to see in his face again.

"B. F. . . ." She stood and walked over to him, taking his hand. "Please tell me what I said that's made you so unhappy."

He cleared his throat, patted Ariel's hand and withdrew his own, turning to look at the distant sea of lights below. "It's kind of a silly story."

"Tell me."

"I used to call Hattie 'Cap'n.' Because she was so bossy, always tellin' me what to do, tryin' to run things. Well, the truth is she *did* run things at home. Anyhow"—he rolled his shoulders as if his back pained him—"when Jane was little, she picked it up, but she'd misunderstood. Thought I was sayin' 'cap'—hat, cap. You see? She kept callin' her that even after I explained that headwear didn't have anything to do with it.

"Damn," he said after a minute, very quietly.

Hesitantly, Ariel put her hand on his shoulder and, after a moment, rested her head on his massive back.

"Laya came to see me the morning of Jane's memorial service," B. F said after a while. "You know Laya, right?"

Ariel nodded.

"She was about Jane's best friend, I guess. She has ... an ability of some kind. Jane didn't want to believe it because she didn't hold with second sight and all that sort of thing, but she did come to believe it, and it gave her the heebie-jeebies. I think, my dear young friend, that you must have some of whatever Laya's got, and I hope you'll use it to find out who did that to my girl."

Ariel raised her head, frowning. "What on earth do you mean by that?"

"I mean, Ariel Gold, that I never called Hattie 'Cap.' Jane was the only person who did that."

forty

The plan, when it came, was obvious. It was such a natural solution that it seemed preordained. True, it had taken longer to conceive than he would've liked, but its pristine beauty was worth the wait. So much of it, after all, had already proved viable.

This time he'd see to it that the ending worked as perfectly as the rest.

He adjusted the sunlamp to cover his body more effectively, applied a little more sunscreen to his face and replaced the eye protectors. A healthy glow, he thought; that was the thing. Ultraviolet rays had to be treated with caution, like so many things.

He smiled to himself. That he'd had the means to effect

the plan all along, it could be argued, was accidental. He knew better. It was because of his prudence, his leeriness of Rodriquez's credentials, that he'd demanded to see proof of the imbecile's claims. To obtain samples of his wares before the fact and, providentially, to have those samples—everything he needed—right here, right now, in his possession. Now all that was required was a little research. The most amazing information, he had reason to know, was readily available if you knew where to look. His ability to put the plan into action was the least of his worries. If a congenital idiot like Rodriquez could do it, a person of his intelligence would have no problem at all.

One of the things that particularly appealed was the misdirection involved. It added an element, he thought, of sophistication, and he'd learned long ago how effective a tool misdirection could be. Nearly four years without a hint of suspicion from anyone save Ariel Gold had given him a profound appreciation for misdirection.

Another advantage was that the plan could be put into effect quickly. Time, he sensed, was running out.

He turned onto his stomach and removed the eye shields. He examined every aspect of the plan objectively. He recognized two or three potential problems. They were fixable. There was a certain amount of chance, it was true, because he couldn't entirely control the actions of another person; even a master player could only force his opponent into so many moves. There would be less chance, he knew, with a simple murder—a bullet at close range, say—but Ariel's death was only the immediate objective. The ultimate objective was what necessitated her death in the first place: his freedom. That objective could only be guaranteed by cunning. By misdirection. By distancing himself.

He glanced at his watch. Another forty-five seconds.

It was interesting, he reflected, how everything was coming full circle, how strangely the decisive events in his life dovetailed. Each event triggered the next, each killing demanded the next. This would be the last. The last pivotal character in the drama who required extinction. He reached for a towel and turned off the sunlamp. There was work to be done.

forty-one

Ariel burned her tongue on too-hot coffee, winced and turned on the shower. Her schedule for the morning had tightened up when the garage had called with the amazing news that her car was finally ready. Plan B was that she would return the rental and taxi to pick up her car. That should put her at the library just about opening time. She'd see what she could find out about Michael and then head for the studio, where the final cuts on Jane's story were being made for tonight—airtime. She was about to slip out of her robe when the door chimes sounded.

A glimpse through the front-door peephole revealed a worried-looking Anita Stroud.

Ariel looked at her watch. She considered pretending there was no one home. She peered again at the fragile, anxious face, and impatience drowned in a wave of guilt. Her greeting was so effusive that Anita looked startled.

"You're certainly chipper," she observed. "I gather it's not too early to be dropping by?"

Assuring her otherwise, Ariel made an effort to smooth her hair, which she hadn't brushed, and invited the elderly woman in.

"How about some coffee? Would you like some?" Silently, she begged Anita to say no.

Anita did. "I've already had my tea, thank you, and I won't take but a minute."

Ariel ushered her neighbor into the kitchen, where sunlight was just beginning to creep through the north-facing window.

"You're sure I can't get you something? I could make tea."

"Ariel, sit down and stop fussing, please.

"Your question about your mother's doctor bothered me," Anita began without preamble. "I couldn't imagine why you wanted to know such a thing all these years later.

And then yesterday Marguerite cleared it up for me. She's been off on a lecture tour, or I'd have asked her about it earlier."

Her look was steady, her voice firm. "First, let me tell you that it's my opinion your mother suffered from Huntington's. It's the same thing, Marguerite told me, that your father had."

"But that can't be." Ariel smiled. "I don't have the gene."

"You've been tested?" Anita guessed. Her face collapsed in relief, and she looked for the first time like the very old woman she was. "You tested negative?"

"Exactly. I don't know what my poor mother had, but it can't have been that or my test couldn't have been negative, could it?"

"Then I was wrong, thank God! Or . . . Well, that's wonderful, Ariel. That's all that matters." Anita pushed herself up.

"What did you start to say?"

"Nothing important." Anita touched Ariel's cheek. "Go on about your business, and come to see me sometime when you feel like a good martini."

"You were going to say something," Ariel persisted. "What?"

Anita stopped. She studied Ariel intently, her eyes narrowed.

"I am going to say this," she decided. "I don't think I was wrong about Gladys's illness. I've since had an acquaintance who died of the disease, and the symptoms are rather distinctive, as I'm sure you know."

"I don't understand."

"Of course you don't." Anita sat back down. "I've given a lot of thought to this conversation, Ariel. I spent most of the night arguing one minute that I was the worst kind of meddler, the next that since I'm the only one left, I have a responsibility. This Huntington's thing makes me realize that something else could come up someday, if not with you then with your children."

She took a deep breath. "I don't believe," she said, "that my friend Gladys Munson was your biological mother. Nor Lawton your father."

"Not—! Why?"

"I'll tell you if you like, but let me be very candid: I have no proof of what I believe."

Ariel's stomach flopped. For a mature woman who didn't remember her parents, who didn't remember her childhood, who had every reason to be grateful if the wretched man she'd read about in her journals wasn't her natural father, she was surprised by how stunned she felt.

"But I saw my birth certificate," she floundered. "It had all the details. The time of birth, the . . . the weight. The address. All that."

Anita nodded. "I'm not surprised; that's what they do. What you have, if I'm correct, is what they call an amended birth certificate. It looks the same as an original. There's no difference, for everyone's protection. I know this because a former pupil of mine, an adopted former pupil, once came to me for advice and I looked into it."

Ariel felt as if she'd been pushed back down the rabbit hole. The hours of filling in the blanks, of finding out who she was, inch by tentative inch, had been a cruel joke. Not only wasn't she herself, she wasn't even Ariel Munson Gold.

"What makes you think they weren't my parents?" she asked.

"There was no one thing, Ariel. Just several little things. That you looked nothing like either of them—and they were both such short people. Gladys was five feet? Five-one? And Lawton wasn't as tall as you are. Also, you were such a natural little scholar. Forgive me, dear. Neither of your—neither of them was stupid by any means, but you were in a completely different world intellectually. And then there were the pictures. There were framed pictures of your poor sister from the time of her infancy. The earliest picture of you, Ariel, was when you were walking. I never asked about that, but I wondered."

Ariel frowned her doubt. The arguments seemed thin.

"I think I may have met your natural mother," Anita said. She sighed deeply, the only sound in the room.

"Not too long after Gladys and Lawton moved in here—you were a toddler then. Remember I told you? I was working in my yard when a woman, a tall young woman, drove up here, to this house. She knocked, and when there was no answer, she started to leave. Then she saw me. She was nervous, trying to act casual. She asked if the Munsons lived here and then if I knew when they'd be back. I offered to relay a message, but she said never mind and mumbled something about her mother having gone to school with Mrs. Munson. She never gave her name. Then, when I told your mother—told Gladys—about the visit, she looked ... well, 'apprehensive' wouldn't be too strong a word. She had no idea who it could have been—or so she said."

Anita laughed a small, tired laugh and said, "I hadn't meant to make this such a yarn! I think I will trouble you for a glass of water, Ariel."

Ariel gave her one and, after a few sips, Anita went on.

"Over time Gladys and I became friends, and one day a few months later I came over here for something, I don't remember what. This young woman was here, sitting in the living room with you on her lap. She and your mother seemed quite comfortable together—it was my impression this wasn't their first visit—and Gladys introduced her. She said Rachel—that was her name—had worked at the hospital where you were born.

"Gladys wasn't accustomed to telling untruths. She turned red as ... Well, there was no mention of having 'gone to school' with anybody."

Anita had been looking into the distance as she recalled her story, and now she turned back to Ariel.

"I wish I could remember her last name, Ariel, but I can't. I'm sorry."

"But I don't understand," Ariel said, puzzled. "What made you think that this Rachel was my mother?"

"You'd have to have seen it for yourself, perhaps. The way she held you. The way she looked at you. She and Gladys—it was as if they had a pact.

"Anyway, the only other time I saw her was on your third birthday. I came over to bring a little gift, and she was leaving as I was arriving. She was excited, and she was crying a bit. Gladys told me later that Rachel had gotten her practical nursing license and that she was moving to Bakersfield to take a position there. It was with a family, and that name

I do remember. It was Teasdale, the name of one of my favorite poets," Anita said. "Even so, it still took me half last night to dredge it up."

"But, Anita, I still don't get it. If I was adopted, why wouldn't my mother have simply said so?"

"On that, too, I can give you a definite answer. You remember I mentioned the pupil who'd been adopted? The one who came to me for advice? Well, I learned then that in California adoption records are sealed, and that one can't get access to one's original birth certificate unless the biological parent initiates a search. I was irate! I felt then, and do now, that keeping adoption from children is unfair, that they have a right to know who their parents are. I happened to mention my opinion to Gladys. She was aghast. She argued that the adoptive parents as well as the natural parents have a right to privacy. I never saw her so vehement about anything. The person who raises the child, she said, who cares for her day in and day out—and the pronoun she used was 'her'—is the parent. Telling a child that she was adopted, she said, was wrong. It would make her feel less loved."

Ariel started to say something, then realized she had no idea what she'd intended to say. After a moment's silence, Anita said, "If you should decide you want to pursue this, Ariel, you might try to contact these Teasdales. I imagine it's too much to expect that Rachel's still there—if, indeed, the family's still there—but they may be able to point you in the right direction."

When Anita had gone, Ariel returned to the kitchen and sat maundering. Her mind was a blank stupor, her plans, so urgent only a short while before, difficult to even remember. She scratched Jessie's chin and stared out the kitchen window. She considered going back to bed. She poured herself a fresh cup of coffee and reached for the telephone.

"There're three Teasdales listed in Bakersfield," the operator announced. "There's a P, a Randall and a T. Which did you want?"

"Could I have them all?"

"I'm sorry. We can only give out one number at a time."

Ariel swallowed sarcasm and asked for P, which turned

out to stand for Pamela, an extremely friendly young woman who immediately concluded that it was her parents Ariel wanted.

"My brother Randy's got muscular dystrophy, and he had nurses for years," said the voluble Pamela, "but he's on his own now. He has his own place and all—a fellow just comes in a few hours a day to see to him. I don't remember a Rachel, but I'm younger so I wouldn't necessarily. Mom probably still has records from when you're talking about, though. She never throws anything away."

Ariel got the elder Teasdales' number, expressed her thanks and dialed again.

The maid who answered said that Mrs. Teasdale was in the garden and asked if Ariel would wait while she was fetched. Ariel did. Minutes ticked by before she heard a breathless "Hello?"

Her query repeated—and supplemented by a handicapped niece invented on the spot—Ariel struck pay dirt. She also guessed where Pamela had gotten her friendly, chatty nature.

"Sure! I remember Rachel," exclaimed Mrs. Teasdale, "although for the life of me I can't bring her last name to mind. Isn't that awful? And she was here two or three years! Wasn't it was Mal-something? Malvern? Oh, this will drive me crazy! Hang on a minute, and I'll look it up and see if I have a forwarding address, okay?"

Ariel was put on hold. She finished her coffee and discovered that the pot was empty. She looked at her watch and then at the kitchen clock, as if the time were going to pass faster there. She opened the refrigerator and closed it and was about to hang up when a click signaled an extension phone being lifted in Bakersfield.

"Sorry to be so long," Mrs. Teasdale apologized, "but I do seem to have an awful lot of records where Randy's concerned."

Ariel eventually, politely, interrupted a dissertation concerning bureaucracy, doctors and insurance to learn that Rachel's last name was Mulkerne.

"Gosh, though, don't you imagine she's retired?" Mrs. Teasdale worried. "She was in her twenties when she was here from, let's see, 'sixty-four to 'sixty-six. So that would make her . . ." Ariel fidgeted while the woman calculated. "Sixty-something?" Math wasn't Mrs. Teasdale's forte.

"Um-hm," Ariel hedged, "but she was highly recommended. Even if she's not interested, I'd like to talk to her. Maybe she can suggest someone else. Did you find a forwarding address?"

"Oh, certainly. Right here. She went to work at a school for handicapped children in Santa Barbara. St. Teresa's. Rachel was so good with children! We hated to lose her—her replacement was a horror, let me tell you! Anyway, Rachel did keep in touch with Randy for a while, but I called him on the other line—another reason I was so long getting back to you—and he hasn't heard from her in years, he said."

Hoping that Mrs. Teasdale's deductive powers were no sharper than her math, Ariel slipped in an offhand question.

"Do you happen to remember whether Rachel ever mentioned her family? Did she have any children that you recall?"

"Oh, I don't think so. Wait, though. Her application form would say. Let's see, the spaces for family and whom to contact in an emergency are blank. The reference she gave was the administrator of her nursing school. Do you want that number?"

Ariel copied it and was in the process of hanging up when she heard a tiny shriek. "Yes? Mrs. Teasdale?" She put the receiver back to her ear. "Was there something else?"

"I almost forgot. Now this could have been a problem! Randy told me that Rachel had married. One of the last cards she sent said she'd married a teacher at the school, at St. Teresa's. Randy didn't remember the man's name, I'm afraid."

The nursing school administrator had died in 1971, but St. Teresa's was still listed in Santa Barbara information.

The personnel director was new and knew of no staff member named Rachel. Ariel was transferred to the gift shop, which was managed by a retired teacher who, she was told, knew everybody who'd ever been at St. Teresa's. Soon, Ariel learned that the former Rachel Mulkerne had married a Gerald Lynley, subsequently divorced Mr. Lynley, who later had died, and moved away. The gift shop manager didn't know if she went by Mulkerne or Lynley after the divorce, but she did know a woman still living in Santa Barbara with whom Rachel had been friendly. She looked up the woman's number and read it off.

Ariel checked the time. One more call, she promised herself. She punched in the number of Rachel Mulkerne/Lynley's friend.

Who didn't answer.

Reluctantly, Ariel headed back to the shower.

forty-two

Ariel dispensed with the rental, waited eons for the cab she'd called and finally retrieved her now purring car, paying out a sum that would've ransomed Farouk. An hour later than planned, she drove to the library, which, fortunately, was en route to the studio. When she left the library, she didn't know if she was physically capable of driving to the studio or anywhere else.

Her first surprise came when she asked for the *Los Angeles Times* microfiche for March of 1989, which, according to the *Times Index*, was when Michael Gold met his death.

"Popular fiche this morning!" said the woman behind the reference desk. "A man was in first thing wanting that same one."

Ariel wound the film according to the diagram on the machine, curious about the coincidence. Somebody else interested in her husband's murder? Unlikely, she concluded, as she watched the newspaper pages flying through March. A lot of things happened in that and every month, and there was no reason to assume that Michael's death interested anyone but her at this late date.

She stopped the machine and backed it up a few pages to the correct date. Scanning slowly, she found the story in the late edition of Wednesday the 15th.

Attorney Michael Gold, she learned, had been shot to death between the hours of nine and eleven o'clock the previous night. His body had been found draped over the steering wheel of his car, which was parked at a construction site in Long Beach. Michael was, in fact, the second victim mentioned.

The first was "a prominent businessman and entrepreneur" named Creighton Arnold, who received the lion's share of the coverage. A resident of Rye, New York, with wide-ranging business interests on both coasts, Arnold had been a client of Michael and the owner of the property where they'd died. There were no suspects; police were investigating.

Two days later there was a follow-up story. The emphasis had shifted. Essentially the same facts were given about Arnold, but police, acting on "reliable information," were looking into allegations that Michael had been involved in certain illegal activities, money laundering foremost among them. Known associates, she read, had included a convicted "drug baron" and a man believed to have been the victim of a professional killing earlier in the year. Michael had been shot three times, Arnold once, and police were speculating that Arnold might have been an innocent bystander who just happened to be with the wrong man at the wrong time.

Ariel rubbed her eyes, swallowed a linty aspirin she found in her purse and found one more reference, a short one.

Michael had been "under observation" by the police prior to his death, according to the article, which went on to say that the crime scene, swarmed over by construction workers the day of the shooting and early on the day the bodies were discovered, had yielded no useful clues.

Ariel was rewinding the film when it occurred to her to look for an obituary. Henry had said she'd been listed as surviving spouse, and morbid though it might be, she wanted to read it.

She was, indeed, named in the brief "survived by" information, along with Muriel Coskey Gold, mother, of San Diego. There'd been a private service locally, a request for donations "in lieu of flowers" to the same college that later benefited from the mother's death, and interment in San

Diego. Ariel was reaching for the rewind knob again when her eye was caught by the name "Arnold" five paragraphs above.

Creighton Arnold was born in Schenectady in 1929, she read, and died, as she knew, on March 14. He was a veteran of the Korean War, an active philanthropist and patron of the arts and an eminent businessman, whose interests ranged from real estate to motion pictures. He was "the beloved husband of Fiona."

Ariel stared at the name. Couldn't be. She reread the birth date. Arnold was sixty when he died. He'd be sixty-four if he were alive today. The Fiona who'd been married to Philip was surely not twenty years older than he? She thought of the photograph in their living room. That woman had looked about Philip's age. Of course, there was no way to know how old the photo was.

Ariel shook the whole ridiculous idea from her head. Pure coincidence, she thought. There must be hundreds of women named Fiona in Los Angeles. Well, dozens. Maybe.

The microfiche flapped off the reel, so hastily did Ariel rewind it before hurrying back to the reference desk. She submitted a request for every *Times* for the first week of February 1993. The obituary appeared on the 3rd.

The artistic accomplishments of the deceased were mentioned, as was her marriage to well-known actor Philip Carroll and the tragedy of her death of heart failure at fifty-two. The information was less detailed and, certainly, less gruesome than Neely's had been. The last paragraph, however, mentioned one thing the detective hadn't. Fiona Morgan's first husband had been a prominent New York businessman whose 1989 murder had never been solved.

Ariel sat in her car in the library parking lot for a full five minutes before she got back out, locked the door and returned to the reference section.

Who's Who in the Motion Picture Industry yielded the information that Philip Carroll had come to fame relatively recently. Beginning in 1986, he'd appeared in several made-for-TV movies and, later, feature films, the bit parts and supporting roles graduating to one or two leads during the run of the successful TV series in which he'd had a continuing role. The review blurbs were respectable, and some of the movie titles struck a faint chord of memory.

An article in a year-old *Us* was primarily pictorial and, her bleary eyes forgotten, Ariel examined each photograph dispassionately. One was a younger Philip at a famous Coronado hotel. What aging he'd done since he'd done well. Ariel thought he might even look better now, and a more recent full-face shot confirmed her opinion. A few lines into the text, she rechecked the photographs, thinking she'd somehow skipped into a different story.

According to the slick copy, Philip had experience in the legitimate theater—news to her—and he was interested in opera, the impressionists and fine wines. The first, Ariel conceded, was possible; the second was a surprise; and the third, she was sure, must be a misprint. She couldn't remember him ever drinking wine, let alone discoursing about it. This Philip Carroll had come from an old East Coast family active "in finance," and he'd graduated from an unnamed Ivy League school. "He did?" Ariel almost blurted aloud. Was her reading of his background that off base?

In *Cosmo* she found publicity shots of Philip in various roles: the suave Jared Toland of *Tulsa;* an unshaven drunk; a scar-faced racketeer; a white-haired, white-mustachioed scientist in a lab coat, clutching a test tube and staring with mad eyes. There were no pictures of Fiona Morgan.

That story glibly reported that Philip "relishes demanding character roles, which he researches assiduously," and that "before discovering a talent for acting," he'd been involved "in such diverse arenas as the hospitality industry and real estate." The implication was that he'd been successful. Ariel wondered what he'd really done all during his twenties and early thirties.

Feeling as if she'd been in the library for decades, Ariel returned the magazines and left, this time for good. She did manage to drive to the studio, although she couldn't have described any part of the trip. She wanted to talk to Henry.

So distracted was she that she'd completely forgotten her altered looks and the effect they might have on the receptionist, a blond, buxom, over-cosmeticized young woman named Tara.

Tara was no less distracted than Ariel, whom she eye-balled unashamedly. "Oh, wow, girlfriend," she said, "you look hot! I mean seriously hot!"

Ariel smiled her thanks and asked again where Henry was.

According to Tara, whose intelligence belied her looks as well as her unfortunate name, Henry had been called away on a personal emergency, to Catalina Island. She anticipated that he'd be out at least the rest of the day.

"I think his son's in some kind of trouble," she confided, still staring as she slashed open an envelope with an improbably long blood-red fingernail. "I sort of overheard him talking to his ex-wife."

Ariel could feel the receptionist's eyes on her back as she wandered into an edit bay and silently watched the fine-tuning of that night's program. It wasn't until the Macaulay segment came up that she made any real effort to concentrate.

She'd seen almost all the footage countless times, but the story had lost none of its poignancy for her. Even now, with half her mind on a four-year-old murder, a new enigma and some woman out there who might be her mother, she found it compelling. Ignoring the covert glances of a producer whose eyes kept zigzagging from the monitor to her face, she viewed a new cut, a screen test Jane had made during a short-lived fling in the movie business. She'd been offered a contract, Ariel had heard, and had turned it down.

Ariel acknowledged a number of insultingly incredulous compliments on her appearance, patted a couple of backs and gave a thumbs-up to an engineer who'd been particularly helpful to her personally. As she wandered out, she glanced again into Henry's office. It was still empty.

Braking at a red light on Santa Monica Boulevard, Ariel tried to bring her mind to bear on Philip Carroll. Her brain cells had all the acuity of pudding. For the twentieth time she went over the extraordinary set of circumstances in which she found herself. Dully, methodically, as if she were watching a slow-motion slide show, she clicked through the facts.

Fact number one, she was seeing a man whose wife had recently died and, two, she'd once asked a police detective for information about the death. Three, the deceased woman's first husband was murdered four years earlier alongside her own husband. Four, Philip had equivocated about one thing, and there was at least a reasonable chance that it wasn't the only thing. Five, whether or not he and Ariel had met previously and whether or not he knew she was amnesic—and for unknown reasons wasn't disclosing knowledge of either—surely he'd known the circumstances of Arnold's death, that the man killed with him was named Gold. Wasn't that coincidence worth even a footnote in a conversation?

And wouldn't that *bloody* light ever change! At that precise moment it did, but the traffic remained frozen. Her eyes smarting from carbon monoxide fumes, Ariel closed the window and looked up at the Mormon temple on her right. If the gilded, celestial figure perched atop it (Gabriel or Joseph Smith or whoever he was) knew anything helpful, he wasn't letting on.

Cursing the smog, the traffic and the dearth of answers, Ariel futilely searched her purse for something to wipe her eyes. She popped open the glove box. There were no tissues, but there was something better: a jury-rigged tape deck she hadn't known was there. When she'd last had the car, one-handed driving had required her full attention, but now diversion was just what she needed. There were even tapes, a half dozen or more. She glanced at the still-stalled traffic and picked one at random. It wouldn't go into the slot. Ariel pushed the ON button. Sure enough, there was a tape already in place. As it began to play, the gridlock broke, and she put her foot on the gas pedal. And nearly rear-ended the car in front of her.

The voice pouring out of the speakers was one she knew very well indeed. Philip Carroll had been caught in midsentence when the tape player had been turned off, and the first words Ariel heard were "... just as glad. The play closed after a week."

Ignoring the horns blaring behind her, Ariel signaled a

turn into the right-hand lane, squeezed in between a Saab and a garbage truck and peeled off into a liquor store parking lot. Behind her, a beige van immediately copied the tricky maneuver. Ariel, who at that particular moment wouldn't have noticed the Budweiser wagon and a full team of Clydesdales, was oblivious. The van drove slowly up a side street, made a U-turn and coasted to the curb. The driver had a clear view of the parking lot.

Ariel cut the engine and ejected the tape. A smudged, hand-printed label read "CARROLL—9/8/89." She plugged the tape back in and rewound it.

The only other voice was at some distance from the microphone. Although it was flat, muffled and somehow "off," it too was familiar. It was the voice on the answering machine at home, her own voice.

Well, she thought, her face as rigid as if it were carved from stone, that answers one question: Philip and I had met before.

She listened. This was an interview, she immediately realized, and it would've been conducted while she was still working for the newspaper. Philip, as shortly became apparent, had recently begun his stint on the nighttime soap that had been his springboard to success—and he'd just married Fiona Morgan. Only six months after her first husband's death, thought Ariel. Interesting.

Staring through the windshield but seeing neither the pedestrians nor the coagulated traffic, Ariel listened to the sonorous voice extol the show's plot, character development and gratifying ratings. Philip had even contrived to wedge in redeeming social values; one of the leads was being played by a Native American.

Ariel's own uninflected voice eventually dammed the flow of hype with a question about Philip's new bride.

"Oh, Fiona's a fine little artist," Philip had enthused. "We're both fortunate in our careers, Ariel, and she's so supportive of mine." He'd worked the conversation back around to himself with a minimum of words. So much for the fine little artist Fiona.

Minutes later, the interviewer had her back in the picture.

"Your wife had a tragedy in her life not long before you

met her—you hadn't met, had you, when her first husband was killed?"

Philip's voice became somber. "No, Ariel, we hadn't."

"Did you ever meet Creighton Arnold?"

"Why, no." Philip sounded puzzled at the turn the interview was taking. "Fiona and I were torn, as you can imagine, about marrying within a year of his death. There are, unfortunately, people who'll misconstrue."

Ariel felt her skin contract at the familiarity of the words. She rolled her window back down and breathed in exhaust fumes.

"But we accepted that it was meant to be," Philip's voice continued, "that we were alive and deserved the happiness we'd found."

Ariel-on-tape seemed to think just about as much of this drivel as did the live one.

"Wasn't there another man killed along with Mr. Arnold?"

Philip's tone had the merest edge of impatience. "Yes. Someone named Gold, I believe."

Another question answered, Ariel thought grimly as her taped voice asked, "Were their murders ever solved?"

"Unfortunately, no. Did you know that I once played the part of a detective . . ." The single-minded actor was back on track, and the rest of the tape was predictably Philip-focused. Rewinding it, Ariel wondered why he hadn't connected his interviewer's name with the second murder victim. Maybe she'd used a false name. Maybe she hadn't given her name. Maybe he was too egocentric to hear it.

That was hardly important now, she thought. The question was: why had the interview been conducted? Maybe it was one of many she'd done during those years, and no significance could be attached to it. Scratch that—the stories she'd found in the scrapbooks were all straight news; she'd been neither an entertainment writer nor a feature writer. And it wouldn't be in the car's tape deck on a fluke. Three and a half years later? Hardly. But the tape was innocuous. There'd been nothing said that was remotely damning, as far as she could tell.

Ariel started the car and drove around the lot to the less

congested side street. Heading north, she began replaying the tape. When she'd gone two blocks, the beige van made another U-turn and followed, allowing a car to feed in between them.

At the intersection of Wilshire and Sepulveda Ariel hit the rewind button. After several attempts she found where the tape had been originally positioned. She listened to that portion again. And a third time.

When she reached home, she didn't stop; she drove straight to Marguerite Harris's house.

forty-three

If you wanted to find out something about a certain unsuccessful Broadway play," Ariel asked, "how would you go about it?"

She'd found her neighbor in her book-filled, paper-strewn study hunched over her computer. Marguerite exited the file with the smallest noticeable regret and faced her unexpected guest.

"Like what, for example?"

"Like who was in the cast, mainly. And what it was about."

"What was the name of the play?" Marguerite was already as involved in the conversation as she'd been in the work she'd set aside.

"Flying Blind. It was staged, I think, in the eighties. Probably early eighties."

"But I remember it!" Marguerite popped from her chair. "I even know who wrote it! Just give me a minute . . ." She ran her finger across a row of books on the far wall of the study and, halfway down, took one from the shelf.

"Who's Who in the Theatre," she exulted, flipping through to the *F*s. "This is the playbill edition, and I think it'll tell us what we want to know."

After a few seconds' perusal, however, she slammed the book shut and replaced it. "Didn't run long enough, I guess." *The Book of 1000 Plays* yielded the same lack of results.

"Look here, though, I can get the information easily enough," Marguerite said, consulting a man-sized, gadget-packed wristwatch, "but not now. It's nearly ten o'clock in New York, and Frank's an early-to-bedder."

"Frank?"

"Eberhardt. You've heard of him? *Flying Blind* was the only flopperoo he ever wrote. I never saw it, but Frank and his wife Betsy are good friends of ours, and I can get what you want tomorrow morning. How's that?"

"Let me ask you this. . . ." Ariel stopped to think. "What if someone, one of the supporting actors, didn't actually appear in the play? If he left the production the day before the play opened? Would his name still be in the playbill?"

Marguerite considered. "Well, I don't suppose they could get the playbills reprinted overnight. They'd just announce that the stand-in was assuming the role for the first few performances. Do you want to tell me what this is about?"

Ariel thought about it. Seriously. She decided she wanted to talk to Henry first.

"As soon as we get the information—or as soon as I can see if it means anything. Do you think there's any way at all I could find a copy of the original playbill?"

The elderly woman gave Ariel a flinty look. Clearly, she wasn't thrilled by the all give and no take. "I can almost guarantee it," she conceded. "Betsy saves the first-night programs of all Frank's plays. She's a one-woman fan club, and I imagine she also has every review about every play he ever wrote. I'll call first thing tomorrow, and if she has the playbill, I'll ask her to fax it. But"—her look turned cagey—"you'll need to tell me the actor's name. I can hardly ask her to fax the whole thing, can I?"

"Would you?" Ariel smiled sweetly. "Just the section with the cast and the bios. And the actors' pictures, of course. Tell her I'll insist on paying for it. Please?"

Marguerite snorted. "I don't think we have to worry about that; Frank Eberhardt's rolling in money. I'll call you when I get the fax, and then you have twenty-four hours to give me a full accounting of all this mystery. I mean it!"

Ariel drove the short distance home lost in thought, frustration and anxiety. The man behind the wheel of the van a hundred yards down the street watched her drive into her garage and enter the house. When he saw the garage door descend and, a few seconds later, the curtains drawn closed, he settled himself comfortably and picked up his car phone.

The subject of his call set her alarm with more heed than usual, gave Jessie a mere pat in passing, and strode to the tape deck in the bedroom. Finding the relevant section of the tape didn't take long; she'd almost memorized it by now. It was just after Philip had deflected the interview from the murders of Arnold and Michael back to himself, and it was Ariel's distinct impression now that he'd immediately regretted the tactic. Her own taped voice was picked up in midsentence.

"—thought I'd prepared for this interview, that I'd familiarized myself with all your roles, but I don't remember your ever playing a detective."

"Well, strictly speaking, I didn't play it." Philip's laugh sounded a little forced, Ariel thought. "There were, um, artistic differences, and I left the production the day before opening. With hindsight, I was just as glad. The play closed after a week."

"I didn't know you'd ever done live theater. Was this here?"

"New York."

"What was the name of the play?"

"Flying Blind." Philip's answers had become curt, and she'd been quick to scent the unease.

"When was that?"

"It was a few years ago, um, Ariel, and it really isn't one of my happiest memories. Let's get back to something more interesting, shall we? Did I show you the—"

As he returned to promoting his TV series, Ariel shut off the machine. Maybe something, she thought, maybe nothing, but it was the only thing on the tape that was remotely provocative.

Antsy as an aspen, she dialed Henry's home number. His recorded message was terse; she left one no less terse. Tapping the plastic receiver, she tried to think if there was anything further she could do. Victor wouldn't be back until tomorrow, and there was no point in leaving another message for him. For now, it seemed, she was at a dead end. Suddenly, she looked at her watch with a start. She'd missed the first two minutes of *The Open File*.

When the phone rang nearly an hour later, the closing credits were still scrolling and Ariel, worrying a cracked fingernail nervously, was second-guessing a couple of editing decisions and watching for her name. She picked up the bedside extension. Her hello brought no response but heavy breathing, and she was just about to slam down the receiver when she realized it was B. F., finding it difficult to get started.

"That was well done," he was eventually able to say. "Let's hope it brings somebody out of the woodwork. Somebody who saw something."

"I'm kind of surprised you watched it." Ariel felt her own throat closing. "I'm glad . . . I'm relieved if you thought it was handled sensitively."

"Yes. Well, that's all I wanted to say. Except take care of yourself. And take me up on my offer now that the show's done." He pulled a Henry Heller and hung up without a good-bye.

Ariel found a tissue and wiped her eyes. She went into the kitchen, made herself a cup of Earl Grey and found the number of Rachel Mulkerne's Santa Barbara friend. This time, she was at home and she was helpful. Without giving herself time to change her mind or even think about it, Ariel placed a call to Spokane, Washington.

"Who did you say this is?" Rachel Mulkerne didn't sound like the doddering "sixty-something" Mrs. Teasdale had envisioned; she sounded like a shocked and alert middle-aged woman.

"Ariel Munson was my maiden name, Ms. Mulkerne."

Ariel forced herself to breathe normally.

"You may remember my adoptive mother, Gladys Munson. You visited her, and me, several times in the early sixties?"

"Well, I'll be . . . ! I don't believe this. Ariel Munson! Oh, my stars! Oh, hold on a minute."

Ariel heard snufflings and a sound like a nose being vigorously blown. Well, she thought, at least she didn't hang up. In fact, she'd sounded thrilled. In moments Rachel was back on the line, her voice nasal, disbelieving and—Ariel hadn't been mistaken—thrilled.

"I just can't believe this! I don't think I'd be any more surprised if Ed McMahon came to the door with a check in his hand. How are you, honey? Where are you calling from? Good glory, you must be in your thirties now!"

Ariel opened her mouth and closed it abruptly. She was being asked her age? She hadn't known what to expect from this phone call, certainly, but this wasn't tracking.

"Uh, yes," she agreed. "Thirty-one."

"I just can't . . ." The voice halted. "Well, I know you probably don't remember me, so I won't keep going on like this. Tell me about yourself! How'd you find me? How's your mother? Why are you calling after all these—"

The voice broke off again, and there followed a deep, profound silence. "Oh, dear," Rachel Mulkerne said, "you're trying to find your parents, aren't you. Your biological parents."

"Ms. Mulkerne, forgive me. I'm very confused. I thought that—Who exactly are you?"

Gently, warily, Rachel suggested that Ariel explain how she'd found her and precisely why she was calling. Ariel did so, without interruption. When she'd finished, she heard a wheeze of breath being exhaled.

"Oh, honey," Rachel said, "I'm not your mother."

The two words carried a quality of sympathy or dismay that Ariel couldn't interpret.

"I was your foster mother for a little while, before you were adopted. I'm so sorry to disappoint you."

"Oh. I see." Ariel made up her mind to ignore the numbing sadness that settled over her like a weight. She forced determination into her voice.

"Is it possible that you could tell me anything about my mother? About my parents?"

Rachel Mulkerne's reply was a long time coming, and

Ariel braced herself for ignorance or rejection. She got neither.

"There's not a lot I can tell you," Rachel said, "but I'll tell you what I can. I don't see any reason not to." Her decision made, she got down to business. "Where'd you say you're calling from, Ariel?"

"Los Angeles. I still live here."

"I don't suppose you could come up here to Spokane? So we could talk in person?"

"I could," Ariel said, "but I couldn't do it for a while. Would you be willing to talk to me now? Please?"

Rachel sighed heavily. When she spoke again, her voice was filled with pity. "I can tell you you're not going to find your mom." There was a silence, a waiting for permission to continue.

"She's . . . not living, then?" Ariel wasn't entirely surprised by the news, but she was surprised by how much worse she could feel than she already did.

"No, honey, she died not too long after you were born, from what I was told. Let me explain this, how I know what little I do."

Ariel waited.

"You were the first of my foster children, Ariel, and one of the last. I found out I wasn't cut out for that scene. It was too painful," Rachel said simply.

"But about you, what happened was this. There was this young woman who'd known your parents, who'd been in a commune with them, she said, where they all lived. Well, she and two men followed your trail to my house somehow. I don't know how, so don't ask. They were in one of those painted vans—are you old enough to remember those?— and I saw it drive by two or three times, with loud music playing and these really scuzzy-looking people in it. When they stopped at my house, I called the police. I had a baby in my care, and I wasn't taking any chances, you know what I mean?"

Rachel stopped for a minute, gathering her thoughts.

"Well, I made the mistake of opening my door. I had one of those chain guards—you know?—so I thought it was safe. One of the men just popped it like it was string. They forced

317

their way in and found you. The woman wasn't mean—well, none of them was, really. They just acted like they had a right to you. Anyway, she was pretty spaced-out, as they said in those days, but she seemed like she wanted me to understand. She said you were her 'sister's' baby and that she'd died. I don't think she meant a real sister; you know how those flower children were. This woman claimed she and her 'brothers' owed it to this 'sister' and to your daddy to get you back."

Excited, Ariel asked, "What did she say about my father?"

"That was all, honey, except something about his not being there when the authorities took you . . . well, she didn't use the word 'authorities.' I cleaned that up. These people didn't have much use for the establishment, let me tell you!"

"What else?" Ariel prodded. "What else did she say?"

"She didn't get the chance to say anything else because the police got there then. When they saw the situation, they put all three of them in handcuffs and took them right out. It was one of the scariest things that ever happened to me."

"Did you ever hear any more about them? About what became of them?"

"No. But you'd think if they were put on trial, I'd have been called to testify, wouldn't you? So I don't know if they were put in jail or what."

"But this . . . hippie woman . . . told you that my mother was dead?" Ariel was trying hard to assimilate the information.

"Yes," Rachel said. "She acted almost like you were hers, though. I guess that's the way it was in communes."

"I don't suppose you know her name? Or could tell me anything that would help me find her?"

"I wish I could, but that's all I remember. Well . . . that's not true."

"What?" Ariel's heart thumped disturbingly.

"I can tell you what she called you."

"What she . . . ? You mean she told you my real name?"

"Well, not the last name. And she didn't really *tell* me

the first one. But when they found you in the playpen, what she said was 'Jessie!' "

Ariel's mouth dropped open. Dumbfounded, she stared at the dog at her feet. Her namesake returned the look curiously.

"Oh, for the . . . ! That's . . . extraordinary!"

Unaware of the consternation her news had caused, Rachel continued, apologetically.

"You were adopted a few months later, and I was as bad as the hippie woman. Young and green. What I did—visiting—was against all the regulations, but I couldn't let you go—boom!—just like that! Never know if you were being loved. I made up this story, but your mom saw through it. She was so glad to have you, she couldn't help sharing her joy with somebody else who loved you, and I knew she'd never report me. I've taken care of lots of kids since then, one way and another, but—I guess it was because you were the first—you were special."

Ariel struggled to regain her composure, to think sensibly. Her eyes still riveted on the shepherd, she asked, "Rachel, when did those people come to your house? What date, do you know?"

"Oh my, honey! Let's see. What year were you born?"

"1961. In June, according to my birth certificate."

"Okay, you were about a year and a half old when I got you, and I hadn't had you but a little while. It was in the winter, I remember . . . Oh! It was December, sometime close to Christmas, because I had a tree! So that would've been 'sixty-two."

"What did the woman look like? Can you tell me anything else about her?"

"She looked like all those people. Long hair. Funny clothes. She was young, maybe nineteen or twenty. The men had long hair, too, but the only thing I remember about them was how much they scared me."

"Where were you living then?"

Rachel gave her an address in Culver City, with only a slight uncertainty about the house number.

Ariel couldn't think of anything else to ask. She was having considerable difficulty thinking at all.

319

"Thank you for telling me all this, Rachel," she said. "I know you didn't have to. And we *will* meet soon. That's a promise."

The night that followed was interminable.

Her glance kept returning to Jessie. What phenomenon of vestigial memory, Ariel marveled, had pulled that name from the hat? It was ironic indeed that she'd once, albeit unknowingly, dredged up a name last heard when she was less than two years old, and now she couldn't remember the previous month.

Ariel paced and tried to read. She checked her alarm system and all the locks twice, calling herself foolish but doing it anyway. Settling on the bed, she watched an old *Combat* segment, sat through but didn't register *The Tonight Show* and was finally, marginally, absorbed by Bette Davis's transformation in *Now, Voyager*. When at last she turned off the bedside lamp, the clock's red numbers clicked over with agonizing slowness. Ariel was sure she didn't miss a single click.

forty-four

Ariel awakened to find that she had, in fact, missed quite a few clicks of the clock. She remembered seeing four-thirty creep by; she remembered a bleary five o'clock. When she'd next looked at the detested red numbers, they read ten-fifteen.

Fighting tangled sheets, she leaped from bed and opened the curtains. Sunlight poured into the bedroom. After splashing her face with cold water—a great quantity of which ended up on her pajamas—she went to the answering machine. It was mute, the message light unblinking. Her heart slowing to what passed for a normal pace these days, Ariel made coffee and went through her usual morning routine, one ear cocked. When the phone rang just after eleven, however, it was neither Marguerite, Henry nor Victor.

"Ariel, hi!" exclaimed Tara, the studio receptionist. "Let

me tell you again how hot you looked yesterday! Will you give me the name of your beautician? I mean, what a miracle worker!"

"Thanks," Ariel said dryly. "I'll give you the number next time I'm down there. What can I do for you, Tara?"

"Mr. Heller called in. He said to apologize for not getting back to you, but there was a complication with his son, and they're still over on Catalina. The kid is in trouble; I was right. But he's not the problem. The problem's the father of the other little boy. One of the kid's front teeth was knocked loose in the fight, and the father's screaming lawsuit."

"Good heavens." Ariel was distracted despite herself. "Sam was in a fight? Did Henry tell you all that?"

"Of course not." Tara didn't elaborate further. "But he did say he ought to be back by late afternoon, and he'd call you then."

The Call Waiting beep sounded, and Ariel excused herself. This time, it was Marguerite.

"I'll have your fax within the hour. Why don't you come on over now, though, and look at something I already have for you."

The beige van was no longer there when Ariel rushed from her house, still zipping her warm-up jacket. However, an equally undistinguished Subaru was now parked sixty feet away, facing the opposite direction.

Minutes later, Ariel was sitting in Marguerite's living room with a cup of coffee, watching through the open windows as Carl mowed the lawn. Thinking he was probably the only man on earth who still used a rotary mower, she inhaled the scent of freshly cut grass with no accompanying gasoline fumes.

Later, she remembered those last few minutes of peace.

"I'm embarrassed to tell you," Marguerite said, thumping a thick book as she came back into the room, "but I had part of what you needed last night. I'd forgotten until Frank reminded me this morning, much to my chagrin." She sat down beside Ariel.

The Mystery and Suspense Plays of Frank Eberhardt. A gift from the playwright, personally autographed. And, voila . . . !" She opened to a previously marked page and handed the book to Ariel. "See anything—or anybody—interesting?"

Ariel read the introductory page of *Flying Blind*. She saw that it was first produced at the Cuthbert Theater in New York on November 21, 1985. She scanned the cast names; there were a couple she knew, but there was no Philip Carroll. Her eyes returned to the playwright's name, and what she saw beneath that stopped her cold. The play had been "presented" by two men, and one of them was Creighton Arnold.

Her "Could I . . . ?" came out a croak. Ariel licked her lips, cleared her throat and, still staring at the name, breathed, "Could I possibly borrow this?"

"I assumed you'd want to. And the Eberhardts are faxing the cast information from the first performance. 'The first of a forgettable few,' as Frank said. I'd have had it earlier, but they were out meeting with their accountants when I called. Tax time, you—" Marguerite stopped, and Ariel, too, heard the faint ringing from the direction of the study.

"No sooner said." Marguerite scurried from the room.

Ariel was seven pages into the script when Marguerite returned shuffling a number of flimsy sheets into order.

"Count yourself lucky," she said, "that Betsy had more than one playbill, or she'd never have been willing to cut one up to send through her machine."

Ariel took the sheaf in unsteady hands and quickly scanned each page. When she came to "Detective Lieutenant Tom Farley," her heart begin to hammer. The clarity of the photograph had suffered in transmission, and the face was different—there was a thick moustache, for one thing—but there was a definite resemblance. Subtract seven years from the present Philip Carroll, she thought, and he'd look something like the photo she held. She looked at the actor's name and frowned in surprise. She felt a stab of disappointment, mixed with relief.

"What's the matter?" Marguerite frowned in empathy.

"I would've sworn . . ." Ariel held out the page. "I know Philip was cast in this role, but the name listed is Adam Shaw."

Marguerite glanced at the smiling actor. "Who's Philip?"

"Philip Carroll," Ariel said, grim-faced. "Do you know who he is?"

Marguerite gave first Ariel, then the picture, a sharp look.

"What do you think?" Ariel asked.

"It's possible. No, it's *im*possible to tell from this. Ariel, what's going on? Is this a story you're working on, or is something wrong? What's Philip Carroll got to do with you?"

Ariel took the photo back. "It is, in a way, a story I'm looking into. Will you do me another favor? Will you call Mr. Eberhardt and let me talk to him?"

Abruptly, Marguerite left the room again, returning this time with a portable phone and a Rolodex card. Wordlessly, her eyes glued to Ariel, she dialed and a few seconds later spoke into the phone.

"Betsy, hi. Thanks for the fax. We're looking through it now. Is Frank still there? Could I talk to him for a minute?"

"Frank," she said after a short wait. "Yes, I know: we don't talk for ages and then it's twice in one day. Listen, I have my friend here, the young woman I told you about, and she'd like to ask you some questions. All right?" To what was apparently a question, she shook her head. "No idea. She's being very mysterious, but I'm not going to get any answers, I can tell, until she gets some from you. Her name's Ariel. Hold on." One eyebrow raised, she handed over the phone.

"Mr. Eberhardt." Ariel gave Marguerite a nod and thanked the playwright verbally. "I won't take much of your time. I'm looking at the photograph of the actor who played the detective in your play. The character's name was Tom Farley and the actor, according to this, was an Adam Shaw. Do you by any chance remember him?"

Ariel listened for a moment and said, "I understand that. But do you remember this man Shaw?"

Several minutes into a long reply, Ariel closed her eyes. Her hand tightened on the telephone.

"I won't repeat it," she eventually said. "I promise. No, I understand. Could you do something for me? Could you—would you—overnight the original of that page from the

323

playbill to me?" She nodded. "Yes, just that one page is all I need. Thank you."

Ariel recited her address and engaged in a short argument about expenses, each insisting on paying. Then she asked one other favor, stressing the urgency, before handing the phone back to Marguerite.

While the old friends were saying their good-byes, she stood and walked to the window.

Outside, Carl emptied grass clippings into a trash barrel. The lawn looked fresh and green, the sky was a glorious blue and Ariel felt like Chicken Little. The illusion of security she'd come to trust had shattered into a thousand pieces, and every nerve in her body was a live wire.

Frank Eberhardt had remembered Adam Shaw, all right. "You don't forget an actor who walks the day before opening," he'd told her, "particularly an unknown getting his first break! They don't do that, believe me. They'd kill to get a role, and I've never heard of another one saying *sayonara* when he got it."

Shaw had not only left the production but, as far as the playwright knew, the world of New York theater. Eberhardt had never heard of him again. But what he *had* heard was that Shaw had been "engaging in a dalliance" with the wife of one of the play's producers, that his having been cast was said to be due to the wife's influence, and that the cuckolded producer had cottoned on to the affair. Word had gotten around, he'd chuckled, that the actor was told to get the hell out of Dodge—or else.

"That's strictly backstage gossip," Eberhardt had cautioned, "as was a rumor that Shaw was blackballed. I wouldn't normally give either story much credence, but it's hard to believe this guy would've quit unless he'd been forced to—or dropped dead. Speaking of which, I'll bet you've heard of the producer ..."

Eberhardt had just then remembered that the producer in question had, in fact, dropped dead rather dramatically.

"Didn't you read about that?" he'd asked. "Big-shot businessman named Creighton Arnold? He was murdered a few years back, and if I'm not mistaken, it was out there. In L.A."

"A penny," said Marguerite after hanging up the phone. She was watching Ariel with a worried expression on her face.

"I've got to sort it out." Ariel turned from the window reluctantly. "And I want to read the play, although I don't really expect it to be of any pertinence at this point."

Ariel reassured her friend and walked home, the book under her arm. It was a powder keg waiting for her to light the fuse.

Halfway through *Flying Blind,* Ariel knew what Victor had said that had been eluding her, the little telltale fact that hadn't jibed. When she closed the book, she knew how Fiona Morgan had really died. And she knew who'd killed her. What she didn't know was why, and what she also didn't know was how to prove it.

She was staring a hole through the living room rug, weighing her options, when the telephone brought her to her feet and squarely back to the present.

Victor was all apology for having taken so long to return her call, but he'd been in the operating room all morning, and another emergency had been waiting when he'd emerged. He was about to embark on a full description of the cyanotic, bee-stung Yorkie when Ariel interrupted.

"Victor, I'd love to hear about it another time, but I'm really in kind of a crunch right now. Tell me, do you remember when I got Jessie?"

"Well, my word, Ariel, don't you?"

"Please humor me, Victor; it's important. How long did it take you to reach Fiona Morgan's husband after she died? Was it right away?"

"Within a couple of days, anyway."

"And I told you specifically that I was going to call him, isn't that right?"

"To get the dog's papers, yes. Is this something about Jessie's ownership? Is there some problem?"

She'd had two full weeks in which to contact Philip, Ariel thought, before she'd woken up in never-never land.

"This next question is even more important, Victor, okay? You remember describing how Jessie came to be at the ken-

325

nel when Fiona Morgan died? How she brought Jessie in to board her?"

"Ariel—"

"Why was Jessie boarded?"

"Because Mrs. Morgan was going out of town, and she didn't want to leave the dog alone." Victor sounded as if he were dealing with a lunatic. "The reason most people board their pets."

Ariel closed her eyes and took a deep breath. "You're absolutely sure she said she was going out of town?"

"Ariel, are you okay?"

"Victor, please."

"That's what she said, yes. Good grief, Ariel, that was ages ago. Why is this important now?"

Ariel played with the phone cord, thinking furiously. "Wouldn't you have a record of when she was there? Exactly?"

"I'd have the date she brought Jess in, sure."

"Would you look it up?"

Victor said something that sounded like a complete non sequitur until Ariel realized he was talking to someone in his office.

"Ariel, I've got to go. I'll have to call you back. I'll look up the date and get back to you as soon as I can."

She put down the phone in frustration and immediately picked it up again. She called Marguerite and asked if she could have Frank Eberhardt's number.

"Well, hello again," the playwright said when she'd identified herself. "I just got your package off, and I've made a start at the other, at checking into the blacklisting rumors as you asked. No luck yet, though."

Ariel explained what else she wanted to know, apologizing for bothering him again.

"No bother. Matter of fact, it's intriguing. And gratifying. I always liked that play, and I never understood why it didn't go. The problem, I think, was with character development. Anyway, that's not what you called to hear about. Let me think. In fact, let me get my working notes from when I was writing it. Hold on."

"Okay," he said when he returned, "you want to know if

the murder scenario would play today, in real life. *Flying Blind* was set in the late forties, when they didn't have security checkpoints in airports. So you'd have to find out whether checked luggage is subjected to X ray these days. I don't know the answer to that, but I do know one thing that could be a problem: they have a test for insulin overdose now. If there was reason to suspect murder, a careful medical examiner might just find the needle mark, and he could test tissue at the site and find traces of the insulin. But, on the other hand, if the injection was made somewhere unlikely—between the buttocks, for example—with the really fine-gauge needles available now, odds are no mark would be found, especially if they weren't looking specifically for it. So, I'd say the only thing the killer would really have to worry about is more sophisticated crime-scene technology."

"Like what?" Ariel was madly scribbling notes.

"Like lividity. You know, livor mortis. The blood settles in the vessels of the lowest parts of the body a few hours after death, and the killer couldn't move the body until lividity was fixed. Then he'd have to be very careful to rearrange the body exactly as it was when lividity ensued because even a slight shift in position might be noticed. I guess it could be done." Eberhardt's voice quickened with inspiration, "The killer could, maybe, take Polaroids of the body from every angle and then refer to them after he moved the body."

"What about rigor mortis?"

"Yes, well, I didn't go into a lot of detail in the script, but that's tricky. As I said, you've had to wait until lividity's fixed and by then the body's pretty well stiff, so you've got to wait for rigor to pass before you pack the body, and you're fighting time—the onset of decay. The timetable can vary a lot, but it can be helped along. Did you want exact numbers on this or are you thinking in general terms?"

"Oh, I need to be very specific," Ariel assured him.

When Eberhardt had detailed the pertinent information, Ariel put down her pencil and said, "One more thing. Do you know the actor Philip Carroll?"

"Well, I know *of* him. Why?"

"Would you say that he and Shaw could be the same man?"

"More and more intriguing," Frank Eberhardt said. "I

couldn't say, but I can't wait for the denouement—which will be soon, I hope?"

When Ariel had hung up, she was even more convinced that she was right. Philip had finally appeared in the play he'd been forced out of, a play no one remembered he'd ever been in, a play that was hardly remembered at all. But this time it had been staged for real. A deadly plagiarism.

She sat down and began to write out everything she knew, as well as all the unanswered questions—of which there were too many for comfort.

On the plus side, she'd caught Philip in a number of lies, explicit and implicit. He'd known Fiona Morgan (in the biblical sense, probably) long before her first husband's death. He'd known Arnold. He'd met Ariel herself, definitely three and a half years ago and probably again little more than a month ago. It was conceivable that he'd forgotten the first time but, unless he was amnesic, too, he'd hardly have forgotten the more recent meeting. And, for what it was worth, he knew that her dead husband's name was Gold, the name of the man who'd died with Arnold.

And what, pray tell, was Philip's real name? Would an unknown actor named Adam Shaw who couldn't get hired in New York reemerge as an unknown actor named Philip Carroll in California? That was one question that might be answered tomorrow when the clearer photo arrived.

There were other questions. Had the backstage gossip about him and Fiona been true? Ariel had few doubts, in view of their later marriage. If he had killed his wife, why? She was filthy rich, for a start. By Philip's own admission it hadn't been a happy marriage, and he'd certainly wasted no time in resuming his social life—she herself could testify to that! But, just maybe, there was another reason.

Ariel came to her feet and paced the room like a housebound cougar. What if Philip had killed Arnold, too? Somebody did. And the murder took place in Los Angeles, where Philip lived. And just maybe Fiona had known about it, had held it over his head. But why would he have waited so long to kill her? She sat back down and scribbled more notes, more questions.

What would have been his motive for killing Arnold? The

murder occurred just about the time Philip was up for the TV series that made his career. If Arnold had once had Philip squeezed out in the East, would he do it again in the West? Would an actor kill to keep that from happening? Frank Eberhardt hadn't meant it literally when he said an aspiring actor would kill for a part, but what if the actor then also got to marry the victim's wife and come into a fortune? A double play. Ariel liked it.

The portable phone shrilled. Her elbow, jerking reflexively, almost knocked it off the table before she grabbed it.

It was one of Victor's receptionists, a girl named Lucy whom Ariel vaguely remembered from her Saturday volunteer work at the orphans' kennel.

"Dr. Pollock said to call," the clear young voice of Lucy said. "He's swamped. It's a real zoo around here today. Haha. Veterinarians' office humor. He said you wanted to know when Ms. Morgan brought your dog in, right? I've got the log here, and it's like I said when you asked before. She arranged to board Jessie for the one night, and she left her January thirtieth at twelve-fifty P.M."

Ariel calculated. That would've been two and a half days before her body was discovered in her home in Los Angeles. Perfect.

She was thanking Lucy and trying to get off the phone when she got an unexpected bonus.

"I talked to her that day, you remember?" Lucy's voice was sad, but there was also a tinge of the vulture.

"To Fiona Morgan?" Ariel asked.

"I can't get over that I might even have been one of the last people to talk to her! The poor woman was so happy and so excited. And so worried that she was running late and might miss her plane to New York. Did you ever figure out why she didn't go straight to the airport? Why she went back home?"

"New York?" Ariel hardly dared to believe her luck. "She said she was going to New York?"

"Uh-huh. Like I told you the last time you asked," said Lucy.

When she'd ascertained that Lucy knew no more, Ariel hung up. Got him! she thought. Should she call the police?

Neely, maybe? She paced in excitement. No, not until she had the photograph. It was Henry she wanted to talk to now.

Magically, the telephone rang. Henry! She snatched it up. She said hello three times to dead silence and then heard a dial tone. She carefully replaced the receiver.

Suddenly, she couldn't stand the confinement of the four walls a second longer. She clipped on Jessie's lead and left her house, unaware that the beige van had returned.

It was parked at the very end of the street in a hedge-shrouded driveway. The house beyond was empty and, from its weathered appearance, the "For Sale" sign in the yard had been there for some time. As the preoccupied Ariel strode away, the driver lowered his binoculars and turned on the motor.

The focus of his attention walked the considerable length and breadth of the neighborhood, her mind churning even faster than her legs.

Where—she kept coming back to the question—did Michael Gold fit into the picture? Okay, he was Creighton Arnold's attorney, presumably only one of many, considering Arnold's multifaceted enterprises. But how could his death have benefited Philip?

Ariel stopped dead in her tracks. It wasn't the late-afternoon temperature drop that caused her to shiver. Maybe, she thought, the police had gotten the Gold-Arnold murder backward. Maybe Arnold had been the intended victim, and Michael had been the innocent bystander who happened to be with the wrong man at the wrong time.

And she'd been Michael's devoted wife, an investigative reporter and expert researcher. Who'd interviewed Philip immediately after he'd married Creighton Arnold's widow (and who'd learned about *Flying Blind* in that interview). Who'd begun patronizing a certain vet at the same time Philip's wife had (coincidence or a ploy to get close to her?) and who, immediately after the wife's death, had jumped at the chance to take ownership of her dog (another coincidence or a legitimate reason to renew contact with Philip?).

She looked at the patiently waiting Jessie. Well, she'd gotten one thing out of the bargain, anyway.

In that moment the significance of her speculations dawned on Ariel, turning her even colder.

Wasn't it reasonable, even unavoidable, to believe she'd put at least this much together before she'd lost her memory? And if Philip knew that then, he still did.

Her feet flying, she made for home.

Henry had left a message in her absence.

Ariel groaned. You might know he'd call the minute she left the house! She listened to the recording, barely able to distinguish his words over the traffic noises in the background. Worse, he sounded as if he'd caught a cold. He was on the road, he said, and couldn't be reached. He wanted her to meet him later, at six-thirty, at Anthony's. Anthony's? Ariel wondered. A new lead on the Macaulay story? Something that sounded like an eighteen-wheeler thundered by on the tape, and part of Henry's next sentence was obliterated. She rewound and, straining, listened again. She heard the word "important," a roar, and then "If I'm late, wait." Whatever followed was lost, except for the last word. Henry had actually said good-bye before he hung up. Would wonders never cease!

Ariel hit rewind and checked the time. 4:43. She called the studio and, as advertised, Henry wasn't there. After leaving word confirming that she'd gotten his message, she hauled out the phone book. A great many calls later, she turned to a fresh page on her notepad and began rewriting all her jottings into a methodical and, she was satisfied, damning précis.

forty-five

The plan was proceeding even more smoothly than he'd hoped, even more smoothly than last time.

Unwilling to trust the blow-by-blow description he remembered from Rodriquez, he'd made a trip to a bookstore. He'd found the technical information he required with ease, in a remarkably informative—and readily available—book called *Armed to Kill*. Rodriquez, he was surprised to discover, had been accurate.

As to the bait, he considered simply repeating what he'd done before. Pretending to be a friend calling for Heller had worked well enough, and in her present state Ariel wouldn't remember. But he'd improved on the ploy, and enjoyed it.

He'd telephoned Heller the previous morning, refusing to give his name but claiming to have information on a recent *Open File* segment. He'd hemmed and hawed and backpedaled and asked many nervous questions about confidentiality. He'd made the man increasingly irritated. He'd also gotten Heller's voice on the tape recorder he'd connected to the telephone.

He'd practiced until he was confident he had the nuances of the voice down pat, the timbre mastered. For an actor of his ability it wasn't that demanding a feat.

Then he'd checked out the restaurant parking lot, which was still as poorly lighted as it had been three weeks before. Some people, he thought, never learn.

Today's most crucial arrangement had been laughably easily. He'd placed the call to Ariel, prepared to deliver his invitation. Never had he been better rehearsed or more up for a role. And then he'd had an inspiration: he'd take his act on the road. Softly, appreciating his little joke, he'd depressed the "disconnect" button.

That she'd left the house before he called again was even better.

He'd driven to a pay phone at a busy intersection. The one-way conversation, held against a backdrop of distracting noise, had been so simple it was almost a letdown. There was no doubt in his mind that the woman would be at the appointed place at the appointed time. Her accursed curiosity would guarantee it—again.

Finally, he'd received a marvelous, unforeseen bonus. Heller was out of town and unavailable to muddy the waters. Getting and keeping Heller out of the picture had been the chanciest part of the plan, and now it wasn't even necessary. If the man had been a partner, he couldn't have been more cooperative!

It really was, he mused, as if this were all preordained, as if it had been given the benediction of his own special gods. That Ariel had been investigating the Macaulay incident was nothing if not providential. It would be natural to conclude that she'd learned too much, that she'd been eliminated because she was getting too close to the killer. The fact that he hadn't even known the Macaulays made it flawless. It was a wonderful piece of irony that Rodriquez's stupidity in killing a perfect stranger had provided the pièce de résistance of the plan.

There was, he'd calculated, yet another curious twist possible. According to the *Open File* segment, police were stymied by the Macaulay woman's death—no motive, no viable suspects—and were leaning toward the theory that it was a case of mistaken identity. She'd been driving a car almost identical to Ariel's. She'd died at the same location and in the same manner that Ariel would die. After tonight, the police might conceivably conclude that Ariel had been the target all along, and he was comfortable with that. Time had proved there was nothing to connect them previously, and there was nothing of consequence now. The truth itself could provide another diversion to keep the police confused.

He laughed aloud. Pulling the strings of all the little puppets on his stage was amusing. He regretted that no one else would be able to admire the Machiavellian niceties of his planning, but then he'd always been alone. Alone and apart. It was one's lot when one had no peers. Alone, he'd consummated plans far more complex. Alone, he'd sustained the most exquisite manipulation for years.

As he proceeded with his preparations for the evening, he remembered those years and their beginning, when he'd made a woman whose only sin was her passion for him an accessory to murder. It had taken infinite subtlety to convince her that murder had been her idea. It had taken endless patience to sow the seeds of guilt and cultivate them; to insulate her, cutting her off from friends one by one; to keep her so off-balance with the reward of approval, the punishment of withholding, that she'd come to believe day was night, truth an illusion.

For three years he'd wielded his weapons with precision. Her vulnerability about her age. His "sacrifice" of fatherhood because of it. His increasing popularity, particularly with women. Her poor health. And then, when he'd achieved almost complete dominance, with the money in his control, he'd begun to notice subtle changes in her demeanor. He'd catch her staring at him, her eyes troubled, doubting, sharper. One moment she'd seem preoccupied, shying away from his touch, the next she'd crave it, mute fingers pleading for reassurance.

He'd watched and he'd listened. Soon he'd learned the reason for the changes. Ariel Gold.

He hadn't even remembered her. She'd been such a non-entity that he'd long since forgotten her and her wretched interview. Then the relentless woman had turned up again. Sneaking around behind his back, undermining his influence, playing the sympathetic friend, she'd gotten too close to the truth. He'd been forced to act, and act he had. Brilliantly. The seeds planted in three patient years had come to fruition.

Oh, if he could live through those interminable hours in New York, he could certainly handle this evening.

Tonight Ms. Gold would pay dearly for her interference. Soon his little drama would reach its inevitable end, and this time he'd be on hand for it. He was confident that his presence would involve little risk. It would be easy enough to disappear in the wake of the pandemonium.

He was smiling as he made the final, cosmetic adjustments. He'd go to bed this night with no uncertainties, the last of his obstacles removed.

forty-six

Henry was in a black mood when he stormed into his office. His son was getting out of hand. His defeated former wife was begging Henry to take over parenting until further notice. The father of the kid Sam had pummeled—for reasons as yet unclear—was still making lawsuit noises. Henry had gotten another ticket driving back from Long Beach, and his desk had acquired whole new layers in his absence.

He glowered at the blizzard of paper and resisted an impulse to push it all into the round file.

Sense prevailed. He shifted several stacks of magazines and newspapers to the floor. He restored phone directories and reference books to their rightful places. He buzzed Tara and, sounding churlish even to himself, demanded to know whether there were any fires that needed to be put out. She answered in the negative, amusement in her voice. She'd seen Henry like this before.

"Your messages are there, Mr. Heller," she told him, "and there's nothing that can't wait."

Henry stared at his desk. Now was the time, he decided, to absorb himself in something mindless. Maybe clearing off this disaster area would bring some sort of order to his thoughts as well. He started sifting through the paper.

Three into the latest batch of messages he found Ariel's.

"About time you called. I'll see you at Anthony's at six-thirty sharp. Don't keep me waiting!" he read.

He buzzed Tara again.

"When did Ariel Gold call?"

"What time does it say on the message slip?" Tara asked, rolling her extravagantly made-up eyes.

Henry hung up. Blasted woman! he thought. Blasted women! Ariel's just assuming he'd show up wherever, whenever, on command, put his back up. He could hardly believe her peremptory attitude, and he definitely wasn't in the mood to be ordered around. He checked his watch. It read 5:55, practically too late anyway. He put the stack of messages aside and tackled the next stratum.

Twenty minutes later he reached the bottom of his in-basket. Much of the contents had concerned matters long since resolved, and the farther he dug the more obsolete the material had become. He was about to toss another handful of message slips when one of them caught his attention.

He buzzed Tara, who was blotting a fresh coat of lipstick in preparation for departure.

"How many times did Ariel call?" he huffed. "What's her problem, anyway!"

"She left one message that I took. It's on your desk. What's *your* problem?"

"Come here a minute, will you?"

Mutinously, Tara stomped to Henry's office.

"What?" she asked. "I'm already late and I'm on my way out the door."

"You didn't take this?" He held out a message slip.

Tara glanced at the paper. "That's not even my handwriting." She looked closer. "That's Ariel's writing, not that I've seen much of it lately. What's the deal with her, anyway? Can I get the same privileges? Just drop in occasionally when I feel like it?"

Henry scrutinized the message. It was very similar to the one he'd already read.

"Got your message. Sorry I missed you here, but I'm on my way to the restaurant—with something hot!"

Sure enough, it was Ariel's handwriting. But there was something peculiar about it.

"Let me see that," Tara said, taking the slip from his hand. "Good grief, Mr. Heller! How long's it been since you cleaned off your desk?" She waved the slip. "Today's the twelfth. This says '17.' '2/17' This message is nearly a month old!" She dropped it, suggested it just might be time Henry got his glasses checked, and sashayed out the door.

Henry turned the note toward him. What was it about the odd handwriting that tugged at his memory? Slowly, light dawned.

That was the way Ariel *used* to write. Before she cracked her head or whatever.

He leaned back in the chair feeling spooked, as if he'd gotten a message from the dead.

"Well, look at that!" Win Peacock's voice cut into his reverie. "I'd always wondered if there was a desk under that mess."

The man, perfectly turned out as always, assumed his debonair, offhand pose against the doorframe. It irked Henry more than usual.

"Don't you have anything better to do than monitor the housekeeping?" Glaring at the message again, Henry swiveled his chair around, dismissing Peacock with his back.

"What's that?" Win asked.

"What it is," Henry muttered to himself, "is a damned

oddball coincidence. What's there about February seventeenth that I can't remember?"

"It's not Valentine's Day. Is it Presidents' Day?" Win began putting on his sportcoat. "Why don't you look at your calendar?"

Henry spun back and flipped through the desk calendar. "A Sunday, assuming we're talking about this year. The message isn't old enough to be from last year. I don't think." He read a jotting on the date in question. "I worked that Sunday, most of the day, as I recall. Then I picked up Sam, I think." He mulled over the calendar page. He couldn't remember anything else about the day.

He leaned back in his chair. "Sunday, February seventeenth. What is it about that date?"

"Why don't you tell me why it matters?" Win asked, waving good-bye to one of the last stragglers behind him.

Henry said, "I found a message slip from nearly a month ago—a message from Ariel, buried in my in-basket. Go ahead, laugh. Get it over with." He rooted around, and finding the current message, held it up. "Today I got a similar message, also from Ariel. She wanted me to meet her at that restaurant, Anthony's." He looked at his watch. "Five minutes ago."

He sat up abruptly, his chair squealing in protest. "Anthony's! That was the date Jane Macaulay was killed at Anthony's! Now, that *is* a damned oddball coincidence!"

Confused but game, Win said, "I'll tell you an even freakier coincidence. Their cars."

"What about their cars?"

"Look-alike classics. Jane Macaulay was in hers when she had her date with destiny."

Henry gave Win a pained look and said, "You want to tell me what you're talking about?"

"Ariel's T-Bird."

"Ariel has a Thunderbird?"

"It's even red, just like Macaulay's was. You didn't know that? As palsy-walsy as you two've been?"

Henry looked at the two messages in his hand for a long moment. His mental radar screen lit up like the Fourth of July. "Good God!"

He leaped from the chair and, pushing Win aside, sprinted toward the exit. Win regained his balance and followed at a run.

"Where are we going and what's the hurry?" he yelled when they reached the parking lot.

Henry ran to his car, unlocked it and said, "Get in if you're going."

They were screeching into the street when Win, buckling his seat belt, said, "Tell me what this is all about, dammit, and slow down! What's with the messages? If I'm going to die on the streets, I want to know why!"

"Both those notes," Henry said through clenched teeth, "indicated I'd called and asked Ariel to meet me. I didn't. Not today and not the day Jane Macaulay, driving a car you tell me is like Ariel's, got blown to kingdom come. At the same place we're still at least twenty minutes away from."

"But I still don't get it." Win flinched as Henry wheeled around the car in front of them, narrowly missing an oncoming Jeep.

"Yeah, well, there're some things you don't know about." Henry spun onto a one-way street, going the wrong direction. "It was the morning after Jane Macaulay's death, unless I'm really off the rails here, that Ariel found out she'd misplaced her memory somewhere or other the night before."

"Misplaced her *what?*" Win braced his feet on the floorboard.

"Her memory. She's amnesic."

"Oh, come on!" Win stole a glance at Henry's profile. "You've got to be kidding!"

"And also"—Henry squinted fiercely as he tried to pinpoint dates—"that was the night somebody broke into her house. And the next night was when that same somebody— or an accomplice—came back and tried to kill her." The car swerved onto a curb and lost a hubcap as Henry steered back into a two-lane street.

Win stopped gaping at the scenery flying toward them and gaped at Henry instead. He said nothing for two blocks as he absorbed the information, his mind racing through the implications.

"The first thing we've got to do," he said, "is check the parking lot. If she's still inside the restaurant, we're okay."

When they reached Anthony's, Henry slammed on the brakes in the middle of the large L-shaped lot. He cut the engine, slung open the car door and pointed back toward the entrance. "You go that way!" he told Win, and sprinted into the darkness behind the building.

He'd run thirty feet when he spotted the car and Ariel inside it, still another fifteen feet away.

"Stop! Ariel, don't move!" he shouted as he ran. He pounded the last few feet to the car and slammed the flats of his hands against the closed driver's window. "Stop!"

Ariel turned, the movement of her head as slow as if she were underwater. Henry could see her huge eyes through the glass. He could also see the key in her raised hand.

"Drop the key, please!" he ordered as he took a step backward. Slowly, deliberately, he reached for the door handle. It was locked. "Open it, Ariel! Get out of the car. Now!"

Ariel looked from Henry to the key. After an eternity, she lowered her arm. She opened the door and, clutching her purse to her chest like a shield, put one foot on the pavement.

"Come on!" Seizing Ariel, Henry half-pushed, half-carried her around the corner of the building, back toward the brightly lighted entrance.

When they reached it, he wrapped her in his arms and held her to him.

By the time Henry's heartbeat had slowed to audible, individual thuds, Win arrived on the run.

"I wonder," he panted, "if we should evacuate the place, just in case it's on a clock this time."

"Yeah. Find the manager and tell him," Henry said over Ariel's head. "Then get on the horn to the cops."

When Win had once again raced away, Henry became aware that Ariel hadn't moved.

"Hey," he said, and held her away from his chest. She looked stunned, remote. A neon sign flicking on and off gave her face a queer, bruised color.

"You're okay now," he soothed, and began to walk her still farther away. "Sorry to scare you, but I think . . . well, I think your car may have been wired. To blow up."

"I know," Ariel whispered.

"You *what?*"

"I saw—"

Whatever she was about to say was interrupted by a commotion at the restaurant door, from which people had begun to surge, herded by a grim-looking woman. In nervously babbling clusters they hurried out, some toward the street and a few, in defiance of the furiously gesticulating manager, scattering back into the parking lot, in the direction of Ariel's car.

"You people," Henry yelled, "not that way! Wait a minute!" He released Ariel and tore after a red-faced man pulling a protesting woman behind her.

Ariel stood where he'd left her, her brain wooden, struggling to function. She saw a lone old man emerge from the restaurant. He was moving much more slowly and cautiously than the rest, and in the wrong direction. Responding to his feebleness, to some half-formed idea of assistance, she took a step toward him and then stopped, openmouthed. The *Cosmo* publicity shot she'd seen the day before appeared in her mind as clearly as if it had actually materialized. This man wore a suit—no lab coat—but the white hair and mustache were precisely those of the mad scientist movie role. Even the eyes were the same.

"Philip?" she breathed, then called out his name. She lurched toward the shuffling old man.

He recoiled. "You!" he snarled. "You get away from me!"

Ariel saw the wrinkled face go rigid, the stooped back miraculously straighten. She saw the hand, incongruously swift, plunge into a coat pocket.

It was then that Win appeared. Like a shot, he placed himself between Philip and Ariel.

"What's happening here?" he demanded.

Ariel registered Win's questioning face as it turned toward her in the same beat that blood seemed to boil from his cheek. He reeled away, clutching his face. There was another swift movement of Philip's arm and an "oomph" of exhalation from Win.

"No!" Ariel cried. She screamed Philip's name, reached out to stop him. The hate she saw in the twisted, old-man face immobilized her.

Philip wheeled around to find his way blocked. With a great thrust, he stiff-armed Henry, knocking him to the ground. For one indecisive second he froze, his eyes pinning Ariel with a desperate loathing, and then, almost tripping over Henry, he bolted. In an instant he'd rounded the building and was swallowed in the gloom.

As if released from paralysis, Ariel moved to Henry's aid. She'd no sooner grasped his arm than she heard a panicked squeal of tires. The sounds that followed were so rapid as to be indistinguishable from one another: a muffled thump, the sickening screech of metal smashing into metal and then a mighty "whoosh" before the night exploded in a blinding convulsion. The pavement bucked as a series of shocks hit, and Ariel was thrown to her knees.

She struggled for oxygen, but it felt as if the breath had been sucked from her lungs. She could hear nothing but the ringing in her ears. She covered her eyes against the afterimage of searing light, and some still-operant part of her mind supplied the information that her glasses were gone. She found air. She found her glasses. She discovered that she felt no pain. Little by little, the world began to right itself. She became aware of Win beside her, bleeding, and of someone pulling at her, trying to get her to her feet. She looked into Henry's face. His mouth was moving, saying something unintelligible, and she realized that the ringing wasn't only in her ears. The piercing wail grew louder, became earsplitting. New, pulsing lights were coming from somewhere, turning them all into a psychedelic, red-and-blue-stained tableau.

Through the scream of sirens and punished tires, there was a great clatter of running feet, and the ground trembled as a fire truck roared by. From directly behind Ariel a voice ordered, "Let's just everybody move this way! Come on! Let's move!" Paramedics seemed to materialize from the ether, as did other men, uniformed in black, and someone—

one of a half dozen policemen—steered the civilians toward the street.

The next minutes were a blur. Ariel peered at the scene around her, trying to make sense of the chaos. The dense cloud of black roiling into the sky from beyond the restaurant. Wide-eyed restaurant patrons and bystanders straining the police perimeter. Henry moving off with a policeman, urgently explaining, pointing back toward her car, toward where it had been. Win being loaded onto a gurney. Paramedics working on one or two people she didn't recognize. Then she saw someone she did recognize. Certain that her nearsighted eyes must be deceiving her, Ariel gawked at the stolid, slightly averted face of Sarge. The muscular cook was some distance away, and he was in earnest conversation with Max Neely.

"Where did Sarge—?" Ariel turned, wondering, expecting to see B. F. At that moment the worst of the noise ceased. The last siren died, and Henry was back at her side, draping a coat over her shoulders.

"How're you doing?" he murmured, pulling a handkerchief from the coat pocket and dabbing at a cut on her cheek that she hadn't known was there. "Do you need a paramedic to check you over?"

Ariel shook her head. "But Win. Is he . . . ?"

"I don't think it's too bad. Nothing vital got in the way. Ariel, who was—?"

He was interrupted when an officer approached and ushered them both to a squad car. They were seated in the back and asked to wait. The door was closed, and the policeman posted himself outside.

"Now tell me," Henry demanded, "who was that guy?"

"His name's Philip Carroll. Henry, what happened? Did the bomb go off?"

"The actor?" Henry was incredulous. "That Philip Carroll?"

"But I didn't turn the key. Did I?" Ariel pulled the coat tightly around her and watched one of the ambulances scream away.

"No, honey, of course not." Henry reached for the door

handle. "I think we'd better get a paramedic to take a look at you."

"No! Stay here!" Ariel clutched Henry's arm. "I'm just ... disoriented. Just give me a minute."

Satisfied that he wasn't leaving, she persisted, "I saw the bomb go off, you see, before it did, while I was still in the car."

"Ariel ..." Henry looked very uneasy.

"I did," she went on as if he hadn't spoken. "I was about to put the key in the ignition, but I saw what had happened. I mean what would happen. I could see myself turn the key, and then there would be this ... holocaust. And then there would be nothing."

Henry relaxed slightly.

"Well, that makes sense," he said. "If I'm right, you were remembering! You were here the night Jane Macaulay's car blew up. See? That's probably what caused the amnesia. You must've been close by. You must've been injured by the impact of the blast."

Ariel considered what he said and began slowly shaking her head. "No, the thing is, I didn't see it from the *outside*. I was *inside* the car."

The front passenger door opened, and Max Neely's huge shoulders and disgruntled face appeared.

"Thanks a lot, Gold. I was going off duty when—"

He took in Ariel's state and the look on Henry's face, and sat down heavily. They all watched as another ambulance departed with a blast of its siren.

"Peacock," Neely said. "Looks like he's going to be okay." He cut his eyes back to Henry. "You up to telling me what's behind this mess? How'd you know the car was wired?"

"I didn't," Henry said. "I guessed."

His explanation was concise, skipping all but the most pertinent facts. Ariel listened as raptly as Neely did.

"But I came here to meet *you*," she protested when he'd finished. "You left a message!"

"Ariel, I didn't. Not tonight and not the night Jane Macaulay died."

Ariel stared at him. "Philip," she said simply. Then, her

voice rising, she turned to Neely. "Philip . . . ?" She saw the answer to that question before he spoke.

"If you're talking about the poor slob that cut Peacock, he's history. Your car is, too, by the way."

"Uh, Neely." Henry shot the detective a warning look. "Go easy. She's kind of—"

"No!" Ariel protested. "I'm all right. What happened?"

"According to a guy close enough to see it and lucky enough to walk away, this character with the knife ran out from between the cars back there, and somebody—one of the customers trying to hightail it—nailed him with his car and then racked up another car or two before he got yours, and it blew. Dynamite for sure, but no more than a couple or three sticks, looks like. The driver might even make it. So, talk to me. You knew this joker with the blade? Who was he?"

"She says Philip Carroll," Henry supplied. "The actor."

"The guy you were asking the questions about?" Neely exclaimed to Ariel.

"What questions?" Henry asked.

Ariel was shaking her head. "Poor Philip," she murmured in disbelief. "But I don't . . . if it was Philip who called me today, who got me here, then it had to be him before, too! What did he have to do with Jane Macaulay? They'd never even met, as far as I know."

"Heller obviously believes," Neely said, "that this scene got played out once before, but the wrong woman died. It was supposed to be you that bought it that time, too."

For a moment there was silence, broken only by the background mutter of the police radio.

"You're saying Jane died in my place," Ariel said quietly. "That he was responsible for her murder."

Surprisingly, the thought of what had been done to Jane gave her the strength of anger, dissipating the nightmarish quality of the last hour.

"Yeah, well, that's all speculation, isn't it," Neely said, rather gently for him. "We've got nothing to back it up."

"But you've got Philip at the scene!" Ariel cried. "And he was in disguise, for God's sake! He was wearing this wig and makeup—it was from a character he played in a movie. I just saw the picture yesterday in a magazine!"

"Yeah," Neely grimaced. "I heard about the getup from one of the bomb techs. But, Ariel, the man was an actor. They call that *in costume*. He could've been on his way to a shoot. Besides," he said with a shrug, "he could've been cross-dressing and not exactly stood out in this neck of the woods."

"What about the knife?" Henry asked. "He did cut Peacock."

"A pocket knife doesn't qualify as a concealed weapon, even if the thing is big enough to gut a shark. So what we've got," Neely continued, "is a corpse who, unfortunately, used to be a prominent man. For all we know, he was just scared sh—scared silly and trying to get to his car. He thought Peacock was trying to stop him and he panicked. At least arguably, that little episode was just a misunderstanding."

"That's not the way it was at all!" Ariel objected. It was then that she remembered Sarge.

"Where'd Sarge go? I saw you talking to him. Did he see what happened?"

"McManus? You know him?" Neely seemed surprised.

"Who's McManus?" Henry was at sea.

"Retired cop," said Neely, "the eyewitness I mentioned. He did see the scuffle, matter of fact. He said none of you did anything to provoke Carroll, but that everybody was in a panic to get away from the joint. When he saw the knife, McManus said, he decided to jump in, but then Carroll took off. He was going after him when he saw the accident. What he saw clears you guys and the driver of the car, too— Carroll ran in front of him and he lost control—but he also didn't see anything to incriminate Carroll. Hey, look, I'd love to hand this one to the Criminal Conspiracy boys all wrapped up—the Macaulay hit, too—but we don't even have anything circumstantial here."

"The tape!" Henry suddenly remembered. "He left a message on Ariel's machine. Even if he disguised his voice, it could still be analyzed!"

"I'm afraid . . . I think I rewound it," Ariel admitted. "If I've gotten any more messages, we're out of luck."

"We'll check it out," Neely said, "but even if we can match voiceprints, all we've got the sucker on is impersonation."

"What about the clothes you were wearing that night, Ariel?" Henry tried again. "Did you save the shirt or whatever it was? Remember? I told you to keep it?"

At her slow nod, Henry explained to Neely.

"If that blood's Jane Macaulay's," he concluded, "and Ariel was close enough to the blast to get the blood on her, it'll prove she was here that night."

"Oh yeah, it might put her here all right but, still, all that proves is she was lured here twice by somebody. We still don't got the who."

"Well, it's not over yet." Ariel looked from one man to the other and set her jaw. "Not 'til the fat lady sings!"

She opened her purse and extracted the notes she'd made earlier. "Maybe you can't connect Philip to attempted murder tonight or to Jane's death either, but you may be able to close more than one case. If I'm right, Philip didn't just kill one person. He's killed four."

"Four!" Neely's somewhat offhand manner vanished.

"What four?" Henry sputtered. "You never said how you even know Carroll. And you *sure* didn't mention why he tried to kill you!"

The police radio came to life in a staccato burst of what sounded like meaningless chatter. Neely reached behind him, detached the transmitter and climbed from the car, propping his elbows on the roof as he talked. Henry and Ariel both fell quiet, trying to hear his brief, murmured responses. All Ariel could see of the detective was his truncated, white-shirted midsection and swirl-patterned tie framed in the doorway. The conversation was quickly over.

Neely leaned into the car, his hands braced against the roof.

"The driver of the car that hit Carroll didn't make it," he said. "He flatlined on the way to the hospital."

"That makes five," Ariel said.

forty-seven

I t's funny, isn't it?" Ariel said as she opened her front door. "I spent all day bent on trapping Philip, and there's not a doubt in my mind he was guilty. But now, with no confession, no proof and no trial, he's as punished as he can get and I just feel . . . sad."

Neely, who'd spotted Jessie rushing headlong to greet them, took a step backward on the porch. "Yeah, well . . ." He waited while Ariel greeted the dog and commanded her to sit before he ambled into the living room and finished his thought. "It's just because we *don't* have any of those things that I'll be stuck on this 'til the Second Coming. Carroll's death'll have to be thoroughly dissected, tonight's attempt on you is an open case, Macaulay's still open and now you want to resurrect Carroll's late wife and a four-year-old double murder just to gum up the works. So why don't we sit down and you tell me what that's about."

Henry arrived just then and suggested they check the answering machine before they did anything else.

The little red light was blinking. The new message was from Frank Eberhardt, and the gist of his news was that of those he'd talked to about Arnold, his wife and the aspiring actor, several remembered the blacklisting rumor, and one person could actually confirm it. "If you want details," Eberhardt had said, "give me a call tomorrow." Ariel dropped into the swivel chair and pushed the Play button again. Sure enough, the playwright's helpful message had all but obliterated the summons to the restaurant. What was left was a second of traffic noise and, over it, what might have been the "eye" sound at the end of the telltale "good-bye." Neely doubted that it was enough to analyze, and hearing even that infinitesimal speck of Philip's voice so spooked Ariel that she couldn't concentrate on the problem. The emotional roller coaster she'd been riding was taking its toll. Her anger had drained away like tepid bathwater, and sneaky spasms of shock kept rippling through her midsection. She wanted to put her head on her arms and go to sleep.

The doorbell rang.

Both men, and Jessie as well, accompanied Ariel into the living room, where Neely, his hand poised on his holster, put his eye to the peephole.

"It's an old guy, a big old white-haired guy."

Ariel hurried to unlock the door.

B. F. merely glanced at Neely and Henry, and he didn't return Ariel's surprised greeting. He stood stock still and looked her up and down, his face drained of color. Then he let out a small groan and enfolded her in a bear hug.

"For one blessed second," Ariel heard him murmur, "I thought you were . . ." He stopped and, clearing his throat, addressed Neely.

"I heard from Sarge," he said, "that Ariel was brought home by a detective. Is that you?"

"Yeah. Detective Lieutenant Max Neely. Who're you?"

"B. F. Coulter. Sarge works for me." His eyes shifted to Henry.

"We were never formally introduced, Mr. Coulter." Henry held out his hand, which, after a brief hesitation, B. F. shook. "I'm Henry Heller, and Ariel works for me."

"I'd like to know"—Ariel slipped out from under a heavy arm—"what Sarge just happened to be doing at Anthony's tonight."

The situation, Neely's expression indicated, was getting out of hand. "It looks like maybe I've got a question or two to ask you, too, Mr. Coulter. Could we all sit down and try to get some answers? I'd like to go home sometime tonight."

"Suits me to sit," B. F. said, and did so. "I've had kind of a bad evening and I'm tired, but I can get my part of this over real fast. Ariel Gold needed watchin' after. Sarge McManus is still one of the best I know in that line, so I asked him to make sure he or somebody as good as him kept an eye on her 'til I could talk her into gettin' out of town for a while. He did, and that's it."

"That is *not* it," Ariel protested halfheartedly. "How long have you been having me watched? I'll bet it was Sarge at the library, too, wasn't it? Checking about Michael's murder? Why didn't you let me decide if I needed to borrow your bodyguard?"

"Obviously," B. F. said, "you did."

"If you two don't mind?" Neely gave them both the fish-eye, then directed his question to B. F. "What's your connection to all this?"

"Jane Macaulay was my granddaughter. Ariel Gold's my friend. Now I'd like to ask some questions. Was this yahoo running around knifing people the one planted that bomb tonight? Why," he asked Ariel, "was he trying to kill you? Which brings up the next obvious question: why'd he kill Jane?"

"It's probable," Neely answered him, "that your granddaughter was killed by mistake. It's possible that the intended victim all along was Gold."

B. F. made a visible effort to keep his face straight and his voice steady. "Then I repeat, why'd he want Ariel dead?"

"Good luck with that one," Henry said. "I've been trying to get an answer for over an hour."

Ariel frowned. "Right now, it almost seems . . . beside the point."

Neely's impatient rejoinder was cut off in the first syllable by a deadly serious B. F. "Don't talk foolishness. Whoever planted that bomb tonight, unless he was some kind of copycat, killed Jane. Period. If the man who killed her's dead, I want to know it. If he's not, I sure as hell want to know that. Whatever you can tell us is very much to the point, and I mean to hear it."

"All right. You're right." Ariel touched B. F.'s hand, but she addressed Neely. "I'll tell you everything I know, but first I'm going to make some coffee."

Neely rolled his eyes in resignation.

Thirty minutes later they were narrowed in incredulity.

Ariel had begun by playing the pertinent section of the interview tape and showing them the faxed playbill photo of Adam Shaw. After she'd read a few earmarked passages in the script, they'd listened as she set forth her theories. Neely had kept his peace throughout. Now he looked set to find every hole in her conjecture.

"Just hold it!" he snapped at Henry, who was about to

bombard Ariel with questions. His gaze slid to B. F., just to make sure they both understood. "This is my show right now."

He turned back to Ariel and placed his coffee mug on the table. "I thought Heller's story about mysterious messages was off the wall, but *yours* makes *his* sound like connecting the dots.

"Let me just recap," he said, folding his arms across his chest, "because I wouldn't want to get any of this wrong. Now according to you, Carroll was once upon a time a struggling actor named Shaw who was up for his big break on Broadway. He diddles the producer's wife to hedge his bets. The husband tumbles that he's been given the shaft—that his wife has, literally—and tells Shaw he's history, maybe also literally. At least he spreads the word that Shaw's persona non grata. Shaw swaps the Big Apple for the Big Orange, changes his name and starts over. Just when he's got another break, this producer turns up and threatens to pull the rug out from under him again. Shaw, who's now Carroll, zaps him. He not only get the TV show, pretty soon he gets the widow, who's now got megabucks."

His head to one side, he asked, "Have I got it right so far?"

"Crudely speaking." Ariel folded her own arms, defensively.

"Yeah, well, guess what: I like it better when I tell it. It almost sounds plausible." Neely propped his elbows on his knees and leaned toward Ariel.

"A few years pass, and Carroll decides he wants the whole bundle for himself. Maybe the wife catches him fooling around and threatens divorce, which leaves him out in the cold financially. Or maybe she's got something on him, like the offing of her husband." Neely was no longer condescending. He was thinking as he went along now. "She could've even been in on that. They were in cahoots before, weren't they?"

He made a tent with his fingers. "Whatever the reason, he wants her gone. So he remembers the murder plot from the play that started all this, planned for him to the last detail, and he borrows it. What makes it swell is nobody remembers he was ever in the play. What the hey! Nobody even remembers the play!"

Ariel, her adrenaline beginning to flow again, took up the narrative, fleshing out what she'd already suggested.

"He lures his wife to New York and takes her somewhere private. He kills her with a hefty insulin overdose—after getting her good and soused, which has the double advantage of making it easier to inject her and increasing the effect of the drug. The fact that she was such a small woman wouldn't help her any in terms of the booze or hypoglycemia either, I imagine. Oh, and neither would her heart problems. Which reminds me—you should check if she was on medication, since certain drugs also exacerbate the effects of insulin.

"In any event"—Ariel took a breath—"she dies. He waits until rigor mortis comes and goes. Now she's flaccid again—and packable. He seals her in a plastic bag, a big garbage bag or whatever, and puts her into a trunk or a large suitcase. In the play," she added as an aside, "it was a footlocker. Then he goes to the airport, checks the luggage and flies to L.A. He has her parking receipt, let's suppose, so he gets her car, drives her home and positions her exactly as she was when she died. Then he 'finds her' and calls 911. He's just flown into town . . ."—Ariel spread her hands, palms up—". . . and she's been here, dead, for a couple of days or more. He's home free."

The questions came hard and fast. Ariel felt like a spectator at a tennis match as she turned first to one man, then another.

"B. F.: "Why insulin?"

Ariel: "Once it's assimilated, it's untraceable. Although, unlike when the play was set, it's now possible to analyze tissue at the injection site for traces—a fact Philip may or may not have known."

Neely: "How'd he know the suitcase wouldn't be X-rayed?"

Ariel: "He could call the airlines and ask, just as I did. In the U.S. checked luggage isn't scanned unless there's a reason to do it."

Neely: "How'd he know it wouldn't be opened?"

Ariel: "Why would it be? And a strong lock would make sure it didn't come open accidentally."

Henry: "But it's always possible there'd be a bomb scare or something and the luggage would be X-rayed. He's taking at least some risk when he claims it."

Ariel: "What the character in the play did was to use a fake name and address on the luggage tag and pay somebody, giving him the claim check, to make the pickup. Then he watched to make sure the person wasn't stopped and took the trunk curbside at his car."

Neely: "You really think it was like in the play? In the murder scene you read us? You think he gave her the shot while they were, um, in the sack?"

Ariel: "Your guess is as good as mine, but exertion just before death *can* accelerate the rigor mortis."

Henry: "Then why wouldn't they have found semen in the autopsy?"

Ariel: "Did they look for semen?"

Neely: "I don't know."

Ariel: "It's also possible the act wasn't culminated."

B. F.: "Okay, y'all explained to me about lividity and how he had to wait until it was set or whatever before he could move the body. But what I don't get is, how'd he know how to fix it so this lividity wouldn't give him away? How'd he make sure the body was in the same position as when she died?"

Ariel: "Eberhardt, the playwright, suggested he might've taken Polaroids before he moved her, but I've been thinking about that. If he didn't get it exactly right, he could always claim that in his shock at finding his beloved wife dead, he grabbed her arm or tried to turn her over or whatever. It would be a natural reaction, wouldn't it?"

Neely: "How'd he get the wife to go to New York in the first place?"

Ariel: "Back to the script. He sent her a ticket along with an invitation by overnight mail. I'm guessing now, but if there'd been infidelity as you suggested, he may have presented the trip as an effort to save the marriage, the enticement of a second honeymoon. My impression was that Fiona was devoted to Philip, and Lucy did say how excited she was at the vet's that day. Plus you told me yourself, Neely, people said she was crazy about him."

Henry: "The key question: how'd he know she wouldn't tell anybody she was going?"

Ariel: "From what I've been told about this woman, she was kind of reclusive, more comfortable with animals than people. She wasn't the type, I think, to confide. At any rate, the timing of the invitation would've left her barely time to pack and get to the airport—hardly time to advertise her plans—and, like in the play, Philip would've insisted that she keep it 'our little secret.' The ticket wouldn't be in her name, of course. In the play it was a code name, but with Philip and Fiona, who knows? It might've been a name they used during their affair, when they checked into hotel rooms."

Ariel wasn't thinking only of Fiona Morgan—charmed by a man she thought wanted her when he simply wanted her dead—when she said, "Philip could be very persuasive. The spontaneity, the clandestine rendezvous, the journey incognito—they'd all be cruelly clever touches, adding to the romance of a tryst back in New York, where it all began. She'd have wanted to believe it."

She gave the men a big, bright smile. "Obviously, though, Fiona didn't see any harm in telling her vet. Thus my witnesses, one hearing her say she was going away and another that she was going, specifically, to New York—and that she was worried about missing her plane. I called the airlines, Neely, and got departure times of all nonstop LAX–Kennedy and LAX–La Guardia flights leaving January thirtieth between one thirty and three in the afternoon—allowing roughly thirty minutes to get to the airport from Victor's, which she left around twelve forty-five. I have the flight numbers."

Henry looked up from the notes he'd been jotting since she began and asked, "Why wouldn't the wife have been suspicious? Presumably, she'd read the play or even seen it."

"The situation was very different," Ariel explained. "In the play the murderer's message was that he was in trouble, his life in danger, and the victim was his lover, who suspected him—correctly—of spying for the Nazis . . . well, you don't need the whole plot. Suffice it to say that it was different."

"What's the timetable?" B. F. asked. "When was Carroll's wife last seen? When was she found?"

"She left the vet's, as I said, at twelve forty-five Wednesday afternoon. She was next seen—her body was next seen—in Los Angeles at ten P.M. the following Friday. Fifty-seven hours later." Consulting her notes, Ariel continued. "The flight takes a little over five hours, so, depending on departure time, she'd have arrived in New York between six forty-five and eight-fifteen in the evening, our time. Let's say she was injected by midnight, which leaves around forty-six hours for her to die, for her body to go through the necessary changes and for Philip to get her back to L.A. and to the house."

"And that could really work?" Henry asked. "Sounds like there'd be a lot of variables."

"You're right, but think about it," Ariel said. "Once she went into a coma, it didn't much matter whether it took minutes, hours or days for her to die. Philip just had to be seen by someone often enough to substantiate his whereabouts, and every eight or ten hours would've been more than plenty. There're flights between New York and L.A. all the time, and it made no difference when he got back to L.A. and 'discovered' the body."

Ariel looked at the men and took a fortifying breath. "Once Fiona died, Philip had no time constraints as far as we know, save one: he had to wait for rigor mortis to come and go, *but* he also had to transport the body before putrefaction was too advanced. Which means the body had to be kept cool enough to slow decay. But . . ." —she held up a finger—" . . . it was January in New York. And then she went into the cold belly of a plane. It's doable."

"Plus you said she was little—thin," Neely supplied. "With people like that rigor generally starts faster, so we're talking about what?" He closed his eyes to calculate. "Twenty-four? Thirty hours after death for it to come and go? And around the same time before she starts to smell? And maybe another twelve before the situation became, shall we say, untenable? A close cut. But if she's kept cool, if the bag she's in is sealed tight . . . you're right, it's doable. And if he did it, the guy had nerve."

"The guy," Henry said, "who baited Ariel to that restaurant tonight and wired her car in a public, albeit dark, parking lot had nerve."

"Which brings us back to the first question," B. F. interjected. "Why'd he want Ariel dead?"

"It's safe to assume I'd guessed at least this much before the amnesia," Ariel said, "and I had a prime-time forum for publicizing it. The only tangible thing I know I had was the taped interview, but maybe I had more—or maybe Philip only believed I did. Maybe it was he who broke in here looking for whatever he thought I had. That's one answer we may never know."

Her eyes widened. "But I just figured out something that's bothered me since my house was first broken into. I couldn't imagine how anybody got in past Jessie and got her shut up in the kitchen. Philip *must've* been the intruder! Jessie *knew* him!"

"The break-ins!" Neely muttered something sibilant under his breath. "I can't believe I didn't think of that! We know for a fact who did the second one, and we know Rodriquez was a military breacher, that he was trained in E.O.D."

"In what?" Henry and B. F. both asked.

"Explosive Ordnance Disposal. Yeah! It's been bugging me how some actor could get his hands on explosives, how he'd know how to wire a car, but if we can tie Rodriquez to Carroll . . ." Neely gave his head a little shake, sighed and abruptly changed the subject. "So tell me, did the guy in the play get away with it?"

"I'm afraid so," Ariel said. "But the victim in the play didn't board an animal. As meticulous as Philip is—was— I don't think that occurred to him. I don't think he even remembered Jessie's existence."

"Yeah, sounds like Carroll's first mistake was he forgot about the pooch," Neely commented sourly.

A tired silence settled, each of them lost in his or her own reverie, when suddenly there was a sharp crack.

"Not quite." Henry frowned at the pencil he'd just

snapped in two. "His first mistake was killing the husband of Ariel Gold, intrepid, never-say-die investigator.

"I cannot believe," Henry said, his anger growing as delayed reaction set in, "that you've been digging into this on your own! Didn't you have sense enough to know that if the man killed any or all of these people, he'd try doing the same to you?"

"Hey!" Ariel flared. "Look who's talking, Fearless Fosdick! Who came flapping up to my car tonight when he thought I was a nanosecond away from . . . from . . ." She found she couldn't say it.

B. F. came alert, his expression thoughtful, as he watched Ariel's jaw relax, her eyes soften.

"The fact that I wasn't going to use the key doesn't change your heroics, does it?" she said. "Listen, until yesterday the worst thing I knew about Philip Carroll was he didn't correct me when I called him by the wrong name, and even the police thought he was clear across the country when his wife died of 'natural causes.' As soon as I suspected otherwise, I did try to reach you."

"So what am I?" Neely asked. "Chopped liver? Anyhoo, enough of this. The only thing that counts is evidence—translation: a ton of legwork."

He slumped in his chair and stared at the ceiling for a long, resigned minute before he asked Ariel for the answering machine tape, the interview tape, the bloody shirt she'd packed away three weeks before and, finally, the list of airline departure times to New York.

forty-eight

When the page from the playbill arrived the next morning, Henry was waiting with Ariel. He'd refused to leave when Neely and B. F. did, sleeping what was left of the night on the sofa. A crick in the neck and aching knees were the rewards of his solicitude, and he wasn't chipper.

"I don't know why you didn't go on home," Ariel said.

"We both know that with Philip ... gone, I'm not in any kind of danger."

"And I don't know what's the big deal about this photograph. Carroll said himself he was cast in the part—we all heard it on the tape. So open the envelope already."

Ariel tore off the tab and pulled out the photo from the playbill. She studied it, Henry hanging over her shoulder.

"I haven't had the chance to check out the guy that you did," he said, "but that looks like him to me, sort of. So with that and the tape, we know he knew a practically foolproof way to kill his wife and get away with it. Maybe too foolproof."

He noticed that Ariel was still staring at the photograph.

"What? You can't tear your eyes away? Just what were your feelings for Carroll, anyway?"

"I'm pretty sure ... He looks younger, and there's the moustache, of course, but it's not just that," Ariel said, too preoccupied to notice Henry's sarcasm or to wonder about the implications. A slow, sad smile spread over her face. "Well, I'll be! If that's Philip, then I'm not the only one who had a little work done!"

Henry was a trifle slow on the uptake. "Carroll had a lift? Well, in his business it'd be more unusual if he hadn't." He waved the page away contemptuously. "But never mind about him. What did you mean about you?"

Ariel went to the secretary and opened a drawer. She handed Henry the graduation photo of the twenty-two-year-old Ariel Munson.

"Notice anything different?" she asked.

"Different from what? Who is that?"

"All me, in one of my Kate Smith phases."

"You were a little, ah, chunky, weren't you?" Henry observed. "Cute hairdo, too, and—wait a minute. Whose nose is that?"

"Mine, originally. I figure my late husband didn't like it and, being a lovesick nitwit, I had it bobbed."

"No kidding!" Henry gave her a frankly sympathetic look. "I like the old one better."

"So do I. Maybe I'll get the job reversed." She put the photo away.

*　　　*　　　*

In the days that followed, a great number of questions were asked of a great many people. With the evidence, or lack thereof, obtaining warrants was tough and manpower tougher, and the legwork, as Neely had predicted, was toughest. He was more frustrated with each report Ariel weaseled out of him.

The first break was tantalizing. A new footlocker, large enough to hold a body, was found in Philip's attic. That the penny-pinching Philip hadn't discarded the trunk was no more surprising to Ariel than the fact that it was obviously inexpensive. It was also defeatingly ordinary and available in any of hundreds of stores in New York and Los Angeles; locating the source was an exercise in futility. There were no tags attached, and there was no trace evidence of any kind inside. There was, however, a barely detectable odor of disinfectant.

No flight, round-trip or otherwise, had been booked in the name of Fiona Morgan, and no records could be found of a credit card purchase of such tickets—again unsurprisingly to Ariel, who knew that Philip had spurned plastic. There was also no canceled check from an airline or travel agent.

Fiona's photograph was shown to the crews of each of the flights that had departed Los Angeles for New York during the afternoon of January 30. Two stewardesses said she looked familiar; they worked for different airlines.

Quite a few people who'd purchased round-trip tickets for the time period in question hadn't made the return flight. All who could be traced were; it was a dead end.

Lucy, Victor's receptionist, hadn't seen whether Fiona was driving when she'd dropped Jessie off. No cab company had a pickup either at her house or at the vet's on the afternoon in question, and none had a record of an airport pickup going to the Carroll house on the night Philip returned. There was no evidence of his having rented a car at the airport.

There was no record of Philip's having checked a footlocker or other large trunk, but airline officials explained that if he'd checked it at the curb, there wouldn't be. Skycaps on duty at the time of his departure from New York were questioned. None had any recollection of a passenger checking such an item for the flight. That didn't mean it hadn't happened, one commented; it just meant they didn't remember it.

The original investigation into Fiona's death had revealed that, while in New York, Philip had stayed at the couple's Rye residence, a secluded estate that, like the one in Los Angeles, was unstaffed. He'd had a meeting with his agent on Wednesday evening, followed by dinner with the agent and his wife. He'd had a conversation with a neighbor, a jogger, very early Thursday morning, and on Thursday afternoon he'd been called back to Manhattan for reshoots on the movie he was making. That same night he'd visited a local Rye pharmacy to fill a prescription for cough syrup, and on Friday morning he'd gotten a haircut in a barbershop a block away. While the facts supported Ariel's theory—they could be viewed as contrived substantiation of an alibi—they also didn't prove anything except that Philip was where he'd said he was.

A search of the Rye house, naturally, disclosed ample evidence that Fiona had been there, but none to indicate that it was recently or that she'd suffered misery and death from insulin shock there.

The autopsy that had been performed on Fiona mentioned no needle mark and no semen. Blood analysis had revealed a high level of alcohol as well as traces of the drug Inderal and, although it was true that both would have accelerated the effects of an insulin overdose, it was also true that the drug had been prescribed by her doctor and that it was S.O.P. for a person with heart problems. What little that had been learned from the body was all there would ever be, for Fiona Morgan had left the mortuary in an urn. The urn was found on Philip's living room mantel; it held dying roses.

If there was anything, anywhere, to prove that Philip Carroll had murdered his wife, the police couldn't find it, and they were no more successful at discovering any connection to Jane Macaulay.

Evidence reconstructed by bomb technicians confirmed that Jane's car and Ariel's had been wired similarly—both primed with electric blasting caps wired to the ignition system, both with three sticks of dynamite taped under the carriage—but minor differences suggested they had not been wired by the same person.

A test of Ariel's stained shirt was positive; the blood matched Jane's. Furthermore, both the spatter pattern and a chemical analysis of the filth on the shirt—which was, in fact, blast debris—made Ariel's proximity to the bombing all but conclusive. That news went a long way toward explaining the contusion on her forehead, and her amnesia as well. It didn't incriminate Philip.

Telephone company records showed three calls from Philip's house to the same public phone during the days immediately before Jane's death—one the day of—but there was no way to determine the recipient. The room Rodriquez had been renting was now occupied by someone else, and a search at the time of his death had turned up only a stash of coke and some hot electronics items—no explosives and nothing that connected him to Philip.

If it had been Philip who lured Ariel to Anthony's on the day Jane was killed, he hadn't done it via his own telephone and, while he had placed a call to her number on the day he himself died, it was made too early to have been the infamous impersonation message.

As to the four-year-old murder of Creighton Arnold and Michael Gold, that trail was icy.

There was one short-lived flurry of excitement when it was learned that Arnold himself had owned a gun of the same caliber as the one used to kill him. That his wife and, through her, Philip had access to it was intriguing, but ballistics tests were impossible because the gun couldn't be found.

Adam Shaw had never been heard from again after he'd walked off the set of *Flying Blind*, and expert opinion was mixed as to whether the man in the playbill photograph was or wasn't Philip Carroll. Shaw had never been in the armed services, he had no record, and no fingerprints could be located anywhere to compare with Philip's. A call to Frank Eberhardt produced Shaw's onetime New York agent, who confirmed that one of Creighton Arnold's minions had advised him to dump Shaw. The agent couldn't remember the reason he'd been given, but he was positive it had nothing to do with illicit sexual activities; that, he said, he'd have remembered. Those connected with the *Tulsa* series had gotten no negative input about Philip from Arnold or anyone else. Either Arnold had been killed before he could interfere or the theory that he was planning to was groundless.

An inquest was held in regard to Philip's death and, as Neely had foreseen, the ruling was death by mischance. The facts in evidence indicated that his were the actions of a man in panicked flight from danger. In the confusion of evacuation he'd misinterpreted Win's approach, blindly striking out at what he'd seen as an impediment. He'd then run directly into the path of a vehicle driven by an equally panicked customer. That vehicle, out of control, had subsequently ricocheted off another vehicle into Ariel's, detonating the bomb. The driver had died as a result of the explosion; Philip had not. He'd been killed by the impact of his skull hitting concrete.

It began to look as if the only death the judicial system would ever be able to lay at the feet of Philip Carroll was his own, and the only positive thing that could be said of the situation was that it was tailor-made for *The Open File.* One entire program was eventually devoted to the mystery.

Two days after Philip's death B. F. paid Ariel a visit.

He seemed reconciled to the likelihood that his granddaughter was the victim of a bungled attempt on Ariel. He believed her theories implicitly, questions no longer plagued him, and the conviction that Jane's killer and the man who'd set the wheels in motion were both dead gave him a kind of peace.

In view of these pragmatic reactions, Ariel was unprepared for what he'd come to say.

When he turned up on her doorstep, he had Stonewall in tow. The instant the dog saw Ariel, he stopped pawing at the big blue bow around his neck, took a flying leap into her arms and proceeded to deafen her by barking in her ear.

"Macaulay doesn't want him," B. F. said, "and I'm gone too much of the time to do him justice. I don't suppose . . ."

Ariel put the dog down, and Jessie immediately began an olfactory inspection, both dogs' tails busily fanning the air.

"It's not just that I know you can take better care of the mutt," B. F. told Ariel, his tone gruff. "I remembered how he took to you, and you saw how he acted just now. It's like he has his own opinion who he belongs to."

He began a nervous pacing and finally came out with what he meant.

"See, it's like the dog recognized you, like somehow, some way, he sees Jane in you. Or senses it. And he's not the only one; so do I."

"What on earth are you trying to sug—"

"Just hold your horses, Ariel Gold. I'm not exactly easy with this kind of thing to start with, so hear me out. All I know is you turned up in my life the very day I knew I'd lost Jane, and I don't think that was coincidence." He tugged at his collar, frowned in concentration and made another circuit of the room. "You don't just look like her, you act like her. God knows I don't understand it, but it's like you were some kind of gift from Providence, and I'm not going to question it and I'm sure not turnin' it down."

Ariel regarded B. F. with growing alarm. She couldn't deny that she'd felt an immediate affinity for him that she could no more explain than she could her strong reactions to Jane's home, Jane's portrait and her husband. She also knew she resembled the woman who died the night she'd lost her own history. But even if she couldn't explain any of it, she knew there had to be a rational explanation. Whatever B. F. was imagining sounded like wishful thinking at best—and just plain unhealthy at worst.

"'All fantasy,'" she said slowly and deliberately, "'should have a solid base in reality.'"

B. F. abruptly sat down.

"That was a quote, wasn't it?" he asked. "You were quotin' somebody?"

"Well, yes," Ariel said. "Listen, B. F., what we're looking at here—"

His sudden broad grin caused her to lose her train of thought.

"What?" she asked. "What's the matter?"

362

"Jane did that all the time. She'd come up with these things that sounded profound, like just because somebody famous had said 'em, they proved whatever point she was tryin' to make. Used to drive me crazy." He was shaking his head, his grin satisfied.

"B. F.," Ariel protested, "please. Don't get weird on me! I don't know what kind of hogwash you've got in your mind, but that's just what it is. Now listen here: as much as I wish I had, I never even met Jane. I had no connection to her, and I'm sure as the dickens *not* her. I'm just me—you're going to have to like me for myself or leave me be."

He ignored her ultimatum. All the unease he'd shown earlier was gone, and he seemed like a man content with things as they were, whatever they were.

"I don't reckon I can talk you into takin' a trip with me right now?" he asked.

"B. F.!"

"I didn't think so. But I'm in and out of town a lot, and now that you've got the animal, it'll give me a good excuse for comin' over here."

Ariel gave up. She rolled her eyes and burst out laughing.

"Lord, B. F., you've never needed an excuse yet to pop in night or day, and I don't expect you ever will. I will take Stonewall, but only if you're absolutely sure Macaulay doesn't want him and only if you can get me a signed paper saying so. I'm not going through *that* mess again!"

forty-nine

On the following Sunday Henry drove Ariel to a tiny spot on the map called Boron, California. Located in the Mojave Desert 120 or so miles northeast of Los Angeles, the town was the last known address of a young woman named Linda Bonner. That was her real name, but it wasn't the name she'd gone by when she tried to abduct a baby named Jessie thirty years before. Then, she'd called herself Dove.

With Max Neely's help, Ariel had gained access to Culver

City police files of the December 1962 kidnap attempt. Within a week after their arrest Linda Bonner and the two men with her had escaped during a routine transport from jail to courthouse. None of them had ever been recaptured. The chances of their ancient address being of any use now were somewhere between slim and none, Ariel knew, but she was going to do her level best to see at least one mystery in her life solved.

Besides, she longed to get away from Los Angeles and the haunting memories, frustrations and dead ends of the past days, and any trip was diverting, especially with Henry at the wheel.

Ariel had spent the better part of one evening telling him about her adoptive status. Henry didn't even blink; he didn't think anything about Ariel would surprise him anymore. The bit about her having unconsciously, as far as she knew, named a dog after herself had given him a good laugh and then intrigued him. Within minutes he was trying to figure out how to work unconscious memories into an *Open File* segment.

As they drove along Highway 14, they didn't talk about Ariel.

They talked about Win, whose stomach wound had indeed been superficial and who had declined corrective surgery on his cheek, apparently deciding that a rakish battle wound might be something he could use to advantage.

They talked about Henry's problems with his son and with his former wife, who was still insisting that Henry take over the raising of what was starting to look like an incorrigible child.

They talked about Ariel's growing menagerie and how Jessie, once she'd established she was alpha dog in the setup, not only didn't mind a cohort but was downright protective of the smaller dog and only snapped at him when he was being especially obnoxious.

When the conversation finally did turn to Ariel, it wasn't about her past but her future.

The wind blowing through the open windows was hot, and Henry took a swig of mineral water and wedged the bottle into the clutter on the seat before he pressed for an answer to his last question.

"Well? What if you don't?"

Ariel turned her gaze from the sere hills to the west and took off her sunglasses, polishing them thoroughly to give herself time. At length she said, "I'm assuming you want a serious answer?"

Henry merely gave her a look.

"Okay. If I never regain my memory, if I never find out any more about myself, I can live with it." Squinting, she replaced the glasses. "I believe I used to be very lonely, Henry, that I had no great urge to live or talent for living. I feel as if I know that woman, but I'm not that woman—do you see what I mean? I don't covet her life or her memories, but I do grieve for her."

Henry had enough sense to keep quiet, and several miles passed before Ariel spoke up again, her tone determinedly upbeat.

"I look at it this way: I'm okay financially, I'm healthy and I'm pretty sure no one wants me dead anymore. With one notable exception, I've made some excellent friends in the last weeks. I've inherited a job I like and, from what you say anyway, I'm more relaxed and a whole lot more fun than I used to be." She flashed a quick grin at Henry's perspiring profile. "So that's the inventory. Onward and upward, et cetera."

Ariel settled back, unsticking her legs from the vinyl seat covers.

"I thought for a minute," Henry said, "that after you got out of your car the other night you were about to have a memory breakthrough." He sneaked a sideways glance. "That maybe, in good old Hollywood style, shock had reactivated your circuits."

"Sorry." Ariel refused to think about the aberrational vision or dream or whatever had occurred in that moment when she'd almost inserted the car key. Like B. F.'s metaphysical mumbojumbo, it gave her the willies.

They'd covered a few more miles when Henry chuckled to himself.

"What? What's so funny?"

"I was just thinking," he said, "about something you said that night in the squad car. 'It's not over yet,' you said, 'not 'til the fat lady sings.' When it was apt, you'd never have said it."

"It's still apt enough."

"What are you, nuts? Break down, Ariel. Buy a mirror."

"Well, thanks, I guess. But I'm not worried about that kind of stuff anymore," Ariel lied. "You know what they say: 'A really busy person never knows how much he weighs.' "

"Oh, good. A pithy saying. We haven't had any of those lately." He passed a truck towing a horse trailer and, his gaze drifting to the stoic equine occupant, he said, "Just don't start looking like one of those emaciated Beverly Hills females. I like a woman with a little flesh on her bones."

Bemused, Ariel glanced at him, then quickly away, just in time to see their exit ahead. "Hey! Slow down. You go east on 58 here."

Thirty minutes later Henry pulled into a Boron gas station and asked about the address Ariel had been given. The girl manning the pumps had no clue but the owner, her grandfather, was a mine of information. The property had been abandoned for years, he said, the land played out. The house on it was all but falling down, and the woman who'd owned it had been buried a year or two back. Having delivered this discouraging information, he gazed sadly into the distance and scratched the back of his neck.

"Um," Henry prodded after a moment of silence, "you wouldn't happen to know who the current owner is?"

"Oh, sure," the old man allowed, "everybody knows Russell."

"I don't suppose you'd know how we could get in touch with . . . Russell?"

"Don't see why you couldn't just drive over to his house. He lives right here in town."

His directions took almost longer to give than to follow, and very shortly they arrived at a modest brick house set in the middle of a patchy yard littered with children's neon-hued plastic toys. A middle-aged man in Bermuda shorts waited on the porch.

"Ray said you'd be over," he called. "I'm Russell Binns. Watch that tricycle. My grandson's made kind of an obstacle course around here."

When Ariel had explained why she was there, Binns smiled.

"Holy smoke," he said, "I haven't thought about those hippies in years. Ma used to threaten me if I went near the place—what they'd set up as a commune—but one or two of the women was right good-looking. I'd heard all the stories about how they were—you know, not too fussy about their morals? It was a temptation, all right." He smiled as if at some secret memory.

"What happened to them, do you know?" Henry asked.

"It didn't take Ma long to wish she'd never rented to them, and she was real glad to have an excuse to evict. When she spotted several little kids out there—grungy-looking, with no adults watching after them and them not in school—that was it. She called the law, and they sent out the child welfare people. I don't know what they found, but the kids were jerked right out of there, and Ma told the hippies to clear out."

"You don't know where they went?" Henry asked it a different way.

"Nah. If I ever did hear, I've forgotten."

"So you never actually met any of them?" Ariel asked neutrally. She was curious about that nostalgic smile.

"Well ..." Binns looked over his shoulder, back into the house. He took a step or two forward and lowered his voice.

"There was this one girl—called herself 'Dove,' of all things. She was the prettiest of the lot, and I did, um, talk to her some." He frowned. "It was about, I guess, eight or nine years ago I ran into her over near Lancaster. She had her a little beekeeping business out in the country. She wasn't using that name anymore and she hadn't aged too well, I hate to say, but it was her."

Back in the hot car, retracing their route to Lancaster, Ariel couldn't believe her luck.

"Don't get too optimistic," Henry cautioned. "She's probably long gone."

Henry was wrong.

367

They saw the wooden roadside stand Binns had described before they saw the house and the apiary in the field beyond. All appeared to be neatly kept. Henry parked in the dusty shade of a huge old magnolia tree, where they sat for a moment looking around. The place appeared at first to be deserted, but then Ariel spotted a figure near the hives, a smallish figure, swathed from head to toe.

They got out and walked over to the stand, where jars of honey were stacked next to trays of neatly aligned candles, tapers as well as animal and flower shapes. A sign overhead, lettered in yellow, simply said HONEY. A smaller sign at counter level claimed that beeswax burned cleaner and lasted longer than paraffin.

"Here comes somebody," Henry said just as Ariel heard the squeak of a screen door from the direction of the house.

A man of about thirty came down the porch steps. He had an unusually sweet smile, and his manner was ingenuous when he asked if he could help them. Ariel returned his smile and asked if there was a woman named Dove living there. Worry rippled across the man's face. His eyes darted toward the figure still working around the beehives and back to Ariel.

"Could I ask you why you want to know that?"

"Please." Ariel reached out her hand and then dropped it to her side. "There's no problem. We mean no harm, honestly. We're just trying to find someone, and we hoped that Dove might be able to help. Will you ask her if she'll talk to us?"

The man looked no less worried, but he did nod. Backing up part of the way, his eyes glued to Henry and Ariel, he went out a side gate, and they watched as he approached the swathed form and conferred briefly. The wide hat turned in their direction, the face beneath it hidden by draped netting. After a few minutes the hat was removed, and the two began walking slowly toward Ariel and Henry. Their hesitance made Ariel think of children approaching censorious parents.

When they came through the gate, Ariel's heart sank. If this was Dove, Ariel couldn't imagine what Russell Binns had meant about her aging poorly. This woman didn't look old enough even to be in her fifties. But as she came nearer, the fine lines around her eyes and mouth became visible and a liberal sprinkling of gray could be seen in her waist-length blond hair. Her skin was pale, and there were deep creases of anxiety between her eyes. The eyes themselves were arresting, a beautiful cornflower blue. They looked fearful. They were also strangely opaque.

"Dove?" Ariel asked.

The woman nodded. She looked poised for flight.

Ariel introduced herself and Henry. "If you've got just a minute," she said, "I'd like to talk to you about some people you used to know."

From the woman's first words, Ariel understood what Binns had meant. What too many years of God knew what experimental drugs had left undamaged physically was all too apparent otherwise. Her voice was tiny, a whisper. "Are you . . . with somebody?"

"No, no," Ariel assured her—benignly, she hoped. "We're just trying to find out about, well, about me. I think you knew me when I was a baby? That you lived with my parents?"

"I did?"

Ariel tried again.

"My name was Jessie then."

"But you can't be." The eyes registered confusion. "Jessie's just a baby and . . ." She stopped and looked at the man in silent consultation. Evidently, it wasn't illuminating.

"What did you want, exactly?" she asked.

Ariel took a chance. She walked to the woman and clasped her gloved hands. "Could we sit down, do you think?"

"Well . . . all right." Dove removed her hands but, shyly, she invited Ariel and Henry onto the porch.

"Will you have some of our special tea?" she asked in her tremulous, little-girl voice. "You'll like it." She disappeared into the house to fetch the drink and was gone so long Ariel was afraid she'd changed her mind about talking to them. The man (Dove's son? Husband?) was utterly mute and clearly uncomfortable. He kept his eyes on the front door and looked as relieved as Ariel felt when Dove finally reemerged.

From somewhere or something, the woman had gained a modicum of courage, and when Henry praised the honey-flavored tea and asked about the apiary, she perched on the porch swing chatting eagerly about the bees and the business. Her guests listened politely, never daring to look at one another.

"What sorts of things did you grow when you were living in the commune?" Ariel asked, completely out of context.

"Strawberries mostly," Dove answered, and then, with a startling abruptness, her voice gained resonance. In a moment of what for her must have been extreme clarity she asked, "That was a long time ago, wasn't it?"

"Yes," Ariel answered, "Long, long ago, and whatever happened then is water under the bridge. I'd just like to know something about who my parents were. Will you tell me?"

"Oh, Annie was fine," Dove breathed. "She was so funny. Do you really like the tea?"

Assuring her that it was delicious, Ariel pressed on. "Her name was Annie?"

"Well, that's what we called her. She said it was a name that suited a cracker."

"Suited a what?" Ariel asked.

"A cracker. You know, a person from the South. *She* said that, though. *I'd* never have called her that."

"She was from the South? Do you know where in the South?"

"I don't . . ." Dove's fine brows drew together in a line of worry. "Texas? Virginia? Somewhere like that . . ."

Ariel sighed. Perhaps they could come back to a geography lesson later. "And my father's name was . . . ?"

"Son."

"Pardon?"

"Son."

"Like . . . ?" Ariel pointed upward.

"No!" Dove giggled. *"S-o-n!* He was so smart, Son was! You wouldn't believe the things he knew!" She retreated, smiling, into some gentle fold of memory.

"What became of them? Do you know?"

"Don't you?"

"I hoped you'd tell me."

"Well, Annie died, of course. She never was all that strong after the birth. Son ... I don't know about Son."

"Do you happen to remember," Henry asked, edging into the conversation and hoping the question wouldn't send Dove's precarious hold on reality back to wherever it usually teetered, "what their last names were?"

The blond head shook a slow, uncertain no.

Knowing it was a futile question, he asked, "I don't suppose anyone has a copy of Ariel's—Jessie's—birth certificate? You or any of your friends from that time?"

Dove looked blank. "Was there one? We delivered you, you know. You were early. Son had said that might happen, and he was right."

"Why did Son say that?" Henry asked.

"I told you, he was really smart. But even he didn't think it would be *that* early, and we couldn't get Annie into town in time." She shook her head, remembering. "By the time you were born she was so weak."

"I don't understand." Ariel frowned in confusion. "If it took so long, why didn't you have time to get my mother to a doctor?"

"Oh, everything went really fast with the first one, but then you took forever."

Ariel and Henry looked at each other.

"The first one?" they asked almost in unison.

"Sure," Dove said. "She came in no time."

For a moment the only sound on the porch was a rhythmic squeak as Dove, oblivious, pushed the swing gently to and fro.

"Are you saying that I had a twin?" Ariel asked when she was capable of speech again. "I have a twin sister?"

"Well, sure." The swing slowed, and Dove looked at first one of her visitors and then the other, her expression growing uncertain. "Jane."

"Jane," Ariel repeated.

Dove's mouth had become an O of anxiety.

"Son had her with him when those people came and took

Jessie," she whispered, apparently again dissociating the child from the adult. "Then, before he came back, they made us leave. I never saw him again. Or the other baby either."

This non sequitur must have reminded her of her jeopardy in regard to the kidnap attempt. She shrank visibly, and she grew increasingly scattered as first Ariel and then Henry urgently probed for more.

When he asked for the full names of the others who'd shared the commune, Dove came to her feet. The abruptly vacated swing bumped the backs of her knees, and she had to clutch the chain to steady herself.

"I have to go now," she said. "Mitchell . . . ?" She threw the man a panicked appeal and before anyone could react, she was gone. The screen door banged shut behind her.

Ariel was halfway out of her chair when Henry caught her hand.

"Another time," he said quietly.

Ariel stared at the door in frustration. Knowing he was right didn't make it any easier.

When the two of them had thanked the taciturn Mitchell and bought a jar of honey for good measure, they drove away in a swirling cloud of dust. It had long since settled by the time either spoke.

"You know it's true," Henry said.

"I know."

"What do you know about Coulter's daughter and son-in-law? Anything?"

"Her name was Suzanne. His was Harrison." Ariel swallowed several times. "He's dead, too.

"I don't think I can stand this. To find out now . . ." She turned her face away.

"You still have a grandfather." Henry handed her a handkerchief, neatly folded and surprisingly immaculate, and waited.

Ariel tried not to cry; she settled for crying as quietly as possible. Finally, drained and swollen-eyed, she said, "It answers so much." She looked at the handkerchief uncertainly and stuffed it into her purse.

"The way I felt about B. F. right from the first minute,

and the way Jane's portrait made me feel. 'Bereaved' is the only way I can describe it. The way Stonewall reacted was . . . And, it's funny, her house—Jane's house—seemed so, I don't know, familiar. Or maybe I'm reaching."

"I doubt it." Henry turned on his headlights. "We did a show once about identical twins who'd been separated at birth. Sometimes when they're reunited, it's pretty amazing the similarities they discover in their lives. Occupations. Hobbies. Tastes. Even marriage patterns—the types of partners they chose."

Ariel looked at him, considering the implications of that. She couldn't seem to focus on one thought before a dozen more intruded. "I wonder . . ." she started, then said, "You know the diaries I told you about? I wrote so much about loneliness. Do you think that was just the circumstances or something deeper? A sense of incompleteness?"

"I don't know. Maybe."

"And, Henry, I just remembered something B. F. told me. He said that when he first got Jane—he said he didn't even know she existed until his son-in-law brought her to him— that she kept saying this one thing over and over. He thought she was trying to say 'yes sir.' Henry, she was calling for me. She was saying 'Jessie'!"

The handkerchief reappeared.

They were a good deal closer to home when Ariel blew her nose with finality and straightened her spine. Beneath the residual quaver in her voice, Henry heard a quiet excitement.

"He's lost so much, Henry, B. F. has. He thought he had no one, and so did I.

"You know," she went on thoughtfully, "Laya told me that whatever reasons I thought I had for getting so caught up in Jane's story, I'd find that there were other, more compelling reasons. I didn't know what she was talking about until now."

And, thought Henry, you still don't.

The twilight had become full night, and he could see Ariel's face only in the occasional flare of oncoming headlights. She looked more at peace than he'd ever seen her. He was sorry it wouldn't last. Once the shock wore off, he knew, the questions would come, and it wouldn't be long before she thought of all the things twinship didn't explain.

She'd need a friend then, Henry thought. Maybe David Friedman. Or maybe Laya. He'd love to hear what that one had to say, just for starters, about what brought two women together at Anthony's Restaurant on one particular night. He could already hear the question in his mind, opening one blockbuster of an *Open File*. He grinned in the darkness as the familiar adrenaline began to surge. Whenever the questions came, one thing was dead sure: he was going to be right there for the answers.

Who was he kidding? He stole a look at the woman beside him and knew the show would never be made. Then he realized something that surprised him considerably.

He was going to be right there anyway.

**POCKET BOOKS
PROUDLY PRESENTS**

BLIND SPOT

Judy Mercer

**Coming Soon in Hardcover
from Pocket Books**

**The following is a preview of
Blind Spot. . . .**

1

Good news doesn't come at 4:00 in the morning.

For those unlucky enough to lie wakeful, that silent predawn black is a lonesome place. Worries nibble at the mind. Old regrets come home to roost. As sleep eludes, just beyond grasp, every minute stretches. The clock ticks. Fears that would seem foolish by day take hold of the imagination, and grow.

It isn't the dead of night, 4:00 A.M., but it can, nonetheless, be deadly. Ask a nurse on the graveyard shift. Ask any priest. It is the hour, you'll learn, when the body's purchase on life is at its weakest, when those sapped by age or illness will often, finally, surrender.

It is an hour when the earth itself is unreliable. Predawn—historically, quirkily, and inexplicably—is favored by earthquakes.

And when the phone rings in the last, dark hours of the night, chances are it's bringing trouble.

It wasn't the phone that woke Ariel Gold at 4:06 A.M., and it wasn't the rumble of a quake. It was, in the first disoriented second, as shocking. She'd been deeply asleep. She'd gone to bed alone. She no longer was. Something cold bumped against her cheek. She jerked awake, still half mired in a nonsensical dream. The noise she heard then was a low, anxious murmur, so close it was like a moist breath on her face, so close it almost stopped her heart. That was when the phone rang.

Later, she questioned whether she could have the sequence of events right: that her dog nudged her awake *before* the phone actually rang. How was that possible? Did telephones emit some sound undetected by human ears in the split second before the ring? Was it coincidence, or did animals have an early warning system for tragedy on the way? The time came when Ariel stopped questioning. Weirder things were entirely, provably possible. Whatever the big German shepherd may or may not have sensed, tragedy had already happened.

"Hello?" Ariel said, her voice hardly audible over Jessie's panting. She stroked the dog's neck, invisible in the dark, but warm, softly furred, and familiar. "Hello?" she asked louder. "Who is it?"

She heard the *thwack!* of a receiver being dropped, banging against something, and snapped on the bedside lamp, squinting against the brightness of the hundred-watt bulb. This wasn't a wrong number; she was somehow sure of that. It wasn't a creep of the heavy-breathing variety either, although Ariel could, faintly, hear the sound of someone breathing. The receiver was evidently retrieved, for the breathing grew loud. It was ragged, the desperate, greedy mouth-breathing of a woman in labor.

"Help me! Oh, God! Help me!"

The voice was a woman's. Thin. At the very edge of a scream. It took Ariel a second to place it. She'd never heard this particular woman sound anything but serene, even detached. "Laya?" she asked. "Is that you?"

Horribly, Ariel's friend had begun to moan. *She's been attacked!* Ariel thought. *Raped.* "What's happened?" she cried, but the moaning, a litany of pain, overrode her. "Hurts!" Ariel made out, and the words "Oh!" and "Please!"

"Stop it," she ordered, "and tell me what's happened."

Laya made a strangling sound and then swallowed noisily, more than once. It sounded as though she were forcing down stones. "I can't," she said. "I can't..."

"You can't what?"

"See!"

"What?"

"Don't you understand English?" The hysteria broke loose then. A flood. "I can't see! I can't see anything! I'm blind!"

2

The kindest thing that could be said about the hospital waiting room was that it was neutral. The muted Muzak that piped in through some unseen speaker was vanilla: white noise, par for Otis ups and downs. The only other occupant of the room was a spent-looking old man. He was snoring quietly, mouth ajar, emitting delicate little puffs as if he were blowing dandelions, and his head had dropped back at an angle that was sure to mean a crick when he woke up. Ariel had seen him earlier down in the emergency room, comforting a woman on a stretcher. A crick, she thought, might be the least of his troubles. He had her sympathy. She didn't know much about her first thirty-two years, but the last one had packed more trouble than most people face in a lifetime.

It was 6:05. The sun was presumably up, but since

there were no windows in the room, it was impossible to know what the new day looked like. Ariel was reluctant to take even a short walk outside for fear a doctor might come looking for her. Paramedics had turned Laya over to the emergency room staff over an hour ago. An hour and twenty minutes ago. Ariel had no inkling of her condition, and she still had no inkling of what had taken place before that horrifying call.

Her race to Laya's apartment had been little short of suicidal. She'd beaten the paramedics, whom she'd phoned en route. The front door had been locked. Frantically, Ariel had felt above the door frame, under the mat, the usual places people keep a spare key. She'd found it beneath a potted plant, a fishtail palm that reigned over a small oasis of palms and succulents in a recess beside the door. Plants were among Laya's few indulgences. She traveled lightly, even in regard to her name.

She was a yogi: Ariel's teacher and her friend, a woman always in possession of herself and, Ariel was sometimes convinced, the secrets of the universe as well. Laya seemed unaware of her quiet charisma and unconcerned about her looks, which were arresting. (Ariel once remarked on her resemblance to Poitier. "Poirot?" Laya had teased. "Wrong accent," Ariel had said, straightfaced.) There was a trace of the West Indies in the tall black woman's cadences, as elusive as its origins. Her graying hair was left to its natural tendencies, and cropped within an inch of her skull, and her wardrobe was utilitarian, the comfortable leggings and sweats of a yoga teacher, or, on occasion, playful: some flowing garment likely to be plucked from a secondhand rack.

Her home was as spartan as a transient's. That morning, in the dense gray predawn, it had appeared abandoned. Ariel had called out. There'd been no answer. Reassuring herself that if anyone had been here—a burglar? a rapist? (a lover who'd turned violent? Who knew? There were chunks of Laya's life about which Ariel knew nothing)—they were long gone, she had made herself go in. It was dark. She was feeling for a light switch, when she heard music—jazz, turned very low. It came, she thought, from the bedroom. So did a faint shaft of light.

At first she saw no one but Arthur, Laya's fat marmalade cat. He was in the middle of an unmade bed, a tightly tucked, unhappy-looking orange mound. Normally the most lethargic of animals, he had his ears back, and his eyes were watchful. His tail switched once, an emphatic arc.

Then Ariel spotted Laya.

She was on the other side of the bed, on the floor with the phone beside her. She was in a sitting position, slumped against the wall, dressed in an oversized T-shirt. Her eyes were closed. She was inert. Ariel was sure for a blank bright moment that she was dead. Then a sprawled leg twitched, the tiniest contraction.

Calling her name, Ariel rushed to kneel beside her. Laya didn't stir. The eyes weren't just closed, Ariel saw; they appeared to be swollen shut. Both dark cheeks bore long scratches. In the stingy glow of the bedside lamp, Ariel could see the welts below each eye: not deep, she thought—the blood beading and beginning already to dry—but angry. There were red smears on the front of the T-shirt.

Ariel reached out, unsure what to do. "Laya!" she said sharply. There was no response at all. She touched her fingers to Laya's neck. The flesh was cool, but the pulse, it seemed to Ariel, beat strongly. Gritting her teeth, she lifted an eyelid. The eye was hideously inflamed, as if it were bleeding internally. Very gently, she let the lid close. There were no other obvious signs of injury. She stood and looked around. Other than an overturned desk chair, there was no sign that anything of a violent nature had taken place.

Ariel pulled the comforter from the bed, dislodging Arthur, who thumped gracefully to the floor and vanished. She was tucking the cover around Laya, when she became aware of the sound of running water. Careful to touch nothing, she went into the bathroom. Using a tissue to handle the tap, she turned it off.

Laya was as oblivious to the noisy arrival of the paramedics as she'd been to Ariel. "Shock," guessed one of the EMTs after a swift glance.

It wasn't until they were lifting her insensible friend to the gurney that Ariel had noticed the small plastic bottle in Laya's hand. It contained eye drops, a generic over-the-counter brand. She'd pocketed it.

In the bedlam of the emergency room, Ariel had

remembered the bottle only at the last minute. The ER doctor barely glanced at it, saying that if the lady's problems stemmed from any kind of chemical burn, he hoped she'd used more than drops. "Should've irrigated with water," he'd said tersely, "and lots of it!" Thinking back to the questions he'd fired at her, Ariel surmised that he'd been more concerned at that moment about his patient's unresponsive state.

She paced the waiting room. It was 6:15. What were they doing that was taking so long? What had been done *to* Laya to make her this way? Every guess was less likely than the one before. Had she scratched her cornea? *Both of them?* Idiotic! Contacts? Did she wear them? Maybe the old, non-air-permeable kind that stuck to your eyeballs like glue if you fell asleep with them in? And when you tried to peel them off . . . Ariel sat down, fidgeted, and got up again. Something had to have gotten into her eyes. Had she had an allergic reaction to soap or some cosmetic? But her eyes looked flayed! An accident, then…some household cleaning solution. Didn't every bleach and detergent and polish caution against contact with the eyes? Why, Ariel asked herself, would Laya be cleaning house at four in the morning? And, surely, even if that was what happened, she would still have been hysterical, as she was on the phone, not…comatose. Out of it. Or whatever she was. Just…gone. *Where?* It was then that Ariel recalled something she'd read in a book about yoga.

It had to do with a thing called *kundalini*. As nearly as she had understood, it was a force or power activated while in a profound trance state. Adepts, she'd read, could stop their own hearts. They could enter into a state of suspended animation. They could curl up on a bed of nails or stroll around on burning coals without pain. *They could escape pain!* Was Laya capable of willing herself, meditating herself, into such a trance?

If she herself were in severe pain, Ariel was sure, in severe distress, and could remove herself to oblivion or bliss or at least absence of pain, she'd be *Om*-ing fit to kill.

She was clutching at straws, avoiding thinking about those facial scratches. What were those all about? *Was* Laya attacked?

What kind of attacker would scratch rather than strike? Or had she been struck? A head blow, knocking her unconscious? Impacting whatever portion of the brain affected vision? The water left running...Someone cleaning off blood? The evidence of attack?

The old man who shared the waiting room exhaled forcefully, one noisy snort. He woke himself up. Smiling sheepishly, he glanced at Ariel and then at the nurses' station and, then, starting slightly, at Ariel again. She smiled back, sympathetic acknowledgment of a fellow passenger in the wait-and-worry boat. He turned pink, and suddenly found his fingers of interest. Lacing them together, he watched himself rub the pad of one thumb against the other. After a good thirty seconds of this fascinating exercise, he blurted, "Excuse me, but you're somebody, aren't you?"

"Pardon?"

"I'll get it in a minute. Somebody..."

Ariel almost turned to look behind her. Preoccupied as she'd been, dressed in last night's wrinkled clothes, her hair at odds with her head and her face bare of makeup, she honestly didn't get it for a second.

"*Open File!*" he cried. "You're the lady from that TV show! A celebrity!"

Wincing, Ariel admitted that the first part, at least, was true. She still wasn't used to being recognized. She found it incredible, at the moment, that she had been. She looked more like a gummy-eyed bag lady, she imagined, than a "celebrity."

In Los Angeles one spots them—celebrities, even legends—regularly, on the street, in the dry cleaner, at the car wash. A major box-office draw blocks the grocery aisle with his cart, studying the ingredients on a cereal box. A sitcom lead sees your look of recognition and gives you a wink as he passes on the sidewalk. The woman rummaging through old linens at the next flea market stall is an Academy Award–winning singer-turned-actress. Ariel wasn't in that league. It was a fact, though, that since she'd gone from producer to correspondent on a network newsmagazine three months before, she did get surreptitious glances and even the occasional autograph request.

"My wife watches your show faithfully," the man said, patting his pockets, pulling out a pen from one and what turned out to be a phone bill from another. "She even tapes it when we go out. We square-dance." He faltered, and seemed to sink into himself. "Diabetes, she's got. Bad. They may have to ampu-tate…"

Ariel took the envelope and scribbled inadequate best wishes. "Tell you what," she said. "When your wife's feeling better, you call the studio, Mr. …"

"Morris. Bobby Morris. Merle, that's my wife."

"Ask for me. I'll arrange a tour of the studio, if you'd like to do that." Jotting the studio number and wishing him luck, Ariel got to her feet. "I need to check on my friend," she said, and started for the nearest nurses' station.

The ER doctor intercepted her. After asking for information Ariel didn't have (like Laya's surname; hospital red tape snarled hopelessly on a patient who'd dispensed with the family name and, it was Ariel's impression, the family that shared it), he volunteered only, "An ophthalmologist is with her now. We've got saline drips going to irrigate the eyes. We'll know more later."

"Tell me what you know now, please," Ariel begged.

The doctor (whose name, Ariel later thought, she must surely have heard or read on his ID badge but didn't remember) considered his reply. Blinking rapidly and addressing his answer through half-closed lids to some point behind her (a nervous and probably unconscious habit she put down to shyness—or having delivered bad news a few times too many), he said, "Chemical burn, of course. Damage to the left eye looks like it might be limited to the outer layer of the cornea." He went through the blinking routine again. "Other eye's not so good. Cornea's cloudy."

Ariel felt herself grow cold. "Which means?"

He tried falling back on his earlier bromide. "We'll know more a little later."

"But what happened?"

He sighed. "What actually took place, you mean? Since the patient's out of it—which is something I have *never* seen in these situations—I can't answer that. We can't get any information from her. I can only tell you that some form of acid was introduced to the eyes." He blinked. "I'm having the contents of that bottle you gave me checked out."

Look for

BLIND SPOT

Wherever Hardcover Books Are Sold
Coming in April 2000 from Pocket Books